Stairway To My Heart

The Bridgewater Chronicles

Stairway To My Heart

MARION MARCHETTO

Marion Marchetto

iUniverse, Inc.
Bloomington

Stairway To My Heart
The Bridgewater Chronicles

iUniverse books may be ordered through booksellers or by contacting:

iUniverse
1663 Liberty Drive
Bloomington, IN 47403
www.iuniverse.com
1-800-Authors (1-800-288-4677)

ISBN: 978-1-4759-3294-2 (sc)
ISBN: 978-1-4759-3296-6 (hc)
ISBN: 978-1-4759-3295-9 (e)

Library of Congress Control Number: 2012910560

Printed in the United States of America

iUniverse rev. date: 06/27/2012

Round her she made an atmosphere of life,
The very air seem'd lighter from her eyes,
They were so soft and beautiful, and rife
With all we can imagine of the skies....

George Gordon, Lord Byron
— *from* Don Juan

Catherine

Chapter 1

April 12, 1890
New York, New York

As I labored through the past eighteen hours, I made a conscious effort to fill my head with thoughts of our little family. The intensity of the labor pains grew stronger with each passing hour. In the twelve years since my son had been born I had forgotten the pain that accompanied childbirth. Thank God for the midwife, Cora, and her daughter Imelda who had taken charge of the situation from the moment of their arrival yesterday around mid-morning. Their tiredness was evident in their faces and I felt guilty from keeping them from their own family and their beds; but not guilty enough to be thankful for their presence here in my own bedroom.

My husband Charlie had taken our son Cal to stay with kindly Mrs. Rosenberg, whose husband had died last summer. Mrs. Rosenberg is the neighborhood grandmother, you know the type - the lady who loves children and spoils them. Her own grandchildren live some distance away, Mrs. Rosenberg's son having married a Southern girl. So she chooses to spoil the neighborhood children when we parents aren't looking.

Charlie had spent most of yesterday at the haberdashery that he had built from scratch into a thriving business. When he finally arrived home it was well past ten o'clock and I had been in the throes of labor for over twelve hours. He had popped his head into the bedroom, took one look at Cora's face, and backed out. He must have slept the night in Cal's bedroom or possibly in his favorite chair in the living room.

I knew I needn't worry about Cal since he liked nothing better than a visit with his favorite neighbor; I'm sure the kind woman would no doubt make the boy's favorite treat, oatmeal cookies, before tucking him into her own son's bed for the night.

My little family slept peacefully while I clenched my teeth to keep from screaming as the labor pains rolled through me like a never-ending tidal wave. Cora and her daughter, themselves showing signs of being weary, took turns at making me comfortable, applying cool cloths to my forehead and the back of my neck. When the pain became almost unbearable I knew that my baby's entrance into the world was imminent.

My body trembled uncontrollably after the baby vacated my womb. I closed my eyes from sheer exhaustion; I had forgotten during the past dozen years since Cal's birth how difficult it was to bring a child into this world. It amazed me that I had the stamina to keep my head upright.

Imelda was extremely gentle as she sponged down my body and applied talcum powder to soothe me before changing the bed linens around me. Her mother took charge of my baby, severing the umbilical cord, slapping its rump to encourage a lusty cry, and finally sponging clean the tiny body before wrapping it in a clean, warm blanket. At long last the swaddled baby was placed into my arms and I gazed in wonder at the delicate features of my daughter.

Yes, a daughter with a slight furring of chestnut hair on her head (like her father), a pair of rosy cheeks, and a tiny mouth already set into a pout. Long lashes framed her closed eyes and her pink lips parted in a gentle sigh as she sensed the security of her momma's embrace.

From the moment I saw her I knew she would be beautiful. That was when I vowed that her life would be far better than mine: she would attend school, have fine manners, and one day be socially accepted by the women who now were clients to a lowly seamstress such as me. She would not be looked down at merely because her parents were immigrants and trades folk.

I placed a kiss on my daughter's forehead, inhaling deeply of her sweet baby smell. My thoughts drifted to memories of my own grandmother back in Ireland, who had been considered a beauty in her youth. With flashing blue eyes, rosy cheeks, and a pout quite like my daughter's, her beauty had been so remarkable that she'd had offers of marriage from no less than eight suitors, among them the son of a local laird. My daughter would share my grandmother's name, I decided.

"Welcome to our family, Cordelia," I whispered. "My beautiful daughter, someday you will become a lady of quality; you will be mistress of a grand house and wife to a wealthy man. I will dedicate my life to making that dream come true. That's my vow to you."

Kevin

Chapter 2

July 1890
Boston, Massachusetts

As a young lad growing up in Boston I would delight in hearing my father's stories. Most of those stories centered around the hard work and perseverance he and his own father experienced as they put together the family business. To hear my father tell it, he went straight from the nursery to the docks of Boston Harbor where my grandfather insisted that Augustus Newkirk learn the business from the bottom up. Father's time on those esteemed docks was rather short in retrospect as grandfather had deemed a minimum exposure to manual labor sufficient for the son who would one day run Newkirk Trading.

But father told other stories too. My favorites were the stories he told about our family's hunting lodge and of the wondrous adventures he and his friends and associates would have there. Father would recount for us the way the men would ride their horses when flushing out the pheasant and guinea fowl before turning their catch over to the chief gamesman. It fell to the gamesman to dress the fowl, see that the cook prepared the finest portions for their victory feast, and oversee the packing of the remainder for the return to the various Boston homes of the gentlemen.

Father's stories also filled my head with visions of stalwart men, having come in from their hunting conquests, sitting in overstuffed chairs before a cheery fireplace as they sipped brandy or cognac from crystal snifters. I envisioned aromatic clouds of smoke from cigars and pipes as the men discussed the events of the day and toasted each other's hunting prowess.

Mostly I imagined a world of men: the cook who was a retired non-commissioned military man; the gamesman and groomsman; the butler, several valets and other male attendants of the gentlemen who would certainly occupy the Spartan servants' quarters while the gentlemen themselves made use of the parlor and perhaps a billiard room. Here was a world without women: no maids, no housekeeper, no governess, and certainly no mother or sisters. This world of manly pursuits dangled beyond my grasp until the day of my twelfth birthday. It was on that auspicious day in July of 1890 that I was summoned to my father's study.

Dressed in my second best set of clothes and having been inspected by mother for cleanliness, I walked down the semi-dark corridor that led to father's private sanctum. With a heightened sense of anticipation I raised my hand and knocked gently upon the gleaming dark-oak double doors that defended Father's Study from intrusion.

"Enter." The directive was delivered by father's gruff voice, a voice accustomed to issuing commands.

My sweaty hand gave the highly-polished brass doorknob a half-twist, enough to unlatch the bolt and grant me access. I forced myself to cross the threshold and pulled the door shut behind me. There I stood, inside Father's Study, frozen to the spot.

"I assumed it was you, boy, but from the way you knocked at the door I feared it was one of your sisters. Put some authority behind that knock next time."

Father adjusted the wire-rimmed spectacles he wore for reading as he looked up at me. He was an imposing figure. A hefty man about forty-five years of age, with hazel eyes and gray-brown hair, even his mutton chops seemed to bristle. In his casual mode of dress, *sans* morning coat which hung on the back of his chair, father's bearing gave him an air of importance that even his perfectly starched and pressed dress-shirt sleeves complemented. These sleeves were folded over at the cuffs and currently displayed his hirsute forearms.

"Come closer, boy."

I placed one foot in front of the other, my chubby thighs rubbing against each other, as I crossed the Persian carpet that covered the center of a highly polished oak floor until I stood in front of father's desk, itself an immovable object which seemed to me almost as large as our formal dining table. During that short passage over the rich-toned carpet I noted the emerald green drapes that hung at the tall windows and two deep, leather chairs that flanked father's desk. Floor-to-ceiling bookshelves filled with various classic tomes as well as maps showing trade routes covered two of the room's walls. At the far end of the room, behind father's desk, was a large gray and black marble fireplace – devoid now of any flames during the heat of this summer's day. I fastened my gaze on a large globe mounted in a copper form that stood to one side of father's desk as I awaited further instruction, running a hand nervously through my hair only to recall that it had been recently cut into a more masculine, short, style.

"Sit down boy, make yourself comfortable. Men don't wait for directions; they give them. Remember that."

I slid into the chair nearest me as father removed his spectacles and carefully set them atop the papers he had been perusing.

"Happy birthday, Kevin." Father smiled at me through his immense mustache.

"Thank you, sir," I replied, sitting up taller in my seat.

"How old are you today, son?"

"Twelve, sir."

"Twelve years old," father sighed, a faraway look momentarily capturing his face. "And what do you make of your sisters?"

"Well, they're girls, sir."

"Yes, they certainly are," father chuckled, a smile forming on his mustachioed lips. "I'm sure you're tired of playing their little girl games, aren't you?"

I vigorously nodded my assent.

"That's about to change, my boy."

"It is?" I could feel a kernel of excitement deep in my chest; as father spoke that excitement grew.

"It's time for you to join the ranks of the men in the family. When I was your age I had already spent two summers working at the dockyard loading and unloading ships. You've been around women and girls long enough. It's time for your first real adventure."

My heart began racing with anticipation when I heard the word 'adventure'. I found myself leaning forward at the edge of my seat. Father stood and came around to the front of his desk. He sat in the chair beside mine and leaned in to me. I inhaled the scent of tobacco that clung to his shirt.

"Now, listen carefully and think about your answer to my question. Kevin, do you feel you can competently ride a horse without assistance? Keep in mind you've only been riding on supervised trails at the riding academy."

"Yes, sir, I'm sure I can ride without assistance. Would you care to watch my next lesson?" I puffed my chest out with pride at the thought that father was interested in my riding.

"I plan to do just that. Now tell me, if you can, what event takes place in this family every September?" He leaned back into the chair's depths, silently daring me to answer incorrectly.

"Your trip to Woodhaven, sir."

"Exactly! This year you will accompany me, Kevin. It's time you learned how to put the meat on the table; to bag the bird, so to speak."

"Really, father? You mean I can ride out with you and the other gentlemen?" My pulse was racing with anxiety and joy.

"Yes, Kevin, it's time for your first visit to The Lodge. I've looked forward to this day for a very long time. Now come and give your father a hug."

"Will we be hunting game?"

"Yes, yes. Most likely pheasant and some other small animals."

"Will there be turkey?"

"Certainly." Father smiled at me.

I dove into his open arms and accepted his bear-like embrace before he gently pulled back and extended his hand towards me.

"Now, we'll shake hands on it. Henceforth, we'll leave those hugs for your mother and sisters."

I placed my hand in his and shook it.

"Keep your hand firm, son. Real men shake hands and that is just like giving your word. It's a sign of honor."

"Yes, sir, I won't forget."

It was all I could do to contain my excitement. After father's dismissal, I did my best to calmly leave his study and close the double door behind me. When I was certain that I was alone in the corridor I let out a loud "whoop" and ran off to share my news with my sisters, Bernice and Sallie.

True to his word, father accompanied me to my very next lesson at the equestrian academy. I dutifully mounted the horse and put the aging mare through her paces. It was a routine that both I and the horse were very familiar with. At the conclusion of the session I walked the horse to where my father and the instructor stood, dismounted, and gave a tip of my cap in their direction.

"Well done, Master Newkirk. Now be sure to brush down Aggie after you've removed the saddle," directed my instructor.

"Poppycock! Don't you have a hired hand to care for the horses?" My father glowered at the instructor who seemed taken aback by the question.

"Why of course, Mister Newkirk. We have two helpers to assist in the stables. But we insist that all of our students learn the proper care involved with keeping such a fine animal." A red flush suffused the man's neck and crept into his cheeks as he replied.

"Now listen here, Norris. I pay your establishment a pretty penny to instruct my son. So far all I've seen is a young man who's been taught to ride an aging and docile nag; a young man who may as well be riding side-saddle like his sisters. Pah! Bring out your most spirited steed and allow the lad to ride him – that is, if you even have such an animal in your stable," father challenged my instructor.

Mr. Norris stepped towards me and jerked the reins from my gloved hands. With a frustrated "Hmph" he himself led Aggie towards the stable. Father placed a firm hand on my shoulder as I moved to stand beside him. Together we waited in companionable silence for Mr. Norris to return.

After several moments, the instructor reappeared leading a beautiful chestnut filly who literally pranced at the end of the leads. A bit of trepidation came over me as horse and instructor approached us. As I turned to father, I was sure my unvoiced concern was evident in my facial expression.

"Nothing to fear, son. Remember, you are master of the horse. You give the commands and the horse will follow."

Father patted my shoulder as I prepared to mount the filly. Mustering all of my waning confidence, I led this spirited horse through the paces of the obstacle course. I drew up before my father and Mr. Norris, keeping a firm grip on the reins.

"Well done, Kevin. Now run the course again, only quicker and with more spirit."

The confidence in father's voice gave me the impetus I needed. I wheeled the horse about and ran the course not once but twice more, giving the filly liberty to pick up speed while I communicated my commands through my hold on the reins. As I guided her back to the stables I heard father's words of pride.

"By Jove, yes! That's the way the son of Augustus Newkirk should ride his horse!"

August 1890

One month later I was again summoned to Father's Study. This time my stride was confident as I moved along the corridor. My knock upon those double doors was self-assured as it announced my immediate entry. Without invitation I approached his desk and seated myself in the same chair that only weeks ago had held an insecure boy.

"You wished to see me?"

I observed father as he set his signature to a set of papers before replacing the pen in the inkwell and using a blotter to take up any excess ink from the signed vellum. Another knock at the door prompted my father to respond.

"Enter."

The double doors once again opened to admit a young man who appeared to be slightly older than I. While his attire was not as fashionable as my own, he was clean and neatly dressed. He stood near the door, hands clasped behind his back, his gaze directed at a spot on the wall above father's head.

"Step forward, lad." Father motioned for him to approach the desk. The young man complied, stopping short of father's desk. "Kevin, this is Paul," father intoned by way of introduction.

"It's a pleasure to meet you, Paul."

I thrust out my hand in friendship, ready to prove how firm my grip could be. Paul in turn appeared flustered at my outstretched hand and immediately aimed a formal bow in my direction.

"It will be my pleasure to serve you, Mister Newkirk."

The young man stood upright once again and I noticed a distinct twinkle lurking in his extremely blue eyes. Only when he brought his hands to rest at his sides did I notice the white gloves that encased them.

"Henceforth, Kevin, you are no longer under the care of Nanny Summers," father informed me. "Paul will serve as your valet, your personal manservant, in the same way that Winsted sees to my needs. In fact, Paul is Winsted's grandson, isn't that correct Paul?"

"Correct, Mister Newkirk, sir."

"Paul has been in training for the past four years and has exceeded my expectations in one so young. I've agreed to give him a try in this position of accountability. If at any time you find his service inferior or his presence unsuitable, you are to inform me immediately. Is that clear?"

"Yes, father." I acknowledged this mantel of responsibility that was suddenly placed upon my youthful shoulders. *"Good heavens!" I thought, "I was now in charge of another person."*

"Very well. I suggest you both go elsewhere and let me return to the tasks here that await my attention." So saying, father once again took up another set of papers and began to peruse them.

Paul and I turned to each other at this obvious dismissal; however, it was Paul who gave me a cue as to how to proceed.

"Perhaps, Mister Newkirk, we should return to your chamber where can further discuss my duties."

Paul signaled me with his eyes that we should exit Father's Study. I rose and led the way although Paul reached the door first and smoothly opened it mere seconds before I could reach for the doorknob.

Paul and I got on famously of course. We adjourned to my room where I learned that all of the men in his family engaged in a life of service to families similar to ours. As a young boy Paul had learned the rudiments of service by listening to conversations between his father and his uncle. His own skills were honed by serving his father when he could. Shortly after his own twelfth birthday Paul entered into training with his uncle who served a well-placed family in Cambridge. Now that he had celebrated his sixteenth birthday he considered himself quite lucky to be appointed to the position of valet to the young Mister Newkirk, that being me of course. We sat on the window seat in my room as Paul divulged this information; just two boys who were about to embark upon a life-changing journey.

"I wish you would just address me as Kevin. I don't feel like 'Mister Newkirk'." I grinned at the fellow, trying to blur the lines of distinction between master and servant.

"I couldn't do that! It's not proper," protested Paul. He sat back and thought for a moment before a smile lit up his face. "When we are behind the closed doors of your chamber I would be honored to call you Mister Kevin but in front of others you must be addressed as Mister Newkirk."

"Wonderful! I agree that you may call me Mister Kevin in private but I wish to be addressed as Young Mister Newkirk among company, in deference to my father."

"A brilliant compromise, Mister Kevin," he acquiesced with such an unyielding expression that we both broke into gales of laughter and became friends on the spot.

The weeks leading up to the annual hunting excursion were filled with a flurry of activity. There were, of course, the usual preparations made whenever father traveled; however, this time I was to travel as well and the idea nearly sent mother into a tizzy, especially since father had taken the liberty of ordering an entire new wardrobe of clothes for me that were to be fitted to my exact, if changeable, measurements. The tailor assured my father that he would take into account any future growth on my part when he was crafting my garments – garments that would more appropriately reflect my status as the son and heir apparent of Augustus Newkirk, head of the Newkirk Trading Company.

In addition to new undergarments, shirts, pants, and jackets I was fitted for a new set of riding clothes. New riding boots and a crop were also ordered. Our butler was kept busy directing the delivery of all these things to the service entrance of our Revere Street house. No sooner had the boxes been delivered than Paul opened them and inspected every item in an effort to uncover even a minute sign of inferior workmanship; when he was satisfied that father's money had been well spent and that all was in perfect order he then saw to the preparation and packing of my things. I was awfully glad to have Paul on hand because I didn't have the faintest idea of how to pack or what I might need while at the family lodge.

Winsted accomplished the task of packing for father with what appeared to be a minimum of effort, having had years to learn exactly what would be required for such an outing. In fact, his task was easier because many of my father's belongings, used specifically for these outings, remained at the hunting lodge from year to year. Therefore, Winsted had ample time to supervise Paul's preparations on my behalf.

Late September 1890

Our travel day, the last Friday in September, arrived. I had so anticipated this day that the previous night found me sleeping fitfully. When a slightly groggy Paul knocked at my door to awaken me it seemed that my head had just hit the pillow and that my eyes had closed only moments before.

"What time is it?" I asked, rubbing the sleep from my eyes.

"Three-thirty," answered Paul as he brushed my jacket.

"In the morning?"

"Yes, in the morning."

I murmured back something unintelligible as I dressed.

"You're to meet Mister Newkirk in the dining room for breakfast. He's already there so you'd best hurry."

I flew through my morning routine with Paul's assistance and a scant three minutes later was on my way downstairs, leaving Paul to deal with the residue of my hurried ablutions.

Cook had prepared a hearty breakfast indeed and father urged me to eat my fill of the numerous dishes that were set before us. While we were thus engaged our bags were being loaded into our coach along with baskets of food for our lunch en route. I was surprised when Mother came downstairs, still in her dressing robe, to bid us bon voyage. Father obligingly kissed Mother's cheek before turning to me.

"Don't dally, son. A quick good-bye will suffice." With that he moved down the path and towards our waiting coach.

"Kevin," Mother began.

"I'll be fine Mother." I reassured her although I did suffer her having to hug me and kiss my forehead.

"Mind your father. Be careful around the horses. If you need something make sure you ask for it." Mother's directives were meant as gentle reminders but to a twelve-year old boy they seemed like admonishments.

"I'll be fine, Mother. I promise."

I squirmed my way out of her arms and hurried out the door after father, who had already boarded the coach. Once I too had boarded, Paul and his grandfather took their places on the seat opposite us. I turned to look back at the house and saw that Mother still stood in the doorway, one hand at her throat, the other in a hesitant wave. It was my sister Sallie who later informed me that once the coach had departed Mother had broken down in tears to see her 'little boy' become a young man.

The coachman's loud whistle and snap of his whip urged the horses forward; we were on our way just as daylight flushed the eastern horizon. In short order we covered the distance from Revere Street to South Street Station. While our baggage was transferred to a special train car that father had reserved for this excursion we took some time to greet father's guests: my Uncle George (my mother's brother), Mr. Woodward (my father's business partner) and his son Robert (a tall, lanky fellow with a pinched expression who was seventeen years of age), and Mr. Hugh Watkins (Mr. Woodward's son-in-law). Each of our guests had their own valet or manservant in attendance as well.

Once everyone had boarded, the servants congregated on wooden benches in the rear of the train car while the gentlemen and I reclined on thickly padded seats. There were drapes at the window but they were held back by some sort of metal piece to keep them from flapping to and fro. I settled myself a short distance from father who was deep in conversation with the other gentlemen. Deeming Robert Woodward to be the closest to my age I took it upon myself to engage him in conversation.

"I'm excited about being included in this year's outing, Robert. Is this your first time traveling to Woodhaven?"

"No."

Robert pointedly continued to look out of the window at the goings on in the train yard. A loud blast of the train whistle announced our imminent departure from the station so I waited a few moments more until the train began to move before attempting conversation once again.

"I wonder how long it will take to arrive at the New Haven station. Care to venture a guess, Robert?"

Robert turned to me and with what equated to an almost sneer replied, "Barring any mechanical malfunction I believe we should be in New Haven late this afternoon. Now be a good lad and find another way to amuse yourself." He then shifted in his seat so that he could eavesdrop on the conversation between our two fathers who sat directly behind us.

Having no desire to force a conversation with such a rude boor I gave my attention to the passing venues directly outside the window. The railway tracks cut through the center of Boston as they made their way to the city limits. Soon we were traveling through the less densely populated areas of Grove Hall and Dorchester as we made our way southward. As the train picked up speed its movements had a slight rolling effect which soon made me drowsy. Whether due to the early hour of rising or to the lack of sleep from excitement I struggled to keep my eyelids from drooping. Everything about this trip filled me with excitement. I didn't want to miss a moment of it. I struggled to keep my eyes open and even deluded myself into believing that I was able to conquer my sleepiness. You can imagine my surprise when I felt a hand on my shoulder gently nudging me awake from my obvious nap.

"Young Mister Newkirk, excuse me. Your lunch is ready, sir."

I rubbed the sleep from my eyes as I corrected my slouched posture; I stifled a yawn and opened my eyes to see Paul standing directly in front of me, one gloved hand on my shoulder, the other balancing a tray of food.

"Your lunch tray, sir," he repeated. "Would you care for a cup of coffee?"

I accepted the proffered tray which held an assortment of cold meats, sliced bread, a generous serving of roasted potatoes, and various condiments. A starched linen napkin, along with flatware, was properly set upon the tray as well. There was a moment of clumsiness as I tried to balance the tray on my knees but a covert glance in Robert's direction showed me the correct method to use and immediately the tray settled securely on my lap.

"I would prefer a cold glass of milk, please."

At my utterance of those words heads momentarily turned in my direction but it was Robert's remark, inferring that my request was more in keeping with that of a young child, which pressed me to amend my original request.

"On second thought I would enjoy a cup of coffee."

Now what was I to do? I abhorred coffee's bitter taste!

Upon his return, Paul removed my used tray and handed me a mug of the imported coffee that put the coins in the Newkirk Trading coffers. In a voice loud enough to be heard by Robert, Paul addressed me.

"I've prepared your coffee to your exact specifications, Young Mister Newkirk. I believe you'll enjoy the blend."

Paul's eyes held that mischievous glint I had come to know during the past few weeks. I took a hesitant sip. That was all it took to convince me that with enough cream and added sugar I could easily consume the entire contents of the cup. Paul had quietly catered to my needs without drawing undue attention to either of us.

Arrival at
Woodhaven, Connecticut

It was almost four o'clock when the train slowly drew to a halt at the Union Avenue Station in New Haven. We were met by two coaches and an open wagon that bore the crest of the Newkirk family. All of the gentlemen, myself included, settled quite comfortably in the larger of the coaches. The servants boarded the second coach which sped off before its passengers could be fully seated, the idea being that the gentlemen's valets would be in attendance when we arrived at the lodge. The driver of the open wagon, accompanied by a stable boy and a gardener, would collect our baggage, secure it, and deliver it to the lodge.

Thanks to Robert, who managed to insert himself between me and father, I found myself sitting next to the coach's window. This suited me splendidly as it afforded me an unobstructed view. As the coachman navigated through the streets of New Haven, I paid close attention to the tightly packed city. As we progressed westward we passed portions of the Yale campus where students scurried to and fro between buildings on their way to class or back to their dorms. Eventually we passed a road known simply as The Boulevard; this it seems was where the city proper ended and the countryside began. A turn onto Forrest Road led us to Amity Road. The coachman kept the horses at a steady pace on this westward leading route and we soon crossed the town line into Woodhaven.

The Village of Woodhaven was an extremely rural area at that time. It was, and still is, nestled between New Haven on the east, Derby on the west, Ansonia to its north, and Milford to its south. The village itself was merely a tiny cluster of buildings although many farms dotted the countryside around the village proper; some of the farms that we passed seemed to be quite busy as the workers brought in their harvest of the day. Several of the farms were dairy farms and I watched with interest as the cows were being herded into the barns as evening approached.

Throughout the journey father and Mr. Woodward discussed the business of their trading company. Robert, who as I mentioned earlier, managed to sit beside father, gave his undivided attention to their dialogue and seemed to mentally file away everything that he heard. Hugh, Mr. Woodward's son-in-law, sat back in his seat. His tweed cap was pulled down over his eyes and it was difficult to tell if he was napping or merely giving the impression of doing so. Like me, Uncle George's attention was given to the passing countryside. After what seemed like an interminably long period of time, he tugged the chain of his pocket watch and clicked open the timepiece, checked the time, and fit the piece back into his watch pocket.

"Not much further to go. Just the other side of this hill and we'll be there." His comments weren't directed at anyone in particular, merely a general observation.

"Truly, Uncle George? I can hardly wait."

My excitement at seeing the lodge, that legendary place of father's stories, was renewed. I stuck my head as close to the coach's small window as possible in an attempt to see further ahead. A moment or two later the coachman guided the horses into a turn that took us onto a well-worn dirt road, over a small wooden bridge that spanned a brook, and onward up an incline.

"Kevin, take particular note of where we are," instructed father, "everything from this point forward belongs to the Newkirk family."

I moved to the edge of the seat in my excitement. Somehow, the knowledge that we were on our own property made quite an impression on me. My head swiveled left and right as I tried to take in everything around me. Across from me Uncle George smiled and chuckled quietly.

"You'll make yourself dizzy with all that back and forth looking about, Kevin."

"But Uncle George, it's all so exciting!"

"I suppose it is," he sighed. "It's been a long day and I, for one, am looking forward to a hot meal, a glass of your father's excellent brandy, and a good night's sleep."

"Me too, Uncle George," I quickly agreed.

"I think perhaps you're a bit young yet for the brandy," chuckled Uncle George.

A quarter hour later we stepped onto the graveled drive before a rustic house surrounded by a veritable forest. The trees were so large that in comparison the house brought to mind those elfin houses I had heard of in fairy tales, although in truth the dwelling was two-storied and fairly large. I counted at least three chimneys. The deep shadows blocked out much of the remaining daylight and I noted that the outdoor lanterns at the front of the house had already been lit. I dallied a bit on the gravel drive as the others made their way indoors watching as the rays of the setting sun touched the leaves of the yellow oaks and maple trees in a final burst of light for this day.

Like a child entering a magical palace, I gazed at the wonders that greeted me once I crossed the threshold. The greater part of the first floor was given over to one huge room partitioned into separate areas by a circular fieldstone fireplace that stood dead-center and whose chimney rose high up and disappeared into the ceiling. Thick wood paneling covered the walls of this great room; the gleaming hardwood flooring created a feeling of warmth and welcome as did the fire burning behind the grate. Three heavy rugs of varied patterns, showing wear and frayed spots, delineated separate areas of this main room. These rugs had once graced our Boston residence; they now were relegated to spending the remainder of their useful lives as floor coverings in a gentlemen's hunting lodge.

Several sofas and overstuffed chairs, themselves showing signs of wear, seemed to have been garnered from attics and storage rooms. In the dim interior light their various fabric patterns gave the room an eclectic appeal. An antique sideboard displayed an assortment of mismatched crystal decanters as well as glasses and snifters in a variety of sizes and styles.

The far side of the room was home to a large rectangular table that was surrounded by eight cane-backed chairs, all gleaming from a recent polishing. The table itself was set for our supper with an odd collection of mismatched china pieces and flatware. Centered on this table were two large oil lamps that were currently giving up sooty trails from their flickering wicks.

A plethora of enticing aromas emanated from an unseen kitchen, making me realize that I was beyond hungry. I was, indeed, ravenous. Before we could enjoy our supper, however, there was a protocol to be followed.

We were met at the front entry by our servants who, in the case of the older gentlemen, took their hats, gloves, and coats. Paul graciously accepted my hat and overcoat into his gloved hands before escorting me up a flight of stairs and into the bedchamber designated for my use. Up ahead I could see father pause while Winsted opened the door of the largest bedchamber. Waiting until I was abreast of him, father caught my arm and addressed me.

"You'll have the room next to mine, Kevin. Nothing fancy, of course, but I'm sure you'll find it adequate. See you at supper."

With a merry wink of his eye, he disappeared into the room where

Winsted waited; the door closed behind him with a mere whisper. A few feet ahead, Paul was already waiting for me inside the next room, standing at attention until I entered before closing the door behind me.

"I've taken the liberty of setting up a pitcher and basin for you, Mister Kevin. You'll find a clean towel beside them. I'm sure you're anxious to refresh yourself after your journey." He motioned towards a small table at the far end of the room.

I removed my jacket, handed it to Paul, and immediately made use of the aforementioned items as Paul brushed my jacket before hanging it in the cupboard. The tepid water felt wonderful as I splashed it upon my face but I was quickly dismayed to find that I had inadvertently allowed some water to drip upon my shirt front.

"Not to worry, Mister Kevin. At my grandfather's suggestion I separately packed a clean shirt for you to wear this evening. It is a custom that your father has often employed and I thought perhaps you would like to do the same."

He pointed to the bed where he had already laid out the clean garment. I noted that it wasn't one of my best but one that had been in use for a while and therefore was bound to be comfortable. I gratefully shed my rumpled and damp shirt and donned the clean one, expressing my thanks to Paul as I did so.

"This is really very thoughtful but I'm afraid my jacket will only make me warm again."

"Not to worry, Mister Kevin. You won't be in need of your jacket again this evening. I'm told that things are quite informal here and it is quite acceptable to appear for supper in just your shirt and trousers."

"Really?" I could barely contain my joy that suck a lack of formality at supper time was acceptable.

"I'm positive, sir. My grandfather assures me that informality among the gents is quite the norm on these outings."

"Whatever would mother say about this?" I wondered aloud.

"It may be that she isn't aware of it, sir."

"Well, if father hasn't felt the need to inform mother of this breach of etiquette, I certainly shan't be the one to tell." I felt like a co-conspirator of sorts at that moment.

Using the brush and comb that Paul had set out for me, I slicked back my reddish-brown hair and inspected my reflection in the pier glass. Deeming myself ready I turned back at the door.

"Have you eaten, then? I should hope so," I inquired.

Based upon the involuntary noises coming from my stomach I could only imagine how hungry Paul must be.

"I recommend the meat pie but I would pass on the dinner rolls. If one were to fall upon your foot you might be relegated to sitting indoors for the rest of the week." Paul was hard-pressed to contain his smile but a wayward wink was forthcoming.

"Perhaps I'll pass the rolls to Robert."

The thought amused me as I stepped out into the hallway, there to meet my father who was emerging from the neighboring room. He gave my attire a cursory nod of his head; I was relieved to see that he too was without jacket. Together we proceeded down the stairs where our guests awaited us in the common room. Within moments supper was announced and we gathered at the table.

"I see you still haven't installed gas lights, Gus," commented my Uncle George as he cut into the steaming meat pie on his plate.

"Absolutely no need for it yet," commented father as he speared a chunk of meat from his own pie.

"I should think it would be very costly, sir," observed Robert as he helped himself to a dinner roll from the breadbasket I passed to him.

"Poppycock, young man! I'm waiting for those electricity wires to be strung up. No sense putting in gas lights when electricity will be the wave of the future. In fact I've already inquired about having electric lamps installed out here before our next annual outing. Cost is no object where comfort is the main goal. Remember that, young man."

I observed the others as I consumed my own meat pie, thinking that the entire dish was a bit on the heavy side: the potatoes were undercooked while the crust simply lay atop the pie's other ingredients and had the distinct taste of lard. Under other circumstances I would have eaten my fill of the dinner rolls but I wisely heeded Paul's warning. I noticed that father also avoided the rolls and kept offering them to our guests who felt obligated to take and eat them.

"I rather like the ambiance of the oil lamps," father commented, "makes the food taste better." He mumbled that last bit so that only those of us at table heard and chuckled.

When our hunger was assuaged we retired to the other side of the fireplace. I sat beside my uncle on one of the sofas and watched the shadows cast by the flames of the hearth as they danced along the wide-planked paneled walls. A footman handed round cigars and brandy to the gentlemen. It was a pleasant feeling, sitting there and watching as the gentlemen talked amongst themselves.

"What do you make of this adventure so far, nephew?" Uncle George sipped at his brandy after declining a cigar.

"It's just grand, Uncle George. I'm really looking forward to the hunt tomorrow." I hoped that my response sounded worldly.

I settled back against the worn sofa cushions as I awaited my uncle's reply. My full belly and the warmth from the hearth were conspiring to lull me to sleep, but I fought to keep my eyes from closing. I didn't want to miss even a moment of this trip.

"Appears to me that you should get some sleep, Kevin. You'll need to be up very early again tomorrow morning."

"I'll be ready, Uncle George. You'll see. Why, I'll be waiting on my horse before everyone else has breakfasted."

We turned our attention to the others who had undertaken a debate on politics. With the men's companionable voices swirling around me I turned my attention to the flames crackling merrily on the hearth. That was the last thing I remembered.

———

My eyelids slowly fluttered open and I found myself disoriented in the blackness that surrounded me. As my eyes adjusted to the lack of light, I realized that I was in bed with the bedclothes pulled over my shoulder.

I had no recollection of how I had arrived there; my last memory was of watching the merrily dancing hearth flames in the common room. My recollections were interrupted by a quiet knock, a gentle tap really, before Paul opened the bedroom door and stepped in.

I feigned sleep, watching covertly through the shadows as he went about his duties. Setting a small oil lamp on the dressing table, he proceeded to withdraw from the clothes cupboard my riding attire and hung the garments on the gentleman's valet stand, placing my riding boots and crop at the base. Since the lodge had no indoor lavatory, Paul placed a clean slop bucket next to the wash table; little did he know that I had never used a slop bucket and had no intention of using one that morning. I would rather face the use of an outhouse than have another person responsible for removing my waste.

Paul next moved to the small fireplace where he stirred the ashes with the hope of finding a live ember or two. Seeing Paul so engrossed in his work gave me an idea. Quietly creeping out from beneath the bedcovers, I stealthily moved across the carpet until I stood a handsbreath behind him.

"Would you like help with that?"

My voice was slightly above a whisper but had the desired effect nonetheless. I laughed to see Paul jump at the sound of my voice.

"Egads, Kevin, you've startle me!"

"I have, haven't I?" The look of consternation on his face initiated another round of laughter on my part.

"You really shouldn't creep up on a fellow like that." He brushed his hands against his trousers without thinking, leaving ashy fingerprints on the dark fabric. "You really gave me a fright."

"I'm sorry. But the timing was perfect." I couldn't contain the smile that lingered on my face.

"Yes, I'm sure it was," Paul smiled in agreement once he had regained his composure.

With Paul's assistance I accomplished the morning routine in record time and donned my new riding garments. Once all was in place I stepped back to glance at my reflection in the pier glass and was quite impressed with what I saw. The tailored cut of the jacket made me appear taller; the boots as well added at least an inch to my height. I tucked the crop under my arm. In my mind I cut quite the dashing figure in spite of the fact that I was merely twelve years of age. Paul double-checked my appearance then gave a nod of satisfaction.

"Enjoy your day, sir."

"I plan to. And how will you occupy your day, Paul?"

"There will be plenty to do, I warrant. Since there are no maids to make up the rooms, that duty falls to the valets. I've been told that we will also assist at table this evening as well. Of course there are our usual duties. Now that I think of all that needs to be accomplished today, I wholeheartedly recommend you begin your adventures at once."

Paul shepherded me closer to the door and held open the portal for me as I stepped into the upper hallway.

"I'm off then," I remarked as I turned back to Paul. "You called me Kevin, you know." I favored him with my best smirk as I jauntily moved towards the staircase.

My excitement swelled during the morning meal. I fidgeted so much at table that father summarily dismissed me and bade me wait outside for the arrival of our mounts. My boots made a loud crunching sound as I paced the gravel drive, keeping my eyes locked on the direction of the stables. The swelling thunder of hooves announced the arrival of the Head Groomsman who directed the horses by their leads. They came to a halt a mere two feet from where I stood, scattering the gravel as they did so.

"You must be Master Kevin. I'm Huckleby," the rider said by way of introduction. A worn felt hat perched on his head while his dull brown riding attire gave evidence that it had seen better days; his boots were spotted with mud. His appraising look made me feel a bit uncomfortable. "Nice riding habit you have."

Before I could respond, a commotion behind me drew my attention to the lodge's front door. My father and the others spilled onto the gravel drive, each brandishing a rifle. I immediately ran towards father with a look of dire apprehension that must have been visible to all.

"Father, what's happened?"

"Why, I don't have a clue son." He looked beyond me to the drive where the horses calmly awaited their riders. "Is there a problem with the horses?"

"The horses are fine, father," I hastened to reassure him. "But are we off in search of thieves instead of game?"

"Thieves? Here? Why do you ask? Have you noticed something awry?" A look of concern settled on father's face.

"The rifles." I pointed to the firearm that was tucked into the crook of his elbow.

"Oh! Ho, ho! So that's it!" Father's laugh was strong and hearty.

"Why are you and the other carrying rifles? Are we in some kind of danger?"

Father hefted the rifle with one hand.

"These are for taking down our prey during the hunt. How did you think we bagged our catch?"

"You mean you kill the creatures?" I could feel myself growing pale.

"Of course, son. You see," he drew me aside as he explained, "two of the stable lads ride ahead of us and flush out the game. Then the rest of us take aim, shoot, and bring down the birds." He placed emphasis on that last phrase. "How do you think the meat you eat ends up on your plate?"

"I…I don't know. It's just there, is all." My response was stammered; I felt queasy as a knot of revulsion tightened around my gut.

"This might be more than you're prepared to handle. Hmm, perhaps you'd rather go fishing in the lake. Huckleby could go along with you. By the time we return, cook will have dressed your catch and prepared us a fine seafood supper." Father seemed content with that idea.

"Noooooo!" I wailed. "I don't want anything to die!"

I screwed up my face to stem the tide of unwanted tears from spilling down my cheeks.

"Hush boy!" I could see that father was visibly irritated with me but I couldn't help myself. "I can't believe my own son would act this way. Hrmph!" The last was uttered *sotto voce*.

"Please father, don't kill any of the animals or fish. Please!"

I lost control of the tears at that point not caring a whit that the other gentlemen had turned their attention towards me. It was easy to see that my crying embarrassed father.

"Kevin, I insist that you remain at the lodge. Find Winsted, he'll give you something to calm your stomach. Now go along, boy." This obvious cover story was spoken in a loud voice as father guided me back towards the front door.

I slowly trudged past the cluster of gentlemen, ignoring the look of superiority on Robert's face and taking solace in Uncle George's concerned expression.

"What's wrong with the boy?" questioned the elder Mr. Woodward.

"Too much excitement, I'm afraid," replied father. "Made his stomach turn sour; I've instructed him to rest for today."

"It's for the best," agreed Mr. Woodward.

"Sorry old chap," Robert called after me. "I'll be sure to shoot a couple of guinea fowl for you." His words led me to believe that he'd heard me pleading with father and that only made me feel more miserable.

From the front steps I watched the others mount their steeds and ride off, whooping and laughing as they followed father's lead. Huckleby, still seated on his own mount, held the reins of the horse I was to have ridden.

"Shame to spend such a beautiful day indoors. I venture Bartley here could use some exercise before I take him back to the stable." Huckleby shifted his weight on the saddle as he spoke. "I've been told that you're quite a good horseman."

I considered Huckleby's offer but shook my head before replying in a voice that sounded forlorn, even to me.

"Father told me to find Winsted."

"Them gentlemen will be clear over the hillock by now. You can meet up with old Winsted a bit later. Reckon he's got enough to keep him busy for the morning."

I cautiously approached the sturdy brown steed named Bartley. Extending my hand towards the horse's nose, I looked him in the eye as I steadily drew near. Bartley lowered his head and allowed me to rub his nose. We were going to be friends! Placing my foot into the stirrup, I pushed off and settled myself onto the saddle, speaking gently to the horse while I did so. I reached over and accepted the reins from Huckleby, who was smiling.

"Got a way with horses, don't you, son? Firm but gentle. That what makes them comfortable."

"Which direction shall we ride in?" I could feel my excitement making a rebound.

"Let's just see where the horses want to go, shall we?"

We set out at a gentle walk until we came to the end of the gravel drive; once the horses' hooves touched ground we urged them into a canter that took us past the stable and the paddock. We followed the uneven contours of the land, coming upon a meadow that was bordered along one side by a stream that bubbled over outcroppings of rocks. Although it was well beyond daybreak the warmth of the autumn sun was dispersed amidst the dense trees that bordered the meadow on its three remaining sides. I followed Huckleby's lead as he reined in his horse and dismounted.

"Lots of sweet grass in this meadow. The horses are quite fond of the alfalfa. It's okay to turn Bartley loose," Huckleby informed me.

I did as Huckleby instructed and watched as Bartley and his equine companion lowered their heads in search of tasty morsels.

"Doesn't the sun reach the meadow?" I asked, noting the tallness of the surrounding trees.

"Not till a bit later." Huckleby stopped for a moment, looked around, and sniffed the air. "Come along, lad. Let's enjoy the quiet."

Together we set off on foot across the meadow in the direction of the stream. It was a further distance away than I had estimated and I quickly grew warm from pushing through the calf-high meadow grasses. At last we reached a point where a large rock pile jutted out into the stream.

"Here we are; the prettiest spot on this property." He motioned to a place atop the pile of rocks. "Sit here. Now turn towards the east. That's right."

I followed his direction, settling my rump atop a flat-ish rock and looking eastward. My curiosity was piqued.

"What are we waiting for?"

"Another moment or two," Huckleby muttered, "wait for it."

I waited and watched. Suddenly the topmost leaves, those that had already begun to turn to gold and yellow, appeared to be lit from within as the sun rose higher and finally surfaced above the treetops. A stray cloud diffused the sun's rays making them appear like ribbons of light connected directly to the heavens. I was awestruck!

"Beautiful, ain't it? A real gift from God."

"Is it like this every morning?" The brilliance of the sun caused me to squint.

"Pretty much. But it's really special this time of year."

"Is this why father likes to come here every autumn?"

Huckleby removed the old hat from his head and tucked it into the side of his boot.

"Why your pa and the other gents come here is not for me to guess. Mostly I think they come here to get away from the women-folk, and to act like young bucks again."

I took some time to really look at Huckleby, noticing fine lines at the corners of his eyes most likely caused by squinting into the sun. Straw-colored hair that had hints of a once tawny color blew in disarray as a morning breeze moved across the meadow. We sat in companionable silence, listening to the gurgle of the water as it rushed to some far-off mysterious destination. At last Huckleby cleared his throat.

"Why did your pa cut you from the hunt so suddenly?"

I kept my head down, pretending to study a bug that was crawling along an adjoining rock.

"Quiet sort, ain't ya? That's alright. Old Huckleby will be here when you want to talk. Look at me boy."

I turned my head up and looked deeply into his pale blue eyes.

"Whatever we say between us," he pointed a finger first at himself then at me and again back at himself, "goes no further. Understand?"

I nodded to show him I understood.

"What you tell me stays here," he pointed again, this time to his heart.

"And what you tell me stays here, Mr. Huckleby." I pointed to my own heart and offered him a tentative smile. He grinned back and the wrinkles at his eyes deepened.

"Looks like we're going to be good friends, Master Kevin."

We spent the remainder of that morning exploring the delights of nature to be found on the property. Huckleby admonished me to take stock of what I saw since the estate would, no doubt, one day belong to me.

From our perch atop our horses he pointed out a small fresh water lake nestled in the northwest corner of the property where fish were always plentiful. Moving on, we guided the horses through dense stands of tall trees. Huckleby showed me how to tell an oak tree from an ash tree. As we moved on we passed small groups of deer that would dash away at the first sign of our horses.

"Most likely skittish 'cause they know the hunting party is out and about," explained Huckleby.

We rode for another hour or two and I was in awe at the vastness of our property. I rather fancied it as a small kingdom where I, a prince, was now surveying what I would one day inherit. While my daydreams kept my thoughts occupied, Huckleby (whom I had relegated to a page in my fantasy) had guided us to the crest of a small hill. Mentally surfacing from my daydreams I could see at the hill's base the long building housing the stable. The horses as well sensed the end of our morning journey and sure-footedly navigated the downward slope of the hill with very little guidance. As we approached, one of the stable boys who appeared only slightly older than myself, ran towards us. He came to a stop just in front of us.

"I'll take the horses, Mr. Huckleby."

"No need for that, boy. We'll bring them in ourselves. You can go back to your chores," Huckleby instructed.

"Yes, sir." The boy nodded to Huckleby, then turned and ran back into the stable.

"I've been told you know how to care for a horse, son. Just lead Bartley into that second stall on the left and have a go at it," Huckleby instructed me.

I did as he asked. Another stable boy appeared from the tack room and took the reins of Huckleby's horse.

"Be sure to rub Smokey down well. An extra lump of sugar for him, too," Huckleby cautioned the lad who led Smokey towards a stall diagonally across from the one I had guided Bartley into.

I set about the care of the horse as I had been taught by Mr. Norris, my riding instructor back in Boston. As I did so I felt the intensity of Mr. Huckleby's observation. He spoke nary a word as I removed the saddle and blanket and handed them to Billy (another stable boy) for transport to the tack room. I then set a feedbag at the correct height so that Bartley could munch contentedly while I brushed him; I felt proud to demonstrate my skills in horse care.

"What is it exactly that you're tryin' to do, Master Kevin?" inquired Huckleby after a few more moments of observation.

I turned to look at the groomsman as he lounged against the wooden frame of the stall, his arms crossed at his chest and a quizzical look on his face.

"I'm giving Bartley a good rubbing after his exercise this morning." I hoped that the irritation I felt at his question was evident in my voice. I turned back to brushing the horse.

"Does Bartley know that?"

"Of course!"

He had succeeded in breaking my concentration.

"You're going through all the correct motions but you're lacking emotion," came Huckleby's response.

"Emotion? We're talking about the horse, right?"

I turned to face Huckleby. He wasn't laughing as I had anticipated; in fact his countenance was a study in sincerity.

"They way you're brushing.....there's no purpose to your

movements. I've seen flies go about their business with more determination."

"Suppose you show me." I hoped my request sounded more like a command.

"Just this once," he conceded.

I held out the brush as he approached but instead of taking the proffered tool from my outstretched hand he grasped my shoulders and turned me around to face Bartley's flank. Placing a weather-worn hand over my smooth and callous-free one, he guided my brush strokes in a firm yet gentle manner. After a moment or two he pulled back, allowing me to continue unaided. A moment later Bartley turned his head towards me, nickered softly, and nudged my elbow with his nose. I jumped back in alarm!

"What's wrong, lad?"

"He...he tried to bite me!"

"No he didn't," Huckleby chuckled. "That's how a horse that enjoys his rub down reacts."

"Are you sure?"

"Who taught you about horses, lad? Your grandmother?" He shook his head. "No need to answer. Talk gently to him while you work. Sets the horse at ease. Has the added benefit of him getting used to the sound of your voice."

I approached Bartley again, patting his back while I resumed working with the brush.

"What should I talk to him about?" My whispered words sounded like a hiss to my ears.

"Don't talk to me. Talk to him."

With that directive Huckleby turned and walked away, most likely to supervise Billy or Denny. I turned back to the horse and addressed him directly.

"I'm sorry Bartley. I have no idea what to talk to you about," I began.

I proceeded to prattle on about all sorts of things as I worked, telling Bartley about my sisters, my expectations about this trip and the accompanying horror I had felt when I learned that the gentlemen were going to kill living creatures for food (Bartley nodded his head at this). I spoke of my studies, winters in Boston, in short I spoke about anything and everything that crossed my mind. When next I looked up from my task I found Huckleby was watching me.

"Well done, Master Kevin. Bartley is much more at ease and will look forward to seeing you again tomorrow." He looked me over, taking in my obviously disheveled appearance. "You must be ravenous. Cook has sent down our midday meal. We'd be honored if you'd join us."

"Perhaps something small," I conceded. "I wouldn't want to take someone else's share."

"Not to worry. There's plenty."

I followed Huckleby to the quarters behind the stable where Denny, Billy, and another young fellow called Stevie were already sitting down at an overly large table that had seen better days. It bore the gouges and scuffs of diners whose chief concern was not the care of fine furniture. From a nearby cupboard Huckleby produced a basket containing a variety of different seasonings and condiments. Noting my raised eyebrows he offered an explanation.

"I take it you've already experienced Cook's culinary offerings?"

I nodded my assent as I set about placing portions of cold meat atop slices of yesterday's bread, taking my cue from the manner in which the stable boys created their own meal. The various jars of condiments and seasonings were passed around the table and in short order I learned the fine art of making Cook's cuisine palatable. So tasty were our sandwiches that I found myself wanting more but recalling my manners I waited until the others declared themselves to have had enough before reaching for seconds. When the meal was done and the table cleared I followed Huckleby into his tiny office, just off the tack room. It had been fashioned from a stall at the back of the stable and was deep and narrow. There were some hooks on the boards where a fellow could place his hat or coat; clean rushes covered the floorboards.

A small wooden table with a shallow drawer served as his entire filing system. Two high back chairs that were held together with sturdy wire provided seating for the Head Groomsman and a single guest. I gingerly sat down on the spare chair facing the table. Huckleby pressed himself against a wall of the office in order to reach the far side of the table and seated himself on the opposing chair. He withdrew a well-worn key from the inner pocket of his jacket and with a single turn unlocked the table's drawer. I watched intently as he withdrew a pair of steel-gray wire-rimmed spectacles before opening a ledger that he placed squarely in front of me.

"Go ahead, take a look," he urged.

"Why?"

"You'll be master here one day. No time like the present to learn about the operation of the place." He pushed the book forward with his finger.

I hesitantly pulled the book closer and let my eyes aimlessly roam the entries. There was line after line of what appeared to be expenditures made on behalf of the lodge as well as the stables. I pretended interest while I perused the entries but none of them made an impression on me. After what I deemed an appropriate amount of time had passed I closed the ledger and pushed it back towards Huckleby.

"Very interesting," I commented.

"Hmph! No concern for what it takes to keep up a hunting lodge and a stable of horses like this one." He slammed the book closed, tucked it back into the drawer, and turned the key once more. "Won't amount to much if you ask me," he mumbled, more to himself than to be heard.

"He was ashamed of me." The words tumbled from my lips before I could stop them. My face suffused with embarrassment.

"Eh?" Huckleby placed his spectacles on the table.

"My father. He was ashamed of me. That's why he cut me from the hunt this morning."

There, I'd let out my shameful secret. I only hoped that the stable boys hadn't overheard.

"Whatever could you have done to make him ashamed of you, son?" Huckleby's voice softened just a bit.

"I asked him why the men were all carrying rifles and…" I stopped to stifle the impending tears I could feel gathering. "I didn't know that a living creature would have to die before we could have food."

"Is that all?" Huckleby came around the table and placed a hand on my shoulder. "That's nothing to be ashamed of, lad."

"It isn't? Then why was he so mad at me?"

I wiped a lone tear on the arm of my shirt.

"Well, there's lots of different types of men in this world," he began. "Many men are like your dad. They work in the world of business and view hunting as great sport. Then there are the men who care about all of God's creatures. Wouldn't hurt nary a fly, those men. And lastly, there are the men who have found a balance in life."

"Which one am I?" I raised my teary eyes up to his kindly face.

"Right now you're none of them. You're just a boy, trying to be a man, who wants to please his father. In time I think you'll be one of those men who finds a balance in life."

"You do?"

"Yes, I do. Tell me Master Kevin, do you read the Good Book?"

"You mean the Bible?"

He nodded.

"I read a passage every evening with mother and the girls and we learn about Bible stories at church on Sunday," I offered.

"Very good. Then you know that God put us here to prosper and multiply. We can't very well prosper without food, can we? So God gave us, men, the means to care for ourselves. He made man to hunt and bring home the food to his family. But only to hunt and take whatever was needed, not to hunt in excess. The wild animals do it all the time. It's called survival, boy. The stronger will feed off the weaker."

"I hadn't thought about that."

"Happens every day, lad. We can't survive on vegetables and bread alone."

I hung my head low as I thought about Huckleby's explanations. It should have been obvious to me that God had created the animals for us to provide meat and poultry. Why else would they be on this earth?

"It's almost time for you to be getting on back to the lodge. The gents will be riding in a-whooping and a-hollerin'. We'll all be workin' tonight to dress their kill."

I stood up and walked with Huckleby to the stable door. There was still something that troubled me.

"Mr. Huckleby? What I told you earlier? You won't...."

"Heavens no, Master Kevin. What I said before stands. Whatever we say to each other remains here." He once more placed his hand over his heart and I knew that my concern for God's creatures would never cause me shame or embarrassment again.

I spent the remaining days of the hunt in the company of Huckleby and the stable boys. Father, relieved that he wouldn't have to cater to my sensitivities, reasoned that my future interests were best served by my learning, albeit at a somewhat early age, how the hunting lodge was maintained. To that end he agreed to let me spend time at the stables.

I learned that Huckleby had been in my family's employ for the past eighteen years, starting out as a gardener on the property. He was given the opportunity to work in the stable when father bought a team of sturdy horses during the summer before his first hunt; father saw the yearly outing as a way to reward current business clients and to impress prospects as well. Huckleby felt at home around the horses, so much so that he made his bed in one of the empty stalls so that if the new horses should become spooked he would be nearby to calm them.

When the footman who handled the lodge accounts at the time had a falling out with the previous cook father fired them both, turning over the jumble of the house accounts to the new groundskeeper. Father also hired another stable boy and promoted Huckleby to the position of groomsman. Upon receiving the promotion and the accompanying raise in wages, Huckleby asked my father to invest the additional wages for him, earning my father's respect (not an easy thing to do).

The groundskeeper who had taken over the accounts for the lodge was just as inept at handling money as was his predecessor. It was Huckleby's ability to balance the stable ledger that eventually convinced father to turn over all of the accounts to the Head Groomsman.

A new cook was hired along with a staff that included a coachman, another footman, and an additional stable boy. With the existing staff there now were a total of seven hired positions. After months of disbursing wages and paying the invoices presented by merchants for the needs of both livestock and staff, Huckleby sat down and outlined a plan that would earn him father's lifelong respect. Huckleby proposed that with a few changes the lodge could easily be self-sufficient and possibly produce a small annual income, thus contributing to the Newkirk coffers.

The proposal was to cut the staff of seven down to three paid positions: one stable boy, the groundskeeper, and Huckleby himself. A cook, coachman, and footman could be hired as needed for family visits or outings thereby saving the wages they would have received. The groundskeeper could do double duty by performing minor repair work that might be required, calling upon professional help only in extreme need.

The next suggestion, of adding a large vegetable garden and a few hens, was inspired. As a former gardener Huckleby would care for this small farm which should produce enough food to provide quite a bit of the staff's sustenance. He personally knew several of the local grocers who agreed to trade meat for the excess produce thereby saving money on the grocery account.

Huckleby had then pointed out to father that since the horses were only kept for hunting parties and the occasional trip into Woodhaven they were not serving a useful purpose most of the time yet their care continued to tax the stable account. He proposed that the horses, which were of fine stock, be bred during the months after the annual hunt; their offspring could then be counted among the stable's assets and either sold at auction or eventually be used by hunting parties to complement the current team. This would bring significant revenue into the stable's account if the plan worked.

Father's response was immediate: "proceed with everything". Eight months later the lodge accounts were in the black, the remaining staff was content, and Huckleby was promoted to Head Groomsman. He was given permission to hire an additional stable boy to take over some of what had been his own chores. At father's direction, the profit that was realized was channeled into upgrading the stable building and renovating the living quarters for Huckleby and the stable boys.

After my initial trip to The Lodge in 1890 and my introduction to the proper care of horses by Huckleby, I returned to Boston with a determination to learn all that I could about those noble steeds. I felt that the proper place to start was with my equestrian instructor, Mr. Norris; however, I soon realized that he had only a cursory knowledge of the different breeds and their characteristics. It became evident that the riding school was merely an easy way for Mr. Norris to make a living from his wealthy clients.

I soon learned that the knowledge I craved was to be found in the Boston Public Library. On those excursions to the library I was accompanied by Nanny Summers. The tight-lipped woman felt it was a wonderful thing that I had taken such an interest in books, only to become dismayed when she noticed that the books I chose to check out all had to do with horses. However, my sisters more than made up for my "boyish interest in livestock" by choosing books that Nanny approved of.

Around that time I also undertook a letter-writing campaign with Mr. Huckleby. While reading my books, I found that I had any number of questions. Father certainly didn't have the time or the inclination to answer my questions and mother knew nothing about horses save that they were beasts of burden. It was Nanny Summers who suggested that I write to Mr. Huckleby.

As a correspondent, Mr. Huckleby was most informative and engaging. He answered each of my questions as fully as possible while giving me glimpses into the workings of our stable. Subsequent trips to The Lodge found me shoulder-to-shoulder with Huckleby. Father smiled approvingly each time our party arrived when, after seeing to the initial comfort of our guests, I would make my way out to the stable. In time I found that I cherished those visits when I could get out to the stable, saddle one of the newest horses, and take to the open countryside.

I loved nothing better than to hunker down over the horse's mane as we flew across the meadow, stopping beside that gurgling brook to watch the sunrise as I had done that first time with Huckleby; I would head back to the stable slowly, allowing the horse to take the lead, in time to share the remainder of the day with Huckleby and the stable boys.

At the end of the day, when father and his guests returned from their hunt I was in place to oversee the flawless execution of their duties by the short-term staff. When our guests believed I was out of hearing range, there were many whispered comments of praise as to what a fine young gentleman I was becoming. Of course this made father proud and he would strut like a peacock, insisting that the footman refill the gentlemen's brandy snifters. I merely stayed in the shadows, watching as Robert Woodward cozied up to father.

Since our first meeting in 1890, I tried my best to give Robert a wide berth. Father and Mr. Woodward had arranged a marriage between Robert and my sister Bernice, more for the sake of consolidating their business than for anything that might pass for love between their two offspring. Bernice wasn't happy about the engagement at first, having fallen in love with another young lad during her coming out. In the end, she consented to the engagement with Robert because, as she put it, "it was her duty to put family first". I had no doubt those very words had been drummed into Bernice's head by mother.

Kevin

Chapter 3

July 1896
Boston, Massachusetts

In May I received my secondary school diploma; one month later I served as usher at my sister Bernice's wedding. It was an elegant affair, attended by the cream of Boston society. No expense had been spared as our family was joined to that of my father's business partner. I remember drinking way too much that day. The hangover I suffered the following day did little to dispel my dismay at the knowledge that Robert Woodward was now a part of our family.

That summer was also the year of my eighteenth birthday. During the past six years I had grown approximately four inches and lost the youthful chubbiness of my childhood, due in part to my participation in field sports. While not overly tall (none of the Newkirk men were), my torso was sturdy and compact, making me a natural defenseman in team sports. My reddish-brown hair was fashionably longer and my tailored clothing hugged my frame. In short, I was the perfect son of Augustus Newkirk, at least in appearance. I stood before the pier glass in my bedchamber as Paul brushed a miniscule piece of lint from my shoulder.

"I wonder what the old man is up to," I mused, referring to the summons I had received to join father in his study. I straightened my cuffs as I spoke.

"Perhaps he'll gift you with another servant," Paul suggested, a sly grin lighting his face.

"Well, she'd better be a good looker then. Wouldn't mind having a maid of my own."

"Has my service been less than perfect, sir?" Paul turned a crestfallen face towards me.

"Don't look like that, old sport. Your service is above reproach. It's just that I've been envious of you for the past couple of years, listening to your tales of bravado with those two girls serving the Monmouth family." I favored Paul with my dazzling smile. "What I wouldn't give for a quick tumble with someone who doesn't have a reputation to uphold."

"What about one of the kitchen girls?"

"No. I don't want my first time to be with someone who can tell the entire household that I'm less than a stallion. I'm thinking perhaps you could arrange for me to meet someone? Later this evening?"

Paul appeared to think about his answer. A wise man never speaks without thinking.

"As luck would have it, I was going to meet my ladyfriend this evening. Perhaps you'd care to join us, sir? Around ten?"

"That would suit me just fine." I looked around the room even knowing that we were the only two present. "The lady should have some experience," I whispered.

"I have a young lady in mind."

I looked back at my reflection, adjusting the way my trousers lay, hoping that my reaction to this kind of talk would go unnoticed.

"I'm sure she'll be agreeable," Paul replied.

"Do you really think so? I hope I won't embarrass myself."

"Just talk with her at first. Like you would to any other girl."

"I don't often talk to other girls."

"I know; you've been busy studying every night when you were in school. But you've put that behind you now. You're free for the summer. You need to celebrate your birthday."

"It's just that every time I see my sister and her husband I think of him…."

"This young lady will be just the ticket to help ease your discomfort when Robert comes to call, especially now that he's married to your sister."

"Yes, well…." I let the comment go unfinished.

It made my skin crawl to think about the arranged marriage between Bernice and that prig Robert. Father had made it perfectly clear that until I was in a position to take my place on the Board of Directors, the marriage between Bernice and Robert would solidify the business. It was clear to everyone else that there was no love between the two; in fact it was nothing more than a business arrangement. Word had it that Robert had already installed his mistress in a luxurious apartment just outside of Boston.

"Thank heavens I won't have to worry about an arrangement of that sort. I could never be tied to a woman I didn't love. Or was at least fond of." I smiled at Paul.

"Then you'll give the willing parlor maid a go?"

"Make it a chamber maid. I want someone with experience in the bedroom."

I made my way downstairs, walking briskly down the shadowy corridor before rapping my knuckles against the study door as I pushed it open.

"Ah, Kevin! Come sit."

Father motioned towards one of the chairs that flanked the desk. I watched as he moved towards a side cabinet and withdrew two glasses and a decanter of his best port. He poured two fingers of the claret-colored liquid into each glass and handed me one. I previously had imbibed several drinks during the annual hunting party but mother and my sisters remained clueless to that fact; a fact that changed with Bernice's wedding day.

"Come now," urged father, "it's time you joined your old man in a drink."

Together we knocked back the port.

"I believe you know why I've called you into my study. Eh?"

"My eighteenth birthday I presume."

I sat back in the chair; lounged actually. I could sense a gift of some sort in the offing.

"We may have discussed this a few times in the past but now it is time for you to make your decision. What line of work, or study, do you hope to pursue?" questioned father.

I had indeed given this much thought over the past year. My ambition was to breed race horses and build a world-renowned stable although I knew father would find that frivolous. In order to placate him I realized I would need to take on the world of business. I chose the words of my response carefully.

"My deliberations have led me to the conclusion that I wish to build my own business and be as successful as you are, father. However, I haven't settled yet on what sort of business that would be. I was rather hopeful that I could continue my education, perhaps a degree in economics, while I evaluated what sort of business would best suit me."

"Well said, son. I was pretty certain I knew what your answer would be and you haven't disappointed me." He reached into a desk drawer that normally remained locked and withdrew a packet of papers which he handed to me. "On the occasion of your eighteenth birthday, and because you have pleased me more than you know, I have two gifts for you. First, I've arranged a place for you at Yale University in New Haven."

"I rather fancied going to Harvard." I allowed a slight frown to form.

"Actually Yale is my second choice; I would rather have had you attend Harvard. But based on the second gift, which you are holding, I thought it the better match." He pointed to the packet I held. "Go ahead, open it."

Carefully I unfolded the sheaf of papers and looked them over with a critical eye. They had been drawn up by Wilson Trent & French, the law firm that represented Newkirk Trading, and they were sealed with the firm's crest. I could scarcely believe what I held. For a full minute I was speechless.

"I don't understand," I managed to say when at last I found my voice. "You've deeded me the entire property in Woodhaven?"

"Why not? You love the place. Something to do with Huckleby and those darn horses." He sat down in his leather chair once again. "The way I see it, you'll attend your classes at Yale and return home to The Lodge in the evening. Paul will be there to see to your needs, you'll have a proper meal, and a proper place to live in. I won't have any son of mine in one of those awful dormitories."

"Feel free to hire whatever staff you deem necessary to see that the place is well run," father continued. "You shouldn't be too lonely as New Haven is quite an entertaining place I'm told. I've increased the accounts for the lodge and stable so that all of your expenses will be covered while you continue your studies. Once you receive your degree the entire responsibility, including funding the house accounts, will be turned over to you. I wanted to deed the property to you now so that you may feel independent during your continuing studies."

"I really don't know what to say, sir."

"Poppycock! Giving you those gifts is one of the benefits of being wealthy. If you have money, you can buy whatever you desire. Don't forget that, son."

"No sir, I won't."

"And I expect that we'll still see you here in Boston for Thanksgiving and Christmas. Your mother would never forgive me if you didn't come home for the holidays. Now be off and enjoy your day. Do you have any special celebrations planned?"

"I sort of do, actually."

"I hope they include at least one young lady."

"I'm working on that, sir."

I tucked the deed to The Lodge in my breast pocket as I rose.

"One more thing; I'll still be bringing my hunting party out in September. No need to worry about us. We're used to roughing it." Father winked at me before motioning me out of the study.

After a family dinner, during which I suffered through the unbearable presence of my brother-in-law Robert, I escaped to Rafferty's Pub where I quaffed an ale or two in the company of friends. Several rounds and some good-natured joking later I took note of the time and knew I needed to depart.

"It's been fun fellas but I must leave."

"What? It's early old chum. I've just ordered another round," responded Phil Evans, my best pal throughout secondary school.

"Surely your mother won't expect you home early tonight," add John Fisher. "Just one more round."

"No, mother won't be expecting me home early. But I promised to meet another friend."

I drained the remaining ale from my mug and set it down on the polished wood bar. From my wallet I pulled out several bills and flung them down on the bar as well.

"That should cover our drinks and be enough to see you two sports another couple of rounds."

"So who is she?" Phil leaned in to me, placed a hand on my shoulder, and whispered.

I remained silent, offering only a knowing smile.

"Good lord, it's not Clara Holmes? She's a looker alright but I've heard she's been with every fellow that winks at her," added John.

"The young lady's name shall remain unspoken," I replied. "A gentleman doesn't bandy about a lady's reputation."

"Unless she's not a lady," snorted Phil.

They laughed and raised their refilled mugs in a silent salute as I made my escape through the pub's rear door. I crossed the street and walked two blocks west until I came to the Concord Hotel. While not a hotel of the first caliber, it was situated in the West End and was wholly acceptable to a man of my station, meaning that it had several of the amenities I required: it was clean, the staff could be counted on for their discretion, and it was not frequented by friends of my family. I approached the front desk and engaged the bespectacled clerk.

"Good evening. I believe you're holding a room for me."

"Under what name, sir?" The clerk peered above the rim of his glasses as he spoke.

"Von Drake," I replied.

The clerk consulted his guest ledger and nodded.

"Room five twenty-three, Mr. Von Drake. Mr. Sterling has already signed the guestbook and is waiting in the suite."

"Thank you." I glad-handed the clerk a five-note to further secure his discretion.

Inside the elevator compartment I pressed the button for the fifth floor. As the device moved upward I decided that I much preferred a better grade of hotel, one where the carpet didn't show signs of wear, where the patrons themselves didn't need to press a commonly used floor button, and where a pleasant lift-operator held open the door for those wishing to enter or exit.

The fifth floor housed several generous suites and I moved swiftly along the dimly lit hallway until I located number five twenty-three. Before I could lift my hand to knock, the door was opened and Paul greeted me.

"Good evening, Mr. Von Drake. I'm so pleased you could join us." His voice was rather stentorian. I could hear female voices giggling behind him.

"Any trouble, Paul?" I inquired as he closed the door behind me.

"None, sir."

"Introduce me to these lovely ladies, then?" I urged, having already set my sights on the voluptuous green-eyed minx who lounged on the sofa. "And for goodness sake don't call me 'sir' or 'mister'."

"Ladies, may I introduce Kevin Newkirk. Kevin, this is Maude Avery." He directed my attention to a tow-headed, slim young woman dressed in a tight dress that clung to her curves. She seemed to slither across the room towards me.

"Ooooh, you must be the birthday boy!"

Her high-pitched voice, although meant to sound enticing, brought to mind the sound of fingernails on a chalkboard. She wiggled her body against mine and brazenly planted a kiss on my lips, ending it abruptly with a smacking sound as Paul peeled her away from me. If she was to be my date for the evening, I was already mentally preparing the calling-out Paul would receive the following morning. Fortune smiled on me, though.

"Maude, darling, behave yourself. Whatever will Kevin think of you?"

"I was only tryin' to wish him a nice birthday. Are you jealous, lover?" She batted her eyelashes at Paul as she spoke, snuggling closer to him.

I moved to the sofa where the other young woman waited. Her green eyes followed my every move as I approached her. Although her clothes bespoke her station (the color was slightly faded from her dress and it was plain to see her worn collar had been camouflaged by a length of lace) they could not diminish her beauty: shoulder length jet black hair, pouty red lips, a pert nose, and above all those emerald green eyes. I came to a halt in front of her and went down on one knee.

"I believe I've fallen into a dream and met an Irish angel." My words were spoken quietly so that only she could hear them.

Her laugh was throaty and the sound of it unleashed a tight heat in the pit of my stomach. When she laughed I glimpsed her teeth which I likened to ivory pearls. She extended her hand in greeting.

"No angel, I assure you. My name is Jeannette." The corners of her mouth lifted slightly.

I claimed her outstretched hand, turning it over so that I could lightly kiss her palm. In return she smiled; a smile that reached her eyes, a smile that smoldered yet fanned the flames of my growing lust.

With the introductions concluded, the four of us spent some time in pleasant conversation, putting away the contents of two bottles of champagne. Mostly it was Maude's glass that seemed to need frequent refills yet I noticed that Jeannette barely sipped at hers. During our conversation I learned that Maude was the parlor maid that Paul had spoken of earlier and she flaunted her superior standing in the hierarchy of domestic staff, putting down the fact that Jeannette was a chamber maid. Jeannette spoke little, allowing Maude to be the center of attention. For that alone I silently applauded Jeannette.

Eventually, Paul shepherded Maude into one of the two bedchambers. I could tell that Paul was embarrassed by Maude's zeal to rip off his shirt. When the bedroom door closed on them I realized I had been holding my breath. Not wanting to appear hasty I resumed conversing with Jeannette.

"Is the champagne not to your liking?" I motioned to the almost full glass that she had placed on a side table.

"Actually, Mrs. Moss, she's my employer, prefers a higher grade of champagne.

"She does?"

I tried to look down my nose at this feminine confection who was quoting her employer in an effort to impress me. We both suddenly realized how silly we were being and simultaneously broke into laughter.

"Mrs. Moss always says....OH!"

I leaned forward and silenced those pouty lips with a sound kiss. She fluttered her long lashes furiously as I began groping at the bodice of her dress. Before she could pull away I drew her into another kiss which she again broke off abruptly.

"Paul assured me you were a gentleman." Her voice had an accusatory tone to it.

"But I am a gentleman," I countered, "one in dire need of a kiss from a beautiful girl."

I gently drew her closer this time engaging her in a lighter, more tender kiss. Instead of pulling away she snuggled closer to me, slowly unfastening the button on my waistcoat and tugging at my ascot. In return I reached for her bodice but she pushed my hand away.

"It's my only good dress," she murmured.

Taking me by the hand, she led me into the unoccupied bedchamber where she carefully removed her dress before she relieved me of my cumbersome attire. Heated kisses led to fevered caresses as Jeannette guided me to the heavenly realms I had heard Paul speak of.

Much later we returned to the suite's living area. We talked late into the night, this time sharing an aperitif that we agreed was much better than the champagne we had imbibed earlier.

"So, you're a rich gent. Funny, you're not all pretentious like I expected you to be." Jeannette rested her head on my shoulder and let out a sigh. "Are you awfully rich?"

"My family is." I leaned over and kissed the back of her neck.

"Wish I was rich."

"What would you do with money?"

"I'd quit my position with Mrs. Moss, that's what. I might not be a high-society lady but I've always dreamed of having my own shop one day."

"What sort of shop?" I continued kissing her neck, moving my lips upward to nibble at her ear before planting a kiss on her nose.

"A millinery shop. That way I could take the money from those rich old cows who don't care a fig about people like me." She placed her hand in my lap as I drew her mouth into another kiss.

"My mother is one of those 'old cows' you speak of," I casually reminded her.

"No, she's not. Anyone who would have a son as handsome and gentle as you couldn't be a cow." She returned my kiss before settling herself across my lap.

"You're quite beautiful, you know. I'm sure you must have a suitor or two who would gladly take you away from your employer." I allowed my fingers to trail along her collar bone to where her own fingers were slowly unfastening the buttons on her bodice.

"No one will have me, I'm afraid. I'm an orphan without a dowry, only hard work to recommend me. My only hope for marriage would be to another servant."

Her fingers entwined with mine as she guided my hand between the folds of her bodice and beneath the chemise to her soft breasts.

"Although we've just met you'll always be my Irish angel, Jeannette," I hastened to reassure her as telltale signs of my desire began to swell. "I promise to always take care of you."

I would have promised her anything at that moment.

"Come then, give your angel a kiss," she invited in a sultry voice.

Her kisses were deep and warm, leading us to only partially remove our clothes as we gave in to our desires once more. I don't recall how long we dozed on that sofa afterward but the muted chiming of a mantel clock alerted us to the lateness of the hour.

"Good Lord, look at the time!" Jeannette leapt up.

Sofa pillows flew to the floor as she searched for her purse. She ran to the room where Maude and Paul were ensconced and knocked at the door.

"Maudie, get yourself out here right now. It's after midnight."

She knocked again. When there was no answer she opened the door.

"Damn! She's already left!"

"But it's only half past midnight," I observed.

"Randolph locks the doors at midnight!"

"Who's Randolph?" I felt a twinge of jealousy.

"The butler," she explained. "There'll be hell to pay. He doesn't like to be woke up for the likes of me."

She hurriedly patted her hair into place, snatched her purse, and made for the door.

"I had a wonderful evening, Kevin. Truly I did. But it will take forever till I reach the house. I really must leave." She blew a kiss in my direction.

"Wait, I'll call you a carriage."

"I suppose I'll pull enough money out of this here purse to pay the driver. No worry, love. I can walk."

"You can't walk about unescorted at this time of night. I won't allow it. Come with me."

I took her by the hand and led her into the corridor where she fidgeted as we waited for the elevator. Together we took the lift to the lobby and stepped out into the warm July air. A nearby carriage for hire approached at my signal.

"Where to sir?" the groggy driver inquired.

"818 Garden Street. And make haste."

I handed Jeannette into the carriage and made to enter as well, but she halted my entry.

"What are you doing?" she whispered.

"Seeing you home, of course."

"No. You must not. I'm in enough trouble as it is." Panic was evident on her face.

"Can you meet me next week?"

"I don't know."

"I'll send word through Paul," I hastened to assure her as she settled into the depths of the carriage's musty interior.

I paid the driver, adding a handsome tip with a strong admonishment that if anything out of the ordinary happened to his passenger I would see to it that he was impressed to work on a freighter bound for Shanghai. The man was highly conciliatory, assuring me that 'the lady' would come to no harm. I watched as the carriage went round the corner, turning only at the sound of a familiar voice behind me.

"Thank you, my dear for a lovely evening." I could hear the sound of a kiss being shared on the far side of a carriage that blocked my view of the participants.

"You know I enjoy every moment of our time together, Gussy." The woman who spoke was being handed into a well-sprung coach with a liveried driver.

"Until next week, Nora dear."

As the coach pulled away I stood face-to-face with my father. Realizing what had just transpired, father let out a hearty laugh and stepped forward, placing an arm around my shoulder.

"Well, son, it seems that we've both had a busy evening." He raised his hand to summon our family coach that had been waiting just out of sight.

"Who was that woman?"

"She's my mistress, son," he admitted matter-of-factly.

"Have you known her long?"

"A while," he acknowledged.

"Does mother know about her?"

"No…and yes. Although I believe your mother knows I have a mistress I'm sure she doesn't know who. Our meetings are clandestine by nature. Your mother understands that a man has needs so she turns a blind eye to Nora's place in my life. But she doesn't know Nora's name or anything about her."

Father settled back against the seat of the coach and continued.

"Your mother and I were parties to a marriage arranged by our families. We like each other well enough. She's given me three handsome children, she plans our society engagements, and she sees to the smooth running of our household. She has kept her reputation above reproach. What more can a man expect from a wife?"

"Love?"

"Poppycock! Love is for young girls dreaming of their Prince Charming. Love is a fairy tale."

"Then why do poets write sonnets?"

"A waste of time if you ask me."

"I don't think I could marry someone I didn't love."

"If you're smart, you'll find a suitable young woman from an acceptable family to provide a Newkirk heir. Love can come later; if it doesn't you'll have your son and you can find a mistress to love you."

"Do you always have your meetings at the Concord?"

"Actually, I own an entire floor there for privacy. I'll leave word with the management that you're free to entertain there on the nights when I'm not using the place. What name do you go by?"

"Von Drake," I replied.

"Excellent! I'm known there as Jack Hunter."

As the coach pulled into our yard on Revere Street, father signaled that our conversation was concluded; together we entered our family home like co-conspirators.

———

I met with Jeannette twice more that month; after that our outings became weekly events on my social calendar. During the quiet times after our lovemaking I learned more about the young woman's circumstances.

On that auspicious night of our first meeting, Jeannette had informed me that she was an orphan. That had piqued my curiosity; I had never known anyone who didn't have living parents. When I pressed her for details she glossed over her time in the orphanage. I gathered that those years must have been dreadful; I gave her my complete attention though when she spoke of how she came to be in her present position.

"Are you sure you want to hear the boring details of my life?" she asked as she snuggled in my arms.

"If it has to do with my Irish angel, than no subject is too boring," I reassured her with a kiss to her forehead.

"Well, then," she drew a deep breath and continued. "I was well into my twelfth year when I met Mrs. Moss. She was impeccably dressed and the matron of the orphanage brought her into the dining hall one day. We were seated at table, devouring the meager share we were allotted, but our eyes all were trained on the high-society lady who was walking around the tables giving us the once over. She stopped a couple of feet away from me and pronounced, "this one", pointing to me as she spoke."

"How crude of her," I commented.

"We didn't realize that at the time, given the way she was dressed and all. Each of us was wishing for someone to love us and make us part of their family."

"How awful."

"Not really awful, dearest, just depressing. You see the little ones get placed quite easily. Most families are more comfortable with a baby or a toddler. The ones over eight years have already become set in their ways. We were also more likely to express ourselves if we didn't like something."

"So this high-society woman just walked in and pointed at you?"

"Yes, she did. The matron told me to stand up and turn around so that Mrs. Moss could see me from every angle. I did as I was taught: I stood up, did a slow turn, then I curtsied to the woman before resuming my seat. That curtsy must have done the trick because the next morning

I was summoned to the matron's office. I couldn't image what I'd done to be called down. Normally only someone who had caused trouble was sent for."

"I can't imagine you causing trouble."

"Oh, I was a model child," Jeannette replied, sticking her nose up in the air.

We both broke out in gales of laughter.

"What happened next?" I urged.

"Matron informed me to pack up my things and thank heaven because I had been chosen by Mrs. Moss to be a companion for her daughter. She also assured me that I was to be treated well and would have many of the same opportunities that the daughter of the house had, especially being included in the daily lessons from the tutor."

"That would seem to speak well of Mrs. Moss," I observed.

"I was overjoyed. I didn't care what the daughter was like as long as I was able to escape from the dreariness of the orphanage. I packed what few belongings I owned and handed the small valise to the driver of the coach that had been sent to collect me. During that drive I thought of all the lovely things I would have someday – a pretty dress, ribbons for my hair, perhaps a doll no longer wanted by the daughter, maybe even a bedroom of my own."

"I much prefer to have you share my bedroom, you know."

"That's obvious. Do you want to hear my tale or not?"

"I'll try not to interrupt." I kissed her nose as she playfully swatted me away.

"The carriage pulled up to the front of the house, dispensed me and my tattered valise, and drove off. I stood there looking at the finely detailed front porch and the inviting front door. The thought briefly crossed my mind that someone should have been there to welcome me, but I shrugged it aside. I didn't care. My new life was about to start. I mounted the porch steps, rang the bell, and waited. Eventually a tall thin man who I assumed to be the butler swung the door open."

"Was that the acerbic Randolph?"

"None other. He peered at me over glasses that perched on his nose. When I attempted to step over the threshold he blocked my way and informed me that 'the servant's entrance was around the back'. Of course I told him that I was expected. He gave me another of his famous dour glances and replied, "You're the waif from the orphanage, aren't you? Been expecting you. You're to be working in the kitchen I've been told. Now be a good girl and go round to the servant's entrance. Won't do to start off on the wrong foot."

"What did you say? Did you set him straight?"

"I immediately told him that there must be some mistake. I was to be a companion to the daughter of the house. He laughed and replied, "That's rich. As if the missus would waste her money on a companion for Trudy. Now get around to the servant's entrance before I come after you with a broom."

"How awful!" I pulled Jeannette closer and kissed her deeply. I wanted her to feel loved.

"Are you sure you want to hear the rest? It's not a pretty story."

"I'm sure. Go on."

"Sure enough, I was to be a servant. I was immediately put to work as a scullery helper doing the jobs no one else would do. Later that day I was given a meal and shown to an attic room that was no larger than a closet and was tucked under the eaves of the roof. By that time I was so exhausted I didn't care, although I reminded myself that at least I didn't have to share the room with another person. I had just finished changing into my nightdress when a knock sounded on my door. Thinking it would be another of the servants I opened the door to see a young gentleman about sixteen years of age leaning against the door frame. He grinned at me, stepped into the room uninvited, and told me to close the door. Introduced himself as Edwin Moss, Mrs. Moss's son. He explained to me that since his mother had 'donated' a large sum of money to the orphanage for me I would receive no wages for my work until the entire sum had been worked off."

I shook my head in dismay as I realized what that young man had intended. As Jeannette continued her story my fears were realized.

"I agreed with him that I should be happy to work off Mrs. Moss's donation and thanked him for stopping by to inform me of that. That's when he told me that he had taken it upon himself to welcome me to the household. Said he had spied me working in the kitchen and had been taken with the sight of me. He came closer and put his hand on my shoulder before leaning in and whispering what he planned to do. His advice was for me to not resist him or he would have me dismissed immediately. What could I do? I had nowhere else to go. I knew no one outside of the orphanage and I certainly didn't want to go back there."

"Did he.....?"

"Oh, yes he did. When he left my tiny room that night I lay on the bed, my body was sore, and all I could do was cry myself to sleep."

"That despicable lout!"

"He was that. Young Edwin became a nightly visitor to my room. This continued on for the next five years. Finally he married a society belle and he set up a home of his own. Although whenever he and his wife came to visit he made it a point to seek me out and take what he considered 'rightfully his'. By the time of his marriage I turned seventeen, I had been elevated to the position of chambermaid, due in part to Edwin's urging. Guess he didn't like the idea of coupling with a scullery maid. That was the only nice thing he ever did for me."

"Well, hopefully things went better after you were in your new position and Edwin was gone from the house." I pulled Jeanette closer into my embrace as I subconsciously tried to protect her from the memories of her past.

"After Edwin's physical departure from the house, Mr. Moss passed away. An awful time it was for Mrs. Moss. Of course Edwin took the opportunity to claim me while the rest of the family was downstairs mourning their loss. Edwin remarked that people grieve in different ways and his way was to use my body to slake his grief. Didn't seem to me like he was grieving while in the throes of passion. However, once Mr. Moss was laid to rest Mrs. Moss's brother moved in. Ryan Andrews is his name. In a money-saving effort he cut the staff who would reside in the Garden Street house preferring to have folks live in their own homes and come in on a daily basis. There were only three of us who would retain our residency: Randolph of course, the cook, and myself. I was expected to be on call at all hours of the day or night since I would be doing double duty as ladies maid as well as my regular duties."

"What an awful time you've had," I replied.

"Don't interrupt me, please. I've got to get this out of me. Now where was I?"

"You were doing double duty," I reminded her.

"Yes, well. Seems that every night, just after midnight, Mr. Andrews would ring for something, an extra blanket, or a glass of milk or, oh, almost anything that had to be brought to his bedchamber; anything to cover the fact that he was just like his nephew Edwin. I would bring the item he requested, be made to take off my clothes and crawl into his bed. This I would have to do of my own free will since he'd told me that he couldn't force me into his bed but if I was there and willing he could do nothing else but take what was offered. I knew that he had the power to boot me out of my position so I gave in. He smiled, did what he wanted, and rolled over. Kept his eyes closed while I redressed myself. Just before I left the room he would call me over to the bed, reach out and tuck a few bills into my bodice before patting my behind and sending me on my way."

"And there was nothing you could do?"

"Not if I valued my position. I had no family. If I had left I would have been on the streets. No, I kept to myself and no one was the wiser that I was building a nest egg."

I was stunned speechless. We treated our household staff like an extension of the family. We respected the staff members as human beings even if their station in life was below ours. Jeannette had continued to talk so I rapidly cleared my head and paid full attention.

"....Caitlyn was readying her trousseau; she handed me almost everything in her wardrobe and told me to 'get rid of these things'. What a waste that would have been! That girl had no sense of what things cost. Well, I did what she wanted. I packed up everything she tossed out with the exception of two dresses that were more tailored than fancy. I kept those aside and brought the remainder to a thrift shop not far from the orphanage. The shopkeeper got the better part of that deal, I can tell you."

"But weren't Caitlyn's clothes worth a lot? I would think a society girl would only be dressed in the finest silks."

"They were fine clothes, indeed. But as I said the shopkeeper got the better part of that deal. I got what I wanted though. Once he'd paid me for the gowns and such, I turned around and haggled with him until I got a price I wanted for some lace and a few basic sewing tools. Still had some money left when I was done." Jeannette smiled as she recalled that episode.

"Whatever did you want lace for?"

"The two dresses I'd kept back, darling. I tucked the remaining money into an old patched pillowslip that I keep beneath the lining in my dresser drawer. That's the money I've been saving to open my own shop and be independent. The lace and such helped me make over the two dresses I had kept aside into a style more suitable to my station."

"Well, you certainly are clever," I praised her. "Now come kiss me and show me how talented you are."

On our third meeting, Jeannette wore the green dress she had been wearing on the night we met; that was when I realized how meager her wardrobe truly was. She alternately wore the green dress with a navy blue one. Somehow though it didn't bother me that she had such a miniscule wardrobe, it was her shining smile and good looks that made one not take note of what she was wearing.

I had wanted to share my good news about attending Yale with her, but I was afraid that she would take the news poorly. Many hours were spent in contemplating how I could bear the thought of leaving her in Boston. At last I had come upon a solution that was nothing short of brilliant. I wanted the timing to be right when I proposed my plan to Jeannette and by summer's end I could no longer control myself. We were at the Concord Hotel, availing ourselves of my father's largesse after a romp between the sheets. I had come to the conclusion that I loved Jeannette and wanted to keep her in my life; my long term goal was to marry her but that would have to wait until my college education was a *fait accompli*. The time was right, however, to set into motion the first part of my plan.

"I really shouldn't have another drop of wine," Jeannette laughingly protested as I refilled her glass.

"Pray tell, why not?"

"It makes me feel wanton."

She placed her pouty lips on the rim of the glass and sipped delicately. Just watching her do simple things sometimes stirred the blood in my veins and this was one of those times. I extricated the glass from her hands, setting it on the night table.

"I believe those lips are needed elsewhere," I murmured into her ear.

She shivered in delight as her hand moved along my stomach, traveling in a southerly fashion. Once free from my embrace, her head followed the trail of her hand as she showered tiny kisses in a line from my stomach and over my abdomen until her mouth found the prize it sought. When Jeannette's work was done and she had drained the final drop of my reserve vintage, we lay side-by-side. I marveled to myself how right it felt to have her in my arms, how comfortably she fit beside me.

"So you'll be going off to college next week," she observed, her voice cracking a bit at the mention of our parting.

"I've become quite accustomed to our weekly meetings, you know." I pushed back a lock of her hair, tucking it behind her ear.

"Me too, darling. But I've always known this day would come."

It was easy to see that she was valiantly trying not to cry.

"I shall miss you, Jeannette." I placed a gentle kiss on her very talented mouth.

"Oh pooh! With all those women in New Haven you'll soon forget me." She rose, turned her back to me, and began putting on her undergarments. I could tell she was holding back her tears. "I'll go back to the Moss household, save my money and one day open my shop. You'll see, Kevin Newkirk, that I will be my own woman."

I reached for my jacket that hung from a nearby chair and from the inner pocket extracted an envelope. I padded over to where she was dressing.

"I have a gift for you." I held out the envelope to her.

She looked at me, then at the envelope in my hand, then back to me. This time she began to cry in earnest. When the tears subsided somewhat, she tried to speak but her words were punctuated by loud sobs.

"I....I thought we meant....something to each other. Did you really....think I would accept your money?"

"Jeannette, my angel, you don't understand," I began.

"Oh, I understand well enough!" Her tearful sobs turned into an angry retort. "You've had your fun, now you're done."

She tried buttoning her bodice but her hands trembled so badly that she couldn't complete the task. At last she gave up the attempt and flung herself on the bed, burying her face in a pillow.

"Jeannette, dearest, please don't cry. I can't bear to see you cry," I pleaded, offering her a handkerchief.

"I was a fool to fall in love with you, Kevin; I knew that you'd leave. But you were kind and caring and I hoped you'd care for me too."

"I love you, Jeannette. Please, look inside this envelope."

I placed the offensive envelope into her hand. Eventually she looked within and discovered my gift.

"Train tickets? I don't understand." Her tears had turned to sniffles now.

"The tickets are for you. Tomorrow you are going to resign your position. You may tell Mrs. Moss that you've accepted another arrangement."

"And just what arrangement would that be?"

"Since my father deeded the hunting lodge to me I find myself in need of a housekeeper. I've been told to hire whatever staff I need for my comfort. And I need you, Jeannette." I kissed her again and tasted the salt of her tears.

"You're serious?" She needed confirmation.

"I'm dead serious," I assured her. "I expect you to take the train down on Sunday. There will be a coach at Union Station that will take you and your baggage directly to the lodge. Huckleby will be awaiting your arrival. He'll show you around and make you feel at ease."

"But housekeeper? I'm not qualified for that!" She dried her tears with my handkerchief.

"This is a unique position, really. I don't know what else to call it besides housekeeper." I grinned at her.

"What would my duties be?" she questioned, very matter-of-factly.

"Since Huckleby already manages the accounts as well as oversees the stables, I need someone to hire and oversee a cook and a scullery maid." I hoped the position sounded tempting.

"That's all I'd have to do?" Her lips lifted into a tiny smile.

"One other thing. I was hoping to put your talents as a chambermaid to good use."

"Oh." Her voice suddenly deflated.

"Especially your talents as a bed-warmer," I whispered in her ear.

"Oh!"

The next year passed in a blissful haze. After long hours of classes and lectures on the Yale campus, I would adjourn to one of several local pubs to lift a few pints before falling into the coach that would bring me back to the hunting lodge. Although the city roads were navigable by motor car, it was the sure-footed horses under the rein of our experienced coachman who brought me home safely. In the dark interior of the coach I was able to catch a nap. When at last I stepped down and entered my humble abode I was refreshed and famished.

Jeannette had hired a local girl who quickly learned my favorite meals. Under Jeannette's direction, we had no wasted food; although I'm sure we ate leftovers on several nights I hardly recognized them as they were transformed into tantalizingly new dishes. Jeannette saw to much of the cleaning and laundry herself although I had intended to hire a scullery maid as well as a parlor maid. My wardrobe and grooming needs were under Paul's supervision when he wasn't paying court to the young cook. In fact, on many a night I could hear a distinctly feminine voice giggling from behind the closed door of Paul's room.

After supper I would hit the books while Jeannette sat in front of the hearth, sometimes darning or sewing, at other times merely sitting and gazing into the fire. When my studies for the night were complete, Jeannette and I would retire to the second floor bedchamber and indulge in the most intense lovemaking I had ever experienced.

While the weekdays passed in a strictly routine manner, I arose each Saturday morning with high anticipation. The weekend was when I could immerse myself in my favorite hobby, horse husbandry. Many long hours were spent with Huckleby, hunched over the worn table/desk in his office as we discussed the requirements for creating a world-class breeding stable. It was my dream that one day the lodge, or Bridgewater as I had named the place, would one day be known far and wide for the high quality of race horses and polo ponies we would produce.

Many times Huckleby and I would share a drink or two at the end of a particularly tedious day. Several times we would finish the bottle as we fantasized about the kinds of horses we would breed. On more than one occasion Huckleby would spin a yarn about some far-off Eastern European breed that I hadn't heard of, telling of the breed's agility and speed. But the most intriguing aspect of these fairy tale horses was the color of their coat. And each time he told the story I would dream that night of a sleek steed racing with the wind; a horse whose coat shimmered like liquid gold as it galloped through the sun-dappled meadows of Bridgewater.

Kevin

Chapter 4

September 1897
Woodhaven, Connecticut

Autumn on the Yale campus is a most beautiful sight: the old stone dormitories with their leaded window panes overlooking courtyards where students scurry to and from their classes; the trees wearing their cloaks of scarlet and orange leaves; the excitement of freshmen arriving on the threshold of their futures. I pulled myself up straight and puffed up my chest just a tiny bit since I was now a sophomore and considered myself a true Eli. In my benevolence I smiled at those freshmen who were exhibiting the usual look of a lost student. Not too long ago I had been one of them.

My class list for the semester was now fixed in such a manner that I had enough time to partake of sports. While I had played football in secondary school, I felt that my sturdy build and compact frame was better suited to rowing. Thankfully, the rowing coaches felt exactly the same and once I had proven my skill at boating maneuvers, I was now on my way to board a trolley that would take me out to the Yale Boathouse. For this purpose the school had chartered one of the commercial trolleys for the entire rowing team eliminating the need for numerous stops en route by non-Eli's. The conveyance was almost full when I boarded but I found a seat next to a tall fellow who smiled as he motioned for me to sit down.

"I didn't expect there to be such a full complement," I remarked as I settled in.

"Neither did I," the fellow responded. He stuck out his hand in welcome. "Name's Cal. Cal Conner."

"Kevin Newkirk." I shook his hand.

"You're not one of the Boston Newkirk's, are you?"

"One and the same," I readily replied.

"I thought you Boston folk all went to Harvard."

"That was my first choice but father had other ideas. Worked out just as well for me, though."

"Have you chosen a major?" I inquired.

"Business economics. My poppa owns a tailoring shop and I'm hoping to expand it someday."

"Say, do you happen to have Professor Winz for accounting?"

"Yes," Cal sighed, "and I'm not looking forward to it. I hear his lectures are very cut and dry."

We chatted about common subjects as the trolley made its way to Derby and the Yale Boathouse. Since this was the first practice for both Cal and I we waited with anticipation as the coaches called out names for each boat. When our names were called and we realized that we would be on the same team, we smiled and clapped each other on the back. There was some good-natured joking amongst the team members that I would soon be cut from the crew because I was the smallest team member, not only in weight but in height. I merely smiled and shrugged my shoulders at their jests. Cal was long of leg and arm and he was placed into position next to me (ostensibly to compensate for my short arms). Once we were in place, the boat was guided out onto the waters of the Housatonic where we practiced working as a team. It soon became apparent to coaches as well as fellow-athletes that I was a storehouse of energy. When a few of the others began to lag behind in their strokes, I was still performing at peak energy. At the end of our practice, the head coach pulled me over and quietly informed me that I was being reassigned to the number one boat and put in the power position. He felt that with my sturdy build I could pick up the slack as others found a much needed breather.

By the end of the day's practice session, we were all very happy to board the trolley for the trip back to campus. As the trolley pulled up in front of the gymnasium Cal, who was seated once again beside me, stretched his muscles.

"I would love nothing more than a good night's sleep," he remarked, "but my roommate likes to have his friends over to our room for his Saturday evening discussions."

"Is he the studious type?"

"On the contrary, his discussions consist of he and several other fellows rolling in during the wee hours, pouring a few rounds of drinks, and discussing how far they've gotten with their respective dates that night."

"See that coach right there?" I pointed to the Bridgewater coach that was standing about a block away.

"Impressive conveyance," remarked Cal.

"That coach belongs to me. Would you care to come along and spend the weekend out at Bridgewater?"

"What's Bridgewater?"

"My home."

"Won't your parents mind you bringing a surprise guest?"

"My parents live in Boston. When I agreed to attend Yale, father deeded this property to me. It's not much mind you, but we do offer all the comforts of home. Proper meals, horseback riding if you're so inclined, and a staff of servants."

"That certainly does sound appealing," admitted Cal. "I'd hate to impose on you though."

"No imposition. Just grab what you'll need for a couple of days and meet me back here in half an hour."

We parted to go our separate ways, Cal back to his dorm room while I ducked into a nearby pub where I put away a couple of pints. As

I was emerging from the pub I spotted Cal walking towards the coach. No sooner had we leaned back against the coach seats and closed our eyes, than I heard my name being called.

"Mister Kevin, wake up. You're home."

I immediately recognized the voice as belonging to Paul. Once I was sufficiently awake I roused Cal by poking his arm.

"Wake up, old chum. We're home."

Cal's eyelids fluttered open and his eyes adjusted to the gathering darkness produced by the ancient trees that surrounded the lodge.

"Don't know what came over me to make me fall asleep like that. Sorry."

"Probably listening to those late night discussions your room mate hosts."

I watched from the gravel path as Cal stepped down from the coach. He turned a complete three hundred and sixty degrees taking in everything around us.

"It's quiet! What a heavenly sound!" he exclaimed.

While he was thus engaged, I turned towards the house to find Jeannette waiting for me with her arms open. I pulled her close, kissing her soundly as I did so.

"Welcome home, dearest," she intoned.

"Jeannette, I'd like you to meet Calvin Conner. Cal and I are on the same crew team."

"Pleased to meet you," Jeannette acknowledged.

"Cal, this is the woman I love. Need I say more?"

Cal placed a kiss on Jeannette's outstretched hand.

"At your service, ma'am," he replied.

"Angel, would you direct that the largest of the spare bedrooms be made up for Cal? I've invited him to spend the weekend, maybe longer."

Jeannette went off to see to Cal accommodations.

"Didn't know you were engaged," remarked Cal.

"Jeannette? Heavens no," I replied. "Jeannette is my housekeeper/bed warmer."

"You'll have to explain to me exactly how that works," Cal smiled as we entered the house.

By the end of the following evening I could see that Cal was anxious over something. I decided to ask outright what was troubling him. He was packing his gear for our return to campus the following morning.

"It's just that I've enjoyed being out here at Bridgewater. More than you can know. You haven't made me feel as though I've intruded in any way; I've been able to wander about and hear myself think. I don't relish the idea of returning to my stuffy campus room and my odious roommate."

"Why not move in here?" I offered.

"I couldn't do that!" objected Cal.

"Why not? We certainly have the room to accommodate you?" I could sense Cal's hesitation. "Was there something about the meals you didn't like?"

"No. Of course not," he replied.

"Then surely you must miss the noise and clamor of New Haven's streets."

"Definitely not that," joked Cal.

"Then what's the problem?"

"It appears there isn't any when you put things that way," agreed Cal.

"Good. Then it's settled. Leave your things here and tomorrow I'll help you collect the remainder of your stuff. This time tomorrow evening you can tell everyone you meet that you're new address is Bridgewater, Woodhaven."

Cal moved in and over the space of the next few months we became fast friends. Jeannette enjoyed his company as well and we both urged him to feel free to bring home an occasional lady friend or two. It was during a particularly snowy evening when we were sitting around the hearth, two old friends sipping father's excellent wine, with Jeannette tucked up on the sofa beside me, that Cal expressed his thanks for our living arrangement.

"Poppa is most pleased to know that I'm saving money by not living on campus."

"I'm happy to hear that. It's not often that I get credit for doing something good."

"It's not every day that a fellow like me meets a good-hearted soul such as yourself," replied Cal.

We were well onto our third or fourth glass of wine when Cal decided to open up about his family. I knew from previous talks that he was from an upper-middle class family hailing from the Irish enclave within The Bronx in New York City but Cal really hadn't given me much beyond that. So when he began his recitation of family history I paid careful attention.

"Did you know that my grandfather came to the states in the late 1820s?" he asked by way of opening the subject.

"That early?" I questioned.

"That's right. He opened a small tailoring business in one of the poorer city districts. Knew what he was doing, the old man. When word of his expertise with a needle and tape measure reached the homes of the upper class Irish his business grew. Finally married my grandmother and had several children."

"So you've got plenty of uncles and aunts?"

"Yes, sort of. My poppa's oldest brother died from some illness or other and one of their sisters died in childbirth. That left eleven of the thirteen siblings still alive."

"Your grandmother had thirteen children?"

Cal nodded as he sipped his wine.

"But only one inherited my grandfather's fine hand with a needle. Poppa took to tailoring like a duck to water. When grandfather passed away poppa took over the business and moved it to a better location. Changed the name to The Elite Haberdashery. He did custom tailoring of course but over time he added a line of gentlemen's ready to wear clothing that he would happily alter for the buyer."

At this point Jeannette sat up a bit straighter and I could tell that her interest had been piqued.

"My mother was a seamstress looking to open her own shop when she met poppa through a mutual friend. After some discussion they both saw that each could profit from the other's business and two months later the merge was made official at their wedding."

"Sounds like a match made in heaven," I commented.

Cal smiled warmly and sipped at his wine before continuing.

"While poppa waited on clients in the store, momma worked in a small alcove in the back of the shop. It was where she created exquisite dresses for her wealthy clients and their daughters. It was a time of hard work for my parents. In order to accommodate the needs of their patrons they would often work late into the night. They agreed that they would make do with the small alcove instead of an apartment that might or might not see them on a regular basis.

Momma would cook up a fast meal on the pot-bellied stove that also provided warmth in the winter. Very often they would work well into the early morning hours by just the light of an oil lamp before falling into their cot, exhausted."

"What a terrible life they must have had!" interjected Jeannette.

"Quite the contrary," answered Cal. "They kept busy with their work; they had a warm place to live and food on their table. And after a period of time, I arrived to keep them company."

"What a sport you were, even then!" I added.

"Well, their living arrangements had to change shortly after I arrived. I was a demanding sort even as an infant."

"Did your mother quit her work after you were born?" inquired Jeannette.

"In a way. Shortly after I was born my parents realized that they would need to have a residence large enough for a nursery – somewhere that I wouldn't be in the way of their work. Together they took stock of their savings. Poppa was amazed when he realized that enough money had been accumulated to outright purchase a brownstone in an adjacent neighborhood. Once our little family had moved into the brownstone, poppa took an option on an empty storefront bordering his current business and expanded the store. He took on a couple of apprentices who moved into the rear living quarters that he and momma had formerly used."

"Sounds like things were looking up," I commented.

"You said your momma went back to work, Cal. Did that happen right after you were born?" asked Jeannette, who was quite interested in Cal's story.

"Not right away, Jeannette. Momma took in laundry and did some mending for a few years but she finally returned to work full time after I began formal schooling. That was until shortly before my twelfth birthday when she presented me with a squalling baby sister. Cordelia was born in April of 1890."

"How sweet," commented Jeannette, "a baby sister."

"Yes, well, a baby sister who cried non-stop it seemed to me. And who momma had trouble disciplining. Of course, in poppa's eyes she could do no wrong."

"Of course," I commiserated with my friend.

"A couple of years later, thanks to poppa's thriving business and momma's careful money management, my parents sold the brownstone at a profit and moved us out to Staten Island. Our house is moderately sized but the quality of the craftsmanship really shines through. They don't build houses like that anymore."

"Did your mother ever open her own dress shop?"

I had been anticipating that question from Jeannette and she didn't disappoint me.

"Not exactly. After I reached school age, momma would see that I was safely tucked behind my school desk each morning before she boarded the ferry into the city. I would watch her as she left the school, one hand holding onto Cordelia, while she balanced her portfolio and portable sewing kit with the other hand. Momma's clients expected her to call at their homes so she spent much of her travel time going between clients. By day's end she would collect me from a neighbor's house, hurrying us to make sure that she had enough time to prepare supper. While I sat at the table and did my lessons, she would feed Cordelia, get her ready for bed, then set dinner on the table before joining poppa and I. Poppa would see to my nightly routine, tucking me in to my bed with a story or two. There were many nights when I would awake and tiptoe part way down the stairs only to see momma doing some hand-stitching on a customer's clothing. There were many nights when I didn't hear her come to sleep."

"I admire her, truly I do," murmured Jeannette, so that only I could hear her.

"Both my parents have a singular goal, though. That's to see that both Cordelia and I have a better life than the one they've lived thus far. I've always had a quick mind with numbers, I must add."

"Must you?" I joked.

Cal smiled.

"At my secondary school graduation I gave the valedictory speech," he informed us. "I received acceptances to several schools, any of which I would have gladly attended. But both momma and poppa insisted that I attend an Ivy League school. Given the proximity of Yale to Staten Island it was a foregone conclusion that once I was accepted I would take my classes here. I argued that Yale was too expensive but momma and poppa said they were glad to make any sacrifice they could to have me associate with a higher class of people."

I merely raised my eyebrows in question.

"Sometimes I have my doubts about that," replied Cal in jest.

"My mother would be happy to hear you think we are from a higher class of people."

"I'll bet," replied Cal.

"What of your sister, Cal? Do your parents hope to find her a brilliant match with a rich husband?" This line of questioning came from my Irish angel.

"Of course. Although Cordelia is still quite young, she has been accompanying momma when she visits her clients, and she is quite adept at copying the mannerisms and affectations she sees. Momma's latest goal is to enroll Cordelia in a fancy school for young women, in the hopes that this will give her a leg up in society."

"Perhaps I can have mother or my sister sponsor Cordelia when she's ready for her debut," I offered.

"That's very kind of you, but we'll need to change Cordelia's manners a bit more before that happens."

Over the course of the following month I exposed for Cal the perks and pitfalls of the privileged life within the Newkirk household. At my request Cal accompanied me to Boston for the Thanksgiving weekend. Any misgivings I may have had about Cal's ability to socialize with the Boston elite evaporated the moment I presented him to my family.

He first met father to whom he offered a firm handshake in greeting; he was unabashed by father's low expectations and Cal's self-confidence immediately set father at ease. Quite appropriately he brought gifts for both my parents: a bottle of fine aged Portugese port for father and a hothouse rose in a very delicate porcelain pot for mother. He graciously greeted my sister Bernice, shook hands with my brother-in-law Robert, and in a most continental fashion placed a soft kiss on my younger sister Sallie's hand.

"Your mustache tickles," Sallie giggled, hiding behind mother's skirts as only an eight-year-old can do.

That Thanksgiving visit was a hit, as I had expected it to be. For Christmas Day I joined my Boston family after celebrating a wonderful Christmas Eve with Jeannette in our woodland hideaway. New Year's Eve was another story altogether.

I traveled by train from New Haven to New York City's Grand Central Station where I was met by Cal. From there we proceeded to my rented suite at The Ansonia Hotel that would serve as my base of operations during my stay in the city. Once I was settled in, Cal took me on a tour of the city before we began our holiday revelry. The highlight of the tour, for him, was his father's business establishment, The Elite Haberdashery. It was there that I finally came face-to-face with the oft-spoken-of Charles Conner, Cal's father.

"Poppa, where are you?" called out Cal as we entered through the shop door, stomping the snow off of our galoshes.

"Cal, is that you?"

A dark curtain that separated the store proper from the back room was pulled aside to reveal an Irish gnome: a jolly man, a bit rotund, with full cheeks touched by a high pink color; a shock of hair that was almost full gray dangled across his forehead; his watery blue eyes were magnified by spectacles that perched atop his nose; around his neck hung a tape measure. He extended a plump hand in my direction and I returned his firm handshake.

"You must be Kevin," he observed. "You're exactly as Cal described you."

"Pleasure to meet you, sir." I returned Mr. Conner's handshake. "Quite a store you've got here."

"You noticed, eh?" Mr. Conner chuckled. "Never a slow season for us. Folks are always in need of fine clothing."

"Are all the garments in the shop hand-tailored?" I inquired, tucking my kidskin gloves into my coat pocket as I perused the displays of various gentlemen's garments.

"Most. I keep a small inventory of ready-to-wear but those are for folks who can't afford the time nor price of hand-tailored clothing." It was easy to see Mr. Conner's pride in his business. "I'm sure Cal has told you the history of our store so I won't waste your time in the retelling. Once Cal has finished his studies he plans to expand the business even further. But the young scalawag won't tell me his plans just yet."

As Mr. Conner spoke I had walked over to get a better look at a few finished shirt samples that were draping some mannequins. Mr. Conner came to stand beside me.

"Go ahead, feel the fabric," he urged.

My fingers skimmed the length of the shirt and I was amazed at the softness of the garment.

"My word, sir; that is without a doubt the finest fabric I've ever felt. I simply must have you make up several shirts for me."

"Hee, hee," chuckled the shopkeeper, "I'd be pleased to do that, Kevin. You look to be about a size fourteen with a thirty-two inch sleeve. Am I right?"

"I can't say for sure," I admitted. "My valet usually orders my shirts for me."

"Let's just measure you, then," he suggested as he whipped the well-worn tape measure from around his neck. "Just as I expected, a fourteen thirty-two," he quipped. "Would you want all formal dress shirts? Or shall I make one or two with the shorter, less formal sleeve length?"

"I don't know," I mused. "Perhaps three of each variety; all from that wonderful fabric," I hastened to add. "You can ship them to my home in Woodhaven."

"I know the address," Mr. Conner smiled as he noted the order on his order pad.

"Let me pay you now, sir." I reached into my jacket and withdrew my wallet.

"I normally charge a bit more but you can have the family discount." Mr. Conner winked at me. "Ten dollars for the lot."

"Why, that's less than two dollars for a shirt!"

"That's right," he chuckled again.

"What has father sold you?" Cal asked as he emerged from the back room.

"Only a half-dozen of the softest shirts I've ever known."

"Consider yourself lucky, my friend. If we stay any longer he'll sell you an entire new wardrobe. We'd best be on our way."

Cal placed a hand under my elbow and propelled me towards the door.

"It was a pleasure to meet you, Mr. Conner," I called out, "you'll remember to have those shirts sent out to Woodhaven?"

"Yes, yes," Mr. Conner nodded as he disappeared into the back room before momentarily popping his head back through the curtains. "You're still coming for New Year's dinner, aren't you?"

"We'll both be there, poppa," answered Cal as we stepped out onto the sidewalk.

It was a rousing New Year's Eve celebration wherein Cal and I, along with some female companions, rang in the new year of 1898. Cal had wisely accepted the offer to spend the night in my suite at The Ansonia. Upon our arising in the late morning, and after having seen to the departure of the ladies who also spent the night, Cal telephoned his parents to say that we would arrive around half past the hour of one.

At exactly one twenty-eight on that New Year's afternoon I had the pleasure of meeting Mrs. Conner and the displeasure of meeting Cal's young sister. At seven and one half years of age Cordelia Conner could be charitably characterized as a contrary child. She refused to shake my hand upon our introduction, instead turning her head in the opposite direction while clasping her hands behind her.

"I don't like you," she pronounced, her dark brown curls shaking to and fro as she spoke.

"Why not?" I feigned surprise at her rudeness.

"Because," was her answer. At that point she turned on her heel and ran upstairs.

"I must apologize for my daughter," began Mrs. Conner, a worried look crossing her face.

"No need to apologize," I replied, "she's just a child."

"A very rude child," Mrs. Conner added. "She's upset because she didn't receive the doll she wanted for Christmas. We've been feeling her displeasure this last week."

Mrs. Conner took my overcoat, hat, and gloves and hung them in the entry hall closet.

"We've explained to Cordy that sometimes a person doesn't receive everything they want but she said that she'd been a good girl and deserved the doll. Since that didn't work I fear she's going to be bad this year," added Cal.

"No matter, she'll get over it," replied Mrs. Conner. "Let's go into the parlor and visit. Cal, why don't you pour our guest a spot of whiskey before dinner."

I followed Mrs. Conner into a small parlor just off the central hallway. Unlike our parlor in Boston this one was filled to overflowing with small knick-knacks and souvenirs of places that the family had visited. The furniture was older but clean and comfy and I found myself completely at home there. Mr. Conner, Cal, and I spent a few minutes in pleasant conversation while Cal's mother returned to the kitchen to see to our dinner.

Later, after I had eaten my fill of a wonderful brisket and a vast assortment of succulent vegetables, I was presented with a large slice of mouth-watering apple pie whose light and flaky crust melted in my mouth. In no time at all I cleaned every last morsel from the dessert plate.

"Would you care for another slice of pie?" inquired Mrs. Conner. She seemed pleased that I had taken two helpings of everything else that was offered.

"Don't let momma fool you, Kevin," offered Cal. "She's the cook, laundress, and housekeeper around here. You name the chore and mom does it. She's what keeps the family going. Only hope I can find a girl like her when I take a wife."

Mrs. Conner had the grace to blush at her son's compliments before being distracted by her daughter.

"Cordelia, please stop fidgeting in your seat," she directed her remark to the youngster.

"May I be excused then?"

"Watch your manners, young lady. We have a guest."

"Is there some reason your sister didn't have any dessert?" I asked Cal quietly.

"It's because I didn't eat my peas," retorted Cordelia. "I don't like peas and I won't eat them."

She turned in my direction and made a funny face to show her displeasure with both the peas and with me. Mr. Conner caught his daughter in the act of doing so and frowned.

"Cordelia, if you won't behave like a young lady in front of our guest, then go to your room and remain there until you are summoned."

"Yes, poppa," Cordelia seemed a bit disheartened at being summarily dismissed from the table. She left the room quietly enough but we could hear her footsteps as she ran up the stairs and slammed shut her bedroom door.

"I'm sorry you had to witness that, Kevin," said Mr. Conner. "Normally she's quite well-behaved."

The remainder of my visit was uneventful. Later, as Cal and I stood on the top deck of the Staten Island Ferry, I questioned him further about his sister's Christmas request.

"What sort of doll was it that Cordelia wanted?"

"It was a porcelain bride doll that she came across in one of mother's magazines. The child has no concept of how much things cost, of course, so she had no idea that momma and poppa just can't afford it right now. Why do you ask?"

"I thought perhaps to purchase one for my sister Sallie. She and Cordelia are quite close in age and I thought she might like a new doll. With Sallie's birthday being in January it will be the perfect gift."

"If you're considering the doll for Sallie, check Macy's store. They have that particular doll in stock," supplied Cal. He sheepishly hung his head as he added, "I was going to buy it for Cordy myself but found that I didn't have sufficient funds."

The next day I found myself in the Toy Department of the R.H. Macy & Company store.

"May I be of assistance, sir?" a timid sales clerk squeaked, bobbing his head as he spoke.

"I'm looking for a particular bride doll that I'm told you may have in stock." I handed the clerk a slip of paper on which Cal had written a description of the doll.

"I know exactly the one you're looking for. It was a popular item this season; seems that all the young misses wanted one. But you're in luck, I have two remaining."

"I'd like to see them both," I directed.

"Certainly, sir."

The clerk scurried to the far side of the department and returned with two large bride dolls in tow.

"Here we are sir, the last two bride dolls." He placed them side-by-side on the counter for my inspection.

The dolls were indeed exquisite. They were similarly dressed in white bridal gowns fashioned from a stiff material that I was informed was taffeta. Each wore a crown embellished with glass stones to which was attached a lacy veil. The dolls' most distinguishing feature, according to the sales clerk, was their movable eyes. "Quite lifelike," the clerk assured me. I didn't think that was necessarily true but I wasn't really knowledgeable as to what a young girl might consider lifelike. The two dolls were, however, quite different when it came to hair and eye color.

"I shall take them both," I informed the astonished sales clerk. "Can you arrange to have them shipped?"

"Certainly, sir."

The sales clerk bobbed his head in affirmation. It was gratifying to see his excitement at making such a sale after the holiday rush.

"I would like the doll with blonde hair to be sent to Miss Sallie Newkirk, 48 Revere Street, Boston. Include a card that says: Happy Birthday to my sister Sallie, Love, Kevin. The doll with the dark hair and green eyes is to be sent to Miss Cordelia Conner at 82 Delafield Street, Staten Island, New York. I should like to include a card with that. I'll write it out myself please."

The card I enclosed with the doll bore the following message:

Dear Miss Conner,

This doll was delivered by mistake to Macy's Department Store. She was intended for delivery to your house on Delafield Street. Sorry for the delay in getting her to you. Please accept my sincerest apologies.

Your humble servant,
S. Claus

I later learned that my sister Sallie was thrilled with her present and thoughtfully placed her doll with the others in her doll collection. Cordelia seemed mollified that her Christmas wish had been fulfilled. Cal presented me with the letter that his sister had penned to Santa Clause in thanks for her present.

Dear Santa Claus,

Thank you for my bride doll. She is very pretty but her gown is last year's style. I can make her a new one, so don't worry.

I know my doll is supposed to look like me since she has brown hair and green eyes but I think I will be a much prettier bride when I get married.

You really should dismiss your navigator because you missed my house by quite a distance.

Thank you again for my doll,

Very truly yours,
Cordelia Conner

My remaining years at Yale passed uneventfully enough. Cal and I spent many nights studying before the Bridgewater hearth. Jeannette saw to the requirements of running the household and to keeping my bed warm on those cold nights. Learning had always come easily for me and so I literally sailed through my classes, leaving me many hours to devote to my first love: horse husbandry.

With Huckleby at the helm, Bridgewater became a first-rate breeding stable, producing the finest and sturdiest work horses for miles around. Many of these animals were kept to accommodate father's annual hunt and were later sold at auction. By the end of 1899, Bridgewater became a self-sufficient estate. Father was greatly pleased when I brought him the news that Bridgewater no longer needed to draw money from the family accounts.

On those school holidays that did not require my presence in Boston, I made the rounds of various race tracks, many times accompanied by Cal and several times joined by Jeannette. At first I simply admired the sleek strength of the various winning thoroughbreds; before long I began to know the breeders of the winning horses, ultimately trying to learn all I could from conversations with them. Still, I wasn't ready to purchase my first thoroughbred.

During my senior year at Yale, a number of things happened. Cal moved into a small apartment closer to campus because he was dating the daughter of a New Haven minister and wanted to be closer to town. Huckleby auctioned off all but four of our sturdiest work horses, adding the funds to our growing account at the New Haven Savings and Loan. And lastly, I gave my stamp of approval to the enlargement of the stables at Bridgewater.

Jeannette, my Irish Angel, had more than proven her worth as housekeeper. Her frugality with household expenditures drew praise from Huckleby – not an easy feat. While Jeannette's execution of her household duties gave no cause for comment, it was her duties as my personal chambermaid that earned her a place in my heart.

From time to time I would surprise her with small trinkets of my affection: an emerald brooch; platinum and topaz earrings; and my personal favorite, a diamond hair clip that she used when she wore her hair in an up-do. This hair clip soon became my personal favorite because she usually wore it, and nothing else, during our intimate moments; when I removed the clip her jet black hair would hang loosely about her shoulders.

My favorite memory of Jeannette is the one from Christmas Eve 1899. A tradition I had begun at Bridgewater was for all of the servants to join me for dinner at the main house. Jeannette would sit at my right and Huckleby to my left. After dinner, the servants would receive their Christmas bonus and then be dismissed for a few days so that they could enjoy the holiday with their own families.

On that particular night Huckleby was last to leave the house. With hat pulled down over his ears and scarf wound around his neck, he crunched through the ice-crusted snow as he made his way back to his quarters on the top floor of the new stable building. Watching his breath on the frosty night air stirred my need for a glass of brandy. I turned away from the window to find Jeannette's outstretched hand holding my drink. It wasn't the brandy though that caused my breath to hitch; it was Jeannette, who stood before me, wearing the sable coat that had been my Christmas gift to her. She looked radiant and happy. That was when I realized that she had secured her hair atop her head with the diamond hair clip.

I moved forward and slid my hands beneath the coat. As I expected, my fingers touched her bare flesh. We both watched the coat glide to the floor and pool at her feet. My fingers traced the outline of her jaw before dipping lower to fondle her full breasts. She in turn placed her arms around my neck and kissed me deeply. I removed the hair clip, allowing her hair to enshroud her shoulders. She trembled slightly as I picked her up and carried her to a carpeted place in front of the hearth where we spent the remainder of the evening enjoying the intimacy of each other's body.

Kevin

Chapter 5

Summer 1900

The new century brought with it a new start for me. In June I received my degree from Yale. On the Sunday of the commencement exercise, my parents, my younger sister Sallie, and a chosen few of our Boston relatives filled an entire row of seats. Afterward, father hosted a celebration dinner at the Taft Hotel where he also had reserved an entire floor of rooms for the family contingent. At the end of our dinner father stood up and made a toast in my honor.

"To my son, Kevin, I raise my glass this evening. Son, you've earned your place in the family business. While I don't expect you to move into a junior partnership just yet, I am pleased to announce your immediate appointment to the Board of Directors of Newkirk Trading. In time it is my fondest wish that you will take my place and partner with your brother-in-law Robert to keep Newkirk Trading alive."

Father raised his glass, as did everyone else at the table, and drank to my health and success. When all were done, I stood up and addressed my father.

"I can't say as I'm surprised at the appointment, father, but I am gratified to receive the position. With my studies at Yale now behind me, I suppose my next question is this: does my seat on the board entitle me to any monetary compensation?"

Father smiled broadly at my question.

"Of course it does! In fact, dear boy, you'll find your salary more than adequate."

———

During the remainder of that summer, I purchased a cozy bungalow set on one of Boston's quiet residential streets. As this would be Jeannette's house, I gave her leave to furnish it as she wished adding only the request for a soft leather chair for myself that would be placed near the hearth.

At last the day came when we left for Boston. As we stepped through the door of Bridgewater Lodge, Jeannette seemed to have trouble holding back her tears.

"Why so sad, angel?"

"This has been the nicest place I've lived in. We've made such happy memories here," she replied as I wiped her tears away with my finger.

"Yes, we have, dearest. But there are thousands more happy memories awaiting us." I kissed her nose and drew her near. "As long we we're together, I don't care where we are."

"I love you, Kevin," she sighed.

"I love you, Jeannette," I replied.

Never had I felt so sure of my emotions. At that moment I silently vowed that I would do everything I could to build a solid future before asking Jeannette to become my wife. Yes, there were sure to be social repercussions but as of late, I found that I had built up a distaste for the ways of high society. It was for the simpler life that I yearned. However, to provide Jeannette the type of life she deserved, I would first require a solid financial foundation. My first steps were the purchase of that small bungalow for my Irish Angel and work at building Bridgewater Stables.

Later that day, after we had arrived at the bungalow on Ash Street and Jeannette had settled in somewhat to our new home (I would be making myself at home there whenever I was in Boston), I took the opportunity to provide her with still one more surprise.

"I can't seem to stop smiling," remarked Jeannette as she put away the final items from the grocery delivery.

"That's good. I love your smile."

"I bless the day that Paul asked Maude to bring along a friend."

"I think somehow we were just destined to meet," I said.

"Perhaps. But God was watching out for me that day."

"And for me as well; after all, he sent me my Irish Angel."

She leaned over to kiss me, a deeply satisfying kiss that began to stir my reactions.

"Before we become distracted," I began, "I have a housewarming present for you."

Jeannette let her hand slide down to the area below my belt and gently grasped my family jewels. Of course my body reacted accordingly. She simply smiled and asked, "Where were you thinking to give me this housewarming present?"

Steeling myself, I grasped her hand and said, "We'll christen the new bedroom shortly darling, but I have another kind of housewarming present for you."

With as much speed as I could muster, I withdrew a folded piece of paper from my jacket pocket and handed it to her. She took it, unfolded it, and stood in complete silence.

"You now have enough money to establish that millinery shop you've always dreamed of," I offered.

"I can't take this check," she murmured.

"Why not?" I countered.

"It's too big a gift."

"And this house isn't?" I smiled at her logic.

"This house is for both of us. For two people. The shop, well, the shop is for me. It's my dream. Not yours." She folded the check and held it out to me.

"Believe me, my dear, the shop is for you, but knowing that your dream has come true and that I had a hand in it, well, that's for me."

Jeannette hesitated for a moment or two before pulling back the check, refolding it, and placing it on the side table. She moved in closer to me and said," I will repay you every penny of the amount on that check. In the meantime, how should I best thank you for your generosity?"

I took her hand, placed it on the area below my belt where it had previously been, and smiled at her.

"Perhaps you should just pick up where you left off?"

July 1907
Boston, Massachusetts

Once again I found myself summoned to a meeting with my father. This time I was to meet with him in his office at Newkirk Trading. I dressed with care that morning, kissed Jeannette, and set out for the headquarters building. The meeting had been called for ten o'clock that morning. I made it a point to arrive no more than five minutes prior to the meeting as father was of the opinion that anyone who arrived more than five minutes ahead of a meeting must not have enough to do except watch the clock.

Father's clerk ushered me into the office while advising me that father had been detained but would be no more than ten minutes late. I was to wait. Thus I found myself seated in father's almost Spartan-like office.

The arm chair I occupied was crafted from a hard wood, the worn spots on its arms and seat giving evidence of its many years of use. Father's chair was similar in style with the addition of a swiveling mechanism. Underfoot, the hardwood floors gleamed from a recent polishing. Father's desk as well had been crafted from the same fine hard wood and it, too, gleamed from a recent polishing. The top of the desk held only an inkwell and a small sheaf of papers in a blue folder bearing the Newkirk Trading logo embossed in gold.

I pulled out my pocket watch, checked the time: 10:04, and replaced it just as father opened the door. He made a beeline for the chair behind his desk, settled himself comfortably, and launched right into the conversation.

"Kevin, do you have any idea why I've summoned you here today?"

"Does it have anything to do with my recent birthday, sir?"

"In a way it does. How old are you now, son?"

"Twenty-nine years and three weeks, sir."

"Have you given any thought to your future?"

Anticipating very little change in my current status, I took a moment or two to formulate my answer.

"I propose to go on as I do now."

"Kevin, you've missed more board meetings than you've attended. And your absence has grown exponentially during the past four years or so. Is it your intention to turn your back on Newkirk Trading?"

"Not at all, father. I've merely had other commitments that I needed to honor."

"Yes, I know all about those commitments. Off chasing horses in some godforsaken backwater place called Kentucky when you should be here tending to business."

"It's true I've been busy trying to establish Bridgewater Stables and I don't trust the purchase of thoroughbreds to anyone other than Huckleby and myself. Since Huckleby is charged with overseeing the stables the chore of traveling falls to me. If it will please you, though, I'll make a better attempt at attending board meetings."

"Bah! No you won't. You're just like my brother Samuel." Father shook his head in despair; I noticed that he now sported a full head of white hair. And there were some fine lines behind the mustache; somehow he had aged when I wasn't looking.

"Sir?"

"Your uncle; my brother. A ne'er do well. Loved to gamble. And drink. And whore around. Died much too young. Thankfully he left no offspring – at least none that I know of. Broke your grandmother's heart."

There was nothing I could offer in response so I wisely remained silent. After father had calmed a bit he looked at me with a shrewd glance and asked, "Interested in raising horses, eh?"

"Yes, sir," I readily answered.

"You've done well with the hunting lodge. What do you call it now?"

"Bridgewater Stables, sir."

"Yes, humph! Well, I've got a proposition for you."

"Sir?"

"I'm prepared to name you Vice President of Foreign Contracts, assuring you a guaranteed substantial yearly salary. You'll only need to show up for one board meeting each year. One requirement is that you maintain an office here. You can time your visits here with your visits to that mistress of yours. By the way, that was shrewd thinking on your part to lend her the money for her business. Always good to diversify."

"Thank you sir, although I didn't think you knew about the millinery shop."

"There are many things you don't know about me, son. Now, in order to keep my high regard there are a couple more requirements to be met by you."

"And those are?"

"I plan to step down at the end of this year as does my partner, Mr. Woodward. We will issue a joint statement naming your brother-in-law as company president. You'll be expected to endorse that announcement."

"I can do that. And the other stipulation?"

"You must marry and produce a male heir to carry on the Newkirk name."

This last request floored me as I didn't feel that I was ready for marriage yet.

"I was thinking about holding off on marriage for a while yet, father. I wanted Jeannette to feel more independent before I broached the subject of marriage."

"You can't seriously be thinking of marrying your mistress! Listen to me, boy. There will be no such shenanigans in this family." Father stood up. His face turned bright red with his ire. "You will marry a young woman of your own social station. Someone with a Boston pedigree. And you will provide this family with a male heir. Is that clear?"

"While I understand the validity of providing a male heir, I do believe I should be free to choose who I will wed."

"Certainly, freedom of choice is a pre-requisite. You'll just need to choose from a certain gene pool. Do not confuse lust for your mistress with your familial duty."

I could feel the turmoil churning within my gut; however, I controlled my emotions and offered my response, "I'll do my best, sir."

"Good. I expect you'll join the family for an outing at Buttermilk Bay. Your mother has agreed to make it a house party and has drawn up a guest list of suitable young women for you to choose from."

Good God! I was going to be the prime stud at a filly farm! Thinking quickly I asked, "Will there be other eligible fellows invited?"

"Certainly not! It's you who need a wife."

"Might I ask that my friend Cal Conner be invited?"

"He's married now, isn't he?"

"Yes."

" I'll see that he and his wife are on your mother's guest list. They can serve as chaperones."

Late August 1907

Securely ensconced behind the steering wheel of my shiny new 1907 Mercedes convertible, I guided the auto across the Bourne Bridge that connected the mainland to Cape Cod. It was a wonderful feeling to be moving along at the high end of the speedometer, approximately forty-five miles per hour, and feel the sun on my face and the wind blowing about my hair. There were few other vehicles on the road that day and I allowed my thoughts to wander back to the wonderful night, and early morning, that I had spent in Jeannette's arms. I had been loath to leave her; she had shown nothing but support for me when I informed her of the reason for this family house party.

"I always knew this day would come," she stated matter-of-factly as she assisted me in donning my traveling clothes. "I am content with whatever time we can have together."

She placed a kiss on my cheek and favored me with a wistful smile. I knew that my life had been blessed when Jeannette and I met, now I was certain of it. Who could believe that we had spent the last ten years as lovers? She was everything I would ever require: adventurous, openly honest, a skillful housekeeper, seriously pretty, and without equal in her bedroom talents. But for her lack of pedigree she would have been the perfect wife.

As pleasant as the thought of last night and this morning were, it was time to put them aside. I turned my concentration to mother's houseguests, all of whom expected me to be gracious. In addition to my parents, my sister Bernice and her obnoxious husband, Robert Woodward, would be in attendance. My sister Sallie and her husband, Professor David Hawks, now lived in upstate New York and distance precluded their attendance. Mother had invited six eligible young ladies from Boston society, all of whom were eminently qualified (by mother's standards) to become Mrs. Kevin Newkirk. I squeezed any thought of these half-dozen wifely prospects out of my mind, preferring to think about reuniting with my college chum, Cal Conner, and meeting his bride of six months. I knew I could count on Cal to guide me in a forthright manner through the maze of beauties vying for my attention.

Once again I lifted my face towards the sun, enjoying the freedom of the open road before me. When at last I turned the motor car onto the drive of our eighteen room cottage located on the shore of Buttermilk Bay, our impeccably dressed houseboy scurried over to open the car door for me.

"Good morning, Jackson," I greeted him cheerily as I unzipped my white overalls and flung them into the back seat of the motor car.

"Your mother is furious, Mr. Kevin. She expected you yesterday." Jackson held my jacket as I slipped my arms into the sleeves.

"Is Paul not here, then?"

"Mrs. Newkirk thought he would be accompanying you, sir, but when he arrived alone she was quite put out."

"Thanks for the warning, Jackson. Now that I'm here I shall soothe mother's nerves."

I buttoned the collar of my shirt while Jackson drove the Mercedes towards the garage, shaking his head as he did so. I proceeded jauntily up the brick-paved path. There, waiting for me at the front door stood Mother, looking like an avenging goddess from Greek mythology.

"It's about time you graced us with your presence," she remarked.

"Good to see you mother." I planted a kiss on her cheek.

"You do realize that I've gone to great effort to arrange this house party for your benefit?"

"I'm sorry, mother, but I was unavoidably detained." I gave her my best sheepish grin.

"Hmph! You sound exactly like your father after he's been with Nora."

My jaw dropped at her mention of father's mistress. Mother gave me a knowing look.

"Certainly I know about Nora. What did you think? I'm a woman, not a fool. Now close your mouth and follow me, the ladies are anxious to meet you." She took a couple of steps toward the morning room before turning to me and whispering, "If you ever disclose to your father that I know about his mistress, I will make your life a living hell."

I was so dumbfounded that I could merely nod my understanding as I followed Mother into the morning room.

"Ladies, you'll be pleased to learn that my son has finally arrived."

Mother's glance took in the assemblage of young women who

immediately trained their eyes on me in much the same way as a pack of hunting hounds sights its prey.

"I'm so glad nothing dire has happened to you. We were all quite worried."

This statement from a tow-headed woman who appeared to be well above the marriageable age earned her a scowl from mother. I could see that mother had mentally struck the girl, whose name was Emmaline Rogers, from the list of serious contenders for my attentions.

After that, I was introduced to the others in turn: Anita Swanson, Patricia Cronin, Elise Bearman, Barbara Wallace, and Margaret Winters. Collectively they were a group of young ladies who had been passed over during their debutante seasons but who were highly marriageable due to their families' connections, one being the daughter of our own Senator Bearman.

So its come to this, I thought. Surely I could do better on my own.

"Ladies," I nodded in their general direction, "Mother, if you'll excuse me I'd like to freshen up after my drive. I won't be long."

I made haste in my retreat from the morning room. Once in my bedroom I closed and locked the door behind me, only to be greeted by a smirking Paul who had been awaiting my arrival.

"I see you've met the ladies," he chuckled.

"Seriously, Paul, can you see me with any of those horse-faced wallflowers? They've been on the shelf so long they've grown long in the tooth."

Paul exchanged my rumpled shirt for a crisp, clean one while I tamed my hair with a bit of pomade.

"Simply choose the least offensive. After all, you still have Jeannette," he pointed out.

"Yes, but Paul, the horses in my stable are handsomer than any children I could beget on those fillies."

"It's quite a dilemma you have, sir." Paul's smile told me that he was happy to be in a position of servitude and not faced with my particular problem. "You do need a male heir, though, and with enough absinthes even those six might look appealing."

Forty-five minutes and three neat whiskies later, I emerged from my room and made my way towards the terrace only to find the ladies gathered around my friend Cal who was regaling them with a story from our undergraduate days. Cal never seemed to change. He was blessed with boyish good looks that seemed to get better as he aged. As he stood with one leg raised on the picnic bench, his eyes held a touch of merriment as he divulged a story of one of our many excursions to Mory's Tavern. His voice was pleasant and when he spoke, he had the ability to make it seem that even in a room full of people he was speaking directly to you. The ladies gave him their complete attention.

From my vantage point in the den I let my gaze wander over the collection of ladies, silently marveling at how they all seemed to be cut from the same template. I was sure Mother had chosen these ladies based on their breeding and gene pool, so they were all quite similar; I decided that I would make my choice based on the sound of their voice since in other respects they seemed interchangeable.

I immediately removed Emmaline from the short list since she had brazenly addressed me without a proper introduction. Anita Swanson was a tall, willowy blonde whose voice was as quiet as a mouse. This was somewhat appealing but could she, I wondered, raise that voice to discipline a servant or a wayward child. Patricia Cronin sported a luxuriant head of black hair that was pulled back in a severe style that played up her overly large doe eyes. I listened as she questioned Cal and was amazed that her voice sounded almost masculine. Elise Bearman, another black-haired beauty, emitted a high-pitched voice that immediately grated on my nerves. Barbara Wallace, whose auburn hair was held back from her face by tortoise-shell combs, spoke only in whispers. Margaret Winters, another blonde, seemed the most outspoken of the lot but I wondered if she would eventually emerge as a controlling wife.

I had just about given up hope when I heard it: the voice of my future wife. I sighed in relief as the sound of this angelic voice fell upon my ears. Who could this sweet voice belong to? Had one of the Buttermilk Six (as I referred to them) perhaps brought along a sister or cousin? I had to find out to whom that voice belonged.

With three quick moves I stepped out onto the terrace and joined the group. Immediately I spotted her, standing apart from the others, on the far side of the terrace. Soft billows of a frothy lawn dress fell from alabaster shoulders. A riot of gleaming chestnut hair was held back from her cherubic face by a ribbon that matched her dress; a pert nose and a tiny mouth complemented her creamy complexion. When she looked at Cal it was evident that her eyes, as green as the hills of Ireland, were full of love. Ah! This must be Rose, Cal's wife. What a lucky bastard, I thought, to have found such perfection. No wonder that he seemed so content.

"Kevin, it's about time you made an appearance. I'm sure that these ladies are bored beyond tears but they've been ever so kind in humoring an old married man." Cal stood up and pulled me into the center of the group. "He's all yours, ladies."

The remainder of that day was spent pleasantly enough but regardless of the activity we were involved in my thoughts strayed to Cal's wife. My curiosity was further piqued when neither Cal nor his wife joined us for dinner. Mother, however, made their excuses when she informed us that "the Conners were having supper with family friends in Hyannis and will be spending the night there."

I was disappointed not to have Cal present at the dinner table but Bernice kept the conversation flowing during dinner as she engaged the young ladies in topics such as fashion and housekeeping. When the gentlemen (father, Robert, and myself) retired to the billiard room for a cigar and brandy I was buttonholed. The campaign to get me married began in earnest.

"Well, son, have you formed an opinion on any of the young ladies yet?" Father took a long pull on his Cuban cigar and blew out a small cloud of smoke.

"I really haven't...."

"Surely one amongst them must stand out? What do you think of Anita Swanson?" Robert queried, helping himself to father's excellent port.

"Well, I...."

"Don't be shy, boy, speak up. I rather fancy that Barbara Wallace myself. She'd be a fine fit with the family, too," Father observed.

"She is rather....."

"No, no. The Wallace girl is too brash," protested Robert. "Anita's beauty speaks volumes on her behalf. Besides, she's as docile as a lamb.

"Poppycock! You're only championing her because she's your cousin, Robert. And at twenty-five she's a spinster. But the family does have money," conceded Father with a shrug of his shoulders.

"Enough! I'll choose my own wife if you please; although I thank you both for narrowing the field for me. Miss Wallace and Miss Swanson are now out of contention.

I crushed my cigar into the ashtray and stalked out of the room.

"Honestly, Paul, I don't care a fig for any of those women. If only I had met Rose before Cal married her I would have swept her off her feet and made her my bride. She's perfect. Pleasant to look at, a lovely voice, and her children would be handsome."

We were back in my room, where Paul was brushing my trousers as I prepared for bed.

"Rose Conner, sir?"

"Yes, Cal's wife. I saw her earlier today on the terrace. I was desolate when she and Cal didn't appear for dinner."

"The young woman, did she have chestnut hair? Green eyes?"

"Yes, that's her all right."

"Ah! That's not Mr. Cal's wife."

"Of course it is. Mother said the Conners were visiting friends in Hyannis."

"That much is true, Mister Kevin. But your mother meant that Mr. Conner and his sister, Miss Conner, were dining in Hyannis." Paul's smug smile indicated that he knew more than I did, which was a rare occurrence.

"You mean that vision of angelic perfection is Cordelia Conner?"

"Exactly, sir."

"Well, I'll be a monkey's uncle! Little Cordelia Conner."

Much to the consternation of my parents I gave only minimal attention to the stable of young women from whom I was meant to choose a life partner. I couldn't help myself. Like a moth drawn to the proverbial flame I found myself drawn to the lovely Cordelia Conner. Her mere presence lit up whatever room she was in, and my smiles came easily when I was in her presence. Next to her beauty the other women paled in comparison. If I was to be forced to choose a wife then I was determined to have some say in the matter. I knew Cordelia could be strong-willed but I didn't see that as insurmountable. At least our children would be handsome. I just needed to convince Cordelia, and her brother Cal, that ours would be a good match. I spoke of my feelings to Cal as we strolled along the shore of Buttermilk Bay, our pant legs rolled up to our knees and the warm sand beneath our toes.

"I can't believe how much your sister has changed since I last saw her."

"That was, oh, several years ago my friend. She's become quite the heartbreaker," Cal agreed.

"It seems that she's captured my attention completely. I'm afraid the other young women don't stand a chance," I admitted.

Cal didn't respond but merely nodded his head.

"By the way, where is your lovely bride?" I inquired. "I'd been looking forward to meeting the girl who finally tied you down."

"Rose wasn't up to traveling in her condition," grinned Cal.

"You sly dog!" I clapped a hand on my friend's shoulder. "When is she due?"

"Sometime in March. I don't get involved in figuring those things out." He smiled.

"We have some catching up to do. How are things at the haberdashery?"

"Excellent. We've rented a small building and installed twelve sewing machines along with two cutting tables. Fourteen employees in all turning out high quality gentlemen's clothing that poppa and his assistants can tailor to the buyer. If all goes well, I'm thinking we can expand to produce ladies clothing in a couple of years."

He stopped and picked up a stone which he skimmed across the water. We walked on quietly for a spell.

"Seriously, Cal, is Cordelia spoken for?"

"She's had a couple of proposals but she turned them away."

"What were her reasons?"

Cal took a deep breath before continuing. "Cordy's goals are twofold. First she seeks to further our family's social standing. Momma supports her on that."

"Quite understandable," I agreed. "And her other reason?"

"That's the tough one, my friend. Cordy says love must be involved."

"Is that all?" I breathed an audible sigh of relief.

"You're serious, aren't you?" Cal stopped dead in his tracks. "My folks would gladly welcome you into the family. They already think of you like a son."

"I'm positive that the Newkirk name could easily elevate your family social status," I offered.

"What about Jeannette? Is she still in the picture?"

"Jeannette will always be a part of my life. Unfortunately, I can't make her my wife as my father has pointedly reminded me. Would that I could," I sighed.

"I'm extremely lucky, then. For I fell in love with Rose at the same time I fell in lust with her," chuckled Cal. "Getting back to Cordy, it's the prerequisite of loving someone that raises doubt about you finding her agreeable to marriage."

"I can be pretty persuasive, old chum. Just leave that to me."

For the third consecutive night sleep would not come. After much tossing and turning I gave up the fight. Donning my silk dressing robe, I made my way downstairs and slipped out the back door and onto the terrace as I done on the two previous nights. An almost-full moon played hide-and-seek with some passing clouds. In the stillness I could make out the sound of the waves in the bay gently lapping at the shore. I filled my lungs with a deep breath, enjoying the silence.

"Peaceful, isn't it?"

The angelic voice wafted towards me from the depths of a shadowy Adirondack chair.

"Quite peaceful," I acknowledged, turning in the direction of the faceless voice.

At that moment the moon emerged from behind a cloud and shone its delicate light on a picture of perfection that stole my breath. If wishing could make something happen, I would be content to be the chair that held Cordelia Conner in its embrace. She was clad in a dressing gown that gleamed like mother-of-pearl in the moonlight. Her eyes twinkled with the light of the stars. *Say something, my brain urged my mouth.*

"Are you finding it difficult to sleep as well?" I eased myself into a neighboring chair.

"On the contrary, I've slept quite well these past few nights."

"I'm happy to hear that." A peaceful silence filled the next few moments. "I hear you're going to become an aunt," I commented.

"Yes, early next year according to Rose."

Again silence ensued as we listened to the breaking waves on the nearby sandy shore.

"It's been a long time since we last spoke."

"I suppose I owe you an apology," she offered. "I was quite a rude child when I first made your acquaintance."

"Yes, you were," I admitted. "But you were merely a child after all. You've grown into quite a courteous young lady."

"Thank you. I think," she replied.

"How are you getting on with the others here?" I changed the topic without preamble.

"I keep clear of them. I know when I'm an interloper."

"But…."

"Please don't apologize for them. I know I'm not of their class. I've heard their whispers when they think I don't hear."

"Does their gossip bother you? I'll send them all away immediately."
I was earnest in my offer.

"Oh, no!" she laughed. "They're only jealous because I'm younger
and have more stylish clothes."

"Right you are on both counts," I agreed. "Perhaps if you gave them
the name of your modiste?"

"They would never agree to work with her." I could feel the smile
in her voice.

"Why ever not? They could certainly use some fresh fashion ideas.
I'll let you in on a secret if you promise not to tell." I dangled the verbal
temptation metaphorically before her.

"Cross my heart."

"They all look frumpishly alike to me." There, I'd said it aloud.

"But they each are unique in their own way." The melody of her
voice gently touched my ear.

"I am obliged to take your word for it. But I must inquire further
why these ladies shouldn't be introduced to your modiste?"

I was fairly sure I knew the answer to my question. She hesitated
briefly before tendering her response in a serious voice.

"I design and sew my own clothes." Her words were whispered.
"Please, Kevin, you can't let anyone know. I would be instantly
ostracized."

Cordelia had used my given name and my spirit soared! Of course
I knew she looked upon me as her brother's friend but I hoped to move
beyond that.

"I think it quite enterprising of you to create your own fashions.
Who better to tailor the garments one wears? Besides, with your
ancestry in the garment industry I would expect nothing less. Never
fear, Cordelia, I shall not inform anyone of your talents if you don't
wish it."

"Thank you." Her whispered response held a note of relief. She rose
from her chair, clutching her dressing gown tightly around her slim yet
curvaceous body. "I must go inside. It's getting late and I'm sure you'd
like some time alone."

Of its own volition my hand shot out and reached for hers, pulling her into my arms as I rose. She yielded slightly. As I enfolded her in my embrace I realized that the fabric separating my hand from her flesh was gossamer thin. With my free hand I pushed back the cascade of hair from her face. It slipped through my fingers like silky moonbeams before I tilted her chin upwards.

"Cordelia Conner, when did you grow into such a beauty?" I murmured against her cheek. Before she could utter a response I firmly kissed her.

She didn't immediately pull away as I expected her to; instead she seemed to melt into my arms. I was mildly surprised to find that she was quite experienced at the art of kissing. Her pliant lips left no room for thoughts of my Irish Angel; it was a wholly engaging experience. I had just allowed one hand to slide down her back when she stiffened, broke off the kiss, and landed a resounding slap to my face that left my jaw tingling from its force. She might be of a slight build but she packed a wallop.

"How dare you?" she panted, backing away from me and falling into the chair.

"I only meant…"

"I know exactly what you meant, Mr. Newkirk," she literally spat out the words. "Just because you're my brother's friend does not give you license to have your way with me."

"Please, Cordelia, lower your voice. Someone might hear you," I implored.

"It's Miss Conner to you!"

She gained her feet once again and dashed into the house, allowing the screened door to slam behind her and leaving me standing in the moonlight, watching her retreat.

The following morning father strode into my bedroom long before I had summoned the energy to rise from my bed. I awoke to see him sitting in a nearby chair until I surfaced from the dregs of slumber.

"Father? What are you doing here? Have I overslept?" I yawned and ran my fingers through my hair.

"Well done, my boy. A bit unorthodox but well done." Father smiled like the Cheshire Cat from a childhood fairytale.

"I have no idea what you're talking about sir. Where's Paul? I need my morning coffee."

I pulled back the bedclothes and yanked on my dressing robe, scratching at the stubble on my chin.

"Your mother is quizzing the young ladies even as we speak and assuring your fiancée that a proper wedding will take place. But I couldn't wait. Tell me, son, who is she? I do hope it's the Wallace girl." Father rubbed his hands together with glee, his face wreathed in smiles.

"Whatever are you talking about, father? I have no fiancée. At least not yet. Where is my morning coffee?"

"Don't pussyfoot around, boy. I saw the entire escapade from my bedroom window. You obviously enticed one of your ladies to meet you on the terrace after the household was asleep. I heard your voices but couldn't make out the words. Yes, it must be the Wallace girl. I know my eyes weren't deceiving me, I saw you kiss her in the moonlight. Did she let you get a bit familiar, eh?"

"Father, please! I did no such thing with Miss Wallace nor with any other of the young women that mother invited." I was still not fully awake and all of this was very confusing.

"Good, good! Deny everything until I give you the high sign. Much better, really. Let the young woman come forward of her own accord." Father rose from the chair but stopped short at the door. "Now don't dawdle, boy. Get dressed and come down to breakfast. We'll announce your engagement this afternoon."

As father left my room, Paul entered carrying a steaming mug of coffee which I downed in two gulps, scalding my mouth in my haste to ingest the brew.

What the hell had happened? My last thoughts before I drifted off to sleep last night were of holding Cordelia in my arms and recalling the kiss we'd shared. Granted, she had treated me like the cad I was but that was a normal reaction from a young woman who had not solicited my advances. Surely all of this could be sorted out. I would speak with Cordelia immediately.

A quarter of an hour later I entered the dining room, hoping to quietly nourish myself for the upcoming scene that I knew would follow. But upon my arrival there I faced not one but six hopeful faces, each hoping that I would name her as the compromised woman that I would wed. I searched the room in vain for Cal and his sister as I mumbled a vague, 'good morning' to the others.

It was the willowy blonde, Anita Swanson, who rose from her seat and walked provocatively towards me. In a shameless manner she leaned against my chest while planting an open-mouthed kiss upon my startled lips.

"Just as I remembered it, darling," she cooed, aiming a sly smile at the others. "I can't wait to become your wife." She hooked her arm through mine and pulled me towards the table. "Let me fix your breakfast plate."

"What's going on? How dare you so brazenly kiss me?" I threw off her arm and backed away from her.

"You enjoyed it well enough last night," she retorted as her phony smile disappeared.

"I didn't kiss you last night," I vehemently denied. "In fact I never laid a finger on any of you." My glance took in all six women.

"I say, what's all the commotion about?" inquired my brother-in-law Robert as he entered the room. "I heard raised voices and thought it best to investigate."

"Oh, cousin, Kevin has compromised me and now refuses to acknowledge his actions," wailed Miss Swanson as she ran towards her cousin for comfort.

"I've done no such thing!" I countered as I backed out of the room pointing at the crying female. "Keep that woman away from me!"

I turned and fled into the parlor as I sought to put distance between myself and the now sobbing Miss Swanson. But I was to find no respite.

"Too bad, son. I'm not overly fond of the Swanson girl but she can adapt to our ways. We'll announce the engagement this afternoon and I'll meet with her father upon our return to Boston." Father tucked his head back into the newspaper he was hiding behind.

"Mother, you must listen to me," I implored of our family matriarch who was sitting across the room. "I did not compromise Miss Swanson last night. She's not the one I kissed out on the terrace."

"But you admit to kissing someone, don't you?" father queried.

"Yes, I...."

"Kevin, dear, just tell us who it is," urged mother.

I looked first to mother, then to father, and back to mother again, noting the look of expectancy on their faces.

"Where's Cal? I must speak with him first."

"Why, he and his sister departed early this morning. He couldn't wait to return to his wife, I imagine. I can't believe his gold-digger sister had the audacity to come here with him. Why do you ask?" inquired mother.

I stood frozen in place. What was I to do? I felt trapped. I looked first at mother, whose talents had orchestrated the events leading up to this moment; a look at father reminded me that this entire affair was not something that I had wanted. Well, they wanted a daughter-in-law and a male heir so I determined that I would give them one. As the wheels of my mind churned to their inevitable conclusion, mother rose from her seat and walked towards me.

"Kevin? Are you all right?"

"I'm perfectly fine, mother. In fact you're both correct. I have decided on my future wife."

"Finally!" exclaimed father.

"I'm sorry she had to leave so early this morning, though. You see, it is Cordelia Conner who I compromised last night on the terrace. It is she who will become my wife."

My pronouncement silenced father; but I was unprepared for mother's reaction. Never had I seen a woman crumple into a swoon and fall to the floor with such grace!

Cordelia

Chapter 6

L et it be said, straight off, that attending the Newkirk party was not my idea. It was momma's.

A few weeks ago, I had been enjoying the bright August morning and had taken my needlework out of doors, settling into a well-worn wicker porch chair. Although I was warmed by the morning sun it had not yet become hot enough to be unbearable. I was concentrating on the intricate embroidery I was applying to the neckline of a peplum jacket that I had recently sewn.

"There you are, dear. I've been looking for you." Momma traversed the length of the porch as she approached me.

"Are you in need of a living model for one of your clients again?" I wondered what sort of outfit I might be called upon to model.

Mother settled into another chair and it was clear that she was excited about something.

"Actually, Cordy, you are being presented with a once-in-a-lifetime opportunity."

"What's his name?"

My words were expelled on an audible sigh. I was weary of momma arranging for me to meet qualified suitors who had a lineage of wealth and social position.

"What makes you think it has anything to do with finding you a suitable husband? Although we'll need to discuss that again at some point. I'm asking you to do something for your brother."

"Is Rose not well? How can I help?" My immediate concern was for my new sister-in-law who was pregnant.

"Rose, bless her heart, is confined with severe morning sickness. Both she and Cal have been invited to a house party and since she is unable to attend she thought perhaps you might enjoy the outing in her place." Momma paused for dramatic effect. "You never know who you'll meet."

"Just as I suspected! You're hoping I'll fall madly in love with the son of a wealthy banker."

"You're under no pressure to fall in love, dear, but if that should happen you'll have raised our social standing as well as having helped your brother."

"I give up! Where is this soiree taking place?"

"It's being hosted by the Newkirks from Boston, at their summer residence on Cape Cod."

"As in Kevin Newkirk? Cal's friend from Yale?"

"So you do remember him?"

"I remember him as looking much like a lump of pasty bread dough," I remarked, noting momma's silence. "Surely you aren't hinting that I set my cap for Kevin Newkirk. Why, he's an old man!"

I was so annoyed that I fumbled a stitch and pricked my finger with the embroidery needle.

"Your brother is the same age as Kevin," pointed out momma. "I shouldn't need to remind you that Kevin Newkirk is exactly the kind of man you need to marry."

"I don't need to marry at all," I countered defiantly.

"Cordelia Catherine Conner, you will accompany your brother to Cape Cod and you will open yourself to any advances Kevin Newkirk may make, within the bounds of propriety of course. Is that clear?"

Momma's voice had become stern but still I remained defiant.

"And if I refuse to attend?"

"Then your father and I will be forced to choose your husband for you. At seventeen years of age you should already have accepted a proposal and be preparing your trousseau."

Thus it was that I had traveled with my brother to Buttermilk Bay and endured the snide remarks of a half-dozen dowdy spinsters whose sole aim was to become Mrs. Kevin Newkirk. They were a pathetic group, really. Each one tried so much harder than the other to compliment and puff up the egotistical bachelor that it was all I could do not to laugh outright. From my place on the sideline (I was not considered a contender) it was delicious fun to watch them fawn over my brother's friend.

My own actions, on the other hand, were similar to those I had previously employed to elicit marriage proposals from Steve Goldman and Horace Davis. It was a time-tested method that women have used for generations: be distant, be aloof, feign disinterest; and arrange a coincidental meeting at a location where the man feels secure. That was all I did.

After our arrival at Buttermilk Bay I noticed Kevin's habit of taking a nocturnal stroll. Biding my time, I waited until the night before everyone was due to depart. True to habit, Kevin arrived on the terrace a few moments after I had taken a seat in the half-shadows where he could conveniently stumble upon me. And stumble he did! Of course the moonlight, the soft sound of the waves along the nearby shoreline, and the occasional call of a night bird, all set the mood beautifully. Kevin and I spoke about various things, all having nothing to do with his search for a wife; when he finally pulled me into an embrace and kissed me, I allowed it of course – before rendering a slap to his jaw for taking such a liberty.

The coup d'etat was our early departure this morning. I wish I could have seen the look on Kevin's face when he realized that mine was the kiss to excite him and that I was the one he would marry. But I remain secure in the knowledge that I'll be seeing young Mr. Newkirk before too much more time passes.

Upon our arrival home I recounted for momma the events that

had transpired during the extended weekend at the Newkirk summer home. Much to my surprise momma was content that my actions would spur Kevin into pursuing me with a proposal of marriage. Momma cautioned me about speaking to Cal regarding any of this: "He'll only tip off Kevin and our plan will be obliterated," she advised. So I resumed my normal routine and gave no further thought to Kevin Newkirk.

September 1907

Momma and I were in the kitchen preparing dinner when we heard muted voices coming from our foyer. Neither of us had heard the front door open nor were we expecting poppa just yet. We exchanged startled looks. Silently, momma motioned for me to grab a heavy rolling pin while she armed herself with a carving knife. Together we stealthily approached the doorway that opened on to the dining room. At momma's signal we stopped and listened.

"I'll attend to that order for your shirts first thing tomorrow morning. I can't tell you how happy I am that you've agreed to have supper with the family. Mrs. Conner and Cordelia will be so pleased to see you."

Momma visibly relaxed when she recognized poppa's voice. We turned and scurried back to the kitchen where we resumed our cooking chores; poppa most likely would have ushered our guest into the living room where he would offer our visitor a finger of brandy.

"It must be a very important customer that poppa has invited for supper," I commented. "I can handle what's left of the cooking duties, momma, why don't you go freshen up?"

"If you're sure you don't mind, dear."

"Not at all. Your place is in the living room with poppa and our guest. Perhaps the gentleman will order a new gown for his wife when he sees you fashionably dressed."

With momma out of my way I set about the final supper preparations, grateful that the roast I pulled out of the oven was a large one and I wouldn't need to prepare still another side dish. I plated the fare on our best serving platter and turned to the cabinet to fetch another place setting, pushing back a strand of my hair that had become displaced in the heat of the kitchen. Beads of perspiration dotted my forehead and I used the back of my hand to wipe them away. I turned towards the dining room to set the extra place but stopped short. There, standing in the doorway, was Kevin Newkirk.

"Good afternoon, Miss Conner."

"Mr. Newkirk." I acknowledged his presence with a nod of my head.

"I would like to have a word with you." He stood, hands clasped behind his back, blocking my movements.

"I'm quite busy, as you can see. Besides, I can't think what you'd want to speak to me about." I kept my head down as I spoke.

"Actually, there are two things I believe we should discuss." He moved around the table and relieved me of the dishes I held.

"Two things?" I questioned. "You must have been doing quite a bit of thinking since we last met."

"First, and foremost, I owe you an apology, Miss Conner. I overstepped my bounds when I kissed you."

"Apology accepted." I turned towards the sink so he wouldn't see my self-satisfied smile. "And the second thing?"

"I'm here to ask for your hand in marriage."

"What of those six high-society women your mother invited to your family's home? Did none of those ladies appeal to you?"

"Next to you they are nothing," he whispered, placing a hand on my shoulder and turning me to face him.

"Surely any one of them would make a better wife for you. After all, I'm not from your social class. Your friends and family would look down on me," I pointed out.

"I don't care about all of that. It's you I want to marry."

That should have been my cue to melt into his embrace but that would never do. He musn't think that I would give in so easily.

"I'm not sure we would be such a good match, Mr. Newkirk," I stated as I pulled back my hand from his grasp and reclaimed the plates for the dining table.

"I've already spoken to your father, if that's what you're worried about. He's given me his blessing. All that remains is for you to say yes."

I could see by the look in his eyes that he truly wanted to marry me. So it appeared that I had won my prize; but I still believed he should work for his.

"This is all very sudden. I don't know how I feel about all of this."

"Will you at least consider the proposal?"

"Well, that I can do. But I don't wish to be rushed."

"Take whatever time you need. I must warn you, though, that my parents are pressuring me to produce an heir. I would like to start on that as soon as possible."

He pulled me closer and I thought for an instant that he was going to kiss me again, but he stopped and gazed into my eyes, trying to convince me of his ardor.

"I've replayed our kiss on that moonlit terrace every moment for the past two weeks. I can't get it, or you, out of my mind. Were you just a vision sent to tempt me? Was that kiss real? I must know."

He gently kissed me there, in the kitchen, with my parents in the next room. Of course I enjoyed it, what woman doesn't want to be cherished by her future husband? But I didn't put my whole heart into the kiss. I was saving that for when I would accept his proposal.

"Do you think you could learn to love me, Cordelia, even a little?" he whispered.

"I'm not sure." My words were murmured.

He pulled me closer still.

"Say you'll marry me and I shall see that you want for nothing."

While I took the time to evaluate Kevin's proposal, he had taken a suite of rooms at The Ansonia Hotel in the city. Every morning, directly after breakfast, he would arrive in front of our house in a motor car with a chauffeur. Some days we would simply drive around Staten Island's more countrified districts, often stopping to take a walk along the shore. During inclement weather he would invite momma and I into the city where we would take afternoon tea at one of the better restaurants.

On several occasions Kevin opened up his suite to our family so that we could dress for an evening at the theater. In an effort to impress me with his wealth he paid for tickets for himself and our entire family, including my brother and sister-in-law. On a daily basis he had fresh-cut flowers delivered to me with a personal note attached.

Small gifts found their way into my possession. At first they were inconsequential: a set of ladies handkerchiefs, a pair of lacy gloves, a delicate parasol. Towards the end of second week the gifts became more elaborate and meaningful: a gold bangle bracelet, a cameo brooch, peridot earrings, jade hair combs. Still I kept him waiting for my answer as he danced attendance on me.

"Another gift has arrived for you, Cordelia," announced momma as she entered my room. "Don't you think it's about time you accepted Kevin's proposal?"

"There remains one problem." I accepted the gift from momma's hands and placed it, unopened, on my vanity.

"And what is that? It certainly can't be lack of money." Momma perched on the edge of my bed as I continued to brush my hair.

"I don't love him."

"Pish-posh. You wouldn't be the first young miss to marry without love. Look at me."

"But you love poppa."

"I do now. But that wasn't the case when we first wed. It was more of a business arrangement. I needed a benefactor to help me get my couturier business off the ground. Your father was already an established tailor. We liked each other well enough so we married."

"But you and poppa love each other now?"

"Yes, we do. Love will grow on a solid foundation of respect and trust. We had those so naturally love followed."

"Do you think that there is enough between Kevin and myself to form such a solid foundation?"

"He appears to love you; we know he respects you. Kevin comes from a good family and has enough money to provide for you and your children. He is respectful, honest, and patient with you. He could easily have been put off by your request to 'think things through'. But mark my words, his patience won't last much longer. If you think to prolong making your decision he'll turn away and choose another."

I turned back towards the vanity and picked up the white box containing Kevin's latest gift. Inside the box lay a heart-shaped jewelers box covered in white velvet. I opened the lid and gasped! There, lying on a bed of white satin, was the most exquisite necklace I had ever seen. It was fashioned of strands of gold that gleamed in the sunlight and was encrusted with white fire opals that glinted with specks of every color of the rainbow. A matching pair of earrings was included. At my gasp, momma stood and looked over my shoulder.

"That gift speaks volumes about Kevin's devotion. It's the kind of gift that a man gives his wife. If you decide against his proposal you must return it."

Momma quietly turned and left my room, leaving me to decide my fate.

———

On that Saturday my parents and I were to be Kevin's guests for dinner at Gino's, a quaint Italian restaurant just two blocks north of poppa's store. Over the years, Signor Gino and poppa had become friends; often they would refer customers to each other's business.

When my brother and I were growing up, momma sometimes left us in the care of Signora Rotini, Gino's wife. It was she and her daughter Lucrezia who did all of the restaurant cooking while Signor Gino played host to his customers. No matter what Signora Rotini was cooking she always had 'just a little bit too much'; somehow, though, her extra portions found their way into our tummies. Both Cal and I were only too happy to have the extra portions. So it was with high anticipation that momma, poppa, and I were eager to visit Gino's once more.

Kevin and his driver arrived at our house with plenty of time for us to board the ferry. I greeted him at the door and ushered him into the front parlor where we awaited momma. She appeared a few moments later and I could tell from her squinted eyes and pinched expression that something was amiss.

"Momma, you seem upset. What's wrong?"

"Oh, nothing that a good rest won't cure," she hastened to assure me, absentmindedly rubbing her temple with her fingers.

"Perhaps we should postpone our arrangements for this evening?" volunteered Kevin, although I could see he had been looking forward to our outing.

"I won't hear of it!" replied momma. "Kevin, I trust that you'll take good care of Cordelia on the ferry ride into the city. Mr. Conner will meet you at the restaurant as arranged. After dinner Cordelia may return home with her father."

"But momma…" I began in protest.

"It's quite all right, dear. No one will look askance at you. Please excuse me, I really must lie down. This headache is quite frightful."

I could hear momma's footsteps on the staircase as she retired to her bedroom. Perplexed, I turned to Kevin.

"What should we do?"

"We should do exactly as your mother directed. We'll go into town and have dinner with your father. After all, he's expecting to meet us at the restaurant," Kevin pointed out. "It is full daylight and there will be plenty of people on the ferry. I'm sure your reputation will remain untarnished."

I thought this through for a few moments, coming to the conclusion that momma wanted to give me time to accept Kevin's marriage proposal in private. Poppa would meet us at Gino's and accompany me back home.

I nodded my assent and Kevin placed my shawl about my shoulders. Approximately sixty minutes later we were alighting from the ferry on the city side. Kevin's chauffeur and hired car brought us to Gino's where Kevin ushered me in. We were greeted by a white-shirted waiter who showed us to our table.

"I hope your mother's headache is soothed quickly. Does she suffer them often?" Kevin inquired sincerely.

"Only when they are convenient," I replied as I sat in one of Signor Gino's plush upholstered dining chairs.

Kevin chuckled at my observation of momma's malady.

"I'm extremely happy that your mother had the headache and not you."

As we were chatting Signor Gino himself rushed over to greet us.

"Buona sera, Cordelia; buona sera, signor." He bowed slightly from the waist as he addressed us. "How beautiful you are this evening, bella."

"Grazie, Signor Rotini." I smiled at my father's friend. Kevin acknowledged the restaurateur with a nod of his head.

"Cordelia, this message arrived just moments ago. It is for you."

He handed me a small cream-colored envelope bearing my name. I immediately recognized the handwriting as belonging to my poppa. I eased open the flap and withdrew the paper within, reading the message and composing myself before turning my attention to Kevin's inquisitive gaze.

"Poppa has been unavoidably detained with business." I handed the note to Kevin so that he could read it for himself.

"Business must be seen to," commented Kevin as he handed the note back to me. "If you're uncomfortable without chaperonage I'll be happy to escort you back home."

There seemed to be real concern evident in Kevin's voice. I smiled and shook my head.

"I feel safe and secure here at Gino's. In fact I spent many hours here when I was growing up. Signor Gino thinks of me as a daughter. He is probably the best chaperone a young lady could have. Besides, there are some things that we need to discuss and it is better that we discuss them in private." I smiled broadly at Kevin, thinking to set him at ease.

"What sort of things would you want to discuss in private? Have you agreed to become my wife?"

"Yes." Suddenly my throat felt parched and constricted. I sipped at the water in the glass before me. "I must begin by saying that I'm very fond of you; I'm hoping that over time the fondness will grow into love."

"I'll work at making you love me, Cordelia." His brown eyes fastened themselves on my face, his posture indicating his attention to my words.

"There are certain goals that I've set for myself and I hope to have those met before we exchange our vows."

"Just name them," he encouraged.

"For momma's sake, I would like to have a formal engagement party, in Boston."

"Done!" He smiled confidently.

"I expect that we'll have our own home, apart from your family home in Boston."

"Done! I already own the lodge in Connecticut and was hoping to build a proper house there one day. You shall have a say in everything." His smile broadened until it almost covered his entire face.

"I will need a new wardrobe to befit my station as your wife. While I am good with a needle and thread I expect to be provided with the finest quality of yard goods to work with."

"At your disposal." His hold on my hand tightened.

"I should like to honeymoon in Europe. You may choose where."

"We shall travel as often as you like. I'll show you the capitals of Europe."

"I desire to have my own set of rooms in our new home. And I want them located in a turret."

Kevin looked at me questioningly.

"I've always yearned for a turret room since I read the fairy tale of Rapunzel," I whispered.

"Then we shall build m'lady the finest turret in the world where she shall reign as the most beautiful princess." Kevin's smile deepened even further, showing the dimples in his rounded cheeks. "Anything else?"

"Just the most beautiful engagement ring in the world, so those high-society girls that were at your parents' summer house can be wildly jealous."

"We shall take care of that immediately."

Kevin reached into his coat pocket and withdrew a small jeweler's box. Nestled within it was the most beautiful ring I had ever seen. Kevin took my hand in his once more and placed the jewel-encrusted platinum band on my ring-finger. I was so astonished that I couldn't speak.

"Do you like it?" He seemed to hold his breath as he awaited my response.

I nodded in affirmation. "It's exquisite!"

"I had it designed just for you. The center emerald reminds me of our Irish heritage. The circle of diamonds speaks to the riches we shall have. And the final circle of light green stones, they are green beryl from Brazil, is for the many children we shall have. I want our home to be filled with happy children."

The ring fit me perfectly. I moved my hand this way and that, captivated by the sparkle of the gems. It truly was stunning. I would be the envy of every woman who saw it.

"When did you have this ring made?"

"I've carried it with me every day for the past week. I had hoped that you would accept my proposal. I've had it with me each day that we've spent together, not knowing when you'd accept my proposal."

I could feel the strength in his hands as they circled mine. At that moment I felt loved.

"You were pretty sure I'd say yes, weren't you?" I smiled at him.

"How could you turn me down when I'm everything you want?" he chuckled.

Signor Gino and his wife brought out a bottle of sweet sparkling wine and proposed a toast to our health and long married life. While Signora Rotini hugged and kissed us both, Gino insisted on choosing our dinner menu himself; we feasted until we thought we would explode.

He brought out a large antipasto, gnocchi in Alfredo sauce,

followed by a succulent veal piccata served with roasted baby potatoes and pearl onions. Dessert consisted of a ricotta cheesecake topped with wild raspberries. Kevin enjoyed a cup of dark espresso coffee while I sipped at a soothing cup of Ceylon tea. The piéce de resistance was our after dinner aperitif: tiny cordial glasses filled with Sambuca in which floated three coffee beans per glass. Signor Gino touched a match to the contents and served them à flambé.

That evening, Kevin and I returned to Staten Island only to be greeted at the door by momma and poppa. Momma's eyes immediately sought out my left hand and she let out a squeal of joy as she pulled me into a hug. Poppa clapped Kevin on the back and welcomed him into the family, insisting on a toast to his newly engaged daughter and her fiancé. Much later, poppa insisted that Kevin stay the night as there wouldn't be another ferry departing until morning. With momma's help I turned down the guest room. Long after we ladies had retired, we could hear Kevin telling poppa about the house he wanted to build for me and of the turret room I had asked for. The last voice I heard was poppa's: "that's my little princess," he remarked.

Cordelia

Chapter 7

Late September 1907
Boston, Massachusetts

The leaves had already turned from their bright green hues to the mottled colors of yellow, orange, amber, and red. The afternoon shadows were quickly shortening when our train arrived at South Street Station. We had been traveling since early that morning. My anticipation had increased as the train ate up the miles between New Haven and Boston until it had grown into a knot in my stomach, yet outwardly I gave no sign of undue distress. Momma and poppa sat directly across from me in the coach car, momma's head drowsing slightly while poppa's fingers turned the pages of the newspaper he was perusing.

I knew poppa hated leaving his store in the hands of his two apprentices but momma had made him well aware that people of quality did not perform menial tasks, such as running a store. To keep momma happy, and to portray to all the world that we were people of quality, poppa turned the store over to his apprentices and joined us as we journeyed to Boston for my formal engagement party. As the train slowed on its approach to the station, I adjusted my gloves and prepared to disembark.

"I wonder if the Newkirks have sent some means of transportation for us?" mused momma.

"Of course they will, dear," poppa reassured her. "After all, they are people of quality."

Poppa winked at me as he said those words although momma failed to see the humor in them. Once we had departed the train, poppa went off in search of our baggage while momma and I scanned the crowds for any sign of a driver attached to the Newkirk family. Suddenly I felt two strong hands grasp my waist from behind and a mustache tickle the nape of my neck.

"Hello, gorgeous," whispered Kevin behind my ear.

"Kevin, how thoughtful of you to meet us personally but quite unnecessary," remarked momma. "I'm sure your driver would have found us."

"No inconvenience at all, Mrs. Conner. I couldn't wait to see Cordelia again." His smile was broad and charming.

"Mr. Conner will be along directly. He's gone off to find our baggage."

"Our coachman has also gone to the baggage area and will see to your things. Mr. Conner can join us at the entrance," offered Kevin.

My arm already rested in the crook of Kevin's elbow and he politely offered his other arm to momma. She gently placed her gloved hand on Kevin's arm and together we strolled towards the entry, attracting the stares of quite a few gentlemen at whom Kevin nodded in greeting. The attention was just the thing momma craved after our journey and she instantly came alive, preening as she daintily placed one foot in front of the other.

Outside, there was a pleasant breeze to cool us after the warm confines of the train. Kevin guided us to the curb where his motor car was parked. By the time he had handed momma into the rear seat, poppa had arrived to join us. He took the seat beside momma thus allowing me to sit up front alongside Kevin.

"One would think that a person of your stature, Kevin, would have a driver."

"Momma!"

"Your mother is quite right, Cordelia. I do have a driver. However, for pleasant outings such as this one I prefer to navigate about town myself."

He shifted the gears of the motor car and we took off down the street.

"Quite a smooth ride on this baby," commented poppa as we traveled along at the high speed of ten miles per hour. "How far is it to your family home?"

"We should arrive there in just under a quarter hour, sir, allowing for the traffic at this time of day," replied Kevin.

The motor car turned the city corners easily enough although momma looked a bit put out after every turn because poppa kept sliding along the seat and brushing up against her side. On purpose, I suspected.

"Wouldn't it be better to slow down on those turns?" momma asked of no one in particular.

I had not previously seen the Newkirk's Boston residence. Thus I was unprepared for the sights of Revere Street. There were exactly five residences: two seemingly diminutive mansions on either side of the relatively short street, but it was the large colonial sitting regally at the end of the cul-de-sac that commanded attention. It was set back from the road by a gated driveway guarded by gas lamps. At the apex of the semi-circular driveway two liveried footmen awaited our arrival.

Kevin handily pulled the motor car to a halt as the footmen stepped forward to open the vehicle's doors. Once we had exited the motor car safely one of the footmen inserted himself behind the wheel and guided the vehicle along the driveway to the rear of the house. The other ran ahead of us to hold open the massive front door.

I marveled at the rich beauty of the entry foyer. Underfoot, gleaming marble floors echoed our footsteps. Overhead an enormous chandelier stood ready to light our path at the first sign of dusk. Fresh flower arrangements graced a pair of elegant side tables.

Kevin guided us into a side parlor where we awaited a formal welcome. We didn't have long to wait. Within moments the brisk tapping of Mrs. Newkirk's shoes on the marbled floor heralded her approach. An under-butler preceded her into the room, holding open the wide door while his mistress sailed through. At her nod he silently retreated.

"Mother," Kevin stepped forward to kiss her cheek. She favored him with a smile.

"I see you've collected the Conners." She nodded in our direction although her eyes never left her son's face.

"You already know Cordelia."

"Cordelia," she replied blandly, nodding in my general direction.

Mrs. Newkirk put forth no outward sign of welcome; thinking, I'm sure, to cut me in front of my own parents. I would not give her that satisfaction.

"The pleasure is mine, Mrs. Newkirk." I met her head-on, neither of us giving an inch. "May I present my father, Mr. Charles Conner, and my mother, Mrs. Catherine Conner."

Momma gave a slight curtsy but poppa stepped forth in an attempt to bow over Mrs. Newkirk's hand. When he realized that her hand was not forthcoming he awkwardly stepped back.

"I hope you've had a pleasant journey," Mrs. Newkirk intoned. "Your rooms have been prepared. One of the maids will show you the way. We dine at seven-thirty. The gentlemen gather for drinks precisely at seven. After we've supped we shall discuss the agenda for the engagement celebration."

With a swish of her skirts she turned towards the door, stopping momentarily to address her son: "Kevin, your father wishes to have a word with you in private. Don't keep him waiting."

The distinct chill that had pervaded the room left with the departure of Mrs. Newkirk.

"Not very amicable, is she?" ruminated poppa.

"Quite rude, if you ask me," quibbled momma.

"Perhaps she's just having an off day," I interjected. "Kevin, please don't keep your father waiting. We'll be fine here until the maid arrives.

Kevin's visage, normally quite jovial, now resembled a thundercloud.

"I must apologize for mother's behavior. I've seen her act this way on only a couple of occasions – when I or my sisters have misbehaved very badly and needed discipline. She is normally an even-tempered woman."

"The problem lies with me, I'm afraid," I admitted. "Your parents don't approve of our match."

"Perhaps we should just call off the engagement and return home," momma suggested. "I had no idea that your parents were against this match, Kevin. You should have informed us."

I was aghast that momma, of all people, felt intimidated by Mrs. Newkirk.

"We'll do no such thing! We are here to celebrate my engagement to Kevin and that is exactly what we'll do," I countered.

I was determined to meet Mrs. Newkirk on her own battlefield. Kevin came forward and put his arm around me.

"You are first priority, Cordelia. Mother and father will have to become accustomed to that. I will see father in my own good time. This may be their house but I'm no longer a child to be ordered about. Now, where is that maid?"

A timid knock sounded just as Kevin finished speaking.

"Enter," called Kevin.

"Mister Newkirk," curtsied a young woman, slightly younger than me. "I've been instructed to show your guests to their rooms. Follow me, please."

She turned and led our small procession out of the side parlor, up a set of marble stairs, and down a long corridor, pausing before two doors at the farthest end.

"Miss Conner, this is to be your room." She opened the door to what appeared to be a bedchamber and beckoned towards me. "Your parents will be next door." She scurried to open the door to the adjoining bedchamber.

"This can't be right. Ellen, are you sure these are the rooms that mother has assigned to the Conners?" Kevin seemed perplexed.

"Positive, Mister Newkirk. These are the rooms the missus had us prepare. Will your servants be arriving shortly?"

This last question was directed towards me and I hesitated, unsure of how I should answer.

"The Conners will be using our staff of servants, Ellen. Since their stay will be a short one it was deemed unnecessary for their staff to make the trip." Kevin answered the maid who nodded her understanding and quietly disappeared from view.

I watched as my parents disappeared into their accommodations before turning to Kevin.

"You seem to be perturbed by our accommodations. Why is that?" I inquired.

"Because the rooms mother has assigned to you and your parents are normally not used unless the other guest rooms are full. These rooms are usually assigned to visitors who mother deems as not socially equal to our family. Of course, you wouldn't know that but I've received her message loud and clear. I intend to have you moved shortly."

Laying a hand on his sleeve I addressed his concerns.

"Please, don't say a word to your mother. We shall be quite comfortable in our rooms. I'll handle this in my own way."

"But I'm incensed! You are about to become one of us. You are to be treated like family; no, better than family." He ran his fingers through his hair in frustration.

"This is best left to the women to sort out." I gave him my best smile (a smirk actually). "Now you'll need to excuse me or I won't be dressed and refreshed in time for dinner. We mustn't keep your mother waiting."

I sailed into the guest room and closed the door behind me, assessing the accommodations from where I stood. The small fireplace contained the flames of a glowing fire which, while it was cheery enough, did little to dispel the chill of the late September afternoon. My portmanteau had been placed on a stand near a tall wardrobe that looked as though it hadn't seen the rub of a polishing cloth in many a long month. I hurried to unpack my gowns, hanging the one I would wear for tomorrow evening's festivities with great care in the wardrobe. My attire for that evening's dinner I draped across the bed before I further explored my quarters.

Behind a somewhat non-descript screen stood a washing table with basin and pitcher. Two clean towels were resting beside the basin. Across the room was an aging dresser upon which stood an antiquated pier glass. At least the bed looked comfortable and inviting. Gingerly I perched upon the bedspread only to realize that the covering was patched in places near its hem. I crossed the room to a small chair and table near the window and made use of those while I contemplated Mrs. Newkirk's actions.

Kevin had been quite up-front with me about the fact that his parents, correct that – his mother, was against this marriage. The elder Mr. Newkirk, after much campaigning by Kevin, grudgingly accepted the fact that I would become Kevin's bride. With his father supporting Kevin's cause, Mrs. Newkirk could do no less than capitulate and agree to hostess our engagement party. Obviously, she didn't have to be happy about doing so nor did she feel compelled to welcome us as her equals. After much thought, I had decided on a course of action and went about mentally preparing to do battle across the dinner table with my future mother-in-law.

Shortly before seven I heard the door of the adjoining room open and close softly followed by a gentle tap on the door to my room. Surmising who it was, I opened the door although I was still in my dressing gown. Standing in the doorway was momma, already dressed for supper in a casual gown of dark blue with Alencon lace at the throat.

"Do you need any assistance, dear?" Momma could see that I wasn't dressed yet.

"No, momma, thank you. We're doing just fine here. In fact, Ellen has been a tremendous help." I smiled at the maid who had earlier escorted us to our rooms and who had been assigned to serve as my lady's maid. There was no need for her to know that I normally dressed and accomplished my toilette without assistance.

"Your father insists that I accompany him downstairs," added momma, "something about 'approaching the lion's den alone', he said."

I noted that poppa had already progressed along the upstairs hallway and was now patiently waiting while momma and I finished our conversation.

"Perhaps you'll meet Kevin's sister in the drawing room," I remarked.

"Good heavens! I hope she's not like her mother. Are you sure you don't need my help?"

"Go ahead, momma, I'll be down shortly," I laughed as I closed the door.

Turning back to Ellen, I gave her my warmest smile and resumed my seat as she skillfully finished repairing my coiffure. Twenty-five minutes later I dismissed the girl, praising her work and promising to tell her mistress how much I appreciated her assistance. Moments later I found my way down the stairs and was directed by the under-butler to the drawing room where the others were already gathered.

The room itself was warm, not only from the fire in the hearth, but from the various heated discussions taking place. I halted at the entrance and perused those in attendance. Seated on a sofa at the far end of the drawing room, like a queen holding court, was Fannie Newkirk. Sitting to her left, in a ladies chair, was momma who appeared to be listening intently to whatever Mrs. Newkirk was saying. Another woman bearing distinct resemblance to Mrs. Newkirk occupied yet another chair, Kevin's sister Bernice no doubt.

Closer to the hearth poppa stood with Mr. Newkirk and another man whose dour expression was deeply etched upon his face. This must be Robert Woodward, Kevin's brother-in-law. Their conversation appeared to be fueled by the brandy that was quickly being consumed from the glasses they held. Between the two groups stood Kevin, looking strangely out of place in his family's house – until he spotted me in the doorway. Placing his untouched brandy snifter on the mantelpiece he made a beeline towards me and took my hand in his.

"Cordelia, you look lovely." He placed a chaste kiss on my proffered cheek.

"I'd begun to think you'd deserted us, Cordelia," observed Mrs. Newkirk in a voice loud enough to cause all conversation to stop and everyone's eyes to turn in my direction.

I calmly crossed the plush carpet that covered the distance between the sofa and the doorway; Kevin stayed by my side thinking perhaps to derail any verbal combat that might ensue. He needn't have worried.

"Good evening, Mrs. Newkirk. I trust that you and momma have found some common grounds for conversation. Kevin, what time is it?"

Kevin looked at his pocketwatch and stated, "Why, it is seven twenty-nine, my dear. Why do you ask?"

"I simply wanted to affirm that I was on time for dinner. I wouldn't want to keep everyone else waiting."

When I turned to face Mrs. Newkirk it was with a look of doe-eyed innocence. Any comment forthcoming from her was interrupted by the appearance of a stiffly dressed butler who announced in stentorian tones that supper was ready. Kevin quietly tucked my hand into his elbow and we led the way into the dining room. We were followed by Mrs. Newkirk on poppa's arm and momma resting her hand on Mr. Newkirk's sleeve. The Woodwards trailed behind. The meal progressed calmly enough with Mrs. Newkirk paying careful attention to the etiquette employed by myself and my parents. At last there was a lull in conversation while our supper dishes were cleared and we awaited dessert and coffee.

"Catherine, I trust your accommodations are suitable."

Mrs. Newkirk tried to sound concerned but I noticed the tone of disparagement in her voice. Bernice had the good manners to busy herself with her napkin. I cut momma off before she could address Mrs. Newkirk.

"Momma isn't one to find fault very easily, however, I find my room barely acceptable, Mother Newkirk. I'm quite accustomed to a larger space at home. One would have thought that a residence of this stature would house more spacious guest accommodations."

"I was addressing your mother, Cordelia." Mrs. Newkirk's words were meant to sting, as filled with venom as they were.

"Oh posh! Mother is too much the gentlewoman to complain to her hostess. But as your future daughter-in-law I feel more comfortable expressing my opinions," I continued, keeping my voice calm.

"Rather ungrateful for someone of your status."

"Cordelia is free to express her honest opinion," added Kevin.

"Fannie, I warned you about putting the Conners up in the north corridor." Mr. Newkirk favored his wife with a shake of his head. One look from his wife, though, caused him to pay undue attention to the folds of his napkin.

"If you would be more comfortable elsewhere, feel free to find other accommodations. I'm sure there are one or two hotels in the vicinity that have rooms available." The smile on Fannie Newkirk's face was more of a sneer.

At this last statement from her mother there was an audible gasp from Bernice that drew everyone's attention towards her. Like her father she sought refuge in looking down at her napkin. I squared my shoulders and addressed my future mother-in-law once more.

"I shall not give you the satisfaction of driving us away from Kevin's family home, Mrs. Newkirk. In future, however, I do expect accommodations that reflect my status as Kevin's wife-to-be; and to have that courtesy extended to my parents as well."

I nodded to a footman who refilled my glass. As I devoted my full attention to the dessert being set before me, I listened to the various reactions to my statement. Fannie Newkirk tried to hide a blush, or was it contained rage, that crept into her face.

"Seems as though you've met your match mother," ventured Bernice.

"Impertinent upstart!" murmured Robert.

"Bravo!" Poppa's encouragement bolstered not only my confidence but provided the impetus for momma to speak.

"My daughter is quite correct, Fannie. Our room is rather more like a closet than a guest room. However, we'll make do since this is just a short visit."

Both Kevin and his father wisely kept silent, preferring to sip their wine as they followed the discourse. Finally, the last dish had been cleared away and we retired to the drawing room for a discussion of the proceedings to be held the next evening.

Mrs. Newkirk, somewhat calmed by this point, took center stage once again as she related the who, where, what, and when of how things would progress on the morrow. Momma asked about the guest list. Mrs. Newkirk confirmed that indeed every one of their acquaintances would be in attendance as they were all anxious to meet the woman who had 'caught' her elusive son. I'm sure she was trying to give the impression that I had somehow trapped Kevin into marriage but I kept my silence. When discussions on the subject of our engagement party had ended, Mrs. Newkirk summarily made her excuses and retired for the evening. Bernice and her husband departed for their own home. Poppa accepted Mr. Newkirk's invitation to visit his study and try one of his imported Cuban cigars. Finding herself at odds, momma also retired for the evening saying that she was tired after our day of travel. I was about to join her when Kevin placed a gentle hand on my arm.

"Must you retire so soon?" He spoke in a low voice, but mother heard it nonetheless.

"I can find my way. Please stay, Cordelia. I'm sure you and Kevin have much to speak of."

Once momma was out of earshot, Kevin pulled me close and tenderly kissed me.

"I've been waiting to do that all day. I admire the way you stood up to mother."

His second kiss deepened a bit and while it was pleasant it didn't cause my heart to flutter. I did, however, open the fan I carried and gently fanned myself. My ploy worked exceedingly well since Kevin believed that his kisses had stirred my passions.

"Perhaps my attentions are a bit too much," he offered.

I didn't respond but demurely looked down at my fan.

"Allow me to show you our ballroom," he suggested.

He gently led me down the darkened main hall and towards the rear of the house. At the far end of the hall he picked up a lighted oil lamp from a side table.

"Just through here. These are actually two large rooms that father uses to entertain his associates but mother has cleverly combined them to form a small ballroom. We used this arrangement when my sisters were married."

I stepped through a doorway and was amazed at how large the space was.

"Will there be enough guests to warrant the use of so much space?" I inquired.

"I expect there will be about two hundred guests in attendance."

"That many?" I had no idea how many friends the Newkirks had.

"Not all are close family friends, mind you, but there are many business associates of father's that needed to be invited for the sake of protocol."

"I see." *Oh, this would make momma so happy!*

Kevin set the lamp down on a sideboard and turned to me. With the shadows playing on his features he looked quite handsome. Any number of young women would have made him a perfect wife, and possibly loved him in the bargain. But he had chosen me, and by extension my family. I vowed to make him proud of his choice.

"Cordelia, dearest, I can't wait until tomorrow evening," he bent to kiss my lips, "until everyone knows that you're to become my wife," he kissed my cheek, "until everyone knows that you are my choice," his kisses trailed along my neck, stopping short at the top of my dress. "Being this close to you is driving me mad."

His hand snaked up to grasp the material covering my breast, giving me a gentle squeeze in the process. My hand automatically reached out to still his.

"Please, Kevin. What if your mother should walk in on us?"

"We're engaged. Soon we'll be married. What's the harm in us cuddling?"

His other hand reached down around my back to cup my derriere while his insistent tongue thrust apart my lips. I allowed him a bit of leeway before inserting my fan between us and taking a step back.

"What's wrong, Cordy?" A puzzled look crossed his face.

"Nothing, really." I plied my fan with a bit of added energy. "It's just that I…"

"Oh, Cordelia!" He attached himself to my mouth once more, pressing against me in the hope that I would notice his passionate arousal.

"I'm sorry, Kevin," I managed to get out between breaths, "it's just that I, well, you see, I'm tired. It's been a long day."

He tightened his hold on me, rubbing up against me in an almost vulgar manner. At last I was able to break his hold.

"How thoughtless of me," he mumbled. "Of course you're tired, especially after you bested mother. We have plenty of time ahead of us."

He grinned as we made our way into the hall once more where he deposited the oil lamp on the side table. Together we mounted the stairs, his hand resting comfortably on my derriere the entire way. I hoped he didn't think I was in any way excited by this. I expected to bid him good-night at the top of the staircase but that was not to be.

"I must insist on seeing you to your chamber, Cordelia. It can be quite dark in the upstairs hall and I wouldn't want you to become disoriented."

At the door to my room, he pulled me close once more, kissing me in the French fashion while groping my bosom, his hips moving of their own volition. After a minute or two of this I decided that was enough and broke it off. His breathing was heavy and ragged.

"Good night, Kevin." I turned and entered the room.

"Good night, dearest," he whispered as I closed the door.

I chuckled silently to myself at the fact that his frustration was so evident on his face. Ah well, I thought, he could go out and visit one of his paramours, of which I felt certain he had several, on the morrow. That should assuage any discomfort he felt tonight. I, for one, intended on sleeping soundly.

———

The mansion on Revere Street was abuzz with activity all of the next day as the ballroom underwent a complete transformation. There were flowers everyone: urns full of every variety and color of chrysanthemums stood before each tall window; potted orange trees and ficus trees were artfully arranged to form small alcoves where guests could find a seat upon any number of long, upholstered benches. At one end of the room was a screened area behind which a full orchestra would be located. Footmen scurried to and fro setting up rectangular tables along one side of the room; two maids then covered these tables with snowy white linen and began setting up several crystal punch bowls and crystal serving cups.

On the second floor of the house one of the larger guest bedchambers had been designated as a retiring room for the ladies in attendance. A half dozen or so screens divided the room into small niches where ladies could find a comfortable seat to escape from the eyes of their friends and family to repair their makeup or coiffures. Two maids were to be stationed here at all times during the evening should any assistance be required.

Mother Newkirk had provided us with a timetable for the events of the evening and it was expected that we would adhere to her guidelines. We were expected to appear shortly before eight o'clock to greet the guests. While I'm sure momma and poppa had every intention of doing so, I intended on making my entrance in my own good time.

Ellen, the maid who had so graciously been of help to me the night of our arrival, had attended to the freshening of my clothes early that afternoon. As evening approached she brought up a tray of food so that I wouldn't have to wend my way through the downstairs preparations. She was also quite helpful in keeping me informed of what was happening.

"Mrs. Newkirk just boxed Jackson's ears for almost tipping over an urn of flowers," she related as I daintily nibbled away at a plate of cold meat and bread and washed it down with a sip of wonderful wine from the Newkirk wine cellar. "Best not to drink too much of that wine,"

Ellen warned, "Mrs. Newkirk will dock my pay if she finds I brought you wine."

"If she does that, Ellen, you are to inform me immediately. I'll make up the difference in your pay myself."

Her eyes widened at my words as I drained the last drops from the wine goblet.

"Yes, miss; very kind of you, miss." She curtsied.

Once she had whisked away the remains of my meal and returned to my room, she brought me another report.

"Irene, that's Mrs. Newkirk's lady's maid, she says that Mrs. Newkirk is already dressed and waiting for the first guests to arrive. We'd best get you ready, Miss Conner."

"What time is it, Ellen?" I inquired from the chair by the window where I sat watching the approach of evening.

"Why, I believe its quarter past seven o'clock, miss. If you're ready I can help you with your dress." Ellen tried not to appear over-anxious but I could see that she had a healthy respect for her employer.

"Let's go over things one more time, shall we, Ellen? My dress is aired and wrinkle-free?"

"Yes, miss."

"I've already got on my undergarments."

"Uh, yes, miss, although they seem a bit lightweight."

"Yes, well, my shoes are clean and ready for my feet?"

"Oh, yes miss."

"You've done an excellent job of arranging my hair so artfully that I could hardly ask for more."

"Thank you, miss."

"I'm powdered, rouged, and laced."

"Yes, miss," Ellen let a small giggle escape her lips.

"So the only thing remaining is for me to put on my dress, have you arrange my headdress, pinch my cheeks, clasp my fan, and await my escort."

"Why, yes miss." She was quite a pretty young girl when she smiled.

"Then we certainly have no need to hurry, do we, Ellen? Why don't you pull up that stool and sit here by me. I should like to know more about you."

"Oh, I couldn't do that miss, it wouldn't be right." Ellen shook her curly head at my suggestion.

"I insist on it. If you don't do as I ask I shall tell Mrs. Newkirk that you were cheeky and impertinent." I smiled at the young maid.

"Oh, please miss, I'll do as you say. Just don't say anythin' to Mrs. Newkirk."

Ellen obliged me by pulling up the stool I had motioned to and placing it about three feet from me. She gingerly perched on its edge. I could see that the girl seemed relieved to be off her feet for a few moments.

"When was the last time you sat down today?" I inquired softly.

"Mrs. Newkirk doesn't like us to take breaks. We're allowed time for our meals though."

"I see." I let my gaze look out over the final rays from the setting sun. "Have you ever seen a more glorious sunset?"

"No, miss. I don't get to see too many sunsets." Ellen's answer was given quite matter-of-factly, without rancor.

"I suppose you don't. How old are you Ellen?"

"I'll be fifteen years next month, miss."

"Have you been in Mrs. Newkirk's employ for a long time?"

"Since I was twelve, miss. I was Miss Sallie's maid until she got married last year and moved away."

"Do you enjoy your position?"

"It's alright, miss. Miss Sallie was always very kind to me."

I heard the unspoken words that Ellen's reply disguised. Ellen was a quiet girl who was always on call it seemed. Dull brown hair tucked under a maid's cap, lackluster blue eyes that seemed to look upon each day as a milestone in a life of drudgery; I wondered where her family was.

"Ellen, do you have any brothers or sisters?" I looked at her straightforwardly.

"Oh yes, miss. I'm the eldest of eight, four boys and four girls my mum had. I really miss the little ones."

"Do you get much time off?"

"I get a half day off each week. That's when I rush home with my pay envelope and buy food for the others. It's so nice to see them happy and fed. But then I have to rush back here and tend to my duties."

I smiled at the girl who, had circumstances been different, might have been me. As I rose from my chair Ellen jumped off the stool.

"Are you ready for your dress now, miss?"

"Yes, Ellen, I'm ready for my dress."

At eight o'clock there came a knock at my door. I nodded at Ellen who went to open it just a crack.

"Mister Newkirk, sir, how can I help you?"

"I've come to collect Miss Conner, Ellen. Is she ready?"

Ellen turned to me and I held up my hand, palm open.

"About five more minutes, Mister Newkirk."

"I shall wait here in the hall, then."

Ellen closed the door behind her. We exchanged a conspiratorial smile and said not a word. Exactly five minutes later, Ellen opened the door and I waltzed into the hallway where Kevin awaited me.

He was dressed in a tuxedo and carried a walking stick that he was currently twirling. When he saw me he ceased the twirling and let out a long whistle.

"I do believe you're the most beautiful woman here tonight."

He held out a hand to me and I placed my gloved fingers onto his outstretched palm.

"Your gown is beautiful. Did you make it?" he made a motion with his hand to encompass my dress.

I nodded affirmatively.

"I don't believe I've seen anything like it."

"It's the latest style in Paris. Father saw it in a fashion catalogue and thought it might be something I'd like. I did, I copied it, and here it is." I did a complete turn so that he could admire the dress from every angle.

"It's stunning. You're stunning. The other women will be green with jealousy," he chuckled.

"You don't think it's too over the top, do you?"

"Not at all." He reached out to touch one of the ruffles that ran vertically down my bodice. "The material is so soft and silky," he marveled.

"Persian silk," I replied.

"Fits like a second skin. Absolutely scandalous!" Kevin's eyes twinkled with merriment.

"Your mother won't approve, you know."

"She'll have a fit. But I approve. And it's my opinion that matters. I wouldn't change a thing." He offered me his arm but retreated a half step as one of the ostrich feathers from my headdress, dyed a light blue to match my gown, hit him in the head. He laughed openly and walked to my other side, offering me his other arm. Together we went downstairs, stopping just short of the ballroom.

"Mother will be quite put out that we weren't here early to greet the guests," remarked Kevin.

"She's the hostess, not us. Besides, it is just past eight o'clock and we are considered to be fashionably late."

I unfurled my feathered fan that had been dyed to match my costume and we proceeded to enter the ballroom. Walking into that crowded room full of Boston's elite was a thrill that I shall never forget. Kevin and I needed to stop every few steps so that he could introduce me to one or another of the Newkirk guests. After the third or fourth introduction Kevin could see that I was having trouble remembering names. He leaned over and whispered into my ear.

"Don't try to remember everyone, dearest. I'll squeeze your hand if it's someone you'll need to pay special attention to."

After that, the introductions went smoothly. The gentlemen were all very polite and seemed to genuinely accept me. It was the women who were the problem. Behind our backs I could hear snide little comments.

"Social climber, that one"; "I heard she'd been compromised";

"Wherever did she get that costume?"; "Scandalous attire"; "Hussy"; "I heard she's with child"; "commoner"; "couldn't even arrive on time"; "wonder how she got him to propose".

Through it all I smiled, especially when I renewed acquaintance with the Buttermilk Six as I'd dubbed them – the young ladies of quality who held no appeal for Kevin.

At last Kevin led me onto the dance floor, gave a signal to the orchestra, and waltzed me around the room to the melody of Strauss's Blue Danube; I noticed smiles on the gentlemen's faces. It was the countenances of their wives that annoyed me. As Kevin's wife I would be held responsible for the way society accepted, or failed to accept, our union. From the bland expressions on the women's faces it was clear to me that they would only begrudgingly accept my presence in their world. When the dance ended Kevin walked with me to the cluster of our parents. I kept a smile on my face the entire time.

"You look lovely, dear," momma murmured as she hugged me.

"Took you long enough to make an appearance," commented Kevin's mother.

"Mother Newkirk, perhaps I could have a word with you, in private?"

"There's nothing that can't be said here, Cordelia."

"Oh, but I believe there is. I'll be waiting in the hall."

I sailed past her and into the hall where a small army of servants was hustling to and fro. A few moments later Fannie Newkirk appeared, looking put out and about to give me a dressing down.

"What seems to be the problem, Cordelia? Is the champagne not to your liking?" Her words were expelled on a huff of air.

"The champagne is not the problem, Mother Newkirk. You are."

"Hush. The servants will overhear."

"Then I suggest we speak privately, perhaps in Father Newkirk's study."

Mrs. Newkirk led the way and closed the door behind us, blocking out the noise of the party just down the hall.

"Speak then," she commanded.

I took a moment to compose myself and met her icy stare with my own.

"I understand that you do not approve of me. You would be much happier had Kevin chosen one of those breeders that you'd hand-picked for him."

"How dare you?"

"I'm not finished." My voice rose slightly and I paused to recompose myself. "This is your home and you may treat me any way you wish. However, I have seen the depth of your love for your son and the way you wish to protect him. But putting out gossip about me can only serve one purpose."

"To make you break off your engagement?" Her tone was hopeful.

"Actually the gossip hurts your son more than it hurts me. I'll have you know that I turned down two previous offers of marriage before accepting Kevin."

"Weren't they wealthy enough?" Mrs. Newkirk pursed her lips.

"Oh, money wasn't the problem. I didn't love them."

"Surely you're not standing there declaring your love for my son."

"I am extremely fond of your son. More to the point, it is me that he has chosen. Would you have your son turned away from the homes of his family's friends simply because he married me?" That statement was met with silence on Mrs. Newkirk's part. "I've heard all the snide comments coming from the ladies of quality in attendance and I seek to put an end to that for Kevin's sake, and by extension your own. I appeal to you for a solution to this dilemma."

Mrs. Newkirk drew herself up as though girding her loins and her facial expression softened just a bit.

"Mr. Newkirk, Kevin's father, would be apoplectic if Kevin, or his bride, weren't accepted into the homes of his associates. Kevin deserves better than you, but since you're willing to put his reputation before your own, I believe we can come to some arrangement."

"I certainly hope so."

"You are an impudent young lady without benefit of social manners, therefore it will fall to me to guide you."

"I'm sure Kevin will be most grateful; as will I." I gave her a shallow curtsy.

"Let's return to the ballroom, together. There are several ladies that need to make your acquaintance. I'll introduce you myself."

Together we returned to the ballroom and true to her word Mother Newkirk took me around to every lady that she deemed to be of the upper crust. I used my best manners, hoping not to embarrass my future mother-in-law. At the end of the evening we stood together, saying goodbye to the departing guests. When the final attendees made their exit, Mother Newkirk turned to me.

"Since you will become a member of this family whether I like it or not, it would be in your best interest to learn the nuances of Boston society. To that end I will insist on a lengthy engagement, at least a year."

"I don't see the reason for waiting, mother." Kevin had walked up to join us, taking my hand in his.

"Cordelia will explain it, dear. I must check on the servants."

We watched as she walked off in the direction of the ballroom, issuing orders to the servants as she went.

"I was hoping for a New Year's Day wedding," Kevin smiled at me. "I see no reason to wait."

"I'll explain everything tomorrow, Kevin. For now, it's been a long and tiring evening."

I smiled contentedly as Kevin placed a hand on my arm.

"Just one question, Cordy. What did you say to mother to win her over?"

"Some things are best left to the ladies, Kevin." I fluttered my fan coyly at him as I climbed the stairs, leaving him to look after me.

"Funny, I've often heard the same thing from father," ruminated Kevin as he shook his head.

I'm sure my fiancé was unaware that I had heard his remark but it gave me cause to chuckle to myself.

The following morning found me still abed long after the sun had risen. Although the warming fire in the hearth had died down completely at some point, the room wasn't terribly cold. I reached for my dressing gown and slipped it about my shoulders just as a knock sounded at the door.

"Come in," I called cheerily.

It was Ellen who entered bearing a tray with some much needed hot chocolate and a plate of sweet rolls.

"Good morning, miss."

"Good morning, Ellen. You may set the tray on the table by the window."

"Yes, miss."

"I assume that you're still assigned to see to my needs?"

"Yes, miss. Shall I set out your clothes for this morning?"

"Thank you." I sipped at the steaming mug of hot chocolate and gave a contented sigh as the creamy richness coated my throat. "Have my parents breakfasted yet?"

"Oh yes, miss. I believe you're the last one to arise this morning."

"I feel thoroughly lazy and decadent. It's not every day that a party is given in one's honor."

I watched as Ellen pulled out a morning dress from the ancient wardrobe and laid it out on the bed.

"After we've finished I suppose you'll need to help me repack my things for the trip home. Will you have time to assist me?" I managed to ask between bites of a flaky, apricot topped bun.

"Perhaps you'll want to speak with Mrs. Newkirk and Mrs. Conner before we ready your baggage."

"Oh, has there been a change of plans? Are we staying on then?"

"I'm not sure of the particulars, miss. You really should speak with your mother."

I noticed that Ellen avoided looking at me and that gave me a moment of fleeting discomfort but I reasoned that if momma and poppa wanted to stay another day that would be perfectly fine with me. Perhaps I could learn more about the family I was marrying in to.

After I had breakfasted, Ellen assisted with my hair which I decided was best left in a casual manner, simply held back by the matching set of jade hair combs that had been a gift from Kevin. At Ellen's direction, I set off to find momma and Mrs. Newkirk who, I was told, were awaiting me.

Upon my entering the morning room, momma stood up and we hugged. Mrs. Newkirk maintained her seated position as she sipped at a cup of something, possibly tea since it did not produce the heady aroma of coffee.

"Good morning, momma, Mother Newkirk."

I sat between them in one of the various comfortable chairs that filled the room.

"Your mother and I have been talking, Cordelia."

"Yes, dear, we have," agreed momma. "Fannie, er, Mrs. Newkirk has explained to me that running a large household, like this one, is quite different from what you and I are accustomed to."

"That's correct. As my son's wife you'll be expected to not only see to the smooth running of all household related activities but you'll be primarily responsible for the household staff and their work. Additionally, you'll be responsible for all household accounts as well. Since Kevin will be kept busy with his position at the firm and with his outside interests, namely those horses he's so fond of, he will have little time or interest in handling household matters."

"She's quite right, dear." Momma bobbed her head in agreement with Mother Newkirk.

"You'll also be called upon to entertain Kevin's business associates. A man should be able to count on his wife to be the consummate hostess, always putting him in his best light," continued Mother Newkirk.

"What we're trying to say, dear..."

"You'll be staying here for the foreseeable future, Cordelia. You'll become my shadow. I will be your role model for entertaining the elite of Boston society."

"This was decided without giving me an option?"

"Of course you have an option, Cordelia," Mother Newkirk gave me a disingenuous smile; "you can marry Kevin after you've served as my apprentice or you can call off the engagement and return to New York with your parents."

I felt as though a boulder had been dropped on me. What could I say? How should I answer?

"How does Kevin feel about this?" I inquired, trying to buy myself some time.

"Kevin's feelings don't enter into this. He's a man, with certain expectations of his future wife. Had he chosen someone from his own class this would not have been an issue. However, he chose you, for reasons beyond my understanding. Therefore, your choices remain as I stated."

Mother Newkirk pursed her lips when she spoke, indicating that there were no alternatives other than those she had enumerated. I looked at her, then at momma. Momma's silence spoke volumes to me. I knew that she wanted me to marry up and become a somebody. Moreover, I knew she wanted this for herself as much as for me. I had already accepted the fact that I would have to marry for social standing and wealth and abandon my search for love. Kevin professed to love me even if I didn't share that feeling on an equal basis. Having turned down two previous proposals I knew that if I broke off this engagement it would be tantamount to societal suicide. It was clear to me what I had to do.

"Mother Newkirk," I smiled at her, "it is a great honor for me to learn at the hand of a well-respected hostess such as you. I will try my best to do you, and my future husband, credit. Momma, I will be staying here in Boston to learn those things that Mother Newkirk has spoken of and to be a credit to our family as well."

I could see momma's shoulders slump in relief as she favored me with a radiant smile.

"You will do us proud, daughter."

"Hmph. We'll begin tomorrow morning. Feel free to spend the remainder of the day with your parents before they leave for home tomorrow."

"There are a couple of conditions, though." I wasn't about to capitulate quite so easily.

"And they are?"

"I would prefer more appropriate accommodations, please."

"Your things are already being moved." Mother Newkirk smiled condescendingly. "I've relocated you to my daughter Sallie's suite. It's a bit more spacious and I think it will suit you."

"Thank you. Now, as for Ellen, the girl who has been attending me for the past two days…"

"Has she not served you well?"

"She has been extremely efficient. Thank you. We also seem to get along rather well. I would like to hire her."

"Ellen is already compensated handsomely," Mother Newkirk stated.

"That may be, but she is compensated by the Newkirk family. I wish to hire Ellen to work for me directly." I hoped that Ellen would be willing but I saw no reason why she shouldn't come to work for me.

"How do you expect to pay her?" It seems that I had piqued Mother Newkirk's interest.

"I have a rather adequate allowance and I shall pay her from my own funds."

"That's true, Fannie. Cordelia has been quite frugal and has amassed quite a savings account in her own name. She can most certainly afford to hire Ellen as her personal maid," added momma.

"Really. Perhaps there is more to you, Cordelia, then I realized. You may certainly hire Ellen if she agrees. Although I can't see how her lot could be much improved. That will leave our staff a bit short-handed but I think we can manage."

"I'm sure we'll all manage quite well," I added.

Ellen was overjoyed to no longer be in the employ of Fannie Newkirk. Not only were her duties considerably lightened, she no longer needed to do double duty as a ladies maid and a maid at large, I had increased her wages by an additional five dollars and allowed her a full day off each week. In return Ellen shared my accommodations, reassuring me that she was quite comfortable sleeping on the chaise longue in the dressing area of my suite.

The following months passed in a blur. I arose each day at dawn and shadowed Mother Newkirk. There certainly was a lot to learn and I applied myself diligently. Within weeks I was able to draw up the menus needed, supervise the housekeeper's shopping list and oversee the household accounts effortlessly. I learned the names of each servant and their duties, realizing that there certainly was more to running a large household than I had been given to expect. Momma had certainly given me a good foundation but in order to economize she and I had done most of the household work ourselves. When Mother Newkirk found me in the laundry one day washing out my undergarments she nearly had a fit.

"A lady never sees the inside of a laundry room, unless it is to inspect the quality of the work being done there." That was one of the commandments according to Mother Newkirk.

Cordelia

Chapter 8

December 1907
Boston, Massachusetts

On a cloud-heavy morning, Mother Newkirk bade me attire myself in my best visiting costume as we were going to pay a call on a very important person. She would not disclose the name of the person we were to visit only that it was someone she held in high regard. Orders had been issued that the car be ready for precisely nine-thirty. As we waited for the chauffeur to bring up the car, Mother Newkirk carefully inspected me from head to toe; I felt as though I was back in school and momma was checking to be sure that I was presentable. Giving a satisfied nod, Mother Newkirk turned her attention once more to the small but prettily wrapped box she held in her gloved hands.

Twenty minutes later the chauffeur drove up to a beautiful colonial house set on a quiet tree-lined street. The morning temperatures hadn't risen more than a degree or two and snowflakes were just beginning to fall as we made our way to the front door. It seems as though we were expected because a maid opened the door to us without our having to ring the bell.

"Good morning, Mrs. Newkirk, Miss," the maid greeted us. "Miss Pickens is expecting you."

"Thank you, Talla. I know the way," acknowledged Mother Newkirk.

We handed our outer garments to Talla who disappeared on silent feet.

"What you are about to witness and hear must never cross your lips, Cordelia," Mother Newkirk admonished before leading the way into a small parlor off the main hallway.

I was floored to think that I was to be privy to one of Mother Newkirk's secrets; perhaps this woman was a distant relative of Fannie Newkirk, I mused silently. The instant we entered the parlor I was struck by the elegantly dressed woman standing by the cheery fireplace. I deemed her to be about the same age as Mother Newkirk; her appearance was one of quiet elegance. She seemed to be awaiting our arrival.

"Fannie, how nice to see you again." The woman held out her hands in a familiar greeting.

"Nora, you're looking well." Mother Newkirk clasped the woman's hands in her own and they exchanged a polite hug. "I've brought along my future daughter-in-law. Nora, this is Cordelia Conner. Cordelia, this is Nora Pickens."

I favored the lady with a shallow curtsy.

"Oh, no need to be formal, my dear," Miss Pickens addressed me. "Please, let's sit down. Talla will be bringing in some refreshments shortly."

We settled ourselves in the comfort of the overstuffed chairs that surrounded a low table.

"I've brought you a small gift in the spirit of the Christmas season. I hope you like it." Mother Newkirk handed the gaily wrapped package to Miss Pickens.

"If you've chosen it, Fannie, then I'm sure it is lovely." Miss Pickens accepted the gift and set it aside, unopened. "So, Miss Conner, you're Kevin's fiancée?"

"Yes, I am."

"Have you chosen a wedding date?"

"No, not yet. Kevin is intent on building our home and having it ready for us to move into. We hope to be married there. Mother Newkirk has graciously extended an open invitation for me to stay at Newkirk House."

"Oh, my, there's no need to embellish the story. I know she's trying to teach you all about Boston society and how to be a society hostess." Miss Pickens gave a dainty laugh.

I looked from Miss Pickens' shy smile to Mother Newkirk's smug one.

"You see, Cordelia, Nora is Mr. Newkirk's paramour," Mother Newkirk explained.

I could feel a blush creeping up my neck at her words. I was speechless.

"Fannie and I have an understanding, dear. Since we share a man, we thought it best to work together to keep him happy." Miss Pickens seemed most comfortable with explaining her situation. "Fannie has him most of the time. I'm blessed to spend time with him at least once a week; sometimes more often."

"Nora is right. Mr. Newkirk simply can't be bothered with the day-to-day affairs of the household. There are times when he becomes frustrated with it all. Those are the times he will claim that he has business to attend to. I know that his business is here, with Nora. She will soothe him, give him the understanding and compassion that he won't accept from me, and send him home in a much better frame of mind."

"But, I'm afraid I don't understand." I looked from Mother Newkirk to Miss Pickens and back to Mother Newkirk.

"It's quite simple, really. My marriage to Mr. Newkirk was arranged by our parents. Although I don't love him, I care for him and respect him. It's Nora, Miss Pickens, who loves Augustus."

Miss Pickens nodded her head in agreement. "Always have, always will."

"Sadly, Mr. Newkirk couldn't marry Nora because she is not acceptable to Boston society."

"Much like you believe that I'm unacceptable. Are you saying that Kevin should keep me as his mistress?" I felt my cheeks redden as my ire rose.

"Not at all, Cordelia. Kevin already has a mistress."

I gasped.

"Did you think that a man of twenty-nine years doesn't have a paramour?" she continued. "I didn't think you were that naïve. You do have some redeeming qualities and we can't discount the fact that Kevin says he loves you; but I thought that surely you understood that marriage isn't always about love."

"What Fannie is trying to say, dear, is that if you work together with your future husband's mistress, like our association," she waved her hand between herself and Mother Newkirk, "it will make for a much easier life for everyone involved."

"Precisely! Thank you Nora." Mother Newkirk inclined her head towards Miss Pickens.

"Let me see if I understand. You want me to go out and befriend my future husband's mistress just to make *his* life easier?"

"You don't have to, of course, but don't you think it wise to know who that person is and how she treats your man?" queried Mother Newkirk.

"I… I don't know. I'd never considered the idea. It's not like poppa ever visited another woman. I'm sure momma wouldn't have let that happen."

"Oh, Cordelia, I'm sorry to be the one to tell you this but yes, your poppa has a mistress. What do you think he does on all those nights when he calls home to tell your momma he's going to be working late?"

"Why he's working on rush orders of course!"

Mother Newkirk and Miss Pickens exchanged knowing glances.

"Your mother confided in me that she knows what he's doing but she has no idea who the other woman is, nor does she want to know."

"She did say that their marriage was more of a business arrangement," I conceded.

"Oh, wonderful, here's Talla with our refreshments," interjected Miss Pickens. "Fannie, you must catch me up on all the latest family news. You know Gussy hasn't a head for those sorts of details. Cordelia, would you like a splash of milk with your tea?"

The visit dragged on for almost an hour while the two ladies chatted about the various goings-on of the Newkirk family. I remained quiet mostly, only answering questions that were specifically directed to me. It amazed me how well Mother Newkirk and Miss Pickens got along. Under different circumstances who's to say that they might not have been close friends.

Once we left Miss Pickens's house we paid calls on several other ladies, mostly wives of Mr. Newkirk's business associates. At the last house, the home of Mr. and Mrs. Harold Farnsworth, I received another amazing piece of news. We had settled ourselves in the Farnsworth drawing room. I was admiring the curio cabinet filled with mementos of the Farnsworth's travels and only half-listening to the two ladies converse.

"Tell me, Fannie, will you be hosting the New Year's Soiree now that all your children have flown the nest?" Mrs. Farnsworth appeared to be on the edge of her seat waiting for the answer.

Mother Newkirk sipped at her tea before answering.

"In truth, Adele, I've decided to put my future daughter-in-law in charge of the affair this year."

I turned from my inspection of an inlaid cigarette box to look questioningly at Mother Newkirk. She seemed pleased that she had been able to unsettle me.

"Oh my gracious! How generous of you, Fannie," responded Mrs. Farnsworth. "We do so look forward to the New Year celebration at your home each year. Cordelia, you'll surely make your mark on Boston society with this affair."

"I'm sure I will, Mrs. Farnsworth. I look forward to welcoming you and your husband at the New Year."

Thankfully my response came through in a calm manner even though my stomach had turned over at least twice at the prospect. On our return trip to the Newkirk mansion I remained silent, although my mind was moving at twice the speed of light.

"You're awfully quiet, Cordelia. I thought you'd have plenty to say after our round of morning calls." Mother Newkirk's voice broke the silence.

"You'll admit that you've given me much to consider, Mother Newkirk. Am I to understand that you want me to assist you in coordinating your New Year's party?"

"Not assist, dear, I'm giving you full charge of the affair, just as I said to Mrs. Farnsworth. I'll supply you with the guest list and give you a budget. The rest is up to you."

"Do you think to embarrass me in front of your acquaintances?" My tone of voice was a bit sharp.

"Not at all. These past weeks you have impressed me with your ability to grasp everything I've taught you. This will be your chance to impress the rest of the family and most of Boston's elite families. Of course you may come to me with any questions you may have. I will be happy to assist you. But it's time to stand on your own, Cordelia."

"I don't trust you. I'm sure somehow you'll find a way to put me in a bad light," I observed as I gazed out the window of the motor car, noting that the falling snow had now covered the roadway.

Mother Newkirk reached out a gloved hand and placed it over mine.

"Look at me, Cordelia." Her voice had softened slightly. "I was prepared to dislike you, nay even prove you not worthy of my son. But you've done everything I've asked, you've taken my instructions well. I'm sure you can handle the New Year's party without my assistance. Take this opportunity to prove to me, and the rest of society, that you are the hostess whose name will be on everyone's lips; whose parties people would pay to be invited to."

I turned to face her and saw sincerity in her eyes. She truly did want me to succeed, if not for my sake at least for the sake of her son.

"Why did you take me to meet Miss Pickens?"

"There didn't seem to be an easy way to broach the subject of a gentleman's mistress. It was quite obvious to me that your mother had kept that kind of knowledge from you and I thought only to save you from the pain of finding out later that your husband, my son, was seeing another woman."

I weighed her response before offering my reply.

"You think it best, then, that I befriend Kevin's paramour?" I almost choked out the words.

"That is for you to decide. Personally, I knew I had to meet Miss Pickens and see for myself what kind of woman Augustus had chosen; to see what it was about her that he loved. Once we had met and conversed, my mind was at ease knowing that she was no threat to me or my family. In truth there have been many times when Nora and I have worked together to suggest that Augustus consult a physician about something or other."

We rode in silence the remainder of the way. There didn't seem to be anything more to be said and indeed I had much to think about.

After the supper dishes were cleared away that evening, and before Kevin and his father withdrew for their brandy and cigars, Mother Newkirk made an announcement.

"Augustus, Kevin, I wish to speak about our New Year's gathering."

"Good heavens, Fannie, it's not even Christmas yet," observed Mr. Newkirk. Mother Newkirk rolled her eyes at his comment.

"You're correct as always, dear, but these things need to be planned ahead of time. They don't just happen. In any case, I've decided to let Cordelia coordinate the entire event this year."

"Splendid!" cried Kevin. "I'm sure it will be a smashing success." He favored me with a fulsome smile.

"Are you sure, Fannie? There will be a great number of my business associates present," interjected Father Newkirk.

"Cordelia is more than ready to make her mark on Boston society." Mother Newkirk smiled in my direction. "I have complete confidence in her."

"This calls for a toast. Let's have some champagne," suggested Kevin.

"I'll pass on the champagne, dear. I'm afraid it's been a long day and I should like to retire." Mother Newkirk sent a suggestive look in the direction of her husband.

"Perhaps I'll join you in a few moments, Fannie. I have an anecdote that I'd like to recount for you," rejoined Father Newkirk.

The two made their 'good evenings' and retired from the dining room.

"Well, that leaves just the two of us," observed Kevin. "I'll forego the cigar if you'll join me in the drawing room, Cordy. I picked up the blueprints for our new house today and I think you should see them. I would welcome your input."

"As you wish, Kevin."

"Jackson," Kevin called out to the footman, "please have champagne brought to the drawing room."

In less than a quarter hour, Kevin and I were seated on a carpet in the drawing room, with a set of blueprints spread out on the floor before us. An ice bucket with a bottle of champagne stood nearby and we sipped the bubbly from two lovely fluted glasses.

"Here's to our new house and to your success as a hostess." Kevin raised his glass and I raised mine in salute.

We evaluated the architect's rendering of our new home, Bridgewater, which was to be built on property that Kevin owned in a town called Woodhaven situated in the neighboring state of Connecticut. The name Bridgewater, he told me, was the name of the horse stables that he had built up and he hoped to carry the name to the entire estate. I had no objection to that so henceforth our home would be called Bridgewater.

The house itself was to be built on a grand scale. The architect had allowed for twelve bedchambers and Kevin pointed out their locations on the blueprints. There was to be the usual number of public areas: dining room, small ballroom, drawing room, billiard room, Kevin's study, a small office for me, a nursery, a wing for servants' quarters, and another for guests. The one thing that made me gasp, however, was a three-story turret attached to the front of the house.

"Can you guess what the turret is for, darling?"

"I have no idea," I confessed as I sipped at my champagne.

"The upper level is to house the nursery. The ground floor will be your office. And the second level will house your bedchamber and dressing area."

Kevin watched my face as he explained all of this.

"All my life I've wanted to sleep in a turret room, like a princess from a fairy tale," I confessed.

"That was one of the requirements you stipulated when you accepted my proposal." He reached over and took the fluted glass from my hand. "I want to make all your dreams come true."

Gently he pulled me closer and kissed me. I placed my arms around his neck and my gratitude for the inclusion of the turret room was evident in the ardor I added to my kiss. This must have fueled his passion for he then trailed a line of kisses down my neck.

"Cordelia, I simply can't wait for our wedding," he huskily whispered. "Let's set the date tonight."

"But your mother…" I began as he nibbled at my ear.

"Mother doesn't understand the needs of a man. I want you as my wife. Soon."

He kissed me again, pushing me back so that I was supported only by his strong embrace. I allowed him to cup my breasts while he rained kisses on my neck but I placed a hand over his when he began to undo my bodice.

"Someone might walk in, Kevin." I protested weakly. His kisses became more insistent.

"We're betrothed. It's not a shame for me to desire you."

He flicked open the buttons in two deft movements and thrust his hand into my bodice, releasing an audible sigh as his fingers fastened on my right breast. His breathing became torn and ragged as he hefted my breast up and down.

"I must have you, Cordelia, don't deny me."

His mouth fastened on mine once again as he plunged his tongue past my lips.

"Please, Kevin, don't do this. Not here," I pleaded.

"A man has needs, Cordelia." His eyes were glazed over with desire.

"What if your parents come in?" I tried to buy time.

"They're similarly occupied right now," he smiled at me, trying to calm my fears. "I'll be gentle if that's what you're afraid of."

"Not here, Kevin, not now. I…I can't. Not tonight."

"Is it your time, then?" He pulled back, removing his hand from my bodice.

"I'm afraid so," I replied, knowing full well that I had at least another week until my menses were due.

"I'm sorry, dearest. Please accept my apology." He seemed crestfallen.

"You had no way of knowing," I replied, straightening my bodice. "If it will make you happy, let us choose a date for our nuptials."

"Yes, yes. What say you to next month?"

"We agreed to be married in our new home, didn't we? How soon can we expect the work to be completed?"

Kevin appeared to give the matter some thought as he refilled our champagne glasses.

"They can't break ground until at least March, and I can offer a bonus to make sure the house is completed within six months. What say you to the latter part of September?"

"That's perfect," I smiled my best smile for him. "I'll have plenty of time to make my gown and hire a household staff."

"While we're waiting for the main house to be built I've already contracted to have the old hunting lodge updated. As it stands, it's not a place that I would bring my future wife to but once it's renovated you can stay there when you visit and we can use it as a base of operations."

"That would be delightful!"

"Perhaps we should take a cue from mother and father and retire for the evening. I have some business I'll need to attend to early in the morning and we should both get some rest."

Later, as I brushed my hair, I chuckled to myself about Kevin's early morning business meeting. I knew he'd be visiting his mistress as soon as the sun was up. Thankfully, he was unaware that I knew of her existence. That was when I decided to take a page from Mother Newkirk's book and find out who my fiancé's mistress was. Perhaps it was time for us to meet.

The following week, with Kevin having returned to Bridgewater to oversee the changes to the old hunting lodge, I deemed it the perfect time to go shopping. I ordered the car to be brought round on a Tuesday morning and with Ellen for company gave the chauffeur the address of the millinery store that I wished to visit. Milady's Chapeaux was located in a pleasant area of the city, where ladies of quality would be equally at ease with wives of working class men. The storefront windows featured hats that were more like works of art sitting atop pedestal bases. Bracing myself for the meeting that would follow, I opened the door upon a wonderland of feathers, ribbons, and gewgaws.

I glanced at each of the hats displayed while keeping my eye on the curtain at the rear of the store. Within moments a woman, slightly older than me, appeared. She was attired in a fashionable dress of light gray wool, a very good choice for a shopkeeper hoping to serve the upper classes although I recognized the style of the dress as having reached its popularity quite a few years past. Her black hair was pulled back into a loose coil at the back of her neck, making the green of her eyes all the more prominent.

"Good morning, miss. How may I be of assistance?" Her voice was quite melodic and she spoke with a lilt that identified her Irish heritage.

"Good morning," I returned her greeting as cheerily as I could. "I've heard many compliments about your creations and simply had to see for myself."

"You're very kind."

"I was hoping to have something made for an upcoming New Year's event. Do you have anything I could look at?"

"Certainly, miss. Did you have any particular color in mind?"

"I'll be wearing a silver-colored dress. I was hoping for something with feathers."

"I don't have anything on display that I could show you," she mused, "but if you'll allow me, I could sketch something for you and see what you think."

"Yes, that would do."

The woman vanished momentarily behind the curtain and returned with a large pad and pencil. She set about sketching a headdress with feathers. I observed her as she worked; her entire focus on the task at hand. She seemed confident and assured as her fingers guided the pencil through the twists and turns of her sketching. After a minute or two she turned the pad towards me.

"Without seeing your ensemble, I believe this is something that would be quite tasteful for you, miss. With your height and coloring we could make up the base of the headdress in silver and attach the feathers, dyed silver and a very pale blue to complement your eyes. It would be most striking."

I was amazed at how quickly the milliner had been able to know what would suit me. She had a definite talent when it came to headgear design; believe me, I have known many milliners but they simply didn't have the talent that this one had.

"It's perfect! I must have it!"

"Thank you, miss. Will you send around a sample swatch?"

"I'll provide you with whatever you need," I offered.

"Once I receive the swatch, I can have it ready in two days."

"Very good." Now came the difficult part, at least for me. "Would you send it to me at my fiancé's family residence, please?"

"I'll just jot down the address."

"I believe you already know the address, Jeannette."

The woman quickly raised her head from the order slip and favored me with a questioning look. I held out my gloved hand to her.

"I'm Cordelia Conner."

She accepted my hand in hers and favored me with a smile.

"I was wondering if I'd ever get to meet you. Kevin, er, Mister Conner, speaks so highly of you."

"I'm happy to hear that," I smiled in return. "There's no need to be formal when you speak of him. You may use his given name with me."

"He's been very kind to me." She lowered her eyes.

"I take it that he's the one who set you up in business."

"Oh, yes! It's something I've always wanted to do."

"Your talent speaks for itself."

"You're most gracious, Miss Conner."

"You must call me Cordelia. After all, we're going to be family in a somewhat unorthodox way."

I took a moment or two to gaze about the store, noting the lovely way Jeannette had showcased her best creations.

"Do you work here alone?"

She nodded her head in affirmation.

"Business has been slow. But I'm sure it will improve over time."

"I know it will. I would be more than happy to recommend your work to people I know."

"There's no need for that Miss Conner...I mean Cordelia."

"Ellen, if you would go ahead and wait in the car for me, tell Jackson that I'll be out directly." I watched my maid depart from the store proper. "Jeannette, I know this will sound rather odd but I should like for us to be friends, without Kevin knowing about it."

"I'm not sure I understand."

"I know that you and Kevin have a relationship. I have no problem with allowing that relationship to continue after our marriage. In fact, I welcome it. There will be times when it will be inconvenient to welcome Kevin to my bed and those will be the times when he will seek solace from you." Jeannette had the good sense to blush prettily as I spoke. "For Kevin's sake, I thought it might be a good idea for the two of us to work together instead of being at odds. What do you think?"

"It's rather a strange idea, if you ask me." Jeannette chewed her bottom lip a bit. "But the idea has merit. Of course we would only communicate when it was absolutely necessary."

I nodded in agreement.

"Since we both know about each other anyway, I don't see the harm in not mentioning our acquaintance to Kevin. He doesn't take a great interest in my shop, only in the accounts. There's no need for him to see the names of my patrons."

"If you ever have need of my assistance, or I of yours, we shall communicate through messages that my maid, Ellen, will be most happy to deliver."

"That would work well, I think. Do you still want the headdress? Or was that merely a ruse to meet me?"

I laughed wholeheartedly at her openness.

"Of course I want the headdress. In fact, I shall pay you for it now. I'll send my maid to collect it when it's ready."

I withdrew some bills from my reticule and handed them to her. On my way out the door I passed a small hat that caught my eye. It was not as fancy as the item I had just ordered but I could see that it would be suitable in a variety of colors as an accompaniment to several of the styles that were part of the inventory of my family's newest venture, a line of ladies clothing.

"This hat, Jeannette, could you possibly make up several in various colors?"

"Yes, of course. But several?"

"Let me explain. My brother has recently gotten involved in the expansion of my father's haberdashery."

"I'm afraid I don't make men's hats." She appeared perplexed.

"No, no. My mother is also a modiste. My brother has rented a small loft where he now employees eight women to sew ready-to-wear fashions that would need only a slight amount of tailoring. He's combined part of the name of my father's business to create this new one. It's called Elite Fashions. There are several costume styles that would be a suitable match for this particular style of hat, with minor variations of course."

"I think I see where you're going. If we took the basic style of hat and changed the decorations to match the fabric and season then your family could sell them with the outfit as an ensemble. Of course we'd have to add gloves to match. I'll work up some samples and we can go from there."

"You can send the samples to my brother. Here is his office address." I wrote it on a slip of paper. "I'll tell him to expect the samples."

"Thank you, Cordelia. You're most kind."

Jeannette was smiling as I departed the millinery store and settled myself in the back of the car where Ellen was waiting for me.

With the holiday season almost upon us, Mother Newkirk spent most of her time directing the preparations for Christmas. At her insistence I accompanied her on her rounds of visits and joined her on those days when she was at-home to receive callers.

Throughout this busy time I also managed to undertake the preparations for the New Year's Soiree. When Kevin was present, mostly on weekends, I quizzed him endlessly on the decorations and entertainment that had been presented in the past. While I definitely wanted something different I knew it needed to reflect positively on the Newkirk family. Eventually, I set my plan into motion, placed orders for refreshments, and hired the entertainment.

By mid-month I had personally addressed each invitation before handing them over to the major d'omo for delivery. The responses came back quickly. One hundred and ten invitations were issued and all were returned with a positive response. This bolstered my confidence immensely.

Swearing Ellen to secrecy, we worked together on my dress for the event. I wanted something spectacular, something on the cutting edge of fashion, something that would establish me as a trend-setter in society. My father had sent me the latest catalogues from the French fashion houses and I pored over these. Borrowing a sleeve design from Tirocchi, a neckline from Callot Seours, and an overall approach by Paul Poiret whose elegant dresses favored the high waistlines that no longer required the use of a corset, I designed a gown that I knew would flatter me from every angle.

My brother Calvin, with assistance from his wife, found the perfect material for me: a thin, almost see-through, film of silver lamé shot through with threads of pure silver. Very expensive but fortunately due to his connections in the world of fashion Cal was able to provide me with five yards of this beautiful cloth. Ellen and I spent hours closeted in my suite where we hand-stitched row upon row of ruching that fell from knee to ankle, ending in a small train in the rear. The bodice fell loosely from tapered sleeves. When at last I tried on the finished garment it appeared that I had fallen into a vat of liquid silver.

"Ooooh, miss, you look exquisite!" cried Ellen.

"Is it too much, do you think?"

"Maybe on someone else, miss, but you have the figure for it. And with the headdress that the milliner sent round you'll be quite the talk of the town."

"Fetch me the headdress, Ellen, I'll try it on."

When Ellen had fixed the feathered piece atop my head, the effect was breathtaking. Jeannette had worked a piece of the same cloth as the dress into a base for three exotic feathers that had been dyed silver (with a hint of blue). I knew in a moment that we had achieved the look that I wanted. With careful instructions to Ellen, the outfit was placed deep into the wardrobe so that it would not be seen by anyone. I was anxious to have my societal debut as a hostess but we still had the Christmas holiday to celebrate.

Kevin arrived back in Boston two days before Christmas and resumed the use of his old quarters which were across the hall from my suite. He spent an entire day bringing me up to date on the renovations of the hunting lodge. Things there were moving along more quickly than anticipated and he hoped that I could join him for an on-site inspection early the following month. He seemed in good spirits and never left my side during that day.

The day before Christmas was different, however. My parents arrived by train and were met by the chauffer. While momma and poppa were settling into their accommodations, much better ones than their last visit, I went in search of my betrothed. Kevin, I was informed, was in his father's study reviewing contracts for the trading company;

he had asked not to be disturbed. No matter, I thought to myself, we would be spending time together at dinner with our families.

As usual when guests were present, Mother Newkirk directed everyone to their places at table. When she directed momma to sit next to me, in the chair that should have been allocated to Kevin, I protested.

"Momma, that chair is normally reserved for Kevin when he's here." I smiled apologetically at my mother who understandingly moved one chair over.

"It's alright, Catherine. You may sit next to your daughter." Mother Newkirk overruled my observation. I looked at her quizzically.

"I'm sorry, Cordelia, but Kevin was called away on business along with his father. They have asked that we don't hold supper for them. I'm sure you understand."

"On Christmas Eve? What sort of business could he possibly have?" I blurted out the question before understanding dawned on me. All eyes were trained on me. "Oh! I'm sorry. I'd forgotten that Kevin did tell me that he might be detained. You're absolutely right, Mother Newkirk. We should proceed without him."

Mother Newkirk nodded her head at me, smiled, and seated herself at one end of the table, giving the signal for our Christmas Eve supper to begin.

How could I have forgotten? I chided myself. Christmas Eve was the time when the Newkirk men visited their paramours. This time was reserved for the Newkirk women and their children to enjoy their supper and entertain any visiting guests. I could understand the elder Mr. Newkirk visiting Miss Pickens on this night but I held out the hope that Kevin would return before the evening was over. Much to my chagrin that was not to be.

We had just retired to the drawing room when the sound of music drew our attention out of doors. Nearing the windows that faced onto Revere Street, we looked through the partially frosted panes to see a group of children accompanied by a tall gentleman who had stopped in the driveway and were now singing a Christmas carol. While we watched and listened to their performance, Mother Newkirk directed the footmen to bring mugs of steaming cocoa and a tray of Christmas cookies out to the carolers. The children's faces were wreathed with smiles as they consumed the warm drink and pocketed the sweets; the tall gentleman walked up to the front door where he greeted Mother Newkirk.

"Thank you for your kindness to the children, my lady. They look forward to visiting here. It's all they talk about for the month of December."

He removed his hat as he addressed Mother Newkirk and it was plain to see that the scarf and coat he wore had seen better days.

"Your children are always welcome here, Reverend. Our family enjoys hearing their angelic voices." She turned to a side table in the entry hall and picked up an envelope that was propped up against a huge vase. "Please accept this small offering from our family. I hope that in some way it will help these children."

The Reverend accepted the envelope and tucked it into his jacket pocket.

"Bless you, Mrs. Newkirk, and all of your family. Without your kind assistance our orphanage could not continue to help the less fortunate."

He made his way down the front steps and rejoined the children as they moved along to the next house down the street. Mother Newkirk stood in the open doorway as she watched the tightly clustered group move away. Eventually she closed the door and returned to us in the drawing room.

"It's a Christmas tradition here on Revere Street," she explained as she rubbed her hands together to dispel the cold. "The local orphanage comes round to sing for those of us who are most fortunate in the hopes of a small donation. It has been my practice for many years to save the funds not expended in the running of the household and set them aside for the orphanage."

"What a charitable act!" exclaimed poppa.

"Exactly what one would expect from a lady of quality," murmured momma, as she looked pointedly at me.

Our supper was finished, our evening visit with my parents complete, and most everyone had retired for the evening. I alone remained in the drawing room, the only light the glow of the dying flames of the hearth, looking out the window at a snow-covered Revere Street, willing Kevin to return to me. I don't know how long I stayed at that window. It might have been minutes or it might have been hours. At last I felt the friendly touch of a mother's hand on my shoulder. I turned to find not my own momma but Mother Newkirk, in her dressing robe, standing just behind me.

"Come along, Cordelia. It doesn't make sense to wait for something that won't happen."

"He'll be back. I know he will." I refused to accept the fact that Kevin would be out all night.

"Of course he'll be back. But not until tomorrow. There's nothing to be gained by gazing out a window at the bleak landscape."

"I don't know if I can accept the fact that there's someone else in his life."

Mother Newkirk remained quiet for a time before lowering her voice and saying, "Come with me, dear."

I turned to her and saw compassion in her eyes. How could I have ignored the fact that her husband was also away for the night? Wordlessly I followed her down the hall and into Father Newkirk's study. She went straight to the liquor cabinet and poured us each a snifter full of brandy.

"I don't let Mr. Newkirk in on the fact that I know Miss Pickens. But knowing her as I do I know he is in good company. Had her circumstances been different she would have been his wife. Who knows who I might have ended up with?" She took a deep draught of the brandy in her glass. "I hear you've made the acquaintance of Miss Harmond."

"Yes, I have." I followed her example and quickly quaffed half of the amber liquid in my snifter. I waited until my tummy felt warm before continuing. "She's not what I would have expected. And she does appear to love Kevin."

"So you see we have nothing to fear. Both Kevin and his father are gentlemen. But as men they have certain needs that need fulfilling. In my case I no longer care to accommodate my husband; in your case you cannot break the rules of propriety to accommodate my son. So tonight we are alone but in the long term they both come home to us. That's just how it works."

We spent the next few minutes in companionable silence. When we had drained our glasses we set them down and silently went up the stairs to our chambers. Before entering my suite I turned to Mother Newkirk and whispered, "Merry Christmas."

"Merry Christmas, dear. Tomorrow will be a better day. Mark my words."

Kevin

Chapter 9

Christmas 1907
Boston, Massachusetts

I awoke on Christmas morning in the bed of my Irish angel. The raven-haired beauty who slumbered beside me was more to me than simply my mistress. She was the woman to whom I turned when I needed validation of my masculinity; that much was true. But there were times when merely being in her presence was enough to soothe me. Take last night for example.

The evening had turned bitter cold with a north wind that moaned through the eaves of the cottage that Jeannette called home. As I slipped out of my overshoes in the outer foyer, I handed her a gaily wrapped package.

"You need to open that package as quickly as possible," I directed as I moved past her through the inner door.

"At least take your coat off first," she replied.

"After you've opened my gift." I clutched my overcoat snugly around me.

Jeannette tore off the ribbon, removed the wrapping and opened the box, extricating the item that lay within. She held it up and inspected it.

"It's rather large for a bracelet," she mused, "and much too small for a necklace. But it is rather pretty."

"It's more of a collar," I explained as I reached inside my overcoat and extracted a small, wriggling form that immediately let out a high-pitched 'arf'.

"A puppy! Oh, he's darling!"

Jeannette cradled the little bundle of sandy-colored curly fur in her arms and cooed to the pup, who turned to face his new mistress.

"I shall call you Brewster," Jeannette pronounced.

The pup sat quietly in her arms, taking in its new surroundings. His ears were a mite large and floppy; eyes the color of liquid chocolate moved me to scratch behind his ears.

"I hope you don't think it presumptuous of me, bringing you a puppy to care for."

We moved to the parlor where I deposited my overcoat on the back of a chair and poured myself a brandy before joining Jeannette on the sofa. She cuddled next to me, nestling her head on my chest as we watched Brewster, who was sniffing about, exploring his new home. In due time, the puppy settled himself on the carpet near the hearth. Jeannette and I spent the remainder of the evening much as any other couple would, catching each other up on the latest events in our lives while I sipped my brandy. When the fire burned down and the parlor began to chill we climbed the stairs to the bedroom.

Jeannette and I had settled under the featherbed and exchanged the first of what I believed would be many kisses when a ball of fur with floppy ears flew across the bed and insinuated itself between us.

"Ooof!"

"Ah!"

"Arf!"

We each reacted to the landing in our own way before at least two of us dissolved into gales of laughter. Brewster began plying us with wet, sloppy, doggy kisses that were meant to convey his joy at having discovered the soft featherbed and us in one exciting action.

Thankfully, Jeannette left the warmth of our bed to pick up the puppy. She moved one of the rag rugs from beside the bed to a cozy corner of the room where Brewster quickly got the idea that the spot was intended just for him. He curled himself up there on the rug and was soon dozing peacefully. Meanwhile Jeannette had returned to my side and we spent the next hour or so becoming reacquainted with each other's bodies. When at last we were overcome by exhaustion we drifted into a warm and peaceful sleep.

Now, in the light of early morning, I thought to arise first and stir the embers in the fireplace hoping that they would ignite the small pieces of wood that I would add. But morning haziness clouded my memory. As I lifted the featherbed from my body a warm moist nose poking under the covers found the back of my knee. Brewster!

How long he had been awake and waiting for us I didn't know but I recognized the look on his face. I hurriedly drew on shoes, pants, and my overcoat, scooped up the puppy, and barely closed the kitchen door behind us before Brewster leaped from my arms into the white snow drift and quickly proceeded to turn it yellow. Once his business was complete, he bounded back to where I stood and gave a joyous 'arf'.

Back in the kitchen he circled my feet and continued to 'arf'. I knew the little fellow was most likely hungry so I searched in the pantry for something that might pass as dog food. As I was peeking into covered dishes and pans I heard Jeannette's padded footfalls in the hallway.

"Ah, so there you are? Whatever are you doing in the pantry?"

"Arf, arf."

"You didn't need to rise, darling. I was just trying to find something for Brewster here to have for breakfast," I replied.

"Arf, arf," Brewster agreed with me as he wagged his tail with glee.

"You won't find any kibble in there, I'm afraid." She reached down and picked up the pup. Together they trooped down the hall and opened the front door where the milkman had left two quarts of milk on the stoop.

Back in the kitchen again, she placed one quart on the table and the other in the icebox.

"Hand me some of the bread from the pantry, it's under the kitchen cloth," she directed me.

I poked about until I found a half loaf of bread and proudly handed it to her.

"Tear off some small chunks and put them in this bowl," she directed as she unstoppered the milk bottle.

Again I did as directed while Jeannette poured some milk on top of the chunks, making sure that each one soaked up some of the milk. As she was doing this Brewster arfed and danced on the floor until she set the bowl down before him. With his head bent, we could only hear the sounds of his tongue lapping the milk as he woofed down the sodden bread. In no time at all the pup had licked the bowl clean and stood there, tongue hanging down, with a grateful look in his eyes.

What a lovely morning it had been; and how I hated leaving that little cottage to go out into the cold and return to my family's house on Revere Street. It was still quite early when I cranked up the motor car and guided it out onto the snow-packed street. In less than twenty minutes I was back in my old set of rooms, Paul was helping me out of yesterday's clothes and into a fresh shirt, and I was enjoying my third cup of coffee, this one laced with a bit of bourbon to ward off the chill.

"Will you be joining the family for breakfast, Mister Kevin?"

"I've already eaten this morning. However, I should put in an appearance of some sort, I should imagine."

"Yes, sir," he agreed.

I made my way to the dining room only to find that the Conners had already breakfasted and mother was directing the removal of the food from the sideboard.

"Good morning, mother," I placed a kiss on her cheek. "Merry Christmas."

"Merry Christmas, dear. Why don't you join us in the drawing room? I'm sure Cordelia would like to give you your Christmas present."

I offered mother my arm and as we crossed the hall we were met by father who cheerfully greeted us. Together we entered the drawing room where the Conner family awaited us.

"Good morning, everyone," father greeted our guests. "Merry Christmas. Sorry I missed breakfast."

"No need to apologize," rejoined Mr. Conner with a wink in father's direction. "Business must be tended to no matter the hour or day. We fully understand."

"Yes, well, shall we enjoy our coffee while we exchange our gifts?"

Mother took the position of honor on the sofa motioning for Cordelia to sit next to her. The others took seats nearby while I preferred to stand near the hearth.

The next hour or so was spent pleasantly while we exchanged our Christmas gifts. Of course mother presented the Conners with a set of crystal wine goblets, thinking to showcase our vast wealth. However, she was totally flabbergasted when Mrs. Conner presented her with a large box. Upon opening it, mother found a stylish dress in a stunning lavender silk.

"I took the liberty of asking your maid for the measurements during our last visit," said Mrs. Conner by way of explanation. "If the garment needs adjustment I can take care of that while we're here."

"You don't mean to tell me that you created this delightful dress with your own two hands?" Mother kept turning the garment over and over and inspecting the fine stitches.

"My needlework has provided me with the means to add to our family's fortune. My creations have been sought after by many of New York City's ladies of quality. I can only hope that you'll find my work acceptable as well." Mrs. Conner seemed a bit shy about her work.

"The dress certainly is exquisite!" commented father. "Can't wait to see it on you, Fannie."

"It's easy to see where Cordelia gets her talent with a needle from," I added.

Mr. Conner presented father with six perfectly tailored new shirts, almost exact duplicates of the ones that I favored. Father was quite pleased with this.

Cordelia then handed me a small package. Upon opening it I found a matched set consisting of a pocket silk and ascot that Cordelia had sewn especially for me in the colors of Bridgewater Stables.

"These are quite lovely, dear." I placed a kiss on her cheek.

"I thought perhaps you could wear these to the racetrack when one of your horses is running."

"Quite thoughtful. I'll do just that." Poor Cordelia had no way of knowing that her gift paled in comparison with the gift that Jeannette had given me the night before. But I was sure that in a few months time I would be receiving the same affection when Cordelia and I were married.

"Kevin, surely you have a gift for Cordelia," mother prompted.

"Yes, I do." I smiled at my bride-to-be and withdrew a long envelope from my jacket.

"Whatever could this be?" Cordelia laughed, as she opened the envelope. "Oh my!" she exclaimed when she perused the sheet of paper.

"What is it, dear? Don't keep us in suspense." Mrs. Conner had moved to the edge of her seat.

"It's a bank account in my name," Cordy whispered. "Thank you, Kevin." She stepped towards me and placed a kiss on my cheek.

"Those are funds for you to use at your discretion when seeing to the furnishing of our new home. I'll expect an accounting of the funds before making additional deposits to the account but I don't foresee any problems."

"That's very generous of you, son," father added.

"I have another surprise for Cordelia as well. I received word just yesterday that the renovations to the lodge will be complete in about two weeks."

"So quickly?" queried Cordelia.

"It's amazing what a bonus will do," I remarked. "Perhaps Cordelia would join me on a visit to Bridgewater at the end of January? You can see for yourself what the place is like and make note of furnishings that need to be ordered. Sorry father, but some of the furniture that was there has been removed and disposed of."

"It was rather ancient stuff," admitted father, "but for a group of rough and tumble guys it was just fine. Certainly can't expect to entertain a lady in those surroundings."

"Well, Cordy, will you agree to an outing at Bridgewater in the near future?" I smiled at Cordelia as I waited for her answer.

Cordelia turned to mother who nodded her silent approval.

"That would be lovely, Kevin. I'll be bringing Ellen along with me."

We spent the remainder of Christmas day attending services. I was proud to have the beautiful Cordelia on my arm as we entered the church. But my attention to the sermon soon drifted as I recalled the genuine happiness of Jeannette and little Brewster when I had left behind me this morning in a cozy little cottage on Ash Street.

At the conclusion of the service we were greeted by friends and acquaintances all of whom expressed their delighted anticipation of our New Year's Eve celebration. Afterwards we trooped over to my sister Bernice's house where we had our Christmas dinner. It was a grand dinner and I enjoyed speaking with Mr. Woodward, my sister's father-in-law and my father's partner. Both he and my father were looking forward to their retirement in a few weeks. My brother-in-law, Robert, took every opportunity to show off his success in the business world by pointing out new acquisitions: art work, new furnishings, and new uniforms for his servants. We allowed him the gloating that he so much enjoyed while we ate at his table, smoked his cigars, and drank his brandy.

The days after Christmas were abuzz with preparations for the New Year's Eve celebration. I decided that this was the opportune time to actually show up at my office in Newkirk Trading and I'm sure I caught my clerical assistant completely by surprise when I did so. There was much camaraderie amongst the associates and we spent many hours lunching at my father's gentlemen's club, toasting his and Mr. Woodward's successes. Those after lunch hours found me at the cottage on Ash Street where I called upon Jeannette to fill the void of those days.

At long last, the final day of the year arrived. I was already dressed in my formal attire when my parents arrived in the drawing room at ten o'clock.

"Mother, you look absolutely stunning! Is that the dress that Mrs. Conner designed for you?" I gave her a kiss on her cheek.

"It is absolutely marvelous. The dress fits perfectly yet feels so light I would swear I had on a nightgown." She turned a complete circle allowing me to see the dress from every angle.

"Son, if Cordelia is half as talented with a needle and thread as her mother, then you've captured yourself a rare gem of a woman. Not that your mother isn't a gem in her own way," father added.

"I must admit that there seems to be a wonderful sense of anticipation on the part of the staff," observed mother. "I rather like the idea of having the N for Newkirk embroidered in silver on everyone's uniform. Wish I had thought of that."

"I take it that you're pleased with Cordelia's work thus far?" inquired father.

"I'll reserve judgment until the evening is over, although I don't foresee any problems."

That was when I looked up and saw my future bride. She was a vision in silver and blue. Her dress was of a style that I had never seen: the top seemed to skim over her body while the bottom exploded in a froth of ruffles. Her hair was pulled back and up and fastened at the back with an explosion of feathers that had been dyed bluish-silver. She carried an ostrich plume fan of matching feathers in her silver gloved hand. Blue topaz earbobs falling from her lobes were the only jewels she wore in addition to her engagement ring. Her feet were encased in silver slippers and when she walked she seemed to glide. I hastened to her side, and taking her hand in mine placed a kiss on those silver-gloved fingers.

"Oh, my goodness!" exclaimed father.

Mother simply raised an eyebrow.

"Is this a sample of your modiste's handiwork?" I whispered, referencing our conversation earlier that year at Buttermilk Bay.

Cordelia nodded her affirmation.

"Then her work will certainly be the envy of every woman in attendance."

At Cordelia's direction we formed a receiving line just outside the ballroom and spent the next forty minutes greeting our guests. Mother and father entered the ballroom ahead of us and it was easy to see from mother's smile that Cordelia had performed well in coordinating this event.

"I can't wait until our home is built and we can welcome guests of our own."

"It's not that far off, Kevin. Have patience. I've learned so much from your mother. I'm really grateful for the opportunity she's given me and for her faith in me by allowing me to coordinate such an important event."

"Then let's not delay a moment longer. I hear the orchestra beginning a waltz and I long to hold you in my arms, even if at a proper distance," I whispered.

And dance we did: waltzes, fox trots, quicksteps, until we were fairly exhausted. When the orchestra took a break, there were strolling musicians who entertained while the guests refreshed themselves with hors d'oeuvres from trays carried about by our uniformed staff.

At eleven-thirty Swenson, our majordomo, made a show of wheeling in a round table upon which a pyramid of champagne glasses had been built. There were oohs and aahs from the assembled guests as they anticipated the midnight hour. Fifteen minutes later two footmen brought out a gaily bedecked ladder which Swenson mounted. Behind him the staff formed a double line that stretched from the pyramid to a serving table where chilled bottles of champagne stood at the ready. At a nod from Swenson, the footman at the serving table popped the first of many corked bottles and handed it down the line to the one closest to the ladder. Swenson, with a grand flourish began to pour the champagne into the topmost glass, being extremely careful not to cause it to move. As he poured, the champagne spilled over the glass and was caught by the row of glasses beneath it, in effect forming a fountain of champagne. The empty bottle was handed off to a footman on his left as another was placed into Swenson's waiting hand.

Soon all of the guests were gathered around the champagne fountain, waiting for the moment when the champagne would overspill the bottom row and pool onto the floor. But they were disappointed because just as the champagne began to fill the bottom row of glasses the champagne stopped flowing. More oohs and aahs broke into a round of applause for Swenson who took a bow.

"How did he learn to do that?" I asked Cordelia.

"Many long hours of practice with water and mops," she replied. "But it was all worth it. I don't believe Swenson will be the same after this." She moved then to stand beside a grinning Swenson and addressed the guests.

"Ladies and gentlemen, thank you for coming and making this New Year's Eve a special one for us all. On behalf of your hosts, Mr. Augustus Newkirk and his wife Fannie Newkirk, please accept a glass of champagne and help us toast the New Year."

The staff scurried to fill their serving trays with glasses from the pyramid and hand them to all of the guests. With barely a minute until midnight, the orchestra broke into a rendition of Auld Lang Sine and there were glasses raised and kisses exchanged, but none more ardent than my kiss with Cordelia who had earned the respect of even the most seasoned Boston hostess.

Late January 1908
Bridgewater

Cordelia and I, along with Paul and Ellen, disembarked from the train at Union Station where my Bridgewater staff waited to greet our arrival. Although the motor car that I kept at Bridgewater enclosed us in its metal cocoon, we soon were chilled. We were most thankful for the fur throws that we pulled over our legs to keep us warm. The late afternoon air turned decidedly colder as we left New Haven and wended our way through the bleak countryside.

Our conversation covered many topics, one being the newly found popularity of the family majordomo Swenson; seems that many of mother's friends wanted to borrow him to re-create that champagne fountain for their own gatherings. As a consequence, Mother's popularity had soared among her set of friends and she graciously agreed to loan out Swenson, with his consent of course, in exchange for social favors.

When our chauffeur at last turned the motor car into the long snow-covered track that was the road leading to the new guest house, Cordelia abandoned our conversation to carefully observe everything around her.

"Is there really a house way out here?" questioned Ellen.

"Of course there is," responded Paul.

"Well a person would need to go a long way just to have supplies brought in. What about food and clothing? It's an awful long way to town," the little maid observed.

"We place orders for what we need and it is delivered." Paul allowed a tone of superiority to creep into his voice.

"I think it's rather nice, actually," interjected Cordelia.

"You do?" Ellen's tone seemed to question Cordelia's sanity.

"Yes, I do. It's quiet and peaceful. I imagine it will be quite lovely in the spring and summer when the trees leaf-out."

"As you say, miss."

"How far is it to the house?" Cordelia directed her question to me.

"Just a bit further. The guest house is set way back on the far edge of the property," I replied.

As Stan, our chauffeur, rounded a small hill the roof of the house came into view.

"Look, there, just to your left," I directed Cordelia. "There's the roof of the guest house."

"And I see smoke spiraling up from a chimney. Heavens, I hadn't realized how cold I was." Cordelia pulled the blanket-like covering up to her chin.

"A nice hot toddy would be very much appreciated," I agreed.

Stan pulled the motor car to a halt before the new gate in front of the guest house. Discarding the fur throws I jumped down to assist Cordelia, holding on to her elbow to offer support on the ice-encrusted walkway.

"Surely someone could have cleared the path, especially since we were expected," observed Cordelia.

"We do operate with a small staff here. Most of us are quite used to navigating the pitfalls of an icy entry," I explained.

We entered the foyer and were met by George, my butler, who took our coats.

"Mister Kevin, if I could have a word with you, sir?"

"What is it George? Can't it wait until we've at least had something to warm ourselves? It's bloody cold outside." I walked over to the circular hearth, the only thing that remained of the former living room, and rubbed my hands together.

"It's Mrs. Michaels, sir." He stood where he was, with our coats in his arms.

"Is she ill?"

"No, sir."

"Good. Then direct her to bring us four hot toddies. Paul and Ellen should have something warm before they undertake their duties," I directed.

"She's quit," intoned George.

"Who's quit?" I was becoming annoyed with the way that George seemed to speak in riddles.

"Allow me to handle this," Cordelia interjected.

"George, is it?"

"Yes, miss." He bowed his head in acknowledgement.

"My name is Cordelia Conner, soon to be Newkirk; but I'm sure you're aware of that. What is your position here, George?"

"I am the butler, miss."

"Am I to understand that one of Mr. Newkirk's staff has left her position here?"

"That is correct, miss."

"Exactly what was her position and how long ago did she vacate it?"

George appeared to mentally calculate how long ago Mrs. Michaels had resigned.

"Mrs. Michaels was the housekeeper, miss. I believe it was shortly after Mister Kevin returned to Boston for the holidays that she resigned."

"And in all this time no one here, you or Mr. Huckleby perhaps, thought to inform Mr. Newkirk that the housekeeper had resigned?"

"Well, actually,......"

"Could not one of you perhaps have posted a note to Mr. Newkirk at his Boston office informing him of the lack of a housekeeper?"

George had the grace to look embarrassed as he maintained his silence.

"Very well, then you shall act as both butler and housekeeper for the time being. We should like four hot toddies immediately. It's been a long, cold ride and we are chilled. Paul and Ellen will see to the personal needs of both Mr. Newkirk and me. We would like our supper served in one and one half hours. Do you have any questions, George?"

"No, miss. No questions."

George turned on his heel and disappeared down the hall. He returned in a few short minutes carrying a tray upon which rested four steaming mugs. Wordlessly, he served us and retreated.

"I must admit that you handled that well," I observed after Paul and Ellen had withdrawn to our personal chambers where they would unpack our belongings before supper.

"It is always best to demonstrate a firm hand with servants from the very beginning." Cordelia smiled at me. "That's from the Gospel according to Fannie Newkirk."

We both dissolved in laughter at that comment.

"If only mother could see how her tutelage has paid off," I observed.

Supper went off uneventfully and after a tiring day of travel Cordelia retired to the second best chamber, the largest being reserved for me as master of the estate. I sat before the fading fire in the hearth, nursing my snifter of brandy, and recalled the many happy hours I had spent there with Jeannette. Although she and Cordelia were physically alike in numerous ways their personalities were totally different. Jeannette had always put my desires ahead of her own while Cordelia took command of a situation and molded it into the form she herself desired. Whereas Jeannette had worked magic with her softly spoken words, the unassailable tone in Cordelia's voice when she had addressed not only George but the others of my staff cemented her authority as equal to my own.

My thoughts moved from tone of voice to compare not only the difference in posture of the two ladies but the turn of their necks, the tilt of their heads, the way they walked and sat, the length of their legs, and so on. As the warmth of the now-dying fire mingled with the haze induced by a second snifter of brandy I recalled memories of Jeannette and me in front of this very hearth after I had removed that diamond hair clip from her magnificent raven curls. The memories were too much for me. I drained the dregs from the snifter and forced myself out the door and into the cold night air. Ah! The outside temperature must have been near zero because I immediately gained perspective about who exactly was in an upstairs bedroom and who was snug in a small cottage back in Boston. I retreated back to the warmth of the house. As I climbed the stairs to my own chamber I tried to envision what Cordelia might look like wearing only a hair clip, but visions of Jeannette jumped to the fore instead. Oh well, I reasoned, if I was to be plagued with visions of Jeannette then I might as well fall asleep and give those visions free reign in my dreams.

Cordelia was up early the next morning and had met with what remained of the staff before I even thought about arising. As I dressed for the day, Paul summarized for me what had transpired.

"Seems to me like Miss Cordelia is going to be a force to be reckoned with," observed Paul as he drew back the window drape and held out my robe for me.

"She certainly made a good start yesterday evening," I admitted, as I scratched at the stubble on my jaw.

"She gathered us all for a meeting this morning at five o'clock."

"At what time?" I sipped at the steaming coffee that Paul had handed me, allowing the warmth to settle in my stomach.

"Five A.M. Cook wasn't even up yet; you know how he likes to sleep in when it's cold."

Paul stirred the embers of last night's fire and placed additional wood on the pile.

"Can't say I blame cook. It is rather cold this morning."

"Looks like it will snow again," Paul observed.

"How did the meeting with Miss Conner go?"

"With the exception of a few of us, everyone has been put on a two week probation period."

"What?" I swallowed the coffee in a gulp and almost choked.

"The stable staff and Stan are fine; she found no fault with any of them."

"She is not to be allowed anywhere near the stables!"

"I believe Miss Conner is aware of that and has no interest in that area. Ellen and I are, of course, above reproach. As for George, Cook, the two footmen, and the maid, they have two weeks to impress Miss Conner with their efficiency or they will be sent packing."

As Paul performed his barbering chores on my stubbly jaw, I thought about what he had just said. Indeed, Cordelia had every right to oversee the servants as long as she did not interfere with my stables and my hand-picked groomsmen.

"Things have been a bit lax around here," I conceded to Paul. "It will be a good time for the other servants to become more efficient; I rather like the idea of having someone take them to task."

Ah, I thought, *Cordelia had learned well from mother. This would be one area of the household that I would happily relinquish.*

The next few days were busy ones, as our architect made the trip out to the country to finalize the plans for the new house. He and the general contractor walked the property, between storms, and he marked his drawings accordingly. Cordelia insisted on having two formal gardens, one being a small park-like setting that was to be set between the guest house and the main house. Around the guest house the contractor suggested a stand of weeping willow trees that would afford not only shade but privacy. Cordelia loved that idea.

"We shall call the guest house Willow Cottage!" she pronounced.

The old stand of trees surrounding the cottage would be taken down and an area cleared for a pond to be created with a small bridge connecting the paths on either side. Cordelia fancied planting an English garden around the cottage. I admitted my ignorance of what an English Garden entailed but gave her free reign in the landscaping.

At the rear of the main house, which would be some distance away from Willow Cottage, there was to be a terraced formal garden. It would be here where we would take our morning coffee on pleasant days, or so Cordelia informed me.

Our architect, Mr. Scola, suggested that the main house be built of white granite which would not only withstand the ever-changing elements but would be a natural complement to the land itself. A large, semi-circular drive terminating in a fountained courtyard would front the house and lead off to the stable area. I gave my blessing to everything.

We then turned our attention to the interior design of the house. For my own suite of rooms I selected a wood paneling that was to cover the walls in a diagonal design rather than the usual vertical one. The wood flooring was to also be of a complementary diagonal design to match the walls. My dressing area was to have two built-in wardrobes; the bathing room was to have a claw-footed tub adjoining a marble sink set between two tall, window fronted cabinets. This area was to be only partially wood paneled, along the bottom, with the upper half of the walls consisting of a large window overlooking the stables. From here I would also have access to a balcony so that I could take my ease when I felt the need for solitude.

Another area of concern to me was my study or office. I wanted to create a place where prospective horse buyers could feel comfortable in their outdoorsy clothes while at the same time allowing them to bask in the elegance of Bridgewater. The study, located directly beneath my suite of rooms, was to be accessed by a concealed passageway that would lead from my dressing area to a sliding panel in the study. In that manner I could attend to business on those early mornings or late evenings when I couldn't sleep. I wanted a large transom window that would overlook the stables here as well. There was to be a lot of wood and leather used in the décor of this room that would be unquestioningly masculine.

The the remainder of the rooms I left to Cordelia who spent much time on the interior design with the architect. While they spent the next two days thusly engaged I removed myself to the stables where a young foal had just made its way into the world. This was of more interest to me than how a kitchen should be laid out or what was the best location for a drawing room window.

As the two week probationary period for the servants drew to a close, Cordelia drew me into a discussion of each servant's merits. It was late in the evening and we sat cordially before the circular hearth.

"I understand you've given your blessing to the final designs the architect has drawn up. Both Mr. Scola and Mr. Johns, the general contractor, are happy. They will both be departing tomorrow," Cordelia began.

"I assume that our visit should be drawing to a close in the next day or two. I'm sure you're anxious to return to Boston."

"There is something further that we need to discuss, Kevin."

"If it has anything to do with fabric or furnishings, I defer to your superior judgment my dear." I smiled at her, wondering what she could have on her mind.

"Nothing quite so trivial, I assure you. I am releasing the house servants from their employment tomorrow. I need to know that you stand behind me on this." Her face took on a serious demeanor as she anticipated my response.

"I agree that the staff here has become accustomed to an indolent lifestyle, but surely they are worthy of redemption."

"I have given them two weeks to mend their ways. They have not impressed me with their efforts."

"There must be at least one or two who could be brought up to snuff," I suggested.

Cordelia shook her head in answer.

"I'll allow that we could find a better cook. I rather miss some of the fare that I've become accustomed to over the holidays."

"It must be a clean sweep." She was not to be deterred.

"Are you sure?"

"Positive."

"I so hate the idea of terminating someone's employment," I ruminated.

"You may leave that to me."

"They are in my employ, Cordelia, I'll see to the matter. I'll even provide a severance to each of them."

"Very well, then I should like to begin interviewing for their replacements immediately. The sooner we have a core staff in place the better equipped they will be to learn our likes and dislikes before moving over to the main house."

"I assume then, that you are willing to stay on here for an additional week or two?"

"Absolutely. I've advised momma that I will be staying and she will travel out to provide companionship for me."

"That would be splendid. I have agreed to breed one of the thoroughbreds to a mare in upstate New York, not far from my sister Sallie's place. I will most likely be gone for at least two weeks, possibly longer."

"I can narrow down the list of prospects and interview them upon your return," offered Cordelia.

"That won't be necessary. You have my permission to hire anyone who can meet your rigorous requirements. After all, you will be overseeing their day-to-day activities."

"I appreciate your support, Kevin."

"Come then, show me how appreciative you are," I answered as I drew her into my embrace and kissed her supple lips. "If we were to share a room this night, no one would be the wiser."

"My dearest husband-to-be, what would that accomplish? We would have nothing to look forward to."

She placed another kiss on my lips, lowered her eyes in a sultry fashion, and left me standing before the hearth with only my memories of another green-eyed beauty for company.

Cordelia

Chapter 10

February 1908
Bridgewater

At last Kevin took himself and his valet off to the far reaches of New York State, leaving me with Ellen to await momma's arrival. For almost a full week the weather delivered storm after storm and delayed any travel, leaving those of us remaining at Bridgewater to entertain ourselves. The remainder of the household staff had been dismissed; while Ellen found it beneath her station to work in the kitchen I certainly did not. There was a time, not too many months past, that I had cooked for myself and my parents. Once Ellen saw that I was not too proud to prepare a meal and clean up the kitchen, she agreed to do the laundry and keep the rooms tidy.

The end of that week saw the sun peek out from the clouds and the temperature rise to just above freezing. I received word that momma had taken a train out of Grand Central Station so I sent Stan with the car to fetch her, reminding him to pile extra blankets in the rear seat so that momma wouldn't catch a chill. In the meantime I busied myself in the kitchen, preparing one of momma's favorite soup recipes so that we'd all have something warm and substantial with which to fill our tummies.

I was in the dining room, setting the table, when I heard the car tires crunch to a stop on the snow-covered gravel driveway. Stan had been instructed to accompany momma to the front door so I wasn't surprised to hear a man's voice on the other side of that entry. I was, however, taken aback by the force of the knock that accompanied that voice; I hadn't known Stan to be that forceful of a man. Wiping my hands on my apron, I drew open the door.

"Momma, you didn't need to knock...." I began.

My words were swallowed as I looked up at a tall gentleman standing beside momma, one leather-gloved hand under her elbow. He was easily the most handsome man I had ever seen. Standing a full head taller than I or momma, his light brown hair peeked out from a smart derby hat that was banded by a dark gray grosgrain ribbon. Hazel eyes that seemed old and wise yet at the same time mischievous were eclipsed by the warmth of the smile that lit his square jaw. His overcoat was neatly tailored and covered him well past his knees. The metal buckles of his galoshes were shiny and neat.

"Oh do let us in already, Cordelia; we're likely to freeze out here in this god-forsaken wilderness."

Momma pushed by me and made her way directly to the hearth where Ellen waited to take her coat and hat.

"Please forgive me, Miss Conner, for showing up unannounced," the gentleman began. I noticed that he lingered in the foyer.

"Do I know you?"

"My name is Nathan Lawson. I'm here in response to the vacancy you have for the House Steward's position." As he spoke, he removed his hat out of respect for my position but I failed to notice that gesture, so enraptured by the sound of his well-modulated voice was I.

"Lawson?"

"Nathan Lawson."

"Oh yes, but you're not expected until tomorrow."

"Let the man in Cordelia. Can't you see that he's freezing out there?" momma called.

"I'm sorry, please come in Mr. Lawson."

I motioned for him to enter just as Stan stepped forward trying to juggle momma's valise with the one ostensibly belonging to our unexpected visitor. Mr. Lawson turned to assist Stan with his burden; once they were inside the tall gentleman turned to me again.

"I was afraid that with the weather being so unsettled it might be prudent to arrive in New Haven a day early. You can imagine my surprise when I met your delightful mother who insisted that I ride out here with her. I apologize if I've caught you unaware."

"Don't be silly, Nate. My daughter assures me that there is plenty of room here now that the renovations are complete," momma chirped in, sounding gracious and welcoming.

"Of course Mr. Lawson, you are welcome to stay the night in light of the weather and the late afternoon hour. We will conduct your formal interview tomorrow, though, as scheduled. Ellen, my maid, can show you to one of the guest rooms. I fear that it will not be warm since we weren't expecting you."

"Please, don't go to any trouble on my account. I can set the fire in the grate myself, if you'll only direct me to the room. I'm grateful to Catherine, uh, Mrs. Conner, for the lift out here and saving me the inconvenience of a hotel room." He flashed me a smile that seemed genuinely nice.

"If you'll follow me, sir, I'll show you to the guest rooms," directed Ellen who had returned to the parlor.

"Please, my name is Nate," he responded to Ellen.

"Nate, then, come along." She moved to pick up his valise but he quickly blocked her.

"There's no need for that, Ellen. I'm quite capable."

Together they went off and I turned my attention to momma.

"Whatever were you thinking?"

"About what dear?"

"Inviting that man to accompany you in the car?"

"He's perfectly harmless. Besides, it saved him the cost of hiring a car to come out here tomorrow. I do believe we're in for more snow." Momma warmed her hands at the hearth as she spoke. "Might I have a brandy, daughter?"

"Help yourself. He called you Catherine," I noted with a bit of frustration.

"Yes, he did. And I called him Nathan. Those are our given names." Momma moved to the sideboard and poured herself two fingers of Courvoisier.

"He is a servant. He is applying for a position here. I hope your actions don't give him the wrong impression."

"I do believe Nathan knows his place. He was quite mannerly."

Fortunately, the pot of soup that I had prepared was deep enough to serve one more. It fell to Ellen to serve us our food after the dismissal of our former servants and as soon as Nathan noted this he insisted on serving us at table.

I must admit that his manner was impeccable. He declined to sup with momma and me at the table, preferring to take his meal with Ellen in the kitchen. Without direction he cleared the table and took it upon himself to clean the kitchen, after which he set himself the task of bringing in more wood for the hearths. He retired for a short while after supper to the room I had assigned to him but just as soon as he heard my footsteps in the upper hall he popped his head out of his room.

"Will you be retiring, Miss Conner?"

"Yes, Mr. Lawson. I should expect that we will begin our interview directly after breakfast. Does that suit you?"

"As you wish, miss." He closed the door to his room as he stepped into the hall.

"Is there something you need, Mr. Lawson?"

"No miss. But in the absence of another gentleman I thought it best to check the various doors and windows and clock down the flue in the living room."

"Thank you, Mr. Lawson. I appreciate that," I softened my tone of voice. It was easy to see that this gentleman was familiar with the routine of a well-run household. "I also appreciate your pitching in to assist at the supper table this evening."

He looked at me with a friendly sort of respect before answering, his hazel eyes reflecting the light from the hall lamp.

"I'll be sure to turn off the lamp when I retire. Good evening, Miss Conner." He gave a slight bow.

"Good evening, Mr. Lawson."

I remained in the hall long after he had disappeared down the stairs. I listened to the sounds he made as he went around, checking the doors and windows, spreading the dying embers of the central hearth, making sure that all was right in every room of the house. Just as he approached the bottom of the stairs I scurried into my own room, thinking to myself that I had perhaps found the perfect House Steward.

———

The following morning was one that I shall never forget. Directly after breakfast, momma sought out the comfort of her warm bedchamber while Ellen saw to the tidying up of my room. Mr. Lawson and I retired to the small library that housed many of Kevin's books on horse husbandry and also served as an office. It felt rather strange for me to sit in the seat of authority behind the desk but Mr. Lawson eased himself into one of the new leather chairs, looking quite comfortable as he did so.

"Mr. Lawson, I've had the opportunity to review your letters of recommendation. Your previous employer and your personal references speak highly of you," I began. "If you are to be placed in a position of authority unequaled by the others on staff, I should like to know more about you, the man."

"Certainly, Miss Conner." He sat up straight in the chair and looked me directly in the eye. "I was born and raised in the small town of Kingsbridge, north of New York City. My mother was governess there to three children; my father is a gentleman's valet. You can see that our family is steeped in domestic service. My parents saw to my schooling and I am a graduate of the Kingsbridge School System. After receiving my diploma I expressed my desire to work in domestic service like my parents. My older sister was already a lady's companion at that time. Her employer agreed to engage me and I served as a page for the household. My promotion to footman came after only three years."

"When did you become valet?"

"My employer at the time knew another gentleman who had need of a valet. On his recommendation, I applied for the position and was hired. Mr. Hastings was a most jovial man and quite easy to work for."

"I see. Why are you applying for this position?" I sat back in my chair and watched Mr. Lawson's face as he spoke. His words came easy enough but it was his mouth that fascinated me. I wasn't sure if it was the curve of his lips or the fact that he had no facial hair that attracted me to him.

"….taken his wife to Europe for an extended length of time. I chose not to follow."

It seemed that I had missed some of what Mr. Lawson had said. But the sound of his voice, a rich baritone, was music to my ears. I mentally chided myself for losing track of his dissertation.

"And you feel capable of handling an entire estate, Mr. Lawson?"

"Yes, Miss Conner, I do. I am exceedingly good with figures and can account for funds in an organized manner."

"You would have no qualms about disciplining another staff member?"

Why did I keep asking these questions when I already knew I wanted to hire this man? And why was it growing unbelievably warm in that cozy room?

"…position is above and apart from the other staff members. My loyalty lies with my employer."

He smiled tentatively at me. His hazel eyes seemed to question my line of inquiry.

"Well, Mr. Lawson, I see no further need for questions." I brought myself back to the current issue. "The position is yours."

"Thank you, Miss Conner. You won't regret hiring me." This time his smile reached all the way to those beautiful eyes of his.

"In the matter of compensation, you will be paid twenty-dollars each month. It will fall to you to hire any staff we may need initially. I will inform you of my requirements tomorrow. I shall have final say on the potential staff of course."

"Of course, Miss Conner." He nodded his understanding.

"This afternoon you may go round to the stables and introduce yourself to Huckleby, the Head Groomsman. He has been handling the accounts for the estate as well as for the stables. It's high time the accounts were separated, although Huckleby has done a splendid job."

"As you wish, Miss Conner."

"There is a smaller wing to this house set aside for household staff. Since you are currently the only one in residence, other than Ellen, you may choose your accommodations. Paul, my husband's valet, also has a room in the servants' wing and Ellen can point that out to you."

"That's most gracious, Miss Conner."

"During your tenure you will be directly responsible to me. If I am not readily available I would expect that you may make a decision on my behalf. Mr. Newkirk, my fiancé, would rather not be involved with household quandaries. If anything needs to be escalated to his level I will be the one to bring it to him. Is that understood?"

"Absolutely, Miss Conner."

"Then I think we'll get along famously. Oh, and please tolerate momma's remarks kindly. She has always sought to better her position in society."

"Is that what your upcoming nuptials are meant to accomplish?" Mr. Lawson's smile faded a bit as he asked that question.

"Yes, it is. However, that is a most impertinent question." I smiled then and extended my hand to him.

"I'm afraid there may be more of those from time to time." He took my hand in his and bowed over it. "Please feel free to use my given name, Miss Conner."

"Well, Nathan, I will happily do that when we are in discussion like this. In the presence of others I believe we should retain the formal use of our titles."

I allowed my hand to rest in his a moment or two longer, noting how large and capable his hand seemed as it cradled mine.

"Thank you, Miss Conner."

He straightened, letting go of my hand. With a smile he turned and left the room, which suddenly seemed colder without him in it. I looked down at the hand that he had so recently clasped in his own and realized that it was my left hand, the one bearing an engagement ring that now seemed gaudy and garish to me.

By the time Kevin returned from his stable-related wanderings, we had a small but adequate household staff thanks to Nathan. Ellen was extremely happy that we now had a maid and a cook. Paul was quick to befriend Nathan, mostly to be able to report to Kevin about his doings I felt. Kevin sat with Nathan for a short while in an effort to know the man who would be second in command of not only Willow Cottage but of Bridgewater in general. Kevin seemed satisfied that the man was honest and forthcoming and commended me on my choice of House Steward.

By the end of February momma and I returned to Staten Island. Ellen accompanied us and was given the guest room for her own use. I had grown accustomed to having her assistance in so many matters that my father joked that I had become one of those snooty society ladies who were featured in the newspaper. Indeed, when we had settled in to our family home once more, the invitations to luncheons, teas, and suppers increased three-fold.

I accepted the invitations and to momma's great delight asked her to accompany me to many of those luncheons and teas. The suppers were entirely different, however, and I accepted only those obligations that I could attend with Kevin at my side.

Between social engagements I pored over the catalogues of the latest styles from the Paris couturiers that poppa brought home. Momma and I spent many long hours debating the merits of a tight-waisted versus a loose-waisted wedding dress and what might be the least offensive, fashion-wise to the society mavens of both New York and Boston.

In the end, I decided that the only one I wanted to please was myself. Kevin had delighted in the fact that my clothes were not 'cut from the same stable blanket' as those of other girls he knew. So I designed my own dress, borrowing heavily from two or three of the major European designers. With momma's assistance, we spent many hours first sketching the dress then creating the pattern for it. Momma took over at that point, saying that I was to involve myself with my trousseau and leave the wedding gown to her. That is precisely what I did.

My brother Calvin, whose wife gave birth in early March to my beautiful niece Myra, brought me bolt upon bolt of beautiful cloth, allowing me to choose the best fabrics before they were delivered to the factory. My sewing machine hummed between social engagements and in no time at all months had flown by.

July 1908

Once we had fulfilled our obligation to attend the Newkirk annual summer outing at Buttermilk Bay, Kevin escorted me to Bridgewater once more. I shall always remember that bright summer day. As we drove up the dirt driveway to the top of the hill where the manor house was to be situated it was easy to see that there was much activity going on. On a lower level of the hillside there appeared to be a tent city, surrounded by trucks of all sizes and colors.

"Whatever is going on here?" I questioned Kevin as we continued past the tents.

"The workmen have decided that it is easier to sleep here rather than go back and forth to their homes each day. By living at the work site they are able to add a full three hours to their work day that would have been spent on travel."

"But what of their families?"

"With the generous bonus I've promised them they seem more than willing to be away from their families," replied Kevin.

"Exactly how generous a bonus?"

"Enough to inspire them to complete our home in record time." Kevin smiled at me in a most suggestive manner. "The sooner the house is ready the sooner I can make you my wife, in every sense of the word."

"Oh, Kevin!" I cried.

"I knew you'd be anxious to reach our marital bed."

"Not that," I replied. "That!" I looked straight ahead at the largest, grandest edifice I had ever seen. "Surely that's not our house?"

"Indeed it is, my dear."

"And to think that those workmen have accomplished so much in the space of only a few months," I added.

"It's amazing what money will buy, isn't it?"

I had no answer for that. None. My eyes took in the sheer enormity of the rock-faced building that filled my line of vision. There at the top of the hill was a small castle, complete with a turret.

"Oh my goodness, it's huge!"

Kevin pulled up the motor car in front of the structure. I sat transfixed as he came around to assist me out of the vehicle.

"Wait till you see the inside. Of course, not all the rooms are finished yet but the unfinished ones are mostly in the guest wing."

He tucked my hand into the crook of his elbow and led me across the threshold. The spaces were open and airy; the grand hallway ran across the front of the house, boasting floor to ceiling arched windows and a flagstone floor. From the grand hallway one could enter straight ahead into the house proper, or from either end have access to the guest wing or the servants' quarters. We visited each of the rooms on the first floor: a lovely ballroom, a formal parlor, a delightful morning room, a drawing room, Kevin's study, a library, a splendid dining room that could accommodate two dozen people. The first floor of the servants' wing encompassed a full service kitchen. Off the kitchen were located the pantry, the laundry, a dining area for the staff, and a stairwell that led directly to the second floor where the senior servants had their accommodations. Kevin pointed out a rather spacious room that was situated between the pantry and a door that led to the kitchen garden.

"Here we are my dear. This will be your office."

I entered a square room with an eastern facing window that would catch the morning light.

"It certainly is spacious," I observed as I walked over to a door within the room. "Ah, yes, here's the water closet I wanted installed."

"I think it's a grand idea, Cordy; a little place to powder your nose." Kevin beamed with pride, thinking that this little water closet was enough to bring joy into my day. Hopefully, he hadn't yet discovered the small addition I had covertly paid the contractor to install. "Shall we see the upstairs?"

"By all means."

Kevin led me through the marble-floored foyer and up a semi-circular stairway to the second floor. More marble flooring along the upper hallway that overlooked the central foyer gave the entire area an airy feeling and as I looked over the balustrade I marveled to think that this house would soon be under my care. But Kevin drew my attention away from the view and towards an extremely large suite of rooms, paneled in a dark wood that had already been rubbed to a high polish.

"This is the master's room," he indicated, puffing up his chest as he laid claim to the space.

"Have you any directions on the placement of furniture? How would you like the bed situated? And your wardrobe?"

"I've already had Paul give my directions to Lawson. By the way, you did a splendid job in hiring Lawson. Very thorough, attention to details and all that. Now come through here, I want you to see the dressing area."

He led me around a corner of the room to a smaller area that would serve as not only a dressing area but a bathroom as well. A large claw-footed porcelain tub had been set in place and a commode already installed alongside a pedestal sink and some very masculine looking wood cabinetry. One entire wall was taken up by a large windowed door that led to a small balcony.

"My goodness, you can see the entire stable area from here!"

"Absolutely true, my dear. I always find peace when I can gaze out and see my horses. But here, let me show you a secret."

Kevin walked over to a door in the dressing area that was partially obscured from view by the cabinetry. He opened it and revealed a built-in passageway.

"This is a short-cut, if you will, down to my office directly below."

"How clever! But I didn't see a door in your office leading to this passageway."

"It is well concealed, that's why. It's located directly beside the bookcase and covered by a sliding panel, not a door."

"Will there be a great need for it's use?"

"I'm sure there will be times when I'll be working late into the night and I won't wish to disturb the household. Or perhaps I may arise early and wish to work on contracts."

"How considerate of you!"

He once again puffed up as my words of flattery hit their mark.

"Now, let's take a look at your personal accommodations."

Kevin took me by the hand and led me out into the hallway. Diagonally across from his chamber was another door which he threw open with a dramatic flourish.

"This, my dear, is where you shall find your own sanctuary."

I must admit that the room almost took my breath away. Where Kevin's accommodations had the rich patina of dark wood, my own space had been painted a soft egg-shell color. There was a marble fireplace; a bank of softly padded window seats beneath the windows in the circular part of the room; a dressing area containing my own claw-footed tub with a screen to shield the commode from view. White painted cabinetry, and a small crystal chandelier completed the space.

"It's positively elegant. And in a turret too!" I favored Kevin with my best smile and pressed a kiss of gratitude on his cheek.

"Your father once told me that you'd wanted to live in a turret like a princess," he admitted, "but since we are to be married I thought the room should be fit for my queen. And look here." He pulled open a closet door in the dressing area to reveal a stairway. "This stairway will lead you directly to the nursery. You won't need to leave your chambers to have access to the children."

"That's perfect," I agreed, "but I shall keep it locked in case our children try to come down here. Is the nursery finished, then?"

"Not quite, my dear. The walls still need some painting and trim work. But I've been assured that all will be complete by the time we are wed."

We spent what was left of that afternoon touring the unfinished guest rooms and the remainder of the servants' quarters. At the rear of the house was a flagstone terrace with stone walls that would afford some privacy. We wandered along the path from this terrace, Kevin pointing out where a swimming pool was to be installed along with a bath house. Further along the path I mentioned that perhaps we could include a koi pond at some future date.

"Whatever you desire, Cordelia," was Kevin's response.

It was a very pleasant afternoon as we inspected the vast amount of work that had thus far been accomplished. By the time we reached Willow Cottage we were both a bit on the warm side as the afternoon temperatures had climbed to near ninety degrees. I was feeling quite wilted.

"Good afternoon, Mr. Newkirk, Miss Conner." It was Nathan Lawson who greeted us with his well-modulated voice - a voice that I had often recalled during the past few months.

"Lawson," Kevin nodded his head in greeting to our House Steward.

"Good afternoon, Mr. Lawson," I returned his greeting. "Is supper almost ready?"

"Cook will have everything ready in under a half hour. She assumed that you both would like to refresh yourselves after your travels."

"Right about that, Lawson. Is Paul upstairs?"

"Yes, sir. He is awaiting you in your room."

"Well then, let's get changed into something not so formal, shall we my dear?"

"You go on ahead, Kevin. There's something I'd like to discuss with Mr. Lawson first."

"As you wish."

Kevin patted my hand and bounded up the stairs. Once I heard the door to his room close I turned to ask Nathan a question.

"Mr. Lawson," I began.

"Please, Miss Conner, I've asked you to call me Nathan."

"Only when we are working alone, Mr. Lawson," I whispered.

He nodded his understanding.

"Have the contractors installed the special item I requested? I failed to notice it when I toured my suite."

"Yes, Miss Conner, the passageway you requested has been completed. I will show it to you as time and opportunity allows."

I nodded my head in understanding, looking deep into those wonderful hazel eyes of his. Lawson's smile was genuine as he took my gloved hand and held it between both of his. I couldn't help but smile in return. Odd, how just a look from him could turn me into a giddy schoolgirl once again.

"It's nice to know that I can trust you to carry out my orders." Good heavens, I found myself blushing!

"Whatever you desire, Miss Conner, you have but to ask and I shall endeavor to fulfill your wishes."

He bowed over my hand.

"Nathan, please let go of my hand." I whispered for fear of being overheard.

"I'm sure Paul is keeping Mr. Newkirk busy, telling him all sorts of things about his horses and stables. May I call you Cordelia?" His lips curled into a smile; I felt a blush rising above the neckline of my gown.

"Yyyes, but only if we are completely alone," I stammered. "I really must go upstairs now."

"Of course, Cordelia." He bowed low once again, this time touching his lips to my gloved hand. "I shall tell Cook to serve within the quarter hour."

I turned and climbed the stairs, aware that his eyes followed me until I was out of his line of vision. I stopped briefly at the door to my room and pressed my own lips to the glove that Nathan had kissed. It was still warm and I could detect his masculine scent on the fabric.

Was I being silly? Possibly. But no other man had affected me the way Nathan did, not even Kevin. I tucked away my thoughts until a time when I could explore them and entered my room where Ellen waited with a fresh towel and a basin of cool water. Fortunately I could explain my blush as a reaction to the warm day and as I pressed the wet cloth to my forehead I smiled to myself, thinking of the way that Nathan had said my name – respectfully yet full of hidden passion.

———

Once Kevin had made certain that I was comfortably settled at Willow Cottage, he and Paul departed for Baltimore where he was hoping to purchase supplies for the stables before they traveled on to Kentucky to pursue negotiations with another stable owner. He informed me that he would be back at the end of August. So excited was he to be underway that he spared no more than a casual kiss for me before making an exit.

Those next few weeks were an opportunity for me to oversee the arrival and placement of furnishings, get acquainted with the staff that Nathan had hired, to meet with the contractors on minor details, and to establish myself in New Haven society.

My first order of business, however, was setting up the servants' wing. As befitted his position, Nathan was awarded the largest room. This also was the one with the best view of the drive. I was busy directing furniture placement in Kevin's study when word reached me that Nathan was insisting that Mrs. Grant take the room allocated to him. I set off for the servants' wing in an effort to settle the dispute.

Wending my way past deliverymen who were coming and going through the large foyer, I made my way along the grand hallway. Picking my way through the kitchen and up the stairway, I could hear Mrs. Grant's voice long before I saw her.

"I tell you again, Mr. Lawson, I won't take the room. It should be yours."

As I reached the top of the stairs I saw them both, standing on opposite sides of the hallway: Mrs. Grant with her legs firmly planted and her arms crossed, a scowl deeply etched on her face; and Nathan, dressed impeccably in a suit, just as firmly planted across from her, a sheepish smile decorating his face as he spied me.

"Miss Conner, thank heavens! Please talk some sense into this woman." He pointed to Mrs. Grant.

"I won't be taking something that isn't rightfully mine," Mrs. Grant declared.

"Enough! Mr. Lawson, please tell me what the problem is," I implored.

"It's quite simple, Miss Conner. I have declined the use of this room and have kindly offered it to Mrs. Grant."

"I see. Mrs. Grant, what is your objection to taking this room as your own?"

"It's not my place to have the best accommodation. I'm only the cook." She glared at Nathan as she spoke.

"Mrs. Grant," I began, coming toward her and putting my arm around her shoulder, "we would never think of you as 'only the cook'. You're so much more. In the short space of time that I've known you I have yet to find anything wrong with even one morsel of the dishes you've prepared. Heaven knows what a great talent you have for creating such sumptuous meals! For the life of me I can't think why you shouldn't avail yourself of a few creature comforts on your off hours, especially since Mr. Lawson seems to have recognized your talents long before the rest of us did. Won't you reconsider? Take the more spacious accommodations? As a favor to me?"

"Well, since you put it that way, how can I refuse?" She turned to me and a tear glistened in her eyes. "I really did want the room, you know," she whispered.

"I thought you did," I whispered back.

"Mr. Lawson, if you would be kind enough to assist Mrs. Grant in moving her things into this room I would be very grateful."

"Certainly, Miss Conner." He gave a bow of his head and nimbly ran down the stairs.

"Mrs. Grant, I shall see to it that you have an extra nice quilt on your bed before the week is out. And a padded footstool as well. I'm sure your tired feet won't mind being set up off the floor."

"God bless you, miss. Miss Ellen was right when she said you was easy to work for."

The woman grasped my hand and did all but kiss it in her show of gratitude.

Lawson

Chapter 11

I must admit that my motive for offering the larger room to Mrs. Grant was less than altruistic. Once we had the hard-working cook comfortably settled into her fine accommodations, I carved out a block of time to move into my chosen chamber.

The bedroom walls were papered in a striped pattern that I found soothing. An armoire large enough to hold all of my clothes occupied the far corner of the room while a deep, upholstered chair was positioned beside a small table. The bed was large enough to encompass most of the remainder of the room leaving space for only a bedside table. A double radiator that was the latest in home heating supported a large window that overlooked what would become, in time, a formal garden.

As I placed my personal belongings in the armoire I recalled the grace with which Cordelia had solved the problem of our lodgings. I smiled at the manner in which she had taken Mrs. Grant into her confidence, rather like a schoolgirl telling a secret to her best friend. I shook my head at the fact that beneath the stern demeanor that she chose to show the servants was still a young girl who should be beset by a dozen suitors. Instead she had agreed to marriage with a man a dozen years her senior simply because her mother wanted to move up in society.

Once my possessions were stowed in their proper places I went to the central linen closet and chose the bed linens I required. While there I spotted a lovely striped quilt in various hues of blue and purple. I added this to the top of my linen pile and returned to the sanctuary of my bedroom.

As I snugged the down pillows into the pillowslips my thoughts turned once more to Cordelia: a beautiful and highly desirous woman who happened to be my employer; a woman whose memory had haunted my thoughts since February last and whose presence caused me to become tongue-tied.

She had filled my imagination from the moment she opened the door of Willow Cottage to me on that snowy January afternoon. Could it only have been mere months ago? Little did she know that I would have done anything, said anything to get her to hire me. I would have agreed to work for half the wages she offered simply to catch sight of her on a daily basis. Fortunately, for my wallet, that was not the case. I fluffed the quilt and tucked its end under the mattress, hand smoothing any wrinkles from its surface. A quick look around assured me that my new quarters were ready for my return later that night.

As I pulled on my jacket a movement on the terrace below the window caught my attention. There, making her way down the flagstone steps, was my Cordelia, most likely on her way to Willow Cottage. I watched her graceful progress until she stopped and turned to look in the direction of where I stood. I took a step back, hoping she wouldn't notice me watching her. She swept the area with her eyes to be sure that no workmen were in the near vicinity. Satisfied that she was alone, she unfastened the top two buttons of her high-necked morning dress.

As she turned I caught a glimpse of the creamy expanse of her neck. How lucky was the slight breeze that kissed her neck with its cooling essence! I couldn't stop myself from watching her as she reveled in the relief that the breeze brought. Suddenly she raised her eyes to my window and laughed before lifting her skirt above her ankles. Twirling once as though caught in some fairy dance she ran the remaining distance to Willow Cottage. Oh, what a coquette! She knew all the time that I was watching her!

With the delivery and placement of the furniture accomplished, it came time to add the touches that would make Bridgewater not just a house but a home. Cordelia saw to the careful placement of draperies and carpets, that Mr. Newkirk's collection of horse ephemera were scattered throughout his study and private chambers, and that stores were laid in for the kitchen and laundry.

Meanwhile, Ellen worked at making Cordelia's room a comfortable haven, filling it with fabrics and ruffles that exuded femininity. Presumptuous though it may seem I took it upon myself to oversee Ellen's work while Cordelia was otherwise occupied.

"The space seems to be coming along nicely, Miss Hughes," I commented from my vantage point near the doorway.

"Mr. Lawson! You startled me."

Ellen dropped an article of clothing that she had been about to tuck into a drawer.

"Sorry. As House Steward it's my duty to show up unannounced."

"Well, the next time you enter this room you'll have to knock, I should think." Ellen seemed a bit put out at my sneaking up on her.

"Yes, well, carry on then."

I allowed myself the pleasure of taking one last look at the place where Cordelia would take her ease each night: the floral patterned chaise in her dressing area; the four-poster double bed with its plump feather pillows where she would lay her head; the lavender chenille bedspread; the padded window seat where Cordelia could sit and contemplate life – where just now Ellen had laid out Cordelia's scarves and ribbons before tucking them away.

"Miss Hughes, would you be kind enough to fetch me a cleaning cloth and some water diluted with vinegar? I see a dirty streak at the top of that window. I fear it is beyond your reach."

"Certainly, Mr. Lawson. I'll the fetch the items right away."

Ellen scurried off in search of the items I had requested. With her out of the room I was free to wander momentarily among Cordelia's things, touching her hairbrush, getting lost in the scent of her perfume – Apres L'Ondee by Guerlain; running the silk of her scarves through my fingers. Her scarves!

I looked down at my hand and realized that I was holding a luxurious peach-colored silk scarf. Turning my head slightly I ascertained that I was indeed alone for the moment. With the deftness of a magician I made the scarf reappear in the pocket of my jacket. And not a moment too soon for I could hear Ellen's footsteps as she approached the turret room.

"Here you are, Mr. Lawson." She handed me the cleaning items as she spoke then turned back to her original task.

With cleaning cloth in hand, I made a great show of rubbing the spotless window glass.

"Hmph," I made a sound to signal my fellow-worker that I was pleased with my own handiwork. "Carry on Miss Hughes."

Back out in the hallway, I made a beeline for the servants' wing. Once there I went directly to my own chamber where I tucked that peach-colored silk scarf beneath my pillow.

———

On the first day of August, Cordelia completed her move out of Willow Cottage and took up formal residence at Bridgewater House. A team of domestics that I had hired for the short term then undertook the cleaning of Willow Cottage. These domestics would stay on through October to provide added staff during the weeks leading up to the wedding and for a month beyond. Work on the rooms in the guest wing was still underway although any noise generated by the contractors was muted by the everyday sounds of the household. I made my morning inspections of the kitchen and proceeded to look in on the other rooms. In all it was an uneventful day with housekeeping being accomplished in a routine manner.

At precisely ten o'clock the following morning Cordelia asked me to gather the staff, including Huckleby and his crew from the stables, into the front foyer. As House Steward I stood at the head of the crowd, just at the base of the semi-circular main stairway. Cordelia herself stood two steps above us all.

"Good morning, everyone. Thank you for taking these few minutes from your work to meet with me. For those of you whom I have not met personally I wish to say 'Welcome'. It is most likely that I will not see most of you on a daily basis; however, I am well aware of the tasks that each of you performs. Thank you all for your hard work in transforming this cold pile of rocks into a home full of welcoming warmth. I'm sure that when Mr. Newkirk returns from his travels he will be most pleased to call this place home."

A nodding of heads greeted Cordelia's words before she continued.

"In the coming weeks we shall be preparing for my wedding to Mr. Newkirk. You will be called upon to serve any number of house guests, both here and at Willow Cottage. Therefore, I am asking both Mr. Lawson and Mr. Huckleby to grant each of you a full day off with pay to be taken during the weeks when Mr. Newkirk and I shall be abroad on our honeymoon."

That announcement was met by the household staff with cheers and applause, shortly after which I dispersed the crowd to return to their duties; likewise Huckleby shepherded his group back to the stables.

Huckleby was called in to Cordelia's office the next morning to review the stable accounts. This was more for Cordelia's benefit in learning about Huckleby's realm. My own review of household accounts was to be held the following morning and I looked forward to it with anticipation.

I remember the date very well, August fourth 1908. The morning dawned with a light fog obscuring the view from my bedroom window. Nonetheless, I washed the sleep from my eyes and proceeded to prepare for the day. My first order of business was to make up my bed as I allowed none of the maids access to my room. I had long ago learned the rudiments of housekeeping from my mother and had no need for a maid to clean my room or make my bed. Once my room had been set to rights I pulled on my jacket, checked to be sure my shoes were polished to perfection, and consulted my pocket watch. It was half past six and I was on schedule.

Turning the key in the lock of my bedroom door, I went about my morning routine of inspecting the drawing room to be sure that all was clean and ready for Cordelia. No fault to be found there. I continued on to the dining room where everything was as it should be and on to the kitchen which was a hive of activity. Mrs. Grant was giving instructions to the two scullery maids who dashed about setting places in the small room set aside as a staff dining room. My own small office, just outside the kitchen door, was my ultimate destination. I nodded in response to Mrs. Grant's cheery 'Good morning'. Since I had relinquished the larger bedchamber to her she couldn't seem to do enough for me.

I unlocked the door to my office and immediately Mrs. Grant was beside my shoulder, following me into the room.

"I've brought you a cup of freshly brewed coffee, Mr. Lawson. Fixed it just the way you like it." She favored me with a broad smile.

"That's very kind of you, Mrs. Grant. What's for breakfast this morning?" My first sip of coffee was always the best and this morning was no exception.

"I've prepared hotcakes this morning," replied the cook. "Lucy, bring in Mr. Lawson's breakfast," she called out to one of the scullery maids.

A young girl of no more than fourteen years appeared in the doorway, holding a tray that was covered with a snowy white linen towel. She set it on my desk and withdrew without making a sound. Mrs. Grant removed the towel and there was the largest stack of hotcakes a man could desire. Six fluffy cakes, piled high, with a crock of butter on the side. Beside the cakes was a heaping portion of crisp bacon. A fork and knife rested on a linen napkin to one side.

"Will there be anything else for you this morning, Mr. Lawson?" Mrs. Grant beamed at me as she made her way towards the door.

"Everything is perfect," I responded, trying to decide how I was going to eat all of the food that she had piled onto my plate.

"Very good, then, I'll be getting back to my stove."

The instant she left my office I allowed the smile to slip off my face. This was the third morning that Mrs. Grant had doubled my portion of food in gratitude for her upgraded sleeping quarters. All I could do was sit and stare at the amount of food in front of me. Not knowing how I was to dispose of it all, I lifted the steaming cup of coffee to my lips and decided that perhaps I needed the coffee most at this juncture.

"Good heavens, are you really going to eat all of that?" the heavenly voice of Cordelia inquired. I looked up to see her leaning against the doorjamb.

"I certainly can't put away this much food. She'll only feed me double again at lunch. At this rate I'll become as rotund as the mayor. Would you care for some?" I honestly hoped to foist off a portion of the meal onto Cordelia.

"It does look rather appetizing," she admitted. "Wait here."

She disappeared only to return a few moments later. Lucy stood just behind Cordelia and I could see she held two empty plates in her hand. Without a word Cordelia motioned for Lucy to quickly transfer slightly more than half of the food from my plate to one of the empty ones. Using the other plate she covered the first one, ostensibly shielding the uneaten food from view. All the while this was happening Cordelia used her body to block the view into my office as Lucy moved past her.

"I've arranged with Lucy to take the surplus food away without Mrs. Grant's knowledge. The staff is welcome to the excess as long as it is consumed out of Mrs. Grant's sight. Once you've finished you should return the empty plate to Mrs. Grant, expressing your thanks for her kindness. Hopefully this will stop soon."

"What an inspired idea, Miss Conner! We spare Mrs. Grant's feelings, the staff gets an extra bit of breakfast, I am spared the agony of gluttony and everyone is happy. Should you ever consider a bid for public office I shall be happy to cast my vote for you."

"I'll be in my office," replied Cordelia. "Please bring the account book with you after you've enjoyed your breakfast." Her conspiratorial smile warmed me as I made short work of the remaining hotcakes and bacon.

True to her word Cordelia was in her office, applying pen to paper as she composed what appeared to be a list of necessary supplies for the servants' wing, when I arrived there. She looked up and smiled as she motioned for me to close the door.

"Shall we have a look at this month's accounts, Nathan?"

I was pleased that she had used my given name and suddenly felt as giddy as a schoolboy. Wordlessly, I handed over my account ledger in much the same way as a schoolboy would hand over his composition book to a teacher. While she took note of each entry in the columns, asking questions here and there, I took the opportunity to openly watch her.

Her morning dress was cut from a bolt of lightweight cotton in a cheery floral pattern. A lock of her chestnut hair seemed determined to stray from the hairpins at the nape of her lovely neck; her pursed lips gave evidence that she was deep in thought. My eyes strayed a bit lower to where her bosom rose and fell with her breaths and I had a momentary vision of her standing before me wearing nothing but the peach silk scarf that now resided in my armoire. Suddenly her eyes lifted and caught me in a stare.

"I'm sorry Nathan, I can't seem to concentrate on the accounts."

"Is there something that I can explain?"

Her face took on a faraway look. She took a deep breath and exhaled it sharply, ending on a sigh.

"Can you explain to me why I'm marrying Kevin Newkirk?"

My mind blanked. Surely she wasn't having doubts? I must have hesitated too long for she sighed again and answered her own question.

"Of course I know why. How silly of me to ask?"

"Is it because you love him?" My mouth went dry as I asked the question.

"Surely you know by now that I don't love Kevin." Her gaze shifted to the misty view outside her window. "I'm fond of him, that's true."

"Then, why the marriage?"

Did I really want her to call off the wedding? What if she left and I never saw her again? My heart began to beat erratically as these possibilities flittered through my mind.

"For the sake of my family," she whispered. "I've already turned down two proposals. Kevin is everything that my mother wants for me."

"You mean Mr. Newkirk is everything your mother wants for herself but can't have."

I don't know where I found the courage to say those words.

"I should be grateful," she continued. "Why, just look at this wonderful estate that I shall be mistress of! Three hundred and fifty acres of land around us; immediate acceptance into both Boston and New York Society; and a turret room of my very own. What more is there?" She looked down at the emerald and diamond ring that almost covered the finger of her left hand, hoping to find an answer there.

"Love. You need someone to love you and for you to love in return." I stood and walked toward the window, watching as the late morning mist dissolved into a dreary summer rain.

"Have you known love, Nathan?"

"Yes."

"And is it as grand as everyone says?"

"Sometimes love can be painful, especially when it isn't returned."

"I'm a simple girl, Nathan. From a working-class family. I don't like pretending to be someone I'm not. I should have accepted one of the other men who proposed, I suppose." She toyed with her engagement ring.

"Did you love one of your other suitors?"

"No. Not love. But I don't think I'm born to be a lady of quality. I was meant to love someone of a lower class than Kevin."

I hadn't heard her move away from the desk. So intent was I on our conversation that she was standing beside me before I was aware of it.

"Could you…" I hesitated, "could you ever love someone like me?" I had to know. I turned to look into her tear-filled blue eyes.

"Oh Nathan, I already do." The words were like a prayer as they fell from her lips.

In an instant I pulled her into my arms and kissed her, tenderly at first. When she put her arms around my neck I deepened the kiss and she responded in kind. She tasted sweet and pure. As my fingers slid down to her waist they felt the warm flesh of her back through the lightweight fabric of her dress, making me realize that she wasn't wearing a corset. The thought of only a few scraps of cloth between us heightened my arousal. Cordelia too felt it and began to giggle, breaking the bond of our kisses.

"Whatever do you find so amusing?" I kept my voice low so as not to draw attention from beyond the door.

"You," she tried to swallow her giggle. "Now you'll have to sit here and think of mundane thoughts before you can go back into the kitchen."

"You little minx," I kissed her nose.

"Seriously, Nathan, what shall I do? I don't love Kevin. It's you I love. I've known it from the first time I saw you standing in the doorway of Willow Cottage, with a dusting of snow on your shoulders." She sat down behind her desk once more and arranged the ledger book in front of her.

"You shall go on as you are. At least for a while. I'll need to think about this."

"Shall we run off together? I must admit I've grown very fond of having servants."

"No. No running off. Although it would be my privilege to serve you every day for the rest of our lives." I turned and smiled at her, hoping to calm her nerves.

"I can wait. I trust you to make the right decision for both of us."

It was after eleven o'clock that night when I concluded my rounds of the manor house. The light rain that had fallen earlier in the day had now strengthened in intensity and in the distance the rumble of thunder could be heard. I stood now just outside the empty kitchen as my mind wandered from thought to thought, amazed at the idea that Cordelia returned my love. What a quandary this was!

Never in my wildest imagination had I dreamed of finding love. I had resigned myself to living the life of a bachelor, visiting a certain madam's house from time to time to find relief from my healthy urges.

Now I was faced with loving someone. It wasn't that her love was unappreciated. I loved her with all my heart. But she trusted me to help her decide her fate. Should she go through with a loveless marriage and become the socialite she was destined to be? Or should we both steal away from Bridgewater? Go somewhere else, perhaps out west to California or Texas? Certainly I could find a position in another household. She was handy with needle and thread and could find work as a seamstress perhaps; or with her organizational skills she could certainly be hired as a housekeeper.

What was I thinking? That would not be the kind of life I'd want for Cordelia. She should be showered with adulation, waited on hand and foot. Her clothes should be on the cutting edge of fashion, created from silk and satin not wool and sackcloth. She should awaken to the sounds of a maid setting down her breakfast tray, not delivering a breakfast tray to someone else. Her hands should be encased in gloves because they were delicate not because they were callused and dry. Could she ever be happy sharing two rooms with someone of my station instead of having a wonderful suite in a turret all her own?

My keen hearing detected movement coming from within the kitchen. Quietly I moved among the shadows until I stood outside the door to Cordelia's office. At once I recognized the noise for what it was: the secret entrance to her office from a concealed stairway that led directly to her turret room. I kept to the shadows until she stepped through the door.

"I was hoping to find you," she whispered as my silhouette was thrown into relief by a flash of lightning.

"I was concluding my evening inspections."

"Is everything to your satisfaction?"

"Yes. We are all safe and secure."

"I couldn't sleep."

In the darkness I could sense her nearness. She placed a hand on my arm.

"Would you like some warm milk? No. Perhaps a glass of Mrs. Grant's sherry?"

"No," she giggled. "Does Mrs. Grant really use the sherry for cooking?"

"Yes, of course. But not all of it." I could feel the corners of my mouth turn up.

"I wouldn't want the kitchen girls to get in trouble because we raided Mrs. Grant's sherry."

"Shall we go into my office, then? We can sit and talk."

"I'd like that."

I led the way to my office, unlocked the door, and ushered her inside. As I made to turn on the lamp she reached out a hand to stop me.

"I like the dark. It makes it easier for me to think."

"As you wish, my dear." I waited to see if she would remark on the term of endearment.

"I love the way you say that, with such meaning. Not at all like Kevin."

I offered her a chair but she refused, going to stand by the small window behind my desk. Another flash of lightning showed me that she was wearing her night robe and my breath hitched momentarily. Her hair was down as well and I ached to run my fingers through it. I went to stand beside her, resting my hand on the small of her back.

"Nathan, what am I to do?" Her voice was small and questioning. I took a deep breath before speaking.

"I believe the best thing for you to do would be to marry Mr. Newkirk." I closed my eyes waiting for her reaction.

"Is that what you really want?" She raised her head and in the space of two lightning bolts I could see that tears had filled her eyes. "You said you love me."

"I do love you, Delia, more than I have ever loved another human being. My life would be desolate without you."

She turned within the embrace of my arm and snuggled against my chest. My other arm encircled her of its own volition.

"Then why would you condemn me to a life without love?"

"There is more to life than love, Delia. You're young and vibrant. You desire so much more than I can give you."

"Then tell me why we shouldn't run away this very night." Her words were more of a plea than a command.

"It is because I love you that I am willing to share you with Mr. Newkirk. He can give you the material things you deserve, the fine clothes, the evenings at the theater, the trips abroad, the servants you would be hard pressed to do without."

"And what of you, Nathan?"

"I will give you the love you need to sustain you. And you, in turn, will give me the love I need to carry on. You will never want for anything with me Delia. I will move heaven and earth to love and protect you from all harm."

"Nathan?" She snuggled against me then.

"Yes, my love."

"I want something."

"What is it?"

"A kiss."

I bent my head and placed a kiss on her forehead.

"Not there."

"No? Then where?" I kissed her nose.

"Not there either."

"Hmm, is it here?" I kissed her cheek. She giggled.

"Not there."

"Then you'll have to show me," I teased her.

She reached up and placed her lips on mine, gently as though she were kissing a baby. I could hold back no longer and claimed her mouth with mine, kissing her soundly while I ran my hands through the silken locks of her unbound hair. I can't describe the taste of her kisses but they were unlike any other I had ever tasted. Her hands had worked their way under my vest and were unbuttoning my shirt. I quickly clasped her hands in mine to stop their movement.

"Delia, you must stop"

"I want to feel you, Nathan. I want to run my hands over your muscles. Please."

Against my better judgment I allowed her to proceed, standing still as she tugged my shirt from my waistband and ran her hands over my chest. When she placed a gentle kiss on my chest I stopped her.

"Delia, my love, you've had your moment of exploration. Now it's time for mine."

I tugged the sash of her night robe and the sides parted, revealing a cotton night shift that seemed diaphanous on her petite body. My fingers toyed with the ribbon that held together the neckline before I untied that too. Slipping a hand inside I marveled at the satiny softness of her skin, so unlike mine. Her breath hitched as my fingers found her breast and gently caressed it. She threw her head back and made a soft sound of contentment.

"The other one too," she whispered frantically, moving aside the material of her shift to expose her other breast.

I could feel her legs tremble as I bent my head and laved first one breast and then the other. It was heaven for me to not only touch but taste the woman I adored, however, I drew upon a well of strength I didn't know I possessed and pulled back.

"Please, Nathan," she whispered to me.

I caught her mouth in a heated kiss that seemed to go on forever. She shuddered in my embrace before going limp. I withdrew my lips from hers and held her to me.

"I think something's happened, Nathan." She raised her face to mine and spoke softly.

"Did I hurt you, my love?" Oh God! Perhaps my hands had been too rough on her tender skin.

"No, you haven't hurt me. But I believe I'm ready for you."

"I don't understand, Delia. What's ready?"

She removed her night robe and let the shift fall to the floor, allowing the lightning to illuminate her naked body.

"I'm ready, Nathan. Will you make love to me?"

"It's too soon, Delia. We must wait until you're married. You will need to prove your virginity to your husband."

She stepped forward to tug at my jacket and vest, moving them off my arms and trying to unbuckle my belt.

"What are you doing, Delia?" I could hear panic in my voice. This wasn't supposed to happen, at least not yet.

"Nathan, I have a confession. I'm not a virgin. You're the only one who knows. Not even momma knows. It was Horace Davis who showed me the delights of making love. Thought he would force me to marry him. I turned him away."

"But, there could be complications," I protested even as I removed my shoes.

"Not if you withdraw before completion."

Another flash of lightning displayed Delia's creamy breasts now standing at attention. In another moment I too was divested of my clothes and I pulled her into my arms.

"Love me, Nate, not just with words but with your whole body," she whispered as we sank to the floor below the window.

———

The storm had abated and hours had passed when I finally opened my eyes to find myself lying on the floor of my office atop a bed of discarded clothing. Delia was cradled in my arms. I looked down at the face of the woman I loved, her hand resting on my chest, her breathing even. I ran my fingers lightly over the sun-dappled skin that only hours ago had been feverishly hot from our lovemaking. That was when I realized that it was almost full morning and the kitchen would be abuzz with activity.

"Delia," I whispered into her ear, "wake up, Delia."

"Mmm," she murmured and snuggled closer to my body.

"Delia, you must wake up." I gently kissed her forehead in an attempt to awaken her.

"Later," she mumbled, waving her fingers in dismissal.

This was proving to be a tough assignment but I needed to rouse her. Using my most professional voice, I spoke directly into her ear.

"Miss Conner, you're needed in the kitchen."

That did it. Her eyes flew open! She looked directly into my face and realization of where we were and what we'd done registered.

"Nate? Tell me we're not in your office, lying naked on the floor." She looked quite like a startled deer.

"Delia, we're in my office, lying naked on the floor, the sun is shining, and the kitchen is in full use."

"Noooo," she wailed quietly.

"Never fear. I've got a plan."

I rose up and began to put on my clothes, taking pains to look as put together as I usually was. Delia too rose and quickly donned her shift and night robe, hugging them close to her body. I looked at my immaculate desk. Too perfect. Withdrawing a ledger book and some invoices from the drawer I scattered them about.

"My hair, its undone!" she lamented.

"It's better left unbound. Keep your head down and let the hair obscure your face. I'll go out first and engage Mrs. Grant. When you sense the time is right, make a run for your office and lock it from the inside. Will Ellen have tried to awaken you yet?"

"What time is it?" she whispered.

"Six fifteen," I announced after consulting my pocket watch.

"I've got fifteen minutes."

"Good. Ready?"

"One more kiss," she begged.

I obliged. Her lips clung to mine for the briefest of seconds before she nodded to me that she was ready. I unlocked my office door, leaving it slightly ajar as I sauntered out into the kitchen.

"Goodness, what time is it?"

"Mr. Lawson, we've been wondering when you'd be ready for your breakfast but no one seemed able to find you."

Mrs. Grant wiped her hands on her apron and turned to pour me a cup of coffee. I motioned with a hand behind my back for Delia to make a run for her office. She was a blur that ducked behind me just before Mrs. Grant turned to hand me my morning brew.

"I couldn't sleep with that storm howling around us last night so I thought it prudent to make use of the time. I've been in my office since three this morning, trying to make some sense of those contractor's invoices."

"Your shirt's a might rumpled, Mr. Lawson. Looks like you might have fallen asleep at your desk." Mrs. Grant winked at me. In a quieter voice she said, "I saw the young thing sneak out of your office just now. One of the new chambermaids I warrant."

"Yes, well......" I almost choked on my coffee.

"Don't worry, Mr. Lawson, your secret is safe with me. After all, you gave me that posh room for my very own. It's my pleasure to cover for ya."

"That's very kind of you, Mrs. Grant, very kind indeed."

Cordelia

Chapter 12

I t wasn't until after the evening meal was behind us that I sought out Nathan in his office. Mrs. Grant had retired for the day to her 'posh accommodations' as she liked to call them. Lucy and Trudy, the two kitchen helpers, were finishing up their work and looking forward to some well-earned rest as well. I nonchalantly walked through the kitchen and knocked at the semi-open door to Nathan's office.

"Enter," he called without looking up. "What is it?"

"I was wondering if you had a moment to join me in my office."

I stood near the doorway, not venturing to walk too close to his desk. The sight of that window and bit of floor behind the desk brought back all sorts of wonderful feelings and I could feel a flush creep above my collar.

"Miss Conner, I didn't realize it was you."

He rushed to stand and in so doing almost knocked over the inkwell. His hands fumbled for a moment but he was able to retain his hold on the elusive item. Looking up at me he grinned sheepishly. It took all of my concerted effort to keep a straight face.

"If you would be so kind as to come into my office, Mr. Lawson, and bring the inventory list with you," I directed.

"Certainly, Miss Conner."

Without hesitation I turned and left Nathan to follow, as any good employer would do. Once in my office I stood behind the door, out of sight of passersby. No sooner had Nathan entered than I pushed the door shut and stepped into his arms. I needed to be held. And kissed. So I took the initiative and pulled his head down. He obliged me with a kiss that was tender yet inflammatory.

"Delia, what are we doing?"

"Kissing, of course."

"I mean all of this. I know I told you that you must marry Mr. Newkirk but are we to go on this way, forever hiding in the shadows. I want to make love to you properly, in a soft bed, not on a hard floor. I don't want you to sneak about in your own home." He pulled away from me a little but didn't let me go completely.

"It was your idea for me to stay with Kevin," I reminded him.

"I still believe that is the prudent thing to do. Not only can he give you things I can't but you'll be in a position to oversee the staff with kindness and fairness."

I nodded at the wisdom of his words but my body craved his touch so much that I wanted to jump out of my clothes.

"Yet you still want to make love to me? On a bed?" The corners of my mouth turned up as I asked the question. I fluttered my eyelashes playfully as well.

"You are meant to lie on a bed of roses and I am meant to kneel worshipfully at your feet," he opined, placing his hand above his heart.

I reached into the pocket of my apron and withdrew a key, tucked it into his hand and closed his fingers around it. He looked at me questioningly.

"Put this in a safe place where no one else can find it. This is the key that will unlock the door at the top of the concealed stairway that leads to my room. I have the only other one."

"I will wear it next to my heart."

"Heavens no. Put it on your key ring with the others. You have so many now that no one will notice one more."

"As always you have a keen mind for solving problems, my love."
He took the key and placed it in the pocket of his jacket, patting it once
or twice to make sure it nestled there securely.

"Come tonight. After you've made your rounds and have secured
the house."

"So soon? I would think you'd be quite sated from our meeting
last night."

"It must be tonight, Nate. I've received word that Kevin will be
returning tomorrow afternoon. In two days time I shall be leaving to
return to Staten Island. I won't be back until just before my wedding
day. Let's not waste what little time we have."

He drew me into his arms then and kissed me, soundly this time.
I loved his kisses. They were deep yet tender. And, God help me, they
weren't as wet and sloppy as Kevin's.

"I shall come to you tonight then," he murmured against my lips
as he pulled me even closer into his embrace. He inhaled the scent of
my perfume.

"Until tonight, Nate. Come as early as you think it is safe. I shall
dismiss Ellen around nine o'clock. I'll leave the panel to the stairway
open in my dressing area. "

"I prefer to err on the side of safety. I shall come up closer to ten
o'clock. If the panel is closed then I shall know you're not alone."

I nodded my agreement before stepping away from Nathan and
moving towards my desk. I nodded at him to open the door to the
kitchen.

"If you'll take charge of procuring those supplies, Mr. Lawson, I'm
sure we'll be in good shape for the remaining month." My voice was
purposely loud so as to carry to anyone still in the kitchen.

"I'll see to it right away, Miss Conner." With a shallow bow he left
my office, leaving the door open.

It was almost nine-thirty before I could convince Ellen that I no
longer needed her ministrations. She seemed determined to talk about
Kevin's return on the morrow. Not so much talk of Kevin mind you
as of Paul. I stopped my thoughts from fantasizing about Nathan for

long enough to really listen to her. When I did, I realized that she had a crush on Paul, Kevin's valet.

"Ellen," I interjected when she took a breath, "how long have you been enamored of Paul?"

"Why Miss Cordelia, I'm not in love with him?" She stopped brushing my hair to make her declaration.

"Then why does Paul seem to be your favorite topic of discussion as of late?"

She seemed to blush rather prettily as I caught her out.

"It just seems a bit lonely here without him, you know. He has such a way of telling a story. Captivating it is!"

"You mean he has such a way with the ladies," I acknowledged. "He's much too old for you, Ellen."

"Not old, Miss Cordelia, just that he's a man of the world. He's seen things. He's been places." Ellen sounded a bit wistful.

"Are you craving excitement, Ellen? Do you wish to travel?"

"I guess I am, Miss Cordelia." She pulled the brush through my curls as she spoke.

"Then I guess there's nothing for it but for you to accompany me on my honeymoon."

"I had hoped you'd say that, Miss Cordelia. I rather fancy seeing those Niagara Falls."

"Niagara Falls? In New York?"

"Yes, Miss Cordelia. The entire household has bets as to where you and Mr. Newkirk will be spending your honeymoon. The smart money says it will be Niagara Falls. Everyone goes there."

"Ellen, I will tell you a secret, but you are not to repeat it. The folks that are betting on Niagara Falls are going to lose their money. Have you put money into the betting pot?"

"No, Miss Cordelia. The others wouldn't let either me or Paul bet. They figure we might have inside information."

"Well, you do now. Ellen we are going to Europe for our honeymoon. We will be sailing two days after the wedding."

"Oh my goodness! Oh my goodness! Oh my goodness!"

Ellen dropped my hairbrush and began dancing around the room. I watched her flit from one side of my boudoir to the other, not knowing what to do or what to say.

"And I'm to accompany you?" she asked between bursts of excitement.

"Yes, Ellen, you're going to Europe with me, although I'm afraid there won't be much time for you or Paul to sightsee as you'll be in charge of our luggage as well as being maid and valet."

"Oh my gosh! I'm going to Europe! Little Ellen Hughes! I'm going to Europe!"

I stood up and grasped her by the waist as she flittered by me. She stopped momentarily to look at me, a grin the size of Boston lighting her face.

"It's true?"

"It's true, Ellen. We're going to Europe. We plan on seeing all the wonderful places of England, France, Italy, and maybe the Riviera."

Ellen let out a most unladylike whoop as I ticked off the countries we would be visiting.

"I'm sorry, Miss Cordelia. I never in the world expected to leave Boston let alone get to live on Staten Island and then here at Bridgewater. But Europe! I'm so giddy I feel faint."

"Perhaps it's best if you retire for the evening, Ellen."

"But your hair…"

"I believe I can wield a hairbrush unaided. Now scoot."

My smile was genuine as I hustled her off towards the door. With her hand on the knob she turned back to me once more.

"Tell me one more time, Miss Cordelia. Please?"

"Ellen, you will accompany me on my honeymoon to Europe. We will be sailing out of New York on September 27th. Oh, and Ellen?"

"Yes, Miss Cordelia?"

"Paul will be accompanying Mr. Newkirk as well."

"Oh my gosh! Oh my gosh! Oh my gosh!" Her hands were aflutter as this extra bit of news took hold. "I… I must go now."

She vanished at last leaving me in a peaceful lull. I could understand her happiness for she had envisioned her life as merely a series of drudgeries. Perhaps Nathan was right. My marriage to Kevin would result in happiness for many people who otherwise might live a dreary existence.

I finished brushing my hair the required one-hundred strokes and set the silver hairbrush back on my vanity. The night had brought about slightly cooler temperatures and I went to stand beside the open window, letting the light breeze caress my face and neck. I listened to the sounds of the night and realized how peaceful this house could be. The neighing of a horse carried on the breeze as even the livestock settled in on this calm night. All that would change tomorrow.

Kevin would return and with him the flurry of activity that always seemed to surround him. We would walk together through the now-furnished house, where I'm sure he would wish to make an adjustment or two to the placement of furniture or accent pieces. Of course he would inspect his office and bedchamber and hopefully be satisfied with their appearance.

I had already alerted the laundress to be prepared for his return. Mrs. Grant had agreed with my suggestions for a welcome-home supper. Huckleby had painstakingly seen to the grooming of each horse in the stable, making sure that all was in tip-top shape.

This time tomorrow I would be fending off Kevin's advances, urging restraint for the final weeks before our wedding. To keep him happy, however, I would accept his wet kisses as they were placed upon my mouth and suffer his hands upon my breasts although I knew his mind would be out in the stables, thinking of his horses.

But tonight would be different. Tonight I would give myself to Nathan, the only man I have truly loved. My lips ached as they awaited his kisses; my breasts ached for his touch; my arms ached to hold him; my body grew warm at the thought of his caresses. I closed my eyes, willing him to appear before the ten o'clock hour.

His hands came around me first, gliding along my waist until they were clasped just beneath my bosom. I leaned back into the hardness of his chest, tilting my head and offering up my mouth to him. He placed a tender kiss first on my cheek before turning me around to face him. His lips claimed mine in another, firmer kiss, sending shivers of excitement down my spine and straight to my toes.

"I didn't hear you come up," I said, hating to move my lips away from his.

"You looked so serene, standing here by the window. I didn't want to disturb you." He drew me closer still and rested his head against mine. "What were you thinking of?"

"Let's not waste our time on my thoughts." I nibbled at his lower lip.

"Would you rather do something else?" Nathan's voice held a note of suggestion.

"I'd like to play a game of pretend."

"I hate games," moaned Nathan.

"You'll like this one. Let's pretend this is our wedding night." My voice had turned husky as I clasped his hand and pulled him toward the bed. He tugged me back into the circle of his arms.

"If this is our wedding night, then you'll need to follow my lead. Allow me."

Nathan scooped me up from the floor and I placed my arms around his neck, savoring the feel of his strong arms supporting me while he pleasured my mouth with his kisses. Gently he placed me on the bed before turning to remove his clothes. I in turn removed my night gown and made room for him. Within moments, Nate had divested himself of his garments and was soon beside me.

"Come to me, Delia, let me love you."

Those were the last words spoken between us as we sank into the raptures of our love.

———

The sun shone brightly on the September morning that I set out for New York. It was time for me to return to my parents' home in preparation for our upcoming wedding. There would be the final fitting of my wedding dress, the packing of my trousseau and my personal effects, and the final round of calls to be made. My head literally ached at the thought of all that remained to be done before I was able to return to Bridgewater and to Nathan.

Kevin insisted on driving his motor car since he had spent much of the past few weeks traveling by train and now wanted to feel the 'freedom of the open road'. Paul and Ellen had departed for New York the previous day on the one o'clock train. Paul had proceeded to The Ansonia Hotel to await Kevin's arrival. Ellen had been met by poppa at Grand Central Station and together they had boarded the Staten Island Ferry for home.

We made ready to depart Bridgewater. I was comfortably seated in the car's passenger seat, my hat secured by not only an army of hat pins but also by a length of chiffon that wound around the hat's crown and was fashioned into a huge bow to one side of my chin. Kevin, nattily attired in a white coverall with matching driver's cap, stepped to the front of the motor car and began cranking the shaft. While he was thus engaged my attention was drawn to the front entryway where I spied Nathan making haste to catch us before we left.

"Miss Conner! Mr. Newkirk!" he called.

Kevin continued cranking away so I acknowledged Nathan's shout.

"Mr. Lawson? Is something amiss?"

"Mrs. Grant asked me to bring this to you. I'm happy to oblige."

He hefted a rather large picnic basket into the back area of the car and placed it on the floor behind my seat.

"Please extend our thanks to Mrs. Grant, won't you?"

I made the mistake of looking up and directly into Nathan's eyes. He returned my glance with one of wistful longing. Since Kevin's return we had been unable to meet privately for even a short conversation. But that brief meeting of our eyes was enough to confirm that our love was more alive than either of us would admit. I diverted my gaze then, breaking the connection between us and reminding myself that Kevin was at hand. When I addressed Nathan again it was with the decorum an employer would use with a subordinate.

"Mr. Lawson, you are in complete charge during our absence. I expect wedding gifts will begin arriving most any day now. Please have them stored in my office. I'll deal with them upon my return."

"As you wish, Miss Conner." A smile toyed with his lips.

"Ah, Lawson," remarked Kevin as he settled himself behind the steering wheel. "I expect the remaining guest rooms to be painted and papered within the week. See that they are fully furnished and ready for occupancy. Miss Conner's family will be returning with her. My own family will be arriving shortly thereafter."

Kevin tightened the strap of his driving goggles as he spoke.

"Everything will be ready for your return, sir."

Nathan stepped back a pace or two as Kevin turned the ignition switch and the motor car bucked forward.

"Just like a stallion being broken to the saddle!" cried Kevin as the motor car roared to life and we sped down the driveway, leaving Nathan and Bridgewater behind us, enveloped in a cloud of automotive exhaust.

———

Back on Staten Island, the final flurry of wedding preparations filled each and every day. Mornings were spent making calls on the women of New York society who now opened their doors to welcome momma and I. Most of the society matrons clucked over me, saying how well I turned out and hoping that in some small way they had influenced my demeanor and manners. Where once momma and I had been relegated to admittance via a side door reserved for servants and vendors, now we were welcomed at society's front door. All because I wore Kevin's ring on my hand.

On alternate days momma was pleased to welcome the younger set of society women, those closer to my own age, who had made brilliant matches of their own or who were recently engaged. Many of these were daughters or daughters-in-law to the women that momma had once served as modiste. Their visits gave me plenty of practice in being a hostess although Ellen was less than happy at being pressed into service as a parlor maid once more.

Afternoons were spent in a variety of ways. Ellen was given the task of packing not only my trousseau but my personal belongings as well. Momma made the final adjustments to my wedding gown. It was a vision of loveliness while being on the cutting edge of fashion. Dispensing with the tradition of a chapel length veil, I had ordered a wedding hat from Milady's Chapeaux in Boston. That particular establishment had flourished over the past several months thanks to several substantial orders from Elite Fashions. I felt rather smug knowing that Kevin's mistress was designing part of his fiancée's wedding costume.

There were several shopping excursions into the city as well to choose gifts for the wedding party. A number of wedding presents were sent to our house as well as bridal shower gifts from a party given by my sister-in-law Rose. I made a point of writing thank-you notes each afternoon in an effort to keep correspondence from piling up.

After supper I kept company with momma and poppa as they discussed the events of the day and their upcoming schedules. My hands were busy during those family evenings as I stitched fine hems on a set of pocket silks for my groom. Yet while my fingers moved through the stitches of their own accord, my mind was free to wander.

Thoughts of Nate invariably crept into my head. I recalled in vivid detail the sparkle in his eyes when he would look at me in a special way; the warmth of his kiss; the feel of his arms when I snuggled into his embrace; the feel of his lean body when he lay beside me; the look of his face – so serene – as he slept alongside me after we'd made love.

Therefore, I was overjoyed when, about two weeks after our return to Staten Island, I received an envelope bearing the Bridgewater crest. I immediately recognized Nate's penmanship and was anxious to rip open the envelope. Instead, I tucked it into the pocket of my skirt. There it remained, quietly calling out to me, during the late afternoon and evening meal.

"Didn't I notice an envelope from Bridgewater arrive with today's mail?" momma inquired as she cut into a warm apple cobbler.

"Yes, you're right momma," I acknowledged as I accepted a small piece of the delicious dessert.

"Was it anything important, dear?" momma continued.

"I haven't had the opportunity to open the envelope yet. I expect it's merely a report from the Head Steward."

"You mean that handsome young man, what was his name?"

"Lawson, momma. His name is Lawson."

"I certainly hope nothing is amiss," offered poppa.

"I doubt that, poppa, or Lawson would have sent a telegram."

"Perhaps you should open the envelope and see," suggested momma.

"Not during our meal, momma. That would be unconscionable."

"We certainly don't mind. Do we Charles?"

"Cordelia can tend to business after supper. I applaud her efforts to make our meal pleasant," replied poppa, holding out his plate for a second helping of cobbler.

All was quiet for a while then momma spoke up again. I could tell she was in the mood for some gossip.

"Cordelia, do you know if that nice Mr. Lawson is seeing anyone?" she finally inquired.

Poppa looked quizzically at momma.

"I was just thinking what a nice catch he would be for Ellen. You could keep both domestics in your employ quite happily. After all, Mr. Lawson is handsome and well-employed," finished momma.

"I really don't feel it's my place to play matchmaker, momma. Now, I believe I'll retire to my room and read for a bit."

I rose, cleared my place at the dining table, and went upstairs to my bedroom, setting the letter from Bridgewater atop my dresser. After I had changed from my day dress into a soft cotton nightshift, I slit open the letter bearing Nate's penmanship and pulled the folded sheet from the envelope. With the light fading from the sky, I read what he had written.

Dear Miss Conner,

I trust this letter finds you in good health.

It is my pleasure to report that the rooms in the guest wing have all been completed per Mr. Newkirk's direction. I have assigned some of the temporary help to preparing these rooms for our guests.

Preparations for the wedding reception are proceeding on schedule. I have verified all orders placed with the various merchants and have been assured of timely delivery of all items.

The Boston contingent is due for arrival here at the end of the week and will be taking up residence in Willow Cottage. I have also assigned staff to see to their needs.

The entire staff at Bridgewater looks forward to your return and the resumption of your duties as the mistress of Bridgewater. There are some things that can only flourish with your touch.

> *I remain your humble servant —*
> *Nathan Lawson*

And there it was. Nate's way of telling me that he missed me and couldn't wait until I returned to Bridgewater. Of course, to anyone else it would appear that his message was merely an update on the status of things at the estate, but I could read between the lines. Therefore, I immediately took pen in hand and wrote my answer, assuring him that he was doing a fine job and that I too looked forward to my return to Bridgewater.

———

September 25, 1908
Bridgewater

Today is my wedding day, I thought as I greeted the morning from the comfort of my bed in my turret room. It was early, not even seven o'clock, and I lay back amidst the pillows that had cradled not only my head, but Nate's as well for the past few hours. We had shared this last wondrous night together; I felt loved and secure in our secret world. Neither of us had wanted the night to end, but end it did. Now, as I took these final moments to relax before the hustle and bustle of my wedding day, I found myself looking with longing at the vase full of cut flowers that sat upon my vanity. It was a large bouquet of mixed flowers that Nathan had brought to me last night; late summer blooms with their vibrant hues intermingled with a few hot-house blossoms that he had appropriated from floral baskets that had been delivered by the florist.

"You should always be surrounded by flowers, Delia," he had said, "even though your beauty far outshines them."

I slipped out from the bedclothes and reached out to touch the blossoms now filling my room with their fragrance. The sun was still low on the eastern horizon and its rays fought to break through the vibrant foliage surrounding the house. From the stables I could hear the muted voices of the stable hands as they went about their business of feeding the horses and cleaning out the stalls. No doubt Kevin would be visiting there shortly, as he did every morning before breakfast. I sometimes wondered if he didn't give more attention to his horses than he did to anything, or anyone, else.

My thoughts were interrupted by a light tapping at my bedroom door.

"Come in," I called out gaily, knowing that it would be Ellen bringing up my morning tea tray.

"Good morning, Miss Cordelia." Ellen's greeting seemed a cheerful as my own. "I didn't think you'd be up just yet."

She placed the tray she carried on a small table near my rounded window seat. The teapot was nestled under a tea cozy, an English bone china cup and saucer were perched next to it. A snowy white linen napkin covered two warm scones that waited for me to cover them with butter and jam. As Ellen set about straightening the room, she filled me in on what was happening below stairs.

"I hope you slept well, Miss Cordelia."

"Thank you, Ellen, I certainly did."

"That's more than I can say for Mr. Newkirk." She disappeared into my dressing area momentarily.

'Why is that, I wonder," I observed as I poured the tea into my cup and stirred in some cream.

"He and the other gents didn't return home until just around sunup this morning. Scandalous, if you ask me."

"Who was he with? Do you know?"

"He was with his brothers-in-law, you know, that nice professor and that awful Mr. Woodward."

I chuckled to myself at her description of my soon-to-be in-laws. She was certainly correct on both counts.

"Paul was up all night waiting for Mr. Newkirk's return. He finally fell asleep around dawn."

"Oh, dear. I do hope Paul will find some time to rest. This promises to be a very full day."

"Not to worry, Miss Cordelia, Paul is accustomed to Mr. Newkirk's crazy hours. At least Mr. Newkirk is now snoring away rather soundly and Paul is downstairs having some breakfast."

"Ellen, would you be certain that Priscilla changes the bedding in here. I would like everything to be fresh for tonight." I had the grace to blush as I issued that directive.

"Why of course, Miss Cordelia! I'll be extra late coming to wake you tomorrow morning, if you catch my drift." She winked at me conspiratorially. "Shall I draw your bath now?"

The remainder of the morning passed rather quickly. As I soaked in the tub I felt extremely relaxed; thoughts of Nathan still filled my head. I allowed myself the luxury of recalling our lovemaking the previous night and to my astonishment found that those memories had stirred me to crave just one more kiss from him. How silly I was being, I realized, when in just a few short hours I would need to devote my energy to my new husband. With Ellen's assistance, I dried off and donned a dressing gown. There was simply no time to think about Nathan. That fact was brought home when a brief knock sounded at my door and momma waltzed in.

"How's my beautiful daughter this morning?" She swooped in and planted a kiss on my forehead.

"I'm perfect this morning, momma," I reassured her.

"Of course you are, dear. This is your wedding day. The day we've all worked so hard to achieve." She broke off a piece of a scone and popped it into her mouth. "What time is the preacher due to arrive?"

"Father Hartigan is due around ten o'clock. We've plenty of time till then." I sat down and poured myself another cup of tea.

"I do hope Kevin pulls himself together by then. He was out rather late last night."

"Yes, I understand he arrived home just before dawn. I should think he's sleeping right now."

"That bachelor party scenario is simply barbaric. There's no need for it at all."

"It's simply an unnecessary tradition. But it's over and done with."

"Cordelia, dear, there's something I need to speak with you about."

"Go ahead, momma."

"In private, if you don't mind." She motioned towards the dressing room where Ellen was tidying up after my bath.

"Ellen, would you be kind enough to fetch us more tea, and another cup for momma?"

"Certainly, Miss Cordelia." She smiled at us as she took away the empty teapot.

Once the door closed behind her, momma put on her serious face and took a deep breath. Obviously what she was about to say carried some weight with her.

"Cordelia, dear child," she began, clasping and unclasping her hands tightly. I could tell she was a bundle of nerves.

"What is it momma? Why are you so nervous?"

"Cordelia," she began again, "tonight will be your wedding night."

"Yes, momma, I'm well aware of that."

"There are certain things that a man, a husband, has a right to expect."

I couldn't help myself. I let out a laugh that caused my mother to blush beet red at first before her righteous indignation found its footing.

"Stop laughing, right this minute. This is a very serious matter that we need to discuss."

"Momma," I tried to control my laughter, "are you trying to tell me what to expect on my wedding night?"

For once momma had nothing to say. She simply opened and closed her mouth much like a fish out of water. Finally, she simply nodded her head.

"Oh, momma, please don't worry yourself. I have no need of 'the talk'." I reached out to hold her hand but she pulled away as though I'd stuck her with a hot poker.

"Cordelia Conner, whatever are you saying?"

"Momma, I haven't been a virgin since I was sixteen." There. I'd let the cat out of the bag.

"Who was he? I'll have to inform your father. They'll pay for ruining my little girl." Her facial features were pulled back into a contorted grimace by her all-consuming fury.

"I won't tell you his name. Suffice it to say that I'm looking forward to my marriage bed."

"You don't understand, do you? Once Kevin finds out that you're not a virgin, he'll annul the marriage. All will be for naught!"

"Hmm. I hadn't thought of that."

"You haven't given yourself to Kevin, have you?"

"Of course not, momma. He has sought surcease from his mistress. He believes me to be untouched."

"And that's exactly what we'll let him think. After the ceremony, you are to come up here to powder your nose. I shall accompany you. All will be well in the end."

"Momma, what sort of subterfuge are you planning?"

"Nothing that hasn't been done before. Now, don't worry your pretty head any further. I have work to do."

Pulling her dressing robe close around her, she flounced out of my room just as Ellen was returning with a steaming teapot and second cup. She looked after momma, shrugged her shoulders, and set the pot on the table before me. Ellen had become accustomed to momma's dramatic ways.

"Shall I pour you another cup of tea, Miss Cordelia?"

"Yes, I rather feel the need right now."

Shortly after ten o'clock that morning, Ellen withdrew my wedding dress from its place in the wardrobe and carefully laid it on the bed. Momma had put hour upon hour of work into the fine stitching and hand-beading that covered the slip-like unstructured first layer of the dress from shoulder to toe. A diaphanous second layer consisting of yards of Belgian lace resting atop the under-layer created a gown within a gown effect.

Starting with my underpinnings, Ellen handed me my off-white chemise. Next the sheer stockings were fastened to a garter belt that cinched my waist with blue ribbons. A full-length slip that momma had created from the softest silk skimmed along the contours of my body. The beaded under-layer of my dress was then carefully drawn over my head and adjusted around my shoulders; the lacy over-garment settled atop all of this, giving the entire ensemble an air of regal elegance. Ellen then made some minor repairs to my coiffure before assisting me with the placement of my hat.

"Oooh, Miss Cordelia, that hat is simply the most beautiful thing that Miss Jeannette has ever created!" cooed Ellen.

"She certainly has outdone herself, hasn't she? Now, no mention of Miss Jeannette's name. Especially within hearing of either of the mothers," I cautioned.

"Wild horses couldn't force me to tell!" replied Ellen.

Indeed, Kevin's mistress had truly outdone herself. The hat itself was wide-brimmed and covered with yards of the same Belgian lace that my over-dress was made from. A large flat bow of soft chiffonese was held in place by a brooch that was borrowed from momma. The hat alone was destined to turn heads; in combination with my gown it was guaranteed to set a style (at least that's what I hoped for). An ornate hat pin, a gift from Jeannette, secured the hat to my upswept curls.

I added the diamond chandelier earrings that Kevin had given me as a wedding gift. They added just the right touch, not too ostentatious but noticeable in size.

I stood before the cheval looking glass and found no fault with the image it showed me: a lady of quality, dressed most fashionably, on her wedding day – the day she would officially become a member of high society.

Was this what I really wanted? Would I be happy in the role of Mrs. Kevin Newkirk? Was I throwing away my chance for future happiness? Could I live my life here, as mistress of this house, sneaking stolen moments with the man I loved?

There was no time to ponder the answers to these questions as the strains of the musicians starting up the pre-ceremony program began. A knock on the door announced the entry of my sister-in-law Rose who had graciously accepted the role of matron-of-honor. She was gowned in rose-colored Belgian lace in a gown styled to complement my own.

"Oh, Cordy, you're such a beautiful bride!"

"Do you really think so?"

"It's so obvious that you're in love."

"Does it show?"

"Oh, yes. Kevin is a fortunate man to have your love."

How should I answer that, I wondered. I merely smiled at her as she handed my bridal bouquet to me. I looked from Rose to Ellen and back to Rose. Their faces radiated their joy on this, my wedding day.

"I'd like just a few moments to compose myself. Do you mind?"

Rose took my cue.

"Ellen, why don't you go on downstairs? Cordy, I'll wait for you in the hall."

At last the door closed, shutting out the rest of the world and leaving me with my thoughts. In a few minutes I would become Kevin's wife. There would be no turning back. I would be bound to him for the rest of my life.

I closed my eyes and thought back to the day when Nathan and I had first acknowledged our love for one another; to the decision that he had made and to which I'd agreed – that I should marry Kevin even though I didn't love him. I searched my mind for the words Nathan had used: "he can give you the things I can't, but I will always be here to love you and protect you".

I could still feel the warmth of his embrace when he had been in this very room, mere hours ago, and showed me the depth of his love; I could still feel the tenderness of his lips on mine as we had parted in the early hours of this morning. Right now he would be standing at the head of our household staff as they, along with our other guests, awaited my arrival downstairs. Turning back to my vanity, I picked up one last tiny item to add to my wedding attire before opening the door and joining Rose in the hallway.

The air of excitement grew as I made my way down the semi-circular stairway and into the foyer. Ropes of flowers adorned the spokes of the staircase. A small spray of cymbidium orchids was fastened atop the staircase newel post. Overflowing baskets of artfully arranged flowers decorated the foyer. Their fragrance was heavenly.

Rose stood near the doors to the small ballroom where my cousin Eloise, also a bridesmaid, waited. My parents stood at the bottom of the stairs.

Momma looked every bit the lady of quality that she strove so hard to be. Her gown was the perfect mother-of-the-bride dress, done in sage green with gold accents; her hat of sage green sported gold-flecked netting and her gloves were also of a matching sage green. She carried a small beaded purse that was tucked protectively under her elbow. Poppa, standing there beside her, was resplendent in his formal tuxedo and high, stiff-collared shirt. His shoes gleamed in the sunlight streaming through the tall windows of the Grand Hallway.

As I descended the staircase they both lifted their faces upward to me: momma's face had a pinched expression attributable to her recent discovery that I was no longer virginal; poppa's smile radiated the wistful joy of a father who is happy to see his daughter well wed yet sad to be losing his little girl. I navigated the last step; poppa extended his hand to me and I placed my own gloved hand into his outstretched palm.

"Are you ready, Cordy?" he asked, choking a bit as he spoke.

"Yes."

Momma nodded at one of the footmen stationed beside the closed ballroom doors. At her signal he opened the doors and after a momentary lull the musicians began to play. Phil Evans, one of Kevin's old friends who was ushering, gave momma his arm and escorted her to her seat. First Eloise, then Rose, walked the short distance to the front of the room. It was time. With poppa beside me we moved forward.

This was the moment I had waited for all of my life. From a very early age I had wanted nothing more than to be a beautiful bride. Now, as I walked through a sea of elegant guests, my dream had come true. Waiting at the end of this walk would be my Prince Charming. I looked ahead and saw Kevin, not by any means my Prince Charming, but the man who had made my childhood dream come true.

As we approached Father Hartigan, who smiled benevolently, my gaze scanned the group of our assembled household staff. They had been given leave to attend the ceremony before going back to their duties. There, at the head of the group, stood Nathan. Tall and lean, impeccably attired, he favored me with a smile that calmed the nervous stomach I didn't realize I had. Only his eyes bespoke his love for me; his eyes, and the rose-colored carnation in his lapel. Ever so nonchalantly I turned my bouquet so that my last-minute addition to it caught Nathan's eye. The moment he spotted the rose-colored carnation that I had tucked into my bouquet, his smile deepened and his eyes sparkled.

The ceremony itself was over in a heartbeat, or so it seemed. I was now Cordelia Newkirk, and officially the mistress of Bridgewater; Kevin's parents were my in-laws, and momma could finally call herself a lady of quality.

Refreshments were served out on the terrace where the mid-day sun shone brightly. A gentle breeze played amidst the dense stands of trees surrounding the house sending intermittent showers of leaves to carpet the ground.

I walked beside Kevin as he introduced me to people whose faces I would most likely forget by day's end. But I smiled and graciously accepted their congratulations even as Kevin downed glass after glass of wine and champagne. Thankfully he didn't seem to notice that I had hardly touched my first and only glass of champagne.

When Kevin began to discuss horse breeding with several

gentlemen, I excused myself. Kevin didn't object to my movements, he was oblivious to everything when speaking of his horses. In fact, just moments later I saw him leading three or four of the gentlemen in the direction of the stables. Looking around I was able to catch momma's eye. She nodded and followed me inside, where she accompanied me upstairs and into my bedchamber.

"I believe everything went well," I observed as I set my bouquet on the window seat.

"All is well so far, you mean."

Momma glided across the room so that her voice wouldn't carry through the open window. She opened her purse and withdrew a small vial that she handed to me.

"You'll need this tonight," she whispered as she tucked the vial into my hand.

"What is this?" I inquired as I took a look at the red liquid contained in the vial.

"Chicken blood."

"What? Why do I need chicken blood?"

"You wouldn't need it if you hadn't thrown away your virginity." Momma ground out the words that seemed laced with venom. "Tonight, after Kevin falls asleep sprinkle this on the sheet. Just a small drop or two will suffice. Then dispose of the remainder. Even if he doesn't see it the staff will, and they will confirm your status as a wife who has consummated her marriage properly. Now put that somewhere safe. You should return to your guests."

The remainder of that afternoon passed pleasantly enough since Kevin lingered out in the stables with his friends. Most of our guests had departed by late afternoon and only our combined families remained to join us for our wedding dinner. We were assembled in our drawing room, awaiting the reappearance of my wayward groom. Kevin's mother was giving me a look that bespoke her exasperation since my father-in-law seemed to be among the missing gentlemen. Having stood all she was about to stand, Mother Newkirk approached me, a phony smile plastered on her face.

"Do something," she whispered to me, "This is your house, do something."

She was absolutely correct, of course. I made my way to the hall where I found Nathan, who was awaiting my signal to announce dinner.

"Mrs. Newkirk," he politely acknowledged me, "may I be of assistance?"

"Mr. Lawson, it appears that Mr. Newkirk has forgotten us. Please send someone to the stables to collect him and whatever other gentlemen are with him."

"Right away, Mrs. Newkirk." His warm smile calmed me.

"And don't call me by that name when we're alone," I whispered heatedly.

"As you wish, Delia." He turned and headed for the terrace where he would find the footmen.

A quarter of an hour later we were interrupted by the men's voices as they engaged in boisterous laughter. Like a group of adolescent boys they spilled into the drawing room. Kevin made a beeline for me although he missed a step or two en route. Reaching my side he pulled me towards him and favored me with a noisy kiss.

"Ah, Cordelia, my beautiful bride, I have come in answer to your summons." He playfully bowed before me.

"Kevin, please, remember our guests," I said through my gritted teeth.

"Oh posh, we're all family."

"You're drunk," I whispered, feeling ashamed that his family should see him like this in his own home.

"Not drunk yet, but I'm going to be."

Over his shoulder I gave the nod to Nathan who, after imparting a worried glance in my direction, immediately announced dinner.

Our wedding dinner was a fiasco. Kevin imbibed more wine, bored most of us with his talk of horses, and nearly caused his mother to swoon when he stated that this very night he planned to plant the seed that would soon become the Newkirk heir. A short time later I led the ladies back to the drawing room while Kevin directed the men to the billiards room.

In the end we ladies were abandoned by the men who had taken up their cue sticks for a round or two of billiards. I begged leave of the ladies around nine o'clock and retired to my room where Ellen patiently helped me to prepare for my new husband's arrival. Once she had left I sat quietly in the chair by my window, looking down at the driveway, thinking how different things might have been if Nathan were my groom and not Kevin. My thoughts were interrupted by a resounding knock on the door before it flew open.

There was Kevin, wearing a silk robe and pajamas. He swayed uneasily as he moved towards me.

"Ah, Cordy, we're together at last. I will finally see you without all those layers of clothes that you hide behind."

I stood up, walked around him, and closed the door. When I turned he was beside me, his hands pawing ineffectually at my nightgown.

"Too many clothes, Cordy. Take them off." His voice was rough and demanding.

"Kevin, please," I implored as I loosened the belt of his robe, "lie down, let me come to you."

"A strip-tease? For me? I didn't think you'd be so willing?"

He removed his robe and sat down on the bed. I could see that he was fighting to stay awake but his eyelids refused to remain open. I moved slowly, seductively around the room buying myself some time. When I reached the bed he was laying on his back, eyes closed."

"Kevin," I whispered, "Kevin?"

No response. I poked his shoulder gently.

"Kevin, wake up." This time my voice was loud.

I nudged him again. In answer I received a loud snore. Then another and another as I realized my drunken lout of a husband would not be able to partake in his own wedding night.

I returned to the chair by the window and looked out at the night while my husband lay in my bed and snored. When some time had passed and I was assured that he would not awaken I walked over to the bed.

Carefully I divested him of his pajamas, throwing them on the floor much as I imagined he would have done had he been a lively participant in our marriage bed. I drew the sheet over him and quietly left him to peacefully dream, presumably about his horses. Proceeding with caution I slid back the panel in my dressing room that led to the concealed staircase, unlocking the lower stairway that led to my office down below. If Kevin awoke I planned to explain my absence by saying that I had trouble sleeping and had gone in search of some warm milk.

But my actions went undiscovered and within moments I was cautiously pushing back the door into my office. The room was dark but I discerned the outline of someone sitting at my desk. One sniff of his clean sandalwood scent identified the trespasser as my own dear Nathan. His head appeared to be down, resting on his chest. That was when I heard a sound that amazed me. My Nathan was quietly sobbing! I moved on bare feet to stand behind him, placing a hand on his shoulder.

"Nate? What's wrong? Are you ill?"

"Delia!" he whispered my name with fervor between sobs, "What have I done?"

Could he be hurt or ill? My heart began to beat rapidly. He turned to face me, taking my hand in his and laying his cheek against it he placed a tear-stained kiss on my palm.

"How can I live now that I've let you marry that poor excuse for a man?"

I pulled him close and placed a kiss on his head, much as a mother would kiss her child, stroking his hair until his sobs subsided.

"I'm here now Nate. Kevin is snoring in a drunken stupor upstairs in my bed." I felt his arms encircle my waist. "This is my wedding night. I don't want to be alone."

Nate stood and drew me into his arms, kissing me with a poignant tenderness as if I was truly his bride.

"Stay with me tonight, Delia. Let me love you. But not here, not like this."

"Surely not in your office?" I chuckled. "I don't think Mrs. Grant will cover for us again."

"We can use your room."

"What if Kevin awakes?"

"We'll use the dressing room. If he wakes he'll be disoriented and hung over. That will give me time to slip away. You'll be where you should be, in your room with your husband."

I nodded my agreement and together we returned to my turret room. The sound of Kevin's snore greeted us as we slipped soundlessly into the dressing room. Satisfied that Kevin would pose no problem, we settled into the chaise and physically expressed our love. Our coupling was sweet and tender and when we were finished I fell asleep in Nathan's embrace. Shortly before dawn he woke me.

"Delia, my lovebird, it's time to wake up."

I stretched and yawned before he kissed me on the forehead.

"It's not morning yet?" I mumbled, noting the darkness outside the window.

"Almost. I must leave you now. It's time you slipped into your own bed."

"If I must," I muttered.

His quiet chuckle reverberated through his chest as he nudged me off the chaise. I hadn't heard him get dressed but he was already fully clothed. One last kiss and he disappeared through the concealed panel, pulling it closed behind him.

I rose lazily and padded over to my vanity table from which I withdrew the vial of chicken blood. Carefully I pulled back the sheet and let two drops of blood fall from the vial. Then I got inspired. Placing a drop more on my finger, I smeared it along the inside of one of my thighs before replacing the vial in the drawer of my vanity table.

Gently I eased myself into bed and rested my head on the pillow. The excitement of the previous day coupled with my nocturnal activities combined to lull me back to sleep. When I awoke it was to the sight of Kevin, propped on one elbow, watching me sleep. He seemed to be unaffected by the amount of alcohol he had consumed yesterday.

"Good morning, Cordy, or should I say Mrs. Newkirk?"

"Kevin?" For some reason my grogginess wouldn't lift but that worked in my favor.

"I fear I owe you an apology, little wife."

"An apology?" My tiredness was leaving me a bit fuzzy and I played it to my advantage.

"I fear I fell asleep before we consummated the marriage. But I intent to rectify that right now."

I allowed him to ply me with kisses before protesting.

"I beg to tell you differently, husband." Kevin drew back and raised an eyebrow in question. "Not only did we make love last night, but we did so twice. You were quite the stallion."

His chest puffed up at my equine reference.

"I swear, Cordy, I don't recall a moment of it," he admitted.

That was my cue to draw back the sheet and show him the proof of our union. He had the grace to look sheepish.

"Oh my dear, I hope I didn't cause you too much pain." He gathered me tenderly into his arms.

"You were gentle, dear husband. But I am rather tender in certain areas this morning."

"Then you shall have a nice long soak in a warm tub." He hopped out of bed and rang for Ellen. "You must rest and have a leisurely breakfast, here in your room, while I make my rounds of the stables."

"I would enjoy the bath," I conceded, "'but I shall take my breakfast in the dining room. There are still guests to entertain and a household to run."

"As you wish, my dear." He pulled on his pajamas just as Ellen knocked upon the door. "Come in," he called.

Ellen popped her head through the partially open door and looked first to me then to Kevin.

"Your mistress needs a warm bath. Please assist her," he directed. Turning back to me he added, "I shall join you in the dining room, my dear. I feel absolutely ravenous this morning."

The warmth of the bath that Ellen had drawn for me was, indeed, therapeutic. I lay in the porcelain claw-footed tub, letting my tired muscles relax while the fragrant lemon oil that had been added to the water softened my skin even as it energized me. When the water began to cool Ellen handed me one of the large monogrammed bath towels. A short time later I was dried, powdered, and dressed for the day. By the time I arrived in our dining room most of our extended family was already seated and enjoying their morning meal. All eyes turned to greet me as Kevin rose from his chair and came towards me. Taking my hand in his, he kissed my cheek.

"Come my dear, sit down and let me prepare a dish for you."

Kevin held out a chair for me and once I was seated he proceeded to the sideboard where various breakfast dishes were kept warm in their serving trays.

"Just some toast please and a cup of tea," I answered my husband before turning to greet the others. "I trust everyone slept well?"

There were murmurs of assent although I noticed that both my father-in-law and Robert, one of my brothers-in-law, seemed a bit hung over.

"I can't believe my little girl is now a married lady," observed momma as she sipped daintily from a china cup.

"I really must compliment Cordelia on a very well-run establishment. I hadn't expected such efficiency from a newly established household."

"Thank you, Mother Newkirk. That's high praise indeed coming from you." I basked in the complimentary remark.

"I would expect nothing less from Cordy," Kevin added between bites of his breakfast sausage.

I favored him with a smile, noting the gusto with which he consumed his morning meal. The remainder of our breakfast passed in pleasant conversation until I made the move to adjourn to the morning room.

"You will excuse us, won't you Cordelia? We need to prepare for our departure." Mother Newkirk accompanied me out into the Grand Hallway where floral baskets still perfumed the air.

"Of course, Mother Newkirk. Do you require additional help?"

"Our servants have everything in hand," she assured me.

"I'll have the cars ready in an hour."

I watched my mother-in-law proceed along the Grand Hallway and disappear into the guest wing. I could anticipate the tumult with not only Kevin's parents but also his sisters and their husbands preparing to depart. Upon my arrival in the morning room I rang for Nathan even as I sat down with momma, Rose having excused herself to sit out on the terrace. Within moments Nathan appeared. He inclined his head deferentially toward momma before addressing me.

"Mrs. Newkirk?" His features remained remarkably composed.

"Mr. Lawson, please send another maid and two footmen to the guest wing. Our departing guests may require assistance. The cars will need to be brought around. Have them ready for ten o'clock." I kept the tone of my voice modulated and professional.

"Certainly. Will there be anything else?"

"That's all for now, Mr. Lawson."

Nathan again nodded to me and went off to deliver my instructions to the staff.

"You seem to have taken to your role of lady of the manor rather well. You've become quite the lady of quality," noted momma as she walked about the room, admiring its décor.

"Are you happy, momma? Now that my marriage has elevated your social standing?"

I felt no rancor towards her, yet all of this was her doing. I settled myself on the settee across from the fireplace.

"Of course, darling. I'm happy for you. You are happy, aren't you?" A look of concern briefly crossed momma's face before being replaced by a smile.

"How could I not be happy, momma? I have this beautiful house, a full complement of servants, a doting husband who showers me with jewels. What more could I possibly want?"

"I was afraid you'd feel incomplete without love. You've always said you would only marry a man you loved. Give it time, Cordy, you'll learn to love Kevin."

I couldn't tell momma that I had already found someone to love, someone who loved me in return; someone who loved me for me, not because I could give him children, although I would be proud to bear his child. But the love that Nate and I shared must be kept secret. No one, especially momma, must know of my liaison with Nate. We would steal whatever moments we could and learn to be content with those.

Momma had been chattering away while I wool-gathered and I now tried to follow her running commentary.

"….even though the house is new. I should think a family portrait, or even one of just you, would fill the space above this mantel quite nicely."

"I promise to give it some thought, momma. I'm sure Kevin will have some ideas as well."

"You're right, of course, my dear." Momma smiled and I could see how proud she was of all that I – we – had accomplished.

"I must consult with Mrs. Grant about tonight's menu and review the accounts before our departure tomorrow. Feel free to walk the garden or further explore the house, momma."

"I think perhaps I'll see to having our bags packed before luncheon. I can't see why we have to be on a six o'clock train tomorrow morning."

We walked down the hall, stopping at the foyer.

"Our ship sails mid-afternoon, momma. We need to be at the pier by noon. We all agreed that Kevin and I would join you and poppa on the return to Grand Central Station," I reiterated for possibly the fifth time.

"Yes, yes, I remember." Momma waved her hand in the air. "In that case I shall lie down while one of your maid's packs my luggage."

She turned and made her way through the Grand Hallway and into the guest wing.

At ten o'clock that morning the Newkirk contingent departed for New Haven and Union Station where their private car awaited them on Track #6. With more than half of our family now en route home I was able to breathe a sigh of relief.

The remainder of that day passed in a flurry of activity for me. I met with Mrs. Grant in my office to review the menus for that night's dinner and for breakfast the following morning. While our supper would be nourishing and plentiful I cautioned her about making the dishes too heavy as we needed to be underway early. I directed that she prepare only hot cereal, an assortment of fruit, and plenty of coffee for the next day's breakfast as we would be setting off long before sunup.

Poppa and Cal had accompanied Kevin on a tour of the property after Kevin's rounds of the stables. The men were still discussing the merits of cross-breeding various breeds of horses when they joined us for supper, however, one look from momma was enough for poppa to quickly change the subject.

While Ellen and Paul saw to the final details of our luggage being prepared, Kevin spent the afternoon ensconced in Huckleby's stable office, reviewing accounts and issuing last-minute directives.

As for me, this would be my final meeting with Nathan to do the same. Nate and I spent quite some time reviewing accounts and inventory for the household.

"I can't think of anything else, Mr. Lawson. I believe we've covered everything. You have full authority to act on my behalf while we are gone." I leaned back in my chair, confident that every contingency had been anticipated.

"When should we expect your return?"

"We'll be back in time for the Christmas holidays. I so want to have a lovely holiday celebration not just for Mr. Newkirk and myself but for everyone on the staff as well."

"I shall count the days until your return, Delia." His voice was almost a whisper as he took my hand in his and placed a kiss upon it.

"As will I, Nate," I whispered in response. "But think of all the wonderful places I'll see! Paris. Rome. London." It seemed that all of a sudden the excitement of actually seeing places that I had only read about took hold of me. "Think of it, Nate. Places I never thought to see will now become real for me!"

"And all of those places will pale in comparison to your beauty, Delia. You will outshine anything Europe has to offer."

"Do you really think so?"

"I'm certain of it."

Lawson

Chapter 13

On the day that Delia, her new husband, and her parents left Bridgewater I opted not to involve myself with their departure. From a private vantage point, I watched the quartet settle themselves in the 1908 Rolls-Royce Silver Ghost Tourer with its three rows of seating. Mrs. Conner of course took the rear-most seat and Delia, bless her heart, climbed aboard and joined her mother there. Delia's father and Kevin Newkirk took the seat directly behind the driver. With the roof extended and the wind shields in place it appeared that the traveling party would be quite cozy even at this early pre-dawn hour. Once Stan, our chauffeur, had ascertained that everyone was comfortable he started up the motor car and slowly navigated the driveway. I watched their progress, feeling my heart become more desolate with each tree and shrub that they passed. Long after they were out of my line of vision, I stood where I was, thinking of nothing, feeling nothing. Eventually, the gray pre-dawn light brightened until the sun was fully above the horizon. I withdrew my pocket watch and checked the time. Six twenty-eight; almost time for the staff to have their breakfast. I would need to make an appearance and consume at least a cup of coffee although I felt no need for immediate sustenance. I was empty inside, not for lack of food, but because I was without hope of seeing Delia for the unforeseeable future.

Turning my back on the window in the turret room, I gazed at the place where she had so recently laid her head. Reaching for her pillow, I pulled it close and held it up to my nose. Her fragrance, a light lemony scent, still clung to the pillow slip and I inhaled deeply of it before returning it to its rightful place on Delia's bed. Her satin robe, thrown haphazardly across the chaise, brought memories of our lovemaking there two nights ago – her wedding night. I could still feel her, the way she nestled in my arms, almost as if she were right beside me.

On her vanity the bouquet of flowers I had brought to her on that day still remained a bright spot in the shadows of morning, although some of the more exotic blooms had wilted. I snapped off the top of a carnation and tucked it into the inside pocket of my jacket. Silly, really, to think that a faded flower would do anything more than perhaps stain the lining of my garment but it made me feel better knowing it was there.

A rustling on the other side of the door leading to the hallway alerted me that other staff members were already about their duties. I hastened to the dressing area and closed the concealed panel behind me. Once through the hidden door I stopped momentarily to lock that portal before proceeding down the stairs. My arrival in Delia's office went unnoticed and I took pains to once again conceal the sliding panel there. Picking up a leather bound portfolio from Delia's desk, I walked out into the kitchen area, pretending that I had arrived there in search of morning sustenance.

"Ah, Mr. Lawson," called out Mrs. Grant, "I wondered when you'd be coming after your coffee. Have the newlyweds departed?" She wiped her hands on her apron and poured a mug of steaming coffee into which she added a small amount of cream and two spoonfuls of sugar.

"I watched the departure myself," I acknowledged as I gratefully accepted the mug of coffee from her hands.

"I would think our work load will be a bit lighter now that all the gentry have left," she observed.

"Perhaps that may be true for you, Mrs. Grant, but there are still the daily chores to be seen to. In fact, I was just looking over the list of things to be done before the Newkirks return from Europe. While you may not be called upon to turn out epicurean delights, you will still be providing meals for our staff as well as a few contractors that have been hired to lay in the gardens for next spring. And don't forget Mr. Huckleby's staff. They are all still in need of nourishment."

"Don't worry, Mr. Lawson, I'll have everyone fed and content. Just no special cakes or crumpets, eh?" The dear woman turned back to her mixing bowls and pans and began to hum a tuneless melody.

The first few days were, indeed, full ones for me. As the senior staff member I took on the things that Delia would normally deal with in addition to my own responsibilities. It fell to me to review the kitchen inventory with Mrs. Grant, to place orders with the various food suppliers, and pay the invoices that were presented.

Delia had drawn up a very specific landscape plan with the head gardener, and for the better part of a week I oversaw the placement of shrubs and flowers that would need to winter in place in order to produce spring blooms. In the area between the main house and Willow Cottage there was to be a large swimming pool centered in a boxwood maze. While the pool had been installed earlier in the summer, the terrace surrounding it was now completed. The boxwoods were planted according to diagram and soon the entire thing looked like it had been there for many years.

Once the initial flurry of activity was complete, I dismissed the temporary staff, handing them their wages with words of thanks on behalf of the Newkirks. Several names I kept in a special file. These were people who had expressed a desire to be called upon in the future. I was positive that there would be holiday celebrations once Delia and her husband returned and advised them that they would most certainly be asked to return.

The warm days of late September gave way to the full foliage of October and soon the chill of November nights lay upon Bridgewater. In the stable area things were run as though it were just another day, with the horses being fed, exercised, and groomed. Huckleby had things there under a tight rein. The only thing missing from the equestrian portion of our estate was Mr. Newkirk's morning visits to his horses.

My days were filled with the various minutiae of overseeing the household. I came to my bed weary each evening hoping that sleep would claim me. Most nights it did. However, Thanksgiving night found me restless and awake.

The resident staff had enjoyed a traditional meal and once the kitchen had been cleaned and the leftovers stored, I granted them all the remainder of the day to be spent in leisure at their own discretion. With the workforce either scattered about the estate or gone to visit friends and families I found myself in search of something to fill my empty hours. Taking up pen and paper I worked at answering personal correspondence that had been set aside. When that undertaking was complete I donned hat, gloves, and jacket before setting myself the task of meandering through the newly established boxwood maze.

Following the gravel path between the shrubberies was an easy enough task; I could see how much fun young children would have running down the pathways, laughing as they went. I could also imagine young ladies and gents purposely losing their way on a summer's night to escape the eyes of parents or chaperones, stealing a kiss or holding hands. Perhaps one night I might even join Delia here to admire the summer stars.

I next followed the path over to Willow Cottage, closed up now that we had no visitors. Peering through a window I saw the dust-cover shrouded furniture, like so many specters, waiting for someone to enter and bring life to the rooms. As I turned to retrace my steps a deer rustled through the wooded area to the side of the cottage, anxious to stay hidden from humans who might do him harm.

My leisurely walk was complemented by a stirring of the wind, bringing with it a cold edge that nipped at my nose. Overhead clouds heavy with moisture began to gather. By nightfall we would have snow. I stopped momentarily before climbing the terrazzo steps leading to the terrace and recalled that auspicious day last February when I first met Delia. I had been so unprepared, not for the job interview but for the way my heart tugged at first sight of her. Up until that point my life had been incomplete, missing a vital piece: someone to love.

I had managed at the time to keep my thoughts professional, knowing that Delia was betrothed. Nothing at that time could have indicated that the most beautiful woman I had ever met was not in love with her fiancé. Delia had kept her emotions well hidden for one so young. Of course her mother had been there as well so what else could Delia have done. But I had sensed an interest on her part that was more than that of an employer. Time had proven me right.

My thoughts were interrupted by the feel of something damp brushing by my nose. A snowflake! Soft and gentle; followed by another and another. The first snow of the season. Again my thoughts turned to Delia, wondering where she was and what she was doing. This was a moment I wished I could share with her, the first snowfall of the season. Most likely she was dancing in Paris or sipping wine in Tuscany, charming everyone she met along the way.

I made my way back to the servant's entrance. By the time I had divested myself of my outer garments and returned to my room the house was surrounded by softly swirling snow, much the same as one sees in a snow globe. I turned the knob on the radiator and in a short time my room was pleasantly warm. The Sherlock Holmes novel that I had begun the day before drew my attention and I passed the next few hours pleasantly absorbed in the twists of the plot. It was late evening before I set down the book, noting that it was time for me to make my final walk-through of the house.

I proceeded along the Grand Hallway, stopping momentarily to observe the falling snow. The darkness of night was brightened somewhat by the fine mantel of snow that already covered the driveway and clung to the shrubs. Everything was peaceful and quiet. My tour of the guest wing was perfunctory, much like my inspection of Willow Cottage earlier that afternoon. Everything there appeared to be in good order.

I next applied my critical eye to the rooms of the main house where, once again, nothing was amiss. I returned to my own room and prepared to turn in, picturing in my mind's eye the subtle way in which Delia had tucked that rose-colored carnation into her wedding bouquet. I'm sure I drifted into a light slumber but deep sleep eluded me and I awoke several times before deciding that the bed was not where I belonged. Pulling on my robe and slippers I padded over to the window that looked down on the terrace, hoping that the falling snow would mesmerize me into a drowsy state. That having failed, I took myself off to the kitchen where I planned to brew myself a pot of tea. Once there, I was surprised to find one of the parlor maids, similarly attired in robe and slippers, pouring a steaming kettle of water into an already warmed teapot.

"May I beg a cup of your tea?" I inquired, trying not to startle the young woman.

"Mr. Lawson, I didn't think anyone else was awake."

"Joan, is it?"

"Yes, Mr. Lawson." She smiled in my direction.

"I apologize if I startled you. Here, let me get the mugs," I offered.

From the cupboard I appropriated two mugs and set them on the table. Joan set out the honey and the cream.

"I'm sorry if my puttering around in here woke you," she filled the mugs as she spoke.

"Not at all. I was having a bit of trouble sleeping." I poured cream into my mug while I noted that Joan preferred her tea with honey. "Since we are being quite informal," I motioned to our attire, "feel free to call me Nathan. But not in front of the Newkirks."

"That's very generous of you, Mr...er...Nathan." She stirred the contents of her cup to dilute the honey. "I find it difficult to sleep when it's this quiet. Always had a full house when I was growing up."

"Large family?"

"Four brothers and one sister. Had to share a bed with my sister." She sipped at her tea, throwing back her head and savoring the brew's warmth as it coated the inside of her throat.

"Having your own room and not having to share a bed must be a great luxury for you."

"A blessing and a curse, I guess."

"How so?"

"I have trouble some nights, knowing that I'm all alone."

I made no comment, sensing where her conversation was going. She was a fetching lass, no doubt about it. Long brown hair lying loose about her shoulders, brown eyes that seemed to smolder in the shadows of the kitchen. Oh yes! I knew what she was after. Wasting no time I finished my tea, washed out my mug, and set it on the drainboard to dry.

"Enjoy your tea. Sleep well," I remarked, making my way to the servant's staircase at the back of the kitchen.

"Nathan, wait," she called.

I turned my head at the sound of my name.

"I'd sleep a whole lot better if there was a handsome man sleeping beside me. No one would have to know." Her voice turned to a husky whisper as she came closer to me.

"Joan, you're a very lovely young woman, and you flatter me immensely. But my heart belongs to someone else. I'm sorry."

"Not someone who works here," she angled for information.

"No, the lady does not work here."

"Can't blame a girl for tryin'. You are handsome and all." She turned back to the table but I caught her last words, "Some lucky girl she is."

Shortly after the first of December word reached Bridgewater that the S.S. Britannia would be docking in New York City in approximately five days. Mr. Huckleby gave orders that all the equipment in the tack room was to be shined and in perfect working order. Mr. Newkirk's horses were groomed to within an inch of their lives. The stalls were swept clean and fresh hay was brought in to line them. Huckleby and his crew were determined that Mr. Newkirk would find no fault in their care of Bridgewater Stables.

At the house I gathered the staff together in the Main Foyer. When all had been assembled I addressed the group.

"By now you've heard the news that Mr. and Mrs. Newkirk are en route home. Before they return I expect every inch of Bridgewater

Manor to sparkle and shine. I myself will inspect every room, every hearth, every cupboard, every window, every curtain and drape. Everything must be spotless and perfect."

The assembled group nodded their heads in agreement as they set off to tackle their various tasks. A flurry of cleaning and polishing, laying in of firewood, clean bedding being carried to the suites, delivery of food supplies, and all manner of related activity filled the ensuing days. I spent hours poring over the household account making certain that every penny was accounted for. December seventh we received word from New York that the Newkirks would overnight on Staten Island with Delia's parents and would I kindly send the cars to Union Station to meet the 2:47 train the next afternoon.

I immediately phoned the florist and ordered a large floral display for the foyer to be delivered early the next morning. The remainder of the day saw me visiting every room and inspecting every inch of Bridgewater Manor. As I suspected, I found no fault anywhere. The house sparkled in anticipation of receiving its mistress.

That night was one of great anticipation for me on a personal level. Self-doubts crowded my mind. Would Delia have changed overly much? Would she remember how much I love her? Would she have fallen in love with her husband or would she welcome me back to her bed?

I turned over those questions in my mind as the night deepened and time passed. When the light of pre-dawn graced the skies, I realized that I had slept not a wink. I quickly dressed and made my way to the kitchen where Mrs. Grant was already issuing orders to the scullery girls. Taking a cup of coffee into my office I reviewed everything once again. It seemed that all was ready.

At nine o'clock the florist truck arrived. I went out front to meet the driver.

"Mornin' Lawson," called the man as he opened the rear door of the truck. Although he was of average size, he seemed huskier because of the large overcoat and muffler he wore along with a knitted cap that was pulled down over his ears.

"Good morning, Jacob. Do you need assistance?"

"Naw, I got it covered."

His gloved hands carefully carried the extravagant arrangement of winter flowers as I held open the entry door for him. He placed the display on the center table of the foyer, turning it a bit to offer its best side for view, before standing back to admire it.

"Uh, Jacob, did you bring that other item I requested?"

"Sure did, Mr. Lawson. I'll be right back."

In the twinkling of an eye, Jacob returned from his truck bearing a small but tasteful arrangement of white spider mums and rose-colored carnations.

"How much do I owe you for this lovely piece?"

"Is it for a special lady? Someone on staff perhaps?" Jacob inquired with a gleam in his faded blue eyes.

"Never you mind who it's for. How much?"

"For you, Mr. Lawson, I'll make a special price of fifty-cents."

From the side pocket of my jacket I withdrew the coins and exchanged them for the flowers.

"Sure hope your lady likes the posies," Jacob remarked as he fired up his delivery truck and drove off.

I scurried inside and, taking pains to remain unseen, carried the flowers to Delia's office where I placed them on her desk. Later that day, while the staff was having a late lunch, I stole away to Delia's office and locked the door behind me. With flowers in hand I ascended the concealed stairway and carefully entered Delia's dressing area where I placed the flowers on a small table near her, our, chaise.

While there I critically inspected the room, noting the perfectly made bed, the drapes open to the late afternoon sun, and the warmth emanating from the applewood fire in the hearth. The sound of a motor car coming up the driveway alerted me that Stan had delivered the Newkirks safely to Bridgewater. I placed another log on the fire before straightening my jacket. The grey mood that had been my constant companion for the past weeks was suddenly gone. Only one thought was foremost in my mind.

Delia was home!

Cordelia

Chapter 14

I leaned my head against Kevin's shoulder, content to let him coddle me and fuss over me in the back seat of the motor car. He had insisted on layering both lap robes over my legs, positive that my fur-lined leather boots were not enough to keep my feet warm. Although I was wrapped in the folds of a full length lynx fur coat with matching fur hat and muff, Kevin insisted on holding me close so that he could share his body heat with me. The cocoon of warmth that I was swaddled in made me drowsy and I must have dozed shortly after our departure from Union Station, awakening as Stan guided our motor car through the wrought-iron double gates that signified the entry onto Bridgewater property.

"Are we home yet?" I inquired, trying to stifle a yawn.

"Almost. Did you enjoy your nap, my dear?"

"I'm afraid I haven't been much of a conversationalist. I can't imagine why I nodded off so easily when I slept so well last night."

Kevin placed a kiss on my cheek and favored me with a smile.

"While I appreciated your parents' hospitality I'm happy to be back at Bridgewater," he commented.

"I imagine you're anxious to visit your horses," I remarked.

"Can't wait to tell Huckleby about my newest acquisitions and draw up a breeding plan." The joy in Kevin's voice was evident.

"I'm looking forward to celebrating our first Christmas at Bridgewater. I can't wait to get the decorating and planning under way."

"You should delegate as much of that work as possible. We have an excellent staff, thanks to you, who can handle most of it."

Kevin took my hand in his and raised it to his lips, placing a gentle kiss on my gloved fingers.

"I'm well aware of our staff's capabilities, dear. With Mr. Lawson in charge I'm sure I'll have all the assistance I might require." There, I'd finally given voice to the name I had longed for months to speak.

"I must insist, Cordy, on you doing nothing more strenuous than lifting a fork at mealtimes."

Try though he might to sound casual, I detected a genuine note of concern behind his words. I met his last pronouncement with laughter just as the motor car came to a halt before our imposing front entrance. As Stan came round to hold open the car door, I reached over and patted my husband's hand.

"Kevin, generations of women have borne children while managing a household. Pregnancy is not an affliction; it's a normal state of being."

I allowed Stan to assist me out of the motor car while I perused the façade of Bridgewater Manor, knowing that somewhere behind one of those many windows was the man I had given my heart to and whose child I now nurtured in my womb. The moment passed all too quickly as Kevin lent me his arm. Together we climbed the steps that had recently been cleared of snow, proceeding through the Grand Hallway and into the foyer. As I stopped to admire the beautiful floral arrangement set atop the highly polished center table my attention was drawn to the footsteps descending the curved staircase. My heart skipped a beat as I recognized the measured tread of the man coming forward to greet us.

"Mrs. Newkirk, Mr. Newkirk, welcome home."

"Thank you, Lawson. It's good to be back," responded Kevin.

At Nathan's signal, a footman approached and relieved us of our outer garments, gloves, and hats before disappearing.

"You both must be chilled after your journey from New Haven. I've had tea service brought into the drawing room for you."

"That's mighty thoughtful of you, Lawson, but I believe my wife is in need of a well-deserved rest. Have the tea brought to her suite," dictated Kevin.

"Please, Kevin, there's plenty of time for rest. In fact a cup of tea sounds perfectly wonderful right now. Mr. Lawson, inform Ellen that I'll be upstairs directly after we've enjoyed tea and a light snack."

"Very well, Mrs. Newkirk. Please excuse me."

Nathan inclined his head in a show of respect and set off to deliver my message. The sight of his receding form was a welcome sight to my eyes but my attention was reclaimed by Kevin once again as he steered me into the drawing room.

A cup of Ceylonese tea was the perfect tonic after our day of travel. A few bites of a light sandwich would carry us until dinner. Thus fortified, Kevin took off for the stables while I adjourned to my turret suite.

I dawdled as I made my way from the drawing room, passing Kevin's very masculine combination office/study, proceeding through the foyer where I noted the high sheen of recently polished wood sideboards and tables. I stopped to admire once more the extravagantly beautiful floral arrangement filling the space with a lovely fragrance.

The gently sloped curving staircase was an easy climb. At the top I turned and looked over the railing, taking in the quiet elegance of this house, my house. Outside, beyond the high windows of the Grand Hallway, dusk was quickly turning to night. I made my way along the shadowy upper hall, pausing momentarily before I pushed open the buffed walnut door to my suite.

"There you are, miss," remarked Ellen who, it appeared, had been waiting for me. "Come have a seat and let me remove those boots for you."

"That sounds heavenly, Ellen. I do believe my feet could use some special attention right about now. First help me out of my traveling clothes. I long for the comfort of my night shift."

Ellen took my rumpled traveling clothes and set them aside while I gratefully slipped into my lavender chenille robe. Following Ellen's direction I sat on the edge of my chaise while she removed my boots and brought my slippers over from the hearth where they had been warming.

"Now don't you move, Miss Cordelia. I've unpacked that lovely violet-scented lotion that you brought back from London and I'll rub some on your feet."

I reclined on the chaise and allowed Ellen's fingers to work their magic. While she rubbed and patted my toes and heels I took a furtive moment to appreciate the lovely little floral arrangement on the side table - white spider mums and rose-colored carnations. I knew without question that it was a silent tribute from Nathan to welcome me home. I wondered if he had spent much time here in my empty chamber or if he had gone on with business as usual.

"There you go, Miss Cordelia, I hope your feet feel more relaxed." Ellen capped the bottle of lotion and tucked it into the cupboard in my bathroom.

"That was very soothing. I didn't realize my feet were so weary."

"If you'd like, miss, I'd be pleased to do that every evening for you," Ellen offered.

"I couldn't impose on you that way, Ellen. You do enough for me."

"Oh, miss, I could never repay you for that wonderful trip to Europe. It was the opportunity of a lifetime for someone in my position!"

I smiled at Ellen's exuberance, aware that her ministrations had greatly relaxed me.

"Will there be anything else, miss?"

"I think I would prefer not to dress for dinner this evening. Please arrange for a tray to be brought up here," I directed.

From my place on the chaise, I watched as Ellen gathered my boots and soiled clothing and pulled the door shut behind her. I released a sigh of contentment. The apple wood in the hearth crackled and the logs shifted. I rested my head against the chaise and drew the fur throw over me. A short nap before dinner would be just the thing to revive me. My last thought as I took a final look at the flowers from Nate was, "I'm home at last".

The morning sun had cleared the treetops and was glinting off the deeply-piled snow when I opened my eyes to the realization that I had slept the night on my lovely floral-patterned chaise. Heavens, I must have been more tired than I realized!

A brief knock announced Ellen's arrival mere seconds before she entered my room. I greeted her entry with a yawn and a stretch.

"You're up bright and early, miss, already waiting on me to bring up your breakfast tray."

She cleared a spot on my side table and slid the tray into position.

"I've brought your hot cocoa, two poached eggs, some Canadian bacon and a serving of bananas and cream. I'll just set the room to rights while you eat."

Ellen turned to make up my bed only to find that it had been untouched during the night. With a concerned look on her face, she turned back to me, then towards the bed, and yet again back to me.

"Miss Cordelia, surely you didn't spend the night in that chair?"

"I'm afraid I did," I responded between sips of cocoa; I had the grace to appear slightly embarrassed.

"You must be all cramped up and just about frozen."

Ellen scurried to the fireplace to stir up the ashes in search of a few live embers. Beneath the gray residue of yesterday's warming fire there did, indeed, lurk some glowing embers that when stirred and fed with pieces of newspaper produced sufficient fuel to eventually ignite two small logs that Ellen arranged on the grate.

"There now, we'll have you toasty in no time, Miss Cordelia."

"Actually, I was quite warm beneath this fur blanket," I managed to acknowledge between bites of toast.

"Are you feeling well this morning? No morning sickness?"

"I feel quite well and hungry to boot."

I made short work of the eggs and bacon while Ellen bustled about laying out my clothes for the day. After I had eaten every crumb and drunk every drop I hastened to change into my morning dress with Ellen's assistance.

We ran into a bit of a problem when she tried to fasten the long row of buttons that ran down my back from neck to waist. The top buttons fit easily enough into their loops but those approaching my waist area couldn't quite close the gap. It was obvious that my tummy had become enlarged by perhaps an inch or two. Several more dresses were tried with similar outcomes.

"Whatever shall we do, miss? You can't go about in your nightshift and robe."

"Here's what we'll do, Ellen. First off I want you to send Stan to fetch Mrs. Warner, the seamstress who has a shop on Temple Street, and bring her back here as quickly as possible. I'll pay double her fee to compensate for closing her shop."

"Yes, miss."

"Then I will need you to fetch the mending box from my office downstairs. Bring it directly here as soon as you can. You may explain my absence today by saying that I'm exhausted from travel. Now go."

I spent the next few hours with needle and thread, pulling out the stitches of several of my dresses. It was my hope that with Mrs. Warner's assistance we could modify a few garments while a maternity wardrobe was being produced. I was up to my elbows in skirts and bodices when the fashionably attired modiste made an entrance into my suite, Ellen hurrying to keep up with her.

"Mrs. Newkirk! Why have I been summoned here on such short notice?"

The woman drew herself up to her full height of maybe five and half feet and tried to look down her nose to where I sat on the padded window seat. She had taken no more than a few steps forward before she was ankle deep in pools of yard goods. Her attitude was arrogance personified so I did my best to recall how my mother-in-law had dealt with merchants of her ilk.

"Dear lady, I have summoned you in this manner because I was under the impression that your talent with fashion and design would highly benefit from counting me among the patrons of your shop. For your inconvenience I have even offered to double your fee." The woman had the decency to shut her mouth even as her cheeks became infused with color. "I returned just yesterday from a sojourn to the capitals of Europe. This morning I find that my clothes no longer fit properly due to the condition in which I find myself."

"You are....enciente?" she stammered out.

I nodded my assent.

"Oh dear! Congratulations, madam. I didn't realize....how may I assist you?"

"Please be seated," I motioned to a place on the window seat. When she was comfortable, I continued. "I plan on hosting several holiday parties in the upcoming weeks. I will need an entire wardrobe to accommodate my expanding girth. Is this something you can accomplish?"

"I can certainly have the necessary underpinnings sent over tomorrow afternoon but the dresses, you understand, will take some time."

Mrs. Warner was angling for some sort of incentive, so I gave her one.

"I will have a list of what I require for dresses, with accompanying sketches, brought to you by my maid, Ellen, when she comes to claim my undergarments tomorrow afternoon."

Mrs. Warner nodded her understanding to me as she rose from her seat.

"Will there be anything else, Mrs. Newkirk?"

"Since I've begun the work of altering a few of my morning dresses, and since you're already here, I had hoped that we could work together on these garments so that I may have something comfortable to wear during the next few days."

"Perhaps madam would be more comfortable remaining in her quarters until suitable garments are ready?"

My temper had reached its limits.

"Am I to understand that you wish me to manage my household

garbed only in a robe and night shift?" I stood up quickly, clutching my robe closer around me.

"Surely you don't expect me, personally, to sew up your dresses?"

"Isn't that your occupation?" I was fuming.

"I'm a shopkeeper." Her chin was raised as she spoke. "I haven't plied a needle and thread in years. That's why I have assistants."

"Ellen, please escort Mrs. Warner to the car and have Stan drive her back to whatever sweatshop he found her in. And watch that she doesn't steal anything on her way out." I turned my back to the woman as I went to stand by the window.

"This way, Miss Warner," Ellen directed her towards the door.

"Where's my compensation?" The woman turned back to ask of me.

"It's obvious that you have no need of money since you've just talked me into taking my business elsewhere. Good day, Mrs. Warner."

Ellen hustled the woman downstairs and I watched as the modiste, now ensconced in the rear seat of our second-best motor car, left Bridgewater. I pitied poor Stan having to tolerate that harridan on the drive back to New Haven. I made a mental note to be sure that our loyal chauffeur received a bonus.

My clothing dilemma was ultimately solved when I sent word to momma telling her of my plight. She contacted several acquaintances in the fashion world of New York City and within three days a trunk full of suitable garments arrived. It was carried upstairs and placed in my suite where Ellen and I examined its contents, much in the same way that children open birthday presents. I was only too happy to hand off to Kevin the invoice that accompanied the trunk. Even with momma's industry discounts the sum was quite substantial. Kevin, still in his first flush of happiness at the prospect of a potential Newkirk heir, declared no amount too high to keep his wife suitably clothed.

"Oh Miss Cordelia, this trunk is a treasure trove of goodies!" exclaimed Ellen.

"Momma has done a magnificent job in putting together this wardrobe. Indeed, it is truly a treasure chest," I agreed as I pushed back the tissue paper that enfolded a stunning morning dress in a rich emerald color.

"That dress suits you perfectly, miss." Ellen gently took the garment from my fingers and hung it in the cherry-wood wardrobe.

"Goodness, momma must have called in every favor owed her in order to garner such a variety of dresses."

We took a few moments to admire everything: morning dresses, tea dresses, visiting costumes, three splendid evening gowns that would neatly see me through the holiday entertaining that was planned.

"Surely these can't be styles for an expectant mother," commented Ellen, removing my 'skinny' clothes from the wardrobe in order to accommodate the new things.

"You're right, Ellen. All of these dresses are in the latest style from The Continent. Bustles are on their way out; as are tapered waists."

"These dresses look very comfortable."

"Precisely. The newer style is cut to drape loosely from a lady's shoulders and skim over her hips. No longer will we need to be trussed up in a whalebone corset just to be fashionable. In fact, the only undergarments needed are a chemise and a garter belt to hold up our stockings."

"Imagine, not having the breath squeezed out of one," cooed Ellen.

"I can wear these dresses well into my pregnancy and still feel fashionable."

"How modern you are, Miss Cordelia! Your friends will all be envious."

"Oh look, Ellen. Here at the bottom of the trunk. Momma even included some matching chemises." I picked up a wonderful lace-trimmed chemise made of raw silk, holding it up to my cheek to revel in its softness.

"It's best I get back to my routine, though. Fetch that morning dress."

Ellen slipped the garment over my head. I watched in the pier glass as the soft folds of lace-trimmed brushed wool draped gently over my shoulders and settled in place, falling gracefully to my ankles. The color did, indeed, complement my coloring. For the first time in over a week my eyes sparkled and my skin seemed to glow.

My arrival below stairs was greeted with a warm welcome. Everyone – maids, footmen, scullery help, laundresses, and of course Mrs. Grant – tried to speak at once and their cumulative voices rose a notch or two as they each sought to be heard above the others.

"What is all the commotion about?"

Nathan's voice commanded attention as he stepped out of his office, causing everyone else to turn silent. That was when he saw me. It was obvious to me that his breathing hitched momentarily but in the space of a heartbeat he was once again the very staid House Steward of Bridgewater Manor.

"Mrs. Newkirk! We were told that you were suffering from exhaustion. We've all been concerned for your health, but it's obvious that you appear hale and hearty."

"Mr. Lawson," I inclined my head towards him before turning my smile on the others who crowded close together. "Thank you all for your warm welcome and concern. Let me set your minds at ease. I have remained in my suite until I had indeed rested from our European travels. You'll be happy to know that I expect the arrival of our first child sometime in June." This was greeted by a clapping of hands before I was allowed to continue, "Now that I've rested I feel better equipped to face our household challenges." I refused to look directly at Nathan so I fixed my sights on our cook. "Mrs. Grant, I'm hoping you have some of those scrumptious lemon cookies hidden somewhere. I find I have a craving for them."

"Never fear, ma'am. I'll whip up a batch right now."

Mrs. Grant turned back to her kitchen, shooing the others out of her way as she moved.

"Get out of my way, all of you. Can't ya see I've got important work to do."

I smiled at her shuffling movements as she disbursed the others.

"Mr. Lawson, might I have a word with you in my office?"

I turned and left the kitchen, heading for my tiny office, leaving Nathan to follow in my wake. Once there I bade him to close the door and have a seat. When we were assured of a bit of privacy, Nate's words came tumbling out.

"Delia, I've been worried sick, thinking that you had contracted some European illness. Then the maids started to gossip and someone brought up the possibility of a pregnancy. I didn't know what to think. I've been beside myself since your return." He ran his fingers through his hair in a show of desperation. Standing up he began to pace, then stopped in front of my desk, planting his forearms on the accommodating piece of furniture. "It's true then, you're pregnant."

I nodded my assent.

"Are you well? The morning sickness?"

"I'm beyond the morning sickness." I reassured him.

He paced some more before returning to his seat. I could see his hesitation before he put forth the most burning question.

"Is....is the child mine?"

I smiled tenderly at this man I loved, reached out and clasped his hand in mine before I answered his question.

"Nate, dearest, please don't worry overmuch. The morning sickness has passed and I've never felt healthier." He visibly relaxed and drew a deep, ragged breath. "I couldn't come downstairs because my dresses were too tight. Now that momma has sent me suitable clothes I'm free to resume my daily routine."

"And the child's father? Tell me Delia."

It seemed that he didn't want to know yet needed to know in spite of himself. I took a deep breath and answered.

"The child belongs to Kevin." His countenance took on a saddened look and he cast his eyes downward. I continued, "Regardless of who the baby's father is, the child belongs to Kevin. Do you understand?"

Nathan raised his head, the light of love shining in his eyes once more. He smiled at me and replied, "Of course, Delia, your child can be nothing if not a Newkirk."

The ensuing days found me consuming dozens of Mrs. Grant's lemon cookies as I directed the preparations for the upcoming holiday season, our first as a married couple and my first as mistress of Bridgewater.

Kevin personally led the stable crew on a hunt to find the perfect Christmas tree. Huckleby guided a wagon full of stable hands and their tools. Kevin, seated on his favorite horse, rode out at the head of the small cavalcade. Paul, much to his dismay, brought up the rear as he guided his mount, one of the stable's gentler horses, in the party's wake. It would be Paul's duty to see to the serving of lunch out in the woods before returning directly home with the empty food basket in plenty of time to draw Kevin a warm bath.

Mrs. Grant and I were reviewing the menus for our first dinner party of the season, three days hence, when Paul returned from the hunt. He recounted to Nathan his morning in the wild but in a voice designed to carry and earn him sympathy.

"I tell you, Mr. Lawson, the cold cut right through me. Six coats wouldn't have kept me warm." He rubbed his hands together in an attempt to warm them.

"Joan," called Nathan to one of the parlor maids, "see that Paul has a hot cup of cocoa." The young woman scurried off to do as directed. "Paul, come into my office with your cocoa. We can talk there."

I knew, of course, that Nathan would offer Paul a finger or two from his personal bottle of Courvoisier brandy. There was no objection on my part with Nathan keeping the bottle in his office cupboard as long as he held the only key to its lock. Nathan was not one to take a daily drink or two; in fact the only time I had seen liquor of any sort pass his lips was on my wedding day, when he had raised a toast to my happiness.

The afternoon sky was quickly welcoming full dusk when a cacophony of men's voices echoed down the length of the windowed Grand Hallway, resounding in most areas of the house. I hurried to the landing at the head of the curving staircase and from there watched as our first Christmas tree was erected in the front foyer. There were all sorts of maneuvers as the stable hands set the tree into a large copper trough that had been brought in earlier. Their main problem, as I saw it, was in keeping the tree standing upright.

Kevin was like a leprechaun, darting around the tree, coaching the others in their work, directing several more men to place the heavy rocks they carried into the trough to hold the tree in place. Still wearing his heavy coat, a woolen hat, three scarves, and boots Kevin at last slowed his pace as he critically eyed the tree. Even from my lofty perch at the top of the stairs I took note of Kevin's red nose, sure that he had gotten frostbite. I was proven wrong the moment he spoke.

"There we go, lads. You've done a marvelous job. What say we go back to the stables and have another round?"

Kevin gave the men no chance to decline the offer as he shepherded them back outdoors. With the door to the Grand Hallway shut tightly once more, I carefully descended the stairs. I was appalled to find the foyer's marble floor covered with slush. Obviously Kevin gave no thought to the common practice of wiping one's feet on the outside mat. No wait, if Kevin had been drinking then I was positive that good manners were the last things on his mind. I had witnessed that all too often on our honeymoon.

Back to the matter at hand. The scotch pine tree was over twelve feet tall and easily five feet in circumference around the lowest branches. Nestled amidst the branches, closest to the tree's trunk, there remained clumps of snow and ice that were only now beginning to melt, forming puddles of water on the floor around the trough.

"Good heavens! What's created this mess?"

Nathan approached the tree from the other side of the foyer.

"You mean who created this mess?" I answered.

"Delia! I mean Mrs. Newkirk. I didn't see you there on the other side of this monstrous tree. Who's responsible for this mess?"

"I'm afraid my husband is to blame, Mr. Lawson. I must also claim a tiny portion of the guilt."

"Surely you didn't drag this tree in here, leaving scuffs on the floor and puddles of melting snow."

"Not directly. But I did watch from the top of the steps as the tree was brought in and set up under Mr. Newkirk's direction." I walked around the tree to stand closer to Nathan.

"I'll see that the foyer is cleaned immediately, even if I have to do it myself."

Nathan was about to rally the household troops when I laid a hand on his jacket sleeve.

"I'd prefer that you didn't clean it yourself, Nathan." My words were spoken in an almost-whisper. He turned to face me and I continued, "I have another task for you this evening, if you're up to it."

He raised his eyebrows in a silent question and I responded with a nod of my head. He nodded his head in answer.

"I'll arrange to have the foyer cleaned immediately, Mrs. Newkirk. Please don't give it another thought."

"Thank you, Mr. Lawson. I believe I'll turn in for the evening. I'd like to read a few pages from the novel I've begun before turning in. I'll leave everything here in your capable hands." I turned and began my assent.

"Thank you Mrs. Newkirk. Enjoy your rest." There was a twinkle in his eyes as he blew me a kiss across the intervening space.

Later that night, much later actually, I heard the concealed panel in my dressing area carefully slide open. In moments Nathan was beside me on the chaise, kissing me passionately as he embraced me. He rained kisses on my lips, cheeks, nose, and other assorted places nearly taking my breath away. I could only revel in the giddy feeling his kisses produced.

"Delia," he whispered as he held me close, "I've been like a man walking through the desert for months without you near."

"A desert full of snow?" I laughed quietly.

"Without you there is nothing for me. I know I shouldn't admit it but I can't help myself. Even when we're not intimate, as we soon shall be, it's a comfort to me simply knowing that we share the same roof over our heads."

I looked up into his loving gaze and sighed.

"I can't begin to tell you how many times in the last few months I regret having married Kevin. We should have run off together."

"Has he hurt you?"

"Not physically, dearest. But to him I am nothing more than a way to gain his heir to carry on the family name."

"Then the honeymoon didn't go smoothly?" He sat back in the chaise, pulling me towards him so that my back was nestled up against his chest. "Tell me about it."

"You'd be bored."

"I want to know everything. Where you went, what you did, what you saw, what you ate. Leave nothing out."

"Good heavens we'll be here till dawn!"

"I have no place to go, except back to my room."

"You know that we visited most of the capitals of Europe."

"Yes: London, Paris, Rome, Berlin, Vienna."

"I would have adored them all. Kevin's father has business acquaintances in all of those places. And they were all so kind to receive us. I believe I've made a real friend in the Contessa Louisa de Gemma. She and her husband have a lovely villa just outside of Rome. We were guests there for about a week. It was she who was the first outsider to notice Kevin's problem with spirits."

"He sees ghosts?" Nathan joked.

"No, silly man. He has more than a passing acquaintance with wine, brandy, and other drinkable spirits." I turned slightly to kiss Nathan's cheek.

"Tell me, Delia, is he an obnoxious drunk?"

"You saw him at dinner on our wedding day. Speaking about bedding his bride to beget his heir. And in front of his mother no less." I sighed deeply before continuing. "After that it was easy to notice how quickly and how often Kevin would consume drinks: with lunch, with tea, before dinner, during dinner, after dinner, and then a nightcap. He came to our bed drunk more often than sober, falling into a stupor to refresh himself. The amazing thing is he never once suffered a hangover.

Always awoke fresh and ready to greet the new day. Seemed like he always had plans to meet with horse breeders, no matter where we went. In fact he's got quite a stable of horses coming across the Atlantic in the spring. I admire his ambition to have the best stable in the country, but I'm afraid I come a distant second after his horses."

"But it was your honeymoon; didn't he take you out to dinner on the Champs-Elysées?"

"No."

"What about sharing a cup of espresso at a bistro in the Campo de'Fiori in Rome?"

"Where's that?"

"Did you not get to tour the public rooms of Windsor Castle?"

"We stayed with another horse breeder who lives in the Cotswolds. Lovely countryside, but nothing more spectacular than what we have here."

"Surely he was by your side on your voyage down The Rhine?"

"Oh yes, that he was. Sadly that was when my morning sickness was at its worst. It pleased him to see me thus, thinking that he had begotten his heir on me. There were some lovely towns that I ached to visit but Kevin decreed that I should stay on the boat, feeling that I might become overstressed. In truth I believe he was rather enjoying the few remaining days of Oktoberfest without his wife at his side."

"Then Vienna, surely. I've heard their opera is unequaled."

"Yes, we did attend the opera as guests of his father's friends. The opera house itself was quite lovely, as was Liesel - the daughter of our hosts. Kevin later explained that it was only polite for him to devote his attention to her since we were staying at their home."

"Oh, my darling Delia! What an awful time you must have had?" He pressed a kiss against my hair.

"It wasn't as bad as all that. To make up for his lack of attention, Kevin would purchase a souvenir for me wherever we went. You saw that lovely fur coat I was wearing when we arrived home? That was to make up for our fleeting trip through Berlin. In London, I was given carte blanche to buy whatever I fancied. Paris saw me purchase an entire new summer wardrobe that will be sent over this spring." I looked down at my abdomen upon which Nathan rested one of his hands. "I do hope I'll be able to wear some of it after our child is born."

"When did Kevin learn of your pregnancy?"

"The ship had just docked in Southampton when the first bout of morning sickness took hold. I thought nothing of it; believed it to be the adjustment from being on an ocean liner to standing on solid ground. By the third day, when the sickness arrived with regularity each morning, I knew I was with child – and so did Kevin. Of course he was thrilled. Cautioned me about doing too much and all that. Then he bundled me into a conveyance and we set off for the Cotswolds, he to talk about breeding horses and I to combat my morning sickness."

"How could he be so crass? If it were our honeymoon I should never have left your side."

"Never??"

"Never." Nate turned me so that we were facing each other. He placed a tender kiss on my lips, murmuring, "Never".

Kevin

Chapter 15

December 1908
Boston Massachusetts

"I *must be the luckiest man in the world,*" I thought to myself as the New York, New Haven & Hartford train pulled into South Street Station. I collected my single valise and threaded my way through the crowd of pre-holiday travelers.

Out on the sidewalk, I turned up the collar of my coat and snugged my hat more firmly in place against the gusty wind that blew in from the north. Gray clouds swollen with moisture were gathering quickly, promising snowfall within the hour. I breathed deeply of the cold, crisp air. Several moments passed as I watched the ebb and flow of people through the station doors. While I usually despised the work at Newkirk Trading that necessitated trips to Boston it was something, rather someone, else that called me into town this trip. My musings were interrupted by a uniformed railway attendant.

"Are you in need of transport, sir?" The attendant was a very polite middle-aged man whose cap and epaulets denoted him as a senior staffer. There was a thin fog that accompanied his words as his warm breath hit the cold air.

"I believe I am." I favored the man with a tight smile, grateful that I didn't have his job.

Within moments I was tucked into the back of a public motor car and the driver was navigating the slushy streets away from the station and towards Ash Street. Jeannette's cottage came into view as the conveyance rounded the street corner. Someone had recently cleared the pathway from the strip of public sidewalk up to the front porch. I paid my fare to the driver and added a generous tip.

"Merry Christmas to you sir," called the driver as I stepped around a pile of snow and onto the path, "and to your wife as well."

Once I had gained the porch, I stomped my feet to remove the snow from my overshoes and immediately heard a dog barking from within. The craftsman-style door was pulled open by the woman who should have been my wife but due to the circumstances of her birth was relegated to being my mistress. Before either of us could utter a word, Brewster jumped up and placed his front paws on my chest. He couldn't contain his excitement at seeing me once again. I patted his head and scratched his ears in fondness.

"Easy boy. Stand down," I attempted to command the canine. To no avail.

"Brewster, down," commanded Jeannette. Instantly, he sat on his haunches and allowed me entrance.

"Jeannette, dearest," I greeted her with a casual kiss.

"Darling, I'm so glad you're home." Her smile alone could brighten up a dreary day.

I set the valise down on the gleaming knotty pine floor before removing my galoshes and placing them in the drip tray near the front door. My coat and hat found themselves a place on the coat tree nearby. Turning toward my paramour I pulled her into my arms and kissed her properly.

"There, now I feel at home," I commented, releasing her once again.

"How long will you be able to stay?" She tucked her hand into mine as we proceeded into the cozy living room. A fire in the hearth contributed heat as did the radiators placed strategically below the picture window. I took my usual place in an easy chair nearby the hearth.

"At least a week or so. I'll need to stop in at the office and sign a few papers then visit with my parents."

"Won't you be bringing Cordelia to Boston for Christmas?"

Jeannette sat down on a stool to remove my shoes and replace them with my slippers.

"It is in Cordy's best interest not to travel overmuch. We're expecting our first child and I wouldn't want anything to compromise her pregnancy." I watched Jeannette's face to gauge her reaction to my news.

"Kevin! That's wonderful! When is the baby due?" Her eyes were aglow at my good fortune.

"Sometime in June the doctor says. Does it bother you that Cordy is having my child?" I reached forward and tilted her chin up so that I could look at her directly.

"I think it's wonderful! It's what you've wanted right from the start. Imagine, by this time next year you'll be a father." Her delight was genuine.

"And, since Cordy will be rather confined to Bridgewater, I'll take advantage of being here in Boston on business much more often." I reached down to take her hand and pulled her into my lap. "Come now, my angel, and give daddy a big kiss. Show me how much you've missed me."

Show me, indeed. Jeannette's kisses were like water to a wilted flower. In no time at all the heat we created with our foreplay soon had us in various states of undress. It never ceased to amaze me that Jeannette seemed to ache for my kisses and my touch and rarely, if ever, seemed sated. Her green eyes flashed with a wild abandon as she shrugged off her shawl and then her day gown. Only when my trousers hit the floor did we hear any objection from Brewster. Jeannette calmed the dog and raced me up the stairs to the bedroom where we shut the door and collapsed on the bed, a tangle of arms and legs as we sought to release our sexual tensions. When at last we had assuaged our needs I found myself wrapped around Jeannette's lithe body, stroking her hair and placing little kisses on her forehead.

"Have I told you how beautiful you are when you lie here, after we've made love?"

"Only a hundred times or so. But you can tell me again. I never tire of hearing it."

"My angel, you are the most beautiful woman in the world. Did you get the presents I sent you?"

"Presents? You sent me presents?" Jeannette asked this with a perfectly straight face.

"Yes, of course. I sent you something from every city we visited in Europe. Surely they've arrived by now." I sat up amidst the bedclothes, anxious to know that she had received my tokens of love.

"What was it you sent, darling?" She lay back on her side of the bed, the sheet covering only one of her lovely breasts.

"There was a long strand of pearls with matching earrings from Vienna. Perfume from France. A fur coat from Berlin."

"Nothing from London?"

"No, nothing from….why you little minx! Making me think that something had gone wrong with the deliveries."

"Kevin, you know that you're the only present I truly want. Now come here and make me cry out in pleasure once more."

She placed a hand on my shoulder and drew me down to her side, letting her other hand stray until I felt my arousal starting once again. Being a gentleman above all else, I was most happy to oblige my lady-love.

I surprised my brother-in-law Robert by showing up in my office at the Trading Company for three successive days. Even though there wasn't much paperwork for me to sift through I spent the time reconnecting with some of the middle-managers and most certainly taking time to exchange pleasantries with everyone who crossed my path. Although Robert sat at the helm of this ship of commerce, it was certainly part of my heritage and I took the time to make his life uncomfortable by posing questions during the annual board meeting.

On Sunday I joined my parents for dinner. Noting how lovely the house looked with all of its Christmas decorations made me pause momentarily and ponder how Cordelia might be decorating Bridgewater. My little hunting party had procured a most wondrous Scotch pine tree and set it up in the foyer. That was my sole contribution to the decorating. The remainder was best left to Cordelia's imagination and flair. I had no doubt that the effect would be splendid.

I arrived at Revere Street a quarter hour before dinner; early enough to partake of father's fine brandy before dinner yet close enough to the actual dinner hour. Now that father was retired I felt sure he would question me at length about the board meeting at Newkirk Trading and I felt disinclined to repeat every detail. He would hear about it soon enough. I found my parents in the drawing room and followed William, the family butler, who announced my arrival.

"Kevin, come join us. There's still time for a brandy before dinner," father invited, not getting up from his chair, merely pointing me in the direction of a credenza along the far wall that held several crystal glasses and a bottle of father's best brandy.

No sooner had I filled my glass than William returned to announce dinner. I offered my arm to mother and escorted her into the dining room while father followed behind. We chatted amiably through the first course until mother could no longer contain her curiosity.

"How is Cordelia feeling, dear?" She smiled at me over the soup.

"She seems quite well, actually. The morning sickness is past. At least that's what she tells me."

"It's unfortunate that she was uncomfortable so early in the honeymoon. She must be extremely fertile to have gotten caught on your wedding night."

Mother motioned to a footman for the dishes to be removed and the next course served.

"I hope she's carrying a son. The Newkirk line must be continued," added father. "I so want to bounce a grandson on my knee and spoil him on his birthday and at Christmas."

As we waited for dessert, mother asked, "Tell me dear, did Cordelia bring any of those new Parisian-style ensembles home? I've heard they're very daring."

"I fear I would have an easier time describing the horses I purchased than to remember any fashion details. You'll simply have to wait a week or so until your visit to Bridgewater. Then you can ask Cordy directly."

After dinner mother excused herself, saying that she wanted to write a letter to my sister Sallie. Father and I returned to the drawing room where we sipped our brandies. We discussed at length the horse stock I had purchased while abroad and talked of my plans for breeding and training race horses.

It was a true pleasure to spend time with my aging father. For the first time I could see the toll his drive and ambition had taken. His demeanor, although gruff, was now tempered by his longing for a grandson; his gaze, once so stern and formidable, now seemed kindly and benevolent rather like that of an aging cleric. Our conversation covered many topics and I was about to refill our glasses when a respectful knock sounded on the door.

"Enter," called father.

"Pardon me, sir, but it's time for your medicine." These words were spoken by father's long-time valet, Winsted, himself seeming to have aged overmuch in the past few months.

"Blast it! I'm not feeling any symptoms so I won't take any of that putrid stuff tonight. Just prepare my room. Kevin, why don't you stay the night? Make your mother happy. She'd love to see you at breakfast."

Winsted, used to my father's blustering ways, merely stood where he was, giving my father time to acquiesce. It was I who broke the silence.

"Go ahead, Winsted, prepare father's room. He'll be upstairs shortly. In spite of father's generosity in offering me use of my old room, I already have my lodging taken care of."

Winsted bowed and closed the door behind him. Once I was sure he was out of earshot, I turned to father.

"What's this about you taking medicine? You seemed fine at our wedding just a few short months ago." I tried to keep my voice nonchalant.

"Fool doctor prescribed a vile tasting medicine for my rheumatism, is all. Nothing to worry about."

"Does mother know?"

"Of course, she's the one who's charged Winsted with being my conscience." He lowered his voice then continued. "Winsted has even delivered a small bottle of the nasty stuff to Nora's house. It's a conspiracy!"

I tried to hide my smirk because I was sure mother had a hand in that. I made a mental note to be sure to keep Jeannette's existence away from Cordelia.

An hour later Jackson, father's chauffeur, deposited me in front of Jeannette's cottage. Although the shades were drawn, a lamp illuminated the interior. Above the chimney I could see smoke curling in the clear night air. This was to be our last night together before I returned to Bridgewater and I looked forward to spending every remaining moment showing Jeannette just how much she was needed and loved.

I climbed the porch steps, turned my key into the door lock, and let myself in. Brewster came trotting down the stairway and watched as I divested myself of coat, galoshes, hat and scarf. In the living room, an open bottle of wine and two glasses stood at the ready beside my easy chair. I sat down and poured the wine. Brewster found his doggie-bed at the side of the hearth and curled into it.

"Kevin, would you pour the wine please?" called Jeannette from upstairs. "I'll be right down."

"Take your time, dearest. I'm quite comfortable."

I felt in my jacket pocket for the small jewelry box that held my Irish angel's Christmas present. I debated giving it to her now but decided to wait for Christmas Eve. So it stayed safely hidden in my pocket. Moments later she appeared in the doorway to the room, wearing the fur coat I had sent her from Germany. At her ears and throat were the pearls I had sent her from Vienna. My olfactory senses were titillated by the scent of the French perfume that was my gift to her from Paris. Her hair had been pulled back and held in place by a certain diamond hair clip. I took one look at her, standing there, and my breath hitched. I rose to my feet like a man who had been mesmerized.

"Come," she invited.

I moved forward until I was standing mere inches in front of her. She was a vision of beauty standing there wearing my gifts. My fingers began at the neckline of the coat and slipped the buttons free one at a time. She lowered her head to watch my actions. When the buttons were undone, I moved my hands beneath the coat to her shoulders and gently slid the garment off of her. The firelight created shadows across her alabaster skin. With a gentle finger I raised her face so that I could look into her eyes. They were full of love and passion. I pulled her close, my lips claiming hers, while my hand removed the diamond hair clip. It fell atop the discarded fur coat. In one swift and easy movement, I picked her up and carried her to our bedroom.

Our lovemaking lasted longer than I had anticipated. It seemed that I couldn't get enough of Jeannette. Her kisses intoxicated me. Her touch inflamed me. And her responses to my own kisses and touches fanned the flames of my passion beyond comprehension. We made love three times that night and yet, when dawn's blush filtered through the window shade, I found that I wanted more. My arms were locked around her slender body. Instinctively my fingers moved across her breasts in a manner that I was sure would arouse her once again. She stirred beneath my machinations and her pelvis began to move against me as she dreamily opened her eyes.

"Good heavens, its morning! Kevin, you'll miss your train if you don't hurry."

"Can you truthfully say you want me to leave?" I pressed a kiss upon her lips.

She shook her head in response.

"Shall I stop kissing you?" I murmured as my lips lingered on hers.

Again she shook her head in response.

"Shall I stop caressing your breasts?" I stroked my fingers over her fully hardened nipples.

"Nnnooo," she whispered on a sigh.

"Should I not suckle at your breasts?" I dipped my head and captured a breast with my mouth, teasing its peak with my tongue. I returned to kiss her mouth once more.

"Tell me, angel, what should I do next?" I kissed the base of her throat as my fingers roamed below her waist.

She was almost incoherent when she begged, "Miss your train. Please."

Lawson

Chapter 16

December 1908
Bridgewater Manor

I t was ten o'clock in the morning on a mid-December Monday when our newly installed telephone filled the air with its insistent ringing. One of my more pleasurable tasks was to answer all calls. Most likely it was a merchant inquiring if we were in need of any household products. So in a most casual manner I lifted the receiver from its cradle and held it to my ear.

"Newkirk residence."

"Lawson, is that you?"

"Yes, sir."

"Lawson, I'm afraid I won't be coming in on the afternoon train. Please inform Stan that I'll be arriving tomorrow and that he should meet me at Union Station at four o'clock in the afternoon."

"Has something gone amiss, Mr. Newkirk?"

"No, no. Nothing's amiss. I've just been detained by business, is all."

"Is there any message for Mrs. Newkirk, sir?"

"No. Just be sure that Stan has the car waiting for me tomorrow at the station."

"Yes, of course, sir."

The click of the phone in my ear signaled the abrupt end of the conversation. I sent word to Stan about the change in plans and went off in search of Delia. At this hour of the morning I knew exactly where to find her. Leaving the foyer where the telephone was located, I paused to enjoy the cheerful atmosphere that the holiday decorations invoked.

Ropes of evergreen decorated with red velvet bows graced the curvature of the stairway. A tall vase of holly was placed strategically near the hall that led to the heart of the house. Of course the focal point of the foyer was the majestic Scotch pine tree dressed now with ropes of ivy and crowned with a blown glass figure of an angel that the Newkirks had brought back from Germany.

As I proceeded down the hallway, I grew a bit incensed at the callous manner in which Mr. Newkirk treated Delia. Now that he was certain she carried a child he thought nothing more about her, going so far as to abandon her here in the middle of nowhere while he took himself off to Boston to conduct "business" with his mistress. He could have at least inquired after Delia's health! I stopped just outside the door to the morning room and took a moment to compose myself: align my posture, deep breath, smile on my face – knock at the drawing room door.

"Come in," called Delia. "Mr. Lawson, just the person I wanted to see." She smiled at me and it was as though the sun had found a home here in this room.

"Mrs. Newkirk, I have a message for you."

"Very well, you first Mr. Lawson."

She motioned for me to close the door.

"Mr. Newkirk has just telephoned. It seems that he's been delayed from returning today. We are to expect him at the same time tomorrow."

"I see," replied Delia. "Hmmm, we shall be short one gentleman for tonight's dinner party. Too bad you couldn't take his place."

"It would be entirely out of protocol, Mrs. Newkirk."

"Nate, please join me here on the sofa."

She patted a place beside her on the sofa. I moved closer to where she sat but remained standing.

"I require your assistance, Nate. Please hand me that basket full of cranberries. I was hoping to entice Kevin into helping me with this simple holiday decoration but now I'm afraid I shan't be finished in time for tonight's party." She looked up at me with those sparkling blue eyes and I knew I'd do whatever she asked. "I guess there's nothing for it but for you to be my assistant."

"Stringing cranberries? Delia, I'm House Steward. I shall fetch you a maid," I offered.

"No. I require your assistance, Nate. Besides, we haven't had much time together since I've returned from Europe." Her lips formed a pretty little pout and that was my undoing.

I pulled up a chair and sat down facing her. Above all there must be no gossip of Delia being too close to another gentleman. We spent the next two hours stringing cranberries for the smaller, family tree that was tucked into a corner of the room. I fervently hoped that no one would walk in and see me thusly occupied! When at last Delia decided that we had strung enough cranberries, it fell to me to drape the ropes around the tree while she directed my efforts. There were all sorts of painted glass ornaments that had been brought back from the honeymoon, along with a spiral tree-topper, reflecting back the rays of the morning sun that were already gracing the branches of this more intimate tree.

We laughed and joked the morning away; in hindsight I can honestly say that while Delia had captured my heart all those many months ago, this particular morning cemented our relationship. We didn't need physical intimacy to become closer; this camaraderie, this joie de vivre was evident in even the smallest events that we shared. In truth, I felt that Delia was my wife and this room was the living room of our house. I would always feel comfortable here, for here was where Delia's light-hearted spirit was most evident.

When the decorations were complete, we stood side-by-side and admired our handiwork. Simultaneously, we turned to each other to say something but instead I put my arm around her and held her close. When she lifted her face to mine I simply had to kiss her. It had been far too long since our last kiss and I took the opportunity to savor every feeling that the kiss evoked. She melted into my embrace and rested her head against my chest when the kiss was done.

"I apologize for that, Delia," I whispered against her hair. "I should not have done that. Someone may have walked in on us."

"I don't care," her voice turned a bit hard.

"But I do. There can never be a question of your faithfulness to Kevin. You must be above reproach." I stepped back from the embrace and resumed my professional demeanor. "At least now I know that you still care for me a little." I smiled in her direction.

"How could you doubt me, Nate?" She turned and moved back to the sofa.

"It's just that you've been busy since your return and I haven't wanted to press you in your condition."

"It's your fault I'm in this condition," she smirked.

"I believe its best that I return to my duties now. Is there anything else you need?"

"There most certainly is. I need you, Nate, in my bed. Tonight. Will you come?" her eyes were bright and her cheeks were rosy as she extended the invitation.

"I thought you'd never ask, my love. I shall arrange everything." I moved to the door.

"Nate, would you please send Joan in here. I'm in need of a cup of tea and some of Mrs. Grant's lemon cookies."

"As you wish, Mrs. Newkirk," I responded, knowing that she hated when I addressed her in that manner.

She stuck her tongue out at me like a ten-year-old girl as I ducked out of the room.

By late afternoon the last of our guests had arrived and had been shown to their accommodations in the guest wing. Cocktails would be served at six-thirty to be followed by dinner at a quarter past seven. At six-fifteen I took up my post in the foyer to direct guests to the drawing room where Delia waited to receive them. From my position I watched Delia graciously welcome each person and thank them for coming. The last couple to make their way to the drawing room was the Bellmans who apologized for bringing along their fifteen year old son.

"Cordelia, you look absolutely stunning!" crowed Edie Bellman. "That gown must be all the latest rage in Europe. I simply must have my modiste make one for me."

Fat chance of looking that good in a similar gown, Mrs. Bellman, I thought. One look at the woman was enough to know that the bustle she still favored at least gave an excuse for her derriere appearing so large.

"Thank you Edie, you always flatter me so," responded Cordelia, as she turned to greet the woman's husband. "Joe, it's good to see you. Kevin will be disappointed that he missed you. He was looking forward to telling you about his new horses."

"Isn't he here, Cordelia? With you two just back from your European honeymoon I would think he'd be hard-pressed to leave those stables of his." Joe Bellman held Cordelia's hand for a trifle too long, giving her an appreciative up and down look.

"Kevin went up to Boston for the annual board meeting and I'm afraid that business has detained him," replied Cordelia smoothly, reclaiming her hand. Turning to the younger gentleman, obviously ill at ease in these surroundings, who trailed after Mr. Bellman, Cordelia inquired, "Who might this handsome young gentleman be?"

"Cordelia, allow me to present my son, Evan Bellman. What do you say, Evan?"

"Pleased to meet you ma'am." The youth, barely more than fifteen, kept looking at his shoes.

"Evan, I'm very glad to make your acquaintance," Cordelia smiled at him. "Mr. Newkirk has been delayed in Boston and won't be joining us this evening. I find myself in dire need of a dinner partner. Will you assume the role?"

"I...I...I don't know." Evan looked up at his father with panic in his eyes.

"'Course he will, Cordelia. He'd be honored to."

With my duties of the moment completed I took myself off to the kitchen to oversee the final preparations for dinner. This was the first dinner party given at Bridgewater since the wedding and it fell to me to be sure that Cordelia was accepted as a hostess of the first caliber in Woodhaven society. There was no room for sloppy service or ill-presented dishes.

"Mrs. Grant, how are things looking?"

"First course is on its way to being served, Mr. Lawson. Second course prepared and waiting."

"Wonderful." I turned and spied the butler. "Mr. Prescott, the wines?"

"They are on the sideboard in the dining room, sir. The footman is in charge of pouring and refilling. I'm on my way to the dining room now to uncork the next complement of wines."

"Excellent."

I turned and made my way back to the dining room entrance, taking up a stand near the doorway to direct the servers. At one end of the table sat Delia, looking radiant and lovely. Gathered around her were a group of guests who represented the best of local society: Joe Bellman, Chairman of the Woodhaven Savings & Loan, with his wife Edie and their son Evan; Humbert Dotson, owner of the Woodhaven Lumber, and his wife Julia; Professor Walter Fairlawn, Yale School of Antiquities, and his wife Helena; Sir Andrew Docket, a playwright, and his guest William Heath; Denis March, co-owner of a New York racetrack, and his wife Bunny, an aspiring actress. I had to admit that Delia was generous with her invitations, excluding no single occupation from mingling with others. The dinner conversation seemed lively and spirited, especially when Bunny March made an effort to draw out young Evan Bellman who clearly was not ready to socialize with the scions of society.

At the conclusion of dinner I led the gentlemen to the Billiard Room where they were offered brandy and cigars. Mr. March initiated a game of billiards with Mr. Heath and placed a hefty wager on the outcome. Young Mr. Bellman stood in one corner of the room, ill at ease since he was not offered a brandy or a cigar. I casually approached the young man.

"Billiards not to your liking, Mr. Bellman?" I inquired.

He shook his head in response.

"I see no reason for you to remain here with the gentlemen. Is there something else you'd enjoy doing?"

The young gentleman raised his eyes to me as a look of relief passed over his features.

"I like to read," he mumbled.

"I have just the thing for you. Follow me."

Together we escaped into the hallway and I led the lad to our library. He made a beeline towards the closest bookshelf and immediately began to peruse the titles. Suddenly remembering his manners he turned back to me.

"Thank you. I should like to remain here if I may."

"Certainly, sir. Will you be able to find your way back to the guest wing?"

"Definitely." He turned his attention back to the shelves of books. Taking that as my cue, I closed the library door behind me and made my way back to the Billiard Room. I offered the gentlemen a refill of their glasses as Mr. Heath, the victor of the first round, challenged Mr. Dotson to a game. Sensing that all was well there for the moment, I took off to find a footman to replace me in the Billiard Room.

The staff was taking a well-earned break when I entered the kitchen. Mrs. Grant was the only one still bustling about the stoves. The maids and footmen were sitting at the large table normally used for their meals.

"Andrew," I called. A young lad of seventeen or so jumped up immediately upon hearing his name.

"Mr. Lawson?"

"Please go to the Billiard Room. The gentlemen are having a rousing round or two. Just make yourself available to them. Ask before you refill their brandy snifters. Offer another cigar. And make sure they know how to find their rooms. Once they have retired for the evening you may do the same."

"I'm on my way," responded Andrew, straightening his jacket as he exited the kitchen.

"Seems like everything went well," remarked Joan, the maid who had served in the dining room.

"Would have been better if Mr. Newkirk had been here to receive his guests," observed Katarina, another maid who had also served at table.

"Mrs. Newkirk did very well, though. I like the way she mixed up the guest list. Didn't have a group of boring people talking about politics or investments. And that Bunny character! Did you see the way she was making eyes at that young Bellman lad?"

"Ooooh, if only I'd seen that!" Mrs. Grant shuffled over to the table where Billy, the other footman, graciously gave up his chair to her. "Imagine, practicing her acting at a dinner party. Tell me, Mr. Lawson, were there any comments about the food?"

"Nothing audible, Mrs. Grant. They were far too busy eating and cleaning their plates to offer more than passing praise for your dishes. However, there were many sighs of delight when the trifle was served. At least three of the gentlemen asked for a second helping."

Mrs. Grant smiled at the praise I relayed to her. "And Mrs. Newkirk? Did she have anything to say about the food?"

"Mrs. Newkirk was delighted that her guests enjoyed the fare." This comment was offered by Delia herself. So engrossed were we with our conversation that we failed to note her arrival into the kitchen.

"Mrs. Newkirk!" I spun on my heels towards her. "Do you require assistance with something?"

"I merely wanted to offer my thanks personally to the staff, and especially Mrs. Grant," Delia inclined her head towards our cook, "for making our first dinner party a resounding success."

Mrs. Grant smiled shyly at the praise so openly given. I watched as Delia lifted her pert little nose into the air and sniffed. A slow smile spread across her face.

"Do I smell….."

"Aye. I've made two batches of those lemon cookies you're so fond of, Mrs. Newkirk. They're cooling on the rack over by the oven," responded Mrs. Grant. "Shall I fetch a couple for you?"

"Allow me, Mrs. Grant," I offered. "You've earned the right to put your feet up for a while."

I reached for a plate and layered the warm fragrant confections in a small pile, covering it with a clean dinner napkin. Delia was fairly drooling at the thought of warm cookies and eagerly accepted the plate.

"Thank you, Mr. Lawson. And once again, thank you all for your superb efforts this evening. If you'll excuse me, I'll retire to my room now, along with this exceptional treat. Good night."

We watched as Delia left the kitchen with a swish of her skirt. I did notice, however, that she hadn't gone more than a few steps before she popped a lemon cookie into her mouth.

"What a lovely lady!" remarked one of the kitchen assistants. "Imagine, coming down here herself to express her thanks for our work.

"I certainly don't mind going the extra mile for her," added Mrs. Grant. "I've worked for a number of wealthy families, and she's by far the nicest lady of the house that I've met. Always willing to listen to my recommendations."

I smiled at Mrs. Grant's remarks, thinking to myself that Delia was indeed very nice to work for. Even had we been no more than employer and employee I would have found it very easy to be loyal to Delia. Her husband, on the other hand, left much to be desired.

Once I had ascertained that everything was in good order, I escorted Mrs. Grant up to her room before entering my own chamber. It would be a good thing, I reasoned, for her to see me enter my room.

Later, much later, I made my final check of the house. Doors locked, fireplace hearths banked, rooms cleaned, stove cool, windows and doors secure, no burning candles left aflame, household staff retired for the night; I plucked several blossoms from the arrangement in the dining room before I closed the door to Delia's office behind me. Gently sliding aside the concealed panel in her office, I made my way up the steps to her turret room. A dim light shone at the top of the steps and I paused, thinking that perhaps this was a sign from Delia that she was not alone.

"Nathan, is that you?" The whispered words belonged to Delia.

"Yes," I answered.

"What's taking you so long?"

In a flash I bounded up the remaining steps, pulled Delia into my arms and kissed her soundly. Her mouth was sweet, no doubt due to the cookies, but there was a sweetness there that no food could camouflage. She circled my neck with her arms and instantly I was in paradise. Delia returned my kiss with one of her own, one that was designed to arouse my passion. My body responded and I picked her up without breaking the kiss and carried her to the bed. She scooted over and made room for me while my clothes seemed to fall away unaided.

We made love not once but twice before either of us were willing to engage in conversation. When at last she snuggled into the curve of my arm, she opened the dialogue.

"I'm so mad I could spit nails!"

"Was it something I did?" I drew away from her slightly.

"Not at you, silly. At Kevin."

"Oh!"

"How dare he miss our first night of entertaining? And for what? Another roll in the hay with his mistress."

God, how I loved it when she pouted!

"How do you know that's where he is? He told me over the telephone line that he was unavoidably detained," I countered.

"Exactly! That's the phrase the Newkirk men always use when they visit their mistresses."

"Ah! And you know this how?"

"My mother-in-law let me in on the secret. My father-in-law has been doing it for years. Besides, I know Kevin's mistress and she is rather clingy." Her lip moved into a very unbecoming sneer.

"You've met Kevin's mistress?!"

"Indeed."

"Why am I not surprised?" I said this more to myself than to her.

"It's a long story, one I shan't bore you with. But thank heavens I've got you here." Delia moved up to kiss me.

"I shall always be here for you my darling." I placed a hand on the spot of her tummy that had begun to protrude, "For you and for this little one growing inside you."

"I'm glad the baby isn't Kevin's!"

"You're not going to tell him, are you?"

"Heavens no! I shall let him think that his potency is unmatched. The whole thing makes me giggle. He goes about preening, accepting congratulations about the pregnancy, when the whole time I know it was you, not him, who got me with child."

"I've heard enough about Kevin for tonight. Let's concentrate on something more at hand," I suggested as I pulled Delia closer to me.

"You always know how to make me feel better," cooed Delia as she kissed me again.

I awoke later, satiated from our love-making. Beside me Delia slept peacefully with the hint of a smile about her mouth. I hoped she was having pleasant dreams. Now that she was carrying my child I felt even more protective of her. There was a feeling, deep inside me, that we should have run off together before she married. Right now we could have been in a house of our own (granted, a small house) and I would be providing everything for her. But my conscience argued that the things Delia had become accustomed to were not the things that I could provide.

I knew she was handy with a needle and thread and could copy the latest fashions, but I would hate to have her washing laundry and working over a hot stove to make our meals. She didn't deserve to be tending to a garden for our vegetables when she should be entertaining her friends during social calls. I didn't want to see her in a slightly frayed coat and cotton stockings; she deserved beautiful furs and silk stockings. And what of our child? Would our child not have a better life as a member of society rather than as the child of one in service?

In the end I watched Delia sleep until almost morning when I slipped out of her bed and donned my clothes. Being careful not to make a sound, I made my way to her dressing area where I discovered the almost wilted flowers that I had brought to her last night. I found a glass nearby the sink and filled it with water, adding the flowers to it. In my imagination the stems seemed to draw strength from the water and I hoped they would perk up. Quietly I slipped through the concealed panel, closing it behind me. In the almost total dark I made my way down the stairs and was back in Delia's office. As it was still rather early, I was able to return to my own room, change my clothes, and emerge from my room just as Mrs. Grant called out a cheery "Good morning!" from her side of the hall.

Most of that day was spent tending to the usual business of running a household. Those dinner guests who had chosen to accept the hospitality of Bridgewater were served a hearty breakfast. One or two of the gentlemen braved the cold to go out for a brisk ride on horseback. Young Mr. Bellman once again closeted himself in the library and remained there almost the entire day. Cordelia gathered the ladies in the morning room where they gossiped over numerous cups of tea while gathered around the cozy fireplace. As I passed by the room I could hear Edie Bellman lamenting the fact that the Fairlawns had returned to town with the Dotsons. Delia offered to take Bunny on a tour of the house, thinking no doubt to leave the other women in peace and quiet. But Bunny deferred after they were joined by Sir Andrew and Mr. Heath. Once Bunny had learned that Sir Andrew was a playwright she expended all of her buoyant energy in convincing him of her natural acting ability of which, I might add, she had very little.

At the appointed hour Stan fetched Mr. Newkirk from the Union Station in New Haven and returned him to Bridgewater. As usual, his first order of business was to visit his stable and receive a report from

Huckleby that all was well and that the gentlemen guests had enjoyed their outing earlier in the day. After that Mr. Newkirk retired to his suite emerging almost an hour later looking refreshed and relaxed, thanks to Paul's efforts and a shot or two of good Irish whiskey. When he joined our guests in the drawing room prior to dinner, he once again availed himself of another dose of whiskey before greeting Cordelia who stiffened slightly as she welcomed home her husband.

During dinner Kevin made his excuses for missing everyone's arrival yesterday; although Cordelia smiled at his words I could plainly see the smirk behind her smile. Bunny March hung on Sir Andrew's every word, as though trying to absorb his patina of laid-back ennui. It didn't help matters that she had chosen a dress that displayed her ample charms to all who cared to look. Sir Andrew's tastes lied elsewhere but Bunny was blithely unaware of that. Her charms did, however, attract the attention of Mr. Newkirk who suddenly seemed fascinated by her stage ambitions.

After the ladies had adjourned to the drawing room, Mr. Newkirk cut short the time for brandy and cigars by announcing that he had been away from his darling wife too long and that he wished to bask in her company. Of course, Mr. Newkirk had consumed copious amounts of wine with his dinner and managed to refill his brandy snifter thrice before making that statement. Paul would most certainly have quite a time handling his charge later!

Once the gentlemen had rejoined the ladies in the drawing room, Sir Andrew and Cordelia put their heads together for a few moments before she addressed those gathered.

"Ladies and gentlemen, Sir Andrew has graciously offered us a preview of his latest play, *With The Dawn*, if we can find it amongst ourselves to choose a lady and a gentlemen to speak the parts." Cordelia allowed her glance to roam over the assembled guests silently encouraging volunteers.

"Oooh, may I read the lady's part?" None were surprised when Bunny March jumped at this opportunity.

"Thank you, Bunny. How kind of you to volunteer," quipped

Cordelia. "Which of you gentlemen will take on the male lead's part?"

Mr. Bellman, after a stern look from his wife, stayed silent. Mr. Heath also kept mum. It was Mr. Newkirk who filled the void.

"Allow me to take the part," he offered. "Since I missed the merriment yesterday I insist that I play opposite Mrs. March."

Once the two actors were given their scripts, I thought it wise for me to busy myself elsewhere. I would send Katarina back in a half hour to refill drinks. The remainder of the evening was uneventful in a business-as-usual kind of way.

Later that night, after our guests were tucked away and the house closed up, I retired to my room. Finding myself not particularly tired, I picked up the book I had been reading and propped myself up against the pillows on my bed. Rather than making me drowsy, the plot of the story kept me so engrossed that I failed, at first, to hear a rather timid scratching on my bedroom door. I glanced at the wind-up alarm clock on my bedside table and noted that the time was 1:48. Thinking to myself that one of the staff had taken ill and wished to be excused from their duties on the morrow, I set aside the book, drew on my robe, and opened the door.

To my utter surprise there stood Delia, silent tears streaming down her face, hair disheveled, and looking quite unlike the mistress of a large estate and more like a frightened girl. I pulled her into the room, closed the door behind her, and buoyed her as she collapsed in my arms.

Cordelia

Chapter 17

I had spent the last several hours more upset than I had ever been. Shortly after we had retired for the evening, there had come a knock upon my bedroom door. Without a moment's hesitation the portal was flung open to allow Kevin entry. He lurched forward, obviously intoxicated, but managed to stay upright as he slammed the door shut behind him.

"Kevin, what a surprise!" I intoned.

"Come here, my love. I need to kiss you." He stood rooted to the spot.

"It's obvious you're drunk, Kevin. Please leave my room." I remained seated at my vanity table where I continued to brush my hair.

"Damn it, Cordy! Come here now!" Kevin's voice went up a notch.

"Lower your voice. At once." I could feel my ire rising. "If you want a kiss then you'll have to come to me."

"Balderdash! You will come when I call you, Cordelia!" He swayed slightly yet remained stationary.

"I will not be summoned like one of your servants!" I threw the brush down and turned to face him. "Or like your mistress!"

"I wouldn't have you for a mistress." Kevin took two steps towards me and I began to feel anxious.

"Haven't you embarrassed me enough?"

He appeared to think this over then shook his head.

"What do you call that public display of affection with Mrs. March earlier? You didn't have to kiss her in front of our guests."

"That was part of the play! I was only reading my lines." His protest was frivolous.

"I don't recall Sir Andrew directing you to give her a full kiss. A peck on the cheek would have done the job."

"But she's quite appealing, in a theatrical kind of way. Wouldn't you say?"

"No, I wouldn't say. You're lucky that her husband is an understanding man." I turned back to the vanity and my hairbrush.

"Ah, Bunny! Bunny of the big bosoms! What a handful, no two handfuls, Denis has in her!!" Kevin leaned against the wall for support.

"I suppose you think I'll forgive you for your actions."

"Of course you will, my love."

I threw down the brush and stood up to face him.

"Get out of my room. Now!"

"Not till you kiss me." He challenged.

"I will not kiss you tonight, husband. Not after you delayed your return home to spend another day with your trollop." I could feel my anger rising to levels I didn't know I had.

"How dare you call Jeannette a trollop!"

"Jeannette, is it?" I feigned ignorance.

"She's a wonderful woman."

"Unlike me, I suppose."

"Damn right! She loves me. She does whatever I ask and then some." His eyes took on a dreamy far-away look.

"Then why isn't she carrying your child?"

"That's what you're for, Cordy." He sounded as though he were explaining something simple to a child. "You're the one who will produce the Newkirk heir."

"Is that my only purpose, Kevin? To produce your heir?"

"Of course not. You're here to raise the child and run Bridgewater." He seemed sure of himself.

"And what of the great love you proclaimed you had for me?" I could feel my emotions rising to the surface.

"Love. Love? I love Jeannette. Would have made her my wife if she'd of had a pedigree. But she didn't and you do. End of story. Now kiss me."

"It will be a cold day in hell before I allow you near me again." It took all of my concentrated effort to hold back the tears that were forming.

"Then keep to yourself, wife!" He spat out the word 'wife'. "You're nothing to me. Nothing more than another filly in my stable." He pushed himself towards the door. "Just provide me with a healthy son. After that feel free to take a lover yourself. But I warn you – I will suffer no public indiscretions."

"Get out!" I yelled.

He managed to get the door open once again before turning to me and saying, "You'll be sorry if you don't kiss me. I'm in the mood for intimacy."

"Get out!"

"Hmm, perhaps Mrs. March will find it difficult to sleep tonight. I might be able to help her relax." He stuck his chin into the air and closed the door behind him.

I was furious! No, beyond furious! I had almost convinced myself that we were in love but that was now a thing of the past. I sat back down, willing my breathing to become normal. Once I got over my fury, recognizing that we would be living separate though close lives, I felt bereft. My marriage was a sham but then I'd known that was true of most society marriages. That was when the tears that had been held back began to stream down my cheeks.

I was alone in this marriage whether or not Kevin would admit it. My responsibilities would not become less because Kevin didn't love me. Quite the opposite. In addition to being mistress of Bridgewater, I would be responsible for raising and educating the child I was carrying.

Why had Nathan not taken me away from here before I married Kevin? We could have been happy together. I didn't care about having servants (although it was nice to call upon others to do the heavy work). Like my mother, I was accustomed to housework. But then mother wouldn't have had the leg up in society that she had so craved. And what of the child I carried? Would he or she not be better off with the privileges of being a Newkirk? Of course I was being selfish. I was pregnant and ought to be allowed some self-indulgence! I needed Nathan.

I needed to see him, touch him, to be held in his arms. I needed to know that I was loved. Drying my eyes with the sleeve of my robe, I left my room. Down the hallway, down the curved staircase, and out to the Grand Hallway I went. I made my way through the dark, stopping momentarily to note that it was once again snowing. At the end of the Grand Hallway I pushed the door into the servants' wing open and climbed the stairs. I stopped when I found myself standing in front of Nathan's bedroom door.

A thin ribbon of light was visible beneath the closed door. I raised my hand to knock but a thin scratching sound was all I could muster. What if Mrs. Grant should see me? What if someone else was about? I put these thoughts out of my head as I listened and heard movement from the other side of the door. Unbidden, my tears began to fall once again. When Nathan pulled open the door all I could do was stand there and cry.

He pulled me into the room and shut the door behind me. I collapsed in his arms.

"Delia! What's wrong?" he whispered, placing a tender kiss on my forehead.

"He….he…he said," I tried to speak between my sobs.

"Ssh, hush now. Don't try to talk. Come, sit here." He helped me into a chair beside his small desk.

"It's KKkkkevin," I managed to say.

"Has he hurt you? Did he strike you?" The concern for me was evident in Nathan's voice. "Look at me." His fingers tilted my face towards him. "Did Kevin hit you?"

"No. No." I shook my head.

"Then what's wrong, darling?"

"He hates me. Told me I was no more to him that one of his breeding horses." I managed to say between sobs that now seemed to be subsiding.

"But you don't love him. You've told me that on several occasions." Nathan handed me a clean handkerchief with which to dry my eyes.

"He claimed to love me. All the time that we were engaged. Couldn't wait for us to be together. And when I accused him of staying in Boston with his mistress he had the gall to tell me that he loves her. HE LOVES HER!"

Wisely Nathan just listened as I continued.

"Told me he would have married her but for her lack of pedigree. Then he told me to take a lover after I gave him his heir. I'm glad this child isn't his!"

For a long time afterward we sat together on his bed, he just holding me until I became calm and collected. When at last I felt that I could face the world, I turned within his embrace and kissed him tenderly.

"What shall I do now?"

"First, Delia, you must never, ever, come to my room again. Under no circumstances. Is that clear?"

I nodded my head. Leave it to Nathan to think of my reputation.

"If you have need of me, send someone to fetch me. I will be at your side in a thrice."

I nodded again.

"Next, there will be no more talk of you taking a lover. You already have a very contented one." He smiled at me and I smiled back. "Let Kevin spout and sputter all he wants. After all, it's his money that's paid for this house and staff. You must remain in control of yourself. Why not become a patroness of the arts? You already know you have superb instincts when it comes to hosting a party. Keep the house filled with guests and you'll find that Kevin becomes a minor irritation at best."

"What a brilliant idea! I shall become the hostess whose soirées everyone wants to attend. Society will be vying for invitations to my salons!"

"You shall dress in the latest fashions. You will set trends. Cordelia Newkirk will be the darling of society!"

"Yes, I'll be the darling of society!"

"But first, we must get you back to your room. I'll escort you downstairs to the kitchen. Let's see if we can't find you some of Mrs. Grant's lemon cookies."

I could feel myself perk up at the mention of those cookies.

"From there you can use the secret stairway to your room. I'll put the panel back in place in your office. No one will be the wiser. Now come."

Nathan took me by the hand and together we set off for the kitchens and Mrs. Grant's lemon cookies.

It was almost dawn before I sank into an uneven sleep. When Ellen arrived to set out my clothes for the day she found me still abed, nestled beneath the quilts.

"Miss Cordelia, are you feeling ill?" She stood beside the bed and placed a hand on my forehead, checking for fever. "Your temperature feels normal," she commented.

"I didn't sleep well, is all," I responded.

"You need your rest, miss, especially now. Maybe it was all that rich food you had at dinner. Or maybe," she picked up the empty plate from atop my vanity, "it was a late night snack of Mrs. Grant's lemon cookies that kept you awake."

"Looks like I've been caught," I said, diving further beneath the featherbed.

"I'll tell Paul to have Mr. Newkirk make your excuses to the guests who'll be leaving this morning. Then I'll bring you a pot of chamomile tea. The other maids will be instructed not to bother you until lunch time."

Ellen bustled about a bit, collected my empty dessert dish, and finally left me alone. She was right. I had the babe to think about and I had earned my rest. I needed to provide Kevin with a healthy child to be raised as a Newkirk heir. With that thought alone remaining foremost in my considerations, I sank against the down pillows, content to know that my duties as a hostess would be relaxed this morning and that Kevin would need to do his part as host. My eyes fluttered to a close as I pictured him making excuses for my absence, preening in front of our guests as he took responsibility for the cause of my growing girth.

Ellen had stirred the embers in the hearth and tiny flames caught at the small, half-burned log on the grate, creating dancing shadows behind the floral, stained-glass fire screen. The gentle warmth pervading the room helped to make me drowsy and I felt myself slip slowly into the oblivion of a deep sleep.

It was cold. There were deep shadows in the horse stalls. I could hear a loud rustling in the stall at the far end of the stable. Close by a thoroughbred nickered softly. The sound was followed by a neighing from the last stall. I pulled my robe tighter around myself to stave off the cold and cautiously moved down the central aisle toward the sound of the rustling. It sounded like the hay was being pushed around. I stopped just outside the stall. By standing on my tiptoes I was able to see over the stall door. There was Kevin, with his trousers around his ankles and his bum exposed. He was bent over one of the workhorses and was moving his hips in a manner that could only be construed as his having intercourse with the animal. I pressed my hand to my mouth, anxious to not make a sound. I was riveted to the spot although I wanted nothing more than to flee and never look back. With a final grunt, Kevin relaxed his stance and patted the horse's rump before resting against the animal. When the mare turned its head, it had the face of Bunny March with her lips pulled back in a horsey kind of smile. That was when I screamed!

The scream woke me from a sound sleep and left me disoriented. Thank God I was only dreaming! I eased myself out of the bed and pulled on my wrapper, going to stand before the semi-circle of windows in my turret room. The driveway was abuzz with the motorcars that would carry our departing guests. The Bellmans were already tucked into their vehicle. Sir Andrew and Mr. Heath were stowing their valises in the boot of their car. Mr. March was conversing with his driver at the far end of the driveway. To the side of the entry stood my husband, with an arm around the waist of Bunny March. Her attention was trained on Kevin; she nodded her head at something he said and the feathers on her hat bounced. Ruby red lips seemed to be permanently etched in a practiced pout although her bleached blonde hair seemed a bit limp.

Kevin surveyed the scene before pulling her close and kissing that pout as his hand strayed to her derriere. How could he! Didn't he think the others would see? Bunny giggled and pulled back a step before turning to ascertain if her husband had caught sight of the kiss. When she began to move away, Kevin reached out and playfully swatted her behind much as he had done in my dream when he had patted the horse's rump. Bunny turned her head back to Kevin and favored him with the exact horsey smile that I had seen in my dreams. That was when I noticed a piece of wheat-colored hay sticking out from her straw-like hair and I knew that my dream had its foundations in reality.

It seemed that Kevin had wasted no time in making good on his threat. But Bunny March! I suppose that was the best he could do on short notice. And she had seemed willing the night before, after Kevin had kissed her during the play re-enactment. Well, I knew there would need to be another discussion between Kevin and myself. If I had been given the directive not to embarrass him then he needed to be discreet as well. There would need to be ground rules.

When Ellen returned to assist me in dressing, I chose with care the dress I would wear. I might be pregnant but there was no need to be relaxed in my attire. I made sure that my hair was perfectly coiffed and that I had a pleasant smile on my face as I made my way to Kevin's study. For just a brief moment I paused in front of the closed door and gathered my courage around me like a cloak. Taking a cue from his own book, I knocked once and flung open the door as I swept in and made my way to the saddle-brown leather chair in front of his desk.

"Cordelia, I hope you're feeling well rested," he intoned as he rose to close the study door.

"I do feel better, thank you." I inclined my head in his direction.

"You missed the departure of our guests but I'm sure they

understood, you being in a delicate condition." Kevin resumed his seat behind the desk.

"On the contrary, I didn't miss the departure of our guests. I merely watched from my bedroom window."

"I see."

"No, I saw. Everything."

"What exactly did you see, Cordy?" Kevin leaned back in his chair, his lips forming into a tight line underneath his mustache.

"I saw you kiss Bunny March. In broad daylight, on our front steps."

"You must have been dreaming." His tone became condescending.

"And I suppose I dreamt about seeing you swat her behind as well?"

"That? That was just a playful gesture."

I took a deep breath before continuing.

"Last night you told me many things, among them that you would 'suffer no public indiscretions' should I decide to take a lover."

"I'll admit to that, yes."

"I believe that the same should hold true for you."

"I beg to differ, Cordy. I'm a man after all."

"You are still my husband, father to my child. You have the Newkirk reputation to uphold although I have no idea why I should care that your name goes unbesmirched. I will agree to turn a blind eye to your indiscretions as long as you publicly play the devoted husband." I paused before continuing. "I've known about Jeannette for a long time."

"Really? How long?"

"Long enough to know that you'll find a reason to return to Boston for Christmas Eve. I've been given to understand that it's a tradition for the Newkirk men to spend the night with their mistress."

"Well, that's a relief!"

"Keep your mistress, Kevin. Have your flings. I will turn the other way. But know this: I will not publicly compromise you. If I hear one word of your openly wooing another woman just to get into her bed, I will destroy your family name. Are we clear?" My stomach was rolling in turmoil as I put forth my own conditions for living under the Bridgewater roof.

"You'll agree to remain my wife and raise the children?"

I nodded in agreement.

"You'll agree to oversee the household?"

I nodded again.

"I shall be generous with the household accounts."

"I expect as much."

"Is there anything else?"

"I've decided to carve out a public role for myself as a patroness of the arts both in Woodhaven and New Haven. There are many struggling playwrights as well as actors who could use the influence of a mentor. There may even be an occasion or two when you might wish to be involved."

"Of course." He seemed to give the matter some thought. "I endorse the idea wholeheartedly. I will stand the expense of any house parties you may plan. We will celebrate our anniversary every year in a public display of affection and loyalty. I will not compromise on that issue."

"Certainly," I agreed.

"Should the child you carry prove to be female, I demand access to your bed until you provide me with a male heir."

"Yes," I sneered at him.

"I will provide for you and the children but I will not tolerate needless extravagance."

"Understood."

"Then we shall proceed as agreed." Kevin stood up to signal the end of our discussion.

Without further dialogue, I left Kevin's study and went directly to my own office where I met with Mrs. Grant to plan the meals for our upcoming Christmas celebration with both Kevin's family and my own in attendance.

———

Momma and poppa arrived during a lull between snowstorms. Although the cold winds blew the snow into drifts, the roads were passable and

Stan had very little trouble retrieving them from the train station. As usual, momma was dressed to the nines with her best, and only, fur coat, high fur-lined boots (a gift I had sent her from Europe), and at least two scarves. In an effort to prove his masculinity poppa's overcoat and gloves seemed inadequate to keep him from becoming chilled, although he wore his hat as far down over his ears as was reasonable. Both had cold noses when they kissed me hello. It gave me a much-needed jolt of family closeness to have them here at Bridgewater, even though it would only be for a few days.

After our supper momma joined me in the drawing room while Kevin, adhering to the guidelines we had agreed to, entertained poppa in grand Newkirk fashion, breaking out a special bottle of port that had been brought up from the wine cellar. Momma caught me up on all the society events of New York City before reminding me, once again, how lucky I was to have married Kevin. She was anxious about my pregnancy, of course, and exuded her relief when I told her that the morning sickness was well behind me. At last, begging exhaustion after her long day of travel, momma retired to the suite I had assigned them in the guest wing. There, another of our maids by the name of Agnieska waited to be of assistance.

Left to my own devices, I made my way to our library. As I went I admired the yards of evergreen garlands that adorned the doorways along that corridor. I stopped momentarily as I felt something odd going on in the region of my budding abdomen. It happened again, almost as though I had swallowed a butterfly that now was trying to escape. My hands moved automatically to the slight swell beneath my dress as I waited for the flutter to return. Indeed, it came again, softer this time but still noticeable.

"Mrs. Newkirk? Can I help you with something?"

I looked in the direction of the voice which seemed to come from the far end of the corridor. A moment later a young woman who couldn't have been more than a dozen years of age emerged from the shadows outside of the morning room. She had a long braid of hair that reached down to the waistband of her somewhat limp maid's blouse.

In her hands she carried a pail of ashes, most likely from the morning room hearth. I searched my brain but couldn't recall her name.

"I'm sorry. You'll think me a ninny I'm sure but I don't remember your name," I admitted.

"I'm Lotte, ma'am." The girl did a quick curtsy.

"Lotte," I repeated the name. "What are you doing here at this hour of the evening?"

"Oh, it's not that late, ma'am. I have another hour or two of duties before I can turn in." She took a step toward me and pointed to where my hands rested on my abdomen. "You've felt the baby move?"

"I'm not sure. Isn't it too early? How would I know?"

"It should feel like the flutter of a butterfly's wings." My face must have betrayed my skepticism because she added, "My aunt is a midwife. That's what she says. The only way to know, though, is for me to feel the baby."

"Feel the baby?" I was beginning to feel alarmed.

"May I?" she asked as she set down her ash-filled bucket. She motioned for me to move my hands and she laid her childlike one atop my slightly protruding tummy. Just then the odd feeling returned. Lotte giggled and withdrew her hand. "Your baby is just saying hello to its momma," she observed.

"You're certain of that?"

"Most certainly, ma'am." Lotte's eyes were aglow with happiness.

"Thank you, Lotte. I thought perhaps I'd eaten something that didn't agree with me." I watched the girl as she picked up the container of ashes. "Lotte, would you do me a favor?"

"Anything, ma'am." She curtsied again.

"Tomorrow morning, after you've had your breakfast, come to my office. Do you know where it is?"

"Yes, ma'am." The smile on her face was replaced by a sad frown. "I didn't mean to be so forward, Mrs. Newkirk. Please don't let me go."

"My heavens! That's not what I had in mind at all. Now hurry along. You should be abed. There is nothing at all for you to worry about, I assure you."

"Thank you Mrs. Newkirk!" The smile returned to her face as she hurried by me, clutching the pail as she went.

"Slow down, Lotte. I would be very upset if you fell and hurt yourself."

"Yes, Mrs. Newkirk."

She slowed to a walk for a few paces then resumed her scurrying as she turned the corner. As for myself, I continued on to the library happy in the knowledge that Lotte would soon be promoted to Nursery Maid.

The next morning, in keeping with my decision of the previous night, I first informed Nathan that I wanted Lotte to become Nursery Maid. I laughed at his confusion when he failed to grasp the duties that would be required in the position.

"But Delia," he questioned, "surely Lotte isn't the right choice for a wet nurse?"

"Nathan, you are being a man now," I cajoled, happy to see a member of the opposite gender become confused by something women so clearly understood. "One can only be a wet nurse if one has recently given birth."

"I understand that, Delia. Then what are Lotte's duties to be? Please explain." He gave me his undivided attention.

"Beginning today, I want Lotte to be in charge of the nursery. She is to be responsible for its cleanliness for now. I will tolerate not even a speck of dust there."

We were interrupted by a shy knock upon my office door, followed by Lotte who presented herself as directed.

"Come in Lotte," I invited.

Nathan stood up and offered the girl his chair.

"Oh, I couldn't, Mr. Lawson," she said.

"I insist," replied Nathan.

Lotte sat on the edge of the chair and waited.

"Thank you for being so prompt, Lotte," I began. "Do you enjoy your position here?"

"Yes, ma'am." She nodded her head earnestly.

"I hear that you are very conscientious in your duties. That is good. After our talk yesterday evening I have decided to give you a promotion."

"Really?" Her eyes became as large as saucers.

"I would like to make you a Nursery Maid."

"Nursery Maid, Mrs. Newkirk?"

"As I was telling Mr. Lawson, beginning immediately you are to be in charge of the nursery. For now you will be responsible for the room's cleanliness. I will tolerate not even a speck of dust. After my baby is born, you will be personally responsible for the nursery linen, keeping the room aired in summer and warm in winter. You will assist the Wet Nurse and the Month Nurse at first: fetching items that may be required, watching over the baby during naptime so that the nurse may have her meals away from the nursery. In time you will be responsible for keeping the nursery neat and the baby's toys clean and in good repair. You will be responsible for the child as it grows, seeing that everything is in its place and that the child's clothes are in good repair. You will alert me if anything is required by either nurse or the child's future governess. In short, you will be my eyes and ears in the nursery. Do you think you can handle all of that?"

"Yes, ma'am. Would I still have my duties as a parlor maid?"

"Only until Mr. Lawson can find someone to take over those duties. Your primary responsibility will be to the nursery."

"It would be an honor to be Nursery Maid, Mrs. Newkirk."

"It would seem that you've been promoted, Lotte," added Nathan, a smile lighting up his handsome face behind his newly acquired mustache.

"Thank you, Mrs. Newkirk; you too, Mr. Lawson."

"I had nothing to do with it," replied Nathan.

"Thank you nonetheless." Lotte stood up, thinking that we were through.

"One more thing, Lotte," I smiled at the young girl, so full of ambition and energy.

"Yes, Mrs. Newkirk?"

"You will find an additional dollar in your monthly pay envelope to reflect your new responsibilities. If you prove yourself, I will consider your wages again in a year."

"A whole dollar? Every month?"

I nodded.

"I'll be rich in no time!"

"Only if you save it for when you get older," I cautioned. "You're dismissed, Lotte."

The girl turned and scurried out of my office nearly colliding with Mrs. Grant who, it seemed, had been lurking outside my office door.

"You may come in, Mrs. Grant," called Nathan. The cook shuffled into my office.

"I was passing by when I heard Lotte's voice. Just listened to make sure she wasn't in any kind of trouble. You know how those young ones can be." She took advantage of the vacant chair and dropped her sizable bulk into it.

"That's very kind of you, Mrs. Grant, to watch out for the young ones," observed Nathan.

"Now don't go getting all up in that mustache of yours," she scolded Nathan and I had to swallow my smirk.

"And what do you make of my promoting Lotte, Mrs. Grant?" I inquired, genuinely wanting to know.

"I think it's a fine thing. She knows an awful lot about babies for someone so young. I've heard she has some gypsy blood in her," whispered Mrs. Grant.

"I'm glad you approve. Now, you may tempt me with a large glass of milk and some lemon cookies and I'll forget the fact that you were eavesdropping on my business." I smiled at the cook.

"Coming right up, Mrs. Newkirk!"

———

The next few days saw the arrival of my brother, his wife and baby. They brought two of their own personal servants for which I was grateful.

While we had a sizable number of household staff they would be sorely taxed if required to do double duty and serve our guests. I had added three more part time staffers for the holiday season and with Calvin's family bringing their own servants I felt that there would be enough staff to handle all of the requirements of both our families.

Two days before Christmas Stan and Richard, a part time driver that we occasionally called upon, collected Kevin's family from the train station. I spent the better part of that morning doing two things: inspecting every inch of Bridgewater before my mother-in-law arrived and bidding Kevin farewell as he accompanied Stan to the train station. In New Haven, Kevin would meet his mother as well as his two sisters and their husbands before seeing them tucked into our cars. Then he would board the train for the trip to Boston where he would meet his father to 'conduct some last minute business' before they returned together on Christmas Day.

While our latest arrivals were shown to their rooms I was able to find some quiet time to myself. I took myself first to the Drawing Room but found that it was devoid of anyone who might provide a distraction for me. Feeling at loose ends, I next went to Kevin's sanctuary – his study. When he was home he disliked my being in that room but during his absence I sometimes found it rather comforting to be surrounded by the masculine décor. The room itself felt like an extension of the stables, housing as it did many small statues of horses and books dealing with horse husbandry.

My fingers lingered over the burled mahogany of the desktop, where only a desk blotter and a desk lamp resided. Kevin's large leather chair looked welcoming so I lowered myself into its seat. From my vantage point I looked around the room, feeling sure that Kevin thought himself a potentate of sorts as he was able to gaze upon his stables through the view from the window beside his desk. My fingers played with the hardware gracing the center drawer of the desk which somehow Kevin had failed to close completely before locking the desk prior to his departure. I knew it was an intrusion of his privacy but I slowly pulled the drawer towards me, thinking I would find some mundane items like the keys to the stable or the household invoices for the month that I had presented to him yesterday.

What I didn't expect to find was a letter from Jeannette, his mistress. In fact, there was more than one letter; several, in fact, that were tied together with a strip of leather that appeared to have come from the stables. The latest envelope had not yet been added to the pile and so was easily opened and laid before me. I knew that Kevin loved Jeannette and that he had provided her the seed money for her millinery business so I deduced that this must be an update on his investment. Clearly there could be nothing wrong with reading what amounted to a business report, I rationalized. I withdrew the scented stationery from the envelope, unfolded the letter, and laid it out on the desk blotter noting the small tight penmanship that filled the sheet. It was the salutation that gave indication that this letter was of a more personal nature.

Dearest Kevin,

It seems like forever since we've been together. I've grown lonely for your company. My bed is cold and friendless without you lying beside me, cradling me in your arms and waking me with your kiss.

In your last letter you said that you and Cordelia are now estranged and this saddens me greatly. I know how much family means to you. Yet I take comfort in the fact that you have a child on the way. I pray each night that Cordelia presents you with a son and that both she and the baby are healthy.

My days at the shop are busy right now with the ladies of Boston all shopping for a new holiday chapeau. It is good for business of course and so I spend most of my evenings making up the creations that will adorn their tresses as they parade into Boston's churches on Christmas Day.

I look forward to Christmas Eve, when I can lock up the shop and hurry home to you. I have a lovely gift for you, my dear. In fact, it will be adorned with my diamond hair clip! I'm sure you can guess what it is.

Brewster has grown into a full size dog now and is quite adept at obeying commands. However, it has been a while since he's seen you so prepare yourself to be greeted in an over-zealous manner.

I count the days and hours until I see you again. Until then, I give you all of my love and affection.

With endless kisses, I remain yours,
Jeannette

At the very bottom of the page there were a few X's to denote kisses. I slowly refolded the letter and slid it into the envelope. It was then that I realized my hands were shaking. Jeannette was not simply Kevin's mistress. She loved him. I had not realized that Kevin's feelings for her were returned in kind. Although I silently wished Kevin and his mistress well, I would nonetheless expect him to be openly loyal to me – his legal wife.

I replaced the letter with the others, pushed the desk drawer shut until I heard the latch clasp, and stood up. My baby chose that moment to move and I felt the flutter deep inside me. Yes, I was loved. I had my baby, I had Nathan, and I had a house full of holiday guests to keep me company. So what if my marriage was a sham. This sort of thing happened all the time. I had once thought to hold out for a husband who loved me but wasn't what I had better, I mused. Within very loose guidelines I was free to live the way I wanted. The fact that I had found love along the way was more than most women had.

I counted my blessings, straightened my afternoon gown, and went off in search of my guests.

———

Our Christmas celebration that year was a bittersweet one for me. My anchor during that time was not momma, who I was beginning to see needed more support that one would have thought, but none other than my mother-in-law Fannie Newkirk.

It was late Christmas Eve, long after everyone else had retired for the night, although not quite midnight. I was sitting in the Drawing Room where shadows were made deeper by the glow of the dying embers in the fireplace. From my vantage point in a deep Queen Anne's chair by the window, I had a perfect view of the side garden buried now in drifts of snow. A cold north wind blew the powdery snow into swirls making me feel cold simply by looking at them. I turned my gaze inwards to the gaily decorated family tree at the far end of the room and to the jumble of presents with their cheerful wrappings that covered a nearby table. From atop the mantle came the sound of the wind-up clock as it ticked away the seconds until Christmas Day. Just then I heard the sound of the drawing room door being opened and the silhouette of a woman became visible.

"Who's there?" I tried to sound authoritative in case it should be a servant coming to check on the fireplace.

"Who are *you*?" came the answer in a voice that I immediately recognized.

"Mother Newkirk? Is everything all right?"

"Cordelia? Is that you?"

"Yes, I'm over here by the window. Are you in need of something?"

Silence for a moment then her voice, now much closer, addressed me.

"I was restless; couldn't settle down to sleep."

"I know the feeling."

There was the soft swish of her robe as she sat down in an opposing chair.

"Shall I light a lamp?" I asked.

"No, somehow the darkness makes this night more palatable."

"Would you care for a nightcap? Our brandy is excellent," I offered.

"That would be rather nice. But let me get it." I couldn't believe that she offered to wait on me.

"I should light a lamp. I wouldn't want you to bump into the furniture."

"Tush! I can see perfectly well by the glow of the embers."

Without further ado she walked over to the sideboard and poured a snifter of brandy for each of us. Before taking a seat she handed one to me.

"Seems like this is becoming a tradition for the two of us," she observed.

"I honestly didn't think he'd go all the way to Boston to be with her," I said. "I could understand Father Newkirk coming down after the rest of the family but for Kevin to intentionally leave home and return to her for Christmas Eve, well, the thought never crossed my mind until he'd stated his intentions."

"His visit to her on Christmas Eve means he doesn't intend to neglect his family, in this case you and the child you carry, on Christmas," replied Mother Newkirk. "Kevin has always prided himself on family coming first as does his father."

Silence for a moment while Mother Newkirk sipped at her brandy.

"This really is awfully good brandy," she observed. "I must ask Lawson where he purchases it and have a case sent up to Boston."

"I believe it's made by a local family," I replied. "I'll have him give you the contact information before you return home."

"That's very kind, dear. Tell me again, when is the baby due?"

"Sometime around the end of June."

"First babies are quite often delivered well after the due date. Wouldn't be surprised if the child was born on Kevin's birthday."

"That would surely make Kevin happy." I was glad of the darkness because it hid the sly smile on my face. Wouldn't it be cosmic payback if the child was born on Kevin's birthday?

"Have you chosen a name for the baby?"

"I thought I would wait until after the holiday season to think about that."

"I've always been partial to the name James myself."

"Any special reason?"

"Let's just say that a boy named James once played a very important role in my life," replied Mother Newkirk.

Her voice sounded quite tender and caring when she spoke the name. So tender, in fact, that I could almost feel her blush through the shadows. I wondered who James had been and how she had come to know him.

"I'll be happy to consider the name along with a few others. The final choice, however, will be Kevin's, I assume."

"I can see that he's most pleased to have gotten you with child so quickly."

"Yes, well, that is one of the main reasons for our getting married."

I downed the brandy from my glass in two large swallows. If I had to stay and talk about Kevin I feared I would be ill.

"If you'll excuse me, Mother Newkirk, I'll retire now."

"Of course, dear. Get plenty of rest and take care of my grandson. Good night."

I made my way down the corridor, up the staircase, and into my room where I rested my back against the closed door.

"Of course she'd think it's a grandson! That whole family has nothing but a line of male progeny on its mind!"

The words came spilling out from my mouth as I shrugged out of my robe, letting it fall to the floor as I walked forward and straight into a huge obstacle. I was ready to scream when a hand was placed over my mouth and a voice whispered in my ear.

"Don't scream!"

I nodded my head to show that I understood and the hand was removed from my mouth.

"Nathan! You nearly frightened me to death!"

I leaned against him until my heart resumed its normal steady rhythm. Strong arms held me close before my head was tilted upwards and a kiss placed on my lips. I melted into that embrace and returned the kiss. A moment later I was picked up and placed upon my bed so gently that it felt like I was being carried aloft by a gentle summer breeze.

"I didn't expect you tonight, dearest," I whispered.

"Did you think I would let a prospect such as this pass us by? We know Kevin won't return until tomorrow."

"I guess I was so caught up with the relatives and their gossip that I failed to recognize this opportunity. Thank you for coming. I do need you with me even if only for a short while."

I watched Nathan divest himself of clothes and slide beneath the featherbed next to me. In no time at all my nightgown was lying atop the pile of his clothes and we were joined in the beauty of our lovemaking. When it was over we lay snuggled together, he raining gentle kisses on my nose and my eyes until I fell into a deep and dreamless sleep.

Sometime later I felt him slip out of bed and heard him getting dressed. I dreamily lifted my eyelids to watch him, silhouetted against the predawn sky, as he pulled on his jacket.

"Ah, you're awake!" he whispered, a smile lifting the corners of his mouth and reaching to his eyes.

"Is it morning already?" I yawned.

"Not quite, but soon." He came to sit beside me on the bed. "Merry Christmas, sweetheart. I have a gift for you."

"I thought you'd already given me a gift last night," I smiled back at him.

"Naughty girl!" He laughed as he withdrew an envelope from his jacket pocket. "This is for you."

I opened the envelope and immediately a slim gold chain with a heart-shaped locket slid into my hands. My initial, C, was carved into the top and a single tiny diamond nestled in the curve of the letter. I was speechless!

"Do you like it?"

"It's breathtaking. But this must have cost you a year's salary!"

"Not quite, darling."

"It's exquisite. Help me put it on?"

I lifted my hair and he fastened the clasp around my neck.

"That's how I love seeing you, you know. Wearing only the locket," he grinned at me.

"Now who's being naughty? But how will I explain it?"

"I'm sure you'll think of something. Kiss me quickly, darling. It's almost time for me to make an appearance in the kitchen."

The kiss was anything but quick and Nathan detested leaving me but he managed to extricate himself from my arms and disappear behind the concealed panel in my dressing room. I pulled the featherbed up and snuggled deeper under it, smiling to myself as I fingered the most beautiful gift I'd ever received. Beautiful because it was given out of love, not duty.

Christmas Day dawned with a weak sun breaking over the horizon and turning the ice-coated trees into a sparkling wonderland. Ellen arrived at her usual time to assist me with my toilette and to tidy up the bedroom. The steaming mug of hot cocoa that Ellen had brought up warmed me nicely and provided a quick bit of nourishment for both myself and the baby.

I had decided not to wear the locket that day as there were sure to be questions about it. Instead, I wore a long strand of pearls with matching earrings to complement the red velvet dress I had chosen for the day. Satisfied with the way I looked, I left Ellen to make the bed and put away my nightclothes, but not before I handed her a small gift box tied with a green satin bow.

"Oh, Miss Cordelia, I wasn't expecting a Christmas present!"

"I certainly hope you like it," I smiled at her.

"May I open it now?"

"I should be quite put out if you didn't."

I watched as she pulled apart the ribbon and lifted the lid of the box.

"I can't believe it! It's exactly the one I was looking at in Paris."

Ellen gently extracted a snow globe that encased a miniature Eiffel Tower and held it aloft for a moment, admiring it, and then turning it over to allow the faux snow to swirl around the Parisian landmark.

"I remember you telling me that you couldn't decide on which snow globe to buy as a souvenir and consequently not buying anything. It was my wish that you have something to remember Paris by and so I bought this for you and packed it myself in Kevin's steam trunk."

"I'm afraid I don't have a gift for you." Her face took on a more sober look.

"Nonsense, you pamper me day and night."

"Only doing my duty, Miss Cordelia." She hugged the snow globe to her chest.

"Yes, but you always have a very bright and optimistic attitude. That means a lot to me."

"Thank you, Miss Cordelia, and Merry Christmas!"

"Merry Christmas to you Ellen," I called as I left the bedroom and made my way down to breakfast.

After a breakfast fit for royalty, the entire family, *sans* Kevin and Father Newkirk, gathered in the Morning Room. We took turns opening presents and exclaiming over the beauty or usefulness of our gifts. Afterward we enjoyed some Christmas pastries that Mrs. Grant had prepared specially for our celebration. It was later that morning when I finally found the opportunity to excuse myself, leaving the others to their own devices. I made my way to my bedroom, closed the door behind me, and kicked off my shoes before sinking onto the chaise. Ah! What a pleasure it was to simply stretch out and relax in the solitude of my room. Through the window I could see that a light snow had begun to fall; not the large pretty snowflakes that indicated a quick snow shower but the tiny snowflakes that heralded a major storm. Within moments the air became dense with snow and I looked up into the sky as the flakes fell faster and faster. They were mesmerizing, as anyone who has lived through a New England snow storm can tell you. I watched until my eyelids became heavy and my last thought was that I would close my eyes and rest for a few moments. I was awakened by a hand being placed on my shoulder; I looked up to see Ellen standing beside the chaise.

"Miss Cordelia, it's time to get dressed for supper."

"I'm sure you must be mistaken, Ellen," I stretched my arms as I tried to stifle a yawn. "We haven't even had lunch yet."

"I looked in on you a while ago. You looked so peaceful that I didn't want to wake you. When I told the others that you were resting they went ahead with lunch. I've brought you a tray with some tea sandwiches if you're hungry." Ellen pointed out a covered dish on my vanity.

"I am rather hungry," I decided now that she had mentioned food. "By any chance are there...."

"Yes," laughed Ellen, "I've brought you a nice serving of lemon cookies. Of course the tea will be cold by now."

I stood up and peered at the clock on the narrow mantle above the fireplace. The hands of the clock were pointed almost neigh onto six o'clock.

"Good heavens! I've slept away most of Christmas Day! Has Mr. Newkirk returned?"

"Oh yes, he and his father arrived shortly after noon. Good thing, too. Seems like we're in for a really heavy snow storm."

I moved to look out of the window and down to the front entrance below. The walkway was completely covered with fresh snow and from the branches on the nearest trees it was evident that over an inch of snow had already fallen. I had a fleeting moment of having missed something while I slept but pushed it aside. Surely it was only the cobwebs of my sleep.

An hour later I was dressed, powdered, and coiffed in my Christmas finery. I gazed upon my reflection in the mirror of my vanity and was pleased with the way I looked.

"One more thing Ellen and then you may have the remainder of the evening to yourself."

"Yes, Miss Cordelia?"

"Would you help me fasten this locket around my neck?"

"It's quite lovely," replied Ellen as she placed the chain around my neck and fastened it. "Is it a gift from Mr. Kevin?

"No. Actually it is a gift from my goddaughter, my brother's child." I centered the locket over my heart and was satisfied that it complemented my gown. "I believe there is going to be wine served in the kitchen with your supper tonight. Enjoy yourself."

"That's very kind of you, Miss Cordelia. Merry Christmas to you!"

Ellen closed the door behind her as she left my room. The sky had darkened from the heavy snow-laden clouds as well as the deepening darkness of a winter's night. I didn't give Ellen's observation of my necklace and locket any more thought because it was just at that moment that the baby within me made a move. I lovingly laid a hand upon my abdomen and smiled. *Merry Christmas to you, little one!* Turning down the lamp I moved into the corridor and down the stairs to join our families for the first Christmas dinner at Bridgewater.

At the bottom of the curving staircase I met up with my sister-in-law Rose who was hurrying to join the rest of the family in the drawing room.

"Cordy, are you feeling rested?" she inquired as she fell into step beside me.

"I had no idea I would require so much sleep," I admitted. "Where is my goddaughter?"

"Sound asleep in our room with one of the maids watching over her."

"Rose, there's something I need to ask you." I placed a hand on her arm to get her attention. She stopped and turned to face me.

"Yes, Cordy, what is it?" Her eyes were luminous and large and were the nicest feature of her face, fringed as they were with long dark lashes.

"I have a favor to ask."

"Just name it," she replied.

"This locket that I'm wearing," I pointed to the item now adorning my neckline.

"It's quite lovely. Where did you get it?"

"I'm putting around the story that it is a gift from my goddaughter. Will you back me up on that?" I waited for a moment or two while she appeared to mull over my request. A sudden smile lit up her face.

"Tell me, Cordy, is it from a secret admirer?" she whispered.

"Yes," I whispered back.

"How exciting! I'll bet it's that playwright that you told us about." I wisely gave no acknowledgement but smiled conspiratorially. "Of course I'll back you up."

"There's no need to volunteer information that might be questioned, you understand, but if the need should arise…."

"I've got your back, sister-in-law. I've never had a secret admirer. What's it like?" she tucked her hand into the crook of my elbow.

"I shall tell you one day, Rose dear, but for now let's not keep the family waiting any longer."

There was no question about my new piece of jewelry since the remaining members of the family were all talking about the snow storm and making guesses as to how deep the snow would get before the clouds moved on. Father Newkirk was standing next to the sofa where Mother Newkirk was smiling shallowly. Kevin, with a quarter-full glass of whiskey in his hand, made a beeline for me the moment I entered the room.

"There you are, my dear." He placed a gentle kiss on my cheek as he tucked my hand around his arm. "I was beginning to fear that you might sleep right through Christmas Day."

"Did you have a pleasant journey home, husband?" I managed a smile in his direction.

"Pleasant enough. Happy to have arrived home before the snow storm began in earnest."

At that moment Nathan announced dinner and I allowed Kevin to escort me into supper. After our meal we returned to the drawing room, each one bemoaning the fact that he or she had overindulged of the sumptuous dishes that had been presented from the kitchen. By mutual consent we retired early, the ladies most eager to divest themselves of their corsets while the gentlemen looked forward to loosening their collars and their belts. Kevin, however, begged my indulgence to stay behind with him in the drawing room for a few moments.

"Cordy, you've outdone yourself in the planning for our first Bridgewater Christmas."

"Thank you, Kevin. I hope you don't think it presumptuous of me to allow the household staff to have wine with their Christmas dinner?"

"Not at all." He stood beside the chair that I had chosen to relax in. "I trust Lawson chose a good wine for the staff, not too expensive but something worthy of the holiday."

"I'm sure you'll catch up with our Head Steward tomorrow and take an inventory. What was it you wished to discuss? Surely more than a compliment or two on how smoothly the staff executed their duties?"

"I wanted to give you your Christmas gift."

"You mean something more than the child growing in my belly?"

"How is my son? Do you think he's healthy?"

"Judging by the movements inside of me, I'd say the child is quite healthy."

"The baby has moved? And you've felt this?" The look on his face was one of pure awe.

"Yes, indeed. Usually the movements come in the late afternoon or in the evening." I waited a few moments and sure enough there was the slightest movement, almost as though the babe could hear what we talked about. "If you'd like, you may place your hand on my abdomen, here," I guided his hand to a spot on my abdomen. "There, do you feel it?"

"Gadzooks! I felt something! That's our baby?" He was grinning from ear to ear.

"Yes, that's the baby."

"A healthy son. What more could a man ask?" He wrapped his arms around me and hugged me with such force that I thought I would lose my breath.

"That will do, Kevin. Let's not forget our arrangement." I managed to extricate myself from his hold.

"Certainly, Cordy, as you wish." He pulled back and straightened his jacket. From an inside pocket he withdrew an envelope, bearing the logo of Newkirk Trading, which he handed me. "Merry Christmas, Cordelia."

I accepted the envelope and withdrew a folded piece of vellum with all sorts of designs and curlicues on it.

"Since you are bearing my son and heir it is only fitting that you own a piece of the family business. I'm giving you one hundred shares of Newkirk Trading. You will most certainly receive a dividend each year. The money is yours to keep as are the shares. I would not want my wife to go about without money of her own."

"That's very generous of you," I replied. "And did Jeannette receive the same gift?"

Kevin's face turned from smugness to contained anger as a bright red hue flushed his cheeks.

"Dammit, woman! Can't you accept the gift for what it is?"

"Of course. I see that it's payment for bearing you a child. I would expect no less from you. If nothing else, you are generous," I sneered.

"Would you rather I showered you with baubles and trinkets?"

"Why give me a gift at all?"

"Because I value your contributions to this family."

"So I'm nothing more than a paid breeding machine. Exactly how many children do you expect me to produce?"

The rage that he held back was simmering, almost to the point of boiling over, when he picked up his whiskey glass and flung it across the room. It shattered into a hundred pieces as it struck the mantel. I steeled myself against the creeping fear that Kevin would turn on me. His breathing was ragged as he brought his temper under control.

"I am the master of Bridgewater, woman. Remember your place. Do not anger me again. Your child has spared you the sting of my slap but you won't always have a babe in your belly. Now take your gift and get out of my sight."

His eyes were glassy and dark, twin portals to the rage that he managed to contain just below the surface. I turned my back to him and swept out of the drawing room. A footman came running towards me.

"Mrs. Newkirk, is everything all right? I heard something break and came as fast as I could." The young man was out of breath as he was, indeed, running.

"Mr. Newkirk has quite foolishly broken a glass that slipped from his hands. Please see that the mess is cleaned immediately."

"Yes, ma'am."

I continued on to my office where I knew that I would find solitude even as the footman continued on to the drawing room. Once I was settled in the tiny room, I locked the door behind me so that there would be no intrusions. Just this once I did not want Nathan coming to me to offer comfort. I threw the stock certificate on my desk and sank into my chair. That was when the tears began in earnest. I let them roll down my cheeks unheeded as I let my head drop to my hands.

Perhaps this crying jag had been a long time coming. Certainly I hadn't cried when Kevin told me that I was nothing more than a brood mare for carrying on the Newkirk name. With the holiday season there had been so much to do that I had barely given Kevin another thought. As my sobs subsided, I dried my eyes on the lace-adorned sleeve of my dress. My breathing calmed as I thought about the child I carried. I sent a prayer of thanks to heaven that my child had been fathered by Nathan. I didn't want to give birth to a child with the Newkirk temper!

I pulled the stock certificate from the envelope and looked at it briefly. With both hands, I crumpled it and rolled it into a ball that I pushed into the drawer. I didn't want to see that awful piece of paper again. Instinctively I placed my hands on my abdomen, as though to shield my baby from the bitterness between my husband and myself. Thinking about the child made me hungry although I had eaten well less than two hours earlier.

Taking care to appear calm, I adjusted my coiffure, dried my eyes, and stepped into the kitchen. I knew exactly where Mrs. Grant kept an ample supply of lemon cookies so I helped myself to a half dozen and made my way to my turret room, determined to enjoy the remaining hours of Christmas Day.

Lotte

Chapter 18

Meine Teuerste Tante Anja,

   *Exciting news. I am promoted to Nursery Maid! All thanks
to you dear auntie. Thanks to what you teach me about what
happens when a woman carries a child and all about the baby's
coming. Because of these things and a chance meeting with the lady
of the house I've made a good impression.*

   *For now my duties will be to keep the nursery spotless - easy
enough until the baby is born. Once the baby arrives I will assist
the Month Nurse and later the Governess. I will also take care of
all the nursery linen. That is a very important job. I will make sure
the room temperature is just right for the baby, not too warm and
not too cold. As the baby grows I will be in charge of his clothing
and his toys too, keeping them clean and in good repair.*

   *I know will be a lot of work for one person but I am anxious
to make a good impression and will be very conscientious in my
duties. Mr. Lawson has hired another maid to take over my duties
in the parlors and she will begin working here tomorrow.*

   I hope that you are in good health. I remain your devoted nichte,
                                        Charlotte

*P.S. Mrs. Newkirk will be increasing my wages by one dollar
each month!*

I blotted the ink on the sheet of stationery that I had borrowed from another of the maids and waited a moment before folding it and placing it into the envelope that was given to me by Mr. Lawson himself, who offered to have my letter posted at his own expense. Surely my guardian angel was watching over me and allowing all of these good things to happen one after another.

It was just past midnight when I finished writing the letter to my Tante Anja, the midwife I had told Mrs. Newkirk about. I knew Tante Anja would be happy for me and write to my mother back in Dusseldorf about my good fortune.

There had been many girls who applied for the position that I was leaving but only two of them had good references. Mr. Lawson had hired a girl of Polish ancestry named Jadwiga and she would be starting work in the morning.

As I climbed into my narrow bed I was grateful for the warmth coming from the radiator near the small window in my attic room. My featherbed was a bit on the thin side but with the afghan that I had brought from Tante Anja's house I was toasty warm beneath the bed covers. I turned out the light and closed my eyes, offering up a prayer of thanks for my good fortune at being employed here in such a fine house with a wonderful lady in charge. It had been a long day that had begun well before dawn for me and I would need to be up and waiting to meet Jadwiga in less than five hours. I don't remember finishing my prayers that night since sleep claimed me rather quickly. Right on time, half past four-thirty in the morning, came the knock on my door from Katarina whose job it was to wake me each day.

I quickly jumped out of bed and was dressed in under a quarter hour. In an effort to get the day underway, I ran down the three flights of stairs in the almost darkness until I spilled into the warmth of the kitchen, where Mrs. Grant and her assistants were already baking for the day. The aroma of fresh bread was simply heavenly. I gratefully accepted a cup of strong coffee with plenty of cream and sugar, drank it down in three big swallows, and went off to Mr. Lawson's office. Mr.

Lawson was seated at his desk, reviewing the household rules with the new girl when I entered.

"Come in, Lotte," he beckoned as I stopped in the doorway. "I should like to introduce you to Jadwiga. Jadwiga, this is Lotte. She will be showing you your duties for the next day or two."

I walked over to the other girl, who had remained seated. She had not even the good manners to turn around and acknowledge my presence. When she did, she presented the dourest looking face I'd ever seen. Her lips were set in a tight line with no hope of a smile. Eyes as dark as midnight, eyebrows that wanted to grow together, jet black hair to match the color of her skirt – all of these things screamed to me of the gypsy heritage that she tried to hide; but my knowing eye saw the intricate patterns in the brightly colored scarf covering her hair.

"Pleased to meet you," Jadwiga enunciated the words carefully.

"Welcome," I replied.

"Lotte, now that Jadwiga is here, you will be giving up your room to her. I've designated another room, closer to the nursery, for you to use."

"That's very kind of you, Mr. Lawson. I can move my things out later this evening."

"No need for that. I've instructed one of the footmen to assist you. In fact, Andrew should be waiting in the hall to escort both of you upstairs. Once the move has been made, then you are free to resume your duties and instruct Jadwiga as you work." He smiled kindly at me.

"Come with me, Jadwiga. I'm sure you'll like your accommodations, the room has always seemed quite cozy to me."

Without a word or a backward glance at Mr. Lawson, Jadwiga rose from the chair and moved past me into the kitchen hallway. Mr. Lawson wiggled his eyebrows at me causing me to giggle. Jadwiga turned to give me a frown, as though I had somehow misbehaved. I sighed and thought to myself that this would certainly be someone to watch myself around.

It was many hours later when I finally crept beneath my featherbed and eased my weary body onto the bed in my new room. The new girl was a difficult person to like. She had informed me, in no uncertain terms, that she could perform her duties very well without too much instruction from a child such as me. There were many things I learned from Jadwiga that day: that she had been an experienced ladies maid in Poland, that she was highly respected by her former employers, that her references were impeccable, that she was eighteen years of age and thought it humiliating that someone of my age (twelve and three-quarters to be exact) would show her how to do her job. I also learned that she had come to America in the hopes of marrying a man who would support her and the children she one day hoped to have. It was almost in the same breath that she had asked furtively if Mr. Lawson had a wife. Thankfully Mrs. Grant overheard that question and put Jadwiga in her place with the terse remark, "Don't go looking too high above your station, dearie, or you'll find that the fall is mighty nasty."

Since Jadwiga informed me, shortly before we turned in for the night, that she did not need me to oversee her work the next day, I looked forward to spending the next day in the nursery. My eyes could no longer remain open so I gave in to sleep and dreamed of ribbons and bows and little baby girls with rosy cheeks.

On my first official day as a Nursery Maid, I had the luxury of sleeping an extra hour. My attire also reflected the change in my status. Mrs. Newkirk had decreed that she did not want any darkness present in the nursery, even in our uniforms. She had thoughtfully provided me with a lovely new grey wool skirt to replace the more severe black one I had previously worn. My white blouses were still serviceable so I quickly donned one of those over my shift before lifting up the new white and grey striped bib apron that I was to wear. I had never had anything new to call my own before and I took an extra moment or two that morning to delight in the feel of the crisp apron and the warm woolen skirt without patches or frayed hems. Satisfied that my hair was braided tightly and that the sleep had been washed away from my eyes, I enjoyed what seemed a leisurely breakfast of toast and tea in the kitchen before proceeding upstairs to the nursery where I was to meet Mrs. Newkirk herself.

I scurried up the main staircase to the third floor where the nursery was located. The polished oak door seemed a bit heavy as I pushed it open but I reasoned that was a good thing. One did not want a toddler opening the door unassisted. Who knew what danger might befall such a curious child!

The morning sun was just above the horizon and the sunlight pervaded this east-facing room. It would indeed be nice to have one's child greet the day with sunshine lighting the room each morning. The semi-circular bank of windows themselves were covered with heavy drapes to block out the cold, but one of the parlor maids had already been here to draw them back and set the radiator temperatures. The walls had been painted a cheery yellow to further complement the morning sunshine. Just off the main bedroom were a small playroom and a bathroom with its own bathtub and water closet. Imagine, not having to share a bathroom with four or five others as the household staff did! The furniture had not been arranged in any fashion and there were boxes and small trunks full of baby clothes and toys that had yet to be put away. I looked forward to being able to bring order out of this chaos.

Directly adjacent to the nursery was another room for the nurse/nanny/governess. This room was not physically located in the turret but adjoined it via a connecting door. I had just put my hand on the knob of that door when I heard movement behind me.

"Good morning, Lotte. I'm sorry if I've kept you waiting."

It seemed to me that Mrs. Newkirk had materialized from nowhere. I knew I hadn't heard the door to the hallway open or close. She must be very quiet indeed!

"Good morning, Mrs. Newkirk." I curtsied out of respect for the lady of the house.

"Have you had a chance to familiarize yourself with the nursery?"

I watched as she glided across the floor to the crib. Her hand trailed delicately over the side railings and she had a far-away look in her eyes.

"I can see that there's much work to be done before baby arrives."

"Yes, there is. But we have some time yet. My baby isn't due to arrive until the end of June."

"If you'd tell me where you would like things to go, I can do the heavy work," I volunteered.

"Lotte, how old are you?"

"Twelve and three-quarters, ma'am."

"What do you hope to do with your life?"

"Ma'am?"

"Surely you don't want to be a domestic all your life. What are your goals?"

"To make enough money to bring my mama and my sister to America."

"Do you plan on getting married? Raising a family of your own?" Mrs. Newkirk looked out the window as she questioned me.

"I..I don't know. I guess so."

"Before you go to sleep tonight, I should like you to make a list for me. Five goals for your life."

"I've never thought about what I'd like to do. I mean, I don't have any skills really."

"Can you sew? Can you cook?"

"I suppose so."

"Five goals, Lotte. I don't care if they seem unattainable to you. Bring them to me tomorrow morning."

"Do you have goals, Mrs. Newkirk?" I ventured to ask.

She was silent for a moment, gazing out the window at the bright morning so full of hope and promise before she answered my question.

"Yes, Lotte, I had many goals," she answered before turning to me. "But like the weather goals sometimes need to be changeable."

"My mother says that dreams can come true," I offered, "especially if one works very hard."

"Keep that in mind, Lotte." She smiled kindly at me. "Your new apron looks very becoming on you. You are just the right person to care for the nursery."

"I dreamt about your baby last night."

"Tell me, what did you see?" Mrs. Newkirk sat made herself comfortable in the maple rocking chair that faced the windows.

"I didn't see the baby's face but I could tell that it was a girl because there were lots of ribbons and bows around the crib."

"You know that Mr. Newkirk is hoping for a boy child, an heir?"

I nodded.

"Don't tell anyone of your dream, at least for now."

Mrs. Newkirk gave me directions on what should be done in the nursery. There were baby clothes that needed to be unpacked and put into the drawers of the chest; linens and receiving blankets to be unboxed and put away. The bathing area needed a good scrubbing as did the floors. Mrs. Newkirk's family was making additional items of clothing and new ones were to arrive each week. Each item was to be hand washed in a mild soap and air dried before I put them away. There was a large cedar closet that would be used for the child's clothing as well. For now we would store the blankets and pillows there until just before the baby was born.

I was also to be responsible for the adjoining nurse's room, keeping it clean and ready for her arrival. By the time Mrs. Newkirk had given me directions for all of this it was well past mid-morning.

"Lotte, I believe it's time for a break."

"Yes, Mrs. Newkirk," I concurred without breaking my stride as I opened boxes.

"Lotte, look at me please."

I turned from the task at hand. Mrs. Newkirk had a grin on her beautiful face.

"Would you be kind and fetch something from the kitchen?"

"Yes, ma'am."

"Tell Mrs. Grant that I require a small pitcher of cold milk and a double batch of her lemon cookies. Don't take no for an answer when she tells you I don't need that many cookies. Do you understand?"

"Yes, ma'am." I curtsied and went down to the kitchen to carry out my assignment.

I returned a quarter of an hour later with a tray full of cookies and a pitcher of ice cold milk. When I entered the nursery I found to my dismay that Mrs. Newkirk was fast asleep in the rocking chair. What should I do?

Certainly she needed her rest. Carrying a child took a toll on a lady's body, according to my Tante Anja. I set the tray on the padded window ledge and resumed my work as quietly as I could, keeping my eye on Mrs. Newkirk should she awake. I was just about to begin scrubbing the bathtub when I heard Mrs. Newkirk call out to me.

"Lotte? Where are you?"

"Right here, ma'am." I stuck my head around the corner of the washroom so that she could see me.

"Come here, please."

I set down my cleaning cloths and the bucket of soapy water. Drying my hands on my apron I came back to stand before my employer.

"Lotte, I'm very cross with you. You should have woken me up when you returned to the nursery."

"I'm sorry, ma'am, but I didn't want to disturb you. You looked so peaceful napping in the rocker."

"It is rather a comfy place," she replied, "however I can see that you haven't had a morning break."

"We're not allowed to take a break until our morning duties are completed, ma'am. Since I wasn't sure what my morning duties were there didn't seem to be a good time for a break."

"I insist you pour yourself a glass of milk and have some of those wonderful lemon cookies. You do like lemon cookies, don't you?"

"Yes, ma'am. But you should have the milk instead of me. For the baby."

"I'll be just fine, Lotte. You've been working non-stop all morning and deserve a break."

At Mrs. Newkirk's insistence, I quickly drank a glass of the milk and made two cookies disappear. I rinsed the glass in the bathroom sink and refilled it, handing it to Mrs. Newkirk before returning to the bathtub and my chores.

"Ah, there you are Delia." I recognized Mr. Lawson's voice at once. "I've been looking everywhere for you." I could hear his footsteps as he moved into the room and stopped near where Mrs. Newkirk was sitting.

"Mr. Lawson, what brings you to the nursery in search of me?" Mrs. Newkirk's voice rang with authority as she questioned the Head Stewart.

"I'm here to inform you that you have a caller waiting in the drawing room." I noticed that his voice took on a more formal manner than from his initial address of Mrs. Newkirk.

"Who would venture on these icy back roads to make a social call I wonder."

"It's Mrs. Fairlawn come to call."

"Helena? How lovely! Someone who isn't family or who isn't making a play for my husband."

"Indeed."

I peeked ever so cautiously around the corner of the washroom. Mr. Lawson had offered his hand to Mrs. Newkirk who graciously accepted it. As she rose I could see her eyes meet Mr. Lawson's eyes straight on and linger for just a moment too long. Then, before I could turn away I saw Mr. Lawson bend forward and place a tender kiss on Mrs. Newkirk's lips. I waited anxiously for her to slap him soundly for taking such liberty but instead she smiled at him. Not just a friendly smile but the school girl smitten with her teacher kind of smile. He tucked her hand into the crook of his elbow as he escorted her out of the nursery.

After they had gone, I moved over to the rocking chair and sat down. As I finished the cookies and milk that Mrs. Newkirk had left, I thought about the five goals she had asked me to write down. I didn't know what the other four would be but I knew one of them was to have a gentleman look at me the way Mr. Lawson looked at Mrs. Newkirk.

Cordelia

Chapter 19

Nathan was kind enough to escort me to the Drawing Room where my caller awaited. As we walked I took the opportunity to quietly scold him for his forthright manner in the nursery however.

"You really should be more circumspect. That kiss, as nice as it was, could have easily been observed." I hoped he didn't notice my slight blush at the mention of his kiss.

"I happen to know that we were alone in the nursery." He smiled at me.

"On the contrary, Mr. Lawson," I purposely used his formal name, "Lotte was in the washroom area of the nursery."

He stopped dead in his tracks, turning to look me straight in the eyes.

"Please tell me you're joking, Delia."

"I kid you not." My eyes held his and never wavered.

"Do you think she heard?"

"Hopefully she was hard at work scrubbing the tub and neither saw nor heard anything."

"If she did, do you think she would tell anyone?" The anxiety in his face was clear for all to see.

"Lotte seems like a trustworthy young lady. As a precaution, however, I shall speak with her."

"Surely you won't...."

"Leave everything to me," I reassured him. "For now I plan on having a nice visit with Mrs. Fairlawn. Please have another place set for luncheon. I'm sure our guest will join us."

"As you wish, Delia," he whispered, giving my hand a slight squeeze before disappearing into the shadows of the corridor."

I patted my hair, took a deep breath, fixed a smile on my face and entered the drawing room. Helena Fairlawn stood a few feet from the hearth.

"Helena, my dear, how nice of you to pay me a call. Is that a new ensemble you're wearing?"

The professor's wife turned at the sound of my voice, favoring me with a happy smile.

"Cordelia, it's so nice to see you again! How are you feeling?" Her gaze dropped from my face to where she imagined my swelling abdomen to be.

"I imagine you're politely trying to spy my growing baby," I laughed.

"Oh dear," she laughed, "was I being so obvious?"

"I don't mind at all," I assured her. "You'll stay for lunch?"

I waved us over to a pair of floral-upholstered ladies chairs where we made ourselves comfortable.

"I'll admit to being famished, the country air seems to have worked up my appetite. But I don't want to intrude on your time with your new husband."

"Kevin normally takes his mid-day meal with the Head Groomsman in the stable office; he so enjoys his equestrian interests."

"Then yes, I'll stay for lunch." She removed her gloves before speaking again. "Cordelia, what were the signs that led you to believe you were enceinte?" Helena's voice had dropped to a loud whisper.

"Other than the obvious signs of feeling full all the time yet being constantly hungry? Or the extreme nausea upon awakening? Or perhaps no longer fitting comfortably in my clothes? Why do you ask?"

Helena looked up and the twinkle in her cocoa-brown eyes was outshone by the sly smile spreading across her delicate features.

"Oh goodness! Helena, are you...?"

"I think so," she admitted. "Everything you've just said rings true except for the morning nausea. I have yet to experience that particular activity."

I leaned forward and clasped Helena's hand in mine.

"I'm so excited for you, my dear. What does the professor think of this?"

"He's delighted, of course. It seems we've been trying for a child forever."

"Then this is truly happy news indeed!"

We chatted and gossiped like two schoolgirls who've been apart for an entire summer. After Nathan announced that lunch was ready we continued our visit over a serving of mushroom and barley soup followed by dainty sandwiches. When at last we dawdled over our tea and it seemed we had covered every topic of importance, Helena brought up another subject.

"Cordelia, I simply must ask you about the style of clothing you've adopted. It's not the usual style for an expectant mother."

"Why Helena, the ensemble you're wearing is perfect for your condition. It appears stylish yet roomy."

"That may be true but I simply can't wear this ensemble every day. And in a few weeks I'm sure it will be quite snug."

"Certainly you'll require a new wardrobe, one that is versatile yet stylish."

I offered Helena the plate of lemon cookies that had been brought up with our tea service. Thankfully she declined.

"I'm not quite sure how to say this, Cordelia," she began, casting her eyes downward.

"Good heavens, my dear, I hope our friendship is solid enough to bear the weight of any question you may have. Ask me anything," I urged.

I took her hand in mine and squeezed it gently. Helena took a deep breath before she continued.

"Walter and I are truly blessed to be expecting a child. But on a professor's salary we are barely able to make ends meet. There really are no extra funds available for an entire wardrobe for me. So I was wondering….."

"Say no more, my friend. I shall ask momma to have some outfits made for you," I offered.

"No, Cordelia, I can't allow that. We aren't penniless!"

"I know that. I'm sorry if my offer gave offense."

"It's just that Madame Warner charged such an exorbitant amount for this morning suit and there is very little room for expansion at the waist."

I kept silent at the mention of Madame Warner.

"Then tell me, dear friend, how I may help."

"I'm quite handy when it comes to sewing. I was hoping that you might have access to a pattern or two that you'd be willing to share. I so admire the less structured style you've adapted."

"I shall write to momma this very afternoon and ask her to send a few patterns."

"Thank you, Cordelia. I was afraid I'd have to hide in my rooms for the next six months."

"That would never do, Helena. Now, before you leave you must come upstairs and see the nursery. Our nursery maid, Lotte, is still at work setting things in their rightful places. I'd love to hear your opinions on the placement of the furniture."

———

Ten days later I prepared for a late morning visit to the Fairlawn residence in conjunction with some other business in town. As Nathan had Bridgewater business to attend to in town as well he offered to drive the car in place of Stan.

I settled into the rear seat alongside a rather large box containing a variety of fashion patterns and a collection of fabrics and trims that were in small quantities and thus of no use in my brother's garment factory. With this treasure chest, I was positive that Helena would be appropriately dressed as the seasons progressed. Kevin was on his way to the stables when he noticed the car being readied for my departure.

"There you are, my dear," he called out as he approached. He leaned into the rear seat and made a great show of tucking the fur throw around me. "Going to call on Mrs. Fairlawn?"

"Yes, and then on to the milliner. I should like to order my Easter hat."

Kevin favored me with a phony smile before stepping back. Nathan was already seated behind the steering wheel.

"Well then, have a lovely day, my dear. Lawson, take care of my wife and her most precious bundle."

"Certainly sir," Nathan responded tersely. He shifted gears and slowly navigated the ice-encrusted driveway. We proceeded until the car neared the end of the extensive driveway, well out of sight of the house and stables. At that point Nathan stopped the car and turned to face me.

"Madam appears to be quite lonely and cold. Perhaps she would be more comfortable in the front seat." His tone was formal but his eyes gleamed with mischief.

"Why Mr. Lawson, I'll have you know I'm a married woman. It would be unseemly for me to sit in close proximity to another gentleman," I answered as I flung back the fur throw and scurried into the front seat.

I had no sooner pulled close the door than Nathan pulled me closer and kissed me deeply. I responded to his passion.

"Delia, it's been such a long time since we've been this close." He nuzzled my neck and found my lips again. "Tell me I can come to you tonight."

While my lips clung to his I shook my head at his suggestion.

"Be patient, my darling. Kevin will be taking a trip to Boston early next week." My gloved hands found their way beneath his greatcoat and were working the buttons on his jacket.

"Another 'business trip'?" He claimed my mouth again, kissing me more deeply this time.

"Yes." I murmured the response into his kiss, feeling his hand on my thigh, high up beneath my dress.

"When does he leave?" Nathan's breath was becoming more ragged as my hands struggled with the last button on his jacket before moving lower to the buttons on his trousers.

"Monday morning," I answered as I moved into position much lower on the seat.

"I don't think I can wait until Monday, Delia."

His hand came down to caress the back of my neck as I set to work. In short order I had consumed every bit of my favorite snack (other than Mrs. Grant's lemon cookies) and brought my head up in time to see the look of sublime ecstasy on Nathan's face. I sat up and straightened my dress where he had raised it. A few moments later Nathan drew me closer, and kissed me deeply.

"Thank you," he whispered.

"Yes, well, I find that I'm not quite satisfied yet. Perhaps we should try that again."

"Not now! Give me a chance to recover." He laughed as he set his clothes to rights.

"I can be a very understanding employer." I gave him a haughty glance before breaking out in smiles. "But I'll expect you to be ready on the journey home."

"Witch! You'll have me thinking about you all afternoon." He restarted the car. "Now sit closer so that I can hold you while I drive."

———

Time passed swiftly. My girth increased steadily and it was no longer deemed proper for me to be seen in public.

Thanks to Lotte, the nursery was ready for the arrival of my baby. Mother Newkirk had chosen the furniture and had it delivered from one of Boston's most prestigious stores. The crib, a rather pompous-looking piece of furniture, was fashioned from prime walnut wood as were the matching chest of drawers and changing table. Each piece was emblazoned with the Newkirk family crest carved in a place of prominence. Kevin, of course, thought the furniture suite was a perfect accolade for his son. The sight of the crib alone made him preen and posture with arrogance.

Mother Newkirk also had seen fit to have several sets of bedding for the crib delivered. These were handmade from the finest brushed cotton and embroidered with the Newkirk family crest. I wondered if family-crested diapers would soon follow.

As the winter snows melted into spring, I divided most of my time between my office (where only the household staff would see my ungainly form) and my turret suite. I allowed myself to be pampered by Ellen. Once each week a vase full of fresh flowers found its way to my room. Nathan had once decreed that I should always have fresh flowers and these quiet expressions of his love and caring were brought to me each week by the young maid Lotte. To all others it must have appeared that Kevin was the sender of those lovely blossoms and I allowed the charade to proceed unchecked.

Dr. Bennett had projected my delivery date as the end of June but Momma, who arrived directly after Decoration Day, was certain that I would deliver early. Lotte simply shook her head in disapproval but kept her silence when Momma insisted on having the Month Nurse arrive two weeks prior to our agreed upon date.

"Has the baby been very active, Mrs. Newkirk?" Lotte asked me one sunny June day as I sat on the chaise beside my open bedroom windows now curtained in light gauze. I held in my hands a small embroidery sampler that I was working on while Lotte took a well-earned break from her duties.

"I feel the baby shifting position every evening, just before the supper hour," I answered.

"That's a good sign," Lotte sighed. She gazed out the window for a few moments, and then continued, "The babe won't be born this month, you know. Your mother is wrong."

"How so, Lotte?" I listened intently for her answer as I had found her to be correct about so many other facets of my confinement.

"You're not large enough yet."

"Good heavens, if I grow any larger I'll outgrow the house," I laughed.

She smiled at my response.

"Your body is holding the baby up high, under your rib cage. Your daughter hasn't yet moved into the birthing position."

"My daughter?" I was secretly delighted with this prediction. "No one can accurately predict the gender of an unborn baby. Besides, even Dr. Bennett is confident that I carry a boy."

"Tante Anja can. She taught me the signs. And don't you remember I dreamt about the baby being a girl." Lotte turned her smiling face toward me. "I'm sure Mr. Newkirk will be disappointed but something tells me you're hoping for a daughter. What will you call her?"

"I haven't allowed myself to consider names for a girl. Mr. Newkirk hopes to name his heir Daniel."

"Your daughter will be born just before mid-July, ma'am. Of that I'm certain," Lotte reiterated before turning to plump my pillows and resume her work upstairs in the nursery.

———

As with all things, time proves us right or wrong. On July ninth I was beset with labor pains. Dr. Bennett shooed Momma from my room, allowing the Month Nurse and Lotte to assist him. At thirty minutes to midnight on July tenth I was delivered of a daughter, whose cry was at first weak but became more robust after a bit of coaxing by Dr. Bennett. Upon hearing the cries of her grandchild, Momma hurried into the room.

"Dr. Bennett," she began, "how is my daughter? And my grandson?"

"Cordelia has had a long and difficult delivery," I heard him say to Momma.

"But Daniel is in good health? I've heard his cries." She tried to peer over the doctor's shoulder.

"The cries of your granddaughter are indicative of a hungry

newborn," he replied, rinsing his hands in a basin of warm water which Lotte immediately removed after his use.

"That can't be, doctor. My daughter was to have produced a son." Momma's voice was full of anxiety.

"Are you questioning my ability to determine a child's gender, madam?" Dr. Bennett inquired as he donned his jacket and straightened his tie.

"No. No, of course not. It's just that....we were so sure of.... You see....Oh dear, what will Kevin say?"

"The child's father has been well into his cups most of this day. Perhaps it's time to summon him," suggested the doctor.

"No," I managed to croak, forcing the words from my parched throat. It seemed difficult for me to muster the energy to speak. "No Kevin. Not yet." I sunk my head against the pillows and opened my hands in supplication. "Daughter," was all I could say.

"Let her hold the baby," instructed Dr. Bennett, "but only for a moment. I've given Mrs. Newkirk something to help her sleep."

The nurse placed a tiny, doll-like creature wrapped in a Newkirk-crested receiving blanket into my weary arms. This baby was tiny and delicate but she was mine.

"Why, she looks like your great-aunt Geraldine from Dublin. Easy to see she favors our side of the family," observed Momma.

I smiled down at the tiny red face and my heart skipped a beat as her fist wrapped itself around one of my fingers.

"Momma, meet your granddaughter, Geraldine Clementine Newkirk."

———

I spent the next six weeks in semi-confinement. The month nurse remained on duty until almost the end of August, well past the time when she could have accepted another position. Of course she was compensated well so she had no real complaints. Geraldine was unwilling from the start to accept my mother's milk so Dr. Bennett put her directly onto a formula, a weak one at first, and she seemed to tolerate that better. Momma hovered over me like an angel, showing great concern in the days directly after the birth. By the second week, however, she would tolerate no amount of protests on my part that I didn't feel strong enough to walk any distance. I, on the other hand, was thrilled with being able to walk from my bed, to my water closet, and back to my chaise, often collapsing onto that convenient piece of furniture. Thankfully Momma spent most of her time in the nursery, making life difficult for Lotte.

Week three saw some of my strength return and I was extremely proud when I could don a loose morning dress and slippers and hold my daughter without fear of dropping her. That was when momma began in earnest to badger me.

"Cordelia, you have had more than enough time to recover from the birthing process."

I was sitting in my chaise, fully dressed, and giving Geraldine her morning bottle. Her eyes were bright and her smile soft as she looked up at me, holding my attention completely.

"It's only been three weeks, momma," I reminded her gently. I didn't like the direction in which momma's remarks were headed.

"Giving birth is a natural thing for a woman. All of your female ancestors were back to their normal routines only days after giving birth. And here you are, surrounded by helpers, still in your third week of recuperation. I don't understand it." Momma shook her head so forcefully that her curls whipped to and fro. She paced as she spoke.

"Momma, please, no disparaging remarks in Geraldine's presence. She can sense your negativity." I wiped at the baby's chin with a soft cloth.

"Pah! She can't tell how exasperated I am with you! You have yet to make your appearance below stairs. Instead you prefer to be holed up here with the Month Nurse and the Nursery Maid." Momma threw herself into a nearby chair and rolled her eyes. "You must steel yourself and undertake your normal duties. I'm sure Kevin will want to try for a son as soon as possible."

I tore my gaze from my daughter's face and looked up at Momma.

"What did you say?"

"You need to stop babying yourself, Cordelia."

"Not that. About Kevin?"

"He'll want to try for a son. That's what this marriage was about in the first place. That's what afforded you the opportunity of being a lady of quality," Momma was quick to remind me.

I turned to look out the window and realized that soon it would be September – almost time for the Newkirk family outing at Buttermilk Bay. Perhaps I could play the baby card and beg off from visiting with Kevin. Then again, the Newkirks would expect to see Geraldine and welcome her into their lair. I was not surprised when, a few seconds later, the door to my suite was slammed shut as momma left the room in a huff. I had more important things to think about than her feelings. We would need to have Geraldine's christening before the Buttermilk Bay gathering. I needed to set those plans in motion immediately. But first a nap was called for. The interlude with momma had drained what strength I'd had.

———

The christening was held on a warm Sunday afternoon eight weeks after Geraldine's birth. St. Stan's Church on Grand Avenue was aglow with the happy faces of the Newkirk Boston contingent; the New York Conners beamed with pride. Even my young goddaughter behaved during the ceremony. Standing as godparents were my brother Calvin and my best friend Helena Fairlawn who was so stylishly attired that no one suspected that she was just beginning her eighth month of pregnancy. Of course once momma learned of Helena's condition she wouldn't even spare a look for my daughter's godmother.

Kevin played the part of the happy father so well that only I was privy to his real emotions. He had forewarned me that this very night I should expect to welcome him into my bedchamber so that he could beget a son on me. I tried to explain to him that I wasn't feeling physically ready yet but he quashed those objections with a simple answer: "Tonight, wife."

Kevin

Chapter 20

After the emotional upheaval of learning that Cordelia and I had failed to produce a male heir to carry on the Newkirk name, I was faced with the ordeal of The Christening. Now, late in the day and with extended family members dispersed to various parts of the estate, I finally found a few moments to myself.

Paul had finished his attentions to my needs and I now sat casually dressed, relaxing in a comfortable chair before the open window in my bedchamber. In the distance I could hear the late day movements from the stables. These underlying sounds were soothing to me. The low murmured voices of the stable hands as they settled the horses in their stalls, the far off sound of metal upon metal as the tack room was set to rights, the quiet nickering of the horses as they bid each other pleasant dreams. All of these were music to my ears. In the distance, still a good ways off, I detected the muted rumble of thunder that heralded a late day storm. I fervently wished that the air would be cleared of the heavy humidity that hung over all of Bridgewater that day.

On a butler's table nearby stood a Waterford crystal decanter filled with Bushmills 1608 Irish Whiskey, just recently imported from their brewery in County Antrim in Northern Ireland. I contemplated pouring myself a fingerful, possibly two, before nixing the idea altogether. I knew that the whiskey would take the edge off of my coupling with Cordelia in an effort to produce the much sought after male Newkirk heir but for some unfathomable reason I hesitated to imbibe.

I noticed the dark clouds in the western sky, rolling in from the Naugatuck Valley as they marched towards the town of Woodhaven. They would soon be right over Bridgewater. Downstairs I knew the staff would be scurrying around to close windows and secure the doors against the coming rain. The stable boys would be taking their positions amidst the stalls in an effort to keep our horses calm. I made a mental note to check with Huckleby after the storm passed.

I watched the storm clouds mingle with the approaching dusk. In the space of two short minutes the skies over Bridgewater became ominous, a dark gray-black punctuated by flashes of lightning. The sounds of thunder reverberated in a rolling serenade. I remember my grandmam telling me that the angels were playing football in heaven every time the thunder sounded. As wind gusts created a maelstrom in the branches of surrounding trees, I felt compelled to seek out Cordelia.

The upper hallway was deep in unnatural shadows as I opened the door to my chamber and stepped out. I crossed the distance between Cordelia's chamber and mine in a few swift steps. The sound of my knock on her door was muted by a passing roll of thunder.

"Cordelia, may I come in?" I shouted above the storm.

The door was pulled open almost immediately and I came face-to-face with Ellen, Cordy's maid.

"She's upstairs, Mr. Kevin, in the nursery." Ellen shouted above the noisy weather as she pointed to the upper floor.

I nodded my head in understanding, turned, and made my way upstairs where I was met with a sight that caused me to pause and linger quietly in the doorway of the nursery. Set back from the bank of windows, the maple rocking chair moved back and forth on its runners as Cordelia controlled its motion. She was holding our daughter in the crook of her arm, humming a lullaby to the infant. She was so absorbed in her task that she failed to notice me and I took these few moments to observe my family.

My family. I turned the phrase over in my mind several times and found that I liked the sound of it. Until this very moment we had, in my mind, retained our individual roles of husband, wife, child. Now these roles merged as I realized we were a family. I moved forward slowly until I stood just inside Cordy's line of vision. The banks of dark clouds beyond the windows chose that moment to let loose their watery burden; almost immediately I could feel the humidity lessen.

Cordy continued to rock Geraldine as the storm played out around us. When at last the rain abruptly stopped and the wind gusts abated, Cordy rose from the rocker and carried our daughter to the crib, gently laying the infant's head upon the monogrammed pillowslip. Already the baby's breathing had fallen into a calm sleep pattern.

"She looks like you," I ventured as I came to stand beside Cordy.

"Momma swears she's the image of great-aunt Geraldine," she replied, her voice slightly more than a whisper.

"She's beautiful," I murmured softly, placing my hands gently on Cordy's shoulders, "just like her mother." At that moment I truly meant what I said.

Cordelia turned to face me, an almost angelic smile playing around her lips. She looked straight into my eyes, searching for something but seemingly not finding it.

"I'll meet you in my chamber in fifteen minutes." Her voice once again had an edge to it. "Lotte is having her supper," she explained.

I pulled her close, tilted her chin up, and tenderly kissed her lips. Amazement set in when I realized that Cordy was returning my kiss. It dawned on me then that her yearnings had been pent up for far longer than my own.

"We're comfortable here. Why move?" I questioned.

"The baby?"

"When she's old enough we'll remind her that she was present when her brother was conceived." I kissed her smiling lips once more, noting the twinkle in her lovely eyes.

It was a leisurely event, our lovemaking, as I rediscovered my wife's many charms. Through it all Geraldine slept peacefully.

We adjourned to my bedchamber shortly afterwards and made love thrice more that night before we gave in to pure exhaustion. Paul's knock on the door the next morning woke me in time to cover Cordelia's nakedness before my valet entered. The look on his face upon seeing Cordy splayed across my naked body, covered only by a sheet, was priceless!

Lawson

Chapter 21

It was the morning after my daughter's christening. Correction, it was the morning after Geraldine Newkirk's christening. I had refrained from attending the church service to keep at bay any speculation of the baby's true identity, although just knowing that she was accepted into the extended Newkirk family made my heart swell with pride. With Delia for a mother, Geraldine would be enveloped in a world of love and motherly protection; with Kevin Newkirk as her father, she would be entitled to a world of privilege that I could not provide. That didn't mean that I wouldn't love or protect her to the best of my ability. In fact, I reasoned, Geraldine was far better off bearing the Newkirk surname.

I had turned my attention to the small pile of correspondence and invoices on my desk when I heard a slight swell in the voices of the kitchen staff. Listening intently I heard Paul's voice as he addressed Ellen, who was on her way upstairs to awaken her mistress.

"No need to rush upstairs, Ellen. I'm afraid your mistress is still abed," he intoned haughtily.

"And how would you be privy to that fact?" Ellen's voice held a bit of sass. "Did you enter Miss Cordelia's room by mistake?"

"There was no need for that. Mrs. Newkirk was sprawled across Mr. Newkirk's bed when I went in to awaken him."

"That's rich!" scoffed Ellen. "Those two haven't been civil to each other since their honeymoon. Them trying to be cute for our benefit just makes me laugh."

"Well, I saw it with my own two eyes!" continued Paul. "I knocked, then entered the room like I always do, expecting to see Mr. Newkirk wrapped around a pillow and snoring the way he does."

"Continue," urged Ellen.

"I stepped into the room to draw the drapes aside and that's when I saw it, er, her. Mrs. Newkirk. My eyes nearly popped right out of my head. There she was, lying face down, sprawled across Mr. Newkirk's body, as naked as a blue jay except for the sheet that the master had thrown over her."

"Well, they must be trying for another baby. I recall Mr. Newkirk as wanting a son. Seems he's not wasting any time getting the missus with child again," concurred Ellen.

The pair moved further into the kitchen to impart their gossip to whoever would listen. That fact was reinforced by Mrs. Grant exclaiming, "Good lord, I can't go through another nine months of lemon cookies!"

I sat perfectly still and looked out the window of my office. Where earlier I had heard the sounds of birds greeting the morning with their song, I now heard a dirge in their warbling; where earlier I had watched the sun rise with the promise of a beautiful day, I now noticed shadows creating pockets of darkness where there should have been light; where my heart had been full of love and hope, there now was a heaviness and a melancholy. Delia had spent the night in the arms of her husband, setting aside the despicable manner in which he had treated her for the past seven months. What if they had patched up their differences? Would she still welcome me into her bed?

My mind went blank. I could neither think about Delia nor could I stop thinking about her. What if Kevin had wooed Delia with promises of jewels or travel to exotic places? Those were certainly things that I couldn't afford. In comparison to Kevin's gifts my tokens of fresh flowers seemed lame and inconsequential. Acknowledging that this line of thought would only lead me to a deeper melancholy I mustered my strength and put thoughts of Delia out of my head. I delved into the matters before me that needed immediate attention and was soon quite busy. It was nigh onto lunch when I sensed a presence in my doorway. I looked up and there was Delia, looking like an angel attired in a day dress of sky blue, her hair fastened atop her head in a loose knot, her eyes dancing with a merriment that I hadn't seen in quite some time.

"Mrs. Newkirk, good morning," I addressed her formally.

"Good morning, Mr. Lawson. How are you this fine day?" she inquired as she breezily moved into my office and sat down on the visitor's chair.

"As you can see, I've been industriously working my way through this pile of invoices and correspondence." I kept my eyes downcast as I motioned to the pile of papers scattered across the desktop.

"Commendable indeed. You must have been quite busy for the past two days. Too busy to see your child christened?"

"Lower your voice! What if someone should hear?" I snapped my head up and looked into her beautiful eyes that seemed to sparkle with a life of their own.

"I'll thank you to keep a civil tone to your words, Mr. Lawson. I am still your employer." Her words were spoken in a stern tone that was underscored with a mischievous note. "In your capacity as Head Steward you could have come to the church with us as a representative of the household staff."

"Why create more gossip?" I ventured before looking away from those lush curves so poorly concealed by the fabric of Delia's day dress. I silently wondered if I would ever behold those curves in their natural state any longer.

"Gossip? What gossip? What has Ellen not told me?"

"Word has it that you were found in the master's bed, sprawled across him in a state of nudity. I've never known Paul to lie about something like that." I couldn't keep the anguish from my voice.

"For heaven's sake, Nathan, the man is my husband. I would think that entitles him to conjugal rights once in a while." She sighed audibly before continuing, "Kevin is in a rush to get me with child again, thinking that this time we'll have a son to carry on the Newkirk name. According to Dr. Bennett I have healed sufficiently to allow for normal relations, whatever that means."

"So you gave him what he wanted?" I was nursing a wounded ego.

"I'm sure Kevin will keep trying until I'm with child once more. Then I'll be free of his attentions." She sat back in the chair with her hands folded primly in her lap.

"Then you and he haven't reconciled? Paul and Ellen both seem to think that the rift between you and Kevin has been mended," I offered.

"Paul only sees what is on the surface. Ellen knows only what I allow her to know. I assure you that I endured Kevin's marathon of love-making in an effort to bolster his ego and provide him with the hope of a male heir sooner rather than later. Once he has his son, I will reject his advances totally."

I felt a heaviness that I hadn't known was there lift from my heart. My spirits soared!

"We shall have to be most circumspect in our meetings," she whispered. "I never know when Kevin will take it upon himself to enter my bedroom."

"Then we are to be separated. For how long?"

"Not as long as you think. I plan to visit your room sometime in the early hours of the morning, shortly after midnight. Will that be convenient?"

"Is that wise?"

"I'm the mistress of Bridgewater. Who is to say where I should or shouldn't be?"

"Then I will await your visit," I smiled at her. Everything seemed to be right in my world again knowing that Delia would soon be allaying my fears as only she could.

That night I completed my rounds of the house in a most expedient fashion. I'm sure I scared a few mice as they scampered through the quieter rooms. The guest rooms were almost full so I didn't give that wing much of a go-through. The same pertained to the kitchen. I knew full well the staff wing was quiet. I quickly returned to my room, closing the door behind me yet leaving it unlocked.

I turned on the bedside lamp for ambiance more than for actual light. A glance at the clock on my desk told me that it was ten minutes past midnight. Delia could arrive at any moment. My nerves began to take over. It had been quite a while since Delia and I were alone, since well before she had delivered Geraldine. In an effort to calm myself, I sat in the chair near the window. From that vantage point, I could see the outline of the gardens below. In the quiet that surrounded me, I could hear every creak of the house and every sound of the late summer insects. Allowing my mind to wander seemed prudent.

I thought back to a time, a mere three weeks previous, when I had found myself in dire need of female companionship. Leaving Bridgewater for a late afternoon and evening, I found myself in New Haven at a club near Long Wharf that was known for its better class of ladies of the evening. Having ordered a drink, I was soon approached by a woman of indeterminate age. She was wearing quite a bit of makeup and had her hair styled in a fashion that framed her face nicely. She was dressed to suit her station: tightly fitted dress with a plunging neckline that showed more of her ample charms than was proper for a lady. I'm sure she reasoned that her buyers would want to preview her merchandise, or at least part of it, before they would lay out their money.

"Hey handsome, what's a nice guy like you doin' in a place like this?" Her voice was low and sultry; she placed a hand on her hip and sort of posed, to be sure I noticed her décolletage.

"I'm simply looking for a pleasant diversion for the next few hours." I smiled at her.

"Care to buy a lady a drink?" she inquired.

I appraised the woman, most definitely a lady of the night: she had no odor about her, other than some cheap perfume; her eyes were clear and focused; her garments appeared clean and cared for, her shoes not worn at the heel. In all, she seemed like a safe bet. After all, a gentleman can't be too cautious!

"Does my lady have a preference for her drink?" I inquired, smiling my almost-best smile at her.

"Whatever you're having is fine with me?"

"Why don't you find us a quiet table while I get the refreshments?" I suggested.

She nodded her head in agreement and I watched her sashay towards the back of the room, stopping only once and turning slightly to be sure I was watching her movements. Satisfied that I wasn't going to run off and leave, she made a great show of sliding into a semi-secluded booth and crossing her legs to show them off.

Moments later I joined her, sliding into the booth beside her rather than across the table. The bartender followed close behind me, setting an ice bucket containing a bottle of champagne and two champagne glasses on the highly polished table.

"I hope you like champagne," I inquired watching a real smile work itself across her tired face.

"A real fancy-man, ain't ya'? I haven't had champagne in a month of Sundays."

"Then allow me to treat you." I nodded to the bartender who popped the cork, making sure that the noise was audible to everyone in the place. The woman beside me began to giggle.

"Ooooh, that's just delicious!"

The bartender retreated to his place behind the long mahogany bar. I passed a glass of the bubbly to her and held mine aloft.

"I should like to toast you, my lady, but I don't know your name. Enlighten me?"

She accepted the glass with both hands, afraid of dropping it.

"Lenore, my name is Lenore," she replied.

"My friends call me Nate. I'm pleased to make your acquaintance, Lenore."

This time her smile was deep and genuine. It appeared that some time had passed since Lenore had been treated like a lady.

"Here's to us, and getting to know each other better, Nate."

I held up my glass to clink with hers. She held her glass aloft with one hand while her other slid gently up my thigh, a sign that she was more than interested in getting to know me. We consumed that bottle in record time as we negotiated – I as the buyer and she as the seller of her wares. When an agreement was reached, I paid for another bottle of champagne and followed her up the stairs to a private apartment.

Ah! The mere memory of the time I spent with Lenore that day, revisiting each and every way in which she gave me pleasure, had worked me up into quite a state. I was more than ready for Delia's late night visit. A glance at the clock told me that I would have to live off of those memories for at least a while longer. I couldn't believe that it was after two in the morning. I reached over and turned out the light. Once more I played out the memories of my sojourn with Lenore, this time allowing myself to become so immersed in them that I no longer cared if Delia found her way to my room.

———

The next morning found me supervising the delivery of Mr. Newkirk's latest purchase of wines. It was my responsibility to catalog each bottle, noting its vintage year and special characteristics, and assign it a numbered spot in the wine cellar where it would age further or be designated as ready for consumption. Mr. Newkirk joined me about half way through the task, more to talk man-to-man than to supervise my work.

"I'm afraid I've gone a bit overboard in my wine purchase this season, Lawson."

"Not a problem, sir. We've more than ample space to accommodate this delivery."

"Didn't want to be caught short during the upcoming holiday season." Mr. Newkirk picked up a bottle and pretended to study the label, turning it over in his hands. I went about my business as I kept a watchful eye on his movements.

"Lawson, have you ever been in love?" The question was put forth in such a calm and serious manner that I was taken aback.

"Why, yes, Mr. Newkirk. I have had the privilege of loving someone," I responded.

"What kept you from marrying the girl? I hope you don't mind my asking."

"She loved another. Or so it appeared." I diverted my attention to the case of wine bottles before me.

"Ah, unrequited love." Mr. Newkirk nodded his head in understanding. "May I confide in you, Lawson?"

"As you wish, sir."

"I'm in love, Lawson."

"One would expect to love their spouse, sir, is that not so?" I was trying to remain objective and see where this conversation was leading.

"The problem is I'm in love with someone other than Mrs. Newkirk."

I held my breath for what seemed to be an eternity before he continued.

"Oh, Mrs. Newkirk is pretty enough, and comes from good breeding. She has been faithful to me, of that I'm sure."

"Pardon my saying this, sir, but what could the problem be?"

"I was in love with this other woman long before I was expected to marry a woman of acceptable family and produce an heir."

"And this other woman, she isn't socially acceptable?"

"She's an orphan, you see. We have no way of knowing who her family was," he explained.

"But you love her nonetheless?"

"Exactly!" He picked up another wine bottle and examined it closely as well. "In an effort to thwart my parents I chose Cordelia, er, Mrs. Newkirk. Sort of flung convention in their faces, you know. But now I fear that I've hurt Mrs. Newkirk."

I drew in an audible breath as he continued.

"She knows I don't love her, even though I pretend to in public. And yet she allows me into her boudoir so that she can give me the son I so desperately need, as she did last night when I knocked on her door unannounced."

Aha! So that was why Delia never arrived in the staff's quarters. Foolish me for thinking her anything but cautious. My heart began to soar even as Mr. Newkirk's thoughts were laid before me in words.

"What shall I do, Lawson? I don't wish to hurt Mrs. Newkirk unduly."

"Well, sir, I should expect that you and Mrs. Newkirk will carry on as you do at present until a son is born. Then you can choose to release her from her vows or ask that she turn a blind eye to your pursuit of true love."

"Well said, Lawson. I couldn't have put it better myself. I knew another man would understand." He clapped a hand on my back in pseudo-camaraderie. "Carry on, Lawson. Sorry to have bothered you." He turned and climbed the stairs from the wine-cellar, leaving me alone with the cases of wine in disarray around my feet.

I pulled up an empty case and sat down upon it, reflecting upon what had just transpired. Mr. Newkirk was truly in love with someone else. Delia had been right about his manipulating her into a loveless marriage. Never again would I question Delia's love or concern for me. Perhaps we could arrange another meeting, if not tonight then soon. My mood had lightened considerably and I found myself actually humming a tune as I returned to the task at hand.

Events conspired to keep Delia and me apart. Geraldine was proving to be a bit more of a problem than any of us had anticipated. At first she was colicky; then there was an ear infection. She also had a problem with digesting her food. For the next month it seemed like we saw more of Dr. Bennett than we had in the six months previous. While

Lotte was extremely helpful, taking the night shift to sit in the nursery, Delia devoted much of her days to caring for our daughter. Most of her household supervisory tasks were shifted onto my shoulders. I was more than happy to share her burden.

Delia's nights were spent alternately between lying beneath Kevin in an effort to provide him a son or in sleeping from total exhaustion. I watched the rosiness in her cheeks vanish. The twinkle in her eyes was replaced by dark shadows. Her vivacity was replaced by an air of lethargy. I watched as she moved from task to task with none of her old joie de vivre.

At last Geraldine was pronounced clear of all current ailments. Delia spent several days confined to her boudoir. Ellen brought her meals and returned with half empty trays. I began to worry, as did the rest of the senior staff, that Delia wasn't eating properly. Each day I made a point of adding a fresh blossom or two to the meal trays, ostensibly to heighten her spirits but also to silently reaffirm my love and concern for her.

It was a brisk, late October day when Delia appeared on the threshold of my office, attired as though she was going for a walk in the park. She looked pale but I felt a short sojourn in the crisp air would bring the color back to her cheeks.

"Mr. Lawson, may I have a moment of your time?"

"Certainly, Mrs. Newkirk. Please sit down." I motioned to the chair before my desk.

"I would prefer if you could accompany me on a short walk to Willow Cottage. I have Geraldine tucked into her stroller and thought the fresh air would do us both some good. Mr. Newkirk is meeting with one of his vendors for stable supplies and I don't care to wait for him."

"It would be an honor, ma'am."

I reached for my jacket and donned it with lightning speed.

Once outdoors, Delia maneuvered the stroller holding our daughter deftly over the path from the rear terrace. Instead of going all the way to Willow Cottage she suddenly veered right, into the maze of boxwood hedges.

"Delia, where are you going?" I kept my voice low on the chance that one of the gardeners was working nearby.

She kept silent and it was all I could do to keep up with her. A moment of caution as I looked around and she was gone from sight. I hurried along the path and at last I caught up to her. There she stood, in the middle of the maze, hands on the baby's stroller, smiling at me in a most mischievous manner. The mere sight of her, head tilted back, straight posture accentuating her figure, caused my senses to quicken. I hurried to her side, pulled her into my arms and kissed her soundly as her arms entwined around my neck. Her kiss tasted like a sweet decadent fruit. It felt so right to hold her.

"Delia," I whispered into her ear, "I've missed you so."

"Don't talk. Kiss me," she instructed, offering her mouth to me again. One kiss led to another and yet another. Before long we were panting with want.

"I must have you, Delia. Soon."

"Or?" she laughed against my lips.

"Or I shall be forced to seek solace elsewhere," I teased.

"One of the maids, perhaps?" her finger traced the outline of my mouth before she set her lips to mine again.

"Never. I would never lie with one of the maids." I nipped her lips with my teeth. She snuggled even deeper into my embrace.

"I have news," she uttered.

"I don't care about news. I want to lie with you again."

"And you shall, my darling, but I want to share my good news with you. I'm with child."

The statement hit me like a lightning bolt.

"What? What did you say?"

"I am carrying Kevin's child. Now shut up and kiss me."

I obliged.

"Am I supposed to be happy with that news?"

"Of course! Now that I'm with child, and it has been confirmed by Dr. Bennett, Kevin will no longer be knocking on my door, unannounced, at all hours of the night."

"Of course," I replied.

"We are free to resume our lovemaking," she pointed out.

"And what of our daughter? Won't you be needed in the nursery?"

"It seems as though most of her health problems are behind her. Lotte can watch over her at night until we find a full time nurse or nanny for her and the new child."

I leaned in and kissed her soundly once more, sweeping her off her feet and twirling her around until we were both dizzy and laughing.

"Will you come to me tonight?" Delia inquired.

"Wild horses couldn't keep me away," I responded.

Through it all Geraldine slept soundly. Delia and I made arrangements to meet later that night before we pushed the stroller and our sleeping daughter back towards the main house. How wonderful life would have been if only Delia was my legal wife! But I could pretend, if that was the hand that life dealt to me. At the terrace, Delia moved swiftly to enter the house with Geraldine. I walked around to the kitchen entrance only to be greeted by Mrs. Grant.

"Don't you look all breathless, Mr. Lawson. Has the wind picked up a bit?"

"It is rather brisk, Mrs. Grant, but I feel quite renewed by my short excursion." I sailed past the woman and into my office where I attacked the paperwork on my desk with renewed vigor.

Cordelia

Chapter 22

Yes, I was indeed with child once more. This time was different, however. After a week of mild morning sickness, I was troubled by that malaise no more. I was fortunate that my condition was not yet too prominent and that I could enjoy the Christmas holidays in Boston that year as my sister-in-law Bernice hosted the round of family functions. We were staying in the Newkirk family residence on Revere Street once again. While I shared a suite with Kevin, I didn't mind the proximity of my husband as I fell into a deep sleep each and every night long before he retired.

With this pregnancy I felt more tired than when I had carried Geraldine. I found myself nodding off earlier in the afternoons. Ellen needed a more determined effort to rouse me from those naps in time to join the family for supper and evening entertainments. Thankfully, the style of dress that I had adopted with my first pregnancy had gained popularity as women everywhere embraced the shapeless silhouette of the new fashions. It thus became quite easy to dress for dinner and the long evenings.

I had chosen to leave Geraldine at home at Bridgewater. She had caught a cold and both Dr. Bennett and I deemed it prudent to not subject her to the frigid December air for the trip to Boston. We had recently hired a new nurse for the baby; and with Lotte to assist as well as Geraldine's biological father in residence, I felt confident that nothing could go wrong.

Once again it was Christmas Eve. Honoring the tried and true Newkirk tradition, Kevin and his father were spending time 'tending to business' in the arms of their respective mistresses. The house was quiet: Mother Newkirk was tucked away in her room, claiming to have a headache; another couple, friends of my in-laws, was occupied elsewhere in the house; I had taken a book from the library up to our room and had made myself comfortable, propped up in bed by several pillows with the book before me. No sooner had I begun to read when I had a very intense craving, for olives. Now why this should be so, I couldn't fathom. I had anticipated craving something sweet as I did during my first pregnancy thus I was caught off guard when the craving for olives accosted me.

Weighing my options, trekking down to the kitchen versus staying where I was and reading my book, I opted to stay put. Thus I relegated the craving to the back of my mind and concentrated on reading. But concentrating was not something easily accomplished. I read a sentence or two and found that I needed to re-read them in order to move on. This craving was proving to be stronger than me so I caved in: setting aside the book, I threw on my robe, slipped my feet into a pair of slippers, and set off to find some olives.

The lights in the hallway had been dimmed, leaving just enough illumination for someone such as myself to navigate without accident. On the first floor, another table lamp illuminated the passage towards the kitchen. I pushed through the doorway and into the kitchen, surprised to see that two of the kitchen helpers were still working. They turned towards me in surprise.

"Good evening, ma'am," the one with her hands in soapy water addressed me.

"Good evening," I replied, knowing that talk of my late night foray into the kitchen would eventually reach Mother Newkirk's ears. "Could either of you help me locate something?"

The two young ladies looked at each other, communicating silently, before the one whose arms weren't immersed in water wiped her hands on a kitchen towel and walked towards me.

"I'll do what I can," she volunteered.

"I must admit that I'm having a fierce craving for some olives. Would there happen to be any just lying about?" I hated having to explain myself and would rather have gone in search of these things myself, but I didn't want either of these young ladies to be blamed for taking something from the larder.

"We have some black olives in the pantry. Shall I fetch you a few?"

"If you'll just show me where they're kept, I can help myself."

"Oh, ma'am, we'd be scolded if we didn't serve you. Wouldn't we, Becky?" she asked the one who was currently washing pans at the double sink.

"True enough," muttered the dish-washer.

I watched as the first young lady disappeared into the pantry. Moments later she emerged carrying a large crock that she set down on a table. She went off in search of a small dish but I could wait no longer. I lifted the crock's lid, plucked a juicy black olive out of the brine, and popped it into my mouth. Ah! At last my taste buds were satisfied.

"Here we go, let me just fix you up a few on this dish."

I watched her dip into the crock with a slotted spoon and place several olives on the small dish. Thinking she was done, she made to replace the crock's lid. I stayed her hand, taking the spoon from her and dipping it into the brine once more. Bringing up another serving of the olives I added them to the dish and returned the spoon to her.

"I think this will do nicely." I smiled at her. "I appreciate your assistance."

"You're quite welcome," she answered and curtsied.

"Good heavens, no need to stand on formality. Now, I'll just take these with me and enjoy them at my leisure."

Grabbing the dish, I turned and made my way through the shadowy halls, where I popped several of the tiny fruits into my mouth at the same time. Fortunately these olives had already been pitted and I enjoyed each bite to the fullest. By the time I regained the upper hallway, the dish was empty.

Just at that moment I heard female laughter from behind one of the bedroom doors. The laughter was answered by a definitely male voice that sounded vaguely familiar. Ah, it was the voice of Mr. Conrad, Mother Newkirk's guest. He and his wife were obviously laughing over a private joke.

I moved to continue my journey before stopping dead in my tracks. That wasn't a guest room I had passed. That was Mother Newkirk's suite. And the male voice was definitely coming from behind that door. I moved closer and pressed my ear to the door.

"Fannie, you get more beautiful every time I see you," the man remarked.

"You're only saying that because it's true," admonished my mother-in-law in a teasing voice.

"Now come here and let me love you once more," he instructed. I could imagine him pulling Mother Newkirk into his embrace.

"Oh, James! Kiss me again. Never stop kissing me," she replied.

I heard the sound of lips sharing a passionate kiss.

"You have the most remarkable breasts, Fannie. They are still as pert and perky as the first time I saw them as a stripling lad."

"Yes, James, you know exactly how to touch them."

I had heard enough. I backed away and continued on to my room, a smirk turning up the corners of my mouth. I was so happy that Mother Newkirk had played my father-in-law's game and had taken a lover of her own. She deserved all the happiness she could get.

As I slid beneath the bedcovers, I wished that I was sliding beneath the naked body of my own lover. But he was in Connecticut, watching over our daughter, while I was here in Boston. Silently I sent my love to him and hoped that he was thinking of me. I closed my eyes with hopes that we would meet in my dreams that very night.

The remainder of the Christmas holiday passed in the usual manner. There was the church service to attend; gifts to open; meals to eat; visits to be made; and gossip to be shared. Once again Kevin gifted me with shares in the family business. This time I gratefully tucked the certificate into my jewelry box until we returned home.

We stayed on in Boston well after New Year's Day. I didn't like being away from home so long but my wishes remained secondary to Kevin's. There was nothing for it but to accompany Mother Newkirk on her rounds of visits and receive her guests alongside her. The only saving grace was that I could beg off of events I didn't truly wish to partake by saying that I felt drowsy. Mother Newkirk insisted in those instances that I retire to our suite and rest, something I was happy to do.

When at last we returned to Bridgewater it was well into January of 1910. The snow had piled up in drifts along the endless driveway. It was only with concentrated effort that Stan was able to keep the car from sliding into those drifts. He was constantly apologizing for each and every rut the tires encountered. Eventually, Kevin voiced his displeasure.

"Must you hit every hole in the driveway?"

"I'm sorry sir, but the condition of the driveway under the ice and snow is full of furrows and ruts."

"Go slower then."

"Yes, sir."

Stan slowed down even further. The tires then turned so slowly that they literally slid along the ice-encrusted drive. We had progressed about two car-lengths when at last we skidded right into a snow drift.

"I'm awfully sorry, sir, ma'am, but there's not much I could do. Never seen the road this bad." Stan shook his head as he got out of the car.

We watched as he walked around and assessed the situation. He stuck his head back in through a window.

"Looks like we're stuck, sir."

"Good God, man, any fool can see that!" Kevin's voice rose with his displeasure. I placed a gloved hand on his arm in an effort to calm him. He took a deep breath and continued. "Hand me the rug from the front seat. We'll wait here while you walk up to the stables. Get back here with a carriage as quickly as you can."

Kevin proceeded to place the additional rug around my feet. We watched as Stan turned up the collar of his coat and pulled his hat down over his ears before jamming his hands in his coat pockets. The ice appeared to be about an inch thick and Stan lost his footing a couple of times before moving to walk along the side of the driveway, part way into the snow drift.

We sat in comfortable silence for a short while, discussing the events of the recent holiday season and how nice it would be for us when we finally could appreciate the comforts of our own home. As we waited for assistance, Kevin noted the lengthening of the late afternoon shadows. He consulted his pocket watch for the time, trying not to be too obvious about it.

"I'm sure Mr. Huckleby will send the best of the work horses with the wagon. Although I'm also sure that they will need to proceed slowly to forestall any undue harm to the animals," I commented.

"Damnation! They should have been here by now. They've had almost an hour to come for us."

"Actually it's quite cozy here, although I must admit that I'm having a powerful craving for black olives," I replied, seeking to turn Kevin's thoughts from the laid-back response from the stables.

"Olives, eh? Not lemon cookies?" he raised a quizzical eyebrow as a slow smile graced his mouth.

"They say each pregnancy is different. I was as surprised by the olive craving as you are."

"I'll instruct Lawson to put in a goodly supply of the best black olives money can buy. If that's what it takes to keep you and our son healthy and happy, it's a small price to pay." He literally beamed at me when he mentioned our son. For all our sakes I hoped he was right.

"Oh, look! Here comes our rescue team."

I pointed straight ahead to where a team of two horses pulled a sleigh across the snow. And there in the driver's seat was Mr. Huckleby himself. One of the stable boys, Denny, was perched in the sleigh atop a mountain of rugs and throws. Huckleby reined in the horses and brought the entire affair to a stop a few feet in front of the car. Denny jumped out of the sleigh and carried two of the larger throws with him as he approached the car.

In short order, we were installed in the sleigh and covered by the rugs and fur throws, some smelling distinctly of horse. As we approached the front entry to Bridgewater we were met by a small army of household staff. Ellen ran forward to assist me but was gently pushed aside by Nathan who handed me up the steps. It was easy for me to see the concern in his eyes but there was no time to calm his anxiety. Once I was safely indoors and divested of my outerwear, Kevin took himself off to the stables with Huckleby et al to see about retrieving our luggage.

"Joan, I should like a pot of tea brought to the nursery immediately. And perhaps a light supper should be ready when Mr. Newkirk returns to the house. And send Mr. Lawson to me after our luggage arrives. I'll be expecting an update on the house. Ask Ellen to bring a change of clothing for me to the nursery as I plan to spend some time with my daughter."

"Yes, Mrs. Newkirk," Joan answered and went off to tend to my requests.

I stood for a moment at the base of the curved stairway, feeling the warmth creep into my extremities. I rubbed my hands together as I mounted the steps; I was beginning to feel weary but I needed to see and hold my daughter. Just when I felt I couldn't make it to the top step, a strong hand reached down to assist me. I placed my hand in Nathan's, smiling up at him as I did so.

"I've been worried about you," he whispered.

"I was never in any danger. Kevin was with me."

"That's exactly what I was afraid of." His smile relaxed me and made me feel slightly better. "Your fingers are as frigid as an ice covered pond." His hand closed over mine and I could feel his warmth spreading into my chilled fingers.

"How is Geraldine?"

"Lotte can fill you in on the details but it appears as though the child has shaken the sniffles that plagued her."

Nathan accompanied me to the nursery but stopped himself from entering. He promised to come to me later with a full report of the household.

"Oh, Mrs. Newkirk!" exclaimed Lotte, "it's so nice to have you home again. Just wait until you see Geraldine. I swear she's grown a full inch since you've seen her."

I moved to the crib where Geraldine was sleeping peacefully. Her eyes were closed and it was easy to see the curl of her eyelashes against her delicate skin. Her breathing seemed regular but her cheeks appeared flushed. I placed a hand on her forehead and was stunned to feel heat emanating through her skin.

"Lotte, call the nurse in here immediately."

"Yes, ma'am." She scurried off to find the woman.

I paced the floor beside the crib, keeping a watchful eye on my daughter. After what seemed an eternity, the nurse appeared pulling Lotte behind her.

"You asked to see me, ma'am."

"Yes. Can you explain why my daughter's skin is hot to the touch?"

"You must be mistaken, Mrs. Newkirk. There's nothing wrong with the child." She turned to the crib and placed a hand on the baby's cheek. "She's resting peacefully. Perhaps she feels warm because of the number of blankets that cover her. Girl, take two blankets off the child." Her instructions towards Lotte were more barked than spoken.

Lotte rushed forward to remove the blankets as instructed. I noticed that her expression looked pinched, as though she were biting her tongue to keep from speaking.

"Thank you, Lotte," I addressed the Nursery Maid. "Would you please go to the kitchen and see what's holding up my pot of tea? When it's ready please bring it to my bedroom and wait for me there."

Lotte looked at me and I could see tears forming in her eyes. She ran from the room to do my bidding.

"That girl," began the nurse, "doesn't know how to respect authority, if you'll pardon my saying so, ma'am."

"Please continue," I requested.

"She questions every instruction I give her and asks me to explain why I want something done. Why, she's only a child. She knows nothing of babies and their health."

"If I recall, Nurse Booker, you came with high recommendation on Dr. Bennett's part."

"That's correct, ma'am," she seemed to preen when I mentioned her qualifications.

"Do you have any children of your own, Nurse Booker?" I inquired.

"That's highly unlikely, ma'am. I'm not married."

"And is not an unmarried woman also likely to be a mother?"

"Not amongst the gentry, ma'am," she pointed out.

"And do you only nurse the gentry, Nurse Booker?"

"I serve where I'm needed," was the haughty response.

"I see." I walked back towards the crib and felt my daughter's skin again. This time there was no question that she was flushed. Her skin was hot to my touch. "Nurse Booker, I suggest that you pack your things and leave Bridgewater immediately. We are no longer in need of your services."

"May I remind madam that I'm here, on a contract, for six months?" Nurse Booker raised her eyebrows in defiance.

"I will remind you, Nurse Booker, that I am mistress of Bridgewater. Your contract will be paid in full. Mr. Lawson will give you a draft for the funds."

"I've never been dismissed before. I shall expect a recommendation from you." The nurse persisted in annoying me.

"There will be no recommendation from me or anyone else in this household. You have until tomorrow noon to leave the premises. We will provide you with transportation into town."

Nurse Booker turned and stormed out of the nursery, slamming the door to her adjoining room as she left. I scooped Geraldine out of her crib and enfolded her into the blanket. She stirred in her sleep but didn't awaken as I navigated the stairway from the nursery to my bedroom below. Sliding back the panel I saw that Lotte was entering from the hallway with the requested tea service in her hands. She stopped in her tracks when she saw me emerge from the concealed panel doorway.

"Mrs. Newkirk, how did you get here?"

The look of perplexity on her youthful face chased away her fear of being reprimanded.

"Lotte, put the tea service on the table," I directed, afraid that she would drop the tray.

She did as I asked before trying to speak up in her own defense.

"I'd like to explain, Mrs. Newkirk," she began.

"Sssh. Let's leave explanations for later. Right now we need to bring down Geraldine's fever."

"As you wish, Mrs. Newkirk."

"I'll need your help, Lotte. Fill the sink with lukewarm water, only about an inch or two of water will do. Then gather two large towels and a soft sponge."

She ran to carry out my instructions while I tried desperately to remember how momma had brought down my fever when I was a child. All I could remember were cool cloths being applied to my body. Lotte returned to my side.

"May I make a suggestion, Mrs. Newkirk?"

"Of course, Lotte."

"I know of a brew that my aunt sometimes uses on feverish babies. I can show Mrs. Grant how to prepare it," she offered.

"Tell me about this brew." I removed Geraldine's shirt and carried her to the sink.

"We'll need raisins and some ginger."

"I believe we have some of those in the pantry."

"We'll need equal parts of both. They must be boiled in a quart of water until only about one fourth of the liquid remains. You'll need to have Geraldine drink it when it is still a bit warm. Tante Anja says it works every time."

I considered this concoction for a few moments. Dr. Bennett certainly couldn't arrive in the next hour or so and this brew seemed innocuous enough.

"I'll bathe Geraldine. You go to the kitchen and find Mr. Lawson. Tell him exactly what you just told me and add that you are to bring the solution to me immediately when it is ready. Is that clear?"

"Yes, Mrs. Newkirk." Lotte left the room and I could hear her hurried footsteps in the hallway as she made her way to the kitchen.

Geraldine, who by now had awakened, began to whimper. I held her close and felt the heat pouring off of her little body. The moment her toes dipped into the tepid water, her whimpering ceased. I placed her in a sitting position and supported her with one hand while with the other I dipped the sponge into the water and squeezed it tightly before applying it in small circular motions across her back and chest. Within moments her whimpers turned to gurgles and she looked up at me and smiled. Again I repeated my motions with the sponge trying to keep from getting wet as Geraldine now decided it might be fun to splash the water with her tiny hands. Obviously, the cool water and her lack of clothing made her feel better.

I stopped sponging her for a moment while I tried to tuck back a loose strand of my hair. That was when she slapped the water and I was treated to a mini-bath. Geraldine began to giggle at my distress.

"My girls seem to be having a good time."

I jumped at the sound of Kevin's voice near my shoulder.

"Goodness, you've startled me!"

"Your door was slightly ajar. I figured it was safe to come in. Can a father get in on what looks like a fun game?"

"Perhaps you'll think differently when I explain exactly what is going on."

"Do tell." Kevin settled on my chaise longue and waited for my explanation.

"Nurse Booker tried to tell me that Geraldine was not afflicted with a high fever but only too many bedclothes. She was rude and impertinent. Furthermore, she treated Lotte with utter contempt."

"Lotte? She's the young Nursery Maid, isn't she?"

"Yes, she is quite knowledgeable about babies for one so young. Her aunt is a midwife and Lotte has assisted her."

"And what of this nurse? I hope you've sacked her!"

"On the spot. Told her to pack her things and be off the premises by noon tomorrow. I told her we'd pay her full contract and provide transportation into town but she would not be receiving a recommendation. Is that satisfactory?"

"Will Lawson be writing her check?"

"I believe so." I wrapped Geraldine in a clean, thick towel and dried her gently.

"I'll get with Lawson. I'd like to speak to the nurse myself before she receives her wages. I refuse to have any child of mine treated so ignominiously."

"Thank you." I felt Geraldine's cheeks again and while the fever seemed to have been brought down slightly it lingered still.

"Here, give the child to me." Kevin held out his arms.

I gingerly handed Geraldine to him, showing him how to best hold her. Once he had her in a firm hold, I stepped away to repair the water damage to my coiffure. In the mirror I watched as Geraldine took hold of a button on Kevin's jacket and tried to turn it much as one would turn a doorknob. It was nice to see them together.

"Cordy, why does she seem to feel hot again?" Kevin asked.

I placed my hand on the baby's shoulder and one touch confirmed that the fever had not abated. Geraldine quieted as the heat within her rose. In less than a minute she began to whimper once more.

"Have you sent for Dr. Bennett?" my husband inquired.

"Yes, I've asked Mr. Lawson to summon the doctor. He should be here shortly."

A tremulous knock at my bedroom door preceded Lotte's return. In her other hand she held one of Geraldine's bottles. This she handed to me.

"How much should she take, Lotte?"

"As much as she will without putting up a fuss, but at least half of what's in the bottle?"

Kevin stood up and handed the baby to me. With Geraldine in my arms I took Kevin's place on the chaise and offered the bottle to her. She began to whimper even louder and pushed the bottle away.

"I thought she might be a bit fussy," offered Lotte, "so I brought a teaspoon of sugar as well."

"How does the sugar bring down the fever?" inquired Kevin.

"Oh, the sugar has nothing to do with bringing down the fever," replied Lotte. "I'll show you."

She took the bottle from my hand, moistened the nipple and coated it lightly with the sugar.

"Try it now," she urged.

Sure enough, Geraldine willingly took the bottle and began sucking noisily. In no time at all she had taken in about a quarter of the bottle's contents.

"Young woman, you're an angel!" boomed Kevin. "Dr. Bennett himself couldn't do better. I'll speak to Mr. Lawson and see that there's a bonus in your pay envelope this month."

"That's not necessary, sir," protested Lotte.

"Tish-tosh! Don't argue with the master, little one. What I say goes!"

We watched as he strode towards the door. He turned back just before exiting the room.

"What a lovely sight – a mother and her child! Carry on!!"

Then he was gone from the room and from caring about Geraldine once again.

By the time Dr. Bennett arrived, Geraldine was dressed in a clean sleep shirt, tucked back under a light crib sheet, and seemed to be sleeping peacefully. The doctor examined her, proclaimed that her temperature was almost normal, and inquired after the treatment we had used. I explained the brew that Lotte had made up and Dr. Bennett gave his approval once he had seen how the child's fever had been broken.

Leaving Geraldine in Lotte's care, I accompanied Dr. Bennett downstairs where he met with Kevin who informed him of Nurse Booker's unprofessional demeanor. The doctor was flummoxed to learn of her actions and vowed not to recommend another nurse without having worked with her personally.

A last visit to the nursery to set my mind at ease and I looked forward to finally resting. Satisfied that all was well, I bid Lotte a good night.

"Mrs. Newkirk?"

"Yes, Lotte," I hoped she didn't want to express her gratitude for the bonus to me again.

"How did you get down to your room earlier? So quickly I mean?"

Only the young can be so forthright with a question.

"I'll let you in on a secret. Come here."

Together we moved to the far end of the room, to a place next to the washroom where the wall was paneled. I placed my hand in just the right spot and the panel slid silently to the side, allowing an opening large enough for a person to slip through.

"When the house was built, I asked for a direct stairway from my room, just below us, to the nursery. I wanted it concealed from view as it was to be used by me and me alone. Now you are privy to the secret. You must tell no one, do you understand? And you are not to use this passageway unless it is a matter of life or death."

"Of course, ma'am, I'll do as you ask. I'll tell no one of this stairway."

"I know that I can trust you, Lotte. You've already earned that trust more than once."

"Thank you, ma'am." Lotte dipped a slight curtsy.

"Since the door is already opened, and since I'm extremely tired, I shall use the passageway. Close it up after me."

I navigated my way down the stairs and once I had the door opened to my room, I gave Lotte a small wave and she reclosed the upstairs door. Back in my room, I kicked off my shoes, and gently stretched out on the bed. In less than a heartbeat, I gave in to the exhaustion of a busy day and slipped into a deep sleep.

Lawson

Chapter 23

I t was well after midnight when I finished making the rounds of the house. Everything was quiet and as it should be. I was restless and knew that sleep would elude me so I returned to my office. A few minutes of shuffling papers proved not to be the distraction I had hoped for. I had, of course, summoned Dr. Bennett immediately when young Lotte had come bursting into my office earlier and explained the situation. Even knowing that Geraldine was being cared for I experienced an anxiety-laden hour.

A short time later, Lotte had returned with additional directions for preparing an old mid-wife's remedy for reducing fever in a child. Once she had explained to Mrs. Grant what was needed, Lotte could be heard telling of how Mrs. Newkirk had put Nurse Booker in her place. I knew enough about Nurse Booker to know that she would never measure up to the requirements that my darling Delia expected. Had I known, however, of her mistreatment of Lotte, the nurse would not have lasted a day in our employ.

Things worked out for the best, however. Nurse Booker had been discharged and would be leaving on the morrow. Geraldine's fever had come down enough so that Dr. Bennett felt sure she would be better by morning. The diagnosis of the fever's cause: it seemed that Geraldine was cutting her first tooth and it wasn't breaking through quickly enough. The doctor had left a liquid medicine to be given to the child should she be in pain.

For now, Lotte had returned to the nursery with Geraldine. Delia had returned to her room and hopefully was recovering from her harrowing day. The crisis had passed.

As I sat there, idly toying with a pen, I was overcome by a powerful urge to go to Delia. I needed to ascertain for myself that she was not too stressed over the day's events. Oh, who was I kidding? I needed to see Delia and hold her in my arms. I needed to express my love to her and remind her that she could always count on my support.

Turning off the lamp on my desk, I stood and left the office, being careful to lock its door behind me. Tonight there were no late stragglers about the kitchen, no one coming in from the staff wing to have a glass of milk to ease them into sleep. For once I felt no need to double check that I was alone before I opened the door to Delia's office, slipped in, and closed it behind me. I made sure the lock was turned from within the office. I strode deftly to the movable panel, stepped into the passageway and climbed the stairs to where my love hopefully was waiting for me.

At the top of the stairs I slid the panel open and stepped through into Delia's washroom. I was greeted by a dark room and silence. Was it possible that Delia had gone upstairs to the nursery? I moved closer to her bed and spotted the silhouette of her outstretched body. She was still wearing her day clothes. With the excitement of arriving home and the near-crisis of Geraldine's fever averted, she must have been exhausted. That certainly wasn't good for the baby she was carrying.

I moved forward in the darkness, pulling a quilt from the quilt rack as I did so. I stretched the coverlet across the bed and pulled it over Delia. Rethinking my plan to leave, I removed my jacket and slipped out of my shoes. I gently eased myself onto the bed next to Delia. She shifted slightly as my weight settled. My head eased down into the pillow. At last I felt at ease.

I must have drifted off to sleep at some point but my internal clock roused me as pre-dawn light crept over the horizon. Delia was still asleep as I slipped back into my shoes and pulled on my jacket.

Retracing my steps of the previous night, I double checked the hallway outside of Delia's office before exiting into the kitchen. Satisfied that my actions had gone unnoticed I made my way to the staff wing to change my clothing and freshen up. My heart felt lighter than it had yesterday. Everything seemed right with the world once more. I bounded up the stairway from the kitchen to the second floor rooms unaware that in the shadows of the pantry lurked the newest addition to our staff, Jadwiga.

———

As the winter months progressed, Bridgewater played host to a creative arts salon hosted by Delia at least once every two weeks. Her favorite playwright was a staple at these affairs. Other guests included budding thespians, poets, sculptors, painters and the like. These salons lasted for days with all of the artists seeming to draw inspiration from Delia. And she, bless her heart, basked in the glow of their adoration.

Throughout this time I was dealing with a threat that I kept to myself. About two weeks after the health crisis with Geraldine, I was in my office writing a check to cover the invoice from the local dairy. I inexplicably felt as though I was being watched. Looking up from the task at hand, I saw Jadwiga standing just outside my office. She appeared to be watching me. As I was about to inquire what she needed, she smiled in an almost seductive manner and moved away. It was a curious occurrence to be sure but I gave it no further thought at the time.

That evening, I noticed that Jadwiga seemed to linger a moment or two after the others retired for the night. There was nothing untoward in her actions. In fact, she rather pleasantly wished me a good night before making her way upstairs.

In the ensuing days it seemed that Jadwiga's presence was more evident. Although she was a parlor maid she seemed to surface in places where she knew I would be. For example, there was the Tuesday delivery of staple goods for the kitchen that arrived at the same time each week. I made it a point of being present when the deliveryman brought in the goods so that I could check the items against the order. For some strange reason, Jadwiga chose this time to empty the ash buckets. She was not obtrusive but merely smiled and nodded and went about her duties.

When the staff sat down to have their meals, I noticed that Jadwiga would choose either to sit directly across from me or, when space was available, to sit beside me. At first I gave no thought to the girl's actions. But when this consistently happened I think I took note on some unconscious level.

During the next month or so I put all thoughts of Jadwiga out of my mind. Delia had increased the frequency of her salons. We now were entertaining all sorts of artists and patrons of the arts, not just for an afternoon of discussion and dinner but sometimes for days on end. With her growing girth, Delia felt more at ease entertaining here at Bridgewater. Sometimes, when drowsiness overcame her, she would quietly slip away to her room leaving the guests to amuse themselves.

On occasion Mr. Newkirk would join the group but he more often than not kept to his study or the stables; he did join the others for meals however. During those times he was often regaled, by the poets especially, with a spontaneous poem composed to the charms of the beautiful Delia. He would chuckle to himself at some of the outlandish prose but smiled and benevolently gave his blessing to all present.

In truth, Mr. Newkirk himself often entertained guests from the world of horse racing and horse husbandry. His never-ending quest to build our stables into the finest in the country occupied him ninety-nine percent of the time. The horsey set, as Delia referred to them, kept to themselves and rarely mingled with the artsy types.

Bridgewater was gaining a reputation among both sets of society. High society may have frowned on Delia and her entertaining friends, but they sought invitations to her salons and weekends nonetheless. The breeders also sought to be invited as word rapidly spread of Mr. Newkirk's largesse with food, drink, and merriment.

I remained in the background, directing the staff, ordering supplies, paying invoices, decanting the wine, listening to the complaints of various staff members, and smiling through it all. The nights I was able to spend with Delia were my sacred haven. We continued our lovemaking even as she entered the sixth month of her pregnancy. Soon, we knew, she would go into confinement, not hostessing any salons until after the birth of her baby.

Throughout this time, I paid only passing attention to Jadwiga. In hindsight, that was not a good thing.

At last Delia had reached a point where she felt she was too pregnant to be seen by anyone outside of the family and staff. She had announced her decision at her last salon and enjoined the guests present to feel free to keep in contact with her through letters. On the morning after I had spent the previous night with Delia, I left my room and was half way down the stairs when I heard Jadwiga's voice call out to me.

"Excuse me, Mr. Lawson?"

I turned where I stood on the stairs.

"Good morning, Jadwiga. Is there something amiss?"

"No, nothing. I have already cleaned the grates and finished laying wood in the fireplaces in the main rooms. I was about to have a bit of breakfast when I saw you."

"You are a very conscientious young woman, Jadwiga." I made to continue on down the stairs.

"I was wondering…" she closed the distance between us until we stood on the same stair.

"Yes, Jadwiga?"

"I was wondering when I might expect a promotion and a raise in my wages."

"You've only been here a few months. It is much too soon to ask for a rise in wages." I put on a rather stern expression at her assertive request.

"That may be true, but my work is exceptional," she countered.

"I wouldn't call it exceptional, but you are a good, steady worker," I conceded. I took two steps down, thinking the matter closed.

"I believe that you'll find a way to grant me that raise and a promotion as well." Her eyes flashed as I turned back to look at her.

"I highly doubt that, Jadwiga. If you continue to pursue this request at this time, I shall be forced to….."

"And I shall be forced to go to Mr. Newkirk and tell him that you're carrying on with his wife." She spat the words out in a hushed voice.

I stood frozen in time and space, feeling the blood rush to my head and drain just as quickly. How could this have happened? I had been as careful as could be not to be seen entering or leaving Delia's office. This couldn't be happening!

"And you have proof of this?" I maintained my calm.

"So it's true," she mused.

"As I suspected. You've allowed your imagination to run wild."

"I've seen you coming out of Mrs. Newkirk's office at all hours of the night," she responded.

"And should you be foolish enough to bring your unfounded suspicions to Mr. Newkirk he would laugh in your face."

"Really?" Her features took on a smirk that I wanted to wipe right off her face.

"You claim to have come from service in highly-respected houses, yet you fail to comprehend the duties of a Head Steward. I'm afraid your gossip will only come back to bite you."

"But one word is sometimes enough to cast one in a suspicious light."

"Young lady, if you want something, come out and say it. I don't have time to play childish games! If you want a promotion, then ask for one and give me good reasons why I should consider it. If you want a raise in your wages, then take on extra responsibilities. We do not tolerate blackmail at Bridgewater." I turned and continued on to the kitchen, leaving her standing there on the stairs. She could either return to her duties or go off and sulk somewhere, in which case she would be dismissed.

Rather than stop for my morning coffee, I pushed past Mrs. Grant and the others, right past my office and strode out the door and into the herb garden. I continued directly to the stables where I knew I would find Huckleby and hopefully Mr. Newkirk. As I approached the stable office I could hear Huckleby directing one of the stable boys. I entered and waited by the door.

"Nathan, what brings you to these parts of the Bridgewater world?" Huckleby stood up and offered me a chair. "Want some coffee?"

"Yes. Please." My words were terse as I accepted the cup. I drank deeply of the strong coffee. My heart had been racing but was now resuming its regular cadence.

"This is quite unlike you, paying us a visit here in horse country," observed Huckleby. "Something's got your dander up."

"Yes, it has. And this time I need to speak to Mr. Newkirk. Do you expect him anytime soon?" I gulped down another mouthful of coffee.

"Almost any minute now," replied Huckleby, checking his pocket watch. "I can pretty much set my watch by the boss."

As if in answer to Huckleby's comment, the outer door opened and closed behind 'the boss'.

"Well, are we having a meeting of the minds?" inquired Mr. Newkirk.

"Mr. Lawson here is in quite a stew. Won't tell me what's wrong. I'll be out in the stable if you need me." Huckleby made his excuses as he vanished through another door to the stable proper.

"Lawson, something has you mightily troubled. I've never seen you outside your domain." Mr. Newkirk sat down in Huckleby's chair behind the desk.

"I'm not sure how to say this, sir. But there is a person on the staff who is trying to besmirch Mrs. Newkirk's reputation."

"You've fired the offender, have you?"

"Not yet, sir."

"Why not? Certainly you're man enough to dismiss someone."

"Oh, I have every intention of dismissing the young woman. I merely thought to gain your advice first."

"A young woman, you say? Which one?" Mr. Newkirk leaned back in the chair, hanging on my words.

"It's the newest parlor maid, Jadwiga."

"The one with the black hair and black eyes? Never smiles, does she? Kind of gives me the creeps."

"Jadwiga feels that she is due for a promotion and a raise in wages, sir. If they are not forthcoming, she plans to come to you with a tale of infidelity on the part of Mrs. Newkirk."

"Preposterous! Cordy is as faithful to me as the sun rising each morning. And who does this maid claim is my wife's lover?"

I took a deep breath before answering the question.

"Jadwiga claims that I am Mrs. Newkirk's lover."

"Ho, ho! That's rich! And she thinks I would believe that?"

"I have no idea what goes on in her mind, sir."

"I happen to have it on good authority that you frequently entertain a lady by the name of Lenore. She loves being treated as a lady, by the way. You've got a way with the women that I wouldn't have suspected. But as for the accusation of you being my wife's lover, that's poppycock!"

"Yes, sir." I was awash in relief.

"I'd like to have a word with Jadwiga. Send her to my office at ten o'clock sharp this morning. Don't tell her why. I'll deal with this myself."

"Thank you, Mr. Newkirk."

"Oh, don't thank me. I'm just happy that you didn't tell Mrs. Newkirk." Mr. Newkirk arose, signifying the end of our discussion. "Thank you for coming to me with this, Lawson. I don't want anything upsetting my wife. After all, she's carrying my son."

"Certainly, sir."

I turned and exited the stable office, making my way back to the house. I wondered what was to become of Jadwiga but I didn't think much about it. Since Delia and I would most likely not be intimate for some months due to her confinement, there really was no chance of our being caught in a compromising situation.

Kevin

Chapter 24

At half past the hour of nine in the morning I concluded my business in the stables, bid Huckleby a good day, and set off for my office back at the main house. The birds in the trees were creating quite a ruckus as they set about building their nests in anticipation of the mating season. The snow had finally melted and was being replaced by individual blades of grass in a show of bravado that would herald a lush lawn. My leather boots beat out a rhythm of sorts as I followed the path from the stables that would take me round to our front entrance. From a vantage point just to the side of the house I had an obstructed view of our driveway. I stopped for a few moments and looked at it with a critical eye.

How did visitors to Bridgewater view the entrance upon their arrival? I wondered. Yes, we had a driveway but it was primitive to say the least. Country living at its worst would be a kind description. As was evidenced last winter it was quite easy for a motorcar to become stuck in the deep ruts caused by ice and melting snow. We needed a more level surface. Something elegant. Hmmm? Cobblestones were common among the gentry, as were crushed stone. Bridgewater must stand out from the rest.

I had always been fond of brick with its myriad striations. I would commission a contractor to pave the driveway all the way to the road in brick. Perhaps a circular bend to the drive as it approached the front entry. Yes, that would be quite the thing. And the colors of the brick would be complementary to the color of the house.

I began my trek indoors only to be stopped dead in my tracks by another idea. We would add a fountain! That would be my gift to Cordelia after she gave birth to my son. A large fountain, on a grand scale, would give Bridgewater just the panache I was looking for. Perhaps a stallion with front legs raised; the water spouting from his mouth. I would call upon our contractors this very week and get things underway.

I was whistling a merry tune as I approached my office. The fountain and driveway must be set aside until this more pressing matter of the parlor maid was dealt with. I poured myself a finger of Bushmills 1608 and sat back in my chair. How was I to deal with an amateur blackmailer? I gave the matter some thought as I drained the glass.

At exactly ten o'clock, a brusque knock sounded on my study door.

"Enter," I called out.

The door opened slightly and the parlor maid slipped in, closing the door behind her. Funny, I had thought her to be much younger. Perhaps it was her work clothing that gave her the appearance of being just like so many others who roamed the halls of Bridgewater. Her black hair was pulled back severely into a knot at the back of her head. She was garbed in a black skirt and dark colored blouse. Serviceable black shoes covered her feet. There was no hint of jewelry although I felt sure she wore some kind of medal around her neck. Most women from Europe did. Her face was devoid of expression but not so her eyes. They were liquid pools of black ink, dark as midnight. I feared they held many secrets.

"Jadwiga, is it?" I spoke first.

"Yes, sir."

"Don't be shy. Step forward. Have a seat." I motioned her to the leather chair in front of my desk.

"I prefer to stand," she enunciated each word in a husky voice.

"I prefer to have you sit."

She perched on the chair's edge, waiting in silence for me to continue.

"You seem to be a quiet person yet I've been told that you quite brazenly threatened to compromise Mr. Lawson."

She turned her face towards me. Not a muscle on her face moved. But her eyes locked on to mine. I waited a moment for her to respond. When she remained silent, I continued.

"I see you choose to remain silent. Then I must conclude, by your silence, that what I've heard is true. We do not tolerate such behavior here at Bridgewater, Jadwiga. There is no place for evil machinations in this house. You will be dismissed."

"It's true. I swear it!"

"What's true?"

"Mr. Lawson and your….." she stopped just short of mentioning Cordelia.

"Go on," I urged.

She shook her head.

"You were going to say 'Mr. Lawson and my wife', weren't you?"

She swallowed hard before nodding her head in the affirmative.

"Why do you say that?"

"I've seen him."

"You've seen him, eh? Doing what?"

"Coming in and out from Mrs. Newkirk's office."

"I see." I mulled over this information, giving her time to think and perhaps add to her statement.

"They are lovers." As she made the accusation she lifted her head and those black eyes seemed to glow with hatred.

"Have you seen them together?"

She shook her head.

"Have you seen Mr. Lawson enter or leave Mrs. Newkirk's private rooms?"

She shook her head again.

"Have you overheard their conversations? Were there words of love and longing exchanged?"

She shook her head yet again.

"I thought not. I will not have you spread vile rumors about my wife!" I jumped out of my chair and came around to where she sat. She shrunk back into the chair as I leaned over and placed my hands on either side of the chair, boxing her in as I did so.

"He is mine," she spat.

"Who is? Mr. Lawson?"

"Yes, he is to marry me."

I stood back a pace.

"Are you with child?"

"No, not yet."

"Has Mr. Lawson been dallying with you? Has he made promises to you?"

"No." She put her head down once again.

"Nor is he likely to do so. I have personal knowledge of Mr. Lawson and happen to know that he is currently paying court to someone else. It seems that your trickery is for naught."

I watched as two tears fell from her eyes and made their way down her cheeks.

"What exactly is it you're after, Jadwiga?"

"I am looking for my husband."

"You're married?"

"No. No. I seek to find a husband," she corrected herself.

"And you thought Mr. Lawson would be the perfect husband, eh? Well he certainly is well paid and some might find him attractive enough." I settled back in my chair and looked at the young woman again, this time paying more attention to the curve of her bosom that was minimized by the type of clothing she wore. It was the lushness of her lips however that caused me to pause. "How old are you, Jadwiga?"

"I have twenty years of age."

"Have you ever been with a man?"

She nodded her head.

"Did you love him?"

"I was young."

"How old were you?" I could feel my nether regions coming alive.

"I was twelve. He was twenty."

"So you are no longer a virgin. How do you hope to lure a man into marriage without your virginity, I wonder." I reclined even further back in my chair.

"There are ways." She smiled at me.

"I'm sure there are," I concurred.

"It has been a long time since Jadwiga has had a man." She stood and walked around the desk until she was standing in front of me, just between my knees.

I kept silent, waiting to see what she would do. Taking my silence as permission to continue, she slowly unbuttoned her blouse. To my surprise she wore no garment beneath her blouse. She came to rest on my knee as she pulled one of my hands to her bosom. Of their own volition my fingers curved around her breast. When I touched her nipple she threw back her head and moaned, long and low; it was the moan of a woman who has been deprived of sexual release for a long time.

All reason seemed to flee from my mind as I greedily helped myself to first one then the other of her taut breasts. In moments my fingers were replaced by my mouth; as I suckled she wove her hands through my hair, holding my head firmly in place. It seemed as though her orgasm came very quickly; she was not to be deprived of her pleasure. With deft hands she quickly unbuttoned my trousers and released my stiff member. She worked her magic for more than a quarter hour, teasing me to the point where I was begging her for release. Another swift movement on her part and she was astride me, riding me in much the same manner that I rode my favorite horse. She was relentless, her talents were many, and when we were finished I was as limp as a dishrag.

She moved back to the other side of the desk, straightening her clothes as she moved. I opened the desk drawer and pulled out my checkbook; I scratched out a check for one hundred dollars and handed it to her.

"Collect your things. You cannot stay here, regardless of how talented you are. Go to the Sherman Hotel in New Haven. Tomorrow you will be contacted by a friend of mine. You will be given a letter of recommendation. I shall arrange a position for you in the home of another friend. Do not make me sorry for doing this."

"I give thanks for your generosity, Mr. Newkirk." She took the check and walked toward the door. "Perhaps we will see each other at your friend's home."

With the early springtime upon us, I put into motion my ideas for enhancing the driveway and installing the fountain. The contractor who handled the building of Bridgewater was placed in charge of the project. I gave him free reign so long as he stayed on budget and produced the finished product to my specifications. With that project in the works, I focused my energies on entering my best thoroughbred, Dublin Prince, as a contender in the Kentucky Derby.

There were entry forms to complete, entry fees to be paid, travel arrangements to be made; in short, all sorts of logistics to be taken care of. Of course there was the need for me to have a new suit of clothing and I would most likely cover the cost of new duds for Paul as well. Huckleby and the stable hands who would accompany Dublin Prince would be wearing uniforms done up in the Bridgewater colors. I had chosen green and black as the colors representing Bridgewater Stables as they were the colors of Jeannette's eyes and hair.

I commissioned my father-in-law to tailor my new clothes as well as Paul's. My brother-in-law Cal had one department of his garment factory working dedicatedly on the uniforms for the stable hands and Huckleby. There were more than two dozen suits made up as I had decided, after seeing the sample uniform, that our stable hands should wear these uniforms on a daily basis and not just when we attended races. I felt it time that our stable looked as professional as possible.

Cordy would have accompanied me on my trips to New York City but she was in confinement. Since I had maintained my rental of an entire floor at The Ansonia I invited her parents to join me there during my visits. It proved to be quite a good idea as my father-in-law was able to devote longer hours to the making of my garments without worrying about missing the ferry back to Staten Island and Cordy's mother took to entertaining her society friends in their suite.

The spring months progressed nicely but I was missing my darling Jeannette more with each passing week. It had been quite some time since I had made the trek into Boston to visit the little house on Ash Street. Often I would find myself attacked by a bout of homesickness for the place.

At the end of April, Cordy was delivered of our baby; she produced another daughter. I was vexed! Not only was I sure of a boy child, but I had even gone so far as to have one of the spare bedrooms redecorated in a more masculine manner.

The child was spare and angular, not at all plump and pink as a girl child should be. She had dark brown hooded eyes, a thatch of reddish-brown hair, and a prominent nose that stuck out of her face rather like the beak on a bird. Cordelia insisted that the child be christened Corinne. I let her have her way. The night after the christening, I brought up my bottle of Bushmills and two glasses thinking perhaps Cordy and I might drink to the health of our latest offspring.

When I arrived in the nursery, Cordy was there as I expected, holding Geraldine and speaking softly to her. The tot had mastered the art of running and walking and slid easily from her mother's arms when she saw me. She wobbled towards me with her arms outstretched.

"Papa," she cried, her voice as quiet as an angel's wings.

"Gerri, come to papa," I encouraged as I set my Irish whiskey on a small side table. I held out my arms and she ran into them, giggling as I swung her high into the air and spun her around.

"Do be careful with her, Kevin, she's such a fragile child," cautioned Cordy.

"Poppycock! She's a Newkirk, isn't she? She'll be fine."

After a moment or two I set the child down in her crib. She clutched my hand until I placed a goodnight kiss on her forehead. With a loud sigh, she seemed to relax under her blanket as her eyes closed. In moments, her even breathing indicated that she was on her way to dreamland.

"What brings you up to the nursery?" Cordy sat in her rocking chair and I pulled up a high-backed chair to join her.

"It's been a grand day. I thought perhaps you'd join me in a toast to our growing family." I indicated the bottle and two glasses that I had carried with me.

"I thought you might be drowning your sorrows in your room, despairing of ever having a son."

"I've given much thought to that," I replied as I poured myself a good shot of the whiskey.

"Only a drop or two for me," Cordy indicated the glass, "I need to have my wits about me if the children need attention."

"Where's that nursery maid? Lotte?"

"She's having her supper at the moment." Cordelia accepted the proffered glass.

"Then let's enjoy the time alone, shall we?"

Cordy raised her eyebrow in a skeptical manner.

"I know you're not ready yet to undertake the making of a son. I merely wanted to spend some time with my family."

Cordy walked over to the two cribs that stood side-by-side. I moved to stand beside her. In silence we watched as our older child, the one who gave us concern with her constant battles with fever and colds, rested her head peacefully on her monogrammed pillow slip. She looked healthier than I'd ever seen her, with a bit of color to her cheeks. Her face had filled out somewhat with the excellent meals that she was fed.

"She'll be a beauty one day," I whispered into Cordy's ear.

"Yes, she'll break hearts," agreed my wife.

In the nearby crib, Corinne moved restlessly. As her head moved around on the pillow the thatch of hair on her head stood up straight.

"Look at her. Her hair reminds me of the feathers on a bird when they get ruffled."

"So it does," agreed Cordy. "And with her angular features and tiny hands she really does resemble a bird."

"Why name her Corinne anyway?" I tossed back the remainder of my whiskey.

"I've always fancied the name."

"It doesn't suit her." I turned my head this way and that, trying to view the child from the best angle. "There's no help for it, she looks exactly like a bird."

"Then we shall call her Birdie, for short."

"Yes, I rather like that. Birdie Newkirk. Has a nice sound to it. Rolls off the tongue easily." I bent down and placed a kiss on her forehead as well. "Sleep well my little Birdie!"

———

Excitement in the stables mounted as we approached the date of the Kentucky Derby. Huckleby himself was to travel with Dublin Prince and he took with him our two best stable boys, all looking resplendent in their new uniforms.

Since Geraldine was nursing a sore throat, Cordy had chosen to stay at home with the children. She hoped that by segregating them Birdie would not catch whatever it was that Geraldine had. I didn't mind her missing the Derby too much as her attention would not be wholly on the horserace but back here with the girls.

Stan drove Paul and me to the Union Station. Once Paul had my baggage secured he handed me the baggage tickets, inquired if there was anything else I needed, and made his way across the station to another train. I boarded my own train with plenty of time to spare. Once on board, I made my way to the club car where I ordered an Irish whiskey. Although the club car didn't stock Bushmills they did offer a suitable substitute. Finding a window seat I made myself comfortable. As the train pulled out of the station, I watched with interest the other trains on the various tracks, fabricating destinations for each one. Just outside of New Haven, the train picked up speed. The countryside moved past the window in a slow blur of vignettes: city limits, suburbs, farm land, more small towns, and finally the entrance to Grand Central Station.

As I easily made the change of trains to the one that would take me to my final destination, I found a newly heightened sense of excitement rising within me. At the final destination would be the Kentucky Derby. One of my own horses, bred from pure thoroughbreds in my own stables, would be running in that race. I thought of Huckleby, my friend and mentor. The man who had instructed me in the arts of horse husbandry was the only man on this earth to whom I would entrust my pride and joy, Dublin Prince. They should already be in Louisville and hopefully Dublin Prince was being treated with care. I knew Huckleby would see to it!

As our train slowed on its approach to the Louisville Union Station, I was reminded of something that I'd read. The station itself covered slightly more than forty acres of land. It was deemed to be the largest railroad station in the southern United States. On July 17, 1905, a fire had occurred in the facility. The structure was unusable until it reopened the following December. Originally, the station had rose-colored windows but after it was reconstructed the windows were replaced with an 84-panel stained glass skylight that became a feature of its barrel-vaulting tower.

I made my way off the train and was met by a porter from the Seelbach Hotel. In short order he had collected my baggage and transported me to the hotel on Fourth Avenue. Although it was a relatively new hotel, having been built in 1905, it succeeded in exuding the charm of a much older establishment while boasting the latest in amenities. The hotel lobby was spacious yet welcoming. Marble floors and mahogany wood trim lent the place an air of plentiful largesse. There were upholstered seats interspersed between large potted palm trees. A deep-pile carpet cushioned the steps of staff and visitor alike. The crowning pieces of this jewel were the murals of Kentucky pioneer days done by artist Arthur Thomas. Indeed, one of the murals was a painting of Daniel Boone telling stories by a campfire. Ah, how Cordy would love this place!

While the porter saw to my bags I casually made my way toward the highly polished wood desk which fronted the room key cubbies. A dapper looking coatless young man with shirt sleeves held in place by garters smiled at my approach.

"Good afternoon, sir. How may I be of assistance?" The clerk's voice was well modulated and his words sounded sincere.

"I've just arrived and would like the key to my room. You have the reservation under the name of Newkirk."

The clerk studied a list of names until he found mine.

"Yes, sir. I have the suite you requested for yourself and Mrs. Newkirk. If you'll just sign the register, here."

He pushed the guestbook towards me, indicating where I should sign. With a flourish I signed my name and entered the date, returning the pen to its holder.

"Your suite is on the third floor, sir. Our finest accommodations I assure you."

With a tip of my head in acknowledgement, I proceeded to one side of the lobby where I was faced with an iron gated lift. The operator was perched on a high stool.

"Third floor," I instructed.

"Yes, sir."

He pulled the iron gate closed then did the same with the latticed door before setting the throttle to the number three. As we approached the floor he reversed his actions and stood back, allowing me egress.

"Good day, sir."

"Thank you. And the same to you."

I stood for a moment, getting my bearings before proceeding to the right of the lift. There, at the end of the corridor, was a cream and gilt door with the number 3A affixed to it. I inserted the key, pushed open the door, and felt immediately at home. The central room or parlor was pleasantly appointed in shades of green and cream. About the room were figurines of previous Derby winners. Prominently placed on the wall between the two bedrooms was an oil painting of the founder of the Kentucky Derby: Meriwether Lewis Clark, Jr., grandson of William Clark of Lewis and Clark fame.

I took a quick look at the two bedrooms, quickly assessing the larger one which I immediately appropriated by placing my hat, gloves, and walking stick upon the bed. Paul would occupy the smaller room of course.

There was a lovely mahogany bar in the parlor and it was to this item that I homed in. The glassware was Waterford crystal and there, as requested, was my bottle of Bushmills 1608. I poured myself a double-finger and let the liquor burn a welcome trail down my parched throat. There was still about an hour until the arrival of my 'wife' and her brother so I picked up the telephone and rang the desk, requesting a light repast and the daily newspaper. Settling myself in a comfortable chair near the window I watched the goings on below me on the street. I must have dozed for a few moments, as the peaceful ambiance of the room was interrupted by a brief staccato knock on the door that I recognized as belonging to Paul.

I covered the distance to the door with long strides, anxious to greet my 'wife'. And suddenly there she was, Jeannette, the woman who would have been my wife but for the tricks of fate. She looked stunning in her travel outfit with a pert little hat sporting a feather and a half veil. I took her gloved hand in mine and led her into the room with Paul stepping in and closing the door behind us.

"You are a sight for sore eyes," I greeted her.

"Posh! I'm tired, dusty, and in need of a bath after traveling on those filthy trains."

"I booked you the best accommodations. Paul?"

"Oh, don't bother the poor man." She motioned Paul back to the bedroom where he was unpacking my bags. "It wasn't the accommodations. It was the train stations, the traffic kicking up dust and in general the public rest rooms that I found obnoxious."

"I'm so sorry you had to travel that way." I kissed her proffered cheek. "I'll ring the desk and ask for a maid to draw you a bath."

"Good heavens, Kevin, I'm not helpless. Who do you think draws my bath when I'm home alone?"

"Why, I never gave it much thought." Indeed, the notion never crossed my mind.

"I've done without servants all my life. I don't need one now." She pulled off her gloves and removed her hat, placing them atop the bureau in the bedroom.

"While that may be true, darling, Mrs. Newkirk would need a maid to draw her bath. Allow me to spoil you, if only for this short time."

"Since you put it that way," she smiled that seductive smile that I found so exciting.

"Paul," I called out.

"Yes, Mr. Kevin." He stood in the doorway, awaiting instruction.

"Ring down to the desk. Explain that Mrs. Newkirk's maid took sick and couldn't accompany her. Request a maid to come and draw a bath for my wife and to assist her in any way she might require. I'll pay whatever they ask."

"Immediately, sir." Paul grinned at us as he stepped away.

Twenty minutes later Jeannette was soaking in a tub of scented bubbles and warm water while her baggage was being delivered. I noted that there were only two bags and questioned Paul as to the number of bags that Jeannette had checked.

"Only the two bags, sir."

"Why, I wonder, when I informed her that we'd be here at least a week?"

"Perhaps because I didn't think I'd need too many clothes to lie next to my 'husband'," answered Jeannette. She was wrapped in a white chenille robe, her hair piled atop her head; she looked damp from the bath and I knew for a certainty that she wore no garments beneath the robe.

"Your hair, you've fastened it with….."

"Yes, so I have," she smiled as she turned to go into the bedroom, giving me a full view of her diamond hair clip.

"I believe we'd best discuss this baggage problem in private. Paul, see that we're not disturbed."

I followed Jeannette into the bedroom. No sooner had I closed the door than she dropped her robe, confirming that she wore nothing else but the diamond hair clip which was soon removed from her hair.

We had arrived on the Tuesday before race day. Each day, after a late breakfast, I left Jeannette in Paul's care and made my way out to the racetrack where I made a point of visiting Dublin Prince and conferring with our jockey, a diminutive man named Red Snapper Jones. We strolled through the stable areas where other contenders were housed, assessing their strengths and possible weaknesses. Jones had extensive knowledge of the other entrants and their home stables. Only one or two were unknown to him. Huckleby, Jones, and I would lunch at a café near the track planning our strategy for the race. Later, Huckleby and Jones would return to their domains while I made the rounds of the taprooms and gentlemen's clubs, hobnobbing with other owners and trainers.

The evenings, though, were all about pleasure. Jeannette and I were privileged to partake of our evening meal at the finest restaurants in Louisville. As race day approached, these establishments grew more and more crowded. The excitement among owners, trainers, and spectators mounted day by day until they reached a crescendo on the night before the race. At Jeannette's suggestion, we dined at our hotel. Paul had secured for us a spot in the small Rathskeller.

Jeannette looked quite fetching that evening, in a simply tailored dress of cream linen and lace. She wore a matching feather arrangement in her coiffed raven locks. With her on my arm, I felt as though I were the king of Louisville. Our descent into the hotel basement brought us to the gracefully arched Rathskeller whose columns created a cathedral-like effect. The entire room had recently been made of Rookwood Pottery (a local pottery company becoming known for its colorful glazes). Jeannette was in awe of the Rookwood pelican frescoes that encircled the archway pillars and planned to incorporate a pelican into the hats she was designing for the upcoming summer.

Our waiter was most helpful, recommending local specialties as well as dishes prepared specifically with a Kentucky Derby theme. Our libations were delivered from the Rathskeller bar, whose most notable feature was the portion of the ceiling directly above it. An enterprising artist had covered the ceiling area with the signs of the zodiac and, while not entirely a new theme, the fact that they were hand-painted in twenty-four karat gold leaf on leather was extraordinary.

We lingered at our table, enjoying an after dinner glass of port, talking about all sorts of things with an ease that I found relaxing. One glass of port led to another and before long Jeannette was leaning forward and whispering naughty suggestions in my ear. When she spoke about taking another bath and pinning up her hair with her diamond hair clip, I hurriedly downed the remainder of my port, grabbed her hand, and hustled her directly to the third floor. Her eyes were looking quite openly at my nether regions as we entered the lift.

"Good evening, sir, ma'am," the lift operator greeted us.

"Third floor, please," I instructed him, allowing my hand to drop to Jeannette's derriere.

Jeannette moved ever so slightly, turning so that she was able to drop her eyelids while her gaze burned through the cloth of my trousers. I began to feel uncomfortable.

"Going to the race tomorrow?" inquired the operator as the lift moved slowly upward.

"Yes," I answered tersely, trying to control the function at the forefront of my trousers.

"I'm looking forward to it," replied Jeannette, her eyes continuing to stare at what I felt must be a huge bulge by now.

"Weather promises to be nice," continued the operator, not realizing that his small talk was making me anxious.

"That's lovely. I have such great plans for tomorrow," answered Jeannette.

She moved to stand in front of me as her hand reached behind her to cup my jewels. I immediately stood straight as a ramrod. We watched as the lift slowed and the operator pulled back the iron gate. Jeannette's hand returned to her purse; she drifted off the lift quite elegantly, leaving me to tip the operator. When I caught up to her she was waiting at the door to our suite.

"You minx!" I pulled her close to me, fitting my body tightly against hers as I kissed her deeply.

"Better hurry. I don't want to waste a minute more," she answered breathily against my mouth.

I fit the key into the door as we stumbled over the threshold together. There was to be no lingering bath that night. We raced into the bedroom, pulling off our clothes as we went, leaving a trail behind us that Paul would have to deal with.

As predicted, the weather for race day was sunny and warm with the stirring of a light breeze. While the general admission area was thronged with elaborately-hatted ladies and gentlemen wearing top hats, Jeannette and I were ushered to our box. I had paid quite a sum of money to reserve this particular box during previous years and it now was known informally as the Newkirk Box. In true Derby fashion, we were dressed to the nines. Jeannette's ensemble reflected the Bridgewater colors: an emerald green dress and short cape that was trimmed in jet-black feathers. Atop her upswept hair perched a large-brimmed black hat banded by green ribbon and adorned with peacock feathers.

In keeping with Jeannette's wearing of Bridgewater colors, I had chosen an ascot of emerald green to match my pocket silk. My top hat of dove gray coordinated well with my morning suit and together I believed Jeannette and I were perfectly matched.

A box attendant came to take our drink order and in moments returned with ice cold mint juleps, another Derby tradition. We sipped at our libations, as we watched the sea of people around us moving constantly like the ebb and flow of the tide. Everyone was eager to see and be seen. A roving photographer for the county newspaper asked us to pose for a picture. I momentarily froze at the request, but Jeannette nodded her consent. I questioned her after the photographer had moved on.

"You realize that his photo will be in all the newspapers," I commented. "Was it wise to fuel a non-existent fire?"

"Please, Kevin, give me credit for my knowledge of right versus wrong. What you didn't see was the way I dipped my head, ever so slightly, just as the young man snapped his picture."

"Meaning?"

"Meaning that whoever sees that photo will merely see a splendid example of my work as a milliner, not my face. It would have been rude for you to not be seen in a photo with your wife, nor would it have been seemly for me to refuse the photographer's request. This way, we 'saved face' for both you and Cordelia."

"Ah, every time I begin to take you for granted you surprise me with another reason why I love you." I leaned over and kissed her cheek.

We had consumed at least three of those wonderful mint juleps by the time the race was ready to begin. The horses were led to their positions. Dublin Prince was in slot number four. His sleek coat shone in the sunlight as Red Jones guided him into position. The jockey was resplendent in the Bridgewater colors. Prince jostled his head in anticipation of the race.

Attendees were quickly finding their seats or taking their places for the opening salvo after placing their wagers at the betting windows. The race was set for a four o'clock start and a large clock on the far end of the track counted down the minutes and seconds. As the clock's hands moved through the final minute, a hush came over the crowd. On the stroke of four, the gates were lifted and the horses shot out from their slots.

Very quickly two or three of the horses took the lead. Two others fell to the last positions within thirty seconds, having given all of their energy to the start of the race. Jones kept a steady pace on Dublin Prince through the first turn before allowing the horse to open up just a bit. As the horses hooves ate up the track, one of the leaders began to fall back. That was the sign that Jones was waiting for. He guided Dublin Prince into the fourth spot and held him steady as they approached the second turn. Steady, steady, through the turn, steady, steady, closing the gap on number two, sidling up to the lead horse, and across the finish line. The cheers of people around the Newkirk Box were hoarse. Jeannette threw her arms around me, kissing me fully and openly.

"You've won!" she cried.

"Not so quick, darling. It was too close to call."

I pulled her into my embrace and held her close as we made our way down to the paddock where Dublin Prince waited alongside Morning Wood, the lead horse. It took some time to arrive at the paddock as we were stopped by people congratulating us on the win. I, however, wasn't so certain. We returned their smiles and waved to the folks who had placed their money on Dublin Prince.

Down in the paddock we waited alongside Red Jones and Dublin Prince. A quick conversation with the jockey told me everything I needed to know. The man was quite sure that Prince had lagged behind by a split second. Moments later a Derby official came down and informed both owners of the official results as they were being announced to the crowd.

"The winner of this year's Kentucky Derby is Morning Wood!"

I watched as the owner of the other horse accompanied his jockey and their prize winning thoroughbred into the winner's circle. The walk *I* had waited so long to take; the walk I would not be taking, this year.

The winning owner came over and shook hands, congratulating us on a close race. He pulled me over to the side, away from the hearing of others.

"Great race, Newkirk, great race."

"Yes, it was a close call."

"Splendid horse you have there. What's his lineage?"

I spent several minutes speaking to Dublin Prince's ancestry.

"Bred him yourself, eh?"

"In our own stables, his sire and mam are still part of our stable."

"I'd like to buy him from you. Name your price."

I was taken completely by surprise. I was shocked.

"Dublin Prince isn't for sale," I managed to respond.

"Of course he is. Every horse has his price. What will you take for him?"

"Why do you want him?"

"To breed another winner of course. With his speed and lineage he'd be a natural for siring a new thoroughbred."

With some clarity returning to my brain, I replied, "As I stated, he's not for sale. But perhaps we can come to terms with his siring one of your mares."

"That works for me. Put the beast to work, I say."

"The mating will be at Bridgewater Stables," I countered, "We get second foal."

"Done." We shook hands. "Why don't you and your missus join us for dinner?"

"Thank you, we look forward to it."

So, in the end, we came in second but with Dublin Prince out to stud we were about to become the most sought-after breeding stable of the decade.

Lotte

Chapter 25

Meine Teuerste Tante Anja,

*Things here are never the same from one minute to the next.
With two babies I am kept busy every hour of every day. Please
understand that being busy does not lessen the enjoyment of my
work as Nursery Maid. With the unending stream of nurses and
nannies that come and go with regularity, I am honored to be the
one constant person in the lives of Geraldine and Corinne (I refuse
to call her Birdie).*

*Geraldine is a delicate child and takes the chill quite easily.
I'm afraid she will go through life as a sickly person. No amount
of caution can be too great on her behalf. I worry about her all
the time.*

*Corinne is the exact opposite of her older sister. Although
she too is slight in build, she is a hearty baby and is beginning
to fill out nicely. I'm sorry to say that her nose is very beak-like
and will most likely never change. She is very difficult to put to
sleep, preferring to sleep once the sun has peeked over the horizon.
Mrs. Newkirk has taken to adding a drop or two of whiskey to
Corinne's evening bottle in the hope of making her drowsy. Sadly,
this has not worked. It falls to me to keep the child company during*

the evening hours and sometimes late into the night so that Mrs. Newkirk may have her rest.

Mrs. Newkirk informed me earlier today that she is has hired a new nanny and that she'll be arriving any day. I'm afraid by the time she arrives I'll be in a deep sleep!

I hope that you are in good health. I remain your devoted nichte,

Charlotte

P.S. Mrs. Newkirk increased my wages by an additional dollar each month! On my fourteenth birthday last month she granted me an entire day off with pay but all I could do was sleep most of it away!!

Many of my dreams during this period are filled with visions of the gentle Mr. Lawson. I know that he is in love with Mrs. Newkirk and she returns his feeling. But I can't help but think how sad it must be for Mr. Lawson to never be able to openly express his love. I don't think I should like to be in Mrs. Newkirk's position either. Imagine having to live in fear of Mr. Newkirk discovering her liaisons with Mr. Lawson. Thankfully in my dreams I am the one with whom Mr. Lawson shares his love. When we go on our dream picnics by the creek we are free to hold each other and share our kisses. We have no fear of being discovered by an irate spouse. Our love is pure and everlasting.

But then I awake and my duties call. I gladly slip into my grey skirt and white blouse, make my way downstairs to the kitchen, and have a quick bite to eat. Some days I consider myself lucky because Mr. Lawson is in the kitchen. I shyly turn away from his glance so that he doesn't see me smile at the memory of my dreams. How lucky Mrs. Newkirk is to be the recipient of his love!

As he turns to answer a question from cook, I look at his fine profile. Sharp angles amidst soft curves combine to make him the most handsome man I've ever seen. Today his hair is in need of a trim yet I like the way it looks, slightly tousled as though he's come in from the outdoors where a breeze has blown a stray lock or two out of place. I try to get closer to where he stands so that I may inhale the aroma of sandalwood that is his signature scent. Wouldn't it be heavenly to wake up to that scent in bed beside me?

I silently wish that he would notice me; but to him I'm just a girl – a child still. But Mrs. Newkirk isn't that much older than me and yet he loves her. I smooth down a crease in my apron, feeling a bit down because I'm so young, when I hear the deep baritone notes of his voice call my name. I turn quickly and find him smiling at me. My heart soars!

"Lotte, would you please take this note up to the nursery and see that Mrs. Newkirk receives it?"

"Yes, Mr. Lawson," I curtsy slightly and when I take the note from his hand our fingers touch briefly.

As I make my way upstairs to the nursery, I foolishly touch my fingers to my lips. His touch has made me feel special, even though it was brief.

I'm in love! With Mr. Lawson! Nathan. Nate. I hurry up the stairs, find Mrs. Newkirk, give her the note, and go about my duties. If only I could get the children into bed and asleep quickly tonight! Then I'd be free to sit quietly in the nursery and dream about Mr. Lawson.

Cordelia

Chapter 26

November 1911

I t has become quite difficult to retain a nanny for the children. Although the women who undertake the position are qualified, they can't seem to carry out my wishes where the children are concerned. Granted young Birdie is quite a handful, having inherited her father's mood swings, yet it would seem to me a simple matter of showing Birdie who retains the upper hand. Sadly, Birdie seems to be the one in charge of the nursery and will only obey Lotte or myself. We are both desperate for a reprieve from Birdie's spirited highjinks. Hopefully, the matter will be settled shortly as I have arranged for a young woman from Yonkers in New York to fill the position. Momma says that the woman, Jenny by name, comes highly recommended by several of her society friends. Jenny had quite a few conditions to be met before she accepted the position, but her references are impeccable and I have a good feeling about hiring her.

There are so many things demanding my attention right now. Thankfully we will be celebrating Thanksgiving with the Boston Newkirks; the children will be staying here with Jenny and Lotte. It seems that Lotte is the only one who can calm Birdie down when she doesn't get her way which is every day. Mostly it gives me a great sense of security knowing that Nathan will be watching out for everyone as he is most capable of doing.

December 1911

This holiday season has taken wings! After our return from Boston and the Thanksgiving holiday which was hosted by my sister-in-law Bernice and her overbearing husband, I geared up the staff for our Christmas ritual of decking the house with holiday trim and setting up the enormous tree in our front foyer. While the larger tree was being placed in the foyer, I summoned the children to the drawing room for the trimming of the smaller tree.

Once the rotund blue spruce had been set up near the drawing room window, I had Jenny and Lotte bring the girls downstairs. Together we females strung the popcorn and cranberries to make the garland for the tree. Of course, Geraldine was more interested in the large tree out in the foyer and kept running into the hallway to check on its progress. Birdie, who had not yet found her feet, crawled along the carpet trying to put everything she could get her hands on into her mouth. Poor Lotte was kept quite busy running after Birdie!

Kevin arrived later that afternoon and dispensed his advice on how the tree should be decorated. When he realized that his advice was being ignored, he abruptly left the room muttering something about being welcomed by the bottle of whiskey he kept in his office. I merely ignored him.

After a while Lotte took Birdie upstairs to change her diaper. Jenny lent me a hand in stretching the final rope of garland around the tree. We stood back and admired our handiwork.

"The tree looks quite beautiful, Mrs. Newkirk," commented Jenny.

"I think it's our best effort," I replied warmly.

"Will there be anything else, ma'am?"

"No, thank you, Jenny. It's well past time for Geraldine to be joining her sister for their evening meal. Why don't you take her upstairs?"

Jenny nodded in affirmation and turned around.

"Geraldine? Geraldine? Now where has she gone off to?"

I watched the nanny search behind the sofa, as my oldest daughter oftentimes liked to hide from us. She was looking behind the drapes when we heard a commotion from the hallway.

"Mrs. Newkirk, Mrs. Newkirk!" one of the maids came running into the drawing room, flushed and out of breath.

"What is it, Agnieska? What's wrong?" A sudden coldness gripped my heart.

"It's Miss Geraldine."

"What about my daughter?"

"She was found outside when one of the gardeners was walking about the house."

"Where is she now? Is she all right? How did she get outside?"

I followed the maid who pointed to the library, the closest room to the front foyer. Running into the room, I found Griswold our gardener standing over my daughter who was lying on the sofa, an afghan hastily pulled over her. He had her hands in his, rubbing them vigorously to try and warm her. She looked so tiny and fragile as she laid there, eyes closed.

"Oh, ma'am, I'm sorry. I didn't know she was outside. If I hadn't stepped between the hedges to straighten the wreath on the window I never would have found her. She was crumpled up in a ball. When I picked her up she didn't answer me when I spoke to her."

"Quickly, Agnieska, call Dr. Bennett." My voice cracked as I spoke.

The maid ran to do my bidding. I turned to Jenny who stood to my side, her face as pale as ash.

"You, Jenny, run upstairs. Send Lotte to me immediately. You are to stay with Birdie. Do not take your eyes off of her for even an instant."

The nanny stood there in shock until I had no choice but to shake her by the shoulders.

"Jenny, snap out of it! Did you hear what I asked you to do?"

Slowly, she looked at me and nodded her head in understanding before she turned and ran up the stairs. Within moments, Lotte was by my side. Her presence calmed me; she was someone I trusted.

"How did she get outside?" was Lotte's first question.

She bent over Geraldine who, I could see, was turning slightly blue around her mouth. Lotte lifted the afghan to look at my baby's feet, so small and devoid of any foot covering. Dear God! She must have gotten frostbite! How long had she been outside? And with only her little dress on, she must have taken the chill so quickly!

"Lotte, can you do anything for her? I've sent for Dr. Bennett," I whispered.

"What's all the ruckus about?" roared Kevin as he ambled down the hallway. He stuck his head into the library. "What's going on?"

"Mr. Newkirk, sir," began Griswold.

"Out with it, Griswold. Have you broken a window?"

"No, sir," tears began streaming down the gardener's face; he could barely lift his head to look up. "I wish I had found her sooner. I don't know how long she was out there. Poor little thing."

"What are you blathering about, Griswold? Cordy, what's going on?"

I stepped back from the sofa so that he could see Geraldine.

"Why isn't our daughter upstairs in the nursery?"

I bit my lip to keep from throttling Kevin in front of the staff. Lotte turned and approached my husband.

"Mr. Newkirk, there's been an accident."

"Accident? Who's hurt?" It was plain for all to see that Kevin had been drinking.

"It's Geraldine, sir. She somehow got out and was hiding in the hedges. She may be suffering from frostbite." Lotte's voice was calm and steady.

Without warning, Kevin raised his fist and slammed it against

Lotte's face. He pushed her aside and moved to the sofa, kneeling beside the child, squinting to focus his vision. Slowly he assessed Geraldine's condition before springing up and slapping Lotte once more. I moved to stand between them and felt the sting of his palm as another slap that was meant for Lotte hit my cheek.

"Enough! Lotte is not to blame." In that moment I hated what my husband had turned into.

"She's through! Do you hear me, girl? Pack your bags and depart this instant!!" His face was blood red with exertion.

"Kevin," I cautioned through swollen lips, "Geraldine wandered outside of her own accord. There is no one to blame."

"She's to blame!" Kevin pointed at Lotte. "She's the nursery maid." His eyes were glazed over with fury.

"Geraldine is Jenny's charge. As Birdie is Lotte's."

"Then discharge them both!" He spat the words at me as he stormed out of the library, his coat tails flapping.

Griswold stood to one side of the sofa where Lotte was bent over the still form of my daughter. It was easy to see that Lotte had taken the brunt of Kevin's tirade from the marks on her young face. There were tears streaming down her face.

"Lotte, please don't cry. I'm so deeply sorry that you've been hurt and I apologize for the way Mr. Newkirk reacted. I'll be sure that Dr. Bennett takes a look at you when he arrives."

Lotte's tears continued unchecked as she reached over to hug Geraldine. When she looked up at me I could see the deep sorrow in her tearful eyes. She began shaking her head.

"Our baby is lost, Mrs. Newkirk."

"Nonsense, Lotte. She's merely asleep. Hopefully she'll stay asleep until Dr. Bennett arrives."

At that moment, Agnieska arrived with the quilt from Geraldine's bed. One glance at Lotte told her all she needed to know. Tears began to well up in her eyes as well.

"I don't know what's come over you two. This is not a time for tears; it is a time for action."

I plucked the quilt from Agnieska's trembling hands. Gently pushing Lotte aside I bent to cover my daughter and keep her warm. That was when I noticed there was no movement of her chest in a normal breathing pattern. I pulled her up into a sitting position to make her more comfortable. Lotte moved to stand beside me, placing her hands on my shoulders.

"Mrs. Newkirk, there's nothing more to be done. Geraldine has left us."

Geraldine! Gone? My daughter was dead? That couldn't be.

"No Lotte, you're mistaken. She's just sleeping, you see. When she wakes up she'll want something to eat. Tell Mrs. Grant to warm up some of that vegetable soup. She'll take the warm broth and feel better." I reached down to hold my daughter. "Gerri, sweetie, it's alright to open your eyes. Momma's right here."

Lotte reached down and pried my fingers from my daughter's lifeless body. I stood up and noticed that everyone else in the room, Lotte, Agnieska, even Griswold, was crying. I moved out of the library and into the front hall where I was accosted by the sight of the large Christmas tree with its bright decorations, the same decorations that had been so enticing to my young daughter. With nary a thought to what I was doing, I walked over to the tree and began to pick those baubles of cheer off of its branches, flinging each one against the walls and marble floor of the foyer. I didn't care what the staff thought of me.

My daughter was dead.

I picked up a lamp from a sideboard and threw it as well against the front door – the door that had so easily beckoned Gerri with its invitation to adventure. When my energy had been spent, I sunk to the floor where I wailed at the loss of my daughter. I had no thought for anyone else at that moment. I allowed the deepest of sorrows to overtake me.

Was it hours, or only moments, later that I felt the comfort of masculine hands take hold of my shoulders?

"Come now, Delia, it won't do for the others to see you this way," a familiar voice whispered in my ear.

I turned my head to look into the eyes of Nathan; he who had always vowed to be there when I needed him.

"Nate...." I began haltingly.

"Please, Mrs. Newkirk," he spoke louder now, alerting me to the fact that we were not alone, "you shouldn't be here, like this." He helped me up from the floor. "You, Agnieska, help Mrs. Newkirk to her room. Assist Ellen in whatever way she requires."

"Mr. Lawson," I began, "thank you."

He leaned forward long enough to whisper, "I'll come to you tonight."

"Mr. Newkirk? I must tell him…"

"Leave Mr. Newkirk to me, ma'am. You have enough to handle."

Nathan handed me over to Agnieska who accompanied me to my chamber on the second floor. There I was coddled by Ellen, who had a pot of chamomile tea brought up. My tears refused to stop. I sat and stared at my tea cup, feeling as though my heart had been ripped from my chest. I longed for Nathan's arms to hold me, to comfort me, to shelter me from the whirlpool of sorrow that was engulfing me.

From afar I heard the bellowing of Kevin's drunken voice as Nathan informed him of Geraldine's death. Then came the crashing of glass as Kevin completed the task I had begun – he toppled the Christmas tree in the foyer and it fell against the marble floor, breaking the remaining ornaments. His heavy footsteps on the stairway alerted me to his coming. My bedroom door was flung open and a very drunk Kevin stood in the doorway. Seeing him there reminded me of our wedding night for he was every bit as drunk as he had been then. Only this time there was fury in his eyes.

"How dare you allow our daughter to move about unsupervised? You bitch!"

He stalked across the room, causing Ellen to back away in trepidation; he came to a halt directly in front of me.

"What've you got to say for yourself?"

My tears began anew as I looked up at him.

"Tears won't bring the child back! This is your fault, bitch!" He pulled back his arm and slapped my face, then slammed his fist into the side of my head twice before he was restrained by his valet Paul who had followed him into my room.

"Sir, you won't bring back Miss Geraldine by doing this," Paul's voice sounded like the voice of reason trying to tell the devil he had lost another soul.

"I'm master here!" Kevin spit out. "Everything you have," he now turned to me, "is because of my generosity. All I asked for was a son. And you've given me puny daughters!"

He reached out for the teapot and flung it against the wall. My perfume bottles were next. They crashed into a myriad of tiny pieces on the bathroom floor. Kevin's fury continued unabated as he moved through my room obliterating everything he thought I held dear. When he was done, he allowed Paul to guide him towards the doorway. He turned and addressed me once more.

"You'll pay for this, wife! I shall ride you every night until you provide me with my son. Is that clear?"

I looked away, ignoring his ranting.

"I shall ride you all night, every night, while you writhe beneath me. And when you've become exhausted I'll ride you still. By God, I'll have my son!"

He stormed out then, confident that he had retained his position as master, leaving me to deal with my sorrow.

Lawson

Chapter 27

That day in mid-December, when Geraldine passed away, was one of the darkest days of my life. I had lost my daughter, my only child, yet I could seek no succor from my colleagues or from the woman who had given me that child. Instead, it fell to me to be the shelter from the storm for the others on staff. Mrs. Grant took to her room, leaving the cook's helpers to deal with providing meals for the family. The maids were unfit for duty as they found it difficult to control their tears. The male members of the staff were so morose that they were unable to fulfill their duties in their normal manner. Yet I was the one they all sought to pour out their grief.

When I first was summoned to the front foyer, I was aghast at the sight that greeted me. There on the floor was Delia, crumpled into a ball, tears streaming down her face; her wail reverberating off the walls, filling everyone's ears. I gently helped her up from amidst the sea of broken glass that surrounded her. As I whispered words of comfort for her benefit, I noticed the marks on her cheek where she had been hit. I assumed that she and Mr. Newkirk had had a terrible row and that he had hit her. Entrusting her to Agnieska's care, I watched a crushed and sorrowful Delia climb the stairs. I turned to the library, where others were congregated.

"Someone, anyone, explain to me what happened."

Griswold stepped forward, his coat lying heavily on his slumped shoulders.

"Mr. Newkirk says it was my fault, sir." He kept his head down and his eyes trained on the floor. "But I don't see how that can be. I was the one that found her."

"Take your time, Griswold. Tell me everything you can remember."

"I was hanging the wreaths over the foyer windows, just like Mrs. Newkirk asked me to. I stepped back to make sure that everything looked all right. That was when I noticed that one of the wreaths didn't line up with the others. So I stepped between the hedges to get closer to the windows. And I found her. Almost stumbled over her, I did. She was lying on her side in the snow. Appeared to me that she had been crouched down low, like she was playing Hide 'n Seek or somethin'. The cold must have got her real quick like. Poor tyke weren't wearin' a coat or anything. Just her little dress. No shoes neither." Griswold shook his head as he spoke.

"I didn't know what to do. So I picked her up gently, talking to her as I did so she wouldn't be frightened. She was so slight, not heavy at all. I brung her into the foyer where folks was doing the decorating. It was that nice maid, Agnieska, who took one look and led us to the library." The man raised his head and looked directly into my eyes.

"I did the best I could, sir. Can't understand why the little lady was outside without shoes or coat." Tears streamed down his weathered cheeks and his lips trembled as he spoke. "And now she's gone. That sweet little girl, so full of life. It's a sad, sad thing."

"You did your best," I murmured. Griswold would never know how my heart was breaking as I listened to the story of how he found my daughter in a drift of snow. "I think you should go to the kitchen. Ask one of the helper's for a cup of hot coffee. Tell Mrs. Grant that she may add a good shot of whiskey to your cup. You've suffered enough for one day. There's nothing more you can do here."

"Thank you, Mr. Lawson. You're a real decent sort, not like himself."

Griswold rolled his eyes toward Mr. Newkirk's office. "Please tell Mrs. Newkirk how sorry I am."

"Leave it to me."

Griswold turned and sauntered off towards the kitchen. Lotte was still sitting beside the still form of Geraldine. It was she who had closed the child's eyes and arranged her quietly.

"How are you feeling, Lotte?" I motioned to her bruised jaw.

"I'll heal."

"I'd like Dr. Bennett to look at you when he arrives."

She nodded her head in acquiescence. I moved closer to the sofa and bent over the lifeless form.

"Poor child, she was never strong," began Lotte.

"Yes, I suppose that's true," I agreed.

"Would you like me to leave you alone with her?"

"Why would you ask that?" My gaze never left my precious child's face.

"I know that she's your daughter," came the whispered response.

I snapped back to reality.

"Who told you that?" I demanded in hushed tones.

"She has the same coloring as you. And when she was near you it was plain for me to see the connection."

"Then Delia, uh, Mrs. Newkirk didn't..."

"No, I realized it on my own."

"Lotte, you musn't let anyone else know of this. It would cause irreparable damage to the Newkirks's marriage."

"Posh!" she smiled at me. "You don't think the Mister gives a fig what his wife does as long as she gives him a son? And don't you think I haven't noticed that there is another door in the passage from the Missus bedroom to the nursery. I don't know where it leads but I can guess."

"Lotte, you must never breathe a word of that to anyone."

"Not to worry, Mr. Lawson. I've no proof of any shenanigans going on. All I know is that there are certain mornings when Mrs. Newkirk is smiling – and I know it's not because the Mister was visiting her. Your secrets are safe with me."

"How can I thank you, Lotte?" The fear of discovery had been lifted from my shoulders. I now had an ally in the house, one who wanted only good things for her mistress.

"A word of warning, though, Mr. Lawson. Don't trust Ellen."

"Mrs. Newkirk's maid?"

"She's close to Paul, the mister's valet. I've overheard them discussing the Newkirks from time to time. What one knows, the other knows. And that leaves everything in Paul's control."

"Thank you, Lotte. You are a true friend."

I pulled the young woman into a warm hug. It was wonderful knowing that Delia and I could trust someone, even one as young as Lotte.

"Isn't she a bit young for you, Lawson?" The words were slightly slurred as they fell from the lips of Kevin Newkirk. "I thought you preferred your women older, and more experienced."

"I….well…..If you are referring to that lady of the evening over on Long Wharf, she is merely someone with whom to pass the time."

"It's me, Mr. Newkirk. I've always wanted to be with an older man," piped up Lotte. "I guess it's our grief over Geraldine's passing that has brought us closer together."

She snuggled closer into my embrace. I rested my arm casually around her shoulder.

"Passing?" questioned Mr. Newkirk, as he downed the remains of his drink.

"Lotte, you'd best leave us alone." I pushed her towards the door. She looked back only once before closing the door behind her.

"What did she mean, Lawson? Why is Geraldine so quiet? Where's the damn doctor?"

"Mr. Newkirk, sir, Geraldine is no longer with us."

"Eh? Don't be a fool, man, I can see her with my own eyes. She's right there." He pointed towards the sofa.

"Yes, sir. Her body is still there. But our Geraldine has passed on."

"Passed on." He glared at the lifeless form of the sweet child again. "Dead. You mean my daughter is dead, don't you?"

"Yes, sir. I'm afraid…."

"You're afraid of what? The dead?" He knelt by the sofa, tenderly brushing back the child's hair from her face. "Who did this to you?" he questioned the unresponsive corpse.

Oddly, I noticed that tears streamed down his face. His shoulders slumped momentarily before they were squared. He stood up and faced me.

"It was Cordy, wasn't it? It's her fault that the child is dead?" His voice came out in a roar that I'm sure could be heard all the way to the stables.

"No, sir. It was an accident," I tried to explain.

"Accidents don't happen! They are caused by carelessness. And it's my wife who was careless."

He moved to the closest shelf of books and picked one up, testing its weight in his hand before he flung it across the room. Again and again he hurled book after book against the far wall, knocking over small items in his path.

As grief and rage overtook him, he flung open the library door and stepped into the foyer, looking left and right for something else to destroy. He noted the debris left by Delia's momentary rage then stepped forward, took hold of a few remaining ornaments, and flung them on the marble floor. The sound of the remaining glass ornaments crashing against the floor seemed to fuel his ire. He mounted the stairway, taking two steps at a time. I could hear his progress as he made his way to Delia's room. I ran off in search of Paul who seemed the only one capable of dealing with Kevin when he was in a drunken rage.

It was later, much later, when I took a few moments for myself. Dr. Bennett had finally arrived and officially pronounced Geraldine's death. His opinion was that the cold air had settled quickly in the child's lungs and had choked off her breathing. The fact that she wasn't wearing any shoes or coat didn't help things. Our efforts to warm her were too little, too late. Mercifully, she hadn't suffered.

After that Dr. Bennett tended to Lotte's bruised jaw, assuring her that she would heal over time since there were no broken bones. By the time he came to visit Delia he was prepared for the worst. And that is exactly what he found. He explained his findings to me as he prepared to leave.

"I'm afraid that Mrs. Newkirk has retreated inside herself, Lawson. That happens to women sometimes when they suffer a traumatic event." He shook his head as he pulled on his gloves. "She's suffered some bruising at the hands of her spouse, again nothing new. She'll recover from that in time. I've given Ellen strict orders that Mrs. Newkirk is to be kept quiet and segregated from the rest of the household until she is more mentally capable. I'll leave it to you, Lawson, to see that my orders are carried out. Nothing strenuous for her at least for a month. I'll check back in a few days."

"Certainly, doctor."

"Will you be making the burial arrangements?"

"I hadn't thought about that. Yet."

"It would be far better if you undertook the arrangements. I don't believe either of the Newkirks is capable at this point." So saying, the doctor took his leave.

Now, some thirteen hours later, I sat at my office desk, an untouched glass of whiskey before me. I stared out the window into the blackness of night. How was I to function when my only child had died? It felt as though a part of my heart had been carved from my chest. And if I felt this way, how was Delia feeling? Should I go to her? Should I remain where I was? I had promised her that I would come to her tonight but was I capable of offering consolation to anyone, let alone the mother of my deceased child? I sat for a while longer, allowing my mind to wander over the memories I held of the times that Geraldine had spoken to me or smiled in my direction. They provided only mild consolation for her loss.

With a weariness that I felt all the way to my bones, I left my office and climbed the stairs to my room. A change of clothes refreshed me and I made my way to the nursery on the third floor. Lotte was asleep in a chair next to Birdie's crib. The bruising on her jaw had turned a horrendous dark color. My heart went out to her. What a shame that she had been the one to bear the brunt of Kevin Newkirk's rage when she was the one who loved both children so much. How bereft must she be feeling at the loss of Geraldine? It seemed to me that Lotte was a friend who would remain true to both Delia and I and for that I found myself extremely grateful.

I carefully moved to the hidden panel in the nursery, pulling myself through the opening. In moments I was in Delia's room. There were no lights but I knew the layout of the furniture and moved quickly to her bedside. As my eyes became adjusted to the dark I saw her figure outlined beneath the bed covers. Her even breathing told me that she was asleep.

I watched her sleep for a few moments, before moving to sit in a chair beside the bed. I gained a sense of peace by merely being there with her. The events of the day slipped away even as the pattern of her even breathing calmed me. Within moments, I too fell into a sound sleep.

———

Geraldine's funeral was held within the fortnight. There were hundreds of callers in the days before the funeral. People from all walks of life, from high society to even the lowliest stable boy, came to offer their condolences. Throughout it all, Delia moved in a dreamlike state. Garbed in black from head to toe, she murmured her thanks to those who were presented to her. Mr. Newkirk, almost sober for once, managed to thank the callers between nips from the flask he kept in his jacket pocket.

The funeral day was overcast with the threat of snow. In a rare moment of consideration, Mr. Newkirk asked if I would attend the church service to represent the household staff and to give a brief eulogy. He felt that since he hadn't been as close to the child as the members of the staff, it was only fitting. I had no other option than to accept the task of eulogizing my own daughter.

In the end, the task was easier than I anticipated. It was simple to recount the joy that Geraldine had brought into the hearts and lives of all who had met her. As I moved back towards my seat, I noticed that for the first time in days Delia's eyes showed that the spark of life still burned in her heart, although it had been deeply buried. The thought that she might come to accept what had happened to our daughter gave me hope that the woman I loved would become whole again.

April 1912

As was customary during the winter months, Geraldine's coffin was placed in the cold storage crypt of the cemetery. It stayed there until spring when the ground had thawed. By that time Geraldine had become a memory in the minds of most people. Mr. Newkirk was away on business, somewhere in the south. The household staff was busy with their daily routines. Delia was under doctor's orders to avoid stress since she was once more pregnant by her husband, who it seemed, had barely waited one month after Geraldine's death. It fell to Lotte and me to represent the Newkirk family at my daughter's internment.

I wasn't sure how I expected to feel, given the fact that my child had been gone for over four months. But as I stood by the side of the small grave and watched the small white coffin being lowered into it, I felt Lotte's hand clasp mine. The warmth of her hand was enough to help me retain my composure. We left Mount Saint Peter's Cemetery sharing a bond that would remain true until our final days.

Lotte

Chapter 28

May 1912

Meine Teuerste Tante Anja,

   Such a sad thing, watching the coffin of little Geraldine being lowered into the ground. Since I had been her maid and guardian, Mr. Lawson asked me to accompany him when the child was buried. It should have been Mrs. Newkirk there at his side but she is once again with child. I pray she will deliver a son so that the dreadful man who is her husband will no longer rant and rave about having a male heir. He already has young Birdie, who is quite independent, to carry on the Newkirk name. Even at her young age she ignores warnings and disobeys at every turn. She is most definitely just like her father, having somehow inherited all of his bad habits – even crying at the top of her voice and throwing tantrums when she doesn't get her way, then smirking when the staff is instructed to give her whatever she wants.

   Mrs. Newkirk has sent to Ireland for a new governess/nurse to take charge of the nursery and of Birdie. Her name is Tess and she is a distant cousin of Mrs. Newkirk. I pray every night that her ship makes good time and that she arrives soon. It has become difficult to keep constant watch on Birdie and finish my duties to my own, and Mrs. Newkirk's, satisfaction.

Mr. Lawson is the one I have much compassion for. Little Geraldine was his daughter (you must remember to keep this secret). Yet he was the one everyone here turned to in their grief. I am happy that in some small way I was able to offer him understanding and compassion. If I were unaware that Mr. Lawson's heart was promised to another, I believe I should want to try to gain his attention for myself. That can never happen. His love for Mrs. Newkirk is easy to see if one but looks beyond the surface; Mrs. Newkirk in turn shares that love. Fortunately everyone believes that her loving radiance is for her beast of a husband.

Since Mr. Newkirk found us in a compassionate embrace on the day of little Geraldine's passing, Mr. Lawson and I have taken pains to be seen together in what might be called 'private moments' – don't worry, Tante, I would not tarnish my reputation. We try to give the appearance of a lackadaisical courtship. Mr. Lawson is comfortable with that and has explained our actions to Mrs. Newkirk. It is enough that he trusts me and I enjoy every moment we share. I find that with each conversation between us, regardless of subject, my esteem for him grows. He is a gentle man, one who considers how his actions and his words will affect others. I can see how easy it is for Mrs. Newkirk to love him. I can only pray that someday I may find such a man to love me truly.

I hope that you are doing well. Please send my enclosed note on to mama. I will be allowed some time off once Tess arrives and I look forward to visiting with you in person. Perhaps I shall ask Mr. Lawson if he would care to accompany me into town. That would give the Bridgewater gossips something to talk about!

I remain your devoted nichte,
Charlotte

P.S. Mrs. Newkirk has rewarded my service with yet another rise in my wages – I am now earning the enormous sum of fifteen dollars each month! Mr. Lawson has promised to take me to the bank in town to open an account on my next day off.

Cordelia

Chapter 29

July 1912

It was a lovely day for an outing. The sun was shining in a cloudless blue sky, the early morning temperatures were hovering in the upper seventies, and the household staff was abuzz with muted conversation as they went about their duties. Momma and poppa had arrived late last night along with Cal, Rose, and their two children. The guest wing was full of artistic types – poets, playwrights, authors – as well as various horse breeders and their families.

From the vantage point of my turret room, I watched an early riding party, composed of mostly the horse breeder set and one or two of their offspring, set out for the far reaches of Bridgewater. A mid-day repast would be brought out to them by the stable lads once Mrs. Grant had overseen the packing of the picnic baskets.

Behind me, Ellen was fussing with the clothes in my wardrobe, choosing and discarding anything she believed would be too confining for my increasing dimensions. I turned to see what progress she had made, only to find that the entire contents of my wardrobe was draped across the bed.

"The blue lawn dress will do nicely, Ellen," I made the selection for her.

"But Miss Cordelia, that would be scandalous. One can see right through the fabric," she objected.

"Tish, tosh! I'll be sitting most of the time. No one will see anything besides my growing belly. It's the most comfortable and the most flattering thing I own for the condition I'm in. Now shake it out and help me get into it."

I stood still as Ellen floated the light-weight confection of sky blue cotton lawn over my head and settled it on my shoulders. Its large circumference hid well my burgeoning belly and I felt rather like a butterfly searching for a place to alight. My hair was pulled back from my face and pinned up so that my neck could feel whatever slight breeze Mother Nature saw fit to grace us with. A large-brimmed straw hat was perched on my head, its blue ribbons trailing down my back. Looking like a renegade cloud, I made my way down the staircase, through the cool dark central hallway, until I reached the double French doors of the morning room that gave directly onto the terrace.

I stopped for a moment to consider the way our guests had grouped themselves together. My sister-in-law Rose was doing hostess duties in my stead and I watched her move effortlessly from group to group, smiling, nodding her head, and being gracious. What a joy she was to have around!

At the far end of the terrace the artistic gentlemen had congregated, most likely discussing their individual art forms and debating which was more popular at the moment. Their followers, those ladies who attached themselves to members of the artistic set in the hopes of having their names in the society pages of the New Haven Register, were frolicking about the lawn. A group of four was diligently whacking their croquet balls through the hoops; others were splashing in the pool and laughing gaily.

Off to one side I noticed Momma and Mother Newkirk, seated beneath large umbrellas that afforded them some shade. They were speaking to the two Schubert brothers – J.J. and Lee – who were most likely talking about the progress on their newest venture. I searched for poppa and my father-in-law but they were not nearby. More than likely they had ridden out with the equine set where they would escape the critical eyes of their spouses.

My friend Helena Fairlawn was perched on the low stone wall of the terrace, visually taking in the assemblage. Her husband, the professor, was engaged in conversation with a visiting author and his spouse, who seemed bored by the entire affair although not bored enough to critically assess the potential of each gentleman present.

I gave an involuntary jump as two strong hands came around my shoulders and a mustache tickled the nape of my neck.

"Don't move, or I shall be forced to kiss you," a definitely male voice whispered in my ear.

"You've already kissed my nape," I observed.

"Ah, but you deserve to be kissed often; and by me." His lips trailed along the back of my neck as he held up the ribbons of my hat.

"Nathan, do stop. Someone may see us."

He spun me around until we were facing each other.

"No one is looking. They're all too busy trying to impress each other."

He dipped his head and caught my lips with his, kissing me soundly. "Ah, no better way to refresh myself than to kiss the woman I love!"

"Nathan! What if my mother-in-law walked in?" I had a moment of panic.

"You could just say you swooned and I caught you," he grinned at me.

"Oh, you are incorrigible!"

"I love you, Delia. Never forget that," he sobered for a moment.

"As I love you," I whispered, raising my head to look deep into those chocolate brown eyes. That was when he dipped his head once more and kissed me again. This time I clung to him, returning his kiss with fervor.

"I must return to my duties," he murmured.

"Will you come to me tonight?" I whispered furtively.

"If you wish it."

"I do, wish it that is."

"Your wish is my command."

He backed away, bowing from the waist. I watched as he disappeared from the morning room before straightening my hat. With supreme self-confidence I stepped through the French doors and onto the terrace, where I was greeted by my guests.

Later that afternoon, after everyone had eaten their fill of fried chicken and potato salad, and after the riding party had returned and refreshed themselves with tall glasses of vodka and lemonade, a large cake was wheeled out to the now shady terrace. There was much joking and a few ribald comments interspersed with good wishes for Kevin's belated birthday celebration. After the cake was served, Kevin gratefully accepted a small mountain of birthday gifts, one being a portrait of him done by one of our artist guests. I knew without doubt that the portrait would soon grace the front foyer.

As twilight settled on our little group, lanterns were placed around the terrace. Gentlemen congregated into small groups as those of us ladies with children moved indoors to tuck our little ones in for the night. Once our motherly duties were turned over to the servants (Lotte and Tess in my case), we returned to the terrace clutching shawls of various sheer fabrics around our shoulders. We waited in anticipation for the arrival of full dark and the pyrotechnic display that would be our evening's entertainment. While our attention was captured by the delightful starbursts overhead, I noticed a few couples slink away towards the hedgerow maze. I smiled to myself at their actions, hoping that their respective spouses were otherwise engaged. I was not in the mood for jealous shenanigans to ruin a perfectly nice day.

Of course I turned a blind eye when Kevin escorted one of our female guests along the path that led to Willow Cottage, beyond the maze. Through it all I kept my attention on the holiday celebration before us. It wasn't until much later, after the pyrotechnics had ceased and only a couple or two still engaged in conversation lingered on the terrace, that Kevin and his paramour of the evening strolled casually out of the maze, up the terrace steps, and directly past the spot where I sat in the shadows. They stopped just inside of the French doors, where I heard their kiss.

"Will you come to me later?" inquired Kevin in what he believed was a whisper.

"I'm looking forward to it," came the reply, followed by a giggle. I was sure Kevin had tickled her.

"You won't have any trouble finding my room, will you?" I heard their sloppy kiss again. "Now go. Don't keep me waiting too long."

I sat there on the shadowy terrace, now devoid of almost all our guests. From the morning room, a feminine form stepped outside and looked around.

She seated herself in a low Adirondack chair next to mine.

"I didn't realize anyone was looking for me," I offered.

"I would have stepped out sooner but your husband and his latest tart were 'making nice' in the morning room."

"Good heavens, did they see you?"

"I had the good fortune of hiding behind your voluminous drapes as they groped and fondled each other. That was rather annoying."

"I'm sorry you had to witness that. I heard them from this side of the door."

"At least they've moved on, for the moment. How can you tolerate his actions?"

I smiled into the darkness.

"Just look at me, Helena. I'm heavy with child and not the most attractive of women at the moment. Kevin did his duty by me, gave me his child to bear, and now is taking his pleasure where he finds it. I won't begrudge him that."

"That's your business, Cordelia. But I can tell you that I wouldn't stand for that with Walter."

"I knew from the start that Kevin didn't love me. Oh, I tried to fool myself into thinking that he did. He only married me so that I could give him a male heir, to carry on the Newkirk name."

"But you seemed so happy at the start of your marriage."

"I was. Or so I thought. I had everything a young woman of quality could want. A beautiful home, servants, money, jewels; even a child on the way."

"Then what happened?"

"Kevin reminded me of my obligation – to give him a son – in return for which I got to keep all the things he provided. If it weren't for him, and his money, I would be working in a sweat shop in New York City, sewing women's clothing."

"Well then, you'll just make the best of it. I know you will." Helena's reassurance was as much for her as for me. "It's been a long day and I'm sure Walter will be waiting up for me. Good night, Cordelia."

"Good night, Helena. Sleep well."

I watched as the silhouette that was Helena disappeared through the French doors, leaving me alone on the terrace. Upstairs in the nursery was my daughter Birdie, most likely snug in her crib and dreaming. Our guests were settling down for the night; those who couldn't sleep just yet were perhaps in our Library choosing a tome to peruse; or in the Billiard Room engaged in a friendly game. The kitchen would still be abuzz with activity, cleaning up after today's events and preparing for tomorrow. On the second floor Kevin would be donning his smoking jacket and savoring a tumbler of Irish whiskey as he waited for his private entertainment to begin. Here on the terrace I sat alone, the very pregnant mistress of Bridgewater. I had no thought of being sorrowful in my solitude; in fact I enjoyed the quiet that enveloped me. I leaned my head back against the chair, closed my eyes, and listened for the sounds of the night.

"Delia, wake up." It was Nathan kneeling before me. "You should be upstairs, in bed."

I pried open my heavy eyelids and saw the concern on his face.

"What time is it?" I managed to inquire.

"It's well past midnight. Why hasn't Ellen come down to find you?" He extended a hand towards me and I placed my fingers in his, using his hold for balance as I stood up.

"I told Ellen that I wouldn't need her this evening. She's probably been abed for some time now, I imagine."

"When I didn't find you in your room I became anxious."

"I must have been more tired than I imagined," I said by way of explanation.

"The heat of the day certainly didn't help any," Nathan concurred.

"Will you still join me upstairs?" I ventured.

"I think perhaps we'd best save that for another evening. You need your sleep."

We stopped at the bottom of the curved stairway. The second floor seemed so far away to me.

"I'll sleep better knowing you're near me," I whispered.

"And I'll sleep better knowing you are actually sleeping," he laughed into the darkness.

I leaned up and kissed his lovely mouth, tasting the lingering bouquet of brandy on his lips. He drew me close and held me against his chest for a few moments before tipping my chin up and kissing me deeply.

"That will have to do for tonight, dearest." He turned and disappeared into the shadows of the hallway.

September 1912

Once again I was delivered of a girl child. So great was Kevin's disappointment that it turned to anger within moments of the child's first cry. Outside the confines of my room I could hear him swearing loudly and throwing everything he could lay his hands on. I turned my attention to the plump bundle that was placed in my arms by Dr. Bennett. Two rosy cheeks, soft brown eyes, and a thatch of reddish-brown hair evidenced her Newkirk heritage. To spite my husband, I named her Katherine, after my mother.

The day after Katherine's birth, Kevin set out on a business trip. We were told that he did not know when he would return, so we christened the baby without her father. The days drifted pleasantly, one into the other and soon it would be Christmas again.

December 1912

The holiday season gave us all pause as we remembered the passing of our dearest Geraldine. I had forbidden a large tree being erected in the foyer. With Birdie dogging my every step we had a lovely time trimming the tree in our drawing room. Nathan saw to the decorations throughout the remainder of the house and by mid-December every garland and swag had been hung. From my small office, I hand wrote our Christmas greetings to friends and family far and near, signing the cards with both my name and Kevin's.

During a break in the weather, Stan drove me into New Haven where I met Helena Fairlawn. Together we shopped at The Edw. Malley Company Department Store, moving from department to department where we chose gifts for our family members. I made it a point to choose something special for Nathan – a wooden-barreled pen and pencil set that he could display on his desk. His other gifts would be given to him in private. Helena and I then spent some time having lunch in the small restaurant on the store's second floor. I made sure to pick up the check since I knew that Helena's funds were limited. In all it was a lovely day spent in the company of a dear friend.

Once more we had a full house: Momma and poppa, of course; the two Schubert brothers and their wives; Sir Andrew Docket, the playwright, and his companion William Heath; Tomas Kohl, an artist from Cos Cob; Alphonse Redder, a rising star in the music world; and a half dozen or so other folk representing the arts. Our guests of honor were the silent film actress Viola Barry and her movie director husband Jack Conway.

I instructed Mrs. Grant to prepare for our Christmas dinner, directing her to include Kevin's favorite dishes. I was sure that after his traditional Christmas Eve celebration with his mistress he would return home with gifts for all. He did not disappoint me. We were gathered in the drawing room when Kevin entered, stopping momentarily in the doorway to peruse those in attendance. He accepted a glass of champagne from a tray and made a beeline for Miss Barry. I was able to cross his path before he reached her.

"Welcome home, dear." I slipped my hand through the crook of his elbow.

"Thank you, Cordy." He reached over and kissed my cheek.

"Our guests are all gathered. There are several who are anxious to speak with you."

"Is that the movie actress, Miss Barry?" he whispered, not too softly.

"Yes, it is. She and her husband," I emphasized the word *husband,* " are anxious to meet you. The Schubert brothers are here as well to provide us with an update on their theater."

I steered Kevin first to greet those we knew before leading him to a small cluster of people surrounding Miss Barry. She was laughing at something Mr. Heath had said but turned immediately when she spotted Kevin and me. As I introduced the two, Kevin exuded more charm than I had ever witnessed as he chivalrously kissed the hand of the lovely leading lady. I left the two of them to become better acquainted.

For a few minutes I drifted amongst our guests, smiling at one, nodding at another, until I made my escape into the hallway. Out there I was able to draw a deep breath, smiling to myself as I realized that almost all of my dreams had come true. I was a hostess who moved among the rich and famous, whose dinner parties were gathering a reputation of their own. Anyone seeking to climb the ladder to success vied for an invitation to my dinner parties; to be asked to spend the weekend or a few days at Bridgewater was an immediate catapult into the societal stratosphere of New Haven. My name was linked to charitable contributions and organizations. I was the mistress of Bridgewater, the loveliest home within a hundred mile radius, whose hospitality was becoming known all the way to the west coast; just this week I had received requests from several actors making the theater circuit asking if they might call upon me and perhaps spend time at Bridgewater. I had closets full of designer fashions and an assortment of jewelry that might rival those of the British monarchy. With a house full of servants to do my bidding, I could devote my time to any leisure occupation I chose. And riding those coat tails was Momma who, in her own eyes, had become a lady of quality.

Upstairs my children slept soundly in the comfort of their own cribs, tended by their governess and their maid. My husband was jovial in his manner even if he did drink too much and chase after other women. What did it matter, I reasoned, when I was dallying with the House Steward? After all, a woman wanted to feel needed from time to time. And the fact that Nathan needed me more than I needed him gave me a sense of power that was lacking in other areas of my life. When I wanted him with me I had only to request his presence and he would come to my room. If I asked sweetly, he would pleasure me in any way I requested. And if I merely wanted his company, he would accommodate that as well putting aside his own needs to cater to mine. He claimed to love me, but I had learned to steel my heart against loving too deeply. I had foolishly thought I loved Kevin at the beginning of our marriage and that had gotten me nothing more than a broken heart. Now, I was in control of my emotions and my favors. Tonight I might grant Nathan the benefit of those favors, or not. He would do as I asked without question.

I'm sure he suspected that his position might be tenuous should he not please me. But since he believed strongly in our love I'm sure the thought failed to cross his mind. I might remind him of that at some point, or not. Regardless of Nathan's position, he filled a need in my life. I needed to be worshipped and adored and in this Nathan excelled. Even now, as he approached the drawing room to announce dinner, his smile when he saw me was genuine and warm.

"Mrs. Newkirk, shall I announce dinner?" he inquired, drawing close to me.

"Yes, thank you Mr. Lawson. But first you must kiss me." I fluttered my eyelashes coquettishly.

"Here? Now?" he whispered.

"Yes. Here. Now."

"But, the others…."

I pulled his head down and kissed him soundly. His hand

involuntarily went around me, drawing me into an embrace. I wiggled against him, causing him to pull back.

"Minx! Look what you've done." We both looked down at the front of his trousers.

"Why Mr. Lawson, I have no idea what you mean!" I smirked.

"You'll pay for this later," he joked.

"Will I?" I teased. "Or will you?"

At that moment, the drawing room door opened, and Kevin's head popped out.

"Ah, Lawson, there you are. Is dinner ready?"

"I was just about to announce it sir."

I noticed that Nathan stood back a pace to hide his momentary discomfort.

"Wonderful!" Kevin disappeared back into the drawing room.

"I'll see you later," I whispered as I turned and entered the drawing room, leaving him standing alone in the hallway.

After we had feasted on our wonderful Christmas dinner and consumed far too much of the wonderful trifle that Mrs. Grant had prepared, we lingered at the dining table where pleasurable conversation sweetened our second cups of coffee.

"Mr. Schubert," began Miss Barry, causing both of the brothers to look up from their conversations. Miss Barry giggled at the confusion her salutation had caused. "I'm sorry, perhaps I should have said Mssrs. Schubert? I understand that your new theater is almost complete. When will the first performances be held there?"

"Miss Barry, feel free to address us by our given names," replied Sam Schubert.

"And you must call me Viola," the actress batted her eyelashes is an exaggerated manner, causing us all to laugh.

"Our first performance is scheduled to open in May. Will you and your husband honor us with your attendance?"

"I don't know," she hesitated. "Jack, darling, are we able to accommodate these gentlemen?" she questioned her husband.

"I'm positive we can be there for opening night," Jack Conway replied.

"Splendid!" concurred Sam Schubert. "We will alert the office to reserve the best box seats for you. What about you Mr. Newkirk? We would be honored to have you and your lovely wife attend opening night as well."

"I'm afraid that I'll be busy overseeing this year's entry to the Kentucky Derby and making sure that all goes well. However, Cordy is free to attend."

"I'll reserve another box for you, Mrs. Newkirk. You may bring a guest or two if you like."

"Thank you, Sam. That's very generous of you," I conceded, thinking how much the Fairlawns would enjoy an outing to the theater.

"Since we are all gathered here at your bountiful Christmas table, I should like to make an announcement," offered J.J. Schubert.

Kevin inclined his head in agreement.

"With the imminent success of our theater, Sam and I are hoping to expand our holdings. To that end we've located a piece of property in downtown New Haven that is a mere few blocks from the Yale campus," J.J. continued.

"How exciting!" exclaimed momma.

"What are you planning to do there?" inquired Jack Conway.

"Will you open another theater?" questioned Sir Andrew, most likely in hopes of trying to have his latest work presented.

"We were thinking of opening another theater but using it as a place where shows could 'try their wings', so to speak."

"I'm not sure I understand the concept," stated Mr. Kohl.

"Since there are so many offerings vying for stage space on New York City's Broadway, we thought it would be beneficial to have a place where producers could present their latest offerings, have them judged by a live audience, and ascertain whether or not the production was indeed Broadway material," Sam Schubert explained.

"I see, sort of like a dress rehearsal for the real thing," I commented.

"Precisely, Cordelia. This would be a proving ground for an author's work, a launching pad for the careers of unknown actors, a place where theater-goers might enjoy a pre-Broadway show at a cost substantially less than a Broadway ticket."

"It has merit," commented Kevin. "In either event, success or failure of the production, you gents as owners of the theater make a pretty penny. Clever, very clever."

"We have one drawback, however," added J.J.

"Ah, here it comes!" exclaimed the heretofore silent Mr. Redder.

"We are in need of backers for the venture," admitted J.J.

"With your fine reputation that should be easy for you to acquire," added Miss Barry.

"While that may be true, our success as theater owners has yet to be established. In other words, our credit is not yet established." Sam Schubert shrugged his shoulders as he spoke.

"Let's not bore the ladies with talk about business," Kevin interjected. "I propose we retire to the billiard room and leave the ladies to their discussions of fashion and such."

At that point, the gentlemen did in fact excuse themselves. Later that evening, I was bidding good night to the last of the ladies who had lingered with me in the drawing room, when Kevin appeared. Once Mrs. J.J. Schubert was out of earshot, Kevin turned, closed the drawing room doors, and came to sit beside me on the sofa. Although he had consumed a good amount of spirits, he was far from drunk.

"It was a pleasant Christmas, don't you think?" he inquired.

We both kept our eyes on the dying fire in the hearth. The embers were still red hot and a tiny flame or two consumed the last small pieces of wood.

"Yes, pleasant enough. I do miss our Geraldine, though," I admitted.

"I should like to try for a son one more time."

"Could it wait until after the holidays?" I was thinking of spending time with Nathan and didn't need the anxiety of whose child I would bear.

"I wasn't thinking about creating the child with you, Cordy?" I turned to find him staring into the fire. "There is someone else who....."

"Has Jeannette agreed to this?" The tone of my voice was sharper than I had anticipated.

"I mentioned it to her last night. She's agreed to think about it." He offered.

"And if she agrees?"

"Then I would spend some time in Boston, at least until she conceived."

"You've already planned it then?" He kept silent. "Am I to raise the child as my own?"

"Only if it is a boy."

"There will be talk," I cautioned.

"We could say he was an orphan. That we adopted him," suggested Kevin.

"Let's cross that bridge when we come to it, shall we?"

I stood up, feeling that this conversation had gone on long enough.

"Before you go, Cordy, I've got your Christmas gift." He reached into his jacket pocket and pulled out a jeweler's box.

"What, no stock certificate in the family business this year?"

"You're a good woman, Cordy. These jewels reminded me of you. I hope you'll wear them to the premiere performance at the Schubert Theater."

"You've already stated that you'll be too busy to accompany me in May."

"I was rather hoping you'd wear them to the opening of the theater here in New Haven."

"You have much faith in those Schubert brothers."

"Yes, I do. So much so that I've offered to underwrite a good fifty-percent of their endeavor in New Haven."

"You did what?" I was astounded.

"It's always good to diversify. Can't keep putting all my money into the horses, you know. But I've made it clear that you, my dear, are to be the 'godmother' of the New Haven venue."

"I'm sure that went over well."

"In fact, Sam Schubert said that he was going to propose the same thing. You've made quite an impression on those two."

"Then I suppose I shall need to order some new outfits to match these jewels."

I opened the box to find a diamond and amethyst necklace with matching earbobs nestled in the velvet lining.

"There's a bracelet that goes with the set," explained Kevin, "but I'll hold onto that until your birthday."

"As insurance that I don't cause trouble between you and Jeannette?"

"Not at all. I expected your acquiescence. I've told you before that I would be open to your taking a lover. The fact that you haven't done so has pleased me. But you are a young woman with needs, and I expect you to choose someone with care. I assumed that was why you invited so many different types of people to your dinners and parties."

Something inside me hardened at Kevin's words. I hadn't realized that he wanted so keenly for me to take a lover. Nay, it seemed that he *needed* me to take a lover if for no other reason than to assuage his guilt at entertaining so many ladies.

"Now that you mention it, I have found one or two of our previous guests who would be acceptable."

"Wonderful! Invite them to dinner next month. I'll ply them with my best whiskey and drop the hint that I wouldn't take umbrage if they were to become intimate with you." Kevin smiled at me.

"How generous of you, husband. I'll look forward to a new liaison." I forced a smile there in the shadows of the drawing room as I turned my back to my husband and made my way to my room.

Kevin

Chapter 30

January 1913

We had weekend guests. The house was full with the usual mix of celebrities, near-celebrities, and artistic geniuses. Normally I paid no mind to the gentlemen, fixing my sights on the ladies present – assessing their openness to a quick liaison even as I evaluated their charms. There was at least one lady in each group who was open to my flirtations and I must admit that I can be quite charming when I choose. This particular weekend was a bit different though. While I still gave my attention to the ladies, I also was evaluating the gentlemen present. Since Cordy had grudgingly admitted that she had an interest in one or two, it fell to me to choose for her the most discreet of gentlemen who would be enamored enough of her to become her lover. I had high standards for the ultimate victor, since I wouldn't let just anyone crawl into her bed.

The one who would ultimately triumph should have impeccable taste in his clothes, a sure sign that he was careful in all aspects of his life. The gentleman should also come from a good family, or at least have no recent scandals attached to his name. That might be difficult since several of these gentlemen were associated with theater or moving pictures. Cordy's lover should also be a take-charge sort, no namby-pamby writers. He should be tall, but not too tall; he must be fastidious in his person; he should be well-versed so as to speak to Cordy's varied interests. Hmm, this choosing a lover for one's wife would be more difficult than I anticipated.

In the end, I decided that it should be Cordy's choice anyway. So, having gathered the several gentlemen in the billiard room, I passed each a glass of my Bushmills whiskey and cleared my throat. They seemed to sense that I was about to say something of great import so they turned their attention to me.

"Gentlemen, I'm sure each of you is well acquainted with my wife, Cordelia."

"Lovely woman," replied one.

"So graceful," commented another.

"If only my wife was as enchanting," remarked a third.

"Thank you all for such kind sentiments. However, I have a daunting task before me. Since I have another to whom I owe my love and allegiance, I have given Cordelia leave to form a liaison of her own. Up to now, she has not done so."

I noticed a look of interest on the faces of at least four of the gentlemen. This made what I had to say easier.

"So, it has fallen to me to see that Cordelia's needs are taken care of. If there be among you any who are so inclined to seek intimacy with Cordelia, please do so. I will not stand in your way. I only ask your discretion to avoid scandal of any sort."

"I say, Newkirk, are you giving us leave to have a go at your wife?" asked one.

"I dare say I am."

"And she is aware of this?" inquired another.

"She is."

"That's quite sporting of you."

"There is another stipulation," I hastened to add.

"Ah, the catch!"

"Cordelia is not to be passed from one to the other of you. You may court her; convince her of your worthiness. She will make the final decision about who she will welcome to her bed."

"Makes sense to me," quipped a literary type dressed in corduroy.

"I dare say she likes poetry, books, music, flowers. Feel free to shower her with trinkets if you think it will help your cause."

"I suppose you expect those of us with wives to turn a blind eye to your own advances upon them."

"Shouldn't be a problem for you, Hal," I answered the gent. "You've allowed your wife to dally in my chamber more than once. I must say she can be quite insatiable."

"Yes, well. You can understand why I look the other way. I'm no longer a young man and my stamina isn't what it used to be."

There was a general round of chuckling as the gentlemen finished their drinks. I could see some of them mentally determining how best to pursue Cordelia.

"One last thing, before we return to the ladies. I will be traveling quite a bit during the next few months. Cordelia shouldn't lack for company or male attention. You are welcome here at Bridgewater as often as you choose to visit."

"Mr. Newkirk, sir, a moment of your time in private?" It was Tomas Kohl, the artist, who put forth the query.

"Certainly, excuse us, gentlemen."

I nodded to the others as I led the somewhat shy artist to my office. Once there he hemmed and hawed for a moment before speaking.

"Mr. Newkirk, I could never hope that Mrs. Newkirk would favor me in the manner that you've just proposed."

"Nonsense, Tomas, you shouldn't take yourself out of the running," I encouraged.

"I have been fortunate to be included with the others on Mrs. Newkirk's guest list. I would however, be indebted for the opportunity to paint her portrait."

"What a grand idea! And how clever of you, Tomas!"

"Then I have your permission, sir?"

"You certainly do. I shall inform Cordelia that I have commissioned you to paint her portrait. I assume there will be a number of sittings involved?"

Tomas nodded his head in agreement.

"Splendid! I shall arrange for the two of you to be completely alone at those times."

"Thank you sir, I work best without interruption."

"As you should, Tomas. I do expect a quality portrait when you have finished. By that time, Cordelia should have become quite comfortable being alone with you. I would suggest that she might be persuaded to take you as her lover."

"Oh, I don't think…."

"Nonsense. In fact, I should like for Cordelia to be portrayed in one of those artistic venues, you know, dressed like a Roman goddess perhaps, with one breast fully exposed," I let my suggestion take root in the artist's mind.

"That would make a most fetching portrait indeed, Mr. Newkirk."

"Then we are agreed. My own goddess, exposing her breast, to be captured by you on canvas for all eternity. I shall hang the painting here, in my office, when it is complete."

"I do believe we are in agreement, Mr. Newkirk."

"Please, use my given name," I offered, "after all we shall soon be sharing my wife."

"How soon may I start?"

I could see the artist almost salivate at the thought of being alone with Cordy. Ah yes, he would be perfect for her. Not too controversial a person, limited contact with our society peers, quiet and unassuming – perfect!

"The sooner the better, Mr. Kohl. I shall inform Cordelia of our arrangement this very evening."

True to my word, I informed Cordy that she should expect to be the recipient of gifts from a select number of men that I had chosen as candidates for her lover. I also informed her that I had commissioned a portrait of her to be done by Tomas Kohl. That seemed to mollify her temper somewhat. I thought it prudent to not discuss with her the details of the portrait but to let Mr. Kohl provide the vision and inspiration for himself.

With these provisions in place I decided the time was right for a trip to Boston. Jeannette had written to me, expressing her acquiescence to my plan to produce a son, and I was anxious to begin as quickly as possible. I looked forward to employing every trick I knew to get Jeannette with child. With luck I would be father to a hearty boy child before the year was out. So with much anxiety on my part, I left Bridgewater behind me and vowed to stay with Jeannette as long as it took to accomplish my goal.

Upon arrival at the train station in Boston, I bid farewell to Paul who would spend his time at our family home on Revere Street. As his taxicab pulled away from the curb and I was about to hail one for myself, I was aware that someone was pulling at my coatsleeve. I turned to find Jeannette. This was a departure from the norm, for usually Jeannette awaited my arrival at home where we would fall into each other's arms. But there she was, fashionably dressed with a fur-trimmed coat, pert hat, and galoshes over her shoes. Her smile was warm and welcoming as she came forward and hugged me. I felt as though I had truly arrived home.

"Kevin, it's so good to see you again. I've missed you so," she whispered into my ear as I hugged her close.

"You must have missed me terribly to brave the cold and wait for me here in the station," I replied.

"It really isn't all that cold. And I do love the feel of snow on my face." She looked up as we stepped out onto the sidewalk, lifting her chin high as the first flakes of a new snow storm drifted down over us.

I raised my hand to hail a taxicab, but Jeannette tugged my elbow in an effort to lower my arm.

"We've no need for a cab," she commented, "follow me."

She led the way along the sidewalk to the end of the block. Stepping out in front of me, she stopped by the side of a shiny black automobile, with high fenders and running boards.

"Here we are!"

I looked about to determine which street corner we were on before looking back at Jeannette.

"Exactly where are we, dearest?"

"Right here," she pointed to the car. "This is my new car."

"I'm impressed," I answered, looking closer at the car. "But where's the driver? Shouldn't he be here awaiting our arrival?"

"Don't be silly, Kevin! I'm the driver. This is my car." She opened the passenger door for me.

I stowed my valise in the rear seat and settled myself in the automobile while she went around to the driver's side and slid behind the wheel.

"I didn't know you knew how to drive," I remarked as she turned the key in the ignition and the engine came to life.

"I've had a few lessons. There really is nothing to it!"

She gently pulled away from the curb and into the line of traffic leaving the railroad station. Once the traffic thinned a bit, she put her foot on the gas and proceeded at what I thought was a bit of a fast pace for a snowy street. Paying little or no attention to the oncoming traffic, she whizzed around corners and merely slowed at stop signs. I surreptitiously clenched my fists as I hid them inside my coat pockets. Jeannette kept up a steady stream of conversation the entire time. I think she mentioned how she had been saving up the profits from her hat shop to buy the car and was given a good deal on this one as the husband of one of her customer's was in the automobile business. I couldn't be sure of the details because my subconscious was too busy praying to whatever saints would listen in the hopes that we would arrive at her house unharmed.

Thankfully, Jeannette did slow down when she pulled into a parking spot directly in front of her cottage. Then, and only then, did I release the breath I hadn't realized I was holding.

'Well, here we are! Home at last," exclaimed Jeannette.

"Yes," I agreed, "home at last!"

Cordelia

Chapter 31

I was furious with Kevin! How dare he give his cronies leave to pursue me? On the morning he left Bridgewater to run off to Jeannette, I languished in bed until I heard the sound of the motorcar carrying him and his valet chug off down the driveway. Pulling on my robe, I stood by the window watching the trail of exhaust from the car's rear. Good riddance! I hoped it would take at least six months, if ever, for Jeannette to get pregnant. A knock on my bedroom door alerted me that Ellen was bringing my breakfast.

"Enter!" I called out.

The door swung open to reveal Ellen, bearing a tray with tea service and a covered dish, hopefully holding a sweet roll or two. I needed something sweet – desperately! What I wasn't ready for was the parade that followed Ellen into my room. Two footmen and one maid, each carrying two floral arrangements, stood just inside the doorway.

"Good morning, Miss Cordelia," Ellen greeted me. "These flowers all arrived for you this morning." She waved a hand at the various vases held by staff members. "Where would you like them placed?"

"Good heavens! Where did these all come from?" I questioned. "Never mind, I can guess." I assumed that Kevin had sent them to make up for his high-handed manner of trying to choose a lover for me during his absence. "Place them there, by the window," I pointed to the window seat. I'll deal with them later."

"There's a card with each vase, ma'am."

"Yes, yes. Mr. Newkirk and I had a spat last night and this is his way of trying to make things right." I turned my attention to the teapot.

"The handwriting is different on each card, ma'am. Perhaps they're not all from Mr. Newkirk," suggested Ellen tactfully.

I watched the footmen and maid depart, closing the door behind them. I turned to Ellen.

"Hand me the cards, one at a time," I instructed.

Ellen moved to the first vase, containing a mixture of yellow roses and daisies: a lovely arrangement, reminiscent of springtime. She plucked the card from amidst the blossoms and handed it to me. The penmanship was definitely not Kevin's and I wondered who might have been so thoughtful.

Dear Cordelia, I spotted these roses and they reminded me of you. Although yellow roses are a symbol of friendship, I'm hoping that we can be more than friends. Sincerely, George Fleming

"George Fleming, how interesting," I mused as Ellen handed me the next card.

The other cards were in the same vein, each more flowery than the last with the sentiments carefully worded, although I knew exactly what sentiment was hidden behind those words. Each of the senders hoped to weasel his way into my bed! The last card was attached to a beautiful hot-house orchid that would eventually find its way into our conservatory. This last must indeed be from Kevin for it would be just like him to find a showy manner to try to regain my good graces. But I was proven wrong.

My dear Mrs. Newkirk, I'm sure that your husband has informed you that he has commissioned me to paint your portrait. I have never had a subject as lovely as you for a model and I'm anxious for us to start. Please join me at your earliest convenience. I shall await you in the library. Your humble servant, Tomas Kohl

"Ellen, am I to believe that Mr. Kohl is downstairs this very minute?" My fury at Kevin was building.

"He's in the library. Says he's content to wait there until you will receive him. What shall we do with the flowers?"

"Disperse them about the house. Better yet, let the staff choose where to put them. Except for the orchid; see that it goes into the conservatory."

"Yes, Miss Cordelia."

" Ring for Mr. Lawson. I want to speak with him."

"Shall I help you dress first?"

"Ring for Lawson. I'll speak to him while I dress."

I didn't care what Ellen might or might not think of me at that moment. I was furious! Nathan would know how to calm me. Ellen rang the service bell that connected to Nathan's office and within moments he knocked at the door. Ellen looked to me, then to the door, then back to me.

"Miss Cordelia, you're not properly dressed," she protested.

"Let him in, for heaven's sake! I'm sure he's seen a woman in a robe before."

Casting a wary glance in my direction, Ellen opened the door to Nathan who had the sense to avert his eyes from me. He walked directly to the windows and kept his gaze trained on the driveway down below. I stepped behind the screen and into the dressing area, from where I could see him by looking into the mirror; he was afforded a partial view of me in the same manner.

"Mrs. Newkirk, how may I be of service?"

"Am I to understand that Mr. Kohl is downstairs in the library?"

"Yes, ma'am. He insisted on waiting for you."

"Then he will have to wait a while longer. Mr. Newkirk has commissioned him to paint my portrait," I offered by way of explanation, "and there are several things I wish to discuss with him before we begin. Provide him with accommodations in the guest wing. See to his needs, and for heaven's sake, be sure the man has had something to eat. These artistic types tend to skip meals."

"Yes, ma'am."

He continued to stand by the window, looking straight ahead.

"Mr. Lawson, you may leave your position by the window. I'm now properly dressed."

He winked at me as he turned, but I was not in the mood for frivolity.

"And what shall I tell Mr. Fleming?" he inquired.

"Mr. Fleming? Is he here as well?"

"I put him in the morning room, Mrs. Newkirk."

"The man must be crazy to be here so early in the day. Why it isn't even mid-morning!"

"He arrived shortly after Mr. Kohl."

"Has he been offered refreshment?"

"Yes, he has. He prefers to await your arrival."

"Then I will be downstairs shortly. Ellen you may take my breakfast tray out, I'm no longer hungry."

Ellen did as I bid, leaving the door open as propriety dictated. Nathan turned to me with a questioning look on his face.

"Delia, what's going on? Where have all these flowers come from? You've never had gentlemen callers, or any other callers for that matter, so early in the day. Is there something I should know about?"

"This is all Kevin's doing," I hissed. "He has given his friends leave to pursue me in the hopes that I will choose one for my lover."

"He's done what?" Nathan's voice boomed out.

"Shh. Not so loud. It's nothing I can't handle."

"No wonder Fleming looked so smug. Why I should…." Nathan's fists clenched automatically.

"You'll do nothing of the sort. You aren't supposed to know anything about this. You must do as I ask."

It took a moment or two for Nathan to bring his temper under control. That was when he reached out and pulled me toward him, kissing me soundly.

"If even one of them lays a hand on you, I'll thrash him and kick his butt all the way to New Haven."

"I believe you would." I smiled up at him. "Now go get Mr. Kohl settled while I dispatch Mr. Fleming."

My first stop was the morning room. I stood in the hallway, looking in through the open door. George Fleming was seated in a chair, looking very comfortable indeed. His gaze seemed to take in the room's furnishings as he seemed to assess how best to make his advances toward me. I flounced in on a full head of steam. He jumped to his feet and straightened his jacket as I approached him.

"Mr. Fleming, what brings you to Bridgewater this early in the day?" I favored him with my most flattering smile.

"Isn't a visit with you reason enough?"

He reached for my hand, pressed a kiss to my palm, and tucked my fingers into his hand. I didn't pull back right away but led him to the sofa.

"Have you had breakfast, Mr. Fleming?" I inquired solicitously.

"Indeed I have, Cordelia," he replied, using my given name in a familiar manner.

"Then perhaps you'd enjoy a cup of coffee or tea?"

"I only wish to feast my eyes on your beauty." He claimed the spot next to me on the sofa. His eyes were bright with anticipation.

"Your flowers arrived this morning. They are beautiful."

"Your beauty outshines even the most beautiful flower. I am overwhelmed by it."

He reached out to clasp my hand in his once more.

"But I'm afraid that they were lost in the veritable hot-house of flowers that arrived along with them." I glanced sideways to gauge his reaction.

"There were others?"

"Oh my, yes. There were all sorts of flowers that arrived this morning. So many; and all quite beautiful. I've had the staff disperse them throughout the house."

"Who else sent flowers?" Mr. Fleming seemed a bit flustered.

"Oh, the usual gentlemen. I believe something arrived from each of the gentlemen who were here when you came to dinner the other night."

"I see," mused Mr. Fleming. He hesitated for a moment, most likely evaluating how best to proceed before he spoke once more.

"Cordelia, let me speak plainly, if I might."

"That would be refreshing," I answered.

"The thing is, I mean to say that…"

I watched his mustache quiver as he tried to phrase his words in a genteel manner.

"Yes, Mr. Fleming, you were saying?" I encouraged.

"Cordelia, your husband has informed us, the gentlemen that is, of his extended absence from Bridgewater as he attends to business," he began.

"Yes, that's true, Mr. Fleming. My husband will be away from home for quite some time."

"Please, Cordelia, I would prefer that you use my given name. After all we are friends, are we not?"

I slanted my eyes as I contemplated the gentleman beside me. He had gone to great pains to make a good impression: neatly combed and freshly shaved, highly starched collar, fashionable three-piece suit. I noticed that the chain of his pocket watch was gleaming, and the shine on his shoes was such that it reflected the morning light. Obviously, Mr. Fleming had taken great care to present himself before me in a most acceptable light.

"We are acquaintances, Mr. Fleming," I corrected him. "I don't feel we know each other well enough for me to use your given name."

That must have been the opening he was looking for. He placed an arm around my shoulders and drew me a bit closer. I stiffened imperceptibly as his fingers began to rub my upper arm.

"You are absolutely right, Cordelia. I apologize if I've offended you. However, I'm here to offer my services as your protector while Kevin is on his travels. I wouldn't feel right knowing you were here, alone, without someone to look after you."

His breathing was becoming a bit ragged as he spoke while his fingers tried to wander down my arm.

"Good heavens, Mr. Fleming! Let me assure you that I am not alone here at Bridgewater. Why I have a household staff of thirty people, my children are upstairs in the nursery, and we have a full complement of employees taking care of the stables. Additionally, Mr. Lawson is here to deflect any harm from myself or Bridgewater. I need only to call out to him and he will be in front of me within moments." I hoped Mr. Fleming took the hint I had so openly provided. Alas, he did not.

"That relieves my mind some, Cordelia, but I was hoping for more." He raised my hand to his lips and pressed a kiss on my fingers.

"I fail to understand what more I might need," I replied, keeping my chin up as I spoke.

"I was rather hoping to assuage your needs on a more personal level. I've always admired you Cordelia, there's no denying that."

"Mr. Fleming, what exactly are you trying to say?" I pulled my hand back.

"Cordelia, please, don't make me say it outright."

"I'm afraid you must, Mr. Fleming. I'm not a clairvoyant."

"I was hoping we could come to some sort of an arrangement."

"Arrangement?" I wasn't giving the poor man an inch.

"Yes, an arrangement. I love to ride and was hoping to make use of the stables in your husband's absence. I was thinking I could come out here every week and stay for a night or two."

"Every week?"

"Yes, that way I could exercise the horses during the day. In the evenings you and I could get to know each other better." He placed a finger under my chin and turned my face so that I had no choice but to look into his eyes. He leaned in closer to me, whispering, "We can learn to know each other much, much better. I could stay in the cottage out back so there wouldn't be any talk; you know how servants love to talk. You could join me there, you see. No one would need to know what transpires behind closed doors."

I allowed him to come a hair's breath away from kissing my lips when I asked, "And exactly what would transpire behind those doors?"

"Ah, Cordelia, I would show you the heights we could reach as we partook of shared pleasures."

He pulled me into his embrace with both arms encircling me, lightly pressing his lips to mine. I gave no response.

"You have inflamed my passions, Cordelia. You must know how much I want you," he whispered. He pressed his lips to mine once more, adding a bit of pressure in an effort to force my lips apart.

"I'm sorry to dash your hopes of riding me like you would one of Kevin's horses, Mr. Fleming."

I drew back and moved slightly away from Mr. Fleming.

"Why, didn't you know? He's given us, the gentlemen who were present here the other night, leave to romance you. He said he felt guilty that you would be deprived of your normal passions in his absence and thus we could present ourselves to you in the hopes that you would choose one of us as your lover."

In one swift move, I grabbed his hand and placed it over my breast, while my other hand grabbed his lapel and pulled him closer.

"Oh, George, I can't believe I have such a thoughtful husband! He knows that I'm normally insatiable."

"Really?" His fingers tentatively squeezed my breast yet I continued to hold his hand there.

"Oh yes. I'm sure even Kevin is unaware of how deep my passions truly run."

"Deep?" His other hand went around me and slipped lower until he had my buttocks in hand.

"Yes, really deep." I looked up into his eyes and found that they had glazed over. I'm sure he was thinking that he was in the home stretch. "How many gentlemen has he given leave to woo me?"

"In all, there were seven, no six, of us." His fingers were slowly trying to lift my skirt from the rear.

"Six! Goodness! That's just perfect." I moved my hands to his vest and began unbuttoning it.

"You can't mean all six of us?" His hand stopped moving along my skirt.

"Not exactly."

"Then you'll choose from among us?"

"Why waste all that passion? It's always been a dream of mine to have two men at the same time." I whispered, moving my hands to the waistband of his trousers.

"Two? At the same time?"

"Yes, just think of it."

His breath was growing more ragged by the second.

"And with six of you, we could alternate nights, or days if you prefer. Two different gentlemen each night. Why I must be the luckiest woman in the world!" My hands had unbuttoned the two top buttons of his trousers, easing somewhat the strain on the fabric as his lust became more and more pronounced.

"Two? Each night?"

"Yes, and when we've tired of that we might try three of you at a time. What do you think of that, George?"

"I...I really don't know what to think."

" Perhaps you'd be willing to play some erotic games with me."

"What...what kind of games?" The poor man was becoming addled quite quickly.

"There are all sorts of things I've heard of. Why we could pretend that you're a police constable and you've just caught me committing a crime."

"What kind of crime?" his grip on my breast tightened. I ran my fingers lightly over his slightly exposed chest.

"Does it matter?" I whispered. He shook his head, unable to voice his response. "Good, because then you, as the constable, would be forced to throw me on the bed in your jail cell. I, of course, would try to escape, but you being bigger and stronger would eventually subdue me."

"I would?"

"Oh yes, and then you'd throw me back on the bed, this time tying my hands to the bedpost above me. When you had me secure, you'd spread me out on the bed and then tie each of my feet to the footboard. And then....."

"And then?" his fingers had crawled up my bodice to the neckline of my dress, bunching it in his fist.

"And then you would proceed to show me exactly how big and strong you were. Do you understand?"

"Big. Strong. Tied up." He murmured, nodding his head vigorously. He was interrupted by a spasm that shook his entire body.

Mr. Fleming stepped back, annoyance evident on his face as reality set in. I stepped back and straightened my garments.

"Look what you've done!"

"I can't say I'm sorry, Mr. Fleming, but you must understand that I don't want a lover." My voice was now devoid of any sensuality. "When and if I do take a lover, it will be someone of my own choice and will be done with the utmost discretion. I can see through Kevin's little ploy of trying to trick me into adultery. It won't work." I moved over to the window. "I'm sure you know the way out. Good day, Mr. Fleming."

There was a good deal of mumbling as the gentleman got himself under control and put himself together. "I beg you, Cordelia, don't let word of this get out. I would be the laughingstock of Woodhaven."

"Good day, Mr. Fleming."

I turned and departed the morning room, a silly smile on my face that fortunately, Mr. Fleming could not see. Not waiting to see to Mr. Fleming's departure, I walked briskly towards my office. Once there, I nodded in Nate's direction and he followed me into the office.

"What happened?" Nate asked, his anxiety quite evident.

"I'll tell you what happened! That man tried to seduce me, in my own home. He tried to convince me that he would be the best choice for me to take as my lover." I moved to sit behind my desk.

"What did you tell him? Surely you didn't allow him any liberties?"

"I allowed him one liberty. One was enough for him to compromise himself and be indebted to me so long as I keep his shameful act to myself."

"Good heavens, Delia, what did you do?"

I spent the next several minutes recounting my meeting with Mr. Fleming. When I was done I felt rather good about it, my anger at Mr. Fleming having cooled somewhat. While I spoke I watched Nate's face become suffused with color at the thought of Mr. Fleming's hands on me. However, he maintained his silence until I had finished my tale.

"I swear to you Delia that I will never again let that man cross the threshold of Bridgewater!" He hands were balled up into fists and I'm sure he felt like punching something, or someone.

"There will be no fisticuffs, Nathan. Not while I am still the mistress of Bridgewater."

"But Delia, surely you can't let such an event go without some sort of retaliation?"

"I believe the proof of my retaliation resides on the front of Mr. Fleming's trousers. I'd like to see him explain that to his wife," I chuckled.

"As you wish," Nate responded on an audible sigh. "What of Mr. Kohl?"

"I will meet with Mr. Kohl in the drawing room after lunch. After all, he has been commissioned to provide a portrait of me. That is more of a business arrangement. I think I'll have my midday meal here. Please inform Mrs. Grant and the others there is no need to set up the dining room. Have something delivered to Mr. Kohl if he desires. I shouldn't want to starve our 'artist in residence.'"

"As you wish, of course." He stood up and made his way to the door before turning back to me. "Delia, be careful. Men don't take kindly to being made to look the fool." With that he left me to think about how I would handle Mr. Kohl.

I spent the remainder of the morning looking over the menus for the next three days, approving the order for more bluing for the laundry room, and writing a letter to momma. So engrossed was I with my business, I was surprised to see Mrs. Grant herself delivering my lunch tray. She set it down on a corner of my desk before availing herself of the vacant chair normally occupied by a guest.

"Please sit down, Mrs. Grant," I invited, since the woman had already done so.

"Very kind of you, Mrs. Newkirk. It's not often I get to rest my aching feet."

"Is there a problem in the kitchen? Are you in need of anything to make your work easier?" I questioned as I buttered a slice of warm pumpernickel bread.

"We can always use an extra hand if that were warranted, but with the master being away it doesn't seem like we'll be needing to prepare quite as many formal meals." She sighed at the thought of a lighter menu.

"That may be true for this week, Mrs. Grant, but I have decided that just because Mr. Newkirk has business elsewhere there is no reason for discontinuing my artistic salons. We will still be entertaining. Additionally, Mr. Kohl, the artist from the Greenwich area will be staying on for a while. He has been commissioned to provide a portrait of me." I managed to convey all of this between sips of a creamy mushroom soup.

"That's splendid, Mrs. Newkirk. A lovely portrait of you in the Grand Foyer. That will be the touch that sets Bridgewater apart," agreed the cook.

"Is there something else I should know, Mrs. Grant?" I queried in a gentle effort to push the hard-working lady back to her chores.

"If I may be frank, ma'am?"

"Certainly."

"Something seems to have gotten into Mr. Lawson today." This was spoken in hushed tones.

"Whatever do you mean?" I feigned ignorance.

"Not so much that he's cross or anything like that, he just looks peeved about something. I noticed he was very abrupt with the younger folks on staff."

"Thank you for bringing it to my attention, Mrs. Grant. I will certainly inquire of Mr. Lawson if something is amiss."

"Here, then, let me take that lunch tray back into the kitchen." The rotund woman grasped the tray of soiled dishes and shuffled towards the door. "I knew you'd like that mushroom soup. Told Mr. Lawson so myself."

Upstairs in my chamber I exchanged my morning dress for a day dress. I hoped to project the image of a confident mistress of her home yet not appear overly adorned. To that end I chose pearl studs and a rope of gleaming pearls as my only jewelry – better too little than too much, a lesson I had learned from my mother-in-law.

Making my way downstairs and to the drawing room I passed one or two of the maids scurrying about their duties. I took the time to stop and chat with each of them, giving praise where it was due. Another lesson learned from Fannie Newkirk: household employees will work that much harder when even a word of praise is forthcoming.

I found Mr. Kohl awaiting me in the drawing room; I sallied forth, making as grand an entrance as I could. He turned away from the window at the sound of my skirts swishing.

"Mrs. Newkirk," he acknowledged me with a slight bow.

"Mr. Kohl, I trust your accommodations are suitable to your needs? Won't you sit down?" I gestured towards a lovely upholstered chair opposite the one on which I seated myself.

"Thank you, but I prefer to stand for the moment." He smiled at me and I could have sworn that a light was turned on, so bright and genuine was his smile.

The drawing back of his cheeks caused the skin around his eyes to crinkle, just a tiny bit, giving one to believe that he was in on some cosmic joke. I had, of course, been in his company several times yet I found it odd to now note how tall he truly was, or that he carried himself with an air of quiet dignity. He was dressed completely in brown, a color that matched his hair and his mustache perfectly. I wondered if that was an unconscious choice so as not to stand out in a crowd.

"I understand that you have been commissioned by my husband to paint my portrait."

"Quite right, Mrs. Newkirk."

"Please, feel free to call me Cordelia. After all, we will be spending quite some time together, I imagine."

He favored me with that warm smile once more.

"And you must call me Tomas," he rejoined.

"Thank you Tomas. Tell me a bit about the portrait you'll be painting."

"Mr. Newkirk has requested a likeness of you that he can hang in his office."

"In his office? How odd?" I mused.

"Not at all, dear lady. Many gentlemen carry with them a tintype of their spouse or sweetheart. In your husband's case, since he conducts much of his business in his office here at Bridgewater, why not have a portrait of his lovely wife?"

"Your reasoning is quite sound Tomas. I am rather flattered that Kevin has chosen you to do my portrait. I have long been an admirer of your work."

"Such kind words from a beautiful lady. The honor of painting you is mine. We begin tomorrow morning, at nine o'clock if you concur. I have taken the liberty of walking through your rooms and find that the angle of the sun in the morning room will be best for what I have in mind. With you standing before the window, the sun's rays should likely catch the color of your hair and create a halo effect."

"I'm far from saintly, Tomas, let me assure you." I chuckled at the intimation of a halo around my head.

Mr. Kohl then bent over my hand, pressed his lips to my knuckles, and raised his eyes upwards beneath his bushy brown eyebrows.

"There's a bit of the devil in each of us it seems." He smiled broadly. "Until tomorrow morning, Cordelia."

———

Ellen brought up my breakfast tray at the appointed hour the following morning, only to find my bed strewn with a myriad of dresses and gowns.

"Good heavens, Miss Cordelia! What's going on?" she inquired as she set my breakfast tray on the small table by the window.

"I've spent the last two hours trying to decide on the perfect dress. Mr. Kohl will begin my portrait this morning. What do you think of the yellow silk?"

"That's quite lovely. But it really doesn't show you off to the best advantage."

"Hmmm. Quite right. But it is comfortable."

"What about the watered green silk? A more formal look for the portrait perhaps. I could pull your hair back and high on the crown and dress it with that lovely feathered comb. Your formal gloves and a fan would give the elegant touch."

"That's perfect!" I exclaimed. "I'm sorry to have created such a mess but I was having the devil of a time trying to decide. It appears that I've created a lot of work for you."

"Nonsense! It's been a while since some of those dresses have seen some use and it was time they were aired out. I'll set things to right after you've gone downstairs."

"Thank you, Ellen. Now let me finish my tea before you tackle my hair."

The next couple of hours flew by as Ellen brushed, curled, and pinned my hair up. I slipped on the watered green silk gown then resumed my seat at the vanity table. Ellen fastened a feathered comb to one side of my coiffure. I donned a pair of emerald and diamond earbobs and a matching necklace that Kevin had once gifted to me. A touch of color was applied to my lips. I pulled on my elbow length gloves, opened my feathered fan, and assessed my reflection in the pier glass.

"You are the epitome of elegance, Miss Cordelia," Ellen commented.

"I rather am," I agreed as I preened a bit before my reflection.

After another long critical glimpse, I felt as though I was ready to present myself for the artist's inspection. I slowly proceeded along the upstairs hallway, carefully navigated the curved staircase, and eventually arrived at the morning room. I entered on the stroke of nine o'clock.

It was evident that Tomas had been here for quite some time. He had rearranged some of the furniture leaving only a single chaise in front of the east facing windows. Several feet away he had placed his easel and paints. He was less formally attired this morning, having left his jacket and starched shirt elsewhere. A painter's smock covered whatever he wore and although it was spotted with a rainbow of colors it appeared to have been freshly laundered. He took my gloved hand into both of his as he greeted me.

"You are a vision of beauty, my dear. It amazes me that you can look so radiant at such an early hour of the day."

"You flatter me, Tomas. But I do so enjoy that flattery."

He escorted me to the single chair and bowed low over me as I seated myself.

"If you will allow me, Cordelia, I should like to position you to take advantage of the natural light."

When at last I was posed to Tomas's satisfaction, he stepped behind his easel and began his work. The remainder of the morning flew by as Tomas applied broad strokes of color to his blank canvas. At the end of two hours, he proclaimed that I had been a perfect model.

"Cordelia, you certainly must have other commitments so I shall release you from your posing for this morning."

He set down his brush and palette before walking toward me. I placed my gloved hand into his outstretched one and rose. My legs were certainly stiff from sitting for such a long period. Tomas took note of the fact that I was momentarily unsteady on my feet.

"A bit of stiffness is the price most models pay when they pose for an artist. I know exactly what to do."

Still holding my hand in his, he led me to the sofa. Surely he didn't think I needed to sit anymore! I was rather puzzled when he turned me to face him and pushed my arms behind me so that I supported myself on the back of the sofa. He then knelt down on one knee, grabbed the ankle of my left foot and positioned it on his unbent knee. Raising my skirt slightly he placed his hands on both sides of my calf and began to rub my leg in a circular motion. Amazingly I felt the blood begin to flow through my leg as his hands worked their magic.

"Now, the other leg," he directed.

Without further instruction, I removed my left leg and replaced it with my right one. This time he didn't hesitate as his hands dove beneath the folds of my dress and captured the lower part of my leg. Again he made circular rubbing motions with his hands.

"I find your hands to be exceptionally soft," I commented, leaning back against the sofa and allowing my head to fall back. "You have such a gentle touch, Tomas. You should have been a doctor."

He merely smiled as his hands kept moving, drawing life back into my stiff muscles.

"Mmmm," I marveled, as I felt his nimble fingers move inexorably higher until I soon realized that they were no longer massaging my calf but had somehow moved above my knee and were softly caressing my inner thigh.

"I hope you're a bit more at ease, Cordelia." His voice was low and sultry.

"Most definitely at ease, Tomas. But I fear you've allowed your fingers to stray a bit."

Instantly his movements under my skirt stopped. As he removed his hands he allowed his fingers to trail against the now sensitive skin of my leg, leaving a trail of fire behind them. He rose and stepped closer to me.

"Perhaps your shoulders are a bit tense as well. Let me ease that tension for you." He turned me around so that my back was to his chest. As his fingers worked the tension away from my shoulders I leaned my head back, allowing him an unobstructed view of my cleavage.

"You certainly have given me much inspiration this day, Cordelia," he whispered into my ear. "I look forward to our session tomorrow."

"Mmmmm, yes," I agreed.

I was so enjoying the massage that I paid little attention to his fingers as they strayed a bit until I felt them outlining the sides of my bosom. The pressure of his masculine touch against my breasts gave my core a quickening feeling, one I hesitated to remark on because it felt so good. However, this could not in all propriety continue. Drawing myself upright, I moved away from this semi-embrace.

"Tomas, I'm afraid you have let your fingers stray again," I remarked lightly, tapping his hand with my fan. He had the good sense to smile sheepishly.

"Your beauty is overwhelming, Cordelia. You can't blame a moth for being drawn to the flame."

"Yes, well, I expect that you'd like to recommence tomorrow morning?" I opened my fan and began to move the air in front of my face.

"That would be perfect. If you would attire yourself as you are today, I can continue from this point."

"Feel free to make yourself at home until dinner, Tomas. I will join you at seven o'clock."

I left the morning room, fanning myself, and wondering from exactly which point Mr. Kohl planned to proceed, his work on his canvas or his play on my legs.

After a restless night, I once again met Mr. Kohl the next day in the morning room. He was ready to begin and directed me to take my place once more on the chaise. Rather than apply himself immediately to his canvas and paints, he spent quite some time arranging me on the chaise. This went on for some minutes before I became annoyed.

"Tomas, your constant moving in circles around me is making me dizzy. Pray tell, what exactly are you hoping to do?"

"Cordelia, if I may be honest for a moment?" He stopped short in front of me.

"By all means, please tell me what the problem is."

"The problem is that with you posed as you are, I cannot provide the type of portrait your husband is desirous of."

I looked at the artist for a moment, trying to determine if this was a ploy to get close to me once more. The look on his face was one of genuine concern so I took the bait and asked, "What sort of portrait has Kevin commissioned?"

It took no more than two or three sentences before I got the mental picture of what Kevin had requested. I was at first furious. Tomas was apologetic when he explained that Kevin had determined the ploy of a portrait the easiest way for me to accept the artist as my lover. Tomas further explained that while he would be greatly honored if I were to choose him, he didn't feel worthy in the least of such an honor.

"Tomas, I thank you for your honesty. I would be grateful if I could take you into my strictest confidences. Would you be willing to help me?"

"I will walk to the ends of the earth for you, dearest lady."

"How much has my husband paid you to paint my portrait in such a lewd manner?"

"Five hundred dollars. Quite a goodly sum for a struggling artist such as I."

"I shall double the sum if you will produce a portrait of my own choosing," I proposed.

"One thousand dollars!"

I nodded in affirmation. He bowed from the waist before speaking.

"I am your humble servant, Cordelia. I will paint whatever you require."

Together we spent the next hour in consultation, refining the details of the portrait I wanted him to paint. When we were done, he set off to do his job. That night, as I lay in Nate's arms, I filled him in on the details, directing him to provide Mr. Kohl with whatever he required to complete his task. For the first time in days, I felt in control of my world again.

Kevin

Chapter 32

Jeannette had evolved into a successful businesswoman who surprised me at every turn. I was in total awe of her ability not only to consistently turn a profit in her millinery shop but also of her ability to navigate her motorcar through the streets of Boston. With her loan to me paid off, she was able to hire a 'hat girl' to run the shop on those days when she went out making deliveries to her most elite clientele. For now, though, the hat girl would need to run the shop on a more or less permanent basis while Jeannette dutifully laid under me in the hopes of my seed finding fertile ground.

Little more than six weeks after we set ourselves to the task of creating a child, Jeannette gave me the news that she thought she was pregnant. A visit to her doctor confirmed the fact that she was with child. I deemed it a cause for celebration. As a tribute to her efforts, I arranged for a private dining room at one of Boston's best eateries. We dined on the finest food and drank only the finest wine, all in moderation of course. Our celebration came to an end only when we both lay fully exhausted and replete on our bed, having eaten our fill and satisfied our lusty yearnings.

I awoke the next morning to an empty spot on the bed beside me where Jeannette should have been. The muffled sounds of her morning sickness in the adjoining bathroom brought a smile to my face. How quickly it seemed that Jeannette became pregnant! With Cordy it sometimes took more than two months for my seed to take hold. That was it! Why hadn't I thought it through before? The blame lay squarely on my wife's shoulders. It was obvious to me that she was not as fertile as I would have hoped.

While Jeannette was thusly occupied, I slipped out of bed and made my way to the kitchen. Brewster managed to leave the warmth of his doggie bed by the stove long enough to pad over to me, lick my hand, and return to his cozy nest. I set a kettle of water on the stove and prepared a tray to bring upstairs. I found the teapot and two cups in the cupboard; next I managed to unearth some breakfast rolls. Setting everything on the tray, I added a pot of jam, some butter from the ice box, a couple of napkins, and some cutlery. When the kettle began to make noise, I knew the water was boiling. I turned down the fire, poured the water over the tea ball in the teapot, and carried the entire thing upstairs just as Jeannette was emerging from the bathroom. The look of awe on her face was something that delighted me no end.

"Good heavens, Kevin, did you hire someone to make breakfast when I wasn't looking?"

"On the contrary, darling, I did this all myself!" I felt proud of my limited culinary skills and allowed myself a smile.

"It appears that you've done very well indeed," she conceded.

She sat down on the bed and I set the tray next to her. Together we broke our fast with jam and bread and steaming cups of tea. In all my years I had never had a more delicious breakfast. That was when I realized that I was content.

There I sat, my dressing robe tied around me, a faithful dog at my feet; my pregnant lover, who should have been my wife, sitting beside me as we sipped our morning tea. Outside the gusts of wind blew swirls of snow past the window yet we were warm and cozy as the heat from the radiator filled the room. I looked down into Jeannette's upturned face, kissed her lips, and whispered, "I love you". Never had I uttered those words with such meaning.

Jeannette whispered "I love you, too". This was where I wanted to be, beside the woman I loved, for the rest of my life. Yet I had an estate full of responsibilities that would sooner or later clamor for my attention.

An hour later I was fully dressed and ready to set off to my office at the trading company. Jeannette descended the staircase and I noticed that she carried her coat and purse.

"Kevin, could you hand me my galoshes? They're near the front door."

"Are you planning on going out?" I inquired.

"Of course. Beth will have opened the shop by now but I really must go in to work. Mrs. Fletcher expects to pick up her latest order tomorrow and I've not finished her hat yet."

"Is that wise? Going in to the shop, I mean?"

I watched her slip on her coat and adjust her hat in front of the small mirror on the vestibule wall. She turned to me with a puzzled expression.

"Because of the baby, you mean?"

"Yes."

She stopped short for a moment, laid a hand upon my sleeve, and looked at me with those emerald eyes.

"You are the dearest, sweetest man to worry about me. Dearest, I'm having our baby. Women have babies all the time. It's a natural thing."

"But you'll be on your feet all day. Surely that can't be a good thing." I held open the door for her as we moved outside.

"I promise to take care of myself. Now let's hurry. Beth will be wondering where I've been."

We made our way to the driveway where the motorcar was parked. I moved to the passenger side thinking to hold open the door for her but she slid gracefully behind the wheel. I braced myself for another wild ride with Jeannette at the helm but to my surprise she eased the car gently through the traffic and pulled up in front of my office building.

"I'll pick you up at five o'clock, shall I?" she questioned as I collected my gloves.

"No need, darling. I'll have a company driver drop me off. It might be closer to six, though. I have a stop to make on the way."

"Alright then. But don't be late. I'm making lamb chops for dinner."

I waited there on the sidewalk as I watched her re-enter the line of cars and navigate across the road until the motor car was out of sight. Proceeding through the revolving doors on the first floor of the Newkirk Building, I bid a good morning to the clerk behind the information desk, strode towards the elevators, and directed the operator to the fourth floor where my office was located.

Miss Fortner was in her usual place behind her desk and looked up at the sound of my "Good morning."

"Mr. Newkirk, I wasn't expecting you." She straightened up in her seat as she tore her attention away from the typewriter in front of her.

"Would you please bring me some coffee, Miss Fortner? I'll be evaluating some contracts this morning and I should like to keep the knowledge of my presence from the general staff."

"Certainly, sir."

The plain-looking woman rose to fetch my beverage and I had the opportunity to assess her as she walked away. Of average height, she was attired in a tweed woolen skirt and matching jacket with a high-necked blouse covering the column of her throat. Her lackluster brown hair, which was pulled into a bun at the back of her head, matched the frames of her glasses. Sensible shoes with a chunky-looking heel seemed to be made for comfort rather than for show. When she walked it was evident that her shoulders were hunched forward, no doubt from spending so much time at her typewriter. From her movements, I gauged her to be in her middle thirties. Her lack of jewelry, with the exception of a tiny pair of gold earrings, screamed to me of her spinsterhood. I wondered if she was content with her lot and why she had never married. I shook my head to clear those thoughts away as I entered my office.

Hanging up my overcoat and resting my hat and gloves in the tiny closet afforded for just that purpose, I turned to my desk. There were several contracts with foreign companies that needed my attention, although none were pressing. I flipped through each briefly and was quite grateful when Miss Fortner entered with my coffee.

"Here you are, Mr. Newkirk," she remarked as she set down the steaming cup along with a napkin. "Will there be anything else?"

"No, thank you." I watched her walk towards the door. "Miss Fortner," I called after her.

"Yes, sir?" She turned towards me.

"I've taken up residence in Boston for the next few months and will be coming to the office on a more or less daily basis."

The news didn't seem to disturb her in the least. She merely waited for me to continue. "May I inquire if what you are wearing is your normal office attire?"

"Yes, sir, it is." She stood up straight as if to preen over her good taste.

From my desk drawer I pulled out my personal checkbook, scratched out the amount of one thousand dollars, and handed the check to her.

"Miss Fortner, if I am to be greeted by the sight of you every day for the next three months, I should like to see you in something a bit less dowdy. You are to collect your coat, hat, and gloves, take yourself to the nearest fashion house, and purchase something a bit less drab. I want to see bright colors on you, do you understand?"

The woman's jaw had dropped and she looked like she could catch flies should any have been buzzing around.

"Go ahead, take the check. I'm giving you the remainder of the day off. Don't worry, you'll be paid for the time. Now go."

Not one to question her good fortune, Miss Fortner stepped forward, snatched the check off my desk and had almost gotten through the door before I offered one last comment.

"And by all means, please do something about your hair."

I turned my attention back to the contracts before me as I heard the door to my office click shut. The contracts themselves were straightforward and boring but I persevered and by the time I had signed the last one it was late afternoon. A call down to the information desk brought the company car and driver to the front door ten minutes later. The driver was a young fellow, a teenager really, who had dropped out of school to help support his family. We chatted as he drove along Seaport Boulevard and I learned that he had eight brothers and sisters, his father worked on our docks as a stevedore, and his mother took in sewing. As the eldest he felt it was his responsibility to add to their income.

At my request we stopped on Gridley Street where I spent some time in The Unpolished Diamond, a quiet establishment run by Simon Greene who had been jeweler to the Newkirk family for well over half a century. It was past closing time when we arrived yet even though the 'closed' sign hung on the window I knocked and was admitted immediately.

"Thank you for waiting for me, Mr. Greene," I addressed the elderly gentleman who locked the door behind me.

"Always a pleasure to do business with you Mr. Newkirk," he replied in a slightly tremulous voice. "I have several items for you to look at."

As he disappeared into the walk-in vault, I noted that Mr. Greene had aged a bit since I'd last seen him. His hair was now completely gray; his glasses seemed to be of a greater magnification making his rheumy eyes appear owl-like. Instead of wearing a business suit, Mr. Greene favored a button-down wool cardigan over his long-sleeved shirt; his trousers bore a sharp crease though and his shoes were highly polished. He returned to the counter bearing several velvet jewelry rolls in his hand.

I spent over half an hour choosing my purchases: a ruby necklace and matching earrings for Jeannette; a sapphire ring for Cordy. My daughters were not to be neglected: a gold bracelet for Birdie and gold studs for young Katie. I directed that the gifts for Cordy and the girls be sent on to Bridgewater with appropriate messages. The items for Jeannette were tucked into the inner pocket of my greatcoat.

"Shall I place these on your account, Mr. Newkirk?"

"The items for Bridgewater should go on my account, of course. But the necklace and earrings I shall pay for now. I should also like to order a bracelet of rubies and diamonds to match these pieces but I shan't be in need of it for at least six months or so."

"How heavy a piece are you looking for?" A gleam appeared in the older man's eyes.

"I want something substantial."

Without a word, the jeweler pulled out from another roll a bracelet of topaz gems and placed it in my hands.

"Perhaps something along the lines of this item?"

I hefted the piece, feeling the weight while I admired the clean lines of the gold links.

"Yes, something exactly like this would do nicely. But not with the topaz, rubies and diamonds."

"I thought you might like the style of bracelet." Mr. Greene smiled as he replaced the item in its roll.

"The lady who receives that is extremely cared for," I commented.

"You won't be surprised then to learn that your father ordered that bracelet. Seems good taste runs in the family."

I smiled in response, waiting while Mr. Greene wrapped my purchases; I returned to the waiting car, directing the driver to Jeannette's house on Ash Street. It was six o'clock when I entered the house, surprised to find it dark. Brewster bounded up to the front door to greet me but seemed a bit put out that I wasn't Jeannette.

Grabbing his leash from the coat tree, I spent time outdoors with Brewster following his trail as he stopped at every shrub and tree within a one block radius. By the time we returned to the house, my nose had turned as red as my cheeks as the temperatures had plummeted directly after sunset. Fortunately, Jeannette had returned home, lit the lamps, and had a meal cooking on the stove.

As Brewster made his way into the kitchen, I divested myself of my outer garments. Following my nose I found Jeannette setting the table for supper. After an exchange of kisses, I climbed upstairs to the bedroom where I hung my suit in the closet, pulling on a more casual pair of trousers and my smoking jacket.

I noted with interest how homey and relaxed the room felt. Heavy drapes were pulled together to block out the cold that seeped in around the window. A large featherbed covered the mattress. Good quality matching furniture, although not of the caliber we had at Bridgewater, gave comfort to our bodies at the end of the day. The other rooms were similarly decorated to provide a feeling of welcome to those who entered – a warm feeling that was somehow lacking at Bridgewater. I realized that I loved this little house; that I could be quite happy spending my days here with Jeannette by my side and Brewster by my feet. Oh, and the baby in the nursery! Yes, I mustn't forget my soon-to-be son.

Later that evening, after we had eaten our supper and retired to the living room, I once again marveled at the simple happiness that filled my heart. There was a glowing fire on the hearth in front of which Brewster now napped. Jeannette sat in one of a pair of overstuffed arm chairs, embroidering a tiny garment intended for our son. I occupied the other arm chair working through the evening edition of the Boston Daily Globe. On a butler's table beside me stood a tumbler full of Bushmill's that as yet remained untouched. In a corner of the living room stood a tall rosewood-encased radio broadcasting a popular orchestra playing live from one of the hotel ballrooms.

From behind my newspaper I watched as Jeannette concentrated her stitches on the piece of needlework in her lap. She was humming along to the tune currently on the radio. Without realizing it, my features had rearranged themselves in a smile. I had no thought of Bridgewater, my wife or children there, or the responsibilities of being the owner of a vast estate. Of course my horses were always in my thoughts, but on this particular evening even they were on the back burner, so to speak. With Huckleby in charge of the stables, I knew there was little chance of anything going askance. I reached into the pocket of my smoking jacket and my fingers closed around the jewelry box that resided there. Now would be the perfect time to present my gift. I made a grand show of folding the newspaper and setting it aside.

"Jeannette, dearest," I began.

"Yes, Kevin?"

She looked up from her stitching and gave me a smile, a lock of her hair falling forward. I stood up and moved to the side of her chair.

"Darling, have I told you how much I love you?"

"Hmm," she appeared to be thinking on the matter. "Not for at least two hours."

"That certainly is remiss of me. I wouldn't want you to question my devotion."

"That would be terrible."

I reached into my pocket and drew out the velvet box.

"I do hope this little token of my love will remind you of my devotion."

"I don't need a trinket to remind me of your affection. Not when I have a part of you growing within me." Her hand strayed to her as yet flat abdomen in a protective manner.

"That is precisely why I wanted to give you a gift. You have already provided me with the gift of your pregnancy. This," I handed her the box, "is merely a small gesture on my part."

Jeannette accepted my gift, running her hand slowly over the lid of the box before opening it. When she finally lifted the lid, a single "Oh" conveyed her delight at the rubies resting therein as they reflected the firelight. "They are beautiful!"

"Will you wear them for me?"

She nodded as she held up her hair and I fastened the necklace around the slim column of her neck. With steady hands she replaced her plainer earrings with the ruby ones, shaking back her hair so that the gemstones winked at me in the dancing firelight.

"They suit you."

"Kevin, there was no need to gift me with more jewels."

"It gives me pleasure to do so." I pulled her into my arms and kissed her lips.

"It gives me greater pleasure to wear them," she murmured against my mouth, "especially when I'm wearing nothing else."

"Perhaps you could give me a preview of what that will look like?" my hands pulled her closer, molding her against my body.

"That would give me the most pleasure," she answered, kissing me fully before leading me upstairs.

The following morning found us both not wanting to leave the warmth of our bed but the morning sickness cut short any plans I had for one last romp between the sheets. I watched Jeannette run into the bathroom, still wearing the ruby necklace and earrings. I removed myself from the bedroom to give her a bit of privacy, pulling on my robe as I sauntered downstairs. The mantel clock chimed nine before I realized that we had lain abed longer than I had planned. Oh well, my work at the office would wait.

It was almost half past the hour of ten when I sauntered through the doors at Newkirk Trading and stopped short in my tracks. It appeared that Miss Fortner had taken my admonishments about style to heart. In place of the mousy brown hair there were highlights of golden blonde. Where before there were overgrown eyebrows there now were shapely arches over her eyes. She wore a navy blue lady's business suit offset by a high-necked ruched blouse in a soft cream color. Gone were the chunky-heeled shoes of yesterday; they had been replaced by a narrow-heeled boot that doubled as a shoe. Her posture had improved greatly as well. I wasn't about to ask the reason behind that but I believe it had something to do with the proper fit of her undergarments. Having married into a family whose business it was to know about ladies fashions, I had indeed learned more than I realized. Adorning the jacket of her suit was a brooch but I spotted it at once as a poor copy of a recent high-end design.

"Good morning, Mr. Newkirk," she looked up from some correspondence that she was typing.

"Miss Fortner," I acknowledged. "It seems that you've become a beautiful butterfly now that you've shed your old cocoon."

"Thanks to you, sir," she had the grace to blush slightly.

"Are there any messages for me this morning?" I smiled at the woman.

"Just one, sir. It's from Mrs. Newkirk?"

"My mother or my wife?"

"Your wife, sir."

"Very good." I accepted the paper with the message from Cordy.

"Will there be anything else, Mr. Newkirk?"

"Yes, actually there is. The young man who drove the company car for me yesterday. Find out what his name is, please. We had a great conversation but I somehow failed to ascertain his name. It was quite rude of me and I should like to make amends for that."

I spent the better part of the remaining work hours ensconced in my office, paying particular attention to the rewriting of one contract that would provide Newkirk Trading with a profitable long-term agreement. The only interruption I had was when Miss Fortner provided me a note with the name of my company driver.

I called down to the Personnel Department and learned that Todd Winslow had been on the payroll for a mere three months, but his father Arthur Winslow had been our employee for almost twenty years. Further discussion with the head of personnel uncovered the fact that the senior Winslow had been passed over for promotion twice although there was apparently no valid reason for having done so. I inquired if perhaps there had been a large number of days away from work but was informed that the senior Mr. Winslow had an impeccable attendance record. By the end of the afternoon I was proud to say that I had requested Arthur Winslow to head up a new team of men in the Receiving Department at our warehouses on Seaport Avenue, a job that would bring the man in from the extreme elements of the Boston Harbor and afford him a raise in his paycheck.

When at last I slid into the rear seat of the company car once more, I nodded at Todd as he held open the door of the motorcar.

"Looks like we're in for another snowstorm," commented Todd.

"Yes, the sky looks a bit threatening. Have you no gloves?" I asked, noticing for the first time his bare hands which appeared raw and rough.

"It's all right, Mr. Newkirk. I'm not all that cold. We've only got one good pair of gloves between the men in the family. It's more important that my pa have them. He's outdoors all day and I'm moving around more."

He guided the car around a stalled vehicle that had gotten stuck in a snowbank.

"It's certainly not fine with me to have my driver present himself with such raw hands. Whatever will people think? That the Newkirks don't pay well?"

I pulled out my wallet from the depths of my jacket pocket, removing two twenty dollar bills. As we approached a traffic signal at which Todd stopped the car momentarily, I handed him the money.

"I expect you to be properly dressed tomorrow. Buy yourself a pair of leather gloves, a suitable hat, and an overcoat of some sort. I've informed the Personnel Department that I have chosen you to be my permanent driver while I'm here in Boston. And when I've departed I expect that you will continue on in that capacity working for my brother-in-law. Is that clear?"

"You mean I won't have to do double duty on the docks?" He eased the car forward once more.

"Quite right. And there will be a bit more money in your next paycheck as well."

Todd was silent for a few moments and I began to wonder if I had rendered him speechless. Just when I was about to inquire if he was all right, he tried to speak. It was then that I realized that he was trying to hold back tears.

"I...I don't know how to thank you, Mr. Newkirk," came his response at last.

"Oh posh! I recognize a good employee when I see one. Besides, I'm sure the extra money will be put to good use."

"That it will, sir. I'm sure my mother will say an extra prayer for you this Sunday, sir."

"Yes, well. An extra voice speaking to the Lord on my behalf will be most welcome."

Lawson

Chapter 33

Spring 1913
Bridgewater Estate

The sky on that late spring morning was a brilliant blue with nary
a cloud to mar its brightness. To my left was the winding fresh-
water creek that flowed through the property. Off to my right and a
short distance away was a copse of trees, the dogwood in full bloom this
day. The meadow grasses were full of clover with dandelions sprinkled
about as though a young wood sprite had dropped them there. Beneath
me was a blanket that had seen better days but was eminently suitable
for today's purpose – a rare day of leisure where my responsibilities had
been shelved. Under the shade of the nearby trees, I'd left my horse to
wander a bit.

Mrs. Grant was kind enough to pack a small picnic basket for me
claiming that it wouldn't be a day of leisure without nourishment. From
the smell of things I was certain that there were cold chicken, a loaf of
crusty bread, and cheese. As tempting as these aromas were, I ignored
them as I lay back on the blanket and allowed the sun to wash over me.
Having removed my jacket and rolled it up, I used that as a pillow for

my head. There didn't seem to be any reason not to close my eyes so I did just that. Within moments I had dozed off.

My dreams were vivid: in them I was lying beside Delia in the full morning light; neither of us was worried that we would be interrupted or that I should hurry to leave her bed. There were only the two of us and I could feel her kiss on my lips as she murmured, "Wake up darling." My dreamy response was to reach out and pull her closer. Only when I felt the solidity of her body in my hands did my eyes fly open.

"Delia! What….?"

I opened my eyes fully and there was Delia, kneeling beside me on the blanket, her gentle laughter at having caught me asleep lighting her face.

"May I join you?"

She didn't wait for my response but flung herself down on the blanket beside me.

"Were you following me?" I inquired as I put my arm around her. "Not that I mind."

"No. I wasn't following you." She turned and smiled at me. "But I found you nonetheless."

"Yes, it would seem that you have. I thought you'd be stuck in the house with the month's end invoices to review." I brushed a strand of hair from her face, feeling more comfortable than I had a right to be.

"The invoices can wait," Delia replied. "The sunshine and gentle breeze just seemed to beckon me, so I had Angel saddled and took myself off for a ride."

"And you followed my trail until you found me. How fortunate!" I leaned over a placed a kiss on her temple.

"There's actually some news I wanted to share with you."

"Really? And you couldn't tell me this news back at the house?"

"Kevin is making ready to return."

I felt the wonder of the day slip away as I turned to lie on my back, my hold on Delia loosening.

"I wish you had waited until I returned to the house to tell me this."

Delia sat up and turned towards me.

"I didn't mean to spoil your day, Nathan. I just felt it was my duty to inform you."

I let out a long sigh.

"I suppose it's something I should know. But really, what good is telling me here, now? I was just enjoying the solitude of the day." I rather felt like a petulant child.

"Kevin will most likely be back tomorrow," she stated matter-of-factly. "That doesn't give us much time."

"Time? Except for changing the menu what exactly needs to be done? You know the first place he'll go will be the stables."

"I'm hosting a dinner party here on Saturday evening, a welcome home party of sorts. I'll be sending out the invitations this afternoon. After dinner we'll have the grand unveiling of the portrait that Kevin commissioned Mr. Kohl to paint." She gave me a sly smile.

"Ohhhhh. You want to see his reaction to exposing your semi-nude portrait in front of guests! You minx." A smile tugged at the corner of my mouth.

"I've already told Mrs. Grant to prepare for a full dining room. Quite a few have been invited to stay on to enjoy the country air."

"So we'll have a houseful to look after," I noted, leaning up on one arm.

"But for now I see no reason why we shouldn't enjoy the remainder of the day out here. It's warm, and quiet." Delia began to unbutton the bodice of her riding vest. "In fact it's so warm I'm afraid I may become faint if I don't divest myself of this riding habit." Her fingers stopped midway along the row of buttons."

"Perhaps you should lay back, Delia, and let me assist you. I'm rather adept at removing a lady's garments."

"Yes, I know," she smiled back at me.

My fingers nimbly undid her blouse and I slipped a hand beneath her chemise as I pushed the blouse away. Delia arched her back, molding her breast to my hand. I leaned down and kissed her lips before leaving a trail of kisses from her mouth to her breast. In a matter of moments we were without clothes, rolling around the blanket.

We spent several hours there on that blanket, watching the sun move across the sky. The picnic basket that Mrs. Grant had so thoughtfully furnished now held only soiled napkins and an empty wine bottle. We spoke of many things: the arts that Delia was endeavoring to nurture, the upcoming dinner party, the rising cost of kitchen staples, and her children. She leaned against me as she spoke, her back to my front.

"I believe I should like to try for another child," she said.

"I thought those days of lying beneath Kevin were over," I remarked.

"They are," she affirmed.

"Surely, you can't be proposing that we...."

"That's exactly what I'm proposing." She turned slightly in my embrace and I could see her smile.

"Is that wise? Look at what happened to Geraldine. She was never really a healthy child."

"No matter. I've got a trustworthy nanny in my cousin Tess and there's Lotte of course. They are most conscientious."

"Point well taken."

"And I should like to provide you with a son," she concluded.

"What purpose would that serve? The child would bear the Newkirk name."

"For now. When the boy was old enough I would tell him who his father was."

"And have him learn that his life was a lie, that he was another man's bastard son?"

"Hmmm. Then the child shall live in ignorance, believing he's a true Newkirk."

I took a moment to consider her plan.

"And what if you bear another daughter? It's highly likely you know," I inquired.

"We'll just have to take our chances, won't we?"

Delia slanted her head and gave me a come-hither look, one I found impossible to resist. I pulled her closer, placed a kiss on her pouty lips, and took a shot at creating a son.

———

Kevin arrived home not one but two days later and went directly to the stables to visit his horses. I followed Paul into the house as he oversaw the arrival of Kevin's luggage.

"It's a true pleasure to be home!" Paul remarked.

"Did you not find things in Boston to your liking?"

"Not in the least. Imagine, working my fingers to the bone every day for the man here at Bridgewater then being unceremoniously told my services wouldn't be required until we returned here. I was 'on loan' to the Boston Newkirks where my position was quite changeable from day to day. Thankfully my grandfather pretended to be suffering from a bad back and I was pressed into service for old Mr. Newkirk."

I found it difficult not to smile at the dilemma Paul had found himself in. Sometimes he failed to remember that he was a domestic and not a member of the family.

"Why did Mr. Newkirk loan you to his family? Surely he was in need of your services as well?" I asked in a leading way.

"He spent the entire time living with Miss Jeannette and her dog. Said he wanted to experience life without cow-towing to rules and regulations." Paul raised his eyebrows in disdain.

"There's a lot to be said for the simpler life," I supplied.

"I've worked long and hard to maintain my position with Mister Kevin to be unceremoniously dumped on his family."

"But you're back now, and that's all that matters," I observed.

I waited for Paul's answer but his only reply was a loud "Hmph!"

———

Saturday morning dawned bright and warm. House guests began arriving shortly after eight o'clock in the morning. In true Bridgewater style, they were shown to their rooms and helped to settle in. We kept a breakfast buffet on the sideboard of the dining room filled throughout the morning so that guests could avail themselves of refreshment as they arrived. Luncheon was scheduled for an hour past noon and we didn't want our guests to feel faint.

The guest list was a mix of artistes from the various genres who normally frequented Bridgewater under Delia's patronage as well as merchants and businessmen and those from what was termed the 'horsey circle' – breeders, investors, and owners of horses. While one group set off for the stables and took out a few of our mounts for some riding exercise, the artistes wandered the grounds around the main house and found whatever inspiration they needed or wanted from the various gardens, wooded copses, or the hedge-maze. Many of the women changed from their travel garb into more light-weight attire and availed themselves of the cooling breezes on the terrace. Two or three of the more adventurous ladies had slipped into bathing garments and caps and made use of the crystal clear pool.

The staff was kept busy; it seemed that every one of our guests was enjoying the fair weather and attentive service. From the vantage point of her bedroom, Delia and I watched the 'horsey circle', led by a jovial Kevin, as they guided their horses down the length of the driveway.

"I'd venture a guess that Mr. Newkirk is pleased with his welcome home party?"

"It would seem that way, yes, Nate. I'm sure we'll have at least an hour or two until he returns." Delia turned to me with a seductive smile lighting up her face. "Let's use it wisely."

"I don't think now would be the proper time, love. It seems we have some late-comers just arriving." I nodded my head at an automobile just pulling up to the front door. "How irksome. I'll need to be on hand to welcome them."

"Oh, let the footmen assist them." Delia turned her head to look out the window. "Good God, that man has the audacity to actually show up!"

I looked out the window and noted that it was the Flemings who had arrived; Mr. Fleming was waiting while his wife emerged from the car.

"You invited the Flemings? After that incident in the morning room a few months back?"

"What could I do, Nate? George Fleming is a friend of Kevin's after all."

"Quite right. But will you be able to keep a straight face when you greet him, I wonder?"

"Why Nathan Lawson, whatever do you mean?" Delia laughed.

"I suppose I should go downstairs. After all, his wife certainly has done nothing to warrant my keeping her at a distance," I observed.

"Are you ready for the great unveiling of the painting this evening? I thought perhaps we should have the masterpiece presented sometime between the main course and dessert."

"Ah, holding everyone captive! Brilliant."

"You'll see to it, then?"

"As you wish, Mrs. Newkirk," I took her hand in mine and kissed her upturned palm. "Now, if you'll excuse me, duty calls."

"I'll be down directly to welcome the Flemings," she called after me as I scurried down the hidden stairway, pulling the hidden panel closed behind me.

Back downstairs, I was just about to enter the kitchen from my office when a footman came running and almost knocked into me.

"Careful lad, you might have hurt us both in your haste," I chided gently.

"Sorry, sir, but there's guests just arrived. We've brought their luggage into the guest wing and offered to show them their rooms but they insisted on waiting in the foyer." The young man let all of this out on a single breath.

"I'll greet them and send word to Mrs. Newkirk."

The footman nodded and stepped back as I passed him on my way to the foyer. I was hurrying down the hallway when I heard Delia's voice, from the top of the curved staircase, address the latecomers.

"Susanna and George Fleming, why I had just about given up on you two," Delia cooed as she descended the staircase.

"I'm sure there must have been some oversight as we were not properly greeted upon our arrival, Cordelia." Susanna Fleming's tone was cool and distant.

"Nonsense, it's well past luncheon, Susanna. I was under the impression that you and your husband had chosen not to grace us with your presence. I was upstairs in the nursery when I heard the commotion of your arrival and now here I am!"

"And why was your Steward not here to greet us properly?" Susanna Fleming turned her haughty gaze to me but before I could utter a word her husband jumped in.

"I'm sure Mr. Lawson has many duties requiring his attention, dear. After all, as Cordelia has pointed out, it is well past luncheon."

Mr. Fleming, it seemed, was trying to placate his wife while giving me unspoken notice that he was on his best behavior.

"Thank you, Mr. Fleming," I responded, nodding my head at him, "however, your lovely wife is correct. It is remiss of us not to have greeted you upon your arrival and I beg your pardon for that."

"I'm sorry for the delay, Mrs. Newkirk," I addressed Delia upon my arrival at the foyer. Turning towards the Flemings I added, " May I escort you to your accommodations?"

"That will be fine," began Mrs. Fleming, but she was interrupted by Cordelia.

"Actually, Mr. Lawson is needed elsewhere at the moment, but one of the footmen will be happy to escort you both."

Cordelia beckoned to the young man who had sought me out moments earlier and he led the way to the guest wing, complimenting Mrs. Fleming on her traveling costume.

"I don't believe Mr. Fleming will give us any trouble during their stay, Mrs. Newkirk," I observed as our guests retreated from the foyer.

"I do believe you're right, Mr. Lawson," Delia answered with a smile.

———

By day's end the temperature outdoors had dropped significantly and a westerly breeze had begun to blow. As the 'horsey circle' made their way indoors to change for supper I heard them comment about the changing weather and a possible storm brewing. Whether or not we were to be cooled by a late spring storm remained to be seen. I did know that the temperature indoors would soon be rising and a tempest brewing with the unveiling of Mr. Kohl's portrait.

As was customary, Delia had arranged the seating so that the 'horsey circle' was clustered together at the head of the table where Kevin reigned supreme. At the table's other end were the artistic group, who looked to Delia to keep the conversation flowing. The lone stand out was a tall, handsome gentleman in military uniform whom Delia had seated to her immediate right. Earlier questioning on my part gleaned the information that the gentleman's name was Josef Weiss, a distant cousin of Delia's sister-in-law Rose, who was en route home and had stopped at Bridgewater to pay his respects. Delia had insisted that since he was family he remain as our guest for several days.

The meal progressed with only a minor interruption when Lotte brought the children downstairs to say goodnight. Delia gave each of them in turn a big hug and a promise to hear their prayers right after supper. Although Lotte 's attention was devoted to her charges she happened to glance up momentarily at the guests seated at the table. From my position near the door I could see her gaze lock with that of Captain Weiss; it seemed charged with electricity although Lotte instantly averted her gaze as any good domestic should.

Having received their mother's hugs and having dutifully kissed their father good night, the children were once again escorted by Lotte out of the dining room. Captain Weiss at last tore his gaze away from the doorway through which they had exited and turned his attention once again to Delia.

"My dear Mrs. Newkirk, I would never have believed you to be the mother of two children." His smile seemed genuine as did his compliment.

"Why thank you Captain, it's rare to hear compliments these days." Delia seemed to preen under the captain's gaze. "However, I do believe it is time for something special."

Delia motioned for me to bring in the covered easel and set it down beside her husband.

"What's this?" boomed Kevin in a jovial manner.

"A homecoming present, dear husband."

"For me?" his tone was incredulous.

"If I might be so bold?" Tomas Kohl addressed Delia as he stood and came around the table.

At that moment understanding dawned on Mr. Newkirk and he began to bluster and make unintelligible noises.

"I don't know; but Tomas, how can you.....No! I won't permit it!"

That was when the fun truly began.

Cordelia

Chapter 34

"Now Kevin, it's only right that Mr. Kohl be allowed to unveil his work. He's spent untold hours with his model in order to capture not only her look but the feel of her soul. He's been quite dedicated to his work," I offered, happy beyond measure to see the look of embarrassment on Kevin's face as he feared the worst.

"Yes, but I commissioned a very private portrait. One that would remain in my office."

Kevin's his face was so red it appeared that he might explode.

"Do go on Mr. Kohl. I'm anxious to see everyone's reactions to your superb work," I directed.

"Yes, please proceed," urged one of our guests.

"Oooh, I can't wait," added Susanna Fleming.

"Very well then," responded Mr. Kohl grabbing the silk that had been draped across the painting.

"I refuse to stay here and witness this abomination! Cordelia, have you no pride?"

I smiled sweetly at my husband as I motioned for Mr. Kohl to proceed.

"Cordelia, I'm begging you…."

"Well done!"

"Bravo!"

"Lovely portrait!"

"Damn nice filly!"

These were the reactions I had anticipated. Mr. Kohl, standing by his painting, basked in the glow of the praise. Kevin had no choice but to look at the painting. Steeling himself against what he might see on the canvas he directed his gaze to the painting. There was a moment of silence on his part as he gazed over the portrait of his favorite filly, Morning Star, as she might look on the day she would win the Kentucky Derby, tall and proud with a circlet of roses around her neck. Intrigued by what he saw, Kevin went up close to the canvas as he cast a critical eye on its subject. He tilted his head first to the left and then to the right before turning to Mr. Kohl.

"Excellent! Superb detail!!" He clasped the artist's hand and pumped it in a congratulatory shake as I rose from my place and walked towards the two men.

"I take it you like my welcome home surprise?" I inquired, placing my hand on the sleeve of Kevin's jacket.

"It's perfect! A splendid gift. One I shall always treasure." He pulled me close and gave me a hug.

"Then I suggest we finish our meal. Mrs. Grant has prepared one of your favorites. I'm sure you'll all enjoy it."

I resumed my seat, leaving Kevin to draw aside Mr. Kohl in discussion over the portrait. Satisfied that I had bested Kevin, I turned to Captain Weiss. Placing my hand on his, I brought his attention around to me.

"My dear Captain, would you be so kind as to humor me this evening?"

"Whatever you require, dear Mrs. Newkirk." A smile brightened his weathered face.

"I'm in need of a rescue. After dinner would you escort me upstairs to the nursery?"

"Your wish is my command," he acquiesced, "besides which I have a favor to ask of you."

"Then our purposes are well served," I replied.

After dinner the ladies retired to the drawing room while the gentlemen accompanied Kevin to the billiards room for brandy, cigars, and a friendly game. As we were leaving the dining table, I made my excuses.

"Please ladies, make yourselves comfortable in the drawing room or wherever you feel most at ease. I will rejoin you after I've heard the children's prayers."

There were nods from the ladies who had children of their own and smiles from those that did not. Captain Weiss held my chair for me as I rose.

"May I join you Mrs. Newkirk?"

"How kind of you captain although I doubt there's anything to interest you there."

"On the contrary. It's been many years since I've seen the inside of a nursery and since I hope to one day have children of my own I should like to see the layout of a modern nursery."

"Well then, if there are no objections?"

I looked towards Kevin who was deep in conversation with several other gentlemen. It appeared he hadn't heard the captain's question although it had been spoken aloud and heard by others. Thus I nodded my head in acquiescence and motioned Mr. Lawson to accompany us. Placing my hand on the captain's uniform sleeve, we proceeded along the hallway and upstairs to the nursery.

"Tell me captain, is it really the layout of the nursery that draws you, or someone else?"

"How astute of you, Mrs. Newkirk. I was hoping to make the formal acquaintance of the children's governess."

"Ah!"

"That is, if you have no objection, Mrs. Newkirk."

We stopped short of the nursery. I turned to face the captain even as Mr. Lawson stood several feet away.

"I assume you refer to Lotte, the young woman who brought the children into the dining room earlier. Am I correct?"

"Yes, she's the one. There's something about her that calls to me."

"Perhaps the fact that she is untouched and pure?"

"I mean her no disrespect, ma'am."

"Very well then, I will make the introductions and let things take their natural course."

Truth be told, Lotte was startled by the entrance of Captain Weiss, Mr. Lawson, and myself. I hastened to set her mind at ease.

"Lotte, I've brought Captain Weiss to meet you," I informed the young woman who came forward at my invitation.

She looked from me, to Mr. Lawson, and finally to the captain.

"Lotte, may I introduce Captain Josef Weiss of the United States Navy." He stood at formal attention. "Captain, this is Lotte Prescott. She has been in my employ for several years and is one of my most trusted employees."

Lotte curtsied at the introduction and when she raised her head it was easy to see that there were stars in her eyes. She was smitten. As for Captain Weiss, it was plain to me that he had fallen head over heels for the young woman.

"Miss Prescott, I am pleased to make your acquaintance. I look forward to getting to know you better." He bowed formally and taking her hand in his, placed a gentle kiss on her knuckles.

"If Tess is up and about, I'll ask her to watch over the children. Perhaps the two of you would like to stroll through the maze," I suggested.

"Oh Miss Cordelia, I couldn't," protested Lotte. "Tess has retired for the night and I shouldn't leave the children alone."

"Hmm, that does pose a bit of a problem. However, I think I may have a solution to this dilemma. Gather round," I included Nate in the discussion, "and listen to my plan."

Lotte

Chapter 35

Summer 1913

My Dearest Aunt Anja,
Please forgive my lapse of duty in writing to you. So much has happened in the past few months that I have not had a moment of time to call my own.
The new nanny, Tess Sulliven, arrived and immediately both girls fell in love with her. She is a lovely young lady, straight from Ireland, who has a gentle way about her; she is a story teller who has many Irish stories and superstitions to relate to both Birdie and young Katie. Tess has had a difficult life, to hear her tell about it. She is one of eight sisters who grew up on the family farm; so she is no stranger to hard work. As the second oldest she has taken care of six of her sisters from their infancy. I'm sure she will be the one to keep the Newkirk sisters in line. Tess is quite as strong-willed as little Birdie. There might be a stand-off between them one day but for now all is calm. I too love to listen to her stories about growing up on the farm in Ireland. In return I share with her some of the stories that mama told me as a child back in Dusseldorf.

Tess and I get along really well. We have worked out a schedule so that one of us is with or near the children at all times. We exchange shifts each week so that neither one of us has night duty all the time.

In looks we are quite different. Tess has flaming red hair shot through with streaks of dark copper and light hazel eyes. Her face is slightly freckled but there always seems to be a smile on her face. She is like a stray shaft of sunlight piercing the gloom when she enters a room. One can't help but smile when she is nearby or when she is humming a tune from 'the old country'. Tess is very grateful for Mrs. Newkirk's sponsorship in coming to America; each month she sends home half of her wages to help support her family back in Connemarra.

Now, dear auntie, I must share with you some exciting news. I think I'm in love. Before you jump to any conclusions, I assure you that it is not the kind and compassionate Mr. Lawson who has been the subject of my foolish dreams. The gentleman who now fills my heart with longing is a distant relative of Mrs. Newkirk. He was here as a dinner guest about a month ago and I caught a glimpse of him at table when I brought the girls downstairs to bid their parents good-night. I immediately shifted my gaze away from him as I had been taught. But to my surprise the gentleman accompanied Mrs. Newkirk to the nursery later that evening. He asked Mrs. Newkirk for an introduction to me and then asked if he could escort me on a walk about the property the next day. Of course I agreed; and with Mrs. Newkirk's permission, we strolled through the gardens the next day.

Oh auntie, he is a kind and gentle man! And he is most handsome too! His eyes are a deep brown, almost the color of liquid chocolate. He is tall as well. Not as tall as Mr. Lawson but tall enough for me so that I need to raise my head a bit when we speak. He told me that he lives in New York State but had stopped here on his way from New London to pay his respects to the Newkirks.

Good heavens, I haven't even told you his name. It is Jozef Weiss. He is twenty-seven years old and a captain in the United States Navy. Jozef was born here but his parents come from Poland so I guess in a way we have similar backgrounds. Sadly, our conversation was cut short because I needed to return to my duties in the nursery. Before we parted Jozef asked permission to kiss me. And I said yes!

It was most divine! Can you believe that I'm fifteen years old and this was my first kiss? I've had my head in the clouds since that day. When I came back to the nursery I must have had my head in the clouds for sure because Tess sat me down and warned me not to get carried away from just a kiss. But it was so heavenly. Jozef had to leave the next day to visit with his family in New York but three days later he was back. Somehow he arranged to stay with us for several days. Duty called him back to the navy base but he has promised to spend some time here this summer. I do think he truly likes me. I know I like him very much. Now that I think about it, I can't believe that I ever liked Mr. Lawson in that way. Next to Jozef, Mr. Lawson seems quite old.

It is getting late and I will need to rest before I go up to the nursery in the early morning hours. We like to both be present when the children have their breakfast. I truly hope I dream about my dear Jozef this night.

Sweet dreams auntie.

I remain your devoted nichte,
Charlotte

Lawson

Chapter 36

What a wonderful summer this has been! With Mister Newkirk gadding about the country on his horse-related trips, I have had the distinct pleasure of spending inordinate amounts of time in Delia's bed thanks to a very clever ruse that she has concocted.

A few months ago, we had as guest a young gentleman who had become smitten with our nursery maid Lotte. Thankfully, Lotte also found that she admired the young man so much that she was agreeable to his courtship. When Delia learned of their mutual admiration, she immediately saw an opportunity wherein we all could have what we desired.

Delia proposed that since Mister Newkirk was so desirous of her taking a lover that she would take him at his word, discreetly of course. Captain Weiss was to play the role of Delia's lover. The good captain arranged to have some time away from his military duties and became an extended houseguest here at Bridgewater. During the day, both Delia and Captain Weiss would engage in flirtatious actions that would suggest to those closely watching that they were carrying on an affair. Each evening at dinner they would manage to touch hands when passing the salt or exchange private smiles as though they both were privy to a secret. Delia allowed the good captain the liberties of holding her hand and whispering in her ear, especially when a member of the household staff was nearby. This was all to give credence to the idea that he was her lover.

The idea was furthered along when Delia would instruct Ellen to leave her early in the evening because she was expecting a 'visitor' in her suite. Those instructions were delivered to Ellen with a sly grin, of course, because we all knew that Ellen would share what she learned with Paul who in turn would tell Mister Newkirk. Furthering the notion of an affair, Captain Weiss made sure that he was seen on several occasions both entering Delia's room in the late evening and leaving it the next morning. In fact there were a couple of mornings when he lingered long enough to be found in Delia's room by Ellen when she came to wake her mistress.

Once Captain Weiss was safely in Delia's room for the night, he was given access to the staircase leading to the nursery where Lotte was on duty. That was where the captain actually spent his night – in Lotte's company.

Meanwhile, I would use the lower level of the concealed staircase to access Delia's room. In this way we were able to spend nearly every night together for almost two months. Of course I made it my business to be well removed before the first light of dawn lit the sky. In this way, even Captain Weiss had no knowledge of what transpired between Delia and me.

At the end of August, we received word that Mister Newkirk had returned not here to Bridgewater but to Boston where urgent 'business' demanded his attention. I remember the discussion that Delia and I had about that business.

It was a hot summer night, with nary a breeze coming in through the open windows to cool our bodies. We lay side by side upon Delia's bed, our eyes closed, our bodies sated. I could barely make out Delia's silhouette near me.

"Nate, I hate to break into our bliss but I'm serious about wanting another baby."

I could hear the anxiety in her voice.

"Is that wise, love?"

"I don't know if it's the wisest decision, but it's one I've given much thought to. I want to have another child with you. I miss Geraldine so much."

"Would it mean that much to you? Having a child of mine?"

There was a moment of silence as I anticipated Delia's answer.

"It would mean the world to me, Nate. We don't know how much longer we'll be together and…."

"Are you going somewhere?" I inquired.

"No, of course not," she hastened to reassure me. "I just meant that we're not getting younger and…"

"Oh, so now you think I'm an old fuddy-duddy?"

I reached out and pulled her close.

"No, no. You're just not understanding what I'm trying to say," she explained.

"Then what exactly *are* you trying to say?" I placed a kiss on her lips as she wound her arm around my neck.

"I…just…want…."

"I know what I want, Delia. You, beneath me. Let me love you again." I continued to kiss her as I moved over her, my movements meeting no resistance. "If it's a baby you want then it's a baby you shall have."

We spent the remainder of that night and every night for the next two weeks making love at every opportunity afforded to us. Thus it came as no surprise to me when in mid-September Delia shared the news of her pregnancy with me.

We were once again laying side-by-side on her bed, the cooling breezes of a late summer night wafting in through the windows. She was nestled in the crook of my arm, tracing my jaw with her fingers.

"I hope our son looks like you," she murmured.

"Really? Perhaps one day that will happen," I sighed as I held her close.

"I believe that will happen in about eight months' time," she informed me as she placed a gentle kiss on my mouth.

I sat up abruptly as though I'd been hit by a lightning bolt.

"Are you sure?"

"Positive," came the response.

"When exactly is this miracle to take place?" I began to kiss her nose, her cheeks, and finally her lips.

"Sometime in May I believe," she managed to say between my kisses.

"Then I expect I'll need to ask my employer for a raise in my wages. After all, I'll be a family man again." I smiled through the dark as I teased her.

"Hmmm, I'll take it up with my husband tomorrow."

"Tomorrow? Tomorrow?" I shook my head at her response.

"Yes. Kevin will be returning home tomorrow. I've been told that he is less than pleased at having another daughter."

"Tomorrow?"

"Yes, tomorrow, Nate. Our time is short so let's not get distracted. Come darling, love me once more," she invited.

That was one invitation she didn't need to issue twice.

———

Delia was right of course. The entire household was in a state of chaos with the return of Mister Newkirk. As always the stables were his first stop. He spent an entire day ensconced there as Huckleby brought him up to date on all the stable-related happenings. After that he closeted himself in his office as he sorted through the mail sitting on his desk.

Paul took the opportunity to speak with me when the master was busy and didn't require his valet's services.

"I can't begin to tell you how wonderful it is to be home again, Nathan." Paul was sitting in the servant's dining room sipping at a cup of coffee.

"Were you 'on loan' again to the Boston Newkirks?" I inquired.

"Yes, but only for a short time. Thankfully Jeannette spent less than twenty-four hours in labor. The boss spent the remainder of that week visiting her in hospital."

I remained quiet; nodding when I thought it was required of me.

"I feel sorry for Mister Kevin, truly I do. Not being able to sire a son makes him think of himself as a failure."

"But that's not necessarily true," I added.

"You're right, my friend; how the rich come up with those ideas is beyond me. At least I was able to move into the little cottage on Ash Street once Jeannette and the baby returned home."

"So you've seen the baby, then?" This question from Ellen as she joined us.

"Tiny, very tiny. But the spitting image of her father," offered Paul.

"Have they named her?"

"Amanda," responded Paul.

"Pretty name, that," conceded Ellen.

I excused myself at that point and left the room although I stayed close by to listen in on their further conversation.

"What's been going on here?" inquired Paul.

There was a moment's hesitation before Ellen answered. I supposed she was making sure that no one could hear.

"Miss Cordelia's taken a lover," Ellen stated.

"She has? Are you sure?"

"Seen him in her room myself."

"Anyone I know?"

"Don't know about that. But he's a nice fellow. Not like any of those that Mister Newkirk tried to saddle her with."

"His name?" urged Paul.

"Joseph Weiss."

"I don't know who that is," mused Paul. "Where's he from? How does she know him?"

"Heard that he's a relation of Miss Cordelia's sister-in-law, that nice Rose lady."

"And they're really carrying on you say?"

"Oh yes, no doubt about it. Couple of times I've gone in to wake Miss Cordelia and he was still in her room, holding her hand and giving her those soulful looks like he couldn't bear to be parted from her."

"And how did Miss Cordelia act?"

"She tried for a while to keep it under wraps, you know, but with Mister Kevin being gone and him giving her leave to take up with someone, she's been a bit more free. But never anything in public more than a look or a smile. Sometimes I've seen them holding hands when they thought no one was looking. The maids are all atwitter over the two – calling them the lovebirds."

That was enough for me to hear. Delia had been correct in her assumption that Ellen would divulge her 'secret affair' to Paul as soon as she could. It seemed that we were in the clear at least for the time being.

A couple of days later Captain Weiss's leave had come to an end. He bid his goodbyes to everyone, especially Lotte who had been given the night off and had spent it in the captain's room. She refused to come downstairs that day, afraid that everyone would know she had been crying.

I felt sorry for the girl. I knew from experience what it was like to lose someone you love, even for a short period of time. But the captain seemed like a decent sort and he had promised to write to Lotte as time permitted.

In a funny twist of fate, Bridgewater was almost devoid of guests the following weekend. With the Labor Day holiday just behind us, we all set our heads to preparing the house and gardens for the upcoming holidays. I was in my office looking over the schedule for the seasonal cleaning. Delia and Mrs. Grant were huddled over the preparatory menus. The maids and footmen were scattered about seeing to their duties. Tess was out on the terrace watching Birdie play with her doll; Katie was napping in her carriage, a gauzy sort of material shielding the infant from attack by nosy insects. The sun was shining, a warm breeze was blowing. Everything seemed right in my world.

Cordelia

Chapter 37

It was a lovely September day, warm sun, gentle breezes; a rare day when we were not expecting guests at Bridgewater for the weekend; the perfect time for planning and catching up on things. I had spent some time earlier in the morning with both of my daughters, Birdie being the attention seeker and pouting every time I held Katherine. But they were both my daughters and I hated showing favoritism so I tried to spend equal amounts of time with each of them.

Kevin had gone off to the stables early that morning returning in time to share with me a pleasant enough breakfast; shortly thereafter he closed the door to his office asking that he not be interrupted until luncheon.

With the Labor Day holiday behind us, I had directed that the rooms in the guest wing be deep cleaned and outfitted with fresh linens. The rooms were to be aired, swept, polished, and in every way prepared for the next round of guests who would be joining us in a few days. We were expecting a comedic couple who would be appearing at the Sterling Opera House in Derby for two nights. Their agent had gotten in touch with me and asked if they could call on us and pay their respects. I recognized it as a couched request for lodging since the couple was young and not flush with funds. Having heard only good things about them, I of course issued the invitation to Burns & Allen (as they liked to call themselves) to partake of our hospitality and perhaps regale us with an amusing story or two. I made a mental note to invite the Schubert brothers to stay with us at the same time. Who knows what might develop when people share time in each other's company?

I consulted my engagement book and found that we would be hosting people from the world of entertainment almost every week through the remainder of the year. At this juncture I thought it prudent to sit down with Mrs. Grant and plan out the menus for the weekly salons. We were thus ensconced in my office when Kevin burst through the door.

"Cordelia, might I have a word with you?" he smiled at me in a way I hadn't seen in a long time.

"Certainly," I acquiesced.

"Mrs. Grant, I would like to have a private moment with my wife."

"Of course, Mr. Newkirk. I've got plenty to keep me busy." The woman rose and shuffled off towards the kitchen, giving me a questioning look with her eyes.

"Thank you, Mrs. Grant," I responded, "we can finish our menu planning tomorrow." I turned to Kevin. "What brings you to the realm of the household's underbelly?"

"I simply had the urge to visit with my beautiful wife," he replied, placing himself on the chair that had held Mrs. Grant.

"Really?" I asked with a healthy dose of skepticism.

"Why not?" he asked cheerily. "You are a beautiful woman, Cordy."

"Obviously my beauty isn't suited to your tastes, though," I responded. "What's behind this display of charm?"

He was quiet for a moment, mulling over whether or not to come straight to the point.

"As you know, Jeannette has been delivered of her child."

"I surmised as much," I conceded.

"Another girl," he sneered.

"Is she well?"

"The child is just what one would expect. Round and rosy, lusty cry when she doesn't get her bottle."

"How like her papa!"

Kevin sighed. "I suppose I deserve that."

I remained silent, waiting for the point to be made; when none was forthcoming, I continued.

"Then Jeannette will raise the girl?"

"Amanda," he corrected me, "the child's name is Amanda."

"What provisions have you made for them?" My demeanor was calm as I began to surmise what he was after.

"Not to fear for them, my dear, they are provided for in every way possible."

"And for me?" I pursued.

"It pleases me greatly that you've taken a lover," he smiled at me. "It further pleases me that no one outside of a few staff members is aware of it."

"It's what you wished, isn't it?" I held my head high, unashamed of my actions.

"It also pleases me that it is someone who is not among our circle of friends. Therefore, I've decided to reward you."

"And what trinket or bauble have you to offer?"

"I offer you myself," he smiled. "Your dalliance with the good captain has come to an end. I am home now. I shall expect you in my bed tonight."

"What if I've been spoiled by Captain Weiss? He was a very thoughtful lover, you know."

"Be that as it may, that episode is past. I am returned home to take my rightful place and exercise my conjugal rights."

"In other words, you wish to try once again to get me with child – a boy child."

"Precisely! Ah Cordy, you know me well." He slapped his thigh with his hand and rose from the chair. "I shall expect you this evening then. Let's say around half past nine?"

I nodded my head in quiet agreement, afraid that if I spoke I would say something I would later regret.

For reasons known only to Nathan and myself, I knocked on Kevin's door at precisely half past nine that evening. And for almost every evening for several weeks until I determined that the charade had gone on long enough. Early in October I announced to Kevin that I was pregnant. He had surmised as much a few days earlier but pretended to be surprised at my news.

Of course Ellen spread the good news that another Newkirk child had been conceived and in short order the entire household staff was abuzz. Now that I was ostensibly carrying Kevin's child, he no longer felt the need for my late-night companionship. I was free once more to entertain in my suite. Nathan resumed his nocturnal visits as we spun dreams for our soon-to-be child. We debated whether the child should take advantage of his position in society and ultimately take up the future reins of Newkirk Trading or be allowed to follow his own dreams. In the end we decided not to decide – leaving the future to unfold without our interference.

Later that month I entered the nursery to spend some time with my daughters. I had brought some scarves and hats that I no longer had use for and gave them to Birdie who loved to play 'dress up'. While she was occupied, Tess brought Katherine over to me so that I could hold her and croon a soft melody to her much as my own momma did with me when I was her age.

"Here you are, Cordelia, this little one is such a joy to care for," commented Tess as she handed Katherine over to me.

"Come to momma, darling," I crooned as Katie snuggled against my neck. "Tess, you look exhausted. Did you not sleep well last night?"

"Oh aye, I slept well enough. But I fear there's something wrong with young Lotte." Tess perched on a chair beside mine.

"Lotte? Is she ill?"

"I'm not sure. She seems perfectly fine most of the time. Then there are days like today when she should have relieved me for the morning but when she appeared late she looked pale and washed out. Seemed to be listless, too. I sent her back to her bed."

"Have you not had your sleep Tess?"

"It's fine Cordelia. Lotte will return when she's rested a bit more."

"That's not like Lotte," I observed, "she hasn't had a day of sickness since she's come to Bridgewater."

"Perhaps the children are too much for her. Birdie can be quite the handful now that she's getting older."

"Yes, well, I should like Dr. Bennett to have a look at Lotte; just to be safe. Tess, I'll stay with the children. You must go have breakfast then take yourself off to bed."

"Thank you Cordelia. I must admit that I'm tired. But I'll skip breakfast if you don't mind."

"As you wish, Tess." I looked down into the sparkling eyes of my daughter as Tess made to leave the nursery. "Tess, when Lotte is rested send her to me."

"Of course, Cordelia."

Later that afternoon, as I reclined on the chaise in my suite, I heard a hesitant knock at the door.

"Come in," I called.

The door opened slightly and Lotte slipped through the narrow opening. She closed the door behind her and stood where she was, partially hidden in the shadows of the room.

"You asked to see me, Mrs. Newkirk?" her voice held the note of a tremor.

"Come in Lotte. Set down here on the window seat."

The young woman stepped forward and took a place on the seat, keeping her eyes downcast and trying to avoid looking at me.

"Tess tells me that you've been tired lately, more so than normal. Is Birdie giving you a hard time?"

"Oh no, Mrs. Newkirk. Birdie is fine. I love her, truly I do!" Lotte raised her head and looked in my direction. I instantly saw what she was trying to hide.

"Lotte, you've been crying. What's the matter?"

I left the chaise and went to sit beside the young woman, putting my arm around her shoulder.

"It's nothing, Mrs. Newkirk," Lotte shook her head as if to dispel something unpleasant.

"Lotte, I don't believe that for an instant. It's plain to see that your eyes are red and that you've been crying."

"Please, Mrs. Newkirk, I can't lose my position here. My mama in Dusseldorf is relying on what I send her every month." Lotte's words were choppy and I felt she might begin crying at any moment.

"There's nothing so dire that I would dismiss you. Now I insist; tell me what's bothering you." I tried to speak in a calm manner hoping to put her at ease.

"It's Jozef, I mean Captain Weiss," she managed to say.

"Has something happened to him?"

"No. No. I wrote to him like I promised and he wrote back to me." I knew this to be true as Nathan was in charge of disbursing any mail received at Bridgewater.

"Then what could have happened to make you so forlorn?"

"Oh, Mrs. Newkirk, I'm so ashamed. I thought Jozef loved me. Truly I did. That's why I let him….I mean that's why we…oh dear, Mrs. Newkirk, I'm going to have a baby!"

The girl wailed as she dissolved into tears. I pulled a lace-edged handkerchief from my drawer and handed it to her. She cried for a good five minutes before she broke into a series of hiccups.

"Lotte, didn't your aunt explain to you how babies are made?"

I would have thought that a midwife would have explained how and where a baby comes from to her young charge.

"I knew it was the man who gives the lady his seed," explained Lotte, "but I didn't know how." She broke into tears again.

"Well, what's done is done. You'll need to write to Captain Weiss immediately and explain the situation. I'm sure he'll do the right thing. After all, he seemed smitten with you."

I tried to console the crying young woman but my words moved her to another round of crying. When the tears seemed to abate somewhat Lotte turned to me again and haltingly offered an explanation.

"I wrote to Jozef. I told him of my joy when I learned that I was pregnant. He wrote back to me at first saying that there was no proof that the child was his. When I wrote back and told him that there had been no one else, he wrote back again. I received his letter yesterday."

She pulled out a crumpled envelope from her skirt pocket and handed it to me. The message was short but to the point.

Dear Lotte,

You are a lovely young woman; the hours that we spent together this summer have been the happiest of my life. I shall never forget you. However, there is no place for you in the life I have chosen. I am engaged to be married to another woman. While I have no true feelings for my fiancé she is well placed to assist me in my military career as she is the daughter of an admiral.

If things had been different, perhaps you and I might have carved out a future together. But ambition is the driving force in my life. There is no place in my future for you or for any children.

Please do not attempt to contact me again.

Thank you for making this summer a memorable one.

J.W.

I silently read the letter, not once but twice, chiding myself for not having kept a better watch over Lotte and the captain.

"What am I to do, Mrs. Newkirk?"

"The first thing is for you to dry your eyes. It won't do you or the baby any good if you are upset."

"Yes, of course. You're right."

"I should like to have Dr. Bennett examine you. It's best we know when to expect the child." I drew a deep breath before continuing. "Lotte, have you given any thought to putting the baby up for adoption?"

Lotte turned her face to me and it froze in a hard look.

"Never! I would never give my child away!!"

"I had to ask. Dr. Bennett will ask the same thing given your unwed state," I explained.

"I'll go back to Dusseldorf if I must. Mama and I will find a way to survive." Lotte stood up, bravely trying to accept her fate.

"There's no need of that. For now you will continue as you have. As time goes by we can put out the story that your child was fathered by a now-deceased serviceman. But we'll cross that bridge when we come to it."

At those words, Lotte flung herself into my arms.

"You are the dearest, kindest lady in the entire world! I should have come to you sooner."

She stepped back, smoothing out her skirt as she turned to the door.

"Our babies are both due in June. Perhaps they will be friends," she whispered as she slipped out of the room, closing the door behind her.

Lotte seemed much calmer after we had our talk, although I now had much to mull over.

Over the following week I discussed with Nathan the advisability of my trying to contact Captain Weiss. As always, Nathan considered the situation from not only Lotte's perspective but also from that of the captain.

"As a man, I'm sure that Josef felt the liberties he was allowed by Lotte gave him unspecified permission to take his ease with her. The fact that he omitted telling her about his previous engagement is often overlooked by men such as he. I'm sure that he toyed with the idea of making Lotte his mistress," offered Nate as we sat together in my office one afternoon not too long after I had learned of Lotte's pregnancy.

"Could he not see that she's just a child?"

"I believe she's almost as old as you were when you met Kevin and lured him into marriage," Nate pointed out.

"Yes, but by the time I was seventeen I was no longer a virgin and quite aware of how men operate."

"You've got me there," he conceded.

"So far Lotte has kept pretty much to the nursery. In addition to you and me, only Tess is aware of her condition," I ruminated. "Lotte seems to be bearing up fairly well."

"Delia, I think you should know that there's talk among the staff that the child you're expecting is not Kevin's. Do you wish for me to put a stop to the gossip?"

Before I could answer we heard the heavy tread of a man's booted foot in the hallway. We both turned to face the door as Kevin stopped just within my office, his head bent in a manner that suggested that he was mentally occupied.

"Cordy, there's a matter of importance that I must discuss with you." He pulled up short when he noticed Nathan sitting across from me. "Lawson! Good, you're here. We can take care of this matter at once."

Nathan rose from his seat and offered the chair to Kevin.

"No, stay seated. I think better on my feet."

"As you wish, sir."

"I've been told that in addition to our own good fortune in conceiving once again that you, my dear, aren't the only one in a family way." Kevin favored me with what he believed to be his most endearing smile.

"Really?" I feigned ignorance.

"I'm surprised that you haven't noticed it yet, Cordy, as you're the one who deals with the staff on a regular basis."

"I'm sure, sir, I would have noticed if any of our young ladies was feeling ill or showing signs of being in a family way," volunteered Nathan.

"Ah, so the little mother-to-be hasn't informed you yet!" Kevin questioned Nathan who merely raised his eyebrows in question.

"Tell us, who is the young lady? I'm sure she must be someone you're intimately acquainted with." I threw the proverbial ball back into Kevin's court.

Kevin merely smiled as he ignored my remark.

"Paul tells me that our little nursery maid is with child. I certainly hope not since I had hoped to initiate her into the intricacies of carnal pleasure but it seems I've missed my opportunity. Lawson, you are one lucky devil!" He clapped his hand on Nathan shoulder in a display of camaraderie.

"Am I to understand that Lotte is pregnant?" I inquired softly.

"Amazing that you haven't noticed her pale face of late, my dear. But then, you have your own delicate condition to deal with."

A light knock sounded at the office door.

"You asked to see me?" inquired a gentle voice followed by the appearance of Lotte herself.

Nathan turned to me with a questioning expression; however, before I could speak Kevin took Lotte by the hand and led her further into my office. In a flash Nathan stood up and offered Lotte his seat. She smiled shyly at his gentlemanly manner.

"Thank you, Mr. Lawson," she murmured as she sat down, placing her hands in her lap.

"I've taken the liberty of inviting young Lotte to join us," Kevin began, a most benign smile lighting up his face. "Lawson, you almost had me fooled there for a moment when you proclaimed ignorance of Lotte's delicate condition."

Lotte's eyes flew to me, a look of fearful anxiety on her face. I tried to calm her by smiling.

"Cordy, you may not be aware of everything transpires below stairs but it seems that Lawson here and young Lotte have been an item for quite some time," Kevin informed us.

Nathan looked at me squarely, mouthing the word "No" behind Kevin's back. Lotte once again became agitated.

"It was shortly after our dear Geraldine succumbed that I found these two in a rather compromising position. At the time they hastened to assure me that all was above board. In fact, Lotte, you'll recall your telling me of how safe you felt with Mr. Lawson since he was so much older than you and how you preferred an older gentlemen. Did you not?"

"Yes, Mr. Newkirk, I do remember saying that," Lotte's voice was quiet and subdued as she answered.

"This is the first I'm hearing of this, Kevin. Are you sure you're not mistaken? After all we were all grieving for the loss of our dear daughter," I managed to say.

"No mistake, Cordy. Lawson here is the father of Lotte's child.

And I'm here to see that he does the right thing." Kevin once again smiled at all of us.

"No, Mister Newkirk, that's not true!" interjected Lotte.

"What a woman! Willing to defend her man to the end," marveled Kevin. "Never fear Lotte, you won't be dismissed. The children love you and you'll be needed more than ever with the arrival of the latest Newkirk. Shall we have the wedding this Saturday?"

"Wedding?" I inquired, coming to my feet.

"Of course, Cordy. Can't have an unwed mother on staff can we? You'll marry the girl Lawson. We'll arrange for living accommodations for you both. Would hate to lose a good maid as well as a trusted Head Steward."

Kevin certainly left no choice in the matter. If both Nathan and Lotte wanted to retain their positions, they would be forced to wed. There was complete silence for a moment or two; it was finally broken by Nathan who tore his gaze away from me. Squaring his shoulders he went down on one knee before a shocked and speechless Lotte.

"Lotte, dearest," he began, choking up as he spoke. He cleared his throat and began again, taking her hand in his. "Lotte, dearest, no words can express my feelings at this time. I hope you will do me the honor of becoming my wife."

"But, but, what about…." began Lotte.

"Dearest, there is no problem that we can't conquer if we are together," he squeezed her hand.

I hoped that she understood what he was trying to tell her. Lotte looked at me as if for approval and I nodded my head ever so slightly. She drew a deep breath, turned back to Nathan, and squeezed his hand in return.

"Mr. Lawson," she began, "I'm sorry, Nathan," she corrected herself forcing a shy smile, "I accept your offer of marriage."

Pulling her up by her hand, Nathan drew her into his embrace.

"Come, come now, Lawson, surely you can do better than that?"

Nathan broke away from Lotte momentarily and turned to face Kevin.

"It would appear that I've already done better, sir. Now if you'll excuse us, Lotte and I would like a moment or two alone."

I watched as my lover put an arm around Lotte's shoulder and escorted her from my office. When they were gone, Kevin sat down in the vacant chair.

"You're mighty pleased with yourself, aren't you?" I queried.

"Some things are best left to the master of the house, Cordy. I'll leave the wedding arrangements to you but I want them married on Saturday."

"What of their living arrangements? Have you also thought about those?"

"Pish, posh! That's the kind of thing I have you for, my dear."

"Have you given any thought that perhaps Mr. Lawson isn't the father of Lotte's baby?"

"Who else could it be?"

"We've had several gentlemen guests over the past month or two who've spent time at Bridgewater," I suggested, as my heart beat rapidly with the impending marriage of my lover.

"No, it's Lawson. I've known him to frequent a certain lady of the evening over on Long Wharf but he hasn't paid her a visit in quite some time. You should have seen them, Cordy, the day that Geraldine died; consoling each other they were but in a quite intimate embrace. No, Lawson is the baby's father. Of that I'm sure."

"As you say, then. I must get busy if we are to have a wedding on Saturday."

"I'll leave you to it, Cordy. Don't overdo though; wouldn't want my unborn son's wellbeing compromised in any way."

Preening like a peacock, Kevin rose and left my office. He seemed content that he had played god with the lives of two of our staff.

Late that night, I heard the quiet movement of the panel in my washroom as Nathan slipped through the opening. In a moment he was beside me, sitting on my bed.

"Delia, what are we going to do? Lotte is beside herself. She's done nothing but cry since I proposed to her."

"What can we do, darling? Surely you understand that Kevin would dismiss you both if you hadn't agreed to a forced marriage?"

"I understand that but Lotte insists that everything is her fault. I don't know what to say to her."

"Poor Nate, trapped into marriage with a pregnant woman." I reached up and caressed his cheek.

"Poor Delia, cheating on her husband with an almost married man," he leaned over and whispered the words against my lips.

"Then make love to me now, Nate. Hold me close. I want to feel your noble heart beating."

———

It was a quiet wedding for Nate and Lotte. The ceremony was conducted by a Justice of the Peace in our Grand Hallway with most of the household staff in attendance. Mrs. Grant had created a lovely cake for the celebration. The staff was given a few hours away from their duties to enjoy the celebration. Kevin surprised everyone by ordering the newlyweds to take one of the cars and drive in to New Haven where he had reserved a two-night stay in a suite for them at the Hotel Duncan. After they had departed, Kevin informed me that both Nathan and Lotte should be paid for their days off. He insisted that both were too valuable to lose.

I spent both nights that the Lawsons were away from Bridgewater sleeplessly staring out my bedroom window. All sorts of thoughts were running through my mind. What were the newlyweds doing? What did they have for dinner? What sorts of things did they talk about? Would they sleep in the same bed? Would they become intimate?

By the end of the second night I was totally exhausted and fell asleep on the chaise. It was there that Ellen found me on Monday morning.

"Good morning, Miss Cordelia. Isn't it nice to feel the warmth of love in Bridgewater again?"

"If you're referring to the newlyweds, yes, I guess so." I slipped into the washroom as Ellen set about getting out a morning dress for me.

"Both Mr. Lawson and Lotte, I mean Mrs. Lawson," she corrected herself, "seem quite happy and content."

"Are they back so soon?" I called out.

"Oh my yes," acknowledged Ellen, "Mr. Lawson showed up in the kitchen right on time to have his usual cup of coffee according to Mrs. Grant."

"How very efficient of him. I take it that Lotte also is on duty up in the nursery."

"Don't know for sure about that but I do know that she's happier than I've ever seen her."

Ellen bustled around the room, humming to herself, while she went about her routine. I left her to her musings and took myself off on an impromptu inspection of every one of the main rooms, forestalling the time when I would be forced to confront Nathan. The last room to be inspected was the morning room. As I approached the French door leading into the room that was awash with sunlight I heard the front doorbell. William, our newly hired butler, hastened to answer the summons. I waited in the shadows of the hallway to ascertain who might be calling.

"Delivery for Mrs. Newkirk," came the voice of a deliveryman.

"Deliveries around the side," responded William.

"Don't think you'll want to take delivery of this gift in the usual manner, if I might be so bold."

"Good heavens, man, what are you delivering?"

"Got me a great big bird cage, real fancy like. You'll have to sign for it," the driver instructed.

"Who sent this delivery, sir?" I inquired, stepping out of the shadows and approaching the front door.

"You be Mrs. Newkirk?"

"Watch your tone of voice," admonished William. Turning to me he said, "I'm sorry ma'am. I told him deliveries should go around the side of the house."

"Not to worry, William," I assured him. Turning to the deliveryman I inquired, "What exactly are you delivering?"

"It's a bird cage, ma'am. Big one. Almost as tall as you are," he doffed his hat when he addressed me.

"Is there a card or something to indicate who sent this birdcage?" I inquired.

"Yes, ma'am, there is, but if you don't mind I'd just as soon bring it in and have you look at the card later. Those birds are like to freeze out here with the wind and all."

"Good heavens! Certainly. Bring the birds and their cage indoors. You may bring them into the foyer."

"Finally, the voice of reason!" the delivery driver muttered to himself as he turned back to the truck he was driving.

After a moment or two of juggling around the front door, a lovely brass cage decorated with intricate scrollwork sat in the middle of the foyer. Inside this huge aviary were two beautiful lovebirds who were eyeing their surroundings.

"Why they're beautiful!" I exclaimed. "William, please show this gentleman the way to the morning room. I think the birds would be happiest there."

"Here's the card that was attached to the cage, ma'am. Now there, butler man, just show me where you'd like the cage set and I'll follow you."

William muttered something unintelligible under his breath as he led the way to the morning room. Once they were out of sight, I hurriedly tore open the envelope containing the card.

Like the love between two lovebirds, I have only one true love. – N

Quickly I jammed the note into my skirt pocket as I heard the deliveryman's voice approach the foyer once again.

"Nice place ya' got here, Missus." He tipped his hat to me, turned and exited through the door that William held open for him.

"I'd be careful about strangers, Mrs. Newkirk," advised William, "that fellow had a shifty look about him."

"I'll be certain to inform Mr. Lawson. Thank you, William."

While the butler went off in the direction of the library, I continued on to the morning room. Closer inspection of this new addition to our household showed me two very colorful lovebirds who managed to flit from perch to perch within their enclosure. The male was most attractive with his bright yellow and turquoise plumage; the female's feathers were nearly identical in color although a bit less bright. I stood and watched them in fascination, unaware that I was no longer alone until a genteel cough from behind me alerted me to another's presence. I knew in a moment who it was, simply by the scent of his aftershave.

"I hope you like your gift."

"They are perfect," I poured all of my excitement into those words. "But it is I who should be giving you a wedding present."

Nathan moved closer and in a lowered voice asked, "May I come to you tonight?"

I tilted my head in a manner that caused my eyes to slant.

"What will your wife say? Won't she miss you?"

"Please, Delia. Don't punish me for your husband's rash actions."

I sobered quickly when I saw how torn up Nate was.

"I'll be in my room all night. Come when you can," I whispered.

"Thank you." He turned and left the room.

It was well after midnight when I was roused from an unplanned nap by the muffled sound of the concealed panel in my washroom being opened. In less than a moment Nate was beside my chaise, kneeling so that we were face to face.

"Delia, are you awake?" he whispered.

"Yes."

"Can you forgive me?"

I could feel his eyes searching my shadowed face for a clue to my mood.

"It's Kevin I can't forgive." I heard his almost inaudible sigh of relief. "You did what I would have expected you to do."

"I never meant to hurt you." He took my hand in his and kissed my open palm.

"How is Lotte?"

"She's fine." His momentary silence told me that he was choosing his words carefully. "We, she and I, had a long discussion on our so-called honeymoon."

"There's no need to recount your weekend," I rushed to assure him.

"Mostly we talked about you; and me; and us."

"Please get off your knees, Nate. You must be terribly uncomfortable."

"Thank you, darling," I could feel his smile through the shadows as he came to sit beside me.

"Now tell me everything. Where you went, what you saw, what you ate for dinner. I'm dying with curiosity." I nestled into his embrace as he held me close.

"Lotte is a wonderful young woman. Very wise for someone of her tender age. Yet in many ways still so naïve."

"Continue."

"She's been well aware of our nocturnal visits, as you know."

"And she's earned my highest regards with her loyalty and devotion," I answered.

"Don't you see Delia? Lotte is not going to stand in the way of our love. She is well aware of how your husband mistreats you and has told me in no uncertain terms that should I wish to continue as your lover she has no objections except…"

"Ah! The conditions are?"

"Only one. That like you and Kevin, she and I put forth a public façade of wedded bliss. Especially when the baby arrives."

Nate was holding his breath in anticipation of my response. I waited a moment or two as I mulled over Lotte's pronouncement.

"Seems quite reasonable to me. She gets the appearance of a happy marriage complete with child and we are allowed to continue on with our affair." I felt Nate's body stiffen slightly. "With her on our side there would never be a problem with you and I in the same room," I continued.

"Affair? Is that all this is to you?" his voice had a slight edge to it.

"Of course not, dearest. I'm sorry for my poor choice of words."

"You must be exhausted. I should leave you to your rest."

"Oh, so that's how it's to be? Before you were married you wouldn't consider leaving my side even if I was pregnant," I teased.

"You can't think…..? Surely you don't think that Lotte and I….?"

"What's a poor girl to think?" I shrugged my shoulders and pouted.

"Don't think I don't know your lips are all pouty, darling. I know just how to tease a smile out of you."

He bent his head and nudged my lips apart with his own until I gave in good-naturedly and accepted his kiss, running my fingers through his hair.

"Took you long enough," I whispered against his mouth, pulling his head down for another kiss.

———

In time we settled into a routine of sorts. When Lotte's turn came for her to take night duty with the children, Nate was sure to be seen entering the nursery so that he might spend the night with his wife. Once the children were settled for the night and fast asleep, he would slip down the stairway to my room where we nestled together until just before morning. Again he would return to the nursery via the same route, and looking as tired and worn as though he had been up half the night with Lotte, he made it a point to await Tess's arrival in the nursery before returning to his own quarters for a quick change of clothes.

Lotte

Chapter 38

May 1914

My Dearest Aunt Anja,

Where do I begin to tell you all that has happened? Of course you must know that once I was wed to my darling husband Nathan I was the happiest woman alive. Even though there is quite a difference in age between us (he is now thirty-four and we celebrated his birthday just a few days ago) I am most comfortable with him. He has been my rock during the past few months and has been a kind husband.

With everything that you taught me about childbirth, I should have recognized the signs that forewarned of my miscarriage. But oh, meine tante, I believe I did not want to see them. When the cramps came that night Nathan was tending to another matter. Even in my pain, I managed to descend through the stairway to Mrs. Newkirk's room and I collapsed on her washroom floor. When next I opened my eyes, I had been laid in Mrs. Newkirk's own bed, in clean nightclothes, and the first person I laid eyes on was my darling Nathan. Of course Mrs. Newkirk and Dr.

Bennett were there as well. They were all very concerned about me since I had lost a lot of blood. In truth, I felt very weak and could barely lift my head.

When I questioned what had happened they all looked from one to the other. "Please," I cried out, "tell me my baby is alright." Tears began to stream down my cheeks as my darling husband came to sit beside me. He took my hand into his and with a gentle voice explained what had happened.

"Lotte, you gave us all a fright. Do you remember anything about the night when you stumbled down the stairs and collapsed in Mrs. Newkirk's washroom?"

"I was in pain. I had terrible cramps." I surprised myself because I couldn't speak above a loud whisper. I'm afraid I knew what was coming and unbidden, my tears began to form.

"Yes, dearest. You were bleeding quite heavily. Dr. Bennett was summoned but by the time he got here the worst had happened." Nathan bent his head then and I could see he was trying to compose himself. When he raised his head I could see tears streaming down his face. "I'm sorry, Lotte. The baby is gone."

I reached out a hand and touched his face. His eyes were filled with a deep sadness. At that moment he gathered me into his arms and together we comforted each other. The emptiness within me was unexplainable. Never have I felt anything so deep and endless. You should know that I would have had a daughter and I had wanted to name her for mama.

I was made to rest in bed for almost three weeks until I regained my strength. After that day when I learned of my daughter's passing, I was physically moved back to my room just outside the nursery. Of course the Newkirk daughters wanted to visit and they kept my waking hours full of chatter and play as they came to sit with me.

Now that I am fully recovered I am able to tell you about the birth of the latest Newkirk child. Just a few days ago Mrs. Newkirk went into labor. The birth was very similar to the birth of her first child, Geraldine. Long hours of contractions lasted through the day and into the next morning. But at last dear Mrs. Newkirk gave birth. There was much excitement when Mr. Newkirk learned that although the birth was more than a month early, he was the proud papa of a healthy, fully formed, boy. At last he has gotten the heir that he has wished for all these years.

Mrs. Newkirk is still abed after the difficult birth but already there is much finger-counting amongst the staff. Most everyone believes that the child was fathered by another gentleman who was guest here for several weeks while Mr. Newkirk was out-of-town on business. But just the other night I overheard Mr. Newkirk, who had come up to the nursery to visit his son, speaking quietly to the babe.

"Funny looking little thing, aren't you, son? Well, I don't give a fig who your real father is. From this day on you're a Newkirk. You'll be raised as a Newkirk and my parents will finally get off my back. My freedom from family was won the day you were born. We need to celebrate that freedom, don't we?" He fell silent for a moment as he gazed at the infant. "What we need is a big celebration! We'll give you a christening party the likes of which this family has never seen. No expense will be spared. The wine will flow, the food will be consumed without end, and guests will come from far and wide to celebrate the birth of the Newkirk heir. I must go and tell your mother of my plans."

With that he turned and left the nursery.

Once I was assured that he had departed, I stepped out from the playroom and gazed upon the little one. Yes, a boy child is a celebration for these rich folk. I'm sure the christening will be one extravagant event.

However, there will be one more thing to celebrate. I believe that when all is said and done, my dearest Nathan and I will be celebrating with everyone else. Perhaps I shan't wait for the christening to impart my news to Nathan. In fact, I think I shall close this letter to you now.

As always and with much love, I remain your devoted niece,

Charlotte
(Mrs. Lotte Lawson)

P.S. In case you haven't guessed, Nathan and I are going to be parents again!

Lawson

Chapter 39

September 1914

Once again Bridgewater was bursting at the seams with family and guests. Both sets of grandparents occupied the best guest suites. Delia's brother and family along with Kevin's siblings and their families took up residence in Willow Cottage. The inner circle of Newkirk friends filled the remainder of our guest wing.

During the week leading up to young Gerald's christening, staff members did double duty, scurrying to and fro to accommodate the needs of our guests. Temporary staff buzzed around the kitchen where Mrs. Grant issued orders like a general commanding her troops. In short, organized chaos swirled around Bridgewater.

I must have walked an extra fifteen miles during those days as I was kept busy tending to one minor crisis after another, usually on opposing sides of the house. By the end of each day, after I had made my final check of the house, I gratefully fell into bed beside my pregnant wife.

Yes, Lotte was with child. My child. I marveled, as I always did, at the wonder of creating a new life even as the gentle rhythm of Lotte's breathing calmed me.

Although the child Lotte had miscarried earlier this year was fathered by another, I had felt the loss as sharply as if the babe had been mine. With the strength of the young, Lotte put her loss behind her and concentrated on giving me the comfort I needed.

"My dearest husband," she had said, "I know your heart belongs to another. That is something I won't ask you to change regardless of the vows we have exchanged."

"I don't deserve your understanding, Lotte. Through my selfish actions I've ruined your life, confining you to a loveless marriage. I should hate me if I were you."

"I don't hate you, husband. Far from it." She had placed her hand gently on my arm. "I would ask a favor, though."

"Name it and it's yours."

"I want another child," she whispered. "I miss that tiny person growing inside me. I feel empty."

I remained silent for a short time, weighing her request against everything I had taken from her.

"Anything but that," I croaked.

"Please, Nathan. When I tend to baby Gerald, knowing that he's your son and that he'll never call me mama, I am filled with despair."

A long-buried sense of guilt deep inside me recalled how loyal Lotte had been to Delia and me over the years. Didn't I at least owe her the one thing of which she had been robbed: a family of her own?

So now, here we lay side by side – Lotte sleeping peacefully with my child growing within her as I tried to sort through the torrent of emotions crashing within me.

Just yesterday Delia had received permission from Dr. Barnett to resume normal activities. Last night she had welcomed me into her arms and her bed once more. Given the fact that we hadn't been together in quite some time, our coupling should have been filled with joy. But for me our coming together had been bittersweet.

As usual Delia was her same delightful self: beautiful, charming, sensual, uninhibited. Yet I found myself assaulted by memory flashes of Lotte: sobbing at the loss of her child, clinging to me until those sobs subsided, burying her face into my shoulder, smiling radiantly when she imparted the news of her pregnancy. These mental images of my little wife intruded on my nocturnal visit with Delia so that she soon sensed my lack of attention and rote movements. I explained these by saying there was much on my mind with the upcoming christening.

I pushed the thoughts of yesterday to the back of my mind and returned to the present. My mind eventually grew as weary as my body and I fell into a sound sleep.

The day of Gerald Newkirk's christening dawned with a layer of dense fog enshrouding Bridgewater. As the family and friends' cars moved down the brick driveway, I made a final check of the preparations for the luncheon that would be served in our ballroom where long tables had been set up. Confident that everything was progressing nicely I made my way to the stables in search of Huckleby.

"Mornin' Nate," he greeted me.

"Huck," I nodded in his direction.

"Off to the big event?"

"Yes indeed. Everything at the house is progressing smoothly. Shouldn't be any problem that you can't handle."

"I'll do a walk through in about forty-five minutes or so. Maybe cajole a sample of dinner from Aggie while I'm there," responded Huckleby.

"Good luck on that score."

"Oh, Aggie Grant and I get along well," he winked knowingly at me, "if you catch my drift."

A short while later I guided my car into the parking lot of St. Stan's. The cool interior of the church welcomed me as I slid into a pew at the rear. I looked around and noted the Boston contingent sitting up front near the altar; the Conners sitting directly behind them. The ladies were all wearing the symbols of their social stations: hats covered with feathers and lace; fur stoles, shawls, and capes; and enough jewels to ransom a small kingdom. The gents sat at attention in their stiff collars, eyes glazed over as their minds ostensibly drifted to thoughts of the food and entertainment that would follow.

At the baptismal font Sallie Newkirk Hawks and her husband spoke the words that marked them as Gerald's godparents. Sallie then held the baby's head over the font and Reverend Hartigan drizzled holy water on his forehead, symbolically washing away any stain of sin on the baby's soul. Through it all Kevin Newkirk, sitting in the pew closest to the font, beamed as he watched his heir accepted into the church.

After the prayers and service were done, Reverend Hartigan and two altar boys walked up the aisle towards the foyer, stopping just behind my pew. A few feet in front of him, but still in the foyer, stood Delia. Until this very moment, I had been unaware of her presence. I watched Delia approach the priest, her eyes downcast and a rosary entwined between her fingers.

Reverent Hartigan spoke the Latin prayers of purification before handing his prayer book to one acolyte and taking a smoking incense brazier from the other. As he wafted the brazier around Delia the scent of the incense filled the air – this was the symbolic purification of the new mother. When this was done, Delia was invited to enter the church proper where Sallie transferred baby Gerald into his mother's arms. I slid from the pew then and left the church. My son, now Kevin's son, was safe in his mother's embrace and in the eyes of God.

———

The remainder of the day was filled with noise, food, activity, entertainment, any number of small crises, and innumerable requests by the gentry. The celebration of Gerald's christening, and the repetitive mention of his being the Newkirk heir, seemed endless. It was well after ten o'clock that night before the last of our guests slowly returned to their accommodations.

In the kitchen the scullery maids were still washing dishes and glassware, the footmen were assisting in drying and storing the pots and pans, leftovers had been re-plated and stored for the morrow. Ellen and Paul at long last made their way to the staff dining room for a late supper after seeing to the care of their charges' clothing: the cleaning and polishing of Kevin's riding boots was assigned to a footman; Delia's requirement of a specific morning dress that had a stain from Gerald's saliva on it necessitated a cleaning and this was taken to the laundress who would have it ready for morning. Mrs. Grant had retired about an hour earlier. I brewed myself a cup of hot tea, laced it with Kevin's best brandy, and retired to my office.

With the steaming brew resting on my desk, I unbuttoned my jacket and eased into my chair. It was marvelous to be off my feet if only for a few moments. I closed my eyes and listened to the routine noises in the kitchen. Finally I heard the scullery girls say an exhausted good night and shortly thereafter one of the footmen popped into my office.

"All done, Mr. Lawson. As tidy as can be."

"Thank you Billy. A good evening to you," I responded.

Finishing up my tea, I stood up and stretched my back, turning down the lamps in the kitchen before I proceeded to make my final rounds of the house. As I proceeded down the main hallway I turned off or dimmed the lamps, allowing enough light to remain. Should any of our guests feel restless they wouldn't bump into a wall or table and cause injury to themselves. My thoughts turned to Lotte and how exhausted she must be. Thankfully Tess had been the one to take charge of Gerald today and Lotte had merely to entertain young Birdie. Oh, who was I kidding? Lotte had the worst of it I was sure. Birdie could be quite a handful!

As I entered the library I made a visual check. Everything seemed in order yet I felt something wasn't quite right. I stepped further into the room. That's when I realized that Delia was seated in one of the elegantly upholstered chairs. Deep shadows camouflaged her presence.

"Mrs. Newkirk, are you all right?"

"Oh, so it's Mrs. Newkirk now?" she smiled at me as she rose from the chair, trailing an elegant silk robe behind her.

"I…."

"I require a word with you, Mr. Lawson," her voice took on that haughty, employer tone. "I wish to commend you on a well-executed performance by the staff today."

She walked toward me, placing her hands on the lapels of my jacket.

"There is, however, one thing that has gone lacking." She bit her lip in an effort to hide her smile behind a fake frown.

"I'm sorry if anything was amiss, madam. Pray tell me what's wrong so that I may speak to the offending party."

I kept my tone professional, as I knew she liked for me to do when she played this game.

She stood on her toes and captured my lower lip between hers, nipping a bit as she did so.

"It's you, I'm afraid. You're the offending party," she whispered.

"How have my actions today offended, madam?"

"You've allowed your duties to come first." She untied the sash of her robe. "You've neglected your employer's personal needs."

"Perhaps madam could instruct me as to how I may make amends?" I tried to keep a smile from my face.

"You may remove my robe," she instructed.

I placed my hands beneath the fabric on her shoulders and tugged the robe, allowing it to pool at her feet. My breath hitched as the moonlight coming in through the window gave evidence of her nudity.

"Delia! Have you gone mad?" I whispered hoarsely as I bent to retrieve the robe from the floor.

"Mad for you, Nate. I couldn't wait for you tonight."

She pulled me close, molding herself against me, kissing me even as her fingers caressed my chest. I felt her unbutton my shirt. My hold on her tightened as she placed her hands on my skin. I took command of the kiss, nudging her gently towards a nearby sofa. Within moments I was shed of my clothes and we were rolling about like two love-struck teenagers. Our joining was heated and frenzied and over quickly. We lay there for a time, wrapped in each others arms. Gentle kisses and touches soon roused us once more. We were fully engaged when I thought I heard a sound out in the hallway. That was when I realized that the door to the room was slightly ajar.

Too late! Delia was fully aroused, as was I. There was no way either of us would stop until fully satiated. Whatever it was – mouse or man – would have to wait until we were finished.

It was almost an hour later that Delia finally bid me good night and climbed the circular stairway to her turret room. I rearranged my clothes, finished my nightly rounds of the house as I stifled involuntary yawns, and at long last returned to the room I shared with Lotte. She would be fast asleep, I knew. These days she often had trouble staying awake past eight o'clock.

As I drifted off into sleep, I thought I heard Lotte sniffling. She did that sometimes when she slept. I hoped she wasn't catching a cold.

Cordelia

Chapter 40

December 10, 1914

A light snowfall made the late afternoon even gloomier than normal for that time of year. But the anticipation of arriving at the Taft Hotel in New Haven dispelled any gloom that surrounded our party. Stan pulled the car up to the front entrance on College Street and hurried to open the door for us. Kevin, on his best behavior, stepped down first and handed me to the recently cleared pavement. A uniformed doorman tipped his hat to us as he held open the heavy wooden entry door. Kevin ushered me in.

Although I had been to several functions at the Taft, each time I entered the Grand Lobby I was awestruck by its grandeur. There was nothing like it in either New York or Boston. With the lobby's white columned walls soaring to a height of three stories and culminating in an ornately golden rotunda on the scale of Grand Central Station, it was enough to give one pause. I smiled at Kevin as he traversed the wide expanse of marble flooring after having deposited me on one of many plush chairs sprinkled about for the convenience of hotel guests. He returned moments later, with the hotel manager in tow.

"Mrs. Newkirk," began the formally dressed manager whose lapel sported a boutonnière, "how nice to see you again. Your accommodations are ready. The members of your staff are waiting to greet you upon your arrival upstairs."

"Mr. Berwyn," I inclined my head in his general direction, giving the feathers of my hat an opportunity to flutter about my head. "I should like to consult with the catering manager after I've settled in. Please send him up to my suite in about an hour."

"As you wish, Mrs. Newkirk. Please allow me to personally escort you upstairs."

Mr. Berwyn managed to stay a step or two ahead of us as he led the way to the lift reserved for those occupying penthouse suites. He called the car and then turned to Kevin with whom he conversed about the weather. Within moments we ascended to the top floor of the hotel, where Mr. Berwyn assured us that his entire staff was at our beck and call. For the money we were dropping at his establishment the staff should be awaiting even our tiniest requests.

We passed by several doors, with Mr. Berwyn noting for us the rooms assigned to various family members. Kevin and I had long ago decided that we would maintain separate suites so that he could entertain the gentlemen while I could do the same for female family members. Consequently our suites were on opposite sides of the floor. The rooms between our suites were assigned to various family members with the room closest to mine set aside for our daughters. Gerald had been left at Bridgewater under Lotte's care, while Tess had accompanied Birdie and Katherine. Although the children were too young to attend the theater's opening night, they were certainly old enough to join their parents at dinner. One was never too young to begin learning the social graces.

Further down the corridor, rooms had been assigned to my Momma and Poppa, Fannie and Gus Newkirk, Bernice and Robert Woodward, and my brother Cal and his wife Rose. Cal's children were also to share the smaller suite with my daughters. Tess was charged with their care as well.

Yes, our party filled the uppermost floor of the hotel completely.

I was quite impressed with the opulence of my suite. The large parlor, which was flanked by two bedrooms, would do quite nicely for my entertaining purposes. I admired the choice of fabrics used in the elegant drapery as well as the upholstery chosen for the graceful furniture.

"Mrs. Newkirk, may I take your coat?" Ellen stepped into the parlor from the smaller of the two bedrooms which I assumed she had already moved into.

"I expect the catering manager to arrive shortly, Ellen."

She nodded as I handed her my coat, gloves, and hat.

"Have all of the family arrived?" I inquired.

"Yes, Miss Cordelia. You and Mr. Kevin were the last ones. Several of the gents have gone downstairs to the tap room. I believe the respective mothers are preparing for this evening's dinner. Tess tells me that the children, with the exception of Miss Birdie, are all napping."

"Birdie is probably planning her choice of outfit for dinner," I smiled at the thought. "Once the catering manager has concluded his business I should like a hot bath. I've become chilled from the drive into town."

I sat down on one of the elegant sofas closest to the small fireplace. As I warmed my hands, I realized that I had indeed become quite chilled on our trip into town. A knock on the door alerted us to the arrival of the catering manager with whom I spent the better part of an hour reviewing the details for this evening's dinner, the various hors d'oeuvres and beverages to be supplied next door at the theater on the following evening, and lastly the after theater party that we were hosting late tomorrow evening in the hotel ballroom. When at last the manager departed, I spent some time relaxing in the warmth of a hot bath. I closed my eyes and let my mind wander.

What was Nate doing at this very moment? I pictured him moving about Bridgewater in the course of his duties, professional yet compassionate when giving orders to the staff. By now Lotte would have seen that Gerald had been fed, bathed, and hopefully been put down in his crib. Would Nate spend his free time in the nursery with Lotte? After all, she was his wife even though the marriage had been thrust upon them by Kevin. There must be some feelings between Nate and Lotte since she now was carrying his child.

Hmmm, I wondered. Lotte's child had obviously been conceived during my confinement with Gerald. It was unlike Nate to succumb to another woman. I knew he had been faithful to me since the day we professed our love to each other. But wait; there was that woman at Long Wharf, the harlot who had slaked his passions when I was confined with my other children. That was it! Of course Nate had been faithful to me; it was just during the months of my several confinements that he had sought ease of his needs. And with Lotte being so near, in his bed, why would he go to Long Wharf?

I leaned my head against the rim of the tub, remembering the last time he and I had been together. Could it only have been the night before last? How tender and caring he had been, how sweet his kisses, how quickly I had been aroused as he lay naked beside me! Deep within me I feel the stirrings of passion as I recalled the feel of his fingers trailing across my skin to be followed by the warm of his mouth. I felt a distinct twitching in my nether regions.

Had I been home I would have summoned Nate to my side. But here I was, in a tub full of rapidly cooling water, miles from my lover with no resource to ease my growing needs. Ah but that would only make our coming together so much more intense when I did return home.

The mere thought of Nate suckling at my breasts caused my nipples to peak. I needed release, now! Otherwise those hard little points would be most obvious to all who cared to glance my way during dinner.

With practiced hand I took the bar of scented soap and wedged it into my private place, thrusting in a steady rhythm as my orgasm neared. I shuddered as my climax peaked, leaving my wet skin to quickly chill. I felt my tensions ease. The relief of sexual release was wonderful.

Heavens, it must be getting close to dinner time. I quickly rose, toweled myself dry, and donned my robe. With a euphoric feeling I opened the door to my bedroom and called for Ellen.

———

At the appointed hour, Kevin knocked on the door of my suite where he was greeted with a curtsy from Ellen.

"Good evening, Ellen. Is my wife ready?"

Before she could answer I swooped out of my bedroom, crossed the parlor, and placed a hand on Kevin's arm.

"You look quite fetching this evening, my dear. I believe I shall be the envy of every gent in the dining room," he complimented me as we made our way downstairs.

Our meal was quite uneventful with polite conversation filling the air above our tables. The pleasant tinkle of glassware, the pleasing aromas of the various dishes we had ordered, and the free flow of wine with our meal all conspired to put our party in a very relaxed mood. Even Birdie and Katherine were on their best behavior. After the children had eaten their dessert, Tess took them upstairs so that we adults could savor our after dinner cordials.

As the conversation moved from topic to topic, I smiled and nodded at appropriate times, allowing Kevin to lead the discussions. Once more my thoughts turned to Nate; seems that my release earlier wasn't quite what I'd needed. I was now becoming aroused once more as I thought of all the wonderfully naughty ways I would torture Nate when I returned home and had him naked in my bed. Therefore, I was quite unprepared for what happened next.

"Cordy," Kevin leaned over and whispered in my ear, "I can only hope that what I'm seeing means that you might welcome me to your bed this night."

"Whatever do you mean?" I was quite perplexed. Had he noticed a particularly comely woman walk by?

He whispered in my ear. "It would seem to me, and a few of the

other gentlemen, that you are fully aroused. Could it be my proximity
has thus affected you?"

I hastily looked down at my chest. The chiffon fabric of my costume
was clinging quite pointedly to those hardened peaks on my chest.
What could I do?

"Good heavens," I had the good sense to lean in to Kevin, "I had
no idea."

I could feel a blush creeping up my neck and suffusing my cheeks.
Kevin cleared his throat and addressed the remainder of our party.

"It seems that my dear wife has had a bit too much wine with
dinner. If you'll excuse us, I should like to accompany her upstairs."

There were several "Good nights" said and many covert winks from
the gentlemen before Kevin propelled me across the Grand Lobby and
to the lift. In no time flat we were exiting the lift on the penthouse
floor. I turned in the direction of my suite but Kevin's hand tugged me
in the opposite direction.

"My suite," he mumbled as he felt in his jacket pocket for the key.

Once inside, he pulled me into his embrace and thrust his tongue
into my mouth while his hands were seemingly everywhere at once,
inside my garments as well as under them. In a thrice his clothes were
on the floor as were mine. As he lifted me in his arms and settled my
legs around his hips I could feel his manhood poking at my entrance.
God help me, I wanted it! No, I needed it! But I needed fortification
first. I motioned to the bar.

"What is it?" he asked.

"Brandy," I managed to squeak out.

"Now?"

I nodded my head.

He leaned my back end against the bar and handed me the entire
bottle. I took several large swallows as the liquid fire warmed my insides
before handing the bottle back to Kevin.

"Bettter?"

I nodded my head once more. He pushed me back against the bar,
taking me there where he stood. I became a wild woman, matching

him move for move. When we were done, we finished the brandy before we made love several times more, trying new positions and using every available space in the suite. We were exhausted by the time dawn broke outside the windows and lit up the New Haven skyline. That was how Paul found us the next morning, entwined in our nudity there upon the parlor sofa.

December 11, 1914

When at last I pulled open my eyelids, I realized that I was reclining on a sofa with a bedspread thrown over me. My sense of feel informed me that I was naked under the bedspread. My sense of taste informed me that I was in need of water to dispel the cottony feeling in my mouth. I pulled the bedspread around me and tried to stand up. That was when my sense of balance informed me that I had consumed too much liquor the night before.

"Ooooh," I moaned softly, reclining once more on the sofa.

"It would appear that you've imbibed too heavily last night, my dear. But the outcome was stupendous!" chuckled Kevin.

I hadn't noticed him in the room; hadn't noticed much else besides the pounding in my head.

"I'll never have another drink!" I vowed, reclosing my eyes to keep the room from spinning.

"Pish, posh! Here drink this," Kevin instructed as he pushed a tumbler full of some awful smelling liquid in front of my face.

"What is it?" I managed to croak.

"Old family recipe for dealing with hangovers. Mother swears by it."

"Your mother?"

"Seems that mother has occasionally over-indulged when father was away on business. Not often, but it has happened."

I'll just bet those times were on Christmas Eve, I thought to myself.

I took the tumbler, emptied its contents, and handed it back to Kevin. As the seconds passed I began to feel slightly more like myself.

"Ah, good, it's working," observed Kevin. "I've had Ellen deliver you a change of clothing. You may use my bedroom to pull yourself together."

"How generous of you," I commented, pulling the spread around me and rising from the sofa.

Sometime later I emerged from Kevin's bedroom, suitably garbed and passably presentable.

"How's the hangover?" my spouse inquired solicitously as he moved to my side.

"Better. What was in that drink you gave me?"

"Perhaps it's best if the ingredients remain a secret." He smiled at me. "I'll instruct Paul to pass the recipe to Ellen. Who knows if you'll need it again someday?" He leaned in and kissed my cheek, putting an arm around my shoulder as he escorted me to the suite's door. "May I come to you tonight?"

"I think not," I replied, keeping my eyes averted. "I'm sure with the theater's opening night celebration and the after theater party in the ballroom that we'll both be too tired."

"Of course," he had the good sense to agree, "perhaps another time."

"Yes, another time," I agreed.

He dropped his hand from my shoulder and I left to seek the comfort of my own suite.

———

A thousand details accompanied the Opening Night of the Shubert Theater in New Haven. Careful planning had gone into selecting the perfect location for the theater – next door to the Hotel Taft which had opened it doors only two years earlier. The Shubert brothers hoped to convey both elegance and excitement with the opening of their venue. Their hard work and dedication paid off.

The opening performance of "The Bell of Bond Street" that Friday evening played to a full house. There was a small room situated behind our theater box where those in our party were met by both Lee and

J.J. Shubert. Although the champagne flowed freely, I was careful to merely sip at my glass. Kevin, who had quite literally funded most of the theater operation, happily accepted glass after glass of the libation as folks toasted his generosity. Before being escorted to our box, Lee Shubert asked for our attention.

"Folks, I'd appreciate your attention for a brief moment."

A gradual silence descended upon our group.

"My brother J.J. and I would like to extend our deepest and most sincere gratitude to Mr. and Mrs. Newkirk whose vision and deep pockets," he chuckled, "have made this venture possible."

A smattering of applause greeted his statement.

"You'll most likely have noticed this covered easel here in the corner." He moved to stand by what appeared to be a covered painting. "Mrs. Newkirk, if you'd be so kind as to join me." Lee extended a hand in my direction.

I moved towards the center of the room, smiling to everyone around me. Lee positioned me next to the easel as uniformed staff passed among us, handing out fresh glasses of champagne. I accepted one gratefully; since I had no idea what was coming I turned my attention toward Lee.

"Mrs. Newkirk has long been a patroness of the arts hereabouts. It was she who brought our ideas for this wonderful theater to the forefront, and I'm sure she had a hand in convincing her husband to help fund our venture. To that end, we will be hanging this likeness," he pulled off the drape from the easel to show a wonderful portrait of me, "in our front foyer. Please join me in toasting Cordelia Newkirk, godmother to the Shubert Theater."

He raised his glass in salute and took a sip.

"Here, here," and other wonderful salutations resounded from around, followed by a small smattering of applause.

Kevin stepped to the forefront to stand beside me. Together we studied the artist's rendition of my likeness.

"I see that Mr. Kohl has done a wonderful job of capturing your most regal side," Kevin commented.

"I don't know when he had the opportunity to paint this," I mused, "we never finished those sittings for the portrait you'd commissioned him to paint."

"If you would allow me," a voice from behind us interrupted.

"Mr. Kohl," I greeted the artist. "Thank you for the lovely portrait."

"It was my pleasure, Cordelia. But to answer your question, I finished the portrait from memory. After all, we had spent quite some time together. Your beauty inspired me. When the painting was complete, I offered it to the Shubert brothers who had been looking for some way to honor you."

"How generous of you, Tomas!"

"For you, fair lady, it is but a token of my esteem." He bent to kiss my gloved hand before turning and walking away.

———

Shortly afterward we were shown to our box. Kevin and I took our seats at the box front; his parents were seated slightly to Kevin's rear while my own momma and poppa were seated directly behind me. Of course momma preened and strutted, reveling in the benefits that my marriage to Kevin had provided for her. Yes, she was now truly a lady of quality.

During the intermission, we ladies took full advantage of the retiring room while the gents milled about the lobby, some smoking cigars while others refreshed themselves with a libation or two. As we rejoined our partners I noticed that Kevin was absent. Pulling Cal aside, I asked after my husband.

"Well, sis, I can't say for sure where he is but he took off to see some of the backstage parts of the theater shortly after the intermission began. I wouldn't worry too much, though, I'm sure he'll return in time for the second act."

As the lobby lights dimmed to signal the resumption of the play, I gratefully accepted my father-in-law's arm as we returned to our seats. It was some time later, with the second act underway, that Kevin returned to our box and took his seat without so much as a glance in my direction. Even though I couldn't see him too well in the dimly lit theater my sense of smell detected the lingering scent of cheap perfume and I knew in an instant where he had been. I merely lifted my head a bit higher and gave my full attention to the players on the stage.

Kevin

Chapter 41

The after theater party that Cordy had put together at the Hotel Taft was stupendous! There were sure to be accolades printed about it in the society news for days to come. I must admit that she is a credit to the Newkirk name. She has elevated our family not only to the top of New Haven society but also has earned us a place in New York society; Boston society has welcomed her as well. Her salons are sought by artists of all genres for the backing of the moneyed elite who are also our guests.

The Taft ballroom had been reserved for us and it was there that we welcomed not only the Shubert Brothers and other members of New Haven's society, but also those connected with providing our evening's entertainment: the producers, director, actors, and anyone and everyone associated with the evening's theatrical production. I made sure that I stood by Cordy's side as we greeted our guests, acknowledging the old dowagers and their husbands graciously. Fortunately, mother and Mrs. Conner swept the oldsters along to more secluded areas of the ballroom where they engaged in private conversations.

A light supper buffet was served before the dancing began. I consulted with the head barman to make sure that an accurate tally of liquor was being kept before I turned my full attention to my personal enjoyment. Earlier, during the intermission, I had had the opportunity to tour the backstage areas of the theater where I was introduced to a buxom understudy who was anxious to make her mark in the theater world. Always one to take advantage of an opportunity when it was presented, I allowed the young woman to privately audition for me. She had provided me with unerring proof of just how talented a mouth she had. Even now, hours later, I could feel the press of her lips where they had last been and a burning need caused me to seek her out.

I found her standing at the side of the ballroom, nearest an alcove that had cleverly been disguised by two sturdy potted trees, where she sipped at the drink in her hand. When she noticed my approach she darted behind the trees. A quick survey of the room on my part confirmed that my actions were unnoticed by the party-goers and I ducked into the alcove.

"Good evening, Mr. Newkirk," she greeted me, a sly smile toying about her talented lips.

"Gretchen," I acknowledged her. "Are you enjoying the party?"

"I am now." She reached a hand down and cupped my family jewels. Her hand felt like a branding iron as I drew in a ragged breath.

"My dear, I'm convinced that you deserve a more prominent place in the theater." I kept my eyes open towards the main ballroom. "Perhaps you'd care to further audition for me."

"Here?" she questioned.

"I was thinking of some place more private. Your room?"

She shook her head in a negative way.

"I share with two other girls. They could return at any time." She favored me with a little pout.

Reaching into my jacket, I pulled out the key to my suite and pressed it into her hand. She wrapped her fingers around it possessively.

"Take this, show it to the elevator operator, and tell him that you are expected," I instructed.

She studied the key.

"Ooooh, the penthouse!"

"Shhh. You leave and go up. I'll wait a suitable time and follow you.

My valet's name is Paul. Tell him that I've sent you up and to make you comfortable."

I turned my back to her and re-entered the ballroom, making sure that I stopped and spoke to a good number of guests who would be sure to corroborate my presence, before I crossed the lobby and ascended to my suite.

Needless to say I found Gretchen very accommodating once we were in private. Much later that evening I walked her to the door and patted her curvy derriere. She was fetchingly rumpled from her 'audition' and I tucked a hundred dollar bill into her cleavage before closing the door on her.

As I turned back to my bedroom, I reflected on my new role as patron of the theater arts. Had I known there were so many benefits to be had I might have taken on the role sooner!

Lawson

Chapter 42

January 1915
Bridgewater

The Christmas and New Year's celebrations were behind us and things settled into a busy routine once more. The opening of the Shubert Theater coupled with Delia's success at being a patroness of the arts ensured that Bridgewater was rarely without guests.

The kitchens were busy, deliveries were almost constant, the laundry was doubled, and I was at times hard-pressed to keep abreast of all that went on. Delia was spending more time seeing to the well-being of her guests, diverting some of the planning and additional paperwork to me. I was still welcomed to her room each night but most nights I watched her sleep beside me, exhausted from her roles as hostess, mother, and patroness of the arts.

Sir Andrew Docket the playwright and his companion Mr. William Heath seemed to have taken up permanent residence in the guest wing. Sir Andrew was writing a play that he was dedicating to Delia. It was based on a song that another guest, Andrew Redder, had written and with which Delia had fallen in love. My guess was that Delia liked the song title, "Stairway to My Heart", because it reminded her of our situation.

It was towards the end of January; Delia and I were snuggled comfortably in her bed, when she turned to me with a request.

"Nate, do you think Lotte would object to helping me with something?"

"Hmmmm?" I was busy nuzzling her neck.

"Nate, pay attention." She moved out of my embrace. "This is serious."

"What is?" I pulled her closer again.

"I'm pregnant." She stated flatly.

"Am I to be a father again?"

"No. I'm positive the baby is Kevin's."

"Then what's the problem?" I nibbled at her ear and she swatted me.

"I don't want the baby."

I stopped what I was doing and looked at her. Her eyes shone in the diluted moonlight and I could tell from the tone of her voice that she was serious.

"Of course you want the baby." I decided on her behalf. "You love children".

"Just send Lotte to me in the morning."

The following morning I watched my wife, large with child, amble out of the staff dining room to meet with Delia. She returned a short time later instructing one of the kitchen girls to set a pot of water to boiling for tea. I followed her into the pantry.

"What did Delia need?" I inquired.

"Mrs. Newkirk asked for my help with a highly personal matter," she replied, stressing the formal use of Delia's name.

I lowered my voice to a whisper.

"She wants to abort the baby she's carrying, doesn't she?"

Lotte nodded as she searched for the right combination of dried herbs that she required.

"And you'll help her?"

"Why not?" Lotte turned away so as not to look at me.

"That would be killing an unborn child," I quietly protested.

Lotte set her lips into a thin stubborn line before turning her gaze on me.

"Mrs. Newkirk asked for my help and I will give it to her. She's been kind to me over the years. This is the least I can do to repay her."

She moved past me, leaving me in the pantry to think about her answer. Later that morning Lotte returned to my office where I found her sitting and gazing out the window. She turned when she heard me approach.

"Is everything all right?" I asked, meaning both she and Delia.

"For now. I have a message for you from Mrs. Newkirk."

Lotte's eyes were bright, as though she was fighting back tears. I settled into the chair behind my desk and nodded for her to continue. On some level I knew that Lotte didn't like the idea of aborting Delia's pregnancy.

"Mrs. Newkirk asks that she not be disturbed this afternoon or this evening. Ellen will see to her needs."

"What will happen to her, Lotte? Will it hurt very much?" I whispered as I leaned across the desk towards her.

"There will be cramping, and yes, some pain; but by this time tomorrow she will be fine." Lotte lowered her head so that she was speaking to her chest. "I feel like a murderess."

"You're not the one who's aborting a child," I pointed out.

"I understand why she's doing it, but rich folk don't understand the importance of life."

"Now, dearest, don't take it so to heart. It's not good for you or our child," I pointed out.

Lotte reached up a hand and dashed away the tears that had begun to fall.

"You're right, Nate. Our child is my first concern. And a healthy child it will be." She tried to smile through her tears.

"How can you be sure?" I smiled at her valiant attempt to muddle through.

"Because he or she keeps me awake half the night, kicking and flailing as though in a hurry to meet us." She placed her hands protectively over the mound she carried.

"I do think it's almost time for you to go into confinement. What say you?"

"Oh no! Not yet. Not until the baby has dropped into position," she protested weakly.

"Well you know best, dearest. Now how about if I fetch you some tea?"

"Chamomile, please."

She smiled at me earnestly this time and I went off in search of chamomile tea.

———

I acquiesced to Delia's request that I stay away from her. She would be in pain, according to Lotte, and I did not wish to add to her discomfort. True to Lotte's prediction Delia was her sunny, cheerful self within a few days. Within a week I was back in her bed and we were happier than before. It was on a frigid night, devoid of starlight or moonlight, when we were roused by a loud knocking at Delia's door.

"Mrs. Newkirk," came a muffled voice.

"Who's there?" questioned Delia as I leapt from the bed, grabbed my clothes, and ducked behind the dressing screen.

"It's Joan, ma'am," came the answer.

Delia dawdled as she pulled on her robe, checking to be sure I was out of sight. She calmly walked to the door, unlocked it, and greeted Joan.

"Joan, what's wrong? Why have you come here in the middle of the night, in your nightclothes?"

"It's Lotte, ma'am. She's gone into labor and it seems like she's going to have a rough time."

"I assume that Mr. Lawson is with her. Has someone sent for Dr. Bennett?"

"I've sent one of the young girls to find Mr. Lawson but no one knows where he is. Please come, Mrs. Newkirk. We're not sure what to do."

"I'll be along directly. Has someone checked Mr. Lawson's office? He sometimes falls asleep at his desk," Delia offered.

She stopped in her tracks, letting her eyes search the darkened bedroom for confirmation that I had already departed. Upon hearing her words I scurried through the sliding panel, leaping over the last steps before sliding back the panel in Delia's office. I had just enough time to duck into my office, spread some papers atop my desk, and settle into a nap-like position before a sharp knock on my office door heralded the arrival of Delia and Joan.

"There; you see, Joan. Mr. Lawson is where I thought he might be," Delia intoned. "Mr. Lawson, do wake up. Your wife has gone into labor."

"Hmm?" I attempted to look bleary-eyed but I could see that I wasn't fooling Delia. I hoped Joan didn't catch on.

"It's Lotte, Mr. Lawson. She's gone into labor. We was all very worried when we couldn't find you. She's been calling for you." Joan elaborated.

"Labor? You mean the baby's coming?" I pretended to appear muddled.

"Mrs. Grant is with her. I've sent one of the footmen to the stables. I believe Mr. Huckleby has sent for the doctor," Delia calmly explained as I pretended to focus my attention.

The three of us trooped back to the servants wing where Mrs. Grant was sitting beside Lotte, who was battling the labor pains. This was the closest I had ever come to a woman giving birth and it pained me greatly to see this young woman, little more than a child really, suffer so greatly. It was plain to see that she was trying valiantly to be brave; between pains she held out her hand to me. I knelt beside the bed, taking her hand in mine.

"Lotte, dearest, I'm sorry that I wasn't here when the pains began." *More than you'll know,* I thought to myself.

"You're here now, Nate. That's all that matters."

She winced as she tried to stifle a pain. I brushed my fingers across her forehead, hoping to ease her nervous tension.

"You'll be fine, dearest. Dr. Bennett is on his way," I hastened to reassure her.

"You'd best be getting out o' the way, Mr. Lawson," cautioned Mrs. Grant. "This is no place for a gentleman."

"I'll be right outside the door," I told Lotte.

"You'll do better to go down to your office," Delia informed me, "it may be quite some time until the child is born."

"As you wish," I murmured, allowing Delia to walk me to the door.

"It's not as though it's your first," she whispered.

"True, but somehow this time is different," I whispered back as Delia closed the door, leaving me in the hallway.

I made a beeline for my office, waiting until I heard Dr. Bennett's arrival to poke my head into the kitchen. The doctor nodded his head in my direction as he made his way to the servants' wing.

Sometime later, I heard a flurry of activity in the kitchen as there was a call for boiling water to sterilize the doctor's instruments. Thankfully, Mrs. Grant, now fully dressed, popped her head into my office and plunked herself into a chair.

"Looks like our little Lotte is going to have herself quite a time with that baby of yours," the woman commented.

"Is she alright?" My heart quickened to think of Lotte in too much pain.

"Doc says the baby is breach."

"Breach?"

"Comin' out feet first. Doc has to turn the baby." Her eagle-eyed look bore into me in an accusatory fashion, as though I'd inflicted torture on my wife.

"Dear God!"

"Oh, she's young and healthy. But I wouldn't be holdin' my breath for a quick delivery."

And with that Mrs. Grant made her way back to the kitchen where she took up her chores.

I sat as still as a statue, not knowing what, if anything, I should do first. Should I go upstairs and force my way into our bedroom? Would Lotte even want me there? Would Doctor Bennett have me removed from the room?

Lotte was in good hands after all: there was the doctor who was being assisted by Delia herself as well as two or three of the female staff members. I had watched in the past as Kevin Newkirk had sat in his office and drunk himself into a stupor when Delia's children had been born; and thought him less than a man when he had done so. Now, I recognized the wisdom of doing just that.

I pulled on an overcoat and was about to see solace in Huckleby's realm when I heard Kevin's voice calling my name.

"Lawson? Where are you man?" he shouted as he entered the kitchen.

"Right here, sir," I answered quietly.

"Going to get some fresh air?" he inquired, noting my coat. "Good. Let's go wake Huckleby and have us a gentleman's discussion."

Together we walked out in the early morning cold, I pulling my coat tighter about me as Kevin braved the elements in a lighter weight jacket.

"A baby's birth, especially your first, can be quite the trying event for us gentlemen," Kevin offered. "Been through it a number of times and it doesn't get any easier."

We spent the next few hours closeted in Huckleby's office, where we put away an entire bottle of Bushmills Whiskey. Mrs. Grant sent us a hearty breakfast followed by a lunch designed to soak up the alcohol we were consuming. It wasn't until late afternoon when I was informed that it was now allowable for me to return to the house and visit my family.

I was met outside our bedroom by Doctor Bennett. He seemed a bit tired but he smiled as I approached.

"How's Lotte, doc?"

"Your wife is fine, Nathan. And so is your son."

"My son? I have a son?" I couldn't keep my joy from creeping into my voice.

"A fine, healthy son," continued the doctor. "Lotte should rest for at least a couple of weeks. She's had a tough time of it."

"I'll see that she does absolutely nothing," I vowed.

"Oh, she'll be up and around when she thinks you're not looking. But don't leave her alone for the first few days. She should have someone around her so she doesn't strain herself."

"Can I see her now?"

I found that I was anxious to visit Lotte and confirm for myself that she was fine. With trembling fingers I tried to smooth the wrinkles from my clothes before running a hand through my hair. I could feel the stubble of my beard and knew that I was a mess.

"Go on, man. Your family is waiting," urged Doctor Bennett.

I opened the door and stood transfixed. Never had I seen such a beautiful sight. Lotte was absolutely radiant. A mountain of pillows at her back supported her semi-upright position. Her naturally curly hair tumbled across her shoulders. The ladies had helped her into a clean robe; the room smelled fresh and sweet as though just aired. But it was the bundle that Lotte held that drew my attention. She was cooing to the child in her arms and her face was wreathed in smiles. Truly the Madonna herself looked thus all those many years ago in Bethlehem.

"Lotte?" I found my mouth dry as I spoke.

"Nathan," she smiled up at me. "Come meet our son."

I gingerly sat beside her on the bed and took my first look at the child. A bundle of reddish flesh with a thatch of fine hair was nestled in a blanket.

"Would you like to hold him?" Lotte questioned me.

"I don't think I should," I whispered, finding that I was apprehensive.

"You won't hurt him," she assured me.

With infinite care I accepted my son, placing my hands where Lotte instructed me so that the child would be supported. I held my breath as his tiny arms flailed about. As soon as I nestled him in my arms the child seemed to calm.

"He already knows his father," observed Lotte with a smile.

"He's so tiny," I murmured, unaware that I had spoken the words aloud. "Hello, son. I'm your father."

"What shall we call him?" asked Lotte.

"I've always liked the name Jonathan. Can we call him Jonathan?" I asked, never taking my eyes off of the wonder that was my son.

"Jonathan is a lovely name. I'd like to give him my dad's name for a middle name," Lotte asked.

"Welcome to our world, Jonathan Wilhelm Lawson," I smiled as I handed the babe to his mother.

Lotte's eyes sparkled as she gazed on our son and for the first time I saw her true beauty. She seemed changed somehow, yet her eyes were still a soft cocoa brown. I noticed now that her hair color matched her eyes exactly. Why had I not seen that before? Her fingers were narrow and tapered yet strong as she held our son. I remembered how she had clung to me on that day when we'd lost our darling Geraldine. Lotte's lips were pursed in a moué as she cooed softly to Jonathan. Suddenly I found myself wanting to kiss those lips; I leaned over and touched my lips to hers, surprising both of us as I did so.

"Thank you, dearest, for giving me a son so fine," I murmured.

"The pleasure is all mine, husband; the pleasure is all mine," she smiled.

Lotte

Chapter 43

June 1916

My Dearest Aunt Anja,

I begin this letter addressing you in English because my dear husband has pointed out to me that since I live in America I should use the American language as much as possible. He also believes that it will be good for our son to speak English only. I promise you that I will not let Jonathan forget his German heritage however. I shall teach him our ways as well as the ways of our employers.

Auntie, our son grows stronger with each passing day. Now at eighteen months he toddles around the nursery following Birdie wherever she goes. She has taken a liking to him and watches over him when he plays with Master Gerald. There are only six and a half months separating the boys and they enjoy each other's company.

Mr. and Mrs. Newkirk have had a small cottage, a caretaker's cottage it is called, built near the guesthouse. They have given this cottage to our small family and now that is where my dearest

Nathan, Jonathan, and I make our home. There are only four rooms but it is cozy and pleasant. I honestly believe that we were given this cottage so that when Jonathan cries or plays in the evening the others on staff aren't disturbed.

Mrs. Newkirk came to our cottage the other day, just after Nathan saw to the placement of our bedroom furniture which was moved from the servants' wing. The desk that had been in Nathan's bedroom was the only item in our parlor except for a rug that I had made. The dear lady commented that we would need more than a bed and a chair. She graciously handed Nathan a check for the amount of two hundred dollars. Oh course Nathan thanked her for the advance on his salary but Mrs. Newkirk said that the money was a gift for service rendered and was not a loan or advance. What a dear lady she is!

Nathan immediately called a furniture store where he knows the owner and was able to get a good price on items for our parlor and for Jonathan's room. We have the crib of course but that boy is growing so quickly. He has a healthy appetite and loves to play. His favorite toy is a wooden whistle that Nathan has carved for him and he carries it about all day long, tooting and marching like a little general. I have to pry it from his hands when he finally falls asleep.

Jonathan now speaks a large number of words, making it known when he is hungry, tired, or just wants to be picked up. Nathan was quite beside himself the first time that Jonathan said "Dada". It was easy to see my dearest husband's pride in our son.

I am grateful every day for Mrs. Newkirk and say many prayers on her behalf. She graciously has allowed our Jonathan to be raised with her own children; he is to be given the benefit of the same education as the Newkirk children. Tess adores him as does Birdie, Katherine, and Master Gerald.

My dearest husband often reads to me from the newspaper, especially when there is news of happenings back home in Europe.

He tells me there is much unrest in our homeland and I worry about mama anew, saying additional prayers for her and the rest of our family every night.

Here at Bridgewater things are always busy. Not a weekend goes by without guests filling the guest wing and oftentimes Willow Cottage. Nathan is kept busy from dawn to dusk and sometimes far beyond seeing to the needs of everyone from the lowest staff member to Mrs. Newkirk herself. The dear lady has become quite the patroness of the arts here in New Haven and is considered the darling of society. I am honored to work for her.

Have I told you how young Birdie likes to play dress-up? That child is quite adept at taking an old dress of her mother's along with some of Mrs. Newkirk's scarves and such, and putting on a fashion show right in the nursery. She has gotten Katherine to play along but that is one little girl who would rather poke her nose in a picture book while her sister is modeling clothes. I think perhaps young Birdie should be a model when she grows up; she is slender and tall – just the look that belongs on a designer's runway.

Well, dearest Auntie, I will now tell you my happiest news. I am again with child and I do pray this time for a daughter. Nathan has asked that we keep the news to ourselves and not let it get out among the staff. He feels that since I miscarried once perhaps it would be best to keep this to ourselves until we are certain that I will have no problems. How sweet he is to think of things like this! Certainly God was watching over me when he sent Nathan into my life.

I close this letter sending you all of my love. I promise to include a photo of Jonathan with my next letter.

Much love to you, auntie.

Charlotte, Nathan,
and Baby Jonathan

Cordelia

Chapter 44

March 1917

Birdie's sixth birthday party created quite a ruckus! Of course the family was there and that accounted for one celebration. However, there were many friends and acquaintances from the world of theater and the arts who sought invitations for their own children. Therefore we decided a second celebration was in order. It was a trying two days during which I was most grateful for Lotte and Tess who kept some sort of order amongst the children. At the end of the two days, all of the children were exhausted except for Birdie. She seemed to be a source of boundless energy. Indeed, she kept the other children totally entertained.

For the adults, however, it was another story. I had never seen our staff looking quite as exhausted as they did at the end of that weekend. Each of us was quite happy to the see the last of our guests depart on that Sunday evening. Indeed, I almost sent word to Nate not to attend me that evening but I longed to see him privately. Nay, I daresay I needed to see him privately.

It had been a while since Nate had slipped through the panel in my washroom. From the moment when Lotte had recently been delivered of her second child, Nate had the misplaced idea that he was needed at Lotte's side now that he was a father yet again. I allowed him his space but earlier today had put the ultimatum to him – either he attend me tonight or make his bed with Lotte. He seemed torn as he listened to my challenge.

I sat at my dressing table, brushing my hair and waiting for his appearance. Only when I heard the panel sliding open did I realize that I had been holding my breath. I turned to smile at his approach. He handed me a small bunch of hothouse roses that he had plucked.

"Some pretty flowers for my pretty lady," he smiled in return.

"Only pretty?" I teased.

"There is no flower that can compare with your beauty, Delia."

He pulled back my hair and kissed the nape of my neck.

"It's been quite a while since we've been together, Nate. I hope you've missed me as much as I missed you."

I turned where I sat and offered him my mouth. He obliged with a deeply sensual kiss. Ah! That was the Nathan I loved so!

"I'm sorry to have kept you waiting, darling," he murmured as he removed his jacket. "Lotte was feeding our daughter and I didn't want to leave until she was finished. She might have needed my help."

"I don't wish to hear about Lotte," I pouted. "I need you too, Nate."

I moved from the dressing table to the bed, where I reclined in a seductive pose. Nate divested himself of his remaining clothes while I took the opportunity to truly look at him. He hadn't changed overly much in the past ten years. Still tall and relatively lean (we all fought a losing battle when it came to Mrs. Grant's cooking), his cocoa brown eyes still held a mischievous twinkle when he looked at me. There were a crease or two at the corners of those eyes that lent him character. That was when I noticed something I hadn't seen before.

"Is that a gray hair I see on yonder head?" I intoned in my most Shakespearean voice.

"What say thee fair lady?" he replied as he clasped my hands in his. "Hast thou seen a cloud hovering over my head?"

His attempt at acting only tickled my funnybone and I laughed. Nate tried to look wounded at my laughter but only succeeded in joining me.

"Really, Nate, when did your hair start turning gray?"

"You're serious?"

I nodded affirmatively.

"I think you're wrong," he stated as he moved over to the mirror above my dressing table.

He moved his head from side to side, making faces at himself as he did so.

"Hmmm, I'll be a monkey's uncle. You're absolutely right, Delia. There are a few of those light colored strands. Hadn't noticed them before but now they seem to pop right out."

"That's what having children will do to you," I observed.

"But your hair is still unmarked," he commented.

"I'm younger than you, darling," I hastened to remind him.

"Well then, come help this decrepit old man into bed. I'm nearly exhausted."

We laughed together as we settled under the bed covers.

"Have you decided how to punish Birdie, yet?" he asked as he gathered me in his arms.

"That child has no boundaries. I'm afraid she'll grow up to be just like her father."

"Well, she certainly has a mind of her own," Nate concurred. "Sometimes she's just as bull-headed as you are."

"She's spoiled, too. I'll need to speak with Tess about Birdie's discipline. She must be made to understand that she can't always have her way."

"Really, Delia, what harm was done? All she did was organize a fashion-show of sorts. Most all of your guests thought it was charming."

"Yes, until they realized that Birdie had raided their guest rooms and 'borrowed' pieces of their clothing. And if that wasn't bad enough she'd had the audacity to remake those clothes into fashions that she dreamed up!"

"She's precocious. She'll outgrow it." He nuzzled my ear. "Just like you did."

"Birdie is old enough to know she's the one the other children look up to," I sighed. "She needs more than what we can give her here."

"Maybe if you spent more time with her, she could learn from you," Nate suggested.

"She needs a firmer hand. Tess has her hands full with Katherine and Gerald. I know she's taking care of Jonathan until Lotte is well enough to return to duty. It's time our Birdie was with other children her own age. She's due to start first grade in September. I must look into schools for her."

With Birdie's immediate future settled in my mind, I reveled in the relaxed lovemaking that Nate and I had come to enjoy.

During the following weeks, I made visits to several schools for young girls that I had hoped would be good for Birdie. Most had already closed their rolls for the upcoming year but were willing to 'find a spot' for my daughter if certain conditions were met – namely if a sizable donation were made to the school. Those schools were immediately stricken from my list; if they were willing to compromise for the Newkirks they would certainly do so for another family whose donation might be larger than ours.

In the end I called Birdie into the morning room where for once I had the company of my husband. We had decided that when it came to the children we would provide a united front. As we awaited the arrival of our daughter, I was calmed by the sweet song of the birds in their gilded cage that occupied nearly an entire wall. Normally the children were not allowed to play here as we liked to keep it as a place of adult sanctuary. My reverie was broken by the tip-tap of Birdie's patent leather shoes as she approached and entered. Upon seeing her father she dipped into a shallow curtsy.

"Father, mother," she acknowledged us.

"Good morning, Birdie," Kevin greeted her jovially.

"Birdie, do you know why you've been asked to come here?" I felt that being direct would be the best way to begin.

"No, mother," she answered, "but I can guess."

"Come sit here beside me, on the sofa." I gestured to a place right next to me.

She walked over and plunked her backside down on the seat and began to swing her feet.

"Don't swing your feet, dear, it's not lady-like," I admonished.

"It makes me happy," she intoned, keeping up the movement of her feet.

"Birdie, please do as I ask. Just this one time."

With an exaggerated sigh, Birdie reined in her feet.

"Birdie," I began again, "this September you'll be starting school. You shall be enrolled in first grade."

"I hate school."

"How do you know when you've never attended one?" inquired Kevin.

"I've heard all about school from my friends. It's a most awful place. Dull, boring. They make you learn all about things that happened centuries ago. All my friends hate it. I'll hate it too." Birdie drew her lips into a tiny pout.

"But it's a good thing to learn about what happened before. After all, you come from the long lineage of a prominent Boston family. Certain things are expected from a young lady who bears the name of Newkirk." Kevin was beginning to sound like his father but I refrained from making that observation aloud.

"Then I'll change my name!" Birdie felt that was the easiest solution to the problem.

"You'll do no such thing, young lady!" It appeared that Birdie could get under Kevin's skin as well. "The only time you'll change your name is when you marry into another family of good background."

Kevin stalked over to a sideboard and although it was a bit shy of the lunch hour poured himself a neat shot of whiskey and tossed it back.

"What your father means, dear, is that as a young lady who represents the best of both Boston and New York society you'll be expected to have a proper education and marry into another society family. You'll want to be the kind of young woman that will attract the right kind of suitors. We can't start too early to see that your education is perfect."

Birdie turned her puzzled gaze at me, appearing to ponder my words.

"I want to be a fashion model when I grow up. Like the models in the magazines."

"Never!" shouted Kevin so loud that both Birdie and I jumped. "You'll go to school, get a proper education, and marry someone suitable. I'll not have you grow up to be a loose woman. Cordy, perhaps you'll do better talking to her without me."

Kevin stalked out of the room, leaving me to address Birdie's latest pronouncement.

"Believe me, dear, you'll see the wisdom of what we say in a year or two. It's a fine thing to take an interest in fashion," I tried appealing to her. "Gentlemen will expect their wife to wear the most up-to-date styles and colors. But those days are quite a ways off. Our first order of business is to get you enrolled in a good school so that you may acquire the basics of education."

"I like when Tess tells stories about the old country," Birdie volunteered.

"Yes, well, that's good too. It's nice to learn about different countries and cultures."

"Will Katherine have to go to school too?"

"Yes, but not yet. She's too young."

"Then I won't go!" Birdie stood up, crossed her arms, and pouted.

"Birdie, you will go to school. Is that clear?"

No response.

"You'll have all summer long to play with your sister and brother. But you will go to school in September and you will learn your lessons."

"Can I go now?"

"You may leave," I told her. "But remember what your father and I have said."

Birdie ran to the door and turned back towards me.

"I won't go to school. I won't!" She paused for a moment. "And I won't get married to some stuffy old man!"

After that she ran through the hallway and I could hear her footsteps running up the stairway. I released my breath, thinking to myself that being a mother wasn't an easy job.

August 30, 1917

After our discussion with Birdie, Kevin and I agreed that she would need to be under strict supervision. We took our dilemma to Mother Newkirk who came up with a workable solution: Birdie would attend an all-girls school in Boston and reside with Kevin's sister and brother-in-law. Bernice and Robert Woodward had no children and readily agreed to have Birdie come and live with them. Additionally, Mother Newkirk would be able to keep her eye on Birdie's progress and lend a hand as needed.

And so, there I stood at the Union Station, watching as Kevin and our six-year-old Birdie climbed aboard the train that would take them to Boston. They settled themselves in the coach, with Kevin allowing Birdie to sit by the window. She refused to turn my way and wave good-bye although I could see that Kevin was trying to coax her into doing so. He kept a smile on his face until the train began to move before allowing his displeasure with his daughter to be seen.

I watched until the train cleared the station, thinking about what the future would hold for my daughter. Would she learn her lessons without the distraction of a brother and sister? I remember her tears that morning as she had to leave her brother Gerald behind. It was almost as though we were torturing her by sending her to Boston and separating her from her brother. She screamed and cried that we were being cruel to her. Of course those childish accusations ripped at my heart, but our decisions had been made and they were in her best interests.

I stood motionless beside the track, thinking back to the times when Birdie's confident manner marked her as a Newkirk. She was strong; she would adjust. When I took note of my surroundings once more, I realized that I was standing alone on the platform. I adjusted my gloves and turned away from the track. Twenty feet away stood Nate, my rock, my lover, my friend. He opened his arms to me and I walked into his embrace. His hug was all I needed.

"When do you expect Kevin's return?" he whispered.

"I'm sure he'll be detained by business for a few days," I answered.

"I love you, Delia."

"I need that love, Nate. But for now I'm content with being in your arms."

"You'll always find what you need here, my love. I promise to be here whenever you need me."

Together we left the station. One part of my life was on a train bound for Boston; the other part of my life was here, with Nate. I would take things one step at a time.

48097359R00338

Made in the USA
Lexington, KY
19 December 2015